# DETERMINATION AND DREAMS

"Someday I'll come back to Magnolia and I'll be rich and famous. Everybody in town will grovel at my feet," Iris vowed, her face etched with fresh rage and hurt and determination. "And you know what? I'll spit on them!"

"Iris, hush!" Laura glanced uneasily about the train.

"You said we'd come back," Iris challenged.

"To clear Papa's name. *Our* name. That's why I must become a lawyer!"

"I'm going to marry a rich man," Iris plotted. "Richer than anybody in Magnolia. Maybe the richest man in the world." All at once tears filled her eyes. Her mouth trembled. "Laura, what's going to happen to us in New York? I've never been so scared in all my life."

"Don't you dare be scared," Laura rebuked. "We can take care of ourselves. And we will succeed . . . for Papa!"

## CATCH UP ON THE BEST IN CONTEMPORARY FICTION FROM ZEBRA BOOKS!

**LOVE AFFAIR** (2181, $4.50)
by Syrell Rogovin Leahy

A poignant, supremely romantic story of an innocent young woman with a tragic past on her own in New York, and the seasoned newspaper reporter who vows to protect her from the harsh truths of the big city with his experience—and his love.

**ROOMMATES** (2156, $4.50)
by Katherine Stone

No one could have prepared Carrie for the monumental changes she would face when she met her new circle of friends at Stanford University. For once their lives intertwined and became woven into the tapestry of the times, they would never be the same.

**MARITAL AFFAIRS** (2033, $4.50)
by Sharleen Cooper Cohen

Everything the golden couple Liza and Jason Greene touched was charmed—except their marriage. And when Jason's thirst for glory led him to infidelity, Liza struck back in the only way possible.

**RICH IS BEST** (1924, $4.50)
by Julie Ellis

From Palm Springs to Paris, from Monte Carlo to New York City, wealthy and powerful Diane Carstairs plays a ruthless game, living a life on the edge between danger and decadence. But when caught in a battle for the unobtainable, she gambles with the only thing she owns that she cannot control—her heart.

**THE FLOWER GARDEN** (1396, $3.95)
by Margaret Pemberton

Born and bred in the opulent world of political high society, Nancy Leigh flees from her politician husband to the exotic island of Madeira. Irresistibly drawn to the arms of Ramon Sanford, the son of her father's deadliest enemy, Nancy is forced to make a dangerous choice between her family's honor and her heart's most fervent desire!

*Available wherever paperbacks are sold, or order direct from the Publisher. Send cover price plus 50¢ per copy for mailing and handling to Zebra Books, Dept. 2806, 475 Park Avenue South, New York, N.Y. 10016. Residents of New York, New Jersey and Pennsylvania must include sales tax. DO NOT SEND CASH.*

# A DAUGHTER'S PROMISE

## JULIE ELLIS

ZEBRA BOOKS
KENSINGTON PUBLISHING CORP.

ZEBRA BOOKS

are published by

Kensington Publishing Corp.
475 Park Avenue South
New York, NY 10016

First Zebra Books printing: November, 1989

Printed in the United States of America

*In memory of Tony Sanchez, whose untimely death deprived the New York City school system of a much loved and intensely dedicated teacher—and for Ellen and Jason.*

# ACKNOWLEDGMENTS

I would like to thank the staffs of the New York Law Library, the Columbia University Law Library, Hilda John and Lita Anderson of the New York University Records Office, Mary Carey of the library of the New York Historical Society, and the library staff at Harvard University's School of Design.

I would like, also, to express my gratitude to the New York Public Library, the Donnell, Mid-Manhattan, and Lincoln Center branches, and the library staffs of the Museum of the City of New York and the Broadcast Museum.

My thanks, too, to Claudia and Brad Dickinson of Claudia's Carriage House in Montauk for generously loaning me their extensive personal library on the history of Montauk. And as always, my thanks to my daughter Susie for diligent research and copyediting assistance.

# Part 1

# Chapter 1

The steamy heat in Magnolia, Georgia in this late May of 1924 was breaking records, exacerbating the almost unbearable tensions that gripped the population of 45,681. In the center of town over a thousand people had gathered on the freshly painted green benches that lined the walks of the Courthouse Square about the lush green lawns dotted with beds of red lilies. Oblivious to the mood of their elders, children splashed happily in the circular water fountain and played leap-frog on the pair of Confederate cannons at the northwest corner of the Square.

These people were outside only because every seat was taken inside the courtroom of the imposing sun-drenched, red-brick, colonnaded courthouse where Jacob Roth was being tried for the rape and murder of fourteen-year-old Tammy Lee Johnson, daughter of a cotton mill supervisor. They were mill workers who served on the late shifts, farmers taking time off from planting cotton, merchants, school teachers, housewives.

Feelings ran high against Roth. He was of German birth—and this was just a few years after the World War. He was a Jew—at a time when the Ku Klux Klan had been resurrected and was a powerful political force.

The spectators who had gained admittance had arrived early in the morning with brown paper bags containing their lunches. They knew that at intervals the courtroom would be invaded by young boys selling lemonade and bottles of "dope"—as Coca-Cola was familiarly known in its home state. No one would vacate a seat when the midday recess was called because the seat could not be reclaimed.

The air inside the courtroom was hot and humid, reeking with the aromas of food, sweat, and Woolworth toilet water, as it had been for the past two weeks. Men sat in shirtsleeves, their ties pulled loose. Women wielded bamboo fans in futile hope of relief.

Today the atmosphere was electric. The defense attorney was concluding his case. The prosecuting attorney was impatient to render his summation. Even the imperturbable, patrician-appearing Judge Slocum seemed tense.

In the first row of benches fifteen-year-old Laura Roth sat clutching the hand of her sister Iris, fifteen months her senior. Both girls were extraordinarily pretty, endowed with their father's eloquent blue eyes and their mother's fine features and "peaches-and-cream" complexion. Like her mother as a young girl, Laura was auburn haired. Iris's lush hair was like her father's, near black.

Each day of the trial the two sisters had sat together, silently ignoring the constant hostile stares of the crowd behind them. Most were strangers. Even their best friends at school pretended not to know them. Only kindly Mrs. Bernstein had come several times to the house—late in the evening when she was sure her arrival would be unnoticed—to bring a pot roast or a tureen of stew. Laura and Iris had become pariahs.

Iris had erupted in fury when even their father's friends from the *shul* had drawn away from them. But Laura understood; they were afraid. Vandals had desecrated the altars at both the Orthodox and the Reform synagogues. The KKK saturated the town with anti-Semitic leaflets. Some Jewish families had received hate letters and several had fled to Atlanta or Columbus.

Now Laura's eyes were glued to Bill McKinley, their father's lawyer. She knew that he wasn't defending Papa the way he should. He wasn't making the jury understand that *Papa was innocent*. Once McKinley had the reputation of being a brilliant attorney—before he became the hard-drinking tool of local politicians. Laura sighed. He was the only lawyer in town who had been willing to take the case.

The mob outside was aware that the trial was nearing an end. What began as a simmering undercurrent was becoming a boisterous demonstration that filtered in through the tall, open windows.

"Bailiff, quiet that crowd outside," Judge Slocum called out sharply. "Tell them to shut up or I'll start issuing contempt summons right out on the Square."

10

"Yes, Your Honor." Sweating profusely, the uniformed man hurried towards the double doors that led to the hall.

The demonstration terrified Laura. Would the mood of the crowd—a demand for conviction—intimidate the jury? She'd overheard whispered predictions that they wouldn't dare bring in a verdict of "Not Guilty." That would cause a riot in this town. The citizens of Magnolia—like everyone in the South—had been reared to believe staunchly that "the sweetest and purest thing on earth" is a young girl. The rape and murder of Tammy Lee Johnson was an attack upon the South's very foundations.

Jacob Roth—known locally as "Jake"—was a small, slight man in his early forties, with handsome features and eyes that had once been warm and compassionate. He had been born in 1880 in a small town in Germany and was a Talmudic student until his parents died and he moved to London. There he learned the trade of shoemaker, met and fell in love with a pretty English girl who came into the East End shop where he worked. They married and in 1901 they left London to emigrate to America. After three hard years on New York's Lower East Side, they had settled in the beautiful Southern town of Magnolia, where life promised to be easier for them. Widowed when his much-loved wife died in childbirth, along with the son she was carrying, his life for the nine years since had revolved around his two precious daughters. Today he sat dazed, in a state of fatalistic resignation that frightened Laura.

Outside on the Courthouse Square, the sullen crowd grew quiet as they heard the judge's warning. McKinley finished his summation. As the prosecuting attorney rose to his feet, the courtroom spectators burst into wild approval.

"Gentlemen of the jury," the prosecutor began, "I beg you to consider the dastardly crime that was committed against fourteen-year-old Tammy Lee Johnson—"

Laura flinched at the fresh outbreak of sobbing from Tammy Lee's mother while the attorney again graphically described the rape and murder and methodically reiterated the evidence presented by his witnesses, laboring over the graphic details.

"He's lying," Iris half-whispered. Laura squeezed her sister's hand, begging her to remain silent.

11

In her mind she saw and heard each witness as he had appeared on the stand. The colored man, a known town drunk, had been cleaned up for his appearance in court:

*"I was goin' out in back behind the store — through that little alley between it and the grocery store — to do my bizness, an' I seen Jake Roth leanin' over the body of that poor lil' girl."*

The woman from the boarding house, who everybody knew was addicted to paregoric, an opiate:

*"Mr. Roth — that man there — rented a room at my house for a day and brought a young girl there. I can't rightly swear it was Tammy Lee because he hustled her by me so fast, but it sure looked like her."*

A policeman had testified that five months earlier he had come into Roth's shoe repair shop to find the proprietor fondling a little girl sent there by her mother with shoes to be repaired. The child's mother, the policeman reported regretfully, had been too embarrassed to prosecute.

"And last but not least," the stentorian tones of the prosecutor intruded on Laura's introspection, "Ralph Brooks testified that he saw Tammy Lee Johnson go into the shoe repair shop, and even though he was working on the road right in front of the store until Jacob Roth closed for the day, he never saw the child come out. And the reason he didn't see Tammy Lee come out —" the prosecuting attorney paused for dramatic effect, "is because Jacob Roth had raped Tammy Lee, and then strangled her with her own petticoat!"

"That's a lie!" Iris shrieked, leaping to her feet. "They're all lies! My father —"

Judge Slocum angrily cut her off, calling to the bailiff to remove Iris from the courtroom. Laura watched in agonized ambivalence. Would Papa want her to go with Iris or to stay? She remained in her seat, noting that the bailiff merely posted Iris at the door with another whispered warning. Her eyes swung to her father's face, and she was glad — this time — that Iris had cried out. Despite his pain Jacob Roth was obviously proud that his daughters steadfastly believed in his innocence.

Finally it was time for Judge Slocum to charge the jurors, and they retired to deliberate before reaching their verdict. *How could they find Papa guilty? The witnesses had all lied.* But Laura trembled at the realization that her father's life was in the hands of those eleven grim-faced men and one seemingly

12

sympathetic woman who had retired to the jury room.

The courtroom was cleared except for the defense attorney and the defendant's daughters. Even the newspaper reporters were forced to leave. Pale and shaken, Iris walked slowly back down the aisle to sit with Laura and Bill McKinley.

"Laura, there's no point in your sister and you staying here," McKinley said uneasily. He always seemed to direct his conversation to Laura, as though fearful of another emotional outburst from Iris. "It's already past three o'clock. The jury won't be in for hours. Maybe days."

"We're staying." Laura was brusque in her anxiety. "Until they close the courthouse for the night."

McKinley sighed and dropped into a chair.

"Your father told me you're both high school graduates now," he said, searching in his jacket pocket draped over a chair before him for a cigarette.

"We were given our diplomas a week ago. In the principal's office," Laura emphasized with a tinge of sarcasm. She had been "skipped" twice, which enabled her to graduate with Iris. "We were excused from classes when Papa's trial opened."

"The School Board wouldn't *let* us graduate with the others." Iris's eyes smoldered. Laura knew how she had longed to go up on the stage of the high school auditorium for the graduation exercises—in her beautiful blue organdy evening dress.

Tears welled in Laura's eyes. Papa had so looked forward to seeing them both graduate. He had been saving up for years so that after high school they could go off to GSCW—Georgia State College for Women. The money for their freshman year was in the bank, and he had vowed to see them through to graduation.

"But you've got your diplomas," McKinley said self-consciously. "That's what is important."

"They wouldn't let Laura make her speech," Iris said. "The principal told her it would be too embarrassing 'under the circumstances.' " Laura had been chosen class valedictorian before her father stood accused, even though the principal had fought against this. He had favored the daughter of a family friend.

13

McKinley reached for a newspaper to fan himself. "I'll go out and pick up some bottles of soda for us." He paused. "If you're determined to stay here?" His eyes moved from Iris to Laura.

"We're staying," Laura reiterated. "We want to be here when the jury comes back." *Don't think about the verdict. They would find Papa "Not Guilty."* "Our father will expect us to be here."

At shortly before 5 P.M., when Laura worried that they would be ordered out of the courtroom for the night, word came through like brushfire that the jury was returning. Judge Slocum emerged from his chambers to take his place. The newspaper reporters and the spectators surged back into the room. Then the jury was brought in and seated. Anxiously Laura inspected the face of each juror, praying for some sign of compassion. Each of the jurors appeared self-conscious and uneasy.

Her heart pounding, Laura leaned forward as the foreman of the jury rose to his feet.

Judge Slocum asked the traditional question.

"Guilty, your Honor," the foreman responded.

Laura's stricken eyes swerved to her father. His own eyes were focused on his two daughters. His lips moved silently as though in prayer.

"Papa, Papa!" Iris wailed and clutched at Laura. "Laura, how could they do that?"

"We'll appeal," Bill McKinley said with a false show of confidence. "We'll take it to a higher court!"

A sudden roar of approval came from outside the courtroom as a reporter called out the verdict through the window to the crowd still milling about the grounds.

"Close the windows," Judge Slocum ordered. "We have a case to finish here."

Too stunned to cry, Laura listened while Judge Slocum sentenced her father to be hanged by the neck until he was pronounced dead. The spectators burst into applause. In a daze she heard Judge Slocum set the day of the hanging as the first Monday in August.

"Girls, you can see your father for a few minutes," McKinley said with an echo of compassion in his voice. "Before they take him back to his cell."

Laura and Iris rushed to their father's side.

"Papa, they can't do this to you," Iris sobbed, burying her face on his shoulder.

"Mr. McKinley says he's appealing." Laura's voice trembled. "Papa, how can we help?"

"It's in God's hands now," Roth said. But his eyes told her he had accepted the verdict as irreversible. "We can only wait and see."

"Papa, they all lied. Every witness." Laura struggled for control. Papa always said that she was the steady one and Iris the firebrand. "Why?"

Jacob Roth placed an arm over the shoulders of each of his daughters.

"You must both promise you will always be close. Laura, take care of your sister," he pleaded. "Iris, listen to her. Stay close," he repeated. "You have only each other now." He gazed with fierce intensity at Bill McKinley, standing uncomfortably beside them. "See that my girls get settled away from this town, Bill. This is no place for them anymore."

"Papa, Mr. McKinley is appealing the case," Laura reminded in desperation. "You're innocent."

"I wish I could have seen you both graduate," their father said wistfully. "That would have been such a wonderful moment in my life."


In a shared conspiracy not to voice their terror lest they fall apart in panic, Laura and Iris walked in grim silence to their modest four-room, white clapboard house only three blocks from the courthouse. They had moved here after their mother died because their father could not bear to stay in the house where they all had been so happy.

As they did each day, the two girls watered their multicolored petunia bed, the rose bushes, and the velvety pansies that were their father's pride. Though the most modest house on the block, theirs was maintained with loving care.

With no taste for food but mentally hearing their father's admonition that they must eat, Laura started supper preparations in the small neat kitchen while Iris went out on the porch to sit on the glider. Both girls were still clinging to McKinley's promise of an appeal. Tomorrow morning, Laura promised herself, she would go to Mr. McKinley's office. Iris and she had a right to know exactly what was happening. A second trial would end differently. Another court — far away from Magnolia — would see through all the lies. Papa would be cleared.

Laura started at the now unfamiliar sound of the phone ringing in the living room. She hurried from the kitchen to respond. Iris was standing at the screen door, her expression a mixture of wariness and alarm.

"Hello —"

"Laura, this is Mrs. Bernstein." She sounded oddly exhilarated. "Your father is not alone anymore. A joint committee from the *shul* and the temple has been in touch with a Jewish organization in New York. An hour ago the committee received a telegram from them. A team of lawyers is already on the way to Magnolia. They'll arrive tomorrow. Not drunken has-beens like Bill McKinley," she scoffed. "Some of the top lawyers in the country. They'll immediately file an appeal with the Georgia Supreme Court for a new trial."

"Will they let us see Papa to tell him?" Laura's face was glowing.

"Rabbi Simon is with him now," Mrs. Bernstein soothed. "Your father knows."


Exhausted, but with fresh hope, Laura and Iris retired early to the small, prettily wallpapered bedroom they shared. Settling in their beds, each tossed aside the top sheet in deference to the hot, muggy night air. Iris had switched on the small electric fan that sat atop their dresser, but it only stirred up the heavy humid air.

Too tense to sleep Laura stared into the darkness and thought about the team of New York lawyers coming to Magnolia to help their father while Iris thrashed about on the adjacent bed. Within minutes her nightgown — like the sheet beneath her — was drenched with perspiration.

Eventually the two girls succumbed to sleep. Laura awoke slowly, conscious of unfamiliar noises in the distance, a cacophony of voices that ignited alarm in her. *The jail. The voices came from near the jail.*

"Iris!" Laura leapt from her bed and leaned over the other to shake her sister into wakefulness. "Iris, get up!"

"It's not morning," Iris objected.

"Iris, get up and dress!" Laura darted to the closet. "Something's happening at the jail!"

"Papa?" Iris's voice was a high thin wail.

"Put on your clothes," Laura commanded. "We have to go over there."

Hearts pounding as they left the house, Laura and Iris saw no sign that any of their neighbors had heard the disturbance. They didn't *want* to hear, Laura thought, her throat tightening. No light showed from the windows of any of the houses they passed as they ran towards the jail while heat lightning flashed across the sky. Were their neighbors asleep? Or were they afraid to come out to face whatever was happening in what had always seemed a decent, God-fearing town?

Illogically Laura remembered her father's distaste for the phrase that had just crossed her mind. He always said God was not to be feared. God was to be revered and loved.

"All the lights are on," Iris said as they cut across the Courthouse Square and approached the ugly brick building. She could feel her terror rising deep within her. "Why are they on like that?"

Now they could hear the prisoners inside the jail—banging on the barred windows with whatever was available. Laura and Iris hurried through the entrance doors and paused in shock. Chairs had been overturned. Phones were ripped from the walls. Nobody was in sight. The banging and calls for help came from the prisoners' cells. With Iris at her heels Laura sped down the hall in the direction of the uproar.

"Get us out of here!" a police officer yelled to the girls. A half-dozen men—all police personnel—had been locked into a single cell right off the interrogation room. "Go look for the spare keys in the middle drawer of the big desk to the left!" He pointed towards the outer office.

"What's happened?" Laura demanded, shouting above the noise. "Where's our father?"

"The mob took him!" another police officer said angrily.

Not because of outrage for Jacob Roth, Laura knew instinctively, but because lawmen had been badly treated. "A bunch of the KKK! Get us out of here so we can go after them!"

Laura rushed to search for the keys. She found the ring, hastily dropped near the entrance, and brought it to the cell. One of the police officers—swearing with impatience—located the proper key and unlocked the door. All six charged down the hall and out of the jail to the police cars parked in the adjacent area.

"Take us with you!" Iris pleaded, as she and Laura followed the men outside. "We got you out! Take us with you!"

But the cars pulled out of the parking lot and onto the road. In impotent fury Laura and Iris watched as the cars—sirens shrieking—disappeared from sight.

"What'll they do to Papa?" Iris was close to hysteria.

"The police won't let them do anything," Laura said, pretending an assurance she didn't feel. They both knew what the Ku Klux Klan was capable of. "And the New York lawyers will be here tomorrow," she repeated in a desperate attempt to reassure herself and her sister. But right now Papa was in the hands of a fanatical mob.

Holding Iris's hand tightly in hers, Laura walked with her sister back into the empty jail. The silence was menacing.

"We'll wait here," Laura said. "The police will bring Papa back."

Laura and Iris heard the police cars returning. In concerted movement they rose from the hard benches on which they had sat for over an hour and hurried to the door. A car pulled up before the jail. The others headed for the parking area. Two police officers emerged from the car.

"Where's Papa?" Iris's voice was shrill.

"Where's our father?" Laura called out as the two men walked towards them, ice cold despite the heat of the night.

"I'm sorry, girls," one of the officers said while the other cleared his throat nervously. "We didn't reach them in time."

"What happened to Papa?" Now Iris's voice was a thin, terrified wail.

"Where is he?" Laura was dizzy with shock. *What did he mean—"We didn't reach them in time."*

"Mr. Roth is dead." The officer was uncomfortable. "We just couldn't get there in time."

"They killed Papa! Laura, they killed Papa!" Iris clutched at her sister.

"Where is he?" Laura asked in a strangled whisper. The lawyers were arriving from New York in the morning. Papa was to get a new trial.

"We took your father's body to the funeral parlor," the second police officer told them. "In the morning you can go over and make the necessary arrangements." He reached into his pocket and pulled out a wallet. "This was your father's. We thought you'd want to have it."

Her hands trembling Laura reached for the wallet and opened it, all the while trying to shut out of her mind the shattering vision of what that mob had done to her father. Her eyes focused on the contents of the wallet. Four dollars in bills, photographs of Mama, Iris, and herself. And the carbon copy of the speech she was supposed to deliver at high school graduation.

"What about those men?" Iris screamed through her sobbing. "Why didn't you bring them in?"

"They all got away." Both officers gazed off into space. "We couldn't recognize anybody behind the robes." They didn't want to recognize anybody, Laura thought. Too many important men in this town belonged to the KKK.

The younger of the police officers cleared his throat. "We'll have somebody drive you home."

"No." Laura's voice was sharp. "We can walk."

*Papa was dead.* Tomorrow Iris and she must talk to the rabbi about Papa's funeral.

"Iris, be quiet!" Laura commanded because Iris was beginning to sob uncontrollably. "Don't let them see you cry."

Laura put an arm about her sister's waist and prodded her across the Courthouse Square. Some day she'd make this town understand what they did to Papa. She'd make the whole world know that Papa was innocent. Tonight Magnolia, Georgia had shamed itself before the world.

## Chapter 2

Conscious of the aching emptiness of their house, Laura walked from room to room to cover the mirrors and draw the shades, as dictated by Orthodox Jewish custom. She could hear her father's cheerful, "Girls, I'm home," hear his voice as he blessed the Sabbath candles each Friday evening, see him conduct the *seder* on the first night of Passover. Iris lay face down on the chintz-covered sofa and cried in grief, frustration, and rage. Sleep was over for the night.

Laura remembered the agony of their mother's death, but this had been eased by the warmth of sympathetic friends who moved in and out of the house with pots and casseroles of food. Friends anxious to offer consoling words to lessen their pain. Both Jewish and Christian friends. Mourning for Papa, they would be alone.

"When can we go to the funeral home?" Iris asked quietly when Laura returned to the tiny living room and dropped into a chair.

"In the morning," Laura said uncertainly. She was frightened by the sudden responsibilities thrust on her. The police officer said they could claim Papa's body and make funeral arrangements. That would cost money. Papa kept some money in the box in the kitchen—to be used for change during the next business day—but that would not be enough to pay for his burial, she guessed instinctively.

"Laura, we'll have to pay for Papa's funeral." Iris—rarely the practical daughter—voiced Laura's own concern. Papa had no insurance. The store was his only insurance.

"Papa has money in the bank," Laura reminded. But how would they get it out? "We'll have to go to Mr. McKinley—" Papa must be buried in the Jewish section of Magnolia cemetery. Beside Mama. When Mama died, Papa had bought a plot for himself as well.

"I'm scared," Iris whispered. "What are we going to do?"

"We'll manage," Laura said with a false effort at conviction. Papa's words to her ricocheted in her mind. *"Take care of your sister, Laura. Stay close. You have only each other now."*

With the approach of dawn the heat wave seemed to have broken. But Laura knew this was only a brief respite. Fog shrouded the house, hovering over the summer flowers and the grass that would soon be parched. Still sleepless, both girls started at the sound of the doorbell, raucous in its intrusion. Not even the milkman or the paper boy had made their rounds as yet.

"Who is it?" Iris asked in alarm while Laura hurried to respond.

Rabbi Simon stood at the front door, his face strained and white. Already word had raced around the town.

"Please come in," Laura stammered.

In hushed tones — as though their communication must be secretive — Rabbi Simon offered his sympathy, telling them how much their father had been respected in Magnolia.

"Then why did they kill him?" Iris burst out. "I wish this town would burn to the ground! I wish they would all die!"

"Rabbi Simon —" Laura forced herself to speak. "We have to bury Papa. Please tell us what to do."

Slowly, conscious that Laura and Iris were still in shock, Rabbi Simon explained what was entailed in laying their father to rest. Laura sensed he was reluctant to bring up the question of costs.

"Papa has money in the bank," Laura told him. "More than enough to pay the funeral home. Our college money." Her voice cracked. "And he has a plot in the cemetery. Beside where Mama is buried."

There was a light knock at the screen door. Bill McKinley came into the living room, nodded to Rabbi Simon, and took each girl into his arms for a sympathetic moment.

"I can't believe what's happened." Slowly he shook his head. "I hope every one of those madmen is brought to justice," he said with more eloquence than he had ever displayed at the trial. "This town has disgraced itself."

"You were Jake's attorney," Rabbi Simon pointed out and McKinley stiffened, interpreting this as a rebuke. "You're familiar with his financial situation?"

"I have his power of attorney, yes," McKinley confirmed.

Now he anticipated the rabbi. "As soon as I heard what had happened, I went to talk with the funeral director. I've told him money will be made available from Jake's bank account to cover all expenses. The funeral must be very quiet." His face was apologetic. "It's best for everybody concerned."

Laura flinched. *Why must it be quiet? Wasn't it enough that they killed Papa?*

For a few moments McKinley and Rabbi Simon discussed what had to be done. Iris shut her eyes, covered her ears in an ineffectual escape from ugly reality.

"Iris and I want to see our father," Laura said with shaky dignity when the men paused.

"This evening," Mr. McKinley comforted. "The funeral director said to tell you to come there around supper time." *When they could walk unnoticed through the streets.* Laura remembered a woman screaming at Iris and her one day at the trial: *"Poor little Tammy Lee's dead, but that maniac's daughters are alive."* "He'll be laid out properly then. Rabbi Simon is helping."

"We'll bury him very early tomorrow morning," Rabbi Simon decreed. "In our faith burial must be quick," he added to remove the implication that this would be a surreptitious event.

"At 6:30?" Mr. McKinley said tentatively. His eyes in a secret exchange with Rabbi Simon.

"At 6:30," Rabbi Simon agreed and turned to Laura and Iris, both taken aback, but understanding the reason for the unconventional hour. "I'll drive you to the cemetery. It's too far to walk in the summer heat."

There would be no services at the funeral home or the synagogue. No mourners other than themselves.

After Rabbi Simon left the house McKinley lingered to explain defensively that he would not be able to attend the funeral.

"I've been called out of town by a client. But I'll be in touch with you girls as soon as I return," he promised with an air of solicitude.

"Yes, sir." Laura understood that they needed Mr. McKinley. He was in charge of their financial affairs.

Laura stood at the door while Mr. McKinley climbed behind the wheel of his car and pulled away. It was hard to

22

pretend to be grateful to him. He had not properly defended Papa.

She stooped to pick up the morning *Magnolia Herald*, tossed on the porch earlier by the delivery boy, and she unfolded it as she walked into the house. With Iris leaning over her shoulder she read the headline: "MOB ACTION SHAMES MAGNOLIA." They read the scathing article condemning the lynching and demanding an investigation. But the newspaper predicted that nobody would be arrested. Nobody would pay the penalty for murdering Jacob Roth.

Her vision blurred by tears, Laura pulled a pair of scissors from a drawer and cut out the half page devoted to the report of her father's lynching. The *Herald* had maintained an editorial silence about the actions of the Klan heretofore, lest their advertising suffer; but now they must take a stand. There it was in black and white: *"The police erred in the way they handled the murder investigation."* Still, Laura could not forget that the *Magnolia Herald* — like its competitor the *Magnolia Journal* — had allowed their readers to assume they believed her father guilty. Any favorable evidence presented at the trial had been buried at the bottom of a back page.

Iris stood grim and silent at the screen door, staring out into the already hot and humid early morning. An old Model-T drove down the road, paused before the house. The driver leaned forward to throw a rolled-up newspaper onto the steps that led to the porch.

"Laura!" Iris called out and darted across the porch to pick up the newspaper. "Somebody threw something—"

"What is it?" Laura hurried to the door.

"It's this morning's *Journal*," Iris gasped as she scanned the front page. "The bastards! The rotten bastards!"

"Iris, don't talk like that." Papa never allowed profanity in the house.

"Read this!" Her hands trembling, Iris thrust the newspaper at her sister. "They don't deserve anything else!"

The *Journal* — which supported the KKK and hated "Jews, Catholics, and 'niggers' " — praised the lynchers for having performed their civic duty, making sure that the New York lawyers did not "connive to clear Jacob Roth of the dastardly crime he committed in our town." The front page article reviled Jacob Roth as a monster who had received the justice

23

he deserved.

"We'll use it to wrap up the garbage," Iris said through clenched teeth. "I'd like to burn the *Journal's* office to the ground. Papa always said the *Journal* was fit for nothing but outhouses."

"You read what the *Herald* said," Laura reminded. " 'A terrible miscarriage of justice.' " All at once she felt a towering sense of direction. "Iris, someday I'm going to be a lawyer. I'll go into court, and I'll prove Papa was innocent. The whole world will know that he didn't kill Tammy Lee Johnson."

Shortly past 6 P.M. — when most working people in Magnolia were home and preparing to sit down to supper — Laura and Iris steeled themselves for their walk through the still-daylight-washed streets to the funeral home. While Laura looked for the housekey — though normally nobody in town ever locked a door except at bedtime — Iris called out that Mr. Massey was coming up the front porch. Mr. Massey was their father's long-time friend, a local pharmacist with a small shop on the other side of town.

Laura walked to the door, pulled it wide in welcome.

"Laura—" Mr. Massey's face mirrored his distress. "It's a terrible thing that happened." He extended a brown paper grocery bag. She saw a bread, a salami, a box of crackers inside. Though a Catholic, Mr. Massey knew from conversations with Papa that during *shivah* mourners were to be relieved of such tasks as preparing meals. "Not just to your father and to you — but to this town. Magnolia has disgraced itself."

"Thank you for coming." Tears filled Laura's eyes. She knew that Mr. Massey, with whom her father enjoyed arguing politics and religion, truly mourned with them.

"I couldn't be at the trial because I'm alone in the pharmacy," he pointed out. Involuntarily his eyes strayed to the door. He was worried that somebody might see him here. He worried that neighbors might remember that Papa and he had been friends and would decide to patronize another pharmacy. "Do you have any family you can turn to?" he asked.

"Nobody," Laura said. "Just Mr. McKinley."

"I don't trust that man." His face tensed. "Please, watch how he handles your father's funds."

"He didn't try to clear Papa," Iris accused. "Those lawyers from New York would have fought for him."

"You'll be laying him to rest tomorrow?" Mr. Massey asked gently. Laura was startled by his sudden smile. "I taught him about Catholicism, and he taught me about Judaism. I know your faith buries quickly."

"Tomorrow morning at 6:30," Laura told him and saw him wince at this strange hour for a burial.

"I'll be there," he promised. "Your father was a fine man." His gaze encompassed both Laura and Iris. "Be proud of him always."


The heat wave had broken. Fog hung low over the cemetery, located along the banks of the mud-colored Chattahoochee. Early morning sounds announced the arrival of a new day. The air was sweet with the scents of roses and wisteria. Their father was not to be buried beside their mother. Rabbi Simon had explained that it would be wise to bury him at an unknown spot lest the grave be desecrated. Incongruously dressed in their tulle and organdy graduation dresses—Laura's sea-green, Iris's sky-blue—because Papa had taken such pride in their graduation, the two sisters stood beside their father's newly dug grave.

Their bare arms were goose-pimple-covered in the sudden drop in temperature, their fragile shoes sodden from the dew that glistened on the grass; but neither girl noticed as they listened to Rabbi Simon perform the brief service. Of all who had known their father, only Mr. Massey was here to say a final farewell. They were aware of Rabbi Simon's frequent anxious glances towards the entrance to the cemetery. He worried about unwelcome spectators.

Laura clung to Iris's hand as they fought back tears. Alone at home they had cried. Laura remembered the anguished minutes when they stood before their father's plain pine casket at the funeral home. The waxen figure in white shroud, *tallit,* and *yarmulka* was not their father. Their father existed now only in their hearts.

The casket was lowered into the ground. Each of the three mourners placed a handful of earth upon it. Now Mr. Massey offered to drive them home. Rabbi Simon was needed at the bedside of a member of his congregation.

"Thank you, Mr. Massey," Laura whispered, still clinging to Iris's hand, trying to communicate strength to her sister.

They drove through the early morning stillness of the town. The stores on Lower Broad—which catered to the millworkers like Tammy Lee Johnson's family—were closed, when normally they opened at 6 A.M. Many were owned by Jewish citizens. Laura suspected they would remain closed for the next day or two.

"Anything you need, pick up the phone and call me," Mr. Massey instructed. "Seven days in the house you're bound to need something." The period of *shivah* extended for seven days.

"Thank you, Mr. Massey," Laura said again, and Iris nodded her agreement.

"Your rent on the house is paid up till June first," he said, embarrassed but determined. "Don't let Mr. McKinley tell you otherwise."

"No, sir," Iris said with unexpected strength.

Mr. Massey parked before the house, walked with them to the door, and wished them well.

"Rabbi Simon said he'll be keeping an eye on you," he said compassionately. "We grieve with you."


Laura and Iris spent the long, empty hours recreating the happy times with their mother and father. Streetcar rides out to Magnolia Park on hot nights; Sunday trips in the rented Model-T, with sandwiches and chocolate milk packed in a bucket of ice; the county fair with its ferris wheel and pink cotton candy; the walk down to the railroad tracks each year when the circus came to town and unloaded there. They sought strength in these memories to face the future.

Alone sitting *shivah* on a pair of wooden crates dug from a cupboard, they hardly discerned between day and night. During the seven days of *shivah* mourners sit on stools that are lower than any other furniture in the house. According to Jewish folklore, this is a sign that the mourners long to be

26

closer to the earth where the departed loved one now lies.

Three mornings after their father's funeral Laura and Iris were startled by the sound of the doorbell. None of their neighbors had come to the house since the night the police dragged their father off to jail. None of their father's friends except for Mr. Massey had come.

With a new wariness Laura rose from the crate and walked to the door. Mrs. Tannenbaum, who lived in a beautiful antebellum mansion far up on Linden Avenue, stood there. Tall, spare, austere, she always was garbed in black since the death of her husband twelve years earlier. Her chauffeured Lincoln sat at the curb.

Mrs. Tannenbaum was from that supposedly elite world of the "German Jews" who belonged to the Reform temple. Papa had left the temple after his first year as a member to help organize the Orthodox synagogue, whose members— mostly of Russian and Polish descent—were less affluent. While of German birth himself he clung to the old traditions, many of which had been discarded by the Reform temple.

"Come in," Laura stammered and pulled the door wide. Mrs. Tannenbaum was what Papa called "one of the temple do-gooders"; although he said wryly that her compassion extended to "how much newspaper space her charity bought her."

"We're all upset about your tragic loss." Mrs. Tannenbaum's air told them she had not come to commiserate. "Something this town will never live down."

"Yes ma'am," Laura said politely while Iris stared in overt hostility.

"I've had a talk with Mr. McKinley," Mrs. Tannenbaum pursued. "He's asked me to speak with you. He felt it would be better coming from a woman—"

"What couldn't Mr. McKinley tell us himself?" Iris demanded.

"That your sister and you are destitute," Mrs. Tannenbaum shot back, her face tightening in irritation. "I've discussed the situation with Rabbi Simon and with a committee of ladies from the temple—"

"Mrs. Tannenbaum, that can't be true," Laura interrupted, struggling to mask the panic that was rising in her.

"Mr. McKinley is selling the shop for us. My father had—"

"The shop has been sold." Mrs. Tannenbaum startled the two girls with this admission. "The money has been attached by creditors. Mr. McKinley tells me your father's bank account has also been attached."

"They can't do that!" Iris's voice soared into shrillness. "Papa owed nothing. He was always proud of paying cash for everything. He had put money away to send us off to GSCW in September. We—"

"There's no point in becoming hysterical." Mrs. Tannenbaum turned from Iris to Laura. "Mr. McKinley is the executor of your father's estate. Creditors have come forward with legal documents. Mr. McKinley's fees are naturally a large item. There's nothing left over. Even the furniture will be attached."

For an instant Laura feared Iris was about to attack Mrs. Tannenbaum physically.

"I think we should talk to Mr. McKinley," Laura said shakily, placing a restraining hand on her sister's arm.

"There's no need for that," Mrs. Tannenbaum brushed this aside. "Mr. McKinley agrees with the committee. It's best that you pick up your lives somewhere else. The committee has collected funds. I have here two train tickets to New York plus twenty-five dollars in cash." She opened her elegant alligator bag and pulled out a pair of envelopes. "I have a distant cousin in New York City. She rents out rooms to working girls. Here is a letter to her, asking her to take you in. Business conditions are good; you'll have no trouble finding jobs."

"We'll find jobs here in Magnolia," Iris challenged, her color high. "At the five-and-ten-cent stores or at—"

"Your name is *Roth*," Mrs. Tannenbaum said coldly. "Who in this town will hire you? Your father was a convicted rapist and murderer. Don't you understand?" Mrs. Tannenbaum's celebrated poise was eroding. "You're putting the whole Jewish community in danger. Nobody wants you here!"

"We'll go," Laura said softly, ignoring Iris's glare of disbelief. "We'll save up money and pay back the committee," she added proudly.

"Laura!" Iris shrieked. "They can't make us run away!"

"We don't want to stay where we're not wanted," Laura

28

told Mrs. Tannenbaum. "Our father was innocent. Anybody in town with a brain knows that. And someday we'll prove it." She extended a trembling hand to accept the envelopes Mrs. Tannenbaum extended. *They didn't have any other choice.* "We'll leave tomorrow." God would understand why they couldn't sit *shivah* for Papa for seven days.

"My chauffeur will come by the house at eight tomorrow morning to drive you to the depot. Mr. McKinley asks that you leave the key to the house under the doormat. If there should be any money due you after the furniture is sold, he'll send you a check care of my cousin in New York. But it's most unlikely that there will be any surplus funds," she warned. "Be ready when Robert arrives with the car at eight."


Laura and Iris were waiting for Mrs. Tannenbaum's car to arrive. Their belongings were packed in the same two brown leather suitcases with which their father and mother had traveled twenty-one years ago. The clothes they would not take with them had been packed in a carton with a label reading "For Betty Lou Davis." Mr. McKinley would understand they were to go to Annie Mae's granddaughter, who had occasionally cleaned for them.

"We should have packed our graduation dresses," Iris said wistfully while they sat at the edge of the sofa, already feeling alien in the house where they had lived for most of their lives.

"We'll never wear them again," Laura said softly, the memory of where they'd last worn them fresh in her mind.

"Mr. McKinley's cheating us out of Papa's money," Iris said for the dozenth time. "I hope he rots in hell."

"That's why he didn't come to the house. He couldn't face us. And it's not just him. It's those awful folks who claim Papa owed them."

A horn sounded out at the curb.

"That's Robert. Couldn't he even come up to the front door?" Iris seethed. "He acts like we were trash."

"Iris, behave," Laura scolded. She took a deep breath and rose to her feet. "We're not saying anything in front of Robert. Let's just act as if he was driving us to the depot because we're going to shop in Atlanta or to visit somebody. I don't want him tattling to Mrs. Tannenbaum about how terrible we feel."

They walked out into the humid morning. Laura locked the door and put the key under the doormat. Each girl clutching a suitcase, they walked down the steps and to the car without a backward glance. They ignored Mrs. Kendrick, standing by her peony bush and staring avidly at them. They were no longer Laura and Iris Roth, who took care of Mrs. Kendrick's three cats when she went to visit her sisters. They were the daughters of a convicted murderer.

Robert emerged from the Lincoln to take their suitcases and store them in the trunk. Laura and Iris settled themselves on the rear seat. Their cap-sleeved cotton print dresses were freshly washed and ironed. By tacit agreement they remained silent while Robert slid behind the wheel again and started up the car.

Papa always said Magnolia was the prettiest city in the South—even prettier than Columbus, Laura recalled wistfully. As Robert drove further up the avenue—past the wide lawns punctuated by the narrow sidewalks mandated by city planners almost a century ago—Laura allowed herself a final gaze at the towering shiny-leaved magnolia trees in sensuous bloom, at the colorful splash of summer flowers that surrounded every house. Papa had loved this town. *She* loved it still.

Robert turned left and the car cut across stately Broad Street, bisected by its picturesque mall—the grass lushly green, circlets of orange-red lilies alternating with tall evergreens. Involuntarily—her heart pounding—Laura gazed towards Lower Broad, straining for a last view of her father's shoe repair shop. The distance was too great, but in her mind Laura saw the small, white brick-fronted store that had been Papa's pride. Not Papa's anymore.

Her throat tightened with fresh anguish. *Iris and she were being run out of town.* But one day she would come back to Magnolia. She'd be a lawyer then. She'd find out who killed Tammy Lee Johnson. She'd make this town admit that Papa had not been guilty. That they had killed an innocent man.

"We're almost there," Iris fretted. "We'll be early."

"It'll be cooler in the waiting room," Laura comforted.

Now the red brick railroad depot, built a few years after the War Between the States, rose into sight. When Iris and she were little, Mama and Papa—and, later, Papa alone—used to bring them here on Sundays to watch the arriving and departing travelers. Iris and she had loved the air of excitement that filled the lofty ceilinged, marble-floored waiting room at these times.

Robert pulled to a stop in the driveway before the depot. He left the car and went to the trunk for their suitcases. Silent and distant Laura and Iris emerged to wait at the curb.

"Have a nice trip, you hear?" Robert said with an unexpected show of compassion.

"Thank you," Laura said politely while Iris—her face white and taut—reached for one suitcase.

As Iris and she walked into the waiting room, Laura shot a glance back outside. Robert was still standing beside the Lincoln. Mrs. Tannenbaum must have told him to make sure they were aboard the northbound train when it pulled out of the depot.

Papa liked to tell them about the long train trip from New York when Mama and he had come to live in Magnolia. He had never imagined in his wildest dreams that one day Iris and she would be traveling alone to New York to live. Like this.

They would be on that Seaboard Airline train when it left Magnolia in twenty-two minutes. *But they would return.*

## Chapter 3

Laura and Iris settled themselves in a seat on the shady side of the day coach, their suitcases stashed on the luggage rack above. They were already sweltering despite the open window. Except for clothes all they took with them from their former lives were Mama's candlesticks—bought when Papa and she were married in London, Papa's pocketwatch and chain—which he had left behind the night he was dragged off to jail—and a cherished collection of snapshots of their mother, father, and themselves.

"I wish we were traveling in the Pullman section," Iris sighed. "I always wanted to do that."

"Papa and Mama came to Magnolia in a day coach." Laura's tone was faintly sharp. Iris was always so envious of rich folks.

"I'll come back one day in my own Pullman car," Iris vowed, her face etched with fresh rage and hurt and determination. "I'll be rich and famous, and everybody in town will grovel at my feet. And you know what?" she demanded with an air of triumph. "I'll spit on them."

"Iris, shut up." Laura glanced uneasily about the car, grateful that the seats around them were not yet occupied. Why didn't the train pull out of the station? How long would they sit like this?

"You said we'd come back," Iris challenged.

"To clear Papa's name." Laura recoiled from the violence that spewed in her sister. "*Our* name."

"I'm not Iris Roth anymore," Iris decided in sudden determination. "From now on I'm Iris Adams."

"Are you ashamed of Papa?" Laura was shocked. Papa had let her change her name from Ida to Iris when she was ten. When Iris cried, Papa would agree to almost anything. "What's wrong with being Iris Roth?"

"Iris Roth lived in Magnolia, Georgia. Iris Adams will live

in New York. Nobody even has to know I'm Jewish. Nobody has to know what they did to Papa." For a moment a fresh surge of grief threatened her composure. Iris lifted her head in defiance. "You said we were going to New York to start a whole new life. Well, I'll be Iris Adams. You be whatever you want."

"I'm not changing my name." This would be traitorous to Papa's memory. "Not ever," Laura retorted vehemently.

"What if you get married?" For the first time in weeks a faint giggle escaped Iris.

"I won't have time for that," Laura brushed this aside. "*I have to become a lawyer.*" Nothing in the world mattered except clearing Papa's name. To do that she would have to be a lawyer.

"I'll marry a rich man," Iris plotted. "Richer than anybody in Magnolia. Maybe the richest man in the world. We'll have a beautiful house, and I'll have my own Pierce-Arrow Runabout. And clothes like Gloria Swanson wore in *Zaza*. Do you know she makes five thousand dollars a week?"

"Iris, you're always reading those dumb movie magazines!"

All at once tears filled Iris's eyes. Her mouth trembled. "Laura, what's going to happen to us in New York?"

"We'll rent a room at that rooming house run by Mrs. Tannenbaum's cousin. We'll find jobs." Laura struggled to sound confident. "This is 1924. Girls all go out and work these days."

"Doing what? We've never worked anywhere."

"We've helped Papa in the shop on Saturdays. We made change and wrapped packages. We can be salesgirls or office clerks. We're high school graduates," Laura pushed ahead with a show of conviction. "We can lie and say we worked in stores in Magnolia. Nobody will bother to write back and ask."

"I'm scared," Iris whispered. "I've never been so scared in all my life."

"Don't you dare be scared," Laura rebuked. "We can take care of ourselves. *That's what Papa would expect us to do.*"

The train chugged northward past endless red-clay fields

33

of newly planted cotton, past orchards where workers picked the first peaches of the season. Other workers bent over stretches of summer vegetables that would appear in town markets the following morning or in baskets atop the heads of colored women selling along residential streets. Not until tomorrow afternoon, Laura remembered, would they arrive at Pennsylvania Station in New York.

At intervals — as the train paused at a depot to disgorge and take on passengers — boys stalked down the aisles of the coach to sell sandwiches and cold drinks. The dining car was patronized mainly by the more affluent Pullman passengers. Warily Laura exchanged coins for sandwiches and cold bottles of Coca-Cola and Nehi, ever conscious of their limited funds. It was taken for granted that Laura — "the steady one" — would handle their money.

The sisters passed the monotonous, sticky-hot hours by recalling their years in Magnolia, as though it was urgent to remember every minute detail.

"I hated being the poorest family on the block," Iris confided as night fell and a porter began to distribute pillows to the day coach passengers. "Remember Sally Lou Edmonds, whose mother sewed for us sometimes?"

"We were in grammar school with her." Laura nodded in recall. Sally Lou had gotten into trouble in her junior year at vocational high. She was supposed to have gone to live with her grandmother for a while, but everybody knew she was pregnant.

"Sally Lou said we were giving ourselves airs by going to the academic high school. She said kids like us always went to the vocational high school."

"Our grandfather on Papa's side was a rabbi in Berlin before Papa was born. Papa would have been a rabbi if his father and mother had not died young and left him all alone. His uncles were doctors." Both uncles had died in the Franco-German war. "Papa grew up believing education was important."

"Money is important," Iris shot back. "If Papa had been a Lowell or a Slocum or a Pendleton, he'd never have gone to jail!" The Lowells and the Slocums and the Pendletons were not just wealthy; they were Magnolia's "first families."

"Iris, we were never millhand or tenant-farmer poor,"

Laura said defensively. "We had everything we needed. Papa saw to that."

"We never even had a car," Iris seethed. "Only when Papa rented one from that man he knew." Papa refused to buy on the installment plan. "Remember how many girls in our classes got their own cars the minute they were sixteen? They had charge accounts at Glover's and Miss Ella's, and bought anything they wanted." Glover's was Magnolia's most exclusive specialty store, Miss Ella's favored by the daughters of the rich.

"We had everything we needed," Laura reiterated, unhappy at this turn in their reminiscences. To talk this way seemed an insult to Papa's memory.

"I hate the way everybody is put onto shelves in Magnolia," Iris went on hotly. "Folks like Papa with shoe repair shops and grocery stores just one notch above the millhands — and then the ones with the stores that sold cheap clothes and furniture. After that the expensive stores — where we just looked in the windows—"

"We've bought at Glover's and Miss Ella's," Laura objected.

"On our birthdays," Iris flared. *Once a year.* And *we* never got invited to the junior sub-deb parties at the country club."

"I never cared about that," Laura admitted. But she remembered how every Sunday morning Iris devoured the society pages of the *Herald.* "Who needed those silly parties?"

"We were friends at school with Beverly Lowell and Elaine Pendleton and the others. But after school we went our way, and the rich kids went theirs." Her eyes were stormy.

"Except for Perry," Laura teased and an instant later regretted it.

"I had such a crush on Perry." Iris seemed suddenly so vulnerable. "And he felt the same way. I know he did. He used to drive me home from school all the time. Remember? In our senior year he got his mother's old car when she bought a new one. He always took the long way round, and we'd stand and talk forever on the front porch."

"Sure." Laura's smile was tender. Papa was pleased that Iris's first boyfriend was "from a fine Jewish family."

"But he never even asked me to go to a movie. He went to all the junior sub-deb dances with Lucy Fast. Her father

35

belonged to the Orthodox synagogue. If we were rich and belonged to the temple, it would have been just great." *He was ashamed to date Iris Roth.*

Nighttime — with the lights in the day coach dimmed — filled Laura with a poignant loneliness that she knew enveloped Iris as well. Night lent a note of funereal finality to the life they were leaving behind. They slept at exhausted intervals. Awaking at dawn they abandoned further efforts at sleep. Within a few hours, Laura realized, they would be in New York. On the train she felt as though they were between two lives. When they got off, they would step out into a strange, frightening world.

Across the aisle a woman pointed out the Washington Monument — rising tall and slender against the early morning sky — as the train approached Washington, D.C. With a rush of excitement Laura and Iris darted to an empty seat on the other side of the car to get a better view of this American legend. Soon the train was drawing into Union Station, and there was a rush of departing passengers.

The same woman told them the train would soon be approaching the Mason Dixon Line. "That's the line that divides the North from the South," she said, enjoying their rapt attention. "I'm from Baltimore myself. Maryland was a slave state, but it stayed in the Union during the Civil War, though my grandfather — like a lot of Marylanders — fought with the Confederate army."

Again at the Baltimore depot there was an exodus of passengers, including their new friend. Laura and Iris said good-bye with a disconcerting feeling of loss.

By the time the train pulled out of the Baltimore depot, the temperature had dropped to a pleasing coolness. The sky was overcast.

"It's cold." Iris was querulous, masking her fear of what lay ahead in minor complaint.

"Let's take sweaters out of our suitcases," Laura said. "We each packed one right on top just in case." She rose to her feet, stared doubtfully up at the luggage rack where a porter had put their suitcases at boarding.

"Can I take that down for you, little lady?" an indulgent

male voice asked and Laura turned around to face a tall, well-dressed colored man carrying a briefcase.

"Thank you, yes." Laura smiled gratefully, and the man swung down one suitcase and then the other after a wordless exchange. "Thank you so much."

"My pleasure," he nodded to Iris and her and moved down the aisle to a vacant seat.

"Laura, he's sitting in a 'white' car," Iris whispered in astonishment.

"Iris, we're in the North," she whispered back. "They don't have separate cars for coloreds up here."

He'd carried a briefcase, Laura noted with respect. He was a professional man. Papa had always talked about the way colored people in the North mixed with whites. It was the one thing he didn't like about the South — the way colored folks had to "stay in their place." But he said that even in New York there were places where colored — and Jews and Catholics — were not wanted. And he used to laugh and say, "Their loss."

When the train stopped at the Philadelphia station, Iris reached for the timetable a departing passenger left behind.

"We're headed for New Jersey now. Laura, we'll soon be in New York!" She squinted in sudden rejection. "Papa and Mama never liked it."

"Papa said New York was a wonderful city," Laura reproached.

"He said it was a wonderful city for rich people. Like London."

"He said it had wonderful parks and museums and beaches—"

"And when Mama and he left those places, they went home to ugly old flats on the Lower East Side," Iris reminded with distaste. "They'd left London because they worked fourteen hours a day and went home to live in one ugly room on Bell Lane."

Both girls had listened so often to stories about London's East End and New York's Lower East Side that they felt *they* had been there. They knew that their parents had scrimped for three years to save enough money to take them to Magnolia, where their father was able to open a tiny shoe repair shop. A neighbor on Hester Street had told them longingly about a childhood in Atlanta. The neighbor mentioned nearby Magnolia, and Mama chose that because she liked the name. They were eager, too, to remove themselves from the squalor of large cities. In Magnolia, the neighbor told them, they could have a house of their own. Even a garden.

"Iris, we're not going to live on the Lower East Side. Mrs. Tannenbaum's cousin has a house on West Twenty-second Street. *We're going to be all right.*"

All at once the railroad car was permeated with an air of anticipation. Passengers were gathering together their belongings, and Laura knew they were approaching their destination.

The train moved underground, traveling in a dark tunnel that was awesome to the two young sisters from Magnolia. Yet despite their apprehension of arriving in a strange city with funds to carry them through no more than three weeks, no matter how careful they were, they were caught up in the excitement that charged through the car.

Clutching their suitcases Laura and Iris left the train and followed other more knowledgeable passengers from the platform into the huge waiting room.

"Laura, it's not like the depot back home!" Iris tried for a flippant tone, but Laura knew she was as impressed as herself.

"We'll have to ask how to get to Mrs. Morgenstern's house." Mrs. Morgenstern was Mrs. Tannenbaum's cousin. Laura stared about the waiting room. "Over there. The information counter."

A man at the information counter told them their destination was about ten blocks south of Pennsylvania Station.

"You can take a bus down or a taxi — it's a short ride." He pointed left. "Just head that way towards the street."

"Thank you, sir." Some folks back home said New Yorkers were not friendly. Not so, Laura thought.

"A taxi would cost a lot," Iris surmised.

"We'll walk." Laura decided firmly. Even ten cents busfare should be saved. Both girls were amazed by the throngs that rushed along the avenue and by the tall buildings that thrust high into the sky. While Laura watched for street signs, Iris maintained a running whispered comment about the dresses, the hairstyles, the makeup of the girls and women purposefully striding past them. *Nobody* dawdled; everybody apparently was late for some important destination. And with each block that Laura and Iris walked in the gray chill of the early afternoon, their suitcases seemed heavier.

"Laura, look at that hat!" Iris swung her head about in admiration. "It's one of those new cloches. I saw a picture of Pola Negri in *Photoplay* wearing one. And did you ever see such short dresses? Nobody back home would have the nerve to wear something like that. Almost up to their knees! And look at all those French heels."

"This is Twenty-second Street." Laura sighed in relief. "The man said to turn right here. Let's watch for the house number, Iris."

Mrs. Morgenstern's rooming house was a narrow, dingy-gray five-story building wedged between two four-storied brownstones that retained a semblance of earlier elegance. Mrs. Morgenstern's building made no such pretense.

"Laura, the houses are all sandwiched next to one another." Iris gaped in disbelief. "Just windows in front and back!"

Together the sisters walked up the low stoop. Laura rang the doorbell. A grossly overweight woman in her fifties—eyes suspicious and wary—admitted them into a narrow dark hallway.

"Mrs. Morgenstern?" Iris asked while Laura put down her suitcase to bring the letter of introduction from her purse.

"I'm Mrs. Morgenstern." She inspected each girl from head to toe with a fast sweep. "You want a room, it's four dollars a week, one week's rent in advance. No men in your room, no cooking."

"We have a letter from your cousin, Mrs. Tannenbaum," Laura said politely, though it appeared this was unnecessary.

"I thought you had a Southern accent." Her own accent hinting of a German birthplace, the heavyset woman pulled the door wide. "How's Millie? We don't write often."

"She's fine." Mrs. Morgenstern was ripping open the envelope. Iris had wanted to open it and read it and then reseal it, Laura remembered. But Papa had always impressed upon them the importance of "doing what's right."

"Unh-hunh." Mrs. Morgenstern nodded briskly when she had scanned the brief content of the letter. "Millie says you

39

want a cheap room. I have another that was just vacated. That one's only two dollars. In advance."

"Yes ma'am." Laura fumbled in her purse for the money. "And we'd like a receipt, please." She sounded apologetic, but Papa had taught them always to ask for receipts.

"I'll put it under your door later." Mrs. Morgenstern shoved the bills into a pocket of her dress. "Follow me."

Laura and Iris struggled behind her up four flights, winded when she finally paused, pointed to a door, and produced a key. She walked inside and pulled a light chain. Laura tried not to show her shock as she stared about the tiny room furnished with a pair of single beds, a dresser with a small lamp, one straight chair, and a pockmarked, much stained wash basin in one corner.

"Your closet is here." Mrs. Morgenstern indicated a minuscule area. "The bathroom is at the far end of the hall. Remember to turn out the light when you leave it." Now she handed the key to Laura. "I'll slide another key under the door with the receipt later. Millie says you'll be needing jobs. Buy *The New York Times* every day," she instructed. "Early in the morning when it first comes out. You can't sleep half the day away and expect to find jobs. Look for the employment section. And go to Macy's and Gimbel's—department stores are always hiring girls."

For a moment after Mrs. Morgenstern's departure Laura and Iris surveyed their new home in grim silence.

"Laura, it's awful!" Iris wailed and crossed the floor to pull up the worn shade. "There's a brick wall just three feet away!"

"We won't stay here long," Laura comforted. "As soon as we find jobs, we'll move."

"We'll buy a hot plate and hide it," Iris said defiantly. "A girl in *True Story* did that."

"Iris, when did you read *True Story?*" Papa let them read *Women's Home Companion* and *Collier's* and *The Saturday Evening Post* and sometimes she and Iris pooled their allowance and bought a copy of *Vogue*.

"Somebody was always sneaking *True Story* into the gym at school." Iris shrugged. "All the girls were reading it."

40

A half hour later Laura and Iris had unpacked their suitcases and put away their modest wardrobes. Mama's candlesticks sat atop the dresser. Then, brushing aside twinges of guilt, they went out and shopped for an electric hot plate at a United Drug Store on West Twenty-third Street. At Woolworth they bought the minimum basic kitchen requirements—to be hidden at the bottom of the closet with their hot plate. Groceries from the A&P were chosen with an eye for their limited facilities. At Iris's insistence—"for good luck"—they bought a small box of Fanny Farmer mints to make their first supper in their new home a bit festive. For two cents they splurged on a copy of the *Daily News.*

After supper—with the dishes washed and concealed and the hot plate cooling—they considered Mrs. Morgenstern's terse instructions about finding jobs. The prospect of job hunting was terrifying.

"We'll say we're eighteen," Laura decided, curled up at the end of one lumpy mattress.

"Both of us?" Iris was skeptical. "But nobody will know we're sisters," she remembered. "I'll be Iris Adams."

"If anybody asks, we'll say we're cousins." Laura knew it would be futile to argue with her sister about the name change. "We'll say we worked as salesgirls in our uncle's department store back in Magnolia."

"At Glover's," Iris pounced. "We worked there for two years—ever since we finished high school. Nobody will bother checking."

"I might be able to get a job as an office clerk," Laura surmised. "I can say I did that back in Magnolia. Office jobs pay better."

"Laura—" All at once Iris's spurt of high spirits evaporated. "Suppose we can't find jobs before our money runs out?"

The atmosphere was suddenly heavy.

*"We'll find jobs.* Remember what Papa used to say? If you want something bad enough and you work at it, you'll get it."

"Laura, Papa was just trying to make me study so I'd get 'A's like you," Iris said in exasperation.

"Let's go down the hall to the bathroom. We'll have to be up early tomorrow."

"How will we ever fall asleep in this—dive?" Iris shuddered. "Back home even the millhands live in houses."

"I told you, Iris—we won't stay here. I'll bet we find jobs in a week," Laura said with shaky bravado. "Come on."

The girls were grateful for the threadbare flannel blankets on each bed because the night temperature was clammy and cold. Despite their fitful slumber on the Seaboard Airline day coach the previous night, both Laura and Iris found sleep elusive. They were aware of unfamiliar night sounds. Raucous voices in the hallways, laughter, cursing. The howl of boats on the river. Fire trucks chasing through the night. In the next room a pair made noisy love—simultaneously fascinating and embarrassing them.

Before the alarm went off at 6 A.M., Laura and Iris were awake. At the shrill intrusion of the alarm they rose to prepare for the day. Last night's chill had been replaced by a blanket of humid heat, their airshaft window giving no indication of the brilliant sunshine that already bathed the city at this early hour.

"You put up tea to go with our muffins," Iris said when they were dressed. "I'll go down and pick up *The New York Times*." This morning Iris seemed to have thrust aside her alarm about their future. Laura sensed an eagerness in her to walk among the big-city girls with their short skirts and French heels and shingled hair. "Okay, kiddo," Iris flipped. "Back for breakfast in ten minutes."

Over tea and muffins the two girls read the job listings, underlining their targets for the day. Then they washed the dishes and hid the forbidden hot plate. They left their room, walked down the dark stairs and out into the strange, frightening city.

Although Laura fought to emulate Iris's pretense of casualness, she was terrified when they approached their first employment agency. Her hands perspiring from nervousness, she filled out an application as Iris did the same. During the next seven hours—stopping only for coffee and rolls at the Automat—the two girls traipsed from one employment agency to another, filling out a stream of application forms.

"Tomorrow we'll go to the department stores," Laura decided when they were heading home, exhausted from endless walking on hot city streets, waiting around in steamy offices.

"Let's stop off at Woolworth," Iris coaxed. "All the girls we saw today were wearing mascara. Maybelline doesn't cost much."

At the end of their second day of job hunting they reluctantly admitted that one of them had to be at home to receive phone calls about possible jobs. Hereafter, one would job hunt in the morning, the other in the afternoon.

Fighting panic at the end of one week—with no solid job prospect for either Iris or herself despite the bustling economy—Laura returned from her morning routine of job hunting with the knowledge that today another week's rent was due. In the afternoon Iris would make the rounds of the agencies while she waited for phone calls.

"Laura!" Iris flung the door wide as her sister approached the door. Her face was luminous. "We've both got jobs!" she shouted.

"Where?" Laura was radiant.

"I'm to report tomorrow morning at Lord & Taylor. I'll be a salesgirl. An hour after I got my call, there was one for you. I said I was you; and yes, I'd be able to start to work at B. Altman on Monday morning. Laura, you said it would happen this way!" Iris flung her arms about Laura while the two squealed with pleasure.

"We won't even have to spend carfare," Laura said with added satisfaction. "We can walk to work."

"Let's celebrate!" Iris swung away from Laura to inspect her reflection in the mirror. "Let's go over to Child's and treat ourselves to pancakes."

"At the end of our first week at work," Laura hedged, her normal caution taking over. "Oh, Iris, we're going to be all right!"

# Chapter 4

Through the hot Manhattan summer Laura and Iris worked as salesgirls and spent as little of their spare time as possible in their almost intolerably cramped and dingy room. Laura discovered the New York Public Library at Forty-second Street and was entranced by its eighty miles of shelves, crammed with more than two and a half million books.

She introduced Iris to the wealth of magazines that could be read there for free. Iris adored *Harper's Bazaar* and *Vogue* and *Town & Country*. Increasingly Laura worried about Iris's obsession that one day she'd "have it all"—clothes from Paris, a Bentley or a Rolls-Royce, an apartment on Sutton Place overlooking the East River. Every day Iris devoured the gossip columns in the *Daily News*. Every night she read herself to sleep with Elinor Glyn's latest sizzling romance, borrowed from their neighborhood library.

Three times in the course of the summer the sisters took the BMT subway to Brighton Beach. On several sweltering nights—unable to sleep—they took a bus up Riverside Drive to the end of the line and back. And they discovered the Staten Island ferry—which Laura dubbed "the working girls' ocean cruise."

Laura worried about Iris's efforts to transform herself into a flapper. She plucked and penciled her eyebrows, had her hair shingled, spent hours learning how to rouge her cheeks to emphasize her high cheekbones—"like Gloria Swanson in *Manhandled*." Another salesgirl at Lord & Taylor was teaching her to Charleston. And constantly she tried to convince Laura that they should move.

"We'll move into a better room when we've sent money back to Magnolia." Laura was firm. "You know that Papa would want us to pay our debts."

On a Saturday morning in late September—when she didn't have to be at work till ten—Laura stopped by the post office to buy a money order for twenty-five dollars. Soon, she promised herself, she would send a second money order to Mrs. Tannenbaum to cover the cost of their train tickets. Her second destination this morning was to sign up for evening classes in typing at the Washington Irving high school. From studying the "Help Wanted" ads she knew she could earn more money as a typist.

Three months later—after a desperate search because New Yorkers were beginning to encounter a housing shortage—Laura and Iris moved two houses east of Mrs. Tannenbaum's rooming house into a larger room with a closet kitchenette and two windows—known as a "studio apartment." They ignored the peeling paint, the seedy furniture, the fact that they shared a bathroom with other tenants on the floor. *It was a real apartment.*

Iris refused to join Laura in the typing class. "I'd hate working in an office." Iris had shuddered eloquently.

Except for their going to a movie once a week at the RKO movie theater at Twenty-third Street and Eighth Avenue, Laura stayed home evenings and practiced typing on the printed chart that stood in for a typewriter. Iris spent her evenings socializing with newly found friends at the department store, including several young men. At least twice a week she chased off to meet one young man or another for an evening at a "speak," but never the same escort more than once or twice a month because the tabs at the booming speakeasies were astronomical for department-store salesmen.

Laura was upset that Iris was reshaping herself in the flapper image.

Iris was seventeen but told her friends she was twenty. She took pride in the amount of "hooch" she could handle without getting "spifflicated." Her skirts were climbing to alarming heights. But when Iris came home one night to announce she was bleaching her magnificent dark hair, Laura screamed at her in such outrage that Iris abandoned this. Like her new friends, Iris complained that their parents' generation had made a mess of the world, that the important thing in life was to have fun — before the whole world blew up.

Six months after Laura enrolled in her typing class she decided the time had arrived to try for an office job. The increase in salary an office job guaranteed was an incentive, but the prospect of working in a law office was the driving force behind her decision. She dreamed of going to Hunter College — free to New York City residents — and eventually becoming a lawyer.

Doggedly determined, she rejected two possible jobs in nonlegal offices until the law firm of Weinstein, Schiffman, and Elkin offered her a job as a receptionist-typist. She was dizzy with excitement as she arrived twenty minutes early for her first day on the job. She would listen and learn everything she could about law. Next September, she promised herself — when she had saved up money to pay for schoolbooks — she would enroll in night classes at Hunter College.

On her first day in the imposing offices of Weinstein, Schiffman, and Elkin, Laura encountered a young clerk named Bernie Hunter. Almost immediately she knew he wasn't like Iris's young men. He worked hard all day, attended law school at night. One of the stenographers admitted to having "a mad, mad crush on Bernie — but all he ever thinks about is law."

In the following weeks Laura learned that Bernie — who lived in the Bronx, where he had been born — had graduated from City College before starting night classes at NYU law school. An orphan, he had lost both his mother and father in the 1918 influenza epidemic. The smitten stenographer also told Laura that Bernie worked harder than any law clerk in the office — staying late every night that he didn't have a class.

"Don't get ideas about him," she warned. "He's in love with his law books."

"I'm not," Laura stammered.

At intervals as her first weeks on the job passed she was conscious of appraising glances from Bernie Hunter. She pretended not to be aware of him except on rare occasions when he asked her to type something for him. He was almost a head taller than she, with rumpled dark hair and probing

46

hazel eyes. She knew that Mr. Weinstein, the senior partner, thought that Bernie "had a great career ahead of him."

On her fifth Friday at the office Bernie dropped a memorandum on her desk. He asked her to type it. Then he asked to take her out for dinner the following evening. Laura was wide-eyed with astonishment and was furious that she was blushing.

"Do you like German food?" His smile was electric.

"I love it," she said, knowing practically nothing of German cooking except from her father's occasional nostalgic descriptions.

Her heart was pounding. *Bernie Hunter had asked her for a date.* "My father was German."

"With a name like Roth," he teased, "I suspected you weren't Irish."

"Are you Irish?" she asked in sudden panic. The first time Papa came home to find Iris talking on the porch to Perry — of whom he approved, he made it clear he expected his girls to go out only with young men of their own faith. *"It saves a lot of grief in this world."*

Bernie's laughter was warm and tender. "My mother and father both came to this country from Russia. Their parents were determined they wouldn't die in a pogrom."

*He was Jewish.*

"We'll go to this little place in Yorkville. Sauerbraten like you've never tasted, and the greatest cheesecake outside of Lindy's."

Shyly Laura reported to Iris over their Friday night spaghetti dinner that she had a date with Bernie Hunter.

"That law clerk you've been mooning over?" Iris asked with a mixture of skepticism and tenderness.

"I haven't been mooning over him," Laura protested. "I just said he was, uh, nice. And he goes to law school at night," she added with a touch of pride.

"He doesn't exactly sound like the cat's meow." Iris inspected her sister with fresh interest. "I could probably fix you up with a blind date."

"I don't want a blind date." With one of those drugstore cowboys Iris talked offhandedly about picking up? "Bernie's taking me to dinner at some place up in Yorkville." She recalled that Yorkville was a section of the Upper East Side where many Germans lived.

"And no gin mill afterwards," Iris surmised.

"Iris, not every girl in New York wants to run to gin mills," Laura said defensively. None of the girls in her office carried on like Iris. Back at school in Magnolia there had been four or five girls everybody knew were "fast"—but she suspected most girls their age had never tasted bathtub gin, never went to a speakeasy, didn't personally know a single "flapper" or "jazz baby"—only those they saw in the movies.

"Okay, baby," Iris drawled. "But when you get bored with flat tires, let 'Big Sister' know."

"Iris, I worry about you," Laura said somberly. "I mean, the way you live."

"How do I live?" Iris's smile blended amusement, defiance, and affection.

"As though you were Clara Bow in *The Plastic Age* or Jacqueline Logan in *The House of Youth.* Running to 'speaks,' staying out half the night with some fellow or other." She hesitated, color flooding her face. Iris and she were so close, yet it was hard to talk with her about some things. "Saturday night three weeks ago you didn't even come home at all." She'd awakened in the morning to see Iris's bed still made up and had been scared to death until Iris walked in two hours later. She'd said something about a party that ended up with breakfast at Child's.

"I was having fun," Iris shrugged.

*"All night?"* Laura's voice was involuntarily shrill.

"We rested in between," Iris giggled. "I'm not talking about just necking. We did everything. Several times," she said with defiant bravado while Laura stared in shock. "Sugar, no fellow bothers hanging around a girl who isn't 'fast.' At least, not any fellow worth seeing." Her eyes inspected her sister with blatant curiosity. "When you're watching a movie with hot lovemaking in it, don't you ever wish you were in bed with the man up there on the screen?" Her mouth parted in laughter as Laura's mouth opened in speechless dismay. "What's the matter? Cat got your tongue?"

"Iris, you're shameful," she protested hotly.

"No, I'm not. I'm honest," Iris said. With girls today, Laura thought, "being honest" made anything all right. "I get all hot and bothered when Rudolph Valentino grabs Alla

48

Nazimova or Gloria Swanson and you *know* what he wants to do even though they don't show it on the screen. But we can't do it with Rudolph Valentino, so we look around for what's next best."

"If we'd stayed in Magnolia, you wouldn't be thinking such things." Iris wouldn't *dare* if Papa was alive. Laura harbored a heavy sense of having failed her sister. "You wouldn't be doing them."

"Laura, you read those books Beverly Jenkins used to smuggle into the gym our last year in school. I used to get hot just reading them. Didn't they do anything to you?"

"I was embarrassed," Laura confessed. "It seemed so awful."

"It's not," Iris said with conviction. "I wouldn't do it with just anybody—I have to like him a lot. But then I close my eyes and feel. I lie back and wait for that sensational minute when we're really together. I mean, when he's in me and I'm about to go out of my mind if he doesn't set off the fireworks. Oh God," she giggled. "I get all worked up just thinking about it."

"I don't think I ever will," Laura whispered.

"You will," Iris promised. "Just listening to you talk about Bernie Hunter, I know you will."

"Don't you worry about getting pregnant?" Up till now she had merely suspected that Iris was doing "unmentionable" things. "Iris, remember Sally Lou Edmonds back home?"

"Sally Lou was a dumb kid, doing it with dumb boys. I wouldn't do it with any fellow who didn't have a condom in his wallet. I insist on my protection."

"That doesn't sound very romantic," Laura said self-consciously.

"Afterwards it's romantic," Iris told her. "When you're almost jumping out of your skin, you're so excited."


As was often the case, little heat warmed the radiators in their drab apartment on this early March Saturday afternoon. Laura was unconscious of this. She was caught up in the miracle of going out to dinner with Bernie Hunter. She had never gone anywhere alone with a boy. A man, she corrected herself with pride. Bernie was twenty-three.

49

She was glad the office closed at one on Saturdays, though Bernie usually worked until late in the afternoon. She relished having the apartment to herself on this special occasion; Iris had to work until six at Lord & Taylor. She had tried on everything both Iris and she owned before choosing the black flannel chemise that Iris had bought at salesgirl's discount at the store—though it meant Iris skipped lunch for three weeks to pay for it. Iris said it was just like a dress designed by Coco Chanel. With it she'd wear the long string of Woolworth pearls Iris and she had chipped in to buy together.

She shot an anxious glance at the clock as she reached for the black chemise. Bernie and she were meeting under the clock at the Biltmore Hotel at six. She mustn't be late. She pulled the chemise over her head—at this moment grateful that Iris was two inches taller than she because on her the length was not the daringly short favored by her sister. She added the Woolworth pearls that hung down to her waist. She'd taken special care with her makeup. Her reflection in the mirror was reassuring. And she looked at least twenty.

Wrapped in her black winter coat—bought in Klein's basement at the end of last winter at a fraction of its original cost—Laura ran down the three dark, narrow flights of stairs and hurried out of the badly lit hallway into the street. Dusk cloaked the city, lending the streets a pleasing grace. Shop windows were lighted now. As she hurried east on Twenty-third Street, street lamps announced the imminent arrival of evening.

With the stone and terra cotta Flatiron building just ahead, she decided to turn north, intent on dropping for a moment into Lord & Taylor—where Iris worked at the first-floor hosiery counter. She wouldn't try to talk to Iris, just walk past and smile. At Thirty-eighth Street and Fifth Avenue she entered the store, her coat open to show off the black chemise and the pearls. Iris's smile and wink as she looked up at Laura from waiting on a customer gave the added stamp of approval.

When she approached the Biltmore, Laura saw Bernie's face light up as he spied her. Oh, Papa would have liked Bernie Hunter.

"You're looking very pretty." He seemed almost shy now.

"Thank you." She glowed with pleasure.

"Is that coat warm enough?" he asked solicitously because the temperature had dropped within the last twenty minutes.

"Oh, yes." Laura's smile was effervescent.

"Let's walk over to Third Avenue and take the bus up. It takes longer than the 'el,' but it's a nicer ride."

For a few moments she was terrified that she wouldn't know what to talk about with Bernie. Her fear evaporated as they headed towards Third Avenue. It was clear that Bernie considered this a special occasion, was eager to make her laugh. He loved the city but was aware of its shortcomings.

"New Yorkers don't need to go to Turkish baths," he quipped. "Any summer day on the subways they get it for free."

Over ginger-spiced sauerbraten in a modestly priced low-ceilinged restaurant with red-and-white checkered table-cloths, Bernie talked about his father and mother and his growing-up years on Arthur Avenue in the East Bronx.

"I slept in our flat on Arthur Avenue," Bernie reminisced, "but most of my living was done in Crotona Park and in the Washington branch of the public library. I stayed on in the old flat after my parents died. With a series of roommates from City College, all of us in need of a cheap place to live."

Bernie talked in a relaxed manner about his father and mother, and Laura agonized over what to say about her own. How could she tell Bernie that her father had been wrongly convicted of murder and then lynched? Instead, she contrived a story about losing her father in a car accident, sounding wistful when she talked about her beautiful hometown. She hated lying to him. Bernie absorbed every word.

At the end of the evening they lingered long at her front door before reluctantly parting. All the while Laura was terrified that this would be one of those rare Saturday nights when Iris came home early. Bernie would never ask her out again if he met her beautiful sister. And she knew—despite all her vows about never marrying—that she would die if Bernie didn't ask her out again.

For a while Bernie took Laura out to dinner once a week. She was an avid listener to his intense conversations about

51

national and world affairs. He was engrossed in the arrest and subsequent trial of John T. Scopes for violation of the Tennessee law which forbade teaching evolution in the state schools. He was intrigued by talk that an Unemployment Insurance Act was under serious discussion in England. He was upset by the recent election of the seventy-eight-year-old General Paul von Hindenburg as president of Germany.

"Laura, I have a terrible feeling about that old man," Bernie confided. "When he was called up before a Reichstag committee in 1919, to defend his refusal to make peace two years earlier, he fabricated the dastardly lie that the 'victorious German army was stabbed in the back by Jews and socialists.' People are gullible—there are those who believed him."

With the arrival of summer Laura and Bernie spent much of each Saturday and Sunday together. With Bernie she went to all the great museums that make up part of the city's richness, packed picnic lunches that they could share in Central Park or on the beach at Coney Island. To Laura he confided his innermost yearnings to be part of the judicial system.

"Laura, you don't know what happens to the poor who try to use our courts. The calendars are so crowded that a person with little funds has no chance of getting a trial in a civil case in less than two or three years. A plaintiff without money can be thrown out of court if he can't produce security or a bondsman. He can be deprived of his rights because he can't pay the cost for his writ or serving process or even entering his suit. In the middle of a case a poor man or woman can be helpless because he can't afford to pay to bring witnesses, or for a stenographer or printer."

"Bernie, that has to change," Laura said earnestly, her eyes flashing. "With lawyers like you fighting the system, it will surely change."

"Laura, we live in such crazy times," he reiterated. "The corruption that infests this city is unbelievable. Most of our politicians are in the pockets of big-time criminals. A man with money and the right connections can get away with anything—"

"It's not just in New York, Bernie. Even in the small town where I grew up, crooked politicians do whatever they like."

She wavered, yearning to tell Bernie—who wanted to dedicate his life to helping the poor and the innocently accused—about how her father had been railroaded to his death. Yet each time she tried, she could not bring herself to speak the words.

With the first crisp days of autumn Laura was seeing Bernie a night or two midweek in addition to much of every weekend. With Bernie's encouragement she signed up for evening classes at Hunter College—joyful that her classes coincided with his classes at NYU. She was wrestling with what to say if Bernie asked her to marry him—and deep within she knew he was gearing himself to ask her this crucial question. How could she marry Bernie when she had years of college ahead of her and then law school? She'd taken a sacred vow to become a lawyer and clear Papa's name. And how could she leave Iris to live alone?

Bernie and she were not like the "sheiks and shebas" of Iris's social life. They saw each other and nobody else. They were in love. Her face grew hot when she was finally able to make this admission to herself. The most they ever allowed themselves, beyond holding hands, was a good-night kiss in the dark hallway when he brought her home. It was unnerving when she admitted to herself that it wasn't enough.

Bernie met Iris for the first time on the eve of Hanukkah, when Laura invited him to the apartment for dinner. On Jewish holidays he was especially conscious of the loss of his parents. *"Mama always made potato latkes at least twice during Hanukkah. Man, were they good!"* To please their father—when she was twelve—Laura had asked a Jewish neighbor to teach her how to make potato latkes. Tears had come into his eyes when she brought them to the table that first dinner.

Bernie arrived at exactly the scheduled time. He was shy at meeting Iris and yet seemed pleased that this had at last happened. To Bernie, Laura understood, this was an admission that they were "serious." She tried not to be nervous as Bernie and Iris exchanged small talk while she went about bringing the chicken from their tiny oven to the table. The latkes were already made and kept warm under a lid. Carrots nestled in a separate bowl.

"Isn't it wonderful that Wyoming inaugurated a woman governor?" Laura said brightly at the first break in the conversation.

"First time in American history," Bernie said with respect. "A woman in Congress in 1917 and now a woman governor." He sighed. "And here in New York we've elected Jimmy Walker as Mayor. Damn it, the man's a buffoon!"

Laura was startled when Iris announced—while Bernie and she sipped at second cups of tea—that she had to meet a friend uptown. A new Valentino movie had just opened.

"Don't do anything I wouldn't do," she flipped and crossed to the closet for her coat.

"I'll help Laura with the dishes, and then we'll go to a movie," Bernie said self-consciously, anxious to reassure Iris that he "respected" her sister. *Did he guess what Iris did?*

In the midst of drying the dishes Bernie stammered out his hope that Laura would consider marrying him.

"When I've graduated law school and have passed the bar exams," he said hopefully. "I'll be making enough money by then to support a wife."

"Oh, Bernie—" Her face was incandescent. For a poignant moment Laura allowed herself to envision herself as Bernie's wife. Then reality punctured the dream. "It would be wonderful—but I can't marry. Not ever. I have to graduate college—and after that law school—"

"Laura, you never mentioned wanting to be a lawyer." Bernie stared at her in astonishment.

"I guess I was afraid you'd laugh at me." She managed a wry smile. "I know how most people feel about women lawyers—but it's something I have to do."

"Your going to college and law school doesn't have to stand in the way of our getting married," Bernie pursued. "You'll *go* to law school, and one day we'll open up law offices together. *Hunter & Hunter, Attorneys-at-Law.* How does that sound?"

"Like a chunk of heaven," she whispered.

"But you must remember, Laura—" He was suddenly serious. "It's very rough for a woman in the legal field. There are less than eighteen hundred women lawyers in the whole country."

"I *have* to become a lawyer. I don't care what it takes," she said with an intensity that communicated instantly to Bernie. "I have to do it. If eighteen hundred have become lawyers, then why can't I?" Her shaky laugh was a mixture of defiance and anguish. "Oh, Bernie, I have so much to tell you."

They sat at the edge of one studio couch, and Bernie listened with compassion — wincing in pain at intervals — as Laura finally told him about those terrifying last weeks in Magnolia.

"I remember the case," he said angrily. "It was written up in the New York newspapers as an example of the terrible injustice in some Southern courts. But I never connected it with you." She always had pretended Iris and she had come up from South Carolina.

"I wanted to tell you. So many times. Sometimes I thought you might have guessed from my name."

"Laura, in New York?" he teased. "Look in the Manhattan phone directory. You'll see how many Roths are in the city."

"We were the only ones in Magnolia. Bernie, they drove us out of town. We couldn't even stay to sit *shivah* for Papa. That's why I have to be a lawyer some day. To go back home and clear Papa's name."

"We'll do it together," Bernie promised. "Not tomorrow or next week," he pointed out gently, "but in time. But until we can do this, let us be together, Laura. Why do we have to wait until I graduate law school? We'll both work and go to school — but we'll be together."

"I have to think about Iris." Laura struggled to be realistic. *She had responsibilities to her sister.* Papa always said she was the "steady one." "It wouldn't be right for me to leave her alone. All we have in this world is each other. I can't desert her."

Bernie hesitated an instant, then smiled reassuringly and put an arm around Laura's shoulders.

"You won't desert her, Laura. She'll live with us." He reached to pull Laura into his arms, and lay his face against hers. His heart pounded against her as they swayed together. "We'll look for a two-bedroom apartment somewhere here in the city. And when we find it, we'll get married."

"Bernie, are you sure?" Laura pulled away to search his face.

"I'm sure." His hands tightened at her shoulders. She was conscious of a surge of passion enveloping them. Her mouth parted expectantly. But all at once Bernie's hands released her shoulders. "Put on your coat and let's get the hell out of here." His voice was almost brusque. "We'll go to Child's for coffee."

## Chapter 5

Iris emerged from the subway at West Seventy-second Street and on the green light, darted across to Broadway and headed north to Seventy-fourth Street. Amy and Ruth shared a studio apartment in the basement of a brownstone between Broadway and West End Avenue. Was Amy serious about quitting her job at Lord & Taylor if she could be a hatcheck girl at The Bombay Bicycle Club or The Town and Country Club or any of the "speaks" in the Forties or Fifties where rich men visited all the time?

Amy said you had no chance of marrying rich if you didn't meet rich men. That wasn't going to happen to her working at Lord & Taylor. It only happened that way in silly love stories. But Laura would have kittens if Iris quit her job to work at a "speak." *Laura was so unsophisticated.*

Pausing at a red light at Seventy-third Street, Iris pulled her short red cloth coat — rising above her knees — closely about her against the deepening cold of the night. She hated New York winters. They were all right for rich women with fur coats and chauffeured Rolls-Royces and penthouse apartments. They didn't have to slog through dirty slush in leaky galoshes and cloth coats. They didn't live in fourth-floor walk-ups with never enough heat and hot water.

One day she'd wear mink and sable and chinchilla, she vowed with grim intensity while she hurried across the street as the light changed. She'd wear sequins and lamé dresses like Gloria Swanson and Pola Negri wore in their movies. She'd shop at couturiers like Worth and Poiret and Lanvin in Paris. She'd be rich and famous and spend winters in Palm Beach.

Caught up in daydreaming, she approached the brownstone where Amy and Ruth lived, aware that behind the fading chintz drapes that masked the two basement windows the party was already in full swing. A phonograph record wailed out the latest popular tune, "Show Me the Way to Go Home." Laughter, laced with the tinkle of ice in glasses, blended with the music. Despite Prohibition somebody always showed up with a bottle of gin or rum.

Amy opened the door, pulling Iris into the apartment with a welcoming grin.

"What took you so long?" Amy chided.

"I had to stay for dinner and meet some flat tire my sister is stuck on. I left as quickly as I could."

"We've got enough hooch to drown in," Amy babbled happily.

"I'd rather drink it," Iris laughed.

In a corner of the room a couple were wrapped in a passionate embrace. Other guests sprawled across the pair of studio couches and fondled drinks.

"Hey, put on something hot," a strikingly handsome young man—a stranger to Iris—ordered the tender of the phonograph. "Put me in the mood!" And then his eyes settled on Iris. She gave him her sexy Pola Negri smile, aware of a sudden stirring *down there*. He wasn't dark and smoldering like Rudy Valentino or Ricardo Cortez, but he would have melted an ice princess.

"Who's that?" Iris whispered.

"Lance Andrews. He's an actor."

"Where did you meet an actor?" Iris asked, surrendering her coat and noting that Lance Andrews was inspecting every inch of her encased in the above-the-knee, low-cut, black-fringed dress. Her unfashionably voluptuous breasts were flattened by a bustbinder. "He's a real sheik."

"He's got a small part in a new play by Noel Coward." Amy glowed.

"Where did you meet him?" Iris persisted. His eyes were on her legs now, displayed to just above the knee in flesh-colored rayon stockings.

"Remember I played sick yesterday to go see about a job at that 'speak' I told you about?" *The job Amy didn't get*, Iris remembered. *Amy really wasn't that attractive*, she judged subconsciously. *Could I have gotten it?*

"I was feeling so lousy I went into that drugstore in the Astor Hotel for coffee. Well," she said with an air of revelation, "that's where all the young actors and actresses looking

58

for jobs hang around. He was sitting on the next stool to me. We started to talk. I told him we were having a party tonight and invited him."

Lance Andrews was walking towards them. "Introduce me to your friend," he ordered Amy without taking his eyes off Iris.

"Iris Adams, Lance Andrews. Now excuse me." Smiling archly, Amy sidled away. She was having a heavy romance with a married man—nobody else interested her at the moment.

Lance dropped an arm about her waist. "Let's go sit in that empty corner. Where have you been all my life?"

Lance—who had been born and raised in Pittsburgh— talked with unexpected bitterness about the difficulties of breaking into the New York theater. Iris was content to listen. Lance Andrews, a Broadway actor, was interested in her!

"I've been in this town five years. I must have auditioned for five hundred parts. I've had bits in four plays." His face tightened. "At regular intervals I'm a soda jerk at the Mayflower drugstore. You have to know somebody to make it big in show business. Go to the right parties. Eat at Sardi's, get ossified at the Twenty-One Club."

"Amy said you have a part in the new Noel Coward play." She lifted one eyebrow with an air of polite inquiry. She'd never even been inside a Broadway theater.

"A rotten three-line part," he said contemptuously. "I'm good. That's not boasting. I know I'm good. Jed Harris said I was good," he pointed out in triumph. "Coward himself said I might be terrific one day."

"You're too young to be cynical," Iris protested. "Cynical" was her latest "new word."

"I love your accent," he murmured, his eyes fastened to her low neckline—the bustbinder not entirely successful in achieving its intended goal. "Where're y'all from?" he asked in mock exaggeration.

"Georgia." Iris knew the charm of a Southern accent on a typical New York male. Her smile was dazzling.

"What's a fair flower of the South doing in this crazy town?"

"My father died in a car crash." She had early adopted

59

Laura's explanation. "My sister and I were alone. We decided to come up North." She was *glad* that old bitch, Mrs. Tannenbaum, had driven them out of town. "Nothing ever happens down there." She shuddered delicately.

"Do we have to stay here?" Lance adopted a stage whisper.

"Not really," she shrugged, her eyes bright. "What did you have in mind?"

"I know this gin mill in the West Fifties that's really the berries. And the apartment I share with another actor is right upstairs." His eyes smoldered as effectively as Rudolph Valentino's. "He's out on tour with *They Knew What They Wanted.*"

"Do you know what you want?" she flipped.

"Isn't it obvious?" He dropped a hand on her knee.

Iris slid from his side and stood up. "Let me get my coat."

They left the party and took a taxi down to West Fifty-second Street. The traffic was suddenly highly congested for a residential crosstown street.

"Half the houses on this block are 'speaks,' " Lance chuckled while they waited for the taxi to move ahead. "I hear Mrs. Cornelius Vanderbilt III — she has that monstrosity of a palace between Fifth and Sixth — curses the cops nightly for not closing them all up."

"Isn't the Twenty-One Club on this block?" Iris asked curiously. She knew it by name only. It was the most expensive, most exclusive, and most fashionable "speak" in all New York.

"It's here." Lance was almost brusque. "And when I move up from my three-line part to the lead, I'll take you there."

The taxi dropped them off in front of a decaying brownstone. Lance prodded her down three steps to a metal-reinforced wooden door. He rang the bell while Iris waited expectantly. First a light appeared above the door. Then a grille opened to reveal an appraising eye.

"Hank knows me," Lance said casually. "I'm in 3-E upstairs."

"Hold it, buster," a terse voice ordered.

Another eye appeared, winked. Suddenly the door swung open. Lance patted Iris on the rump. "Inside, baby."

They went through the usual series of doors and then arrived at the bar. There was a restaurant beyond the bar, but Iris was certain they would not linger there. They settled themselves at a small corner table and ordered drinks. Under the table Lance's knee was pressing Iris's.

"The stuff they give you here is garbage," Lance warned, "but Hank takes my IOUs."

"Tell me about the play you're in," Iris coaxed. "I've never known an actor before."

"It's another of Noel Coward's bits of fluff." His smile dismissed it as inconsequential. "I'd like to get a role I can really dig into, but today nobody gives a damn for serious theater. Oh, once in a while something worthwhile comes along. Thank God for Eugene O'Neill."

"Did you ever think about acting in movies?"

"That's pure shit," he said contemptuously. "There's a lot of money in Hollywood but no talent."

"I bet you'd be great in pictures." She was serious. He was good-looking and he had sex appeal. Wouldn't it be wild to be married to a movie star? "And don't knock money." Maybe Laura would settle for a poor slob like Bernie Hunter. *Not Iris Adams.*

"I don't knock it." He grinned. "It's what puts spice in my life. That and other things—" A hand crept under the table now, settled on her knee, fondled. "I knew the minute I set eyes on you that you'd be a hot baby."

"I have to be home by midnight," she warned. "Tomorrow's a working day."

"So we'll swig down our drinks and cut out," he promised.

Lance lived in a fifteen-dollar-a-month studio-and-kitchenette apartment with walls papered with theater posters. There were a pair of studio couches, two cheap maple chests, a club chair, and a phonograph that sat on the floor. Records filled a sagging orange crate.

"What would you like to hear?" Lance asked, helping her out of her coat and allowing one hand to caress her rump.

"Have you got 'Lady, Be Good'?"

"If you'll be good to me?"

"I'll be *terrific* to you," she boasted, slightly giddy from her one watered-down drink downstairs. *Lance Andrews was special.* "Provided you observe the rule."

"What rule?" His eyes were wary.

"I don't want to get pregnant."

"I'll be equipped," he laughed and reached into the crate to find the record. "Throw back the covers and get comfortable."

While Lance put the record on the phonograph, Iris pulled her dress over her head with one sweep and tossed it across the club chair, shed her teddy and pearls.

"Don't ever wear one of those things," Lance laughed and helped her out of her bustbinder. The Gershwin music flooded the room in potent invitation. "What crazy fashion designer decided women should be built like men?" His large muscular hands reached to imprison the rich spill of her breasts.

"A fashion designer who hates women," Iris guessed. Knowing that the sight of her nude except for stockings and pumps was arousing him to frenzy.

"Shall we cut the opening act and get down to the real show? I don't have to tell you what you do to me."

"I'm available," she drawled and draped herself on the studio couch in a seductive pose while he began to strip. What were Laura and Bernie doing this minute? Probably sitting in a movie and holding hands. *What a waste.*

"What's that perfume you're wearing?" he asked, lifting himself above her.

"The new Richard Hudnut," she said. The cologne — she couldn't afford the perfume.

Her hands closed in at his shoulders while his mouth burrowed at her throat and a hand moved between her thighs. To the provocative music and lyrics of "Lady, Be Good," Lance's mouth trailed from throat to one taut-nippled breast, to pelvis. All senses alert, Iris waited expectantly, remembering scraps of whispered girlish conversations about sexual variations. Lance Andrews wasn't one of those one-tune men she'd known so far. Tonight her education was being extended.


In flannel nightgown and robe Laura huddled under a blanket and sipped hot tea against the night cold because by ten o'clock the heat in their brownstone was off for the night. Fighting yawns though her mind was too active for sleep, she waited impatiently for Iris to come home. At the sound of her sister's familiar light knock Laura hurried from the studio couch to the door.

"You'll never guess who I met tonight," Iris bubbled, managing to pull off her coat and kick off her shoes simultaneously. "An actor named Lance Andrews. He's in a Broadway play."

"Iris, Bernie and I are getting married!" Laura flung her arms about her sister in a burst of exuberance.

Iris was suddenly somber.

"You're awfully young."

"I'll be seventeen in April," Laura scolded. "Lots of girls get married that young. And you'll live with us," she hurried to reassure Iris. "Bernie doesn't mind a bit."

"No," Iris rejected. "You and Bernie can live in his apartment up in the Bronx. I'll find somebody who'll move in here with me." She sighed. "I can't pay the rent alone on my salary."

"Iris, I won't marry Bernie unless you move in with us." Laura's happy mood ebbed away. The prospect of Iris on her own was alarming. "That's the way it has to be. Bernie understands that."

"Laura, that's nuts!"

"I'll tell Bernie I can't marry him," Laura said quietly. She was in love with Bernie, but Iris was her sister. She'd promised Papa to look after Iris. Even if it meant losing Bernie. But the prospect of his walking out of her life was devastating. "I'll tell him we can't get married until—" she searched her mind, "until I'm twenty."

"You really want to marry him?" Iris asked.

"Yes—" Laura's face was luminous. "I never thought I'd feel that way ever. Bernie's wonderful." Not one of Iris's drugstore cowboys.

"Then marry him," Iris pushed. "I'll be okay."

"No," Laura said in what Iris always called her "bulldog voice."

"I couldn't stand living way up in the Bronx," Iris sulked. "Spending forty-five minutes twice a day on the stupid subways."

"We'll look for a place in Manhattan." Laura felt a surge of relief. Iris wouldn't fight it. "Bernie said it would be too much to travel to the Bronx when we're going to school three nights a week."

Iris left the apartment-hunting to Laura and Bernie. She would move in with them, sure—but that didn't mean she'd stay there. She was ambivalent about Laura's imminent marriage. She had envisioned Laura and herself marrying rich, important men. Living the kind of lives that would make everybody in Magnolia turn green with envy. Bernie was okay, even kind of good looking—but he'd never be one of the richest men in the country. Still, Laura would be set for life. She wouldn't have to worry about her little sister.

While Laura and Bernie spent every available moment in search of an apartment in the growingly difficult housing situation, Iris spent her free time with Lance. He'd told her how he'd been orphaned by the time he was five, had been shifted from one set of relatives to another through his growing-up years. At high school graduation five years ago he had hitch-hiked to New York, vowing to be rich and famous before he was twenty-five. He'd read every play written in the past forty years, talked with mesmerizing intensity about his contempt for "commercial theater." His voice filled with reverence when he spoke of Stanislavsky and the Moscow Art Theater.

Rehearsal money was low, but at the end of his second week in rehearsal Lance took Iris to a late supper at Sardi's rather than to The Tavern on West Forty-eighth Street where the owner allowed "regulars" to run up tabs when their funds were low.

While Lance complained about the long, boring hours of sitting around at rehearsal to wait for his three lines, Iris watched the stream of Broadway actors and actresses arriving at Sardi's after their performances. She was enthralled when the glamorous star of a new play that had just opened that evening strode in with her entourage, to be greeted by loud applause from the diners.

"She's such a bitch," Lance whispered in amusement. "I hear the cast is ready to pitch in to hire somebody to bump her off."

"She wears such gorgeous clothes," Iris whispered.

"So would you if you had her salary. But the word is she's

heading for Hollywood when the play closes."

"Who's that?" Iris spotted a vaguely familiar face. From the pages of *Vogue*, she recalled.

"Marilyn Miller," Lance said, "and the man at the next table is—"

"John Barrymore!" *She, Iris Adams, was sitting in the same room with John Barrymore!*

From Sardi's Iris and Lance walked up to Fifty-second Street to his apartment.

"I can't stay too late," she warned while he prodded her up the narrow stairs. "Tomorrow's a work day."

"I'm going to miss you those seven weeks on the road," he whispered hotly at the apartment door.

"I'll miss you," she said truthfully. She had never known anybody like Lance. He vowed someday he'd see his name up in lights—and she believed him. Wherever they went, women turned to look at Lance.

"Go shower while I fix a drink," he ordered, thrusting the door open. "We've got to make up for those seven weeks I'll be out on the road." His eyes were dark with promise.

Lance walked into the kitchen. Iris dropped her coat on a chair, headed for the bathroom, and turned on the "hot" faucet in order to steam up the room. Now she began to strip. Lance kept perfumed soap and dusting powder on a wall shelf—especially for her, he insisted. For a moment—while steam began to take off the chill—she wondered about the other girls before her during the five years Lance had been in New York.

"Don't stay in there all day," Lance called with a hint of promise in his voice. "There's gin and me waiting for you out here."

"Five minutes," she stipulated, pulling on a shower cap, enjoying the knowledge that she made him passionate. He'd even taught her how to take care of herself—"so we don't have to have that goddamn rubber between us."

With an exhilarating sensuality she soaped herself, then moved under the hot spray until every vestige of perfume soap was gone. She stepped out of the tub and reached for the thick towel—that bore the name of a plush Chicago hotel—to pat herself dry. Liberally dusting herself with the Elizabeth Arden powder, the faint scent clinging to her, she dropped the towel to the floor and reached for the door. She knew Lance's ritual.

"I Want To Be Happy," a huge three-year-old hit, was playing softly on the phonograph. Lance stood in the center of the room, dancing naked with a filled cocktail glass in each hand.

"Come make me happy, baby," he ordered, holding out a drink. "You have such sex appeal," he drawled. "You ought to be a Ziegfeld girl."

"I'm not tall enough," she demurred, but excitement coursed through her as she imagined herself in the role.

"In the three-inch heels those girls wear you'd be tall enough," he insisted.

They sipped at their drinks, inspecting each other with blatant passion. *Could* she be a Ziegfeld girl? Somebody said they made a hundred dollars a week. She'd be too scared to try. And Laura would just die.

"Some day we'll guzzle champagne," he said, taking her glass from her and depositing it along with his own atop a chest. "The best."

Then came the signal for them to "get the show on the road." The record was stuck in the groove. He lifted the arm of the phonograph and returned to her. Her tongue darted about her full lower lip while her eyes focused on his pelvis. Wow, was he hot! She was conscious of a muscle low within her moving in response.

He took her face between his hands and brought his mouth down hard on hers, his tongue thrusting between her already parted lips. She placed her hands at his hips as he moved tauntingly against her. Damn, why did he have to play games? *She wanted him in her right this second.*

"Torrid," he approved when his mouth finally left hers. "That's my baby."

With one playful push he shoved her along the length of the studio couch, sat at the edge and ran his hands down her body. Up and down. He knew he was driving her up the wall. Her own hands reached to fondle him, impatient to break his control. Later they could play games.

"And what does my baby want?" he mocked.

"You," she said. "Lance—"

"All yours," he promised and dropped his mouth to a hardening nipple while she murmured approval.

"Don't bite," she reproached as her body arched beneath him.

She closed her eyes as his mouth slid down from her breasts to toy briefly at her navel and she cried out softly as he reached his ultimate quarry and probed deeply with his tongue.

"Lance, now," she gasped imperiously. "Now!"

She sobbed in relief when he lifted himself above her and the hard mass invaded. They rocked together, perspiring despite the chill of the room, reaching for the cataclysmic moment of total union.

"Oh Lance," she murmured when they at last lay motionless, spent. His face pressed against her shoulder, his body heavy on hers. "You are sensational."

"Don't go away," he teased. "That's only the first act."


In mid-February — when it seemed they must settle for an apartment in Brooklyn or the East Bronx, which Iris loudly rejected — Bernie ran into a City College friend whose parents were giving up their long-held apartment on the Lower East Side to join the rush to Florida.

"We're not going to Palm Beach," Mr. Tarlow explained to Laura and Bernie while his wife brewed tea in the kitchen and hovered over poppyseed cookies due momentarily to come out of the oven. "To Miami," he said with an air of great anticipation. Half the population of the country was rushing to Miami, Laura thought in gentle amusement. She'd read somewhere that Atlanta was so upset about this migration that the city had organized a campaign to keep their citizens from defecting.

"We won't have to worry about another cold winter." Mrs. Tarlow's voice drifted in from the kitchen. "And we'll have a place to live down there. My sister and her husband bought eight years ago — before the prices all went *meshuggah*."

"They could sell for a fortune," Mr. Tarlow said. "But if they sold, where would they live?"

"It must be a wonderful satisfaction to own property." Bernie's tone was longing. "A piece of earth that belongs to you."

Over tea and golden poppyseed cookies the four talked

about the pleasures of being a homeowner. Laura felt a rush of pride in Bernie's knowledge as he talked about how Henry Flagler had discovered Florida back in the early nineties and had built a real-estate empire that eventually was to reach from Palm Beach to Key West.

"Then around 1920 Carl Fisher started building Miami Beach. He's created a great resort out of a swamp. He built land in the water. Star Island and Belle Island. But I'm sure he didn't anticipate—nor want—the real-estate mania that's taken over in the last two years." Laura sensed that if Bernie was not so dedicated to becoming a lawyer, he would have gone into the real-estate business. He had the kind of vision that drove men like Flagler and Fisher to create cities.

"In Florida," Mr. Tarlow told Bernie and Laura, "my brother-in-law says they call Carl Fisher the 'King of Miami Beach.'"

"But the boom in Miami is already slipping," Bernie warned. "The sucker money is disappearing."

After an hour's visit Laura and Bernie wished the Tarlows well and left their apartment in jubilant spirits. They would have a place to live. They could set their wedding date.

"Let's sightsee a while," Bernie said when they emerged into the February coldness. "Then we'll go over to Ratner's on Delancey Street for supper." He reached for her hand. "We can afford to celebrate on the day we've found our first apartment."

As they roamed about the streets of the Lower East Side, Laura remembered Papa talking about the brief period when Mama and he lived here. Her boss talked fondly about such stellar Yiddish restaurants as Moskowitz and Lupowitz, the Cafe Royal, and Ratner's. The secretaries talked about the bargains to be found at the Lower East Side pushcarts and the small crowded shops. Bernie had bittersweet memories of his early childhood somewhere on Hester Street, before his parents made their way up to the East Bronx, escaping the noise, the congestion, the painful summer heat of their first home in America.

With tender amusement Bernie watched Laura's astonishment at this almost totally Jewish neighborhood. She tried to conceal her unease, a spiraling sense of inadequacy. She knew about the basic Jewish holidays. And in Mama's absence Papa had lighted the Sabbath candles every Friday at sundown. Papa had talked with ethnic pride about such New York Jews as Bernard Baruch and Isidore Strauss—who had moved up from peddling to owning his own tiny store in Talbotton, Georgia and had gone on to found the great Macy's at Herald Square in New York. But she was not steeped in Jewish lore as were many New York Jews.

"My Georgia *shiksa*," Bernie laughed when Laura admitted that she had never tasted lox or gefilte fish. "You'll learn."

Laura and Bernie searched happily for the bare essentials in an inexpensive furniture store that offered the new "easy-little-payments" installment plan, though Laura had some misgivings about incurring debts. She remembered her father's conviction that people should live within their means. But Bernie insisted that the furniture in his apartment— bought thirty years ago by his parents on Grand Street—was too decrepit to make the trip from Arthur Avenue to Jefferson Street.

They scheduled their wedding for the last Friday afternoon in the month, with Weinstein, Schiffman, and Elkin agreeing to their taking the afternoon off. They would be married at City Hall because that was the easiest and least expensive way.

"Later we'll be married by a rabbi," Bernie promised.

The wedding date had been chosen at Iris's suggestion. Since the rent on the Twenty-second Street apartment was paid for the week, Iris could spend the weekend there and allow Laura and Bernie to have the Jefferson Street apartment for their "honeymoon."

"On our first anniversary," Bernie vowed, "we'll go to Niagara Falls for a whole week."

"In February?" Laura laughed. "We'll need ice-skates."

At agonizing intervals Laura reproached herself for being selfish in marrying Bernie. She ought to think only about the vow she had made when Papa died to take care of her sister. *She wasn't doing that.*

Yet Laura knew she couldn't deny herself the joy of marrying Bernie even if it meant she was thinking of herself instead of Iris and Papa. Papa would have respected and loved him because he had such deep feeling for people and their needs. He was dedicating his life to the cause of justice for the poor. Bernie would help her clear Papa's name. They'd work together for that — when they were both admitted to the bar and practicing as attorneys. She wasn't deserting Papa by marrying Bernie.

Iris called in sick that Friday so that she could be with Laura and Bernie at City Hall. Bernie was bringing a college buddy as his "best man." Iris, Laura said sentimentally, was her "maid of honor."

"Sugar, do you know how long it is since I've been a 'maid'?" Iris giggled and Laura frowned in reproach.

Somewhat ill at ease, Laura and Bernie left the office at noon. Bernie had already transferred his belongings to the Jefferson Street apartment. He would dress, meet his friend, and together they would pick up Laura and Iris. Laura knew Bernie harbored a wistful hope that Iris and his friend Mannie — a bright young accountant — would be attracted to each other. She knew, also, that he would be disappointed. All Iris talked about was Lance Andrews. He was due back from his road tour in two weeks.

Laura was touched to discover that Iris had gone to a florist shop and bought a tiny cluster of pink rosebuds to serve as a bridal bouquet. She knew Iris just managed to survive from paycheck to paycheck. She had not allowed herself to buy anything new for her wedding except a pair of Holeproof silk-faced stockings because she was intimidated by the weekly installment payments on their furniture.

Laura was overwhelmed when Iris presented her with a lace-trimmed black chiffon nightgown bought at Lord & Taylor — "at my salesgirl's discount."

"Iris, do I dare wear it?" she whispered with a proper blend of shock and anticipation.

"You'll wear it," Iris insisted. "Men love sheer black nightgowns."

Laura and Bernie were married in the typical two-minute ceremony at City Hall. Afterwards Mannie treated them to an early dinner at an Italian restaurant in Greenwich Village, where the food was good, the atmosphere romantic, and the prices sensible. With a knowing glance at Mannie — while he still happily alternated between zabaglione and espresso — Iris suggested that they take the subway together since she was unfamiliar with the downtown subways.

"Sure—" Mannie's face lighted for an instant, then he understood that Iris was contriving to leave the bride and groom on their own. "In a few minutes." He dug enthusiastically into his zabaglione again.

Iris was relieved that the rush hour had passed, and they found seats at the end of the car and settled down to the noisy ride. When Iris made it clear that she was hurrying to a date, Mannie was philosophical.

"Then I'll go straight on up to the Bronx. You don't need me to walk you to your house?"

"No, thanks, you stay on the train." She wished he wouldn't look at her with those cow eyes. She hadn't been out with anybody since Lance left on tour. But Mannie could become a pest if she took him home with her. Better a cold shower, she told herself, than having to brush off Mannie afterwards.

As the train rumbled uptown, Mannie reminisced about his days at City College with Bernie. "I don't know why we loved the damn school the way we did. It was ugly and rundown. The best thing about it," he said with respect, "was Professor Morris Raphael Cohen. Bernie worshipped him. Most of us did."

It was kind of crazy to think of Laura as married. *Her little sister.* Bernie and Laura would go to that shitty little flat on Jefferson Street, and it would be beautiful to them because they would share a bed. In a way she was glad Laura was married. That left *her* free.

"I think it's terrific the way both Bernie and Laura plan to be lawyers. Don't you?" Mannie sounded wistful.

"Sure," Iris agreed.

"Did you ever think of going on to college?" Mannie was curious.

"Only if they guaranteed I'd learn how to become a millionaire," she flipped. "I've got expensive tastes."

Then the train pulled into the Twenty-third Street station. "Oh, here's my stop," she said with relief. "See you around."

Iris rose to her feet and rushed up the stairs towards the exit and out into the cold night air. It would be strange to be alone in the apartment. She could have invited Mannie up.

She knew he was all worked up. It was nutty the way she was getting all hot and bothered thinking about Laura and Bernie in bed.

She was glad Laura was married, she reiterated silently. Laura would forget all that garbage about going through college and on to law school. Within a year she'd be pregnant. Then she'd be all wrapped up in Bernie and the baby. Not for her. *Not for Iris Adams.*

She reached for her key as she approached the house. She'd pack up everything Sunday morning. Laura and Bernie would come over to help her move. She was suddenly restless at the thought of an empty weekend. She'd cut herself off from everybody since Lance walked into her life. To hell with that. In the morning she'd call Amy.

She hurried up the dark staircase despite a strange reluctance to go into the apartment. In all her life she had never spent a whole night away from Laura. Not true, she mocked herself. But when she was out all night — partying, she knew she'd come home and find Laura there.

Approaching the apartment door she saw a note shoved beneath. She frowned. The landlady knew she wasn't moving until Sunday. The rent was paid up for February. She reached for the scrap of folded paper beneath the door and then unlocked it. Inside she read the brief message.

"Guess what? I'm home. Call me. I've missed you like hell! LANCE."

## Chapter 6

Iris closed herself in the phone booth at the United Cigar Store, dropped a nickel into the slot, and dialed. Lance and his roommate had their own phone—a business expense, Lance said. She waited impatiently for him to answer. *He was so anxious to see her he had come all the way down to the apartment.*

"Lance here," his voice announced in a provocative drawl.

"What the hell are you doing in New York already?" According to his postcards the play was doing well.

"The bastard director wouldn't give me room to play the part the way I wanted to play it. But I got a week's salary and train fare home. Come up and console me."

"I'll be there in half an hour." Iris was jubilant at this turn of events. Belatedly she realized that Lance must be depressed at losing the part. Or was he? He'd bitched all along about playing such a small part.

Iris rushed back to the apartment to change from her moderately conservative "maid of honor" dress into the short black fringed chemise that Lance said made her look sexier than Clara Bow. Why wouldn't he take a crack at Hollywood? Maybe she would go out there with him if he did. Laura was married. *She* was free as a bird.

Lance opened the door at her knock and drew her into a heated embrace. "Oh baby, I've missed you—" He reached to help her out of her coat. "I have a flask of gin. Want a drink?"

"Later," she parried. Had Lance been sleeping with some girl in the company all these weeks? Anyway, so what? Now he was here. "At the moment I have other needs."

"That's my girl." His smile was dazzling. "I'll help you take off your clothes," he said seductively.

Later—much later—they sprawled on the studio couch and sipped at slightly warm gin because Lance had no ice in his icebox. The phonograph was blaring, "I found a million-dollar baby in a five-and-ten-cent store."

"What's been happening in all the weeks I've been away?" His eyes were appraising.

"The usual," she shrugged. She'd never tell him she hadn't been near anybody else in all that time. "My sister got married this afternoon. At City Hall."

He lifted an eyebrow. "Then you don't have to go home tonight."

"Not if you promise me my teddy and stockings will dry on the radiator before I have to go to work tomorrow morning," she giggled.

"If they don't, we'll put them in the oven." He sat up. "If your sister got married this afternoon, you didn't go to work?"

"No. I called in sick." Iris read his mind. "And maybe I'll still be sick tomorrow."

"Sensational," he approved. "We'll make up for all the weeks I was away."


Though Lance worried about his financial state—*God knows when I'll land another part*—he took Iris to Reuben's for cheesecake and coffee late the next evening.

"It's important to be seen," he murmured when they were seated and had given their order to the standard Reuben's grouchy waiter. "I can't afford Sardi's right now, but Reuben's is the next-best place to be seen."

"Lance, you're good," she encouraged, covering his hand with hers. Without ever having seen him in a play she was convinced of this. "You'll find a part."


On their second evening as man and wife Bernie took Laura over to Delancey Street for a dairy dinner at Ratner's. His knee pressing against hers under the table, he talked about his parents, who had moved to the East Bronx to give their only child a better life. But through the years he had sensed that they missed the excitement of the Lower East Side Jewish culture.

"I think for my parents," he said seriously, "assimilation

was frightening. They wanted to be Americans, yes. They were fiercely proud of being Americans. But they also were scared that somewhere along the road their Jewish roots would be lost."

"Iris and I always knew we were Jewish, but we didn't really think about it." Laura searched her mind for the words to explain her growing-up years in Georgia. "I mean, it was part of us—but kind of beneath the surface. We observed the Jewish holidays, and Papa made it clear that he didn't want us to go out with boys who were not Jewish. And we knew how much the Ku Klux Klan hates Jews—" All at once she was cold and trembling remembering those awful final days in Magnolia. "But we didn't understand until Papa was accused of murdering that little girl that folks in town hated Jews."

"Laura, that's not true of everybody in Magnolia." Bernie reached across the table to take her hand in his. "These terrible things are always the work of a few insane fanatics. They whip the population into a frenzy. It's like a disease that runs out of control."

"Even the Jewish families were afraid to come near us." Laura hurled out her words with fresh rage. "I told you about Mrs. Tannenbaum—"

"Mrs. Tannenbaum was an arrogant, insensitive old bitch." He shook his head in distaste. "But you told me a Jewish committee fought to bring new lawyers into town," he reminded gently. "They *had* to remain undercover, Laura—they were frightened for their lives. And you told me your father asked his lawyer to help you settle out of Magnolia. He knew you couldn't survive in that town."

"Bernie, I wish you could see Magnolia." Suddenly she was caught up in a surge of homesickness. "It's so beautiful and quiet and peaceful. Most of the time," she amended bitterly. "I'd never before seen it like it was then."

"We won't always live on Jefferson Street," Bernie promised. Without her saying a word, Laura marveled, Bernie knew how she missed the sunlight and grass and flowers of Magnolia. He knew she hated the noisy, crowded streets, the pushcarts, the gagging aromas of chickens being singed, fat rendered. "In little more than a year I'll be out of law school. Mr. Weinstein says they'll put me on the firm's legal staff. I'll get a big raise. I'll stay with them until you're through law school and have passed the bar exams," Bernie plotted. "Then we'll open our own office."

"Bernie, can it happen like that?" She searched his eyes for reassurance.

"It *will* happen like that," he said with conviction. "We'll *make* it happen."

On Sunday evening—as planned—Laura and Bernie met Iris at the old apartment to help her move to Jefferson Street. Laura was conscious of a sense of relief that Iris and she again would be under the same roof. Together—like Papa said. But tonight when Bernie reached for her beneath the mound of blankets, she was uncomfortable in the knowledge that her sister was on the other side of the thin wall that divided the two minuscule bedrooms.

Laura and Bernie settled down into a routine that revolved around work, night school, and muted lovemaking. Many nights—long after Bernie lay asleep beside her—Laura waited for the sound of Iris's key in the door. Only then would she allow herself to sleep.

She worried that Iris was seeing so much of that actor-friend, Lance Andrews. In late May—on the night she lit the *yortsayt* candle for her father—Iris came home all excited because Lance was about to start rehearsals in a new play in which he had an important part. After the rehearsal period the company would go on the road for seven weeks. Iris was sure he'd become a star once the play opened in New York.

When Lance's company left for the out-of-town tour, Iris came home directly from work most nights, lounged around the tiny, constricting apartment over the weekend. Laura knew that Bernie secretly chafed at their lack of privacy. Any show of affection between them now had to be confined to their bedroom.

Bernie was much less secretive about his outrage at Iris's habit, acquired since leaving Magnolia, of littering the tiny apartment with sweaters, fake jewelry, shoes, stockings, all left wherever she tossed them. At home, Laura acknowledged to herself, Papa—loving as he was—would not have allowed such behavior.

"Laura, talk to her," Bernie railed repeatedly. "You're not her maid! And why can't she help with the cooking and

76

cleaning? You work, too."

Anxious to alleviate the tensions between Bernie and Iris, Laura hurried to pick up after Iris before Bernie noticed the latest littering. When Bernie offered to wash supper dishes, mop the kitchen floor, or sweep, she lovingly pushed him aside. How could she let Bernie do these things when Iris lay around the house reading her magazines or listening to their new radio?

Iris was furious that Bernie was adamant about her not smoking in the communal areas of the apartment. She refused to believe Laura's explanation that smoking caused breathing difficulties for Bernie. She also derided his warnings—when she talked about the popular speakeasies—that bootleg liquor was causing blindness and death.

"Newspapers trying to be sensational," she quoted Lance's reaction to grim statistics.

To Iris, Laura unhappily realized, Bernie was a "flat tire," a "pushover." He'd never become rich or famous, Iris's criteria for a suitable husband.

With each passing day Iris seemed to grow more short-tempered. Laura asked herself if Iris was in love with Lance. She just said he was "swell," "hep," "keen." Never that she was in love with him. Did Lance know that Iris was Jewish? Would Iris ever marry out of their faith? Of course, she was Iris Adams now and talked airily about being an atheist.

On a sweltering night when Bernie remained late at the office, Laura hovered at a window studying for her evening summer-school course. Iris, too, was late in coming home and she was alone in the apartment. In this heat—with loud querulous conversations reverberating off the fire escape and intensifying the street noises—Laura felt no hunger.

She thought wistfully of summers in Magnolia, where the torpid valley heat could be brutal. But they could sit out on the porch in a rocker in the evening with a tall glass of iced tea and wait for a breeze. It was quiet there on the porch – none of the screeching of tired kids who should be asleep but couldn't sleep in the badly ventilated boxes that passed for bedrooms. In Magnolia the air was sweet with the scent of roses and honeysuckle. Lightning bugs darted about the lawns with the arrival of dusk. Somewhere along the block a soft Southern voice often scolded an exuberant child for trying to catch a lightning bug to be imprisoned briefly in a jar.

*"You wouldn't like it if somebody stuffed you in a jar!"*

She started at the sound of the doorbell.

"Iris?" she called, hurrying to the door. Bernie wouldn't be home for at least another hour.

"Yeah—" Iris sounded impatient. She was hot and tired from being packed in the subway, Laura sympathized.

"I've already sliced some tomatoes and cucumbers and I'll open up a can of salmon," Laura greeted her consolingly. "And there's a pitcher of iced tea in the icebox."

"Do you have to sound so damn cheerful?" Iris scowled as she walked into the room. Shoulders drooping, her dress clung wetly between her shoulder blades.

"Take off your stockings. And put on that pretty cotton chemise you bought on Orchard Street last week," Laura encouraged, heading for the kitchen.

By the time Laura had a cool supper on the table, Iris had changed to the chemise and was trailing barefoot into the kitchen. Her face grim, she dropped into a chair and reached for her fork.

"Hell, I can't eat." She threw down the fork. "Laura, you've got to help me—"

"What's the matter?" Laura stared anxiously.

"I hate working in Lord and Taylor. I have to find another job." Then she burst out sobbing. "No, that's not it," she paused. "Oh Laura, I'm pregnant."

Laura's throat constricted in alarm. Iris was always so confident it could never happen to *her.*

"Are you sure?"

"Of course, I'm sure," Iris sniffled back. "I'm almost three weeks late." She slumped over the table, scared yet defiant. "And Lance is down in Baltimore or some place. Laura, you've got to find a doctor for me."

"What about your friend Amy?" How would she find a doctor for Iris? Laura's mind was in chaos. How much would it cost? A lot of money, that they didn't have. "Would Amy know somebody?"

"Maybe if she was in town," Iris conceded. "But she got sick of New York and went home. She said she'd write—but she hasn't so far. I don't know where her folks live. Laura, you know these women in the house—you talk to everybody," she pursued with a hint of frenzy. "Lots of girls get pregnant—and then they aren't anymore. You've got to find me a doctor."

"Lance and you could get married," Laura tried soothingly.

"God, Laura, neither one of us wants a baby." Her voice was raised in exasperation. "I'm not even nineteen yet. I don't want to be tied down with a kid."

"Will Lance pay for the doctor?" Laura struggled to be practical.

"Just find one," Iris repeated. "Then I'll worry about the money."

*Iris pregnant? Iris having an abortion? Girls died from that.* Laura felt sick at the thought of some doctor scraping away what would have been Iris's baby. "Mrs. Katz down on the second floor said something once about a woman doctor around the corner," Laura said slowly. "She'll be sitting on the stoop in this heat."

"Don't tell her it's for me," Iris warned. "Say it's for a girl in your office."

While Laura went downstairs, Iris put away the food. Lance and she had gotten careless, she reproached herself. In their frenzy they didn't remember that one of them had to take precautions. She wouldn't be put in this kind of spot ever again.

She crossed to the icebox and reached for the pitcher of iced tea. How would she find out Lance's address? He'd have to come up with the money. Laura was smart. She'd know how to reach him.

She poured the tea into a tall glass and walked into the kitchen to look out the window. She spied Laura walking slowly towards the corner with Mrs. Katz. Laura was talking to her and Mrs. Katz was nodding as though she understood. She wasn't the first girl to get caught, Iris told herself with shaky bravado.

Iris listened for sounds of footsteps on the stairs. What was taking Laura so long? All she had to find out was the name and address of that doctor. Then she froze at attention. That must be Laura coming up the stairs. She darted to the door, pulled it wide just as Laura arrived—breathless and perspiring—at the landing on their floor.

79

"Well?" Iris hovered, almost accusingly, in the doorway.

"Put on your shoes and stockings," Laura said. "We're going to see the woman doctor around the corner. Mrs. Katz says she sometimes takes care of girls in trouble."

"Did she say how much?" Already Iris was hurrying to her room.

"You'll have to ask her, Iris."

Iris put on stockings and shoes and reached for her purse. She glanced at herself in the mirror that hung over the dresser. Thank God she didn't look any different. She'd hate being pregnant, sticking out like that. Would it hurt? But the doctor wouldn't do it now—they always waited for the money first.

She'd make Laura come with her, stand right there while the doctor did it. *How much would it cost?* If you had money, life was so different. You didn't have to worry about things.

Laura was standing by the door, pale and scared.

"Don't look like that," Iris said with false bravado. "I'm not going to die. Real doctors know how to do these things. I'm not about to use a clothes hanger."

"Mrs. Katz says Dr. Fink takes care of a lot of the women in this neighborhood when they have their babies." Laura paused while she locked the door. Her voice dropped to a whisper. "And sometimes she—she helps girls who're in trouble." Laura prodded Iris down the stairs.

"What'll I tell her?" A woman doctor, Iris thought with unease. She had never seen a woman doctor.

"Tell her your boyfriend is an actor, and you two can't afford to get married now." Laura sounded matter-of-fact, but Iris knew she was a shambles inside. "Dr. Fink won't be concerned about that. Just tell her you're sure you're pregnant, and—and you can't have the baby."

When they arrived at the doctor's second-floor offices, three women sat on the clean but worn sofa, all in varying stages of pregnancy and discussing earlier deliveries. Iris thought they stared suspiciously at her when Laura and she came in and sat in a pair of chairs across from the sofa. Then she saw the youngest of the women inspect Laura's left hand, eyes dwelling on Laura's wedding band. Iris realized the woman thought Laura was pregnant. The assumption was strangely comforting.

Iris picked up a copy of *Collier's*, flipped pages, and pretended to read. God, how long would they have to wait?

"I should have left a note for Bernie," Laura said with belated compunction. "He'll be worried."

"He won't be home till late," Iris surmised. "When he stays at the office, he's never home before nine or ten."

Iris shifted restlessly in her chair. If she was rich, this would be *nothing*. Without money in this world you were in a torture chamber. Would Lance find the money for the doctor? Could Laura and Bernie borrow it from their bosses? Bernie was always bragging about what terrific people they were.

One by one the other women went into the office as the doctor appeared in the doorway and beckoned them inside. She didn't look like a doctor, Iris decided. She looked like one of the buyers at the store. Nice, she comforted herself.

Finally the last of the three patients had gone. Dr. Fink stood at the doorway with a questioning smile. She didn't know which one of them was a patient. Iris rose awkwardly to her feet, managing a faint smile.

"Me," she said flippantly and walked into the inner office.

At a gesture from the doctor Iris sat beside the desk. For a few moments Dr. Fink was occupied with writing down her name, address, and age.

"And what seems to be the problem?" she asked, reassuring in her matter-of-factness.

"I'm pregnant," Iris told her. "And there's no way I can get married now."

Dr. Fink sighed slightly and pushed back her chair. No arguing, Iris thought with relief. The doctor knew why she was here.

"Undo your teddy and lie down on the table there," she instructed.

"How much will it cost?" Iris forced herself to ask.

"Let's first see if you're pregnant." The doctor's voice was unexpectedly gentle as she stood beside the table and pulled on a pair of rubber gloves.

"I'm pregnant," Iris told her. "I'm three weeks late. I'm never late."

Iris hoisted herself onto the examining table after lifting her chemise to unbutton her teddy. She lay back and waited while the doctor separated her thighs and began to probe.

"Stay right there, please." Her tone was impersonal now.

A few moments later the doctor was probing again, her face inscrutable.

"All right. Button your teddy and come sit down again."

Iris was in a nervous sweat when she settled herself back in the chair by the doctor's desk. What would she do if Dr. Fink asked for an awful lot of money?

"You're not pregnant," Dr. Fink said briskly. "You girls are always so ready for a D & C." She smiled at Iris's blank stare. "A euphemistic phrase for an abortion. I shudder to guess how many needless abortions are done every year. Take a long walk," she ordered. "I guarantee by tomorrow you'll have your period."

With an air of disbelief Iris paid the doctor's modest fee and hurried out to report to Laura.

"I hope she knows what she's talking about," Iris whispered while Laura and she walked down the stairs to the street. "Why did she tell me to take a long walk?"

"I don't know, but you take that long walk," Laura ordered.

"If nothing happens tomorrow," Iris warned, "I'll go back there and pull out every hair in that woman's head."

"I believe her." Laura's serenity was irritating. "You walk, and I'll go home and wait for Bernie."

Iris awoke to a steamy morning even before her alarm clock rang. She heard Bernie whistling in the bathroom. First Bernie went into the bathroom, then Laura, then she. Laura and Bernie had to be at the office before she left for the store. Then all at once she was wide awake. The first twinges of menstrual cramps had asserted themselves.

That nutty doctor was right, Iris thought with a surge of relief. She wasn't pregnant. But the next time she saw Lance she'd be wearing a chastity belt!

# Chapter 7

Iris walked out of the employees' entrance and into the waning late July sunlight. The heat wave that had assaulted the city for the past week had mercifully broken. Subconsciously she remembered that both Laura and Bernie would be at school tonight. Maybe she'd splurge and have a beef pie at the Automat instead of eating at home.

"Iris, baby!" She whirled about at the sound of Lance's voice. "Hey, you look spiffy."

"What are you doing in town?" Subconsciously Iris tensed, the nightmare of her suspected pregnancy all at once vivid in recall.

"Is that a way to welcome me?" he reproached and pulled her close, ignoring passing stares. "Let's go up to my place and talk about how much we missed each other."

"You can take me to the Automat for a beef pie and iced tea," she told him. He lifted an eyebrow in mocking reproach. "I've been standing on my feet since ten o'clock this morning—except for my lunch hour." She glanced up appraisingly. "You still haven't told me why you're in town. You weren't due back for another three weeks."

"The director and I had a difference of opinion," he drawled. "The bastard was ruining the play. We kept fighting about it. He told me to do it his way or get the hell out. So I came home. This is the time of year new plays are being cast. It was the smartest thing I could do." But Iris heard a hollow bravado in his voice.

"Lance, I'm sorry." She felt a stir of genuine compassion. This was the play he had expected to make him a star.

"We could buy some cold cuts and take it to the apartment," he said while they waited for a red light to change to green.

"Lance, we have to talk," she warned. No matter how she felt she'd vowed she wasn't going to sleep with him again.

One scare like she'd had was enough.

"Okay." His voice was casual, but his eyes were guarded. "We'll go to that deli on Sixth Avenue. I do my best talking over pastrami and rye." His arm moved about her waist.

Why didn't Lance forget about Broadway and head out for Hollywood? If he asked her to marry him, she'd go with him. She didn't want to spend the rest of her life selling stockings at Lord & Taylor.

"Is your roommate still out on the road?"

"That's the story of his life." Lance grimaced. "But as long as he keeps sending in his share of the rent, I don't give a shit."

They shopped at the Sixth Avenue delicatessen, then headed for Fifty-second Street. In the narrow stairway of his building Lance paused for an unnervingly passionate kiss. That was all he'd get, Iris vowed as they pulled apart.

"Oh kiddo, did I miss you." His hand lovingly fondled her rump.

"I had a little incident while you were away," she told him haltingly as they climbed the stairs. She had meant to tell him when they were settled in his apartment.

"What kind of incident?" he demanded.

"I was sure I was pregnant," she told him. He stopped dead on the stairs. "My sister took me to this doctor. A woman doctor," she mocked because Lance made jokes about professional women. "I don't know if it was because she poked around the way she did—or I just wasn't pregnant. Anyhow, the next morning everything was okay."

"Baby, we were always so careful." He was shaken. "Maybe we waited too long before you took care of yourself. Hereafter we'll—"

"No more, Lance. That scared the hell out of me. That's what I wanted to tell you."

"Iris, we'll be careful," he insisted.

"We won't need to be careful," she said bluntly, "because you're not getting in anymore." She fought against adding, *not unless we're married.*

"It must have been tough on you," he commiserated. "But it was just a false alarm."

"No more, Lance," she reiterated stubbornly. "Just necking from now on."

Lance reached for his key, slid it into the lock.

"There are ways we can make each other happy," he reminded. "I promise to send you right through the roof—and you won't ever get pregnant."

"Just that way?" She was conscious of a surge of heat.

"Just that way," he promised. "Come on inside and let's get hot!"

Iris saw Lance almost every evening. She knew he was certain she would relent soon, get over what he called her "nutty attitude." But no matter how much she wanted to, *she wouldn't.*

She was exhilarated by the sudden shift in their relationship. Before the "big scare" Lance had always led; she followed. Now she was conscious of a new power over him. Was it strong enough to make him marry her and go out to Hollywood? He'd have a chance to become a movie star. She daydreamed constantly they'd be rich! Their pictures would be in *Photoplay* and *Modern Screen* and *Movie Weekly.* Louella Parsons would write about the dashing new movie star, Lance Andrews, and his beautiful young wife. Back in Magnolia folks would see her photographs with Lance and recognize her. The kids Laura and she had gone to school with could eat their hearts out.

She felt imprisoned by her job behind the hosiery counter at Lord & Taylor. She envied the chic women who emerged from the rows of chauffeured Lincolns, Cadillacs, or one of the expensive foreign cars that the very rich were importing. They shopped without ever looking at price tags. She had to give up lunches for five weeks to buy a cheap new dress.

When she left the store at the end of each day, Lance was waiting for her. On hot nights they'd stop at the deli and then walk up to Central Park to picnic on the grass. Once a week he took her to Sardi's—occasions they both relished. Once he took her to El Fey Club to see Texas Guinan—though she was nervous that the club might be raided and their picture plastered across the front page of the *Daily News* or *Mirror.* Another night they went to the Casino-in-the-Park to hear Eddie Duchin at the piano. Lance had confided that he'd been a heavy winner at the nightly poker games on tour. But he became increasingly bitter as summer blended into autumn.

"Every office in town is casting," he complained on a chilly Sunday evening in late October while they sipped coffee in the Automat at Times Square. They were waiting for an acceptable hour to appear at a prestigious "show biz" party to which Lance had been invited. "I can't even get a reading, damn it."

"It's still early in the season," Iris comforted. Lance was educating her in theater lore. "There'll be lots more plays."

"If something doesn't break soon," he said, his voice tainted by frustration, "I'll have to start looking for a job soda-jerking again. I learned long ago that in this stinking business you have to keep a healthy cash reserve." He slammed one fist against the cafeteria table. "Damn it, I'm a good actor. Jed Harris said I was good, but he wouldn't let me read for his new play. From what I hear around town, there's a great part for me in it."

"Lance—" Iris hesitated, groping for the right words. "Maybe it's time you took a stab at Hollywood."

"Baby, you know what I think about Hollywood," he said contemptuously.

"Maybe just for a while," she pushed. "I mean, you've walked out on two plays, Lance—" Her voice trailed away, but her eyes commanded appraisal.

"You think the word's around town that I'm hard to handle?" Angry color tinged his cheekbones. "You think that could be it?"

"Don't you?" she challenged, her heart thumping. *Lance, go to Hollywood. Take me with you.*

Iris watched while Lance squinted in reflection.

"Scofield and I had some rough words on the last deal," he conceded. "The son-of-a-bitch swore I'd never work in another Broadway play. I didn't believe him." His eyes were glazed with shock.

"You don't need New York theater. You've got as much sex appeal as Rudy Valentino had." The whole country had gone into wild mourning when Valentino died suddenly in August. "Hollywood is looking for somebody to take his place." Iris was as devoted to the movie magazines as she was to *Vogue* and *Town & Country*. "You could be the one. You

86

could be an important movie star! Riding around Hollywood in a Mercedes Benz or a Hispano-Suiza. Living in a gorgeous mansion in Beverly Hills."

Abruptly he pushed back his chair. "It's time to go to that party."

"Lance, do I look all right?" The party was being given by some post-debutante enamored of theater. Iris knew the type—she read about them in magazines and tabloid gossip columns. They went to dinner at the Palais Royal or the Rendezvous or to Petroushka, then on to dancing at the Trocadero or the Four-Hundred Club. On Friday or Saturday nights they went up to Harlem to the Cotton Club or the Alhambra Ballroom. They were mad about Ethel Waters and Bill "Bojangles" Robinson and Duke Ellington. In addition to theater people, Lance said, there were apt to be members of Social Register families like the Rockefellers, the Whitneys, and the Astors.

"You look sensational," he approved, his eyes sweeping over her black chiffon dress with its Paris-decreed uneven hem, her superb legs, her satin pumps with Baby Louis heels. He grinned. "Would I take you there if you didn't?"

They left the Automat and walked up to Central Park South, then across to Fifth Avenue, and up to the elegant East Sixty-third Street limestone-fronted townhouse. A solemn-faced butler admitted them into the wide entrance hall dominated by a pair of antique Spanish Corinthian columns and took their coats. The conversation and laughter that drifted through a pair of French doors at the right told them the party was in full swing, as Lance had planned. *I hate being the first one at a party.*

With the faint smile she had cultivated as being "chic and sophisticated," Iris walked with Lance into the large reception room. Their hostess greeted them effusively, though Iris suspected she had no recall of having met Lance. It was sufficient that he was "a member of Actors' Equity." She pointed them in the direction of the bar and crossed to the piano, where several people clustered around the pianist.

"That's Richard Rodgers," Lance whispered. His eyes swept around the room an instant later, his face brightening. "There's Tallulah Bankhead. She's marvelous." His eyes moved on, seeking someone who might be the bearer of useful theatrical gossip. "Hey, my old buddy Ralph Lane's here." He reached for Iris's arm. "Ralph and I worked together in the Catskills two summers ago. We run into each other making rounds."

Ralph also had spied Lance and his face broke into a broad grin as he charged forward.

"Lance, I don't see you around much," Ralph said warmly. "Of course, I was out on tour for a while, and now I'm going into rehearsal again in a couple of weeks."

"Great!" Lance slapped him across the shoulder. "What are you doing?"

"The new Jed Harris play," Ralph said. "The juvenile lead." Iris saw Lance stiffen, though he contrived to conceal his shock. He had been praying for that part. "It's the part I've been waiting for since I landed in New York."

"Ralph!" a huge-eyed little ingenue called from across the room. "Come over here and tell this character I really have been cast in the Jed Harris play!"

"Let's get out of here," Lance said tersely. "Jed Harris said I was good. Why in hell wouldn't he let me read for that part?"

They left the room, collected their coats from the butler, and walked out into the crisp night air. Lance was grim-faced and silent until they reached the corner and turned down Fifth Avenue.

"Let's go have coffee somewhere," he said and paused, frowning. "Not to the Child's at Fifth Avenue and Fifty-ninth." This was the deluxe Child's, almost as favored by New York's smart set for early morning breakfast parties as Reuben's. "Let's go down to the Times Square Child's."

"Okay," Iris agreed softly. Instinct told her this was not the moment to talk.

They walked in silence for almost a block.

"I should have got that part," Lance smoldered. "I'm ten times the actor Ralph will ever be." He looked down at Iris with a new respect. "You knew I'd screwed myself by walking out on those two companies.

"It seemed like it," she said softly, her head down.

"It was just rotten luck," he said savagely. "I was right both times."

"You don't need Broadway," Iris soothed. "You can go out

to Hollywood. Show them you don't need them, Lance."

He frowned in silence while they waited for a light to change.

"If I go, will you go with me?"

Her face glowed.

"Oh, Lance, wouldn't that be sensational!" But now the glow ebbed away. "But how could I? I mean, I have a job here. I don't know if I could find one out there—"

"Sure you could," he encouraged, prodding her across the street as the light changed. "They've got department stores in California."

She didn't *want* to work in a department store in California, or anywhere else. She wanted to be the wife of a rich and famous movie star. Lance might be the closest she'd ever come to that.

"I couldn't take a chance," she said wistfully. "Here in New York I have Laura if something goes wrong." Like when she thought she was pregnant.

"Out there you'd have me," he reminded.

"Maybe." She was blunt. "How do I know you'd feel the same way if you're running around with all those gorgeous actresses?"

"We'll get married," he said and grinned. "It just might work."

"Then I'll go with you," Iris flipped, her air of amused anticipation concealing a surge of triumph. She'd push Lance right up to the top, she gloated inwardly And if they decided to get divorced later, so what? Being a divorcé would be exciting.

As casually as they might have planned a trip to Coney Island, Iris and Lance discussed their trek to California over hot cakes and coffee in his favorite Child's. He had money for the train trip for two. The rent would be the same for one or two, he shrugged. If it took a while to "make connections" out there, he'd find a job as a soda jerk.

"I've got a few names to call," he said in rising optimism. "Even some good reviews to show."

"Lance, you'll make it." Iris's smile was dazzling. "I read in some movie magazine that Hollywood producers have a lot of respect for Broadway actors." She paused, her mind charging ahead on half a dozen paths. "We can get married at City

Hall like Laura and Bernie. Fast and cheap," she laughed. No question about their being married in a church. She knew Lance wasn't Jewish. A couple of times when he was drunk he'd made cracks about Jewish producers. "I'll tell Laura tonight."

"But Iris, to go off to California with somebody you hardly know!" Laura protested. "Three thousand miles away!"

Iris had known Laura would be upset that she was marrying Lance. An actor, non-Jewish, and unemployed.

"I've known Lance almost a year," she pointed out. She just never brought him home because she knew Laura wouldn't approve. Hell, Laura knew she'd been sleeping with Lance—she'd thought she was pregnant by him. "I've known him as long as you knew Bernie when you got married."

"Iris, I worry about you."

"Don't," Iris said gaily. "I'm doing great. We'll go out to Hollywood, and Lance will become a movie star. And Bernie and you will come out and stay with us in our big house in Beverly Hills. I'll write every week," she promised. "And once every month I'll phone."

"Iris, we don't have a phone," Laura laughed shakily.

Laura was remembering that they had never been apart except for the two nights of her "honeymoon." Not once in their lives had they been in separate towns. Now Iris was putting the whole country between them.

"You told me Bernie's getting a raise. You'll be able to afford a phone." Iris determinedly brushed aside a seeping uncertainty.

"Laura, I don't want to spend the rest of my life behind a hosiery counter. *I want to be rich.* Someday I'll drive into Magnolia in a chauffeured limousine, and I'll make everybody in that rotten town sick with envy."

"Iris, Magnolia did a terrible thing to Papa—and to us," Laura said slowly. "But not everybody in Magnolia is bad. Remember Mrs. Bernstein? How good she was to us? And Papa's friend, Mr. Massey. And Rabbi Simon—"

"They let Papa be convicted!" Iris blazed with fresh outrage, as though the trial was yesterday. "They lynched him! They drove us out of town! I wish the whole town was dead!"

For a moment Laura seemed to reel before her sister's anger. Laura had been living in New York for almost two and a half years, Iris thought impatiently; but she was still the same small-town girl she'd been when they came here. Bernie and she lived in a whole different world from Lance and herself. And suddenly she realized how much Laura missed Magnolia. She'd love to be back in that bible belt town.

"Laura," Iris pushed herself back to the present, "Lance doesn't know I'm Jewish. Tell Bernie not to say anything. We're going to be married in City Hall, anyway," she shrugged, "so why does he have to know?"

"Iris, how can you lie to him like that?" Laura reproached. "It seems the wrong way to begin a marriage."

"I don't need to add problems to my life. I'm an atheist — that's all Lance has to know." Lance knew they lived on the Lower East Side because that was where they could find a cheap apartment. It had nothing to do with their being Jewish.

Ten days later — in the late afternoon so that Laura and Bernie would have to take off only three hours from work — Iris and Lance were married at City Hall. This time it was Laura who brought along a small bouquet of pink rosebuds. Iris suspected that Lance was having some last-minute misgivings. He was tense and unsmiling when the judge pronounced them man and wife.

"Relax," she mocked as he bent to kiss her. "You're not going to jail. Only to California."

They left City Hall and walked up to Chinatown to have an early wedding dinner at the Oriental on Pell Street. Normally when Laura and Bernie treated themselves to dinner in Chinatown, they patronized the cheaper first floor and basement restaurants, but this was an occasion that merited an "upstairs palace."

There was much elation among their small party when Iris read aloud the message in her fortune cookie: *"You are taking the first step towards fantastic success."*

"You see," Iris said in triumph, "even the Chinese know!" She turned cajolingly towards Laura. Her sister had managed a festive smile since they left their apartment for City Hall. Laura smiled with her mouth but not with her eyes.

"Hey, that cookie should have been mine," Lance protested. "You switched with me."

Poor Laura, Iris commiserated inwardly. Laura would never go on to law school. She would probably never finish college. Laura had cashed in her dreams for marriage to Bernie.

"Tomorrow this time we'll be aboard a grubby day coach, but we'll be bound for California." Iris was dizzy with elation. She reached for Lance's hand. "Our lives are just beginning."

## Chapter 8

Laura hurried up the stairs from the subway station as the first December snow hit the ground in dollar-sized flakes that hinted at a minimum of four or five inches. With one gloved hand she tugged at the collar of her straight black coat that reached decorously just below her knees. Bought off a rack at S. Klein, it was hardly adequate for the raw cold of the early evening. With the other hand she pulled the black-felt cloche—becoming to her delicate features though unflattering to so many wearers—more snugly over her short hair.

She was grateful that this was Friday—she'd been abnormally tired this week. Thank God, she had no class tonight. And Saturday the office closed at one unless there was some crisis.

Bernie had gone directly to his Friday night class at NYU. She'd have time to stretch out for twenty or thirty minutes before he got home. Long enough to read a few pages of the new Hemingway—*The Sun Also Rises*—that Bernie had bought her for Hanukkah. Now she forced herself to plan tonight's supper. Reared on Southern cooking she was making an effort to learn to prepare the Jewish-style food that Bernie liked.

She stopped at the bakery a block from the apartment to buy a loaf of *challah*, which always graced their Friday night dinner table. With the *challah* in tow she went into the fish market a few doors down. Fish had become a Friday night tradition. Last night's carrots, glazed in honey, could be reheated in minutes. For dessert, a pudding. Her face softened as she remembered Bernie so patiently explaining to his "Georgia *shiksa*" that the pudding on the Sabbath was to remind those about the table of the dew-covered manna that fell from heaven to feed the Israelites during their forty years of wandering in the wilderness.

Approaching their Jefferson Street tenement Laura

93

thought worriedly about Iris. There had been no letter from her for almost two weeks. It was six weeks today since Iris's wedding, yet she still felt an anguished sense of loss at her sister's absence. Sometimes she forgot for a moment when she saw a particularly attractive dress or coat in a department store window and thought, "Oh, I must tell Iris tonight."

Though she had no real interest in movie magazines, she read them religiously since Iris went out to California. She worried about the stories that came out of Hollywood — wild parties involving alcohol, drugs, and indiscriminate sex.

Ever since the Fatty Arbuckle scandal four years ago — and the unsolved murder of movie director William Desmond Taylor that same year — Hollywood was regularly reviled as a "den of iniquity." Lurid stories circulated about the secret gatherings of actors and actresses, directors, cameramen — even extras — where marijuana and opium and morphine were in use.

Laura's eyes lit up when she discovered a letter from Iris in their mailbox. She hurried up the stairs, impatient to read Iris's latest news. She knew that Iris and Lance were living at the Washington Hotel on Washington Boulevard — "it's only six blocks from the M-G-M studios." Iris had written about the colorful pastel bungalows that lined the residential streets, about the palm trees that soared six stories high. She loved the perennial summer weather — "people go swimming on Thanksgiving!" But between the lines Laura read Iris's dissatisfaction with what was obviously a sleazy hotel, its sole good feature the low cost of its rooms.

"Something good is finally happening," Iris wrote and Laura could envision her sister's excitement. "Lance has a part in a new movie that starts shooting right after Christmas. Remember that girl we liked in the Jackie Coogan movie *Old Clothes?* Lucille LeSueur. They've changed her name now to Joan Crawford. Well, Lance was in a Shubert show with her two years ago. He ran into her on the street, and she introduced him to an M-G-M director. We're both terribly excited. This is the break Lance has been waiting for."

In their tiny bedroom Laura read and re-read Iris's typically short letter, then changed from her good office clothes into the emerald-green wool chemise that Bernie particularly liked. Later she would protect it with an apron. Right now all she wanted to do was stretch out on the bed for a little while. She reached for the Hemingway novel, then abandoned it. Of their own volition her eyes closed.

She awoke with a start to realize she'd slept for almost half an hour. She could still have supper ready by the time Bernie came home from school, she comforted herself. But as she reached for her kitchen apron in the closet she was caught by a red-circled day on the calendar hanging on the closet door. Her heart was suddenly pounding. Most days in the morning rush she ignored the calendar. And at night she was involved in the rush to prepare supper, to collapse afterwards in heavy studying. But that precise red circle told her that her period was almost two weeks late.

She tied the apron about her waist and walked out into the kitchen in an aura of unreality. For the last week she'd been fighting sleep during the day. She was embarrassed at the office because she was running so often to the ladies' room. Along with that reminder on the calendar, unmistakable signs—*She was pregnant.*

She was enveloped in a rush of conflicting emotions. A wonderful tenderness in the knowledge that she was carrying their baby. *Bernie would be so happy.* But she had vowed to go through college and law school. To become a lawyer and one day to return to Magnolia to clear Papa's name. Guilt battled with joy within her. She was only eighteen years old— Bernie was only twenty-five. *They could afford to wait.* She was abandoning her vow made the morning Papa died.

It wasn't enough that Bernie would be a lawyer. For Papa *she* had to be a lawyer, too. The lawyer who would prove to the world that Jacob Roth had been an innocent man.

Wracked with anguish, Laura forced herself to deal with the mechanics of supper preparations. First the rice pudding, which must go in the oven a good fifteen minutes before she put the fish on a burner on top of the stove to simmer into tenderness. Then boil the potatoes. Only when she heard Bernie's steps coming to the door would she reheat last night's glazed carrots.

Had she been wrong to marry Bernie? Wrong to believe she could have marriage and a profession? A hand involuntarily rested on her stomach. Their baby — Bernie's and hers — grew within her. Papa's grandchild. Tears welled in her eyes. How Papa would have loved this baby!

With food on the stove and in the oven she brought out the brass candlesticks — Mama's candlesticks — and set in the candles. She could not light the candles at the traditional arrival of sunset. Instead, she would light the candles and say the blessing when Bernie and she sat down at the supper table.

Her face lighted at the familiar sound of Bernie's footsteps on the landing. Her heart was pounding when she opened the door for him. He would be so happy when she told him she was pregnant — despite their plans to wait.

"The snow's coming down like it means never to stop," he reported when he had kissed her. "You'll need galoshes when you go to the office tomorrow."

"Your feet must be wet," she scolded. "Change into slippers."

"They're dry," he insisted.

"Take them off," Laura ordered.

"Bossy wife," he complained good-humoredly and allowed her to prod him into the bedroom.

"I'll get your slippers." She flipped the light switch and walked to the closet. They'd have dinner, and then she'd tell him. *No.* How could she wait all through dinner? She'd light the candles, and then she'd tell him.

"If the snow keeps up this way all night, nobody will be going to work tomorrow," Bernie prophesied, bending to unlace and remove his shoes.

"That would be nice." She brought his slippers to the side of the bed. "Take off your socks, too."

"Yes, Mommie," he teased and her heart began to pound again at the appellation. He removed his socks, slid his feet into the slippers she held for him. "You look so beautiful tonight. There's a special kind of glow about you."

There ought to be. How could she wait another minute to tell him? She lifted her face to his. "Bernie, I'm pregnant."

For a moment he seemed immobilized.

"Honey, are you sure?" He was simultaneously ecstatic and nervous.

"I'm sure," she whispered.

"Laura; this won't change anything for us." He pulled her into his arms, his face against hers. He always knew her every thought. "You'll go on to college. You'll become a lawyer. We're young and strong—we can handle it."

"Bernie, how can I go to school?" Tears stung her eyes even while love for their unborn child surged through her.

"The professors are going to stop you because your belly's sticking way out?" he teased. "When do you figure the baby will be born?"

"August, sometime."

"You see?" he said triumphantly. "God's on our side. You'll be able to finish up this school year. When the new term starts in September, you'll go on to school again. I'll be out of law school then—I'll stay home with the baby the nights you go to classes. Oh, Laura, this is the most wonderful moment of my life."

"Bernie, do you think it'll work?" She lifted her face to his.

"Of course," he promised, his mouth reaching for hers, tender at first, then passionate.

"Bernie, I have to watch supper on the stove," she protested, pulling away even while her body responded to his.

"Let's turn it off. We'll eat later." He ran a hand across her still-flat belly with a touch of wonder on his face. "It's all right now, isn't it?" he asked in sudden concern.

"It's all right," she reassured him. "It'll be all right for months yet." She pulled him toward the bedroom.

## Chapter 9

To Iris the California days seemed to blend one into another, each little different from the day before. Except for the two days in May when the whole world was caught up in the wonder of Captain Charles A. Lindbergh's flying 3,600 miles nonstop—from Roosevelt Field in Long Island, New York to Paris—in thirty-three and a half hours. Alone in a tiny monoplane. Fascinated by the feat, Lance clung to the radio as the news flashed around the world. In Paris Lindbergh was welcomed by over 100,000 people, and the details were dutifully reported by the press.

In that same month in Hollywood the Academy of Motion Picture Arts and Sciences was founded, with one of its main functions to recognize outstanding film achievements and present annual awards to be known as "Oscars." Lance complained that the film business was giving itself airs.

Now on a July afternoon—in a bright-red bathing suit that Lance said was "short enough to make any man under eighty ready to jump you"—Iris lay across the sofa in their newly acquired apartment and read Laura's latest letter.

The day was steamy hot. Perspiration glistened about Iris's throat, lending a glow to her California tan. If Lance had not been out with their third-hand temperamental Ford, she would have driven out to the beach. Edna Kane, the old character actress who lived below them, had taught her to drive when she'd complained that Lance wouldn't. In return she joined in playing at intervals what Edna called a bastard form of mah-jongg, the game that the country had gone crazy over.

It still seemed unreal to Iris that Laura was pregnant. Sometime next month—August—she expected to give birth, Iris recalled as she slowly read Laura's large sprawling handwriting. Bernie had finished law school and would shortly take the bar exams. Already he had been accepted on his firm's legal staff, with a substantial raise in salary.

Laura was happy that they'd moved from the Jefferson Street apartment to one in Borough Park, Brooklyn. Their living room windows overlooked a whole block of private houses. *"Such nice houses, Iris, and just one or two families living in them—almost like back home. And the most beautiful gardens. Papa would have loved them."* She'd finished her school term, "even though I'm popping out like crazy," and insisted she'd be back in school for the fall term. That was now, Iris told herself. Once the baby was born, Laura would forget about school. She'd become another Brooklyn housewife. Poor Laura.

She'd have to buy something sensational for the baby. *Her* niece—or nephew. It seemed unreal. She'd bet anything that Laura hadn't planned on having a baby. Not when she was so bent on staying in school. Wasn't Bernie hep enough to make sure she didn't get pregnant? Of course, Laura would never even think about an abortion.

Sometimes she missed Laura so damn much she wanted to pack up and head back for New York—but there was nothing back there for her. *Lance had to make it big.* She'd been writing Laura about Lance's success in pictures. He really wasn't doing all that great—three shitty parts in eight months and his salary for those bit roles didn't pay much. The last one landed on the cutting room floor at the insistence of the male star. The director had given him some baloney about how the male star and he were too much alike. *"Damn it, Iris. So we both have dark hair, hairy chests and balls! He couldn't stand knowing I'm one hundred times the actor he'll ever be!"* They were surviving on the money Lance was earning for extra roles and occasional bits. He never stopped bitching about that. He wouldn't admit it, but she was sure he'd lost two or three more parts because he'd opened his big mouth to the wrong people.

He refused to look for jobs as a soda jerk "between pictures"—he said it would spoil his image. She knew he was teed off because she didn't go out and land a job at May's or I. Magnin's. Maybe she could get a job—but instinct warned her not to, even though she was bored to death at sitting around doing nothing. Lance would take every cent she earned and blow it on the "big impression" he always talked

99

about having to make in Hollywood.

Lance had a reading this afternoon for a part in a new movie that was supposed to be prestigious. *"All I need is one great Part, Iris — it doesn't have to be large, just flashy — and I can name my own price with these jerks out here."* Lance might be contemptuous about Hollywood, but he was greedy for Hollywood money.

Restless, not sure when Lance would be home from the reading, Iris reached for the new issue of *Vogue* and sprawled on the sofa to read. Some day they'd have a palace of a house out here and their own swimming pool, she fantasized. She'd wear the most gorgeous clothes. They'd travel regularly to Europe aboard the *Aquitania* or the exciting new *Ile de France* — in the best suites, of course. They'd stay at Claridge's in London and the Crillon in Paris. When they were in Paris, she'd shop for dresses at Poiret and Lanvin and Chanel.

Iris sat up at the sound of a key in the lock. Lance thrust open the door and charged inside.

"Baby, we're on our way!" he chortled, swinging her off her feet. "That small but meaty part we're always talking about? I persuaded that new agent I met last week to send me over to test for it. It's mine!" He set her down and smacked her on the rump. "And don't worry about this one landing on the cutting room floor. The female star has the 'hots' for me."

"Lance —" Did he think he could dump her for some over-heated bitch who could help his career?

"Nothing's going to happen," he laughed. "I'll play along until the picture's edited and my part hasn't been cut. She's forty-two pretending to be twenty-three. So I'll pat her on the ass and squeeze her boobs when nobody's looking." He slid a hand down the front of her dress. "Do you want to make love or go to the tea dance at the Cocoanut Grove?"

"The tea dance," Iris laughed. "We can make love any time."

When Lance came home early from the studio on the second day of shooting, she knew he had lost the part.

"What happened?" she asked as he crossed without a word of greeting to the kitchenette cabinet where they kept a bottle of gin. In Hollywood liquor was as easily attainable as in New York.

"The old bitch didn't stand up for me!" he exploded. "The part really wasn't that sensational, but it could have been. I tried to make that bastard of a director understand how it ought to be played. The way a young John Barrymore would play it. I—"

"You opened your big mouth again!" Iris shot back. "Lance, when will you stop fighting with directors? You did it in New York, and now you're doing it in Hollywood!"

"All you give a shit about is the money!" He turned his back to her and fixed himself a drink.

"That's why you came out here, Lance," she reminded. "God knows, you have no respect for the industry."

"I can act circles around ninety percent of the actors out here." He glared at her, daring her to defy him.

"So what?" she jeered. "You have to know how to handle people. Directors. Maybe if you *were* John Barrymore, you could get away with that temperamental act. But you're not."

"I'm good," he said unsteadily. "Nobody out here sees it."

"Lance, they will." She walked to him and thrust her hips against his, meaning to comfort him in the only way she knew. "Just learn not to talk back."

"Out here it's all a matter of luck. Russian roulette," he jeered, but already he was aroused. "Let's go into the bedroom—"

Tomorrow she'd make him get up early and go over to "extra" casting. They needed the money. He'd sulk, but it was better than jerking sodas around town.

On a hot early August morning Laura lay back against the pillows in her bed in the maternity ward of the Brooklyn hospital. Exhausted but radiant, she cradled her newborn son in her arms while Bernie hovered lovingly above them.

"He looks just like you," Bernie decided.

"No, no," Laura laughed. "Like you." Her eyes grew wistful. "I wish Iris was here to see him." Her voice dropped. "I wish Papa was here."

"If the stock I bought last week keeps going up, we'll be able to go out to California next summer."

"Bernie, I worry about your buying stock. I don't understand how people can make so much money gambling that way." She was enthralled that Bernie's salary kept going up in a way they had never expected to happen so quickly. It was happening to everybody. Yet it scared her that every month he put more cash into the stock market. She'd rather he bought a car—that was something they could see.

"Laura, everybody in the country is in the stock market," he protested gently. "We're in an economy where people like us can become rich in a few years if we handle our money right." He reached for one of Jonathan's tiny hands. "We'll buy a house of our own in five years," he predicted. "You'd like that, wouldn't you?"

"Oh Bernie, yes."

Once home with the baby, Laura rejoiced in Bernie's continued insistence that she return to night school when fall classes began.

"Unless you're afraid to trust Jonathan with me," he teased. "You know better than that," she scolded, her eyes aglow with love.

Bernie was wonderful with the baby. Despite her concern at his losing sleep he got up to sit with her while she nursed Jonathan at his 2 A.M. feeding. He was always ready to change a diaper or just to hold his son. How many men in Borough Park—or anywhere else in the country—would bother changing diapers? She wouldn't even mention it to anybody but Iris. That was considered women's work.

With a nagging sense of guilt she left Jonathan in Bernie's arms while she left for her first class of the new school term. School was a break in her daily routine that she discovered she enjoyed. Most of her days were spent caring for Jonathan, shopping for groceries on Thirteenth Avenue, preparing meals.

Bernie insisted on buying her a washing machine, though she was nervous about buying on the installment plan. He argued that they could easily afford the five dollars down and eight dollars a month. And Bernie provided her with liberal housekeeping money, from which she managed to save each week—bills carefully tucked away in a dresser drawer beneath stockings and teddies—to be a surprise for Bernie when she had accumulated an impressive amount.

When notification came through that Bernie had passed his law exams he bought her a Royal portable typewriter. She cherished the prospect of being able to type for Bernie.

Over her protests — because she was reluctant to leave Jonathan even in the care of Mrs. Goldstein, who lived next door and was three times a grandmother — Bernie took her to the Warner theater in Manhattan to see Al Jolson in *The Jazz Singer*. The reception of the "first talking picture" had been sensational.

Riding back to Brooklyn on the BMT Laura thought how her father would have loved the movie. She envisioned the beautiful smile on his face, the tears in his eyes, if he could have seen Jolson — wrapped in his tallith — sing *Kol Nidre* in the synagogue.

The world would have seemed a perfect place if Iris had not been at the other side of the country.

Iris awoke slowly and swung over on one side. All at once she remembered that Lance was not in bed with her. He was on location in Catalina, doing a bit part in a movie being shot out there. He was beginning to make cracks about his "lazy wife." He couldn't understand why she didn't go over to apply for a job at I. Magnin's. *"You'd get a job there in a minute, Iris."* But she had not come out to California to work behind a hosiery counter again.

She was drinking coffee and flipping through the latest issue of *Photoplay* when somebody knocked on the door. Tossing aside the magazine and with cup of coffee in one hand she went to answer.

"Iris, I've stopped hangin' around the house waitin' for my agent to call me," Edna — small, nondescript, and fiesty — announced. She had not worked in close to two years, she'd admitted a few days earlier. She lived on the modest income from stocks her husband had left her. "So I'm not getting any more character roles. I've still got studio contacts. I can get 'extra' work. Come along with me," she urged. "You're sick of just sittin' round the house. You'll get a kick out of bein' an 'extra.' "

"You think I'd be hired?" Iris was simultaneously startled and intrigued.

"Honey, you're a gorgeous lookin' broad." Edna was emphatic. "You'll be hired. But first," she said with an elfin grin, "let's have a little nip." She reached for the flask tucked inside her garter. "See what you young things with skirts over your knees are missing? No place to hide your hooch."

With much trepidation Iris accompanied Edna to the studio. To her astonishment and elation Edna and she were both hired for three days of "extra" work beginning the following morning. She left the apartment each morning with a sense of adventure ahead. She relished the long hours on the set, absorbing every sight and sound. Suddenly she realized how bored she had been these last months. And she felt a charge of satisfaction at the prospect of earning money of her own.

"We'll be workin' again," Edna promised when they arrived home after the third day's work in Edna's beat-up Ford roadster, which she declared was her prize possession. *"I'd give up food before I'd give up my wheels."*

"It *was* fun," Iris acknowledged while they walked into the apartment house. "Lance will be shocked right out of his socks." She remembered he was due home from Catalina tonight. *She hadn't missed him the least little bit.*

She was in the shower — an hour later — when she heard the apartment door open.

"Iris?" Lance yelled.

"I'm in the shower," she called back over the sound of the water. The bathroom door cracked because she never closed it when she was home alone. "Be out in a minute."

She turned off the faucets, stepped past the shower curtain onto the bathmat. Lance was coming towards her, stripping en route.

"Get back in the tub," he said, his eyes resting appreciatively on her wet nudity. "After those rotten days in Catalina I need some cheering up."

He stood immobile for a few moments while she obligingly soaped him. Then he reached to pull her hard against him, his mouth hungry on hers. The spray of hot water — because Iris loathed cold showers — was oddly arousing.

"Let's get the hell out of here," he said, his mouth releasing hers. "I thought I was too goddamn tired to do anything — but that was before I saw you."

"Let's dry up first," she began, but Lance was pulling her down to the bathroom floor. "Lance, not here," she protested.

"What's wrong with here?" he challenged and lowered himself above her.

Later—while they sprawled across the bed with a bottle of gin beside them—Iris told him about the "extra" work.

"You didn't mind it?" His smile was quizzical. He damned "extra" work as a fate worse than death.

"It was fun," she shrugged.

"The money will come in handy," he approved. "Game for more of it?"

"Sure. Edna says we'll pick up lots of work through her contacts."

At least once a week Edna invited Iris and Lance for dinner at her apartment. Hating to cook and prone to cold cuts Iris welcomed these invitations. After they'd eaten, she'd do the dishes while Edna and Lance talked about the business. She was satisfied just to listen.

Everybody was excited about the future for talking pictures, though Edna pointed out that most producers and directors figured they would never replace silent films.

"It's a fad," Edna insisted. "Remember a few years ago how everybody said radio would kill the movie business? More people than ever go to the movies because they want to see how the rich live and dress and play—and make the same mistakes they make, only in more comfort."

"They go," Lance pinpointed, "because most of them are too scared to be part of today's 'flaming youth.' They want to see hot petting parties and beautiful jazz babies doing the Charleston and cars and more cars." His voice grew bitter. "And in the theater people run to see shit like *Abie's Irish Rose*. That damn play has been running since August, 1923!"

As Iris had expected, Lance withheld his own salary from the household money as she continued to work two or three days every week at the studio. This she could accept; she enjoyed the hours at the studio, the camaraderie among the "extras," the excitement of being close to stars she knew heretofore only from movie magazines. But she made a point of never seeking work at the same studio as Lance.

Early in the spring Edna was delighted to run into an old acquaintance in the studio commissary, where Iris and she had gone for lunch.

"Dennis, my God!" she squealed in pleasure. "I haven't seen you in a dozen years. You're still hangin' around this town!" She turned to Iris. "I was workin' regularly back in those days. Dennis was just startin' out in the business. All starry-eyed about makin' pictures."

"I still am," he said humorously. "The way I see it, the best is yet to come." Iris decided he was in his early thirties, his trim figure making him appear taller than he was. There was a Ronald Coleman charm about him. "I'm directing now."

"Hey, that's great, Dennie." Edna's eyes widened with respect.

"Dennis!" a studio bigwig called across the room. "Get your butt over here, will you?"

"He's travelin' in fast company," Edna whispered when he had excused himself and hurried to join his friends. "Wow, am I impressed!"

Letting herself into the apartment, Iris remembered that Lance would be working till all hours tonight. He had three lines in the new Joan Crawford movie. *"Joan wangled it for me. She knows I'm terrific. It could be the beginning of a real roll of luck."*

She changed from the smart I. Magnin dress—whose price tag had elicited shock from Lance—into pajamas, made herself a cheese sandwich and coffee, and settled herself in bed. She was physically tired from the long hours of standing about the set, though always exhilarated from the experience. But her earlier conviction that Lance Andrews was sure to become a major movie star was faltering.

She had finished eating and was listening to the radio and reading the current issue of *Vanity Fair* when the doorbell rang. She put down the magazine, stepped into what Lance called her "floosey mules," and headed to the door. Lance must have forgotten his keys.

"You'll never guess who just called me," Edna chirped as she pulled the door open. "Dennis!" Iris stared back blankly. "Dennis Drake, the guy we met in the commissary today. At least, that's his Hollywood name. Back in Chicago, he told me once, it was Dennis O'Reilly."

"What did he want?" Iris beckoned her inside.

"Lance not home yet?" Edna made a point of not coming into the apartment when Lance was home unless specifically invited.

"He'll probably come trailing in around midnight. Have some coffee with me."

"Dennis wants to talk to you," Edna said with a smug grin, following her out to the kitchen.

"What for?" All at once Iris was wary.

"Relax, baby," Edna chuckled. "He's not trying to climb into your bed. I made sure he knows you're married. This is strictly professional. He wants to talk to you about a part in the movie he's going to do. Iris," her voice deepened in excitement, "he said you were a girl with great bones. That means he thinks you'll photograph sensationally with good camera treatment."

"Edna, I'm not an actress—" But her mind was suddenly racing.

"Honey, for movies first you have to be beautiful. Then they worry about the acting. I think my young friend Dennis wants to create his own star. That could be you."

"Edna, it's crazy—"

"This is the town where crazy things happen. He wants to see you in his office tomorrow morning at nine. You be there."

## Chapter 10

Iris sat in a chair facing Dennis Drake — at his desk in the small, starkly unadorned office — and listened to him with uncharacteristic gravity.

"You understand, Iris?" he reiterated. "I'm not making any wild Hollywood promises. But if you're willing to do exactly as I say, I think you have a real future in this business."

"I'll do whatever you say," she agreed. She knew he wasn't talking about hopping into bed with her. "You run the show."

"I'm having a small part written in for you in my next picture. Just a few lines," he added quickly. *He knew she was scared shitless.* "I'll ask Edna to coach you. She'll be paid for it. I want Nat to see you in action." Nat Blumberg was head of Sunrise Films.

"Okay." Her heart was pounding. *Dennis Drake thought she could be a movie star.*

"Nat's dying to spring somebody new, somebody different on movie audiences. If I can bring this off," he acknowledged, "then I'll be Nat's fair-haired boy. I'll be able to write my own ticket in Hollywood."

"Great." She managed a shaky smile. She wouldn't say anything about this to Lance. Not yet. If it turned out to be awful, he'd never stop riding her about it.

"We start on the picture in ten days. There'll be four or five days' work for you. You'll get a call from the studio about when to report. In the meantime, I want you to take dancing lessons—" He was scribbling an address on a piece of paper. "The studio will pay for it. And you need a new hairstyle. Something smarter. Come in tomorrow morning and ask for Adolpho. I'll tell him what I want. You have to stand out from the others in this town — more than one more pretty face."

In a haze of incredulity Iris left Dennis Drake's office and hurried to where Edna waited for her in the Ford roadster.

"You look like you've just discovered you have the winning ticket in the Irish sweepstakes," Edna greeted her. "Give, give!"

Iris reported on the exchange with Dennis while Edna nodded in satisfaction at intervals.

"I'm scared to death," Iris confessed. "I was never even in a school play."

"It's a cinch," Edna comforted. "I'll work with you. It's like playing a game. You're just being somebody else. And with your looks, they won't expect Ethel Barrymore."

"Don't say anything to Lance about this afternoon," Iris warned. "If things work out, then I'll tell him."

Iris told Lance that her new hairstyle had been the inspiration of one of Edna's cronies and pretended that she had several days of "extra" work coming up while she started the dancing lessons. Lance had a bit part in a Western and loathed it. Still, it was better than soda-jerking, he conceded.

Her first day on the set with Dennis Iris tried to appear confident. She made a point of being friendly to the crew as well as the cast and sensed that Dennis, who was clearly respected by his cast, was pleased. At the end of the day she left the studio exhausted from tension yet exhilarated that she had come through without any major catastrophe.

Edna, who'd worked as an "extra" for the day on another movie being filmed on the lot, was waiting to drive her home.

"How do you feel?" Edna grinned slyly.

"I was feeling terrific," she admitted. "But now I have to go home and tell Lance. It was bad enough when I was doing 'extra' work."

"He'll like the extra money coming in," Edna surmised. "That jalopy of his is always in the shop."

As Iris had expected, Lance was already in the apartment when she arrived. He'd had a morning appointment with a new agent and was stretched on the sofa with a gin and tonic in one hand.

"Christ, if they offer me one more bit part in a Western, I'm leaving town," he grumbled. "What's for dinner?"

109

"Hamburgers and salad." Here he was lying stretched out doing nothing—probably for hours—and he had the nerve to ask her, *"What's for dinner?"* She hesitated, gearing herself for what had to be said.

"Something nutty happened today." She kicked off her shoes and sat on the arm of the club chair. "Somebody didn't show up on the set so I got promoted from 'extra' to a bit part."

Lance swung his feet to the floor. *"You?"* His voice skeptical. "Who did you sleep with, Iris?"

"You've got a nerve!" Her eyes darkened in anger. "You know I don't play around."

He deliberated for a moment.

"Okay, so you fell into shit and came out a star," he drawled. "Enjoy your big moment, baby."

"I'll be working again tomorrow." She rose from the chair and headed for the kitchen. "I'm in another scene."

"Don't burn that hamburger," Lance called after her, burning with jealousy. "You know I like it rare."

After he saw the rushes on her first bit part, Dennis ordered Iris to lose weight. She stared at him in shock.

"You think I'm too fat?"

"The camera adds ten pounds," he said briskly. "I want you to take off fifteen: I want the cameras to pick up those great cheekbones and jawlines without an ounce of fat."

"Okay," she said softly.

"You're all set for my next two pictures," he told her. "They're just to fill Sunrise's commitments to the theaters. But I'm working on Nat to trust me with a major film. You'll tag along, baby," he encouraged.

Lance was sullen and argumentative when Iris and he were together, even though she played down her "run of good luck." She was aware that he was avoiding "extra" work on the strength of her checks. He was full of derision for those in Hollywood who predicted that "talkies" would soon take over the industry, but Dennis was intrigued with the new medium. Dennis was sure the day would come—not right away, of course—when moviegoers would ignore theaters that did not provide talking pictures.

Iris was impatient at how long it took to lose fifteen pounds—she wanted it to happen overnight. But she was determined to *make* it happen despite the agony of depriving herself of her cherished sweets, the calorie-rich salad dressings and the hamburgers dripping fat that had been standard fare for Lance and her. In four weeks, she promised herself, she'd be as slim as Laura. "The prettiest toothpick in Magnolia," Papa used to call Laura and urged her to drink Ovaltine three times a day. As the pounds began to melt away, she saw in the mirror what Dennis meant. Her cheekbones were elegantly outlined. Her eyes seemed enormous. And as she slimmed down to thoroughbred sleekness, Iris cannily began to change her style, becoming less the flamboyant flapper and more the smart young sophisticate. She studied *Vogue* and *Harper's Bazaar* with a passion.

She wrote Laura about the possibilities that lay ahead. "It may not work out at all, Laura—but I'm so thrilled at having this chance."

Walking up the stairs to the apartment—her dress clinging wetly between her shoulder blades on this humid July night—Laura heard the radio. Bernie must have come home early. Mrs. Goldstein never played the radio when she sat with Jonnie. She was always afraid she'd wake him.

Thank God for Mrs. Goldstein. Bernie had insisted he could always get home from the office in time for her to leave for classes, but she had seen the way his bosses were piling work on him. And Mrs. Goldstein was pleased to be earning a little extra money for presents for her grandchildren.

Despite her tiredness Laura smiled while she waited for Bernie to respond to the doorbell.

"You didn't expect to find me here yet," Bernie surmised while he opened the door. He reached to kiss her. "The heat get you down?"

"It's awful. I almost fell asleep in class." At least tomorrow was Saturday. In the hot weather Bernie tried not to work later than one o'clock. Maybe they would take Jonnie and run out to Brighton for a few hours.

"Go sit down in the living room, and I'll bring you a glass of ice-cold lemonade," Bernie ordered.

111

"Let me go look in on Jonnie first—"

"Jonnie's fine. You saw him four hours ago. Sit," he threw over his shoulder and headed into the kitchen. "Guess what?" he called to her ebulliently. "I'm off tomorrow. All day."

Laura stopped dead, then detoured to the kitchen.

"What do you mean? Why is the office closing?"

"Laura, be grateful," he chided. "Never ask a question like that." He poured lemonade into a glass, returned the pitcher to the refrigerator.

"Bernie, why will the office be closed tomorrow?" she persisted.

"Because, my love, I have a special assignment." He handed her the glass, dropped an arm about her shoulders, and prodded her down the tiny hall to the living room. "And you're going with me."

"Where are we going?" Bernie loved to tease her.

"Out to Montauk. Mr. Weinstein is loaning me his Studebaker."

"Where's Montauk?" She dropped onto the sofa and kicked off her shoes while Bernie adjusted the electric fan to direct the air to her. She squinted in thought. "Out on Long Island somewhere?"

"One hundred and twenty-five miles out into the Atlantic. We can drive it comfortably in about four hours." He was pleased he would have a chance to drive. He had learned to drive at Mr. Weinstein's instructions when he first began to work for the firm. On occasion, in addition to being their hardest-working young attorney, Bernie filled in as Mr. Weinstein's chauffeur. Each time they considered buying a car of their own, Bernie decided to invest in the stock market instead. "We'll leave around six in the morning and get back around ten or eleven at night."

"Must we leave so early?" Laura reproached. "Jonnie sleeps till past seven."

"Jonnie will stay here with Mrs. Goldstein," Bernie said firmly. Laura's mouth opened in shock. "I've already talked to her. She agrees with me—it's time you had a day off."

"Bernie!"

"Don't you trust Jonnie with Mrs. Goldstein?"

"You know I do." Laura protested.

"Then it's settled. Mrs. Goldstein will sleep over so it won't matter how late we come home. And stop fretting," he scolded. "You can phone once or twice during the day and check in."

"It'll be wonderful to get out of the steaming city," Laura admitted. A whole day alone together would be like a miniature honeymoon. "Bernie, what's this assignment?"

"Mr. Weinstein is sending me out with papers to be signed by a wealthy client who's staying there for a month. He's involved with Carl Fisher's new development in Montauk. Fisher and his associates bought almost ten thousand acres out there—with nine miles of waterfront. I hear it's one of the most beautiful stretches of beach anywhere in the world. Fisher is vowing to make Montauk 'the Miami Beach of the North.' He's been working on the new project since early in '26."

"So that's why you're sparkling like a Christmas tree," Laura laughed.

"I'm dying to see what Fisher's doing with the land."

"Let's go look in on Jonnie and then go to bed," Laura said. "If you mean it about leaving at six." *She had never been away from Jonnie for a whole day and evening.*

"In the car at six," Bernie said exuberantly. "We'll pack breakfast and lunch and have dinner at Gurney's Restaurant in Montauk—on the firm's expense account. Mr. Weinstein says it's a great place for fish—and we can stare at the ocean while we eat." Bernie knew that to her dining out was one of the great pleasures of the universe—but one in which they seldom indulged. Bernie was determined to make every dollar they could save earn more on the stock market.

By 6 A.M. the next morning—already humid at sunrise—she and Bernie were in Mr. Weinstein's Studebaker.

"This early we'll miss all the traffic." Bernie radiated enthusiasm. "When we're out on the south shore, we'll park somewhere and have breakfast." Laura had filled a thermos with coffee, and they'd bought onion rolls at the neighborhood bakery. "Did I tell you last night?" he asked as he stopped for a red light. "Carl Fisher bought a group of houses out at Montauk that were designed by Stanford White back in the early 1880s. 'Summer cottages' with nine or ten bedrooms," he grinned. "I really would love to see them."

113

"Bernie, if you weren't a lawyer, would you want to be an architect?" Laura asked curiously. He always seemed to light up when he talked about famous houses. She remembered his excitement when he showed her the Century Club and the Villard houses in New York—also designed by Stanford White.

Bernie thought for a moment.

"Not an architect," he said. "Maybe a real-estate developer in the style of Carl Fisher. Maybe someday—when we're both established as lawyers and with a killing from the stock market—we'll get out of New York. Move down to Magnolia. We can practice law down there as well as in New York."

"Oh, Bernie!" Laura was awed by the prospect.

"Maybe we'll move into real-estate developing on the side," he pursued. "In real estate everything is in the timing. It's not just having the money to buy. It's knowing *when* to buy. *What* to buy. *What* to build."

"Bernie, you'd love Magnolia. And it'd be so good for Jonnie. And," Laura said, her face luminous, "we'll clear Papa's name. Together, we'll be able to do that."

"In time, Laura," Bernie said gently. "All in good time."


Bernie decreed that their first hour or two in Montauk belonged to them. Later he would contact Mr. Moncrief. Now they walked hand in hand along the magnificent stretch of beach. The sky was a cloudless blue reflected in the sea. The only sounds were those of the gulls cawing in flight and of the waves crashing against the white sand.

Laura was astonished that they were the sole occupants of the beach.

"Bernie, where are all the people?" After all, this was a resort town.

"Probably up at Montauk Manor," he surmised. "We'll get a look at it later." He chuckled. "We sure as hell can't afford to stay there. Or perhaps everybody's out fishing."

Later they discovered the well-populated bathing casino, and the long ocean boardwalk. From here they walked a block into the new center of town.

"See that?" Bernie pointed to the impressive seven-story granite-trimmed red-brick building that dominated the area.

"That's the Carl G. Fisher Office Building. It's an exact replica of his Florida office."

Laura's eyes swept over the handful of low Tudor stores that comprised the center of town.

"How strange to put so tall a building here!"

After a picnic lunch they sought out the "summer cottage" where Mr. Moncrief was vacationing with family. Moncrief signed the necessary papers, and then in a burst of proud proprietorship he took them off on a guided tour of the town. They saw the Tudor gabled Montauk Manor high on a hill — with 178 guest rooms and a dining room capable of seating 500. They drove past the colonial mansion, set on fifteen rolling acres, that was the home of Carl Fisher. He proudly showed them the new homes that were being constructed in every imaginable style — yet all fitting in with the landscape.

They drove from the rolling green knolls down to the yacht basin Fisher had created and his new Star Island in Lake Montauk.

"Fisher expects Montauk to become the new harbor for New York City," Moncrief confided. "The harbor can accommodate forty-seven ocean-going liners. Passengers coming from Europe can save a whole day's travel by disembarking here."

While the two men talked, Laura grappled with the realization that Bernie's heart was in real-estate developing. Bernie wanted to build.

"Bet you didn't know we have Stanford White cottages here," Mr. Moncrief said. "They were built back in 1881 and 1882 for people like Robert W. DeForest of Southern Pacific Railroad. For a while after the original owners died off, they just sat around in neglect. Then Carl came out and bought up some of them for his friends."

Laura and Bernie were delighted when Moncrief contrived for a personal tour of one of the houses. They were swept up in admiration for the elegant staircases, the multitude of fireplaces, the wood-paneled ceilings.

Finally Mr. Moncrief drove Laura and Bernie back to his house, where they had left the Studebaker.

"Don't rush back to the city," he encouraged. "Spend the rest of the afternoon walking on the beach. We don't have air like this back in New York. Have dinner at Gurney's and watch the sunset. Nothing can quite match the sunrises and the sunsets over the ocean at Montauk."

Walking with Bernie on the clean white sand again—after a phone call to Mrs. Goldstein—Laura was conscious of an inner excitement. She had thought she knew Bernie so well. That there was nothing new to learn about her husband. But here in Montauk she had looked into his soul.

Her mind focused on what Bernie had said about their going to Magnolia someday. Practicing law there, buying a house, venturing into real estate.

"Bernie, did you mean what you said earlier?" Laura asked. "About our going to Magnolia to live someday?" *She would go back as Laura Hunter.* Nobody would know her.

"I meant it, Laura. I promise," he emphasized quietly. "When the time is right, we'll go to Magnolia."

# Chapter 11

Early in the fall Iris received a letter from Laura that bubbled over with excitement. In her own letters Iris had not bothered to mention the titles of the movies in which she had small roles—she considered them of little consequence. But Laura and Bernie had gone to the neighborhood Loew's and had seen her.

"Suddenly there you were, Iris! I was so excited at seeing you, I started to cry. You looked just beautiful. And you were *good*. I'm so proud of you. I told all my neighbors and the students in my classes to go see my sister in *The Constant Heart*."

Late in November Dennis phoned Iris and told her to come to his office the following morning.

"Be there around nine," he ordered.

"Sure," she said. Something in his voice told her this meeting was special.

Iris arrived at Dennis's office at nine sharp. The whole studio knew he was at his desk by 7 A.M. when he wasn't on the set directing. Rumor said that he was battling with Tom Chase for the directing chore on an important new movie.

"Iris, come on inside—" He stood in the doorway, his smile magnetic, his bearing confident. He'd got the picture, Iris guessed.

"You look like a cat who's raided a fifty-gallon fish tank," she giggled while he shut the door behind them.

"Close to that," he grinned. "I'm directing the biggest production Sunrise has ever put on film. And there's a juicy part for you in it."

"Oh, Dennis!" She glowed with anticipation—but an instant later alarm took root in her. "Do you think I'm ready for it?"

"I'll make you ready. I showed Nat what you could do with that last part. He likes the way you look on the screen. Sit down, baby," he said. "I don't want you to fall on your face."

"Why would I fall on my face?" But she sat in the chair he indicated.

"I've convinced Nat to put you under a five-year contract—with the usual six-month options." He paused, his smile teasing her. "Starting at seventy-five dollars a week. If you do the job I expect, I'll make sure they up your salary."

"Oh, Dennis!" Iris leapt to her feet and flung her arms about him. "I can't believe it!"

"Believe it, Iris," he said and kissed her. Suddenly it wasn't the usual, casual kiss; it was a passionate embrace, disconcerting to both. "You let me down," he tried to laugh it off as they pulled apart, "and I'll beat your tail to ribbons."

Iris hurried back to the Ford, ordering herself to forget that heated moment in Dennis's arms. It didn't mean anything. Nothing had changed; they had a business arrangement.

She'd had a fight this morning with Lance about taking the car. But he didn't need it and why should she wake up Edna to drive her to the studio? When she got back to the house she found Lance at the dinette table playing solitaire. God, she hated the sound of the cards being shuffled. When he was mad or bored, he played solitaire. He played it a lot lately.

"Hi—" She crossed to the gas range and put a light under the coffee pot.

"I thought you were working today." Lance finished off a game. "You said you had to go to the studio."

"Lance, the craziest thing happened." She reached for a coffee cup. "Want some coffee?"

He shook his head and began to shuffle the cards again.

"What crazy thing happened?" He was mildly curious.

"I had this appointment with Dennis Drake." She braced herself to tell Lance. "He says that Sunrise wants to put me under contract for five years. Starting at seventy-five dollars a week!" Her elation broke through her determination to be casual. Compared to what she had earned at Lord & Taylor, that was a fortune. Even the workers at the Ford Motor Company—the best paid manual workers in the country—earned only 62.5 cents an hour. Bernie with his great law degree was earning forty dollars a week. "Lance, I can't believe it!"

"You've got something going with Drake!" Lance pushed back his chair and leapt to his feet. "That's how you've been getting these bits all along!"

"I barely know Dennis," she protested hotly. "He said Nat Blumberg had seen the rushes on that last bit I did and told Dennis to sign me up. Dennis—"

"Forget it," Lance ordered. "I don't want my wife playing around with some studio big cheese. I know what goes on."

"I *won't* forget it." She gaped at him in disbelief. "Seventy-five dollars a week! Every week."

"I said to forget it." He moved menacingly towards her, a hand raised. "You do what I say or—"

"You touch me, Lance, and I'll castrate you!" She grabbed the bread knife that lay on the counter.

"Put down that knife, you little nut." But he lowered his hand. "And you get on the phone and tell that bastard you don't want his lousy contract. You know about those six-month options. He'll screw you till he's had enough, and then they'll drop the option. Those contracts don't mean a damn."

"I'm signing the contract, Lance." She struggled to sound calm. How could he expect her to turn it down? "I won't throw away this chance."

"What kind of actress do you think you could ever be?" he taunted. "You act with your tits and your ass. You have no brains—just a body." His face flushed with rage. "I've had enough of this fucking town. I'm taking the car and going back to New York. I never should have listened to you about coming out here. And when you find the time," he said bitterly, "take yourself to Reno and get a divorce."


Morning sunlight filtered through the blinds and elicited a muttered protest from Iris. Then all at once she was awake, remembering the fight with Lance yesterday morning. He'd slammed out of the apartment and still hadn't returned at bedtime. Edna said he was probably in some gin mill getting ossified.

She turned to the pillow beside hers. Lance hadn't come home last night. She lay immobile while her mind digested this. Had he meant it about going back to New York? About a divorce? In a burst of movement she left the bed, crossed the room to the closet. His clothes were gone. She opened the drawers of the chest that normally contained his shirts, socks, and underwear. All empty.

In sudden suspicion she hurried to the kitchen. Most of the cash they kept in a jar in the cabinet for daily expenses was gone. She didn't have to go out to the parking area to know the car was gone.

Okay. It wasn't a tragedy. All she had to do was wait for Dennis to call her to come in to sign the contract. She was about to become a Hollywood starlet. She didn't need Lance anymore.

Dennis phoned her the following morning and told her to come to his office immediately. Edna had left for a day's extra work at another studio. Iris explained she'd have to call a taxi.

"Don't bother," he said briskly. "I'll send over a studio car."

Within thirty minutes the big black studio car had picked her up and delivered her to the lot. Churning with excitement she hurried to Dennis's office. He had the contracts on his desk. He called in a secretary to witness the signing.

"You're old enough to sign a contract?" he asked belatedly.

"By a few months," she laughed. *She was under contract to Sunrise Films. On salary as of today.*

"Let's go over to the commissary and celebrate with an early lunch." He felt smug about this deal, Iris told herself. It would be terrific for both of them.

Over lunch Iris told him about the breakup with Lance.

"Are you upset?" He was solicitous.

"No," she admitted. "It was long dead between Lance and me. I'll get a divorce somewhere along the line." She shrugged vaguely.

Dennis squinted in thought.

"Everything's going just right for us, Iris. The new picture starts shooting in Reno in two weeks. I want you to head out there tomorrow and establish residence. While you're sitting out the divorce, you'll be working. The studio will pay for everything. Nat likes his starlets to be unencumbered." He grinned. "And you're seventeen. That's what the publicity department will tell the world."

"Okay." Iris felt a surge of satisfaction. Dennis meant to make her a star. Anything he said was okay.

"We're great for each other, Iris. In a year—two at the most," he prophesied, "you'll be Sunrise Films' brightest young star. And Nat Blumberg will eat out of my hand for bringing you to him."


The morning was gray and cold, the kitchen windows steamed over as heat rattled in the radiators. Jonathan was sleeping late this morning, for which Laura was grateful. She had been able to spend almost two hours studying for her French exam tonight, the final class before the winter school break. Now she sat at the table with a cup of steaming coffee at hand and re-read Iris's letter.

She had worried about Iris's marriage from the very beginning. She had suspected Iris was marrying to get away from her job, reaching for something better in the world. But if Iris was in Reno sitting out a divorce, at least she was financially safe. Seventy-five dollars a week was an enormous jump upward. And she sounded so confident about the future. It was amazing to realize that her sister was on the way to becoming a movie star.

Laura started at the sound of the doorbell.

"Just a minute," she called, hurrying to respond. She remembered Bernie's admonition as he left for the office to take a long nap with Jonathan in the afternoon. She was always sleepy in the first weeks of pregnancy. Hopefully Jonathan would have a little sister.

Laura opened the door and smiled at plump Mrs. Goldstein standing there with a cinnamon-laced coffee cake.

"Bernie's favorite, darling. It's just from the oven," Mrs. Goldstein beamed. "I thought maybe you'd like a piece now with some coffee."

"I'd love it," Laura pulled the door wide. "Come in and have some with me. I have fresh coffee on the stove."

"You're feeling all right?" Mrs. Goldstein asked solicitously. She had known about the new baby only hours after Bernie. Even before Iris received word.

"I'm fine." Laura went to the cabinet to bring down the pretty china that Mrs. Goldstein liked. "Just the crazy sleepiness."

"You're going to keep on with the night school?" Mrs. Goldstein's face betrayed her concern. "That subway trip into the city four nights a week." She clucked in disapproval. "Such a strain on you."

"I'm just so glad I'll be able to finish out the term. And start the next one." She laughed. "Bernie says we plan well." But the baby—like Jonathan—had been an accident. Two beloved accidents.

"Bernie's a good man." Mrs. Goldstein had enormous respect for a man who allowed his wife—*"a mother already"*—to go on to college.

"The best," Laura said tenderly. Not only did she love Bernie; she respected him for his wonderful mind, his compassion, his involvement with the needs of the world.

He was so upset by the inadequacies of Mayor Walker, by the corruption that pervaded the city government. And now he worried because Herbert Hoover—a Republican—would be inaugurated as the thirty-first president next March. Hoover talked hopefully about wiping out poverty; he promised "two chickens in every pot and a car in every garage." Though millions of Americans believed the Republican party would keep the economy healthy, Bernie was a diehard Democrat.

Laura's eyes fell on the letter on the table. She often talked to Mrs. Goldstein about Iris. "The letter was from my sister—" she sighed. "Bad news and good news."

Mrs. Goldstein listened sympathetically while Laura talked about Iris's blooming career and about the imminent divorce.

"Laura, it's best this way. Now, before she's tied down with children." Mrs. Goldstein was somber. "I don't understand young people today. We're living in crazy times. Nobody wants to take on responsibility. They all spend, spend, spend. Like the world is going to end tomorrow, and they're scared to death they won't enjoy every minute left to them. Not everybody," she conceded. "I look at Bernie and you, and I'm proud of this country. In Russia what young girl can think about going to school and becoming a lawyer?"

Laura's face lighted at sounds from the smaller bedroom. "Jonathan's awake," she said, a lilt in her voice. "Let's go take him out of the crib."

Back from Reno—divorced and with her first important film role behind her—Iris was introduced by Dennis to her new dramatic coach. She was being groomed for the young leading role opposite a major male star and Dennis demanded that her wardrobe take top priority at the studio. She knew that Dennis was counting on her success to win the position of Nat Blumberg's number one man.

Dennis left the studio each day to meet Iris at his cottage for an evening of intensive work. He planned to rehearse her in every scene of the movie before the cast went before the cameras. At times when he yelled at her, impatient that her every gesture be right, she bit her lip to keep back the angry retorts.

Two nights before the cameras were set to roll on the new picture Dennis and the coach worked with her till close to eleven, when the coach rebelled.

"Dennis, enough already," he complained. "I have to be up at seven tomorrow morning. Knock it off for tonight." He turned to Iris. "Come on, I'll drive you home."

"No," Dennis said. "I'll work with Iris for another hour. You go on."

The coach left. Dennis collapsed into a chair and ordered Iris to go through the scene again.

"And watch yourself," he said sharply. "You can't move out of camera range."

Exhausted, Iris began to go through the scene again.

"Hold it, Iris!" Dennis leapt to his feet, tense and determined. "I've got it now. You're doing just one wrong thing. You're playing the whole scene on one key. It's got to be built up slowly. Now pretend I'm Ken." Ken was the male lead. "The camera's rolling. Let's do the scene."

Miraculously she understood what Dennis wanted from her. She felt a new lightness. Begin softly, her mind commanded, and build up to the kiss. *She knew what Dennis wanted.*

But when Dennis pulled her into his arms and his mouth reached for hers, they forgot the Hays Office decree that kisses should run no longer than ten feet of film. This was clearly the version shot for the European audiences, who expected their love scenes to be torrid.

"Stay here tonight," Dennis whispered when they broke for air.

Her smile was suddenly dazzling. "I thought you'd never ask."

At six sharp Dennis's alarm clock was a raucous intrusion. He reached across to silence it.

"I'll phone in to say I'll be in late," he told Iris. "We'll work this morning on your first scene. I want it exactly right."

"I'll make us breakfast," Iris offered. "Scrambled eggs, toast, and coffee?"

"That's good enough." His eyes were oddly contemplative. "Why don't we simplify our lives and move you in with me?"

"Sounds great." Excitement charged through her.

"After breakfast, we'll drive over to your apartment and you can pack up," he said.

"That won't take long," she laughed. Everything was working out sensationally. Dennis and she would be together every hour of the day. He'd be her director, her teacher — her lover.

All at once Iris was no longer on the fringe of Hollywood. She was part of the magic circle that lunched at the Brown Derby, went to dinner with Mary Pickford and Douglas Fairbanks at Pickfair, danced in the elegant Patent Leather Room in the Ambassador Hotel, partied almost nightly with Hollywood's biggest stars. Dennis said the socializing — all slavishly reported by Louella Parsons — was important to her career. Still, Dennis and she were both at the studio every morning before 7 A.M.

Iris was a mass of nerves as she dressed for the screening of *The Velvet Lady* in which she played her first major role. Before the screening — at the Sunrise Films screening room seating three hundred people, they were to attend a dinner party at Nat Blumberg's house in Beverly Hills. At the dressing table that Dennis had added to the bedroom as a surprise for her, she sat in a black satin teddy and focused on her makeup. Her dress — black chiffon splashed with silver sequins — lay across the oversized bed in which Dennis and she had made tumultuous love only an hour ago. The dress, like the chinchilla cape she was to wear over it — had been borrowed from the studio wardrobe.

The sneak preview in San Bernardino had been a wild success. The audience—seeing *The Velvet Lady* as a second, free movie—had obligingly written comments on cards distributed at the end of the film. Most of them had commented on her performance. *"Iris Adams is gorgeous!" "Iris Adams the best thing since Pola Negri and Gloria Swanson." "Wonderful movie. Let's see more of Iris Adams."*

She had been so excited that she'd forgotten the time difference and had phoned Laura in Brooklyn after the sneak preview. She'd awakened Laura at four in the morning. But Laura was so pleased to hear about the new picture that she hadn't minded.

For a few moments Iris was caught up in a surge of homesickness. God, she wished she could see Laura! She'd never even seen the baby, and he was already over a year and a half old. And Laura expected to give birth again in July. It astonished her that Laura kept on with night school—but then she was always as tenacious as a bulldog once she made up her mind about something.

Dennis said Nat was sure to tear up the old contract and up her money to three or four hundred a week after tonight's screening. Wouldn't Laura be amazed when she heard about that?

Yesterday she had gone out and bought herself a brand new Packard runabout. The monthly payments were high, but she could afford it. From the automobile dealer's she had gone to I. Magnin and bought a beautifully tailored tweed coat to be sent to Laura, because she remembered how Laura and she used to freeze in their cheap Klein's basement coats in the New York winters.

"Iris, shake a leg," Dennis called from the doorway. "Nat's got a thing about everybody being on time."

As 1929 moved along, Hollywood grew increasingly apprehensive about the effect of the new talking pictures on the movie business. Those who had been so sure it would be only a passing fad were reconsidering. In February MGM premiered *Broadway Melody*—a huge box-office success—followed by *Hollywood Revue* of 1929, offering such stars as

Marie Dressler, Norma Shearer, John Gilbert, Laurel and Hardy, and Joan Crawford.

Suddenly every studio was preparing to take the plunge into talking pictures. But the new medium presented monumental difficulties. Movie companies were fighting desperately for delivery of sound apparatus, even to the point of some convert hijacking. And with the arrival of sound, more sophisticated literary properties were required. Studios sent scouts to New York to buy Broadway plays and popular novels that could be coverted into screenplays.

Studios were pushing their stars to work with diction coaches. Determined to keep pace with the changing scene, Dennis hired one of the best diction coaches in Hollywood to work with Iris. She rebelled after the first lesson.

"Dennis, this is crazy!" she wailed. "If I try to talk the way he wants me to, I'll sound like such a phony. I don't play classy Broadway actresses, so why try to sound like one?"

"Baby, it's important to speak well," he cajoled. "Some of the top stars have had hysterics the first time they heard their voices on discs."

"Dennis, what's so hard about talking dialogue?" Iris shrugged away his concerns. "I'll listen carefully to myself when I'm studying my lines. If there's a word I don't understand, then I'll just ask you," she said triumphantly.

"You'll do a lot of dancing in the new picture," he told her. He grinned. "You Charleston as well as Joan Crawford in *Our Dancing Daughters*." He sighed. "But you should be working with a diction coach."

"Dennis, do you see anything wrong with the way I talk?" Iris challenged. "Does anybody point at me and say, 'Oh, God, what a terrible voice'? I play sexy flappers," she pinpointed, draping her arms about him. "Now when do we start on my first talkie?"

"I worry about your Southern accent," he admitted.

"Dennis, everybody out here loves it," she laughed. "What's to worry about?" *The Velvet Lady* and the movie that followed were breaking box-office records. There was even talk that *The Velvet Lady* would be nominated for an Academy Award.

Within three weeks Iris was involved in fittings and publicity shots for the new film, and there was talk of sending her on a promotion tour. *Refuge* was to be made in four weeks on the studio's highest budget to date. While the story centered around the character Iris would play, the cast was bolstered with Broadway names brought out to insure that Sunrise Films' first talkie would have acceptable voices.

Early in July Iris came home from a long, tense day of shooting to find a telegram from Bernie. Laura had given birth to a seven-pound, three-ounce daughter, to be named Kate in memory of their mother. Iris immediately phoned Bernie at home and plied him with questions about Laura and their new daughter.

"Like Jonathan, Kate's the image of Laura," he said with pride, "except that Jonathan has my dark hair. Actually," he laughed, "that makes him the spitting image of you."

Sitting at the edge of the oversized bed in Dennis's bedroom after putting down the phone, Iris made a silent vow to go to New York to see Laura and the children once the new picture was in the can. She'd made three pictures in a row and the studio would have to let her off for four weeks, she resolved.

She'd travel in a drawing room of her own, she decided. Edna would go along as her secretary. She dallied briefly with the thought of flying. With the new air-rail combined service it was possible to travel coast to coast in forty-eight hours. No, she rejected this—she felt safer on the train. What was the fun of becoming a movie star, only to die in an airplane crash?

"Let's call it a night." Dennis yawned as he walked into the bedroom with a scotch and soda in one hand. "The damn alarm goes off in five hours."

Stimulated by the conversation with Bernie, Iris was suddenly amorous.

"Dennis, you don't need a drink tonight," she said seductively. Dennis wasn't much of a drinker. He drank only when he was tired and wanted a solid night's sleep. "I'll make you sleep." Her smile was a provocative promise as she rose to her feet and began to undress.

"I'm beat," he warned, but his eyes were focused on her with what she recognized as arousal.

"Poor baby, I know how to resuscitate you," she laughed as she kicked aside her dress, teddy, and stockings and crossed to the bed. "You worry too much."

All through the four weeks of working on *Refuge* — brought in right on schedule — Dennis had refused to allow the cast to see or hear the daily rushes. Iris was faintly in awe of her co-star and supporting cast, most of whom had heavy Broadway credits. The atmosphere on the set was different from what she'd known in the past, more reserve, less kibbitzing. Dennis, too, seemed different on this picture. He was different even at home — except in bed. Then he was the old Dennis.

Now, at last, Iris rejoiced as she sat in the darkened Glendale movie theater chosen for the first sneak preview. She was about to see herself in her first talkie. The Friday night audience seemed in a festive mood.

"When's this thing going to be over?" she whispered impatiently to Dennis. The scheduled film seemed to be endless.

"In a few minutes, Iris." His voice was tense. He sat silently in his seat, shoulders hunched.

Nat Blumberg sat on the aisle on the other side of Dennis. Both men had seemed grim and uncommunicative since they'd left Hollywood in a studio limousine. They had a hell of a lot of money riding on Sunrise's first talkie, Iris consoled herself.

Finally the feature film was over. The announcement came on the screen that a sneak preview was to follow. An aura of anticipation hovered over the audience.

When Iris appeared on screen, whistles came from the seats ahead. She broke into a cold sweat while she waited to hear her first lines of dialogue, her mouth involuntarily preparing to form the words in unison with the sound. But then the first line in her opening scene penetrated her consciousness. She felt sick with shock.

"Dennis, that doesn't sound like me!" she protested.

She was aware of a few titters that rippled through the audience. *She hadn't said anything funny*. She glanced at Dennis. He was staring hard at the screen, his mouth set. Ice-cold with alarm Iris watched the movie. She sounded different from the others. *She sounded awful*.

Twenty minutes after the film had begun, Nat Blumberg lumbered to his feet and moved into the aisle.

"We'll reshoot all her scenes," he said in a furious whisper to Dennis. "That's the only way to save the picture. Adams is through at Sunrise Films."

*Part 2*

# Chapter 12

Laura dressed in nervous haste. With her compulsion for promptness she was determined to be at Grand Central Terminal at least half an hour before Iris's train was due to arrive this afternoon—just in case it should be early. Now she studied her reflection in the mirror on the bedroom-closet door. From Iris—and the endless copies of *Vogue* and *Harper's Bazaar* that Iris had bought even if it meant going without lunch—she'd learned to dress smartly.

The image in the mirror was reassuring. Her simple black sheath—worn with a single strand of pearls—skimmed her slender body lovingly, highlighting her translucent white skin. Her hair—fast mellowing from its original auburn into a tawny brown—was worn in a chic bob. This afternoon's reflection was remarkably different from the Laura Roth who had arrived in New York slightly over five years ago.

Laura wished that the late September weather was unseasonably cold so that she could wear the exquisite tweed coat Iris had sent her from California. *Poor Iris.* She was pretending to be both brave and amused that her bonfire of a success had been extinguished in one ugly gust.

Bernie had understood right away, Laura remembered while she left their bedroom to look in on Jon and Katie, both asleep in their small room across the narrow hall. He'd warned *her* that she would have to work to lose her Southern accent before she ever walked into a courtroom to try a case.

*"It's sweet and charming and appealing, but it'll create the wrong image in court. It's rough enough to be a woman lawyer. You can't sound like a Georgia belle."*

Why didn't those monsters in Hollywood give Iris a chance to dump her accent before they dropped her option? She said there was nothing for her in the movies anymore—unless some bit part came up for a girl with a Southern accent. Suddenly nobody was making silent pictures anymore. For Iris the dream was over. *"I'm twenty-two years old and my career is finished!"*

Laura lingered a moment before Katie's cradle, another at Jon's crib. These were precious moments, when both children were asleep and she was suffused with love for them and their father. She was so lucky. She mustn't be impatient about how long school was taking. She was a senior at Hunter now. Next time this year — God willing — she'd be in law school.

Already Bernie was working with her on elementary points of law. There were lawyers — men and women — who'd never gone to law school. They'd "read law" with a seasoned lawyer and then took the bar exams. And she learned from the typing she did for Bernie.

She worried about his discouragement at the cases the firm threw his way — real-estate closings and divorce suits. Bernie yearned to work to change the legal system to help the poor. One day, she reminded herself with anticipation, they would open their own law office. *Hunter & Hunter, Attorneys at Law.* The time would come when they could go down to Magnolia, search the records, discover a way to clear Papa's name.

Laura started at the sound of the doorbell. That would be Mrs. Goldstein, coming to sit with the children while she went into the city to meet Iris. She hurried to respond.

"I just nursed Katie," she told Mrs. Goldstein. "If I'm not back in time for her next feeding, I left a bottle in the icebox. Jon and Katie are both sleeping."

"Don't hurry home," Mrs. Goldstein encouraged. "Better you should miss the rush hour."

On the BMT en route to Manhattan, Laura thought back to her arrival in New York with Iris five years ago. Both of them scared of the future, grieving for Papa. How terrible Iris must feel about what happened in Hollywood. Just last week she'd read an article in *Time* about how so many fine actors and actresses were being thrown out of work by the talkies. John Gilbert was supposed to be the latest casualty.

Iris admitted she had saved nothing from the weeks when she was earning so much. *"The car dealer repossessed my car when I missed the last three payments. I needed the cash to buy my ticket back to New York."* Once she was washed up in pictures, Iris wrote, Dennis wanted no part of her. *"He said the smart thing was to get the hell out of Hollywood."*

Laura checked her watch as the subway rushed through the tunnel into Manhattan. In fifty minutes — if the train was on time — she'd see Iris. They'd not seen each other in almost three years. It seemed unbelievable.

Iris would have to sleep on the living room sofa. She would hate living in Brooklyn — but it would only be until she got her life together again.

Snatches of last night's conversation with Bernie filtered into her mind. *"Laura, she's going to have one hell of a time adjusting. She went so fast from selling hosiery in Lord & Taylor to Hollywood stardom. Knowing Iris, it'll be rough on both of you."* Iris wouldn't have any trouble finding a job, Laura comforted herself.

At Grand Central Laura learned that the train was to arrive on schedule. She took her place at the gate to wait. Iris was traveling on the celebrated Twentieth Century Limited. The car dealer might have repossessed her Stutz Torpedo, but Iris was returning to New York in a deluxe Pullman car.

The handful of those waiting grew into a festive crowd within the next twenty minutes. The famous red carpet was unrolled on the platform and the train was pulling into the station. As the passengers began to emerge, Laura sought eagerly for Iris. Then she spied her, sleek and beautiful, in a simple jersey dress in the style made popular by Coco Chanel. A fur coat was slung over one arm. She *looked* like a movie star, Laura thought tenderly.

"Laura!" Iris called out exuberantly as she spotted her in the crowd. "Oh, Laura!"

They clung together in a poignant surge of relief and pleasure. Two sisters separated for too long.

"Iris, you look wonderful." Laura's face was radiant with affection as she inspected her. "That California tan is so becoming." It made her eyes seem an incredible blue. "But you're so thin."

"No more than you," Iris laughed. "You were always the family string bean." Her eyes moved over her sister's figure. "You've filled out in the best places," she approved. "Marriage agrees with you." She reached forward to hug Laura

135

again. "I can't believe you're a married woman with two children!"

"And in a year a married woman with two children and a college degree," Laura said softly. A few minutes ago it seemed that Iris and she had been separated for such a terribly long time. Now—with her sister beside her—it seemed only yesterday that she had seen Iris off for California.

Iris turned to the porter, hovering close by with her two Vuitton valises bought in a burst of extravagance some weeks ago when Dennis had promised to take her to San Francisco.

"Just leave them here," she instructed the porter and reached into her purse for a tip.

"Would you like to stop for coffee before we go home?" Laura asked. She recoiled from the prospect of shoving themselves into the BMT at rush hour with those two large valises. "The trains will be mobbed right now."

"Let's go for coffee," Iris said. "We'll check the bags here at the station and come back for them. And no subway to-night," she said airily. "We'll wait till the traffic lets up and then take a taxi." Laura held back words of reproach for such extravagance. Today was special.

Over beef pies and coffee in the nearby Automat Laura and Iris chattered animatedly about the intervening years. Iris was almost matter-of-fact as she told Laura how she had tossed around her weekly salary. A five-hundred-dollar watch for Dennis for his birthday. Pure-silk sheets for their bed because Dennis said silk was sensuous. Her mink coat. Her gorgeous wardrobe. For a few moments Iris allowed her bitterness to show through.

"Laura, I was earning seven-fifty a week while we were making *Refuge*. In four months it would have gone up to a thousand. By the end of the year, Dennis said, it'd be up to two thousand a week. That's more than the president of the United States earns! How could the bubble burst like this?"

"Bernie said the timing was bad," Laura comforted. Why couldn't talkies have held off for a few years until Iris had earned—and put aside—a lot of money?

"Part of it's my fault." Iris tightened one slender hand into a taut fist. "Dennis tried to make me work with a diction coach. *I just didn't understand.*"

136

"Everything will work out." Laura contrived for an aura of optimism. "Right now we've got a lot of catching up to do."

Laura tried not to be aware of the steady click of the taxi meter. *The trip to Borough Park would cost a fortune.* Iris asked endless questions about Jon and Katie. She rebuked herself for coming east without bearing gifts.

"Iris, they're too young to know," Laura laughed. "Just love them."

"How's Bernie doing?" Iris asked.

"He's impatient for a raise. But actually he's doing well. Young lawyers just out of school are willing to work for almost nothing, just to get the experience. Even those from law schools like Harvard and Columbia."

Laura was pleased that Mrs. Goldstein made a fuss over Iris. She knew that other neighbors, too, were intrigued at the prospect of having a young Hollywood star in their midst.

"Bernie phoned," Mrs. Goldstein reported. "He said he should be home by ten."

Mrs. Goldstein returned to her own apartment and Laura took Iris into the tiny bedroom where the children slept. The faint spill of light from the hall illuminated their faces. Iris stared with an aura of awe and disbelief and pleasure.

"Laura, I can't believe it," she whispered. "Your son and daughter. My nephew and niece. I can't wait for tomorrow," she said in a burst of exuberance, "so I can pick them up and hold them."

Over coffee they sat on the sofa—which later would become Iris's bed—and continued to rehash the years. Exactly at ten Bernie arrived. He greeted his sister-in-law with affection. Laura told herself that this time there'd be none of the old friction between Bernie and Iris.

As Laura had expected, Iris was recognized by avid neighbors on the street and in the shops. They didn't realize her Hollywood career had been aborted. Iris casually explained she had taken a year off from pictures to work at losing her Southern accent. *"It sounds just ghastly in talkies."*

But after the first few days Iris recoiled from the waves of local adulation. Her career as a movie star belonged in the

137

past.

"It's dead, dead, dead!" she lamented to Laura.

Laura watched in concern while Iris closeted herself in their small apartment, pretending to be content to listen to the radio, to read the magazines Laura brought up for her from the candy store, and to play with Jon—who adored her, and to fuss over "my darling little Katie."

Bernie was shocked when Laura told him that Iris's entire savings consisted of a hundred and five dollars. *"Do you know what it cost her to travel on the Twentieth Century Limited?"* She was conscious of the unspoken questions in his mind. When would Iris go out to look for a job? When would she move into her own apartment? Laura knew, too, that he was uncomfortable that Iris wandered around the apartment day and night in her seductive Hollywood negligées. *"She's like a girl I might meet in a fancy whorehouse—if I was the type to go to them, which I'm not."*

In mid-October Bernie reminded Laura that the department stores were already hiring Christmas help. Why didn't Iris go to Lord & Taylor? She'd been well liked there.

"Bernie, she's terribly hurt. She needs a little time. Be patient with her," Laura pleaded. She commiserated with Iris, feeling her pain. *To go back to selling hosiery in a department store after being the hottest young star of the year.*

Bernie was troubled in these final days of October. The daughter of one of the partners in the law firm had just returned from six weeks in Europe. She talked about the rise of Hitler in Germany and how he ranted about the "Jewish menace," the "Jews of Wall Street who are ruining America." In Berlin, three hundred Nazis attempted to attack a synagogue; mounted police had to use clubs to disperse them.

Bernie was upset, too, by heavy breaks in the stock market, as headlined by The *New York Times*—though word had come through immediately after the October 4th break that the "big boys" were involved in a new wave of buying. There seemed to be an epidemic across the country to "get into the market." But most of their funds were tied up in stocks—bought, as customary, on margin, and Bernie was uneasy.

On the night of October 23 Bernie and Iris quibbled over what programs to hear. Nervous about the state of the stock market, Bernie wanted to listen to the news. All three networks were giving over considerable time to the news of the plummeting stocks. Since noon, stocks on the New York Stock Exchange had been taking catastrophic tumbles.

"I want to hear Rudy Vallee," Iris sulked.

"I need to hear the news." Bernie was unnaturally terse. "The market's going through some awful craziness."

Suddenly Laura was anxious. "Bernie, are we in trouble?"

"We could be," he conceded.

On Thursday, October 24, investors were frantically dumping shares. Margin calls were beginning to cause panic. Then in the afternoon there appeared to be a recovery, but rumors of financial ruin were rampant. Even several suicides were reported in the newspapers and on radio newscasts.

On Monday fresh disaster arrived. Brokers were besieged by orders to sell. By Tuesday morning—despite a statement by President Hoover that U.S. industry was sound—it was clear the market was in a state of panic.

In midafternoon—while Jon and Katie were napping and Iris was in the bathroom washing her hair—Laura was startled by the sound of a key in the door. She hurried forward to see Bernie walk into the apartment. His face was ashen, his eyes anguished. Laura knew without his saying a word that they had been wiped out.

"How could I have been such a damn fool?" he asked Laura, humble, angry at himself. "I was so damn greedy. I wanted enough to buy a house for us. Free and clear, I told myself," he said bitterly. "No mortgage. But I bought stocks on margin."

"Bernie, we'll be all right," Laura comforted him. "We're young. We can wait to buy a house." But she knew that property had become almost an obsession with him. "And we have our savings account."

"Not anymore," he whispered in anguish. "I pulled out everything to try to meet the margin call." Laura gasped in shock. *Conservative, cautious Bernie?* "It was useless. Hate me, Laura!" he said with sudden strength while she tried to assimilate the knowledge that their savings account—their emergency fund—was gone. "I've acted like a goddamn idiot!"

"We'll be all right," she insisted, pulling him into her arms.

But her heart was pounding. She had been so smug at the way they were putting money away. Life had seemed so *good*. "We'll manage. And I have a little surprise." She managed the semblance of a confident smile. "I've been saving a few dollars every week from the house money. When it reached five hundred, I was going to tell you. It's up to four hundred and seventy. But not to go into margin," she laughed shakily. "For our emergency fund."

"How did you do this?" He was amazed and touched.

"I shopped carefully. I cut corners. And each week I put another few dollars under the mattress."

"Tomorrow," he said tenderly, "put it into the bank. Only scared old ladies put money under the mattress."

"Into postal savings," Laura stipulated. "The government I trust."


Laura was bewildered that so many people appeared unaware that the country was in trouble. On a cold November Sunday night — while Iris lounged before the radio and listened to "Amos 'n' Andy," Laura and Bernie discussed this over coffee in the kitchen.

"How can so many people go on with their lives as though the country isn't in trouble?" Laura demanded. "I know a lot of people haven't been hurt, but they listen to the news on the radio. They read newspapers. They have to know how many people have lost every cent they owned in the stock market. We're all right," she emphasized for the hundredth time because Bernie never ceased to blame himself for their own losses. "But so many are in trouble."

Bernie sighed. "Things are going to get a lot worse before they get better." He paused for a moment. Iris — absorbed by the radio program — was laughing loudly in the living room and couldn't hear their conversation in the kitchen. "Laura, when's Iris going to start looking for a job? She can't spend the rest of her life hovering over the radio or reading *Vogue*."

"I'll talk to her," Laura promised. She knew Bernie was not concerned that their food budget was larger than normal. He was truly anxious about Iris's future. "I saw her looking at the *Help Wanted* ads in today's *Times*."

"Iris won't find an ad that says, 'Wanted: beautiful young

movie star,' " Bernie said bluntly. "She'll have to take what she can find."

"Maybe she'll go into the city tomorrow and look," Laura encouraged. "Bernie, she's not happy just sitting around this way." She wished desperately that she knew what to say, what to do to wash away the anguish she saw in her sister's eyes.

By the first of December the automobile industry was facing serious problems. Henry Ford had cut prices as a "contribution to the continuation of good business," but the market was saturated. Over a million used cars sat on secondhand lots. The Stutz Motor Car Company — makers of the car that seemed to epitomize the decade — went into bankruptcy.

New York stores reported the sales of radios were off by fifty percent, yet there was a boom in expensive motorboats. Houses with mortgages and cars bought on credit — by people no longer able to meet the payments — were being repossessed, yet there were the super-rich who had been unscathed by the market collapse and who were preparing to head for Palm Beach in their private railroad cars.

Other wealthy families — hard hit by the Crash — were firing their maids, butlers, chauffeurs. Manufacturers were cutting back on production, laying off workers by the thousands. Suddenly unemployment was soaring.

Three weeks before Christmas — bored with radio, restless in the confines of the small Brooklyn apartment — Iris went into the city in search of a job. She was unnerved to discover that the department stores had long waiting lists of would-be employees.

"They won't even let me fill out an application," Iris reported furiously. "What the hell is going on in this city?"

"Try other stores," Laura encouraged, but she was worried. "Or maybe the restaurants. You could be a hostess."


Iris went into the city half a dozen times in search for a job. The only offer she got was as a waitress in a smart restaurant. The salary was nonexistent; she was to work for tips. In addition, the owner made it clear that she was to occupy his bed on demand. Up until now she had been subconsciously sure that she would find a job once she could bring herself to accept something less than Hollywood stardom. Suddenly she was scared.

Feeling herself caged she prowled about the Brooklyn apartment; she was too distraught to lavish her usual affection on Jon and Katie, sharp with Laura and Bernie. Maybe she should have stayed in Hollywood. At least she would have picked up extra work.

On an early January evening Bernie arrived home with an unfamiliar air of joviality. Yet Iris sensed a self-consciousness underneath his high spirits. Was he about to tell her to get the hell out? *Laura wouldn't let him do that.*

Iris waited warily for some announcement from Bernie. She knew that Laura, too, felt strange undercurrents in him tonight. He followed his usual evening routine of helping Laura put Jon and Katie to bed while she made her customary trips into the kitchen to make sure supper wasn't burning.

Finally Bernie and she sat down at the table while Laura sliced the pot roast. Bernie smiled as he leaned towards her.

"I've been saving some great news. I had lunch today with Mannie. Mannie Schwartz. Remember him, Iris? You met him at our wedding."

"What about Mannie?"

"He's an accountant with a big firm. Doing well," Bernie said with respect. "Anyhow, he has this very rich client. A society woman who travels the resort circuit." Normally Bernie had only distaste for what he labeled "parasites." "Her companion just eloped and she's in a hurry to hire a replacement. She's scheduled to leave for Palm Beach in three days. In her private railway car. She's the widow of Cyrus Latham."

"Latham Cough Syrup?" Iris was suddenly alert.

"That's right," he nodded. "She has no children, no immediate family. She's always traveling. She needs a companion to start immediately. Someone young, she specified, and pretty. And able to handle herself in fancy surroundings." He grinned unexpectedly. "I don't think you'll have any problem there."

"What should I do?" *Palm Beach. In a private railroad car.* She was conscious of Laura's excitement. Laura knew she'd die selling hosiery again. "Should I phone her?"

"Mannie remembered you well," Bernie said with relish. "He made an appointment for you to see her tomorrow morning. She keeps an apartment in the Ritz Tower, though she's seldom there. She's always traveling."

Alternately excited and depressed, Iris dressed for her appointment with Mrs. Latham. Instinct told her to wear nothing flamboyant or daring. She chose an elegantly simple black wool shift, omitting the usual splash of costume jewelry, and over it her mink coat. Her one hockable possession. She wore a flattering black-felt cloche bought at Bullock's new showplace store on Wilshire Boulevard in Beverly Hills. Inspecting her reflection in the mirror, she was pleased.

At five minutes before ten she stood before the entrance to the Ritz Tower, torn between hostility that she had been put in a position where a job as companion would be a "lucky break" and anticipation at the prospect of moving into the world of high society.

At exactly ten o'clock she was at the door to Mrs. Latham's apartment. She was admitted by a sullen-faced elderly maid who escorted her down a carpeted hall to the door of Mrs. Latham's bedroom. Clad in a white satin negligee bordered with white velvet, Mrs. Latham, a tall, corpulent woman with drooping jowls and suspicious dark eyes, reclined on the bed.

"Come inside and close the door," she ordered. "I don't want the maid hearing everything we say."

"Yes ma'am," Iris said with Georgia-bred politeness as she closed the door behind her.

"Turn around and let me get a good look at you," Mrs. Latham said, taking mental inventory of the chic shift, the mink coat. "I don't want somebody who looks like a frump. After all, you'll frequently be my dinner companion."

"I can understand that." Iris made an effort to appear deferential. She'd meet rich men at Palm Beach. *Very* rich.

"How do you know Mannie Schwartz?" All at once there was a guarded quality in Mrs. Latham's voice.

"He went to college with my brother-in-law." For a moment Iris didn't follow her thinking.

"What's your brother-in-law's name?"

Iris hesitated a fraction of a second, understanding dawning.

"Bart Hunter." "Bernie" sounded Jewish.

Mrs. Latham considered this for a moment, then smiled.

"I gather he's broadminded about his friends. It's not that I don't like Jews. I always look for a Jewish accountant and a Jewish lawyer. They're smart. But socially it can be embarrassing."

"One of Bart's close friends at Harvard Law School," Iris improvised, "was a colored man." Mrs. Latham raised her eyebrows. "Some Ethiopian prince."

"My companion must have an impeccable family background," Mrs. Latham pursued. "I move in rich and important circles. And after my last experience," she said with disdain, "I must have a promise that her replacement will remain with me for at least one year."

"That would not be a problem with me," Iris assured her.

"Where did you get the Southern accent?"

"I was born and raised in our old family home near Atlanta," Iris fabricated. "When Mother and Daddy died in a car crash, my sister and I were so distraught we moved up to New York. I married a Broadway actor and went with him to Hollywood. The marriage didn't work out." She smiled wistfully. "I divorced him and came back to New York." The old bat was impressed by the "Broadway actor" husband.

"Have I met you somewhere?" Mrs. Latham squinted at her from beneath outrageously mascaraed eyelashes.

"No. I'm sure I would remember you." Iris debated for an instant. "You may have seen me in a movie. I took a fling at pictures." She shrugged. "It was boring after a while."

"I remember now." Mrs. Latham's smile was condescending. Clearly, in Mrs. Latham's circle movie actresses were of a lower social level—except, perhaps, for Gloria Swanson, who was married to a Marquis. "You were in that movie, *The Velvet Lady*. The Southern accent didn't set well with the new talkies," she surmised. "Too bad." Iris could sense the wheels turning in her head. *The old bitch knew she was desperate.* "I think you'll be fine as my companion. All your expenses will be paid. You won't need to lay out a cent except for your clothes. We'll travel by private railway car. We'll be staying at The Breakers in Palm Beach. When the season ends there, we'll go to The Homestead at Hot Springs. Can you be ready to leave day after tomorrow?"

"I couldn't accept a position that didn't include a salary." Iris was polite but firm. "And I'd like to know what my duties will be."

For an instant Iris expected Mrs. Latham to order her from the room. Then her prospective employer managed an indulgent smile.

"You young girls today," she twitted. "So bloody independent. All right, I'll pay you twenty-five dollars a month. As for your duties, you'll do the usual companion things—caring for the luggage, making hotel arrangements. Actually, you'll have a marvelous paid holiday."

Iris hesitated. Latham was a witch—but she was rich. They'd stay at the most expensive hotels, travel in her private railroad car, meet the best people. She guessed that Mrs. Latham was not Old Society, but her money bought her entrée into the best places.

"I can be ready to leave the day after tomorrow," Iris assured her.

*She was escaping Brooklyn.* No more sleeping on a sofa in Laura's living room. And to the devil with that promise about staying with the old bat for a year. After all, it wasn't a written commitment.

Long ago she had told herself she was not looking for a knight on a white charger. Rather, a rich husband behind the wheel of a paid-up white Rolls-Royce. In Palm Beach she'd have a chance of landing one.

## Chapter 13

In the dank cold morning Iris and Laura arrived at Grand Central Station fifteen minutes later than anticipated though ten minutes before the Florida express was scheduled to depart. The rush-hour traffic coming into New York — and this time it was Laura who insisted on a taxi — had been horrendous. Grand Central was bulging with southbound travelers.

"It's going to be warm down there." Iris realized Laura was trying not to show her unhappiness that they would again be so far apart. "All that gorgeous sun!"

"Laura, let's say good-bye here," Iris said cajolingly, her eyes skimming the crowd. She was nervous that Laura might unwittingly say something to Mrs. Latham that contradicted the background she had constructed for herself. "I'll get a porter to carry my suitcases to the train." She didn't have to worry about waiting at the gate; she had a special permit to allow her to go through directly to Mrs. Latham's private car. "You don't need to fight your way through this bedlam."

"Iris, write me," Laura ordered, fighting tears as they embraced. "And take care of yourself."

Approaching Mrs. Latham's private railroad car, a respectful porter at her heels with her luggage, Iris heard her new employer screeching invectives at someone inside the car.

"Why can't your office do anything right? I told Mr. Ashford the car was to be supplied with my usual gin and vermouth and fresh caviar."

"I'm sorry, Mrs. Latham." A young woman was fighting to conceal her exasperation. To intimidate Mrs. Latham could cost her her job, Iris suspected. "I wasn't told. But the dining car on the train is said to be superb."

"Go on," Mrs. Latham said peevishly. "Go back to your office and forget that you've left me stranded this way."

Iris stood back while Mrs. Latham's harried visitor hurried from the car, now attached to the regular train. The porter waited politely for Iris to board, then followed with her luggage.

"Oh, thank God, you're here," Mrs. Latham greeted her tersely. Iris noted the approving inspection of the Vuitton luggage while she tipped the porter. "Run ahead into the train, will you please, and tell the conductor I must see him immediately."

"Yes, Mrs. Latham."

Before Iris retired for the night in the minuscule bedroom provided for Mrs. Latham's companion, she vowed to make her escape from this harridan at the earliest possible occasion. Mrs. Latham was traveling without a maid, hence Iris was pressed into this service as well, assuaged with vague promises about employing a maid once they arrived in Palm Beach. She had brewed endless pots of tea for Mrs. Latham in the kitchenette of their private car. She had ironed for her, sewed on buttons, even washed her silk stockings. She had drawn a bath for her employer in the marble tub in the railroad car's bathroom and had cleaned the tub — at Mrs. Latham's instructions on emerging.

Now she lay in her bed and fought against tears of rage. Mrs. Latham enjoyed humiliating her. Her memory shot back to the morning when Mrs. Tannenbaum had invaded their house with orders that they leave Magnolia. *She'd get back at both of them one day.*

From a blend of exhaustion and the soothing rhythm of the train's wheels Iris fell asleep. She awoke to the strident sound of a buzzer somewhere in the room. For a moment she was puzzled. Then she remembered; Mrs. Latham was buzzing for her morning pot of tea.

The morning was devoted to Iris's learning to play contract bridge.

"In Palm Beach everyone plays," Mrs. Latham told her in injured reproach. "I assumed you knew how to play."

Early in the afternoon Mrs. Latham announced they were approaching the West Palm Beach station.

"Martin will be there with the car to drive us to The Breakers," she said with satisfaction. "He drives for me every season."

Iris was intrigued by the exotic scenery that reminded her

147

of California. Everywhere, it seemed, there were towering palms, tropical bushes, bougainvillaea, tall magnolia trees. Her California wardrobe, she reminded herself, was perfect for Palm Beach. She was impressed, too, by Mrs. Latham's casual complaint that since the new Breakers had been built she was charged six thousand dollars a month — *"but that does include meals."*

"I do wish they'd do something down here about all the palm trees," Mrs. Latham sighed. "They get so monotonous."

The train was skirting what Mrs. Latham called Lake Worth — "though it's not truly a lake but a sea inlet." The day was summer hot, the water — like the sky — a brilliant blue. Across the water was Palm Beach. And everywhere glorious scarlet hibiscus bushes.

As they descended from the private railroad car, they saw Martin running towards them with a pair of porters in tow to help with what he must have known would be voluminous luggage, though Mrs. Latham's five steamer trunks were arriving separately. Minstrels — local Negroes wearing black Eton suits and straw hats and playing banjo, cornet, and ukulele — serenaded them. Iris was conscious of the almost tropical seductive warmth that was reminiscent of the summer heat in Magnolia, yet unlike the Southern California climate that was almost always followed by cool evenings.

"Martin, Palm Beach gets hotter every season," Mrs. Latham scolded, as though he were personally responsible. "Get us to the hotel before I pass out."

Iris was awed by her first view of The Breakers. An enormous and sumptuous Italianate hotel, it was surrounded by marble terraces, magnificent fountains and pools. Mrs. Latham had told her that the original hotel had burned to the ground in 1925 and the new seven-storied, twin-towered structure of 450 rooms, costing over six million dollars, had been completed by the end of 1926.

"The Breakers is the finest hotel anywhere in the world," Mrs. Latham said complacently. "Right on the ocean. It's like the Excelsior on the Lido in Venice. Wait till you see the marvelous ceilings in the public rooms. The Doge's Palace in Venice was the model for the ceiling of the Gold Room and the Palace Davanzate in Florence for the dining room ceilings. And the food!" She gestured blissfully.

Walking into the great hall — with frescoes on its vaulted ceilings — Iris decided this was more impressive than any Hollywood set. She felt cheered by the splendor of the hotel, which surely reflected the bank accounts of its guests. Since Mrs. Latham always slept late she would have much of the mornings to herself. And she would not waste them.

She'd read in the New York gossip columns about the fast marital pace among those who inhabited Palm Beach during the season. Wives and husbands were discarded with a regularity that shocked much of America. Let her be visible — in the cobalt-blue backless bathing suit that had been an eye-catcher at Malibu — to one of those temporarily unattached multimillionaires. *All she needed was one.*

Once they were settled in their four-room oceanfront suite, Mrs. Latham ordered Iris to unpack for her. The five steamer trunks had arrived the day before. Mrs. Latham fussed endlessly over what to wear down to dinner this first night, then made her decision.

"Press this one, Iris. But first, run me a bath like a dear girl," Mrs. Latham purred.

At last Mrs. Latham announced that she was ready to go downstairs to dinner.

"But first help me with my jewelry," she told Iris. Tightly corseted beneath her blue-velvet Lanvin gown, she reached into the sewing basket on her dresser, lifted out a tray, and scooped up a diamond-and-turquoise necklace, earrings and bracelet as casually as though they had been bought at Woolworth.

In an ivory-chiffon dinner dress that dramatized her California tan, Iris walked beside Mrs. Latham into the handsome multiwindowed dining room. She forced herself not to stare upward at the magnificent chandelier hanging from the carved and inlaid domed ceiling. She wasn't Iris Roth from Magnolia, Georgia. She was Iris Adams — Hollywood actress.

As they were led to their table, Mrs. Latham stopped at intervals for effusive greetings with old aquaintances. At each pause Iris waited beside Mrs. Latham with a faint, aloof smile.

"Darling, this is my beautiful new companion," Mrs. Latham introduced Iris, almost as an aside.

149

Only six months ago she was being heralded as Hollywood's next young star yet nobody recognized Iris Adams, she thought with bitter humor. Palm Beachers were more addicted to the Broadway theater than to movies. And in Palm Beach society a companion was merely one step above a lady's maid. Still, at intervals, she was conscious of curious male glances from neighboring tables.

After a seven-course gourmet dinner Iris accompanied Mrs. Latham to Colonel Bradley's Beach Club. The deceptively modest white clapboard house, surrounded by a neat lawn, contained the green-and-white octagonal gambling room where, Mrs. Latham confessed, she liked to dally briefly at the roulette table each night of the season.

"We'll have lunch here often," Mrs. Latham promised. "For years, before George Lamaze opened the Colony, it was the only place important people cared to be seen. My dear, the food is marvelous. But now," she said, her eyes gleaming with anticipation, "let's go down the corridor and play roulette."

Iris was grateful that tonight Mrs. Latham lingered only long enough to lose three hundred dollars at roulette without batting an eyelash. That was more than Bernie earned in a month, Iris thought with involuntary distaste. She could hear Bernie's voice at the dinner table a week ago:

"We're two nations these days — the 'have's' and the 'have-nots.' The average American worker earns less than fifteen hundred dollars a year. The farmers — who feed the nation — are starving to death. Their income is way down, their property values have dropped; but they have to pay the same taxes and the same mortgage payments."

"I'm exhausted from the train trip, Iris. Let's go back to the hotel and catch up on our beauty sleep," Mrs. Latham said archly, glancing sidewise at a handsome young croupier. "We'll be here tomorrow night."


Their lives quickly fell into a pattern in Palm Beach. Mrs. Latham slept late in the mornings. This was the time when Iris sunned herself on the luxurious stretch of beach that was The Breakers' property. Once Mrs. Latham was awake and awaiting her breakfast tray, she demanded Iris's presence in her bedroom.

Iris wrote endless letters dictated by her employer — inconsequential, gossip-ridden notes to acquaintances thus far absent from the Palm Beach scene. Mrs. Latham was impatiently critical of her large, sprawling handwriting. She followed through on reservations for Mrs. Latham at The Homestead in Hot Springs. She made embarrassed complaints daily to the management in behalf of Mrs. Latham — complaints totally devoid of foundation but graciously received. She re-made Mrs. Latham's bed each morning with the silk sheets that filled one steamer trunk and which the hotel maids were not allowed to touch. She pressed Mrs. Latham's silk stockings because the lady would not tolerate a single wrinkle. And she listened to Mrs. Latham's endless mindless chatter.

Before lunch at the Colony or the Beach Club or the Embassy, Iris trailed along with Mrs. Latham for pre-luncheon cocktails at the Addison Mizner designed mansion of one or another of her acquaintances. Addison Mizner's brother Wilson was a partner in Hollywood's new Brown Derby. It seemed to Iris they were always thrown together with the same very rich, very dull group, who were at least twice her age.

There were plenty of young women, Iris acknowledged inwardly. Women in their twenties who had inherited — or married into — huge fortunes. The richest women in the world were here at Palm Beach. But Mrs. Latham moved in older circles.

After lunch Mrs. Latham liked to shop on elegant Worth Avenue or at Mrs. Hamilton's delightful shop on the Via Mizner. Iris was amused by the young, sugary voiced saleswomen who cleverly cajoled bored resort visitors into lavish purchases. She saw in their eyes the same blend of contempt and envy she'd felt herself when selling hosiery at Lord & Taylor in New York.

Later in the afternoon Mrs. Latham played contract bridge. If a fourth was needed, Iris dutifully filled in — usually to be scolded by Mrs. Latham.

"Really, Iris, you must do something about your bridge-playing."

Around six they moved on to someone's house to drink gin

with French vermouth and fresh lemon peel or tall glasses of gin with lime and ginger beer or a Scotch whiskey. Iris was ever astonished at the informal clothes. The men, in white linen trousers and canvas espadrilles, looked as though they had spent the past hours playing tennis or fishing in the Gulf Stream—which they had. The women wore pajamas or wide-bottom white or navy jersey pants with brightly colored sweaters and sandals. Mrs. Latham looked grotesque in orange or green or purple pajamas.

Whenever a man—young or old—seemed eager to pursue a conversation with Iris, Mrs. Latham intervened.

"Darling, do bring me a drink. And call the hotel to see if anyone has phoned me from New York."

Before descending to the hotel dining room each evening, Mrs. Latham underwent an elaborate beauty ritual, with Iris in charge of the application of an assortment of Elizabeth Arden beauty creams and cosmetics. After dinner they went off to the Patio or Marguery's or the Oasis or the Everglades, usually ending up at the Colony and leaving only when Mrs. Latham declared herself exhausted.

By the end of their first two weeks in Palm Beach Iris was reviling herself for having fallen into this trap. *How the devil would she survive this boredom for three months?*


With a casual show of interest Iris gazed at intervals about the dining room as she ate her solitary breakfast. She mustn't be obvious, she warned herself. But where was the wealthy bachelor or divorcé she had been so sure of finding here at The Breakers? She was aware of furtive glances now and then—but always from a man accompanied by a woman. Rarely did she see a man alone.

She mentally froze at attention when she saw a tall, spare man in his early fifties—the knickers told her he was headed for the golf course after breakfast—being seated a few tables away. He carried himself with the air of a man accustomed to having his way with the world. A recently arrived guest, she assumed, despite his deep tan.

She dropped her eyes to her coffee when she saw the man's scrutiny focused on her. *He was asking the waiter who she was.* For a moment she allowed her gaze to tangle with his. Her heart began to pound. Was he here alone—or did he have a wife sequestered in their rooms?

She debated about dallying over a second cup of coffee. No, if he was unattached, he'd make a move to meet her. The way his eyes lingered on her legs assured her of this.

She returned to the suite and changed into her cobalt-blue, backless bathing suit, then covered it with a cerise cape for the brief walk from hotel to beach.

Arriving there she smiled in recognition at a pair of Mrs. Latham's acquaintances.

"Isn't the sun marvelous this morning?" she said gaily, buoyed by the brief encounter in the dining room.

"Rather," the younger of the two women shrugged and dismissed her. The other woman ignored her.

Stung by their rebuff Iris settled herself on the beach. These women—young and old—were such bitches. One minute they were friendly, the next looking right through you as though you didn't exist. They didn't give a shit about anybody else's feelings. Being rich gave them the power to do as they pleased.

And yet, Iris thought in sudden realization, despite their constant air of gaiety, these women weren't truly happy. She could read the discontent in their eyes. She'd heard it in careless phrases. *She would change places with them any day.*

As she lay on the beach along with sundry other bodies she allowed her restless mind to dwell on the men who came to Palm Beach for the season.

Whether in their twenties or sixties, most were slim and muscular. They were so serious about running a mile up and down the beach each morning, swimming far out into the rough Atlantic. Later they would play tennis or golf with the same seriousness. Instinctively Iris knew they were industrial giants, financiers, scientists. Men who owned oil wells, factories, chains of stores.

After a prudent interval Iris settled herself beneath a beach umbrella. In an hour, she reminded herself, she had to be back in their suite. *Who was that man in the dining room this morning?* Weaving romantic fantasies about being pursued by a millionaire business tycoon she drifted off into a semi-slumber induced by the heat of the morning sun.

"I say, you are the most smashing girl around these parts."

A deep masculine voice with a British accent brought her into instant wakefulness. She opened her eyes to gaze up at the solitary diner. He'd abandoned the golf course early.

"Do I know you?" she asked with impersonal politeness yet managed to convey a glimmer of interest. Closer to sixty than fifty she decided now. At close range she could see the paunch that standing ramrod stiff didn't hide. Nor did his deep tan camouflage the slightly bloated features that hinted at too many late nights spent at the gambling tables and swigging down too many gin and tonics. And his eyes could be cold as steel or lecherous.

"You know me now," he drawled and dropped into a beach chair that flanked her chaise. "I'm Peter Cranford. If you prefer to be formal, Lord Peter Cranford." His eyes rested on the high rise of her breasts.

"I'm Iris Adams." She shrugged in the faintly disinterested manner of the Palm Beach women. "I'm playing at being a companion to Mrs. Latham. Elvira Latham," she pinpointed. "Her husband founded Latham Cough Syrup."

"Nasty stuff," he recalled with a shudder. "My late wife was partial to American patent medicines. One sneeze and she was calling a servant to bring the bottle of Latham's."

He was letting her know he was unattached. So what if he was old and kind of weatherbeaten. He was a British lord, and he was rich.

"Before this I was a Hollywood actress, but I got bored with that, too. But at least it got me away from Georgia and the old plantation."

"Let me take you to lunch today," he pursued.

"I can't," she said with a show of regret. "I have to lunch with Mrs. Latham." She could see him here on the beach tomorrow morning.

"Where are you lunching?" he asked.

"The Everglades," she told him. "Mrs. Latham adores their turtle soup."

"I'll see you there," he told her. "You're not going to escape from me now."

Iris was enthralled by the way Peter Cranford manipulated his way into their lives. Mrs. Latham was ecstatic at their being escorted everywhere by a British lord, known to many of the Palm Beach set who included European resorts in their travels.

"Palm Beach is becoming *so* international," Mrs. Latham gushed at regular intervals. "But Peter *does* have a reputation for being rather naughty." Iris was aware that Mrs. Latham preferred to ignore reality; in her eyes Lord Cranford was enamored of her.

No longer did Iris relax on the beach each morning. She arose early and hurried downstairs for her rendezvous with Peter. His manservant, Dobkins, met them at the rented Stutz with a wicker basket containing their breakfast, prepared by the hotel staff. They preferred to share this meal away from the curious eyes of other guests. At intervals they paused in the Stutz for amorous pursuit on the back seat. But Iris rejected Peter's impatient pleas to consummate their relationship.

On a morning exactly five weeks after their first meeting, while they clutched at each other on the back seat, Peter showed his irritation at the lines drawn by Iris.

"I always thought you American girls were so open and adventurous," he reproached. "Here I have the keys to this marvelous house. You don't have to worry about becoming pregnant," he chuckled. "I have three children. I'm past the stage where I'll have another."

"Peter, no," she insisted. *Not unless he married her.* "I adore you," she said with a wistful smile, "but I promised myself I'd never sleep with a man until I was married." He didn't know she was divorced. She leaned towards him, her blue eyes guileless and passionate at the same moment. "But you can kiss me—" She lifted her face to him, mouth parted provocatively.

"Let's go back to the hotel." His face flushed in anger. Then he paused, his hand on the ignition key. "You'd look marvelous in a diamond necklace," he drawled. "We could go down to Worth Avenue and pick up something for you to wear to dinner tonight." His smile was ingratiating, his eyes daring her to refuse.

"No, Peter." But her heart was pounding. *He was hooked enough to buy her a diamond necklace.* "I couldn't accept such an expensive gift."

155

His eyes turned hostile as they met hers. He didn't believe she was a society belle from Georgia, who had taken a fling at pictures and now at being a companion. He thought he could dangle a diamond necklace before her eyes, and she'd hop into bed with him. *No.* Not that the prospect of owning a diamond necklace wasn't a potent invitation.

"Let's go back to the hotel." He stared sullenly ahead as he started up the Stutz.

After this episode Iris had thought Peter would disappear from their lives. But he remained their faithful escort, though now he ordered a breakfast tray sent to his suite and did not appear until lunch time. For almost a week Iris did not see him alone. *What was his game?* She was conscious of the curiosity of those who were part of their inner circle. Mrs. Latham might not be aware, but the others knew that Lord Peter Cranford was madly smitten by her young companion.

Mrs. Latham was becoming bored with Palm Beach and already talking about their departure for Hot Springs in two weeks. Panic brushed Iris at intervals. Once they left Palm Beach, would she ever see Peter again?

At a cocktail party on an afternoon when crystal rain assaulted the earth and apathy overtook the guests, Peter leaped to his feet and demanded their attention.

"Hear ye, hear ye!" he declaimed in stentorian tones. "Why do we put up with this ghastly weather?" It had rained for the past twelve hours, and they knew the steamy heat that would come when it ceased. "Why don't we all fly down to Nassau for a few days?"

"Oh, I would never fly in this weather," Mrs. Latham objected.

"Nor I," the wife of a multimillionaire industrialist agreed. "But why don't we run down there on the *Elvira?*" Iris had seen the *Elvira,* one of the most luxurious of the yachts on the Palm Beach scene. "Ralph keeps it docked here for the whole season, though he's always dashing back to New York by train on business. The crew's on stand-by. Let's all go pack a bag and take off for Nassau!" she coaxed ebulliently.

In moments it was agreed that the party would transfer itself to the yacht for the trip to Nassau.

"Nassau is marvelous," one guest assured the others. "All

those charming houses built by Loyalist refugees after the American colonies won their freedom. They're painted in delicate pastels, and they have delightful screened balconie."

"And we must sail on a glass-bottomed boat. That's one of the pleasures of Nassau," another contributed.

They'd have dinner on the yacht and breakfast in the morning in Nassau. Amid much gaiety they parted to go to their respective homes to prepare for the trip.

In her bedroom Mrs. Latham chose, discarded, and chose again the clothes for the Nassau jaunt. Iris brought forth the endless tissue paper that must be utilized in packing each dress.

"Iris, I've just remembered," Mrs. Latham said casually. "I should be receiving a phone call from my broker tomorrow morning. You'll stay here to receive the call. I'll manage alone on the yacht," she said with an air of indulgent generosity, a glint of triumph in her eyes. She was not unaware of Lord Cranford's interest in her companion. "Just write down whatever Mr. Silberman tells you. If he calls."

"Yes, Mrs. Latham." Iris struggled to hide her rage.

When Mrs. Latham had left for the yacht Iris paced impatiently about her bedroom. She was tempted to call Laura in New York and talk for an hour. But Mrs. Latham checked every item on her bills. The old skinflint was sure everybody was out to cheat her.

She would soak in a hot tub drenched in bath salts and then get into one of her Hollywood negligées, Iris decided. And very late she would call to the dining room and have a dinner tray sent up. Once this rain stopped it was going to be bitchy hot. She'd throw open the windows and have a table set up there.

Lying back in the tepid bath water with the scent of roses permeating the air, Iris thought about Dennis. He had not given a damn about her once she wasn't useful to his career. She had not been in love with him, Iris assessed. She'd been attracted by what he could do for her. And he was great in bed. God, she was beginning to feel like a virgin again!

Out of the bath she patted her delicate golden body until every drop of moisture had been absorbed, then reached for the box of dusting powder. Suddenly she thought of Lance, who was aroused when she allowed him to run the puff over hèr. It was weird to feel passionate alone this way.

She brought out the black chiffon nightgown and matching negligee that she had worn in *The Velvet Lady* and had filched from the studio wardrobe. She had brought it along for a possible more auspicious occasion and she laughed quietly to herself as she envisioned the waiter wheeling in her dinner and finding her like this. But waiters at The Breakers were trained to be discreet.

She had written to Laura only once since they arrived in Palm Beach. With an unexpected surge of homesickness she went into the sitting room and sat down at the desk.

She was startled when she heard a key turn in the door. Had Mrs. Latham decided not to sail to Nassau? She turned around to face Peter Cranford, a triumphant grin lighting his face, a bottle of champagne tucked under one arm, a pair of flute glasses and a corkscrew in his hands.

Her heart pounding, she pretended indignation. He'd discovered she was not on the yacht, and he bolted.

"How did you get in?"

"A romantic maid and an extravagant tip," he laughed. His eyes devoured the sight of her in the black chiffon negligée. "That damnable battle-ax meant to keep us apart. Wait till she discovers I got off before the yacht sailed!"

"Peter, you can't stay here," Iris said sweetly.

"Dinner is being sent up. I gave instructions. It may be the only time all season we'll have a chance to dine alone."

"When I'm dressed like this?" she scolded. "What will they think of us?" Her mind grappled with the possibilities this rendezvous offered. If she couldn't persuade Peter to marry her tonight, it would never happen. But she wasn't sleeping with him. If she did, he'd never marry her. "And somebody's sure to tell Mrs. Latham."

"Fuck Mrs. Latham," he said, then grimaced. "No! That's a terrible thought."

"Peter, you can't stay here," she repeated.

"You can't send me away," he clucked. "I gave up Nassau for you. And dinner's coming up. We can at least have dinner tonight." All at once he was playing "Mister Charm."

"All right," she acquiesced. "Just dinner. But let me go change into something more respectable. And you," she emphasized. "You stay right here."

When the waiter wheeled in their dinner cart, Iris was demurely dressed in a turquoise-silk dinner dress. Peter had already refilled his champagne glass twice. Iris clung to the first. It was enough that the heat dulled her mind. Too much was at stake not to have her wits at their sharpest.

Tonight Peter was determined on conquest. He talked about his country estate outside of London, his Mayfair townhouse, about his triumphs at polo—though Iris suspected these were far behind him. She sat across the table from him while rain fell without ceasing outside.

"Let's have more champagne," he said when dinner had been finished and all vestiges removed.

"Peter, I've had my quota," she scolded. "And I think it's time for you to go back to your rooms."

"How can you send me away when I'm dying to make love to you?" He reached for her hand and pulled her down to the sofa beside him.

"Tomorrow we'll make love," she comforted. His arousal was oddly exciting. *If she married Peter Cranford, she'd be Lady Cranford* with a townhouse in Mayfair and a country estate outside of London. That was better than being a movie star. "In broad daylight on the back seat of the Stutz," she emphasized. Meaning with the usual limitations.

"Damn it, Iris, I'm not some schoolboy satisfied with tidbits." His face was flushed, his eyes glittered. "You make me feel like twenty-five again. No woman's done that for years."

"Peter, I've told you. I mean to go to my husband without ever having slept with another man." Her eyes held his, straining to implant her message. "I adore you," she confessed prettily, "but I can't sleep with you."

He hesitated, frowning in champagne-fogged thought.

"We could get married, Iris. Let's do it!" He slammed a fist on one thigh. "What the hell! We're both unattached. I can do what I want with my life. I've been a widower for eight years. Iris," he said with mocking seriousness, "will you do me the honor of becoming my wife?"

"When, Peter?" Right now the champagne was talking. How would he feel tomorrow?

"In the morning." He leapt to his feet. "I'll take you away from that old monster. She'll come back and have hysterics," he laughed and reached for her. "Iris, I want to love you from head to toe."

His mouth reached hungrily for hers, his hands moving greedily about her breasts. His hips thrusting against hers in impatience.

"Peter, no," she ordered when a hand slipped between them to his crotch. "Not until we're married."

"We'll be married tomorrow. I know a little place where we can —"

"Peter, you don't get in until I'm your wife," she interrupted. Don't let him change his mind now. "That's the rule." But she allowed her body to nuzzle his. He might be pushing sixty, she thought subconsciously; but right this minute he was as hard as twenty.

"Pack your bags and let's get out of here!" One large hand fondled her breast. "I know where we can be married ten minutes after midnight." His face was alight with anticipation.

"Where?" She was skeptical.

"Onboard the midnight boat to Havana. The captain can marry us. And bring along that bit of black fluff you were wearing when I arrived. It reminds me of a girl I had in a French brothel when I was sixteen."

"I'll bring it," she promised. "Come help me pack."

She debated an instant about calling Laura. No. She'd call her tomorrow from Havana. *Laura, guess what? I've married again. I'm Lady Cranford!*

# Chapter 14

In the black chiffon nightgown that Peter had ordered her to put on as soon as they were alone in their luxury hotel suite in Havana, Iris tiptoed from the bedroom into the sitting room, where the late morning sunlight was a welcome intruder after last night's dreary rain in Palm Beach. Peter snored on their bed. He had fallen asleep while she was undressing. She ought to be exhausted, too, after their marathon wedding night. At first the captain had been reluctant to marry them, but Peter had been persuasive. For a while she'd thought he was too ossified to perform, but after much sweating and grunting he achieved his climax. He was too drunk to suspect he was not the first.

She was grateful that the switchboard operators were bilingual. Now she waited impatiently for Laura to pick up the phone in Brooklyn.

"Hello." Laura's voice answered with that familiar little eager lilt.

"Laura, I'm in Havana," Iris bubbled.

"Cuba?" Laura was startled.

"Havana, Cuba." Iris gave it the Spanish inflection. "We came on the overnight boat. I can look down on the harbor right here from our suite. Iris—" She took a deep breath. "I'm married again. He's an English lord. I'm Lady Cranford."

Iris calmly answered Laura's rush of questions. As she had expected, Laura was upset that she had known Peter only a few weeks, that he was almost three times her age, and that they would be sailing for England within a week.

"All at once Peter can't wait to take me home and show me off," Iris giggled. "Thank God, his three married children haven't made me a step-grandmother!"

Laura was anxious for Bernie to come home so they could discuss Iris's marriage, but he wouldn't arrive for hours yet. It had alarmed her when Iris put a whole country between them. Now she would soon put an ocean between them.

Iris seemed genuinely happy. *"Laura, I'm set for life. I'll never have to worry about money again. And if Peter kicks off, I'll inherit part of the estate."*

Iris insisted her new husband was really a British lord. People she'd met in Palm Beach — well-known socialites with impeccable backgrounds — had known him in London and Paris and Rome. Iris said they'd eloped to Havana and that his manservant was packing for him and would meet them in New York to sail with them on the *Berengaria*. *"Wouldn't I just love to send a note to the society editor of the* Magnolia Herald, *announcing my marriage to Lord Peter Cranford of London and Kent! But I can't do that. I buried Iris Roth when we left Magnolia. But someday, they'll know, Laura. You just wait and see."*

"Mommie," Jonnie had awakened from his nap. "Mommie, can I have a drink of water?"

"Coming, darling." Laura hurried into the children's bedroom.

Iris said she'd be in New York for a day. They'd have lunch in town. *"We'll come in one evening and sail the next midnight. I won't have time to run out to see the kids."*

The day seemed endless. Bernie didn't arrive home from the office until she had fed Jonnie and Katie and put them to bed. She heard the key in the door as she turned out the light in the children's room.

"You look tired," she commiserated in greeting. She knew tension in the office was acute since the firm had fired their office boy and one stenographer.

"How do you make a seventy-two-year-old widow understand that there's no way for her to recover funds when her bank's gone under?"

"Oh Bernie, how awful." Bernie didn't tease her anymore about keeping their savings in Postal Savings. Not with more and more banks closing their doors.

"I'll look in on the kids for a minute while you get

162

dinner on the table." He smacked her gently on the rump. "The family jewels."

"Bernie, I had a phone call from Iris. She was down in Havana—"

"Still bitching about her boss?"

"She got married last night." Laura took a deep breath. "To some British lord. She'll be living in England."

"Good lord!" Bernie grinned. "No reference to Iris's lord."

He listened absorbedly, the visit to the children's room temporarily aborted, while Laura told him what she knew about this latest turn in Iris's life.

"Iris insists he's not some phony." Laura tried to sound unworried. "Some of Mrs. Latham's rich friends know his family. He's almost three times her age, of course."

"Iris is like a cat," Bernie joshed. "She always lands on her feet. Laura, don't worry about her," he cajoled. "Iris will be fine. She'll love being Lady Cranford, even if the old boy is part of the deal. And you'll see her," he comforted. "En route to Palm Beach or wherever else the rich visit."

"It's unreal." Laura forced a laugh.

"What's real isn't very pretty." All at once Bernie was somber. "President Hoover tells us the bad effects of the Wall Street crash are almost over, but try to explain that to the millions who've lost their jobs. But let me go see my kids." He strived for a more cheerful mood.

Over dinner they talked about Hoover's insistence that government support for the farmers, laborers, the unemployed would only destroy the true American spirit. In case of real disaster voluntary relief organizations should handle the situation.

"Damn it, Laura. We have people going to bed hungry in this country! Little children! The government has an obligation to help. I heard today that the Salvation Army is preparing to open up breadlines. I know Hoover organized famine relief all over Europe after the war. When's he going to take some action about feeding our people here at home?"

"Bernie, I've been thinking about school. I don't think it's the right time for me to start law studies." Bernie insisted his job was not at stake. But that was today. "I don't think we should lay out all that money."

"You're starting law school in September." A nerve quivered in his eyelid. "I went to NYU law. You'll go there. Besides," he teased, "how can we deprive Mrs. Goldstein of the money she'll earn taking care of the kids?"

"It seems wrong to spend when so many people are hurting." Laura was troubled. They ought to save every cent when business was so bad.

"You'll go to school. I won't hear of anything else," he said firmly.

Laura sat across the luncheon table from Iris in the lofty ceilinged Salle de Cathay of the St. Regis while Lord Peter Cranford slept in an elegant suite seven floors above them.

"Peter will sleep till dinnertime," Iris said. "But it's just as well," she added with candor. "You wouldn't like him. He's arrogant and snobbish as hell. He knows how British titles fascinate most Americans. But he's *rich*. I'm not kidding myself, Laura. I could never be happy and poor."

"It seems crazy that I won't even meet your husband." Laura was faintly reproachful. "And at midnight you'll be on a ship bound for England."

"On the *Berengaria*." Iris chuckled. "Peter says all socially important people sail on the *Berengaria*." Then—fleetingly—she seemed frightened and vulnerable. "I'm scared to death of meeting Peter's two daughters and his son. They'll hate me on sight. Peter says they have such contempt for Americans."

"I wish you'd be living here in this country."

"Laura, stop worrying like that. You're supposed to be impressed. Papa would disapprove because Peter isn't Jewish, but he'd be impressed that his daughter married into British nobility. Peter will probably live to a hundred, but I'm his wife—when he kicks off, I'll inherit along with his three children. *I'll never be poor again.*" She reached across the table to cover Laura's hand with hers. "You know what I'd adore to do? To send an item to the society editor of the *Magnolia Herald*. 'Iris Adams, née Iris Roth, marries Lord Peter Cranford.' But if it ever got back to Peter that

164

his new bride is Jewish, he'd die."

"Iris, I just want to know that you're happy."

"I'll send you snapshots of our townhouse in Mayfair and the country estate in Kent," Iris promised. "You'll know I'm happy."

"Promise you'll write often." It was still unnerving to Laura to know they'd be separated by an ocean.

"I'll write every week. And Peter's always traveling. Before you know it, we'll be back in New York and having lunch somewhere fabulous. No," she corrected, "next time I'll come out to Brooklyn. I have to see Jonnie and Katie. And Bernie," she added belatedly. "How is Bernie?"

"Terribly worried about the economy." Laura had been surprised that Bernie was so realistic about Iris's marriage. He understood it was important to Iris to live well. "It's frightening, the way people are losing their jobs. Bernie said he saw a breadline here in the city. He said it was awful to see those men — scared and humiliated — standing patiently in line for a bowl of soup and a slice of bread."

"Bernie's job is all right, isn't it?" All at once Iris was solicitous.

"The firm's laid off the office boy and one of the stenographers, but Bernie thinks the rest of the staff will be kept on." Laura tried to brush away apprehension. "Bernie says only a few of the very rich have been hurt. They keep on with their lives as though nothing is wrong in the country."

"In Palm Beach people were talking about Barbara Hutton's debut in December. Columnists are saying it'll cost at least fifty thousand dollars."

Laura winced.

"Can you imagine how many meals that would provide for hungry families?"

"I'm glad we had a chance to be together today." Iris pointedly rechanneled the conversation.

"When you left for Palm Beach with Mrs. Latham," Laura managed a shaky laugh, "I was afraid I wouldn't see you for ages."

"We've come a long way from Magnolia in just a few years," Iris said with satisfaction. "I'm married to a British lord, and you're on your way to law school. We've done all right, kiddo!"

To Iris, the midnight sailing of the baroque *Berengaria* was like a movie premiere—though this was an off-season crossing. Reporters hovered on the trail of celebrity passengers. Flashlights exploded as one great name after another appeared. Peter seemed to be enjoying the excitement, yet at intervals she suspected he was dreading—as she was—a confrontation with his family. Dobkins had been impassive when Peter introduced her as the new Lady Cranford. British servants, she surmised, were trained to conceal their feelings.

Peter and she went directly to their suite, where Dobkins was already unpacking in the bedroom he assumed would be his master's. Peter traveled with twenty-five suits, four topcoats, four-dozen shirts, two-dozen pairs of shoes, and fifty ties. And Dobkins had managed to acquire a case of champagne for the crossing.

Iris reveled in the luxury of having her own bedroom, even while Peter apologized that she must travel without the services of a maid.

"I'll be your ladies' maid," Peter murmured fatuously when they were alone in her bedroom. "I'll help you dress. I'll draw your bath. I'll scrub your back. And with the least encouragement I'll join you in the tub." A tub that provided both fresh and sea water.

On their second night out a young American approached Iris and diffidently asked if she was Iris Adams.

"She was, young man," Peter snapped with an air of reproof before Iris could reply, but she had seen a momentary glint of pleasure in his eyes. "Now she's Lady Cranford. She's put that ridiculous Hollywood business behind her."

They were seated at the captain's table along with other prestigious passengers with names that Iris recognized from newspapers and magazines. Life aboard ship for the six-day crossing appeared to revolve around dining. Peter encouraged her to invite attractive young people to their suite for champagne each evening when he grew bored with the dancing. It was as though, she thought, Peter was trying to regain his youth with her.

166

When they left the ship at Southampton, Iris wore a smart but simple tweed suit under her mink coat. Peter's children could do nothing to undo their marriage, she told herself defiantly. She was Peter's legal wife—whether his children approved or not.

Iris was impressed by the cream-colored thirty-room, six-storied Regency mansion that was Cranford House, in the Mayfair section of London. Here she was introduced to the staff of nine as their new mistress.

"Don't worry, my love," Peter whispered while he pinched her rump. "You won't have to do a thing. Mrs. Hawkins handles everything."

Not until a week later did she meet Peter's two daughters, Eleanor and Melinda, their husbands, and Peter's son, Roland. Perfect Hollywood casting for the disapproving British offspring, Iris thought with a flicker of humor, relieved that she wasn't afraid of them, as she had feared.

After an unimaginative dinner in the gloomy, tapestry draped, wood-paneled dining room, the family retired to the ornate, awesomely large drawing room for coffee. Peter reached for Iris's hand.

"They won't linger," he whispered and then bristled as Melinda's voice filtered to them.

"Eleanor, it's these crazy times. Nancy Cunard is off to France with her black lover, and Father brings home an American adventuress as his wife."

"Really, I don't know which is worse," Eleanor said and then managed a semblance of a smile as she realized her father and new stepmother were approaching. "Father, will you be staying long in town?"

"I can't say," he told her, his own smile malicious. He knew, Iris surmised, that his daughters and son were impatient for his departure from London.

Peter had intimated to Iris that they would not see much of his family. They had disapproved of him for years. His marriage was the ultimate disgrace. Iris was relieved when their guests left.

"I ignore the bloody young bastards," he confided in triumph over Manhattans at the Embassy Club the day after the familial dinner at Cranford House. "Eleanor made the supreme sacrifice and invited us to a family dinner a week from Friday. I declined," he said with relish. "I told her we'd be at the country house."

The life Peter enjoyed revolved around reading the London *Daily Mirror* after breakfast in his room, then deciding upon what social activities would be most amusing for the balance of the day. Though certain circles of British society were closed to Peter—and Iris sensed that his behavior even before their marriage had shut these doors—they regularly received invitations to luncheons, cocktail parties, dinners. They dined at Boulestin's or the Eiffel Tower. They danced at the Kit-Cat or the Grafton Galleries, or the Embassy Club—where the Prince of Wales did the Charleston every Thursday with Mrs. Dudley Ward. Later they went to Ivor Novello's club or the Silver Slipper or the "43"—despite fears that it might be raided.

Since the London season didn't commence until the first of May, Peter decreed that Iris and he must take off for Paris. Before their departure he took Iris shopping at Harrod's for the Harris tweeds and Chanel jerseys he deemed suitable for the new Lady Cranford.

Though it was understood that the London season would be observed as usual, Peter admitted to annoyance at the change in the London spirit. Suddenly wealthy Londoners—though personally unaffected by the alarming increase in unemployment—were making a show of concern. In the rich homes in Mayfair it was considered vulgar to appear extravagant. Some households ceased to serve champagne. Dinners were reduced to two courses, with no canapes beforehand. Some even closed up parts of their mansions and discharged some of their servants.

In Paris—still the hub of the international set—Peter and Iris settled in at the elegant Crillon in a two-bedroom, balconied Louis XV suite that looked out on the Place de la Concorde. They encountered several of Peter's friends who had been in Palm Beach during the season. They all congregated at Fouquet's or the Ritz Bar for cocktails, dined at Maxim's, went night after night to the Ambassadeurs or to the Grand Duke to hear Bricktop, the celebrated American Negro singer.

Peter took her to the finest fashion salons—Vionnet, Chanel, Poiret, Lanvin—and allowed her to buy with no limits. Surreptitiously — at the salon of Coco Chanel — she arranged for an elegant black suit and a turquoise sheer wool dress with the new longer skirt and high waistline — to be shipped off to Laura. A graduation present. Peter could afford it, she told herself.

She wished wistfully that he would dally with her in one of the fine jewelry shops. She adored diamond and emerald and ruby necklaces and earrings and bracelets but they were an investment as well. If she had bought herself diamond earrings in Hollywood, she would have had something to exchange for cash. *Without money you were nothing.*

Soon Peter was bored with Paris. He was drinking too much, gambling too much. Now when they returned from the evening's social activities, he stalked to his own room and slammed the door shut.

"We'll leave for London in two days," he decided on a late April night when they'd arrived at their hotel suite after a party given by Elsa Maxwell.

"All right, Peter." Iris masked her disappointment. She adored Paris and the exciting parties. Like Maxwell's party tonight. She had been enthralled at meeting Cole Porter, the Aga Khan, and Scott Fitzgerald all in one night. Of course, Peter had spent most of the evening talking with Sir Oswald and Lady Cynthia Mosley. "But tonight was such fun."

Peter was not going directly to his room tonight. He settled himself on the sofa in their sitting room and removed his bow tie.

"Too many Americans at this damned party," he said superciliously and then swung around on the sofa to call towards his bedroom. "Dobkins? Where the devil are you?"

Dobkins appeared instantly.

"Yes, your Lordship?"

"I won't need you anymore tonight. And tell Edwina to clear out, too." Edwina had been appointed Iris's personal maid at their arrival in London.

"Yes, your Lordship." Dobkins headed for Iris's room to dismiss Edwina for the night.

Iris heard a low exchange between them and then a door opening and closing at the far end of the hall. Peter and she were alone. He was in an amorous mood. He had not

169

made love to her for almost three weeks and she had been vaguely disturbed by his lack of interest. She kept telling herself she was his wife; he couldn't do anything to change that.

"Change into one of those French whore costumes," he snapped at Iris and rose to his feet, discarding his jacket.

"Yes, darling."

She started towards her room, swinging seductively in the newly fashionable, high-waisted long evening gown bought at the salon of Vionnet. This was a Peter she understood. Other times she felt uncomfortable with him.

Freshly drenched in Chanel 5, she was standing nude in the black-satin high-heeled mules Peter had personally shopped for her and pulling the black chiffon nightgown over her head when Peter came into the bedroom.

"Get rid of that thing," he ordered and reached to wrench the nightgown from her. "Come on, Iris. Show me how good you are."

"You're impatient, darling," she scolded lightheartedly and lifted her mouth to his.

He kissed her roughly, then drew his mouth away to nuzzle at one ear. His hands moved about her breasts, his hips thrusting against hers. His passion, she realized, was all in his mind.

"Peter, take off your clothes," she whispered. "Or let me." Already her hands were at his stiffly starched evening shirt. He liked it when she helped him undress.

"You're always ready," he chuckled, yet she sensed a kind of anger in him.

"I can't wait, darling." She sounded like a character in a Noel Coward play, she thought. That's what Peter wanted of her. "Even at the party I was wishing we were here. Like this."

"I saw the way you were looking at all those men!" His eyes glittered while he stripped off his trousers. "Like you were dying to hop into bed with every one of them."

"That's not true!" He liked to pretend he was jealous. She didn't believe him. It gave him a crazy kind of satisfaction to know she belonged to him. "Why would I need them when I have you?"

"I want to own you," he said with savage intensity.

"Every inch of you." He reached with one hand to smack her on the rump.

"Peter, that hurt." She was startled.

"Hit me," he said. "Hit me hard."

"Don't be silly." She reached to slide her arms about him, nuzzled against his slim body. Only the faint paunch gave away his age. That and the lines in his face, the sagging jawline that spoke of too much night life. "I don't want to hurt you. I want to make love."

"Damn it, help me!" he yelled. "Make me hot, you little bitch!"

"Let's go to the bed." All at once she was frightened. "It'll be all right in a few minutes," she promised. *This Peter was a stranger.*

They lay together on the silken coverlet, and she tried all the little things that usually pleased him. She whispered the stupid entreaties he relished while his mouth and his hands roamed down the length of her. She cried out in a pretense of passion when his hands parted her thighs and his tongue invaded her. But when he lifted himself above her, she knew their efforts were futile.

"Damn you!" He swung himself away from her and off the bed, reached to pull her roughly to her feet. "You're like a chunk of ice!"

He slapped her hard across the face and while she gaped at him in shock, he flung her to the floor. She cried out as his foot kicked against her ribs.

"Peter, no," she begged when he hovered over her with a fist clenched in fury. "Don't hit me." Her mind flashed back to the one time Lance had lifted his hand to her. But this wasn't like with Lance. She was in a strange country, without money to take her back home. And who would believe her if she told them Lord Cranford had beaten her?

"You're my wife." He yanked her to her feet, threw her across the bed. "Turn over, you little whore!"

Numb with fear, Iris swung over on her face. His hand flailed heavily at her rump, again and again, while she whimpered in pain and terror.

"On your back," he ordered at last, his breathing heavy, his face contorted. "It's going to be great now. Like I was

171

twenty again."

He lifted himself above her and separated her thighs. In a haze she was aware that now his passion was genuine. She lay passive while he thrust himself within her, intent on achieving his goal. At last he lay limp above her for a few moments, grunting. Then he lifted himself from her, crouched at her side.

"Iris, forgive me," he pleaded. "I drank too much champagne. It won't ever happen again. I swear." He brought her hand to his mouth. "Tomorrow morning we'll go shopping," he cajoled. "I'll buy you a diamond necklace. You'll wear it for dinner at the Boeuf. You'll be the most beautiful woman there. Everyone will stare at you. And I'll tell them all, she's Lady Cranford. My wife." He lowered his mouth to her breast. "You've made me very happy, my darling."

A diamond necklace. That could help her forget the ugliness of tonight. It wouldn't happen again — Peter swore it wouldn't. It was like he said — he was bored with Paris and he drank too much. He was upset that he had lost control that way. *It wouldn't happen again.*

She couldn't go back to America. Mrs. Latham would never take her back. She'd be sleeping on the sofa in Laura's apartment with no money even to buy herself a lipstick or a pair of stockings. There were no jobs back home. *People were standing in lines for a bowl of soup and a piece of bread. She had to stay with Peter.* The diamond necklace. It would be her emergency fund.

## Chapter 15

Laura inspected her reflection in her closet mirror. She was grateful this was an unseasonably cool June day that allowed her to wear the sheer turquoise wool dress that Iris had sent her from Paris. She felt a delicious quiver of pleasure at standing here in a dress designed by Coco Chanel. Her eyes swung compulsively to her diploma already framed and hanging above the chest of drawers. How proud Papa would be if he could know!

Ever conscious of the Depression, she'd tried at intervals to convince Bernie that she should take time out before going to NYU law. But she had been accepted at the law school—which had graduated its first women lawyers at the turn of the century—and Bernie insisted she'd enroll as scheduled. She glanced at the clock on the bedroom night table. Bernie would return in a few minutes from his Sunday afternoon walk with Jonnie and Katie. He was taking her to the Plaza for tea to celebrate her graduation. Dinner was unthinkable on his salary, he conceded.

She sat at the edge of the bed and reached for Iris's most recent letter. Iris wrote that Peter and she would be in London till late June, when they'd leave for St. Tropez. In August and September they would be in a rented palazzo in Venice.

*"I would have liked to stay in Paris, but Peter insisted we had to be back in London for the opening of the Season. That means endless parties and pub crawling—though both Peter and I are considered beyond the pale for some of the duller parties. And in June we must stay for Royal Ascot Week and the Marlow Regatta."*

Iris bubbled about her girl friends—Diana and Elaine and Sandra, all of whom had married rich, titled men. When in London they met each day for luncheon at the dazzling new Dorchester or at Claridge's or the Ritz, and shopped with what Iris called luscious extravagance at Harrod's or Selfridge's or at the currently fashionable small shops.

*"Did I tell you that when Syrie Maugham—she's the terrific interior decorator who used to be married to Somerset Maugham— became Gordon Selfridge's lover, he gave her an unlimited charge account at his store? Wow!"*

Iris sounded bitter that she had so little access to cash. She said she rarely had more than three or four pounds in her purse—she signed "chits" for everything. Laura smiled in sympathy. Iris was an independent soul—she resented having to have Peter pay every small bill for her.

At the sound of the bell Laura rose from the bed and hurried into the narrow hallway and to the door. She automatically guessed it was Mrs. Goldstein. Bernie had his own jaunty signal.

"I baked bread." Mrs. Goldstein smiled and extended a plate. "I know Bernie and you like my rye."

"We love everything you bake," Laura said affectionately, walking with Mrs. Goldstein to the kitchen. They'd made the small friendly room their special place in the apartment. "Let's have coffee while we wait for Bernie and the kids. And we won't stay in the city more than a couple of hours," she promised. Every night she thanked God for Mrs. Goldstein's presence in their lives.

"Stay," Mrs. Goldstein urged. "What else have I got to do? I have to hear more about Mrs. Gurfein's diabetes or Molly Rosen's arthritis or Mrs. Kaufman's high blood pressure?"

Laura and Mrs. Goldstein talked about Katie's two new teeth and Jonnie's excitement over his prospective birthday party next month. It would actually be a party for Katie too, since they had been born just five days apart. Though physically much alike, they approached life in a different fashion—Jonnie was intense and outgoing, Katie, cautious and reserved except with the family.

"Such a beautiful dress you're wearing," Mrs. Goldstein admired. "The one Iris sent you from Paris," she recognized. "A dress like that will be fine fifteen years from now. Quality counts."

174

They'd finished their coffee and Mrs. Goldstein was insisting *she* wash the dishes when Bernie appeared with the children. Katie was rebellious at being relegated to the stroller after taking her first few steps a week ago. Jonnie suppressed a yawn.

"You're tired, Jonnie," Laura clucked tenderly. "Bernie, you kept them out such a long time."

"I'm almost three," Jonnie reminded. "I can walk a long time."

"They'll go to bed early tonight," Laura laughed and reached to kiss each in turn. "You be good," she ordered.

Enveloped in a glorious sense of adventure Laura and Bernie left the house and walked towards the Fiftieth Street BMT station.

"One of the great things about New York," Bernie mused as they climbed the stairs up to the elevated platform, "is that for a nickel you can take yourself into another world."

On the train Bernie talked about the possibility of the repeal of Prohibition. Though he seldom drank, Bernie considered the Eighteenth Amendment an abomination that had brought on the worst violence the country had ever seen.

"And it keeps a lot of lawyers busy," he added wryly. "Not that I'm about to defend Al Capone. Times may be hard, but I've seen Mr. Weinstein turn down more than one racketeer."

They left the subway at West Fifty-seventh Street and walked east towards the Plaza. Laura relished this brief interlude in a world far beyond their reach. In a haze of pleasure she inspected the smart attire of the women they passed. Women who shopped at Bergdorf's and Bendel's. Even the buildings in this part of town wore an air of affluence.

All at once Laura felt a tightness in her throat. A shabbily dressed man—his expression a blend of humiliation, anguish, and sullen rage—was approaching strollers with an outstretched hand. Two well-dressed men rushed past with eyes straight ahead. Bernie was already reaching into his pocket for change.

Breadlines were appearing in every large city in the country. Children were starving. Thousands of homeless were building huts of cartons and bits of cast-off wood and tin along the Hudson River, beneath Riverside Drive.

Laura remembered Bernie's seething contempt for President Hoover's comment last month regarding the soaring unemployment in the United States: *"I am convinced we have now passed the worst."* And she remembered Will Rogers' comment: *"There has been more 'optimism' talked and less practiced than at any time in our history."*

Bernie reached for Laura's hand, knowing what she was thinking and feeling.

"We'll walk in Central Park before we go back to the subway," he said. "Pretend we live in one of those fancy apartment houses with a view of the park." He squeezed her hand. "I think my wife has a taste for high living." Laura knew the compassion beneath his effort at raillery.

"Bernie, when will this craziness end?" she asked, feeling so helpless in a hurting world.

"Soon." He tried for an air of conviction. "At least we have a governor who's trying. Roosevelt's concerned about unemployment and relief. He's even fighting to set up a plan for unemployment insurance. He has a solid chance of becoming the Democratic candidate for president in thirty-two."

"That's so far away." How would people survive till then? "Mrs. Goldstein said something earlier that scared me. She said, 'the only people sure of their jobs are civil-service workers.' "

"Laura, the country will always need lawyers."

"How many people will be able to afford them, the way things are going?" Laura challenged.

"I know a terrifying number of people are suffering. But many more are leading their normal lives. We'll be all right, Laura." Bernie paused, his face somber. "I worry about those others—the ones who've lost their jobs and don't know when they'll find another. Some nights I can't sleep. I remember the people walking around with newspaper in their shoes because they can't afford to buy new ones. I see men and women in hock shops, and I know

176

they're pawning what's left of their possessions to put food on their tables. *I know what they must feel.* It's so rotten it makes me physically sick sometimes. But today," he said with determination, "belongs to us. We're having tea at the Plaza. We're celebrating my beautiful wife's college graduation."

All through the hot New York summer Laura studied under Bernie's tutelage, absorbing the kind of details that came from actual practice rather than the classroom. She clung to the knowledge that the first woman to apply for admission to the bar, back in 1869 — Myra Bradwell of Chicago — had studied law only with her husband, a distinguished attorney. There were many lawyers who'd never set foot in a law school. If the cost became too much for Bernie and her to handle, then she'd drop out and study with him.

Laura was simultaneously thrilled and terrified when she started classes at NYU Law School in September. She had registered as L.R. Hunter rather than as Laura Hunter, in a subconscious attempt to lose herself among the predominantly male student body. She was grateful that her professors were not affronted at having a woman in their classes but outraged at the same time that some of the students showed varying degrees of contempt.

"Honey, what do you want to bother your pretty little head about such things?" an amorous fellow student cornered her at the end of the first week of classes. "Nobody — not even other women — take women lawyers seriously."

Laura made it clear she was married, a mother, and a future attorney. She constantly fought against guilt that she was in the classrooms stimulated by her studies instead of home caring for Jonnie and Katie. But she cherished the hours she spent with the children, grateful that on weekends Bernie spent much time watching over them so that she could study.

With the approach of Hanukkah and Christmas a parade of parcels — shipped from Harrod's in London — arrived. Iris had hoped Peter and she would go to Palm Beach in January—which meant they would spend a few days in New York and she could see Laura and Bernie and the children. But this wasn't to be.

*"Peter says Palm Beach is definitely out this season. The pound is beginning to fall and nobody can guess how low it'll hit."*

Iris had written about their stay in St. Tropez, about Venice in August and autumn at Cranford House in Kent. She reported that Peter spent most of his waking hours at the gambling tables or at all-male hunting parties at various country estates. He enjoyed showing her off at glittering dinner parties and balls, but much of the time she was on her own.

*"Laura, don't worry—I'm being so discreet it's painful. I know Peter's children are just waiting to catch me in an affair so they can run to him with it. I'm so chaste I belong in a convent! Peter's sixty and having his troubles in the bedroom, but I'm there like a good little wife when he's in the mood. Which, thank God, isn't often."*

Laura was disappointed that she would not be seeing Iris. She sensed, too, that Iris was growing bored with what she called her "lush celibate life."

Bernie lifted an eyebrow in astonishment when he saw the expensive Hanukkah-Christmas gifts—exquisite clothes for the children, fine cashmere sweaters for Laura and himself, a collection of Waterford crystal—that had arrived from Iris.

"Some of the British may be hurting," he said wryly, "but obviously not the upper crust."

Laura was jubilant when she completed her first year at law school with high grades.

But with the approach of the new school year she was nervous about laying out money for tuition. Salaries in general had dropped to forty percent of what they'd been in 1929 and Bernie had taken a thirty-percent cut.

"You're enrolling for your second year," he insisted. "We'll manage. And I'm not going to be fired—I'm handling more work than anybody in the firm."

Still, Laura was anxious. For the last year a familiar

sight on many street corners in cities across the nation had been shabbily dressed men and women selling apples for a nickel—a touching effort to earn rather than to beg.

Iris wrote that life among her own social set was changing little because of the unstable economy in England, though foreign investors were alarmed and withdrawing funds and government securities were plummeting.

*"Of course, Peter and his friends are grumbling about higher taxes, and there's talk now of death duties. A few clubs have closed. It's still hard to find domestic help. I read in 'Queen' that despite all the cries about unemployment girls don't want to work as servants. Oh, yes, I'm serving in a soup kitchen once a week. Peter thinks I'm out of my mind."*

Laura managed a wry smile as she envisioned her beautiful sister, wearing one of her chic Paris frocks, on duty at a London soup kitchen. She remembered Iris and herself, standing in grief and shock before Mrs. Tannenbaum while the arrogant old woman told them they were destitute. Iris would never have to worry about money again. She prayed that Bernie and she would survive the Depression without the desperation that was inflicting so many.

For Laura the months seemed to speed by with almost alarming swiftness. Late in February she and Bernie celebrated their sixth wedding anniversary. Bernie bought twenty-five-cent top balcony seats and they went into New York to see the new Elmer Rice play, *Counsellor-at-Law.* Iris had sent them a set of Wedgwood china. After lengthy admiration Laura decided this must be placed on high shelves in the kitchen out of the range of Jonnie and Katie's reach.

Jonnie was excited about starting kindergarten in September, the same month that Laura would enter her last year of law school. It was a heady realization.

On a balmy spring day Laura and two women classmates sat in a coffee shop near the campus during a break between classes and pondered over the discrimination they would face after they passed their bar exams.

"We know women lawyers never make it into big business," Laura reminded. "We know we'll never be able to do business at the clubs." Women were socially ostracized from this useful arena of operation. "We have to face the fact that the public — and that includes women — are wary of women lawyers."

"I've been warned already," one of Laura's classmates contributed, "that if you know steno, don't tell your boss. If you do you'll never get a chance to do anything else."

"Making it as a woman lawyer is a lot harder than making it as a woman doctor," Laura's other classmate emphasized. "And there are a lot more of them around. Maybe we chose the wrong profession."

"We'll graduate, pass our bar exams, and join a law firm. Even if we have to work for nothing," Laura said earnestly.

"That's all right for you," one of the girls pointed out and the other nodded. "You've got a working husband. But after they've helped me through law school, my parents expect me to pay my share at home." She sighed and shook her head. "We're nuts. Where will we find jobs when we earn our degrees and pass the bar exams?"

"We're not nuts," Laura insisted. "We're fighting for our futures. The Depression can't last forever."

"From your mouth to God's ear," the other girl said softly.

Like many in the troubled nation Laura and Bernie clung to the conviction that Franklin D. Roosevelt — chosen as the Democratic presidential candidate earlier in the month — would turn around the economy of the country. The Republicans were sure to lose at a time when even New York, the richest city in the country, could afford to give only $2.39 a week for relief to a family of four.

In England some of the ultra-rich showed their recognition of the terrible state of their country by going off meat for a few weeks. Some ladies served at soup kitchens and ran social clubs for the deprived. But the upper-class British — after an earlier pretense of "tightening their belts" — were dedicated to pretending that life was, indeed, "normal." Dances, balls, houseparties, flitting to and from European capitals, filled their days and nights.

Some English were nervous about the growing threat of dictators. Japan had set up a puppet republic after occupying Manchuria and had moved on to occupy Shanghai. In Germany — where five million were unemployed and thousands lived in tents — Hitler had received 13 million votes in the recent presidential election, though Hindenburg had won. Italy was ruled by the Fascist dictator, Mussolini. And in England Sir Oswald Mosley with his newly formed British Union of Fascists sought to emulate both Hitler and Mussolini.

Iris was irritated by Peter's friendship with Sir Oswald. She was more irritated by his recent fondness for everything German — including Hitler. Like many around the world she was horrified by Hitler's Jew-baiting tactics.

"Hindenburg is an old man — eighty-four years old. He can't control Hitler. I tell you," Peter had said with a fanatic gleam in his eyes, "Hitler is the future of Germany!"

On this mid-October afternoon Iris left the Elizabeth Arden salon on Bond Street and hurried to the waiting Bentley. She resented Peter's having dragged her away from all the partying on the Lido ten days ago. They had been at Cranford Hall only three days when he took off for Germany. He was due back sometime today.

Peter had gone to Munich for a private meeting with Hitler. From there he was to go to Berlin for three days. She suspected he had been intrigued by stories they'd heard about the nightclubs in Berlin that catered to homosexual and lesbian patrons. *Darling, I understand they're marvelously amusing.*

Iris leaned back against the gray-leather upholstery of the Bentley and instructed Reginald to head for Kent. Thank God, Cranford Hall — where Peter insisted on staying for weeks at a time — was within driving distance of London. She suspected that Reginald reported her destination to Peter every time he drove her alone. Was Peter afraid she would take herself a lover? Much as she would have liked that, she didn't dare.

She ought to be happy, she scolded herself. She had everything she'd always wanted. Gorgeous clothes, big houses, endless parties. Peter and she went to the best nightclubs and restaurants and to the theater. They traveled to the smart places in Europe. She had danced with the Prince of Wales and the Aga Khan. *Why couldn't she forget those ugly, painful nights when Peter came to her bedroom?*

Peter would probably be in a good mood today, she comforted herself. He usually was when he came back to Cranford Hall after a holiday. She tried to gear herself for a possible amorous mood. He hadn't touched her for months — she'd hoped he'd found permanent diversion elsewhere.

He was so violent when he made love — and each time he swore it wouldn't be that way again. If she sold her diamond necklace, she mused, and the other pieces he'd given her as peace offerings, she'd have enough to pay her passage back to New York and to live for a while. *But what about when the money ran out?*

Although Laura insisted they were doing all right despite the Depression, at intervals Iris worried about Laura and Bernie and the children. She wished she could send Laura a sizeable chunk of money after Laura admitted Bernie's salary had been cut a second time.

They left the city behind and moved out into the English countryside, beautiful in autumn dress. She'd have to pretend a warm welcome home for Peter in front of the servants. All the time she lay beneath the wonderful hands of that masseuse at Elizabeth Arden's, she had thought about Peter's homecoming. If she could be sure that *this time* he wouldn't hit her, she wouldn't feel so rotten right now.

Reginald turned off the public road onto the acreage that surrounded Cranford Hall. Soon the ivy-covered Tudor mansion with its tall brick chimneys, its bays of mullioned windows, rose into view. Peter was home. She saw his Horch — that passion of his for everything German — sitting before the entrance to the house.

She hurried into the entrance hall with the semblance of a welcoming smile. Dobkins stood at the head of the first flight of stairs, a glint of reproof in his eyes. Dobkins thought she should have remained at home to welcome "the Master," she told herself with ironic amusement.

"His Lordship would like you to come to his rooms immediately," Dobkins said. He always managed to convey a lack of respect for her despite his show of required deference.

"Thank you, Dobkins."

She went to her own rooms to find that Edwina had laid out the bias-cut, white-satin evening dress Peter had personally chosen for her at Molyneux's Paris salon last April. Of course Edwina was following Peter's instructions, a private message that he meant to make love to her. He said the white satin dress made him feel sexy. Not that it helped. He couldn't do a thing until he'd smacked her across the butt at least a dozen times. *Hard.*

"Shall I draw you a bath?" Edwina asked.

"*Please.*" *How much did Edwina know about Peter and her?*

While Edwina disappeared into the bathroom, Iris undressed and slipped into a robe. When Edwina emerged, she dismissed her, dallying in the tepid perfumed tub. Let Peter wait.

Had he ever tried to hit his first wife? Gossip told her that Peter and Eleanora Cranford had lived separate lives from the time their younger daughter was a toddler. They appeared together only on ceremonial occasions. His wife would never consider divorce despite Peter's unfaithfulness. Perhaps he hadn't wanted a divorce. Having a wife was a convenience.

She walked into her bedroom and pulled on the white-satin evening gown without bothering with undergarments. A glance in the mirror told her she looked radiant as she slipped her feet into high-heeled white-satin shoes. That was the result of this afternoon's facial. She swiftly redid her makeup, touched her earlobes and then her throat with the Chanel's that Peter claimed was an aphrodisiac, and left her room for his.

She hesitated before his door, assumed a festive air, and knocked.

"Come in," Peter called. Iris sensed an undercurrent of excitement in his voice.

Iris opened the door, walked into Peter's sitting room,

and froze in shock.

"Iris, shut the door!"

"Peter, what is this?" she demanded, her eyes blazing. Each of two nude girls—local village tarts, Iris's mind grasped instantly—sat cross-legged on a carved walnut William and Mary chair. They eyed her with wary curiosity.

"A welcome-home party," Peter drawled. "We'll tie up the girls, wallop them, and we'll both be as passionate as hell. I'll send you right out of your mind!"

"*You* are out of your mind, Peter." She was trembling in rage.

"Iris, take off your dress and let's play," he coaxed, reaching for her wrist.

"No!" Color stained her cheekbones.

She saw the instant of hesitation in his eyes. He didn't dare strike her. The two tarts sitting there would be witnesses. *How much had he paid them?*

"Sit down on the sofa and watch," he ordered, reaching to remove his belt.

"Peter, I won't have any part of this," she told him, her eyes clashing with his. "You've gone too far this time."

He ran his tongue over his lower lip, turned to stare at the girls. His breathing was heavy.

"Go back to your rooms and wait for me," he said tersely. "I won't be long."

Iris, with an instinct to pack up and leave, left Peter's rooms and rushed to her own. But alone in her room she knew she would not leave.

She couldn't go back to sleeping on the sofa in Laura's living room—or in some cheap airshaft bedroom if she was lucky enough to find a job in New York. Here she was Lady Iris Cranford. *She would remain Lady Cranford for the rest of her life.*

She would wait until Peter considered himself sufficiently aroused to make love. Perhaps this time he wouldn't hit her.

# Chapter 16

While Bernie hovered over the radio and listened to the returns on this cold election eve of 1932, Laura went through the nightly ritual of putting Jonnie and Katie to bed. Both were adept at ruses to delay the ultimate moment. Laura was grateful that tonight they fell asleep after only a few minutes of her reading to them. She knew most people were convinced Roosevelt would win, yet she was anxious to know that the country had voted in a Democratic president.

She covered Jonnie and Katie, kissed them, tiptoed from the room, and closed the door behind her. Bernie kept the radio so low, lest it keep the children awake, that she could not discern the trend of the returns.

"It's going well," Bernie greeted her. "Hoover's leading in only six states."

"We won't know until tomorrow," Laura surmised. "The waiting's going to be awful."

Roosevelt's convention promise, "I pledge you, I pledge myself to a new deal for the American people," had brought hope to those who were in despair. His humanity, his eloquence, his confidence were contagious. Even his campaign song—"Happy Days Are Here Again"—created an atmosphere of new optimism. Still, no one expected instant miracles. It was sufficient to know that changes lay ahead if Roosevelt was elected.

Though their alarm clock would awaken them at 6:30 A.M., Laura and Bernie remained at their radio till well past midnight. Laura was in the kitchen making yet another pot of coffee when a jubilant shriek from Bernie propelled her into the living room.

"Hoover just conceded!" he chortled. "Roosevelt is our next president!"

The nation awoke the next morning to headlines heralding Roosevelt's victory. As predicted, he had won by a landslide. Sitting in the kitchen over breakfast on this dreary morning that carried a threat of rain, Bernie somberly reminded Laura that it would be months before Roosevelt would take office. The last March inauguration because this past March the Twentieth Amendment — providing that new presidential terms would begin on January 20 — had been submitted to the states for ratification and was certain to be adopted.

"We won't have a new deal for a few months," Bernie reminded. "I wish to hell the Twentieth Amendment was already in force."

"But once Roosevelt's inaugurated," Laura said softly, "we'll have an administration that cares about the workers — about the farmers."


"I won't need you any more tonight, Edwina," Iris dismissed her maid when she was dressed for the evening's dinner party in honor of Sir Oswald Mosley.

"Good night, your Ladyship." Edwina smiled gratefully.

Peter complained that she spoiled Edwina, that she set a bad example for the rest of the staff, but it seemed absurd to keep her awake until two or three in the morning. Peter complained about everything. The "arrogance" of today's servants, the National Government, the stupidity of the unemployed.

If it hadn't been for this ridiculous dinner tonight, they would have stayed at Biarritz for another two weeks. At Biarritz Peter spent most of his time gambling — sparing Iris from playing the adoring young wife for most of each day.

Iris surveyed her reflection in her dressing-table mirror. The new gray-velvet Molyneux — which reflected his costumes for *The Barretts of Wimpole Street* and had been bought at his new salon on Grosvenor Street — emphasized her perfect figure. Her emerald necklace and earrings provided a dramatic contrast. She picked up her chinchilla cape, which Edwina had laid across the bed earlier, and

186

walked into her private sitting room.

The door was thrust open, and Peter stalked inside. She frowned. Why couldn't he bother to knock?

"Why didn't you wear black?" he scolded. "And your pearls."

"Would you like me to change?" she asked sweetly, knowing they must leave in a few moments.

"It's too late. I'd like to talk to Oswald before we sit down to dinner. He must be as furious as I am about those nasty demonstrations." Hordes of so-called "hunger marchers" had marched last week on Buckingham Palace, only to be forced back into Trafalgar Square by mounted and foot policemen. Just yesterday the demonstrators had attempted to send a group of fifty jobless men and women to the House of Commons with a petition signed by a million, demanding abolition of the "means test" and restoration of the cuts in unemployment benefits and social services. "It's the stupid Communists who foment all these riots."

It was going to be a dull political evening, Iris surmised, full of fanatical talk about Hitler and the wonders he was creating in Germany. She tried to erase from her mind the blatant anti-Semitic remarks that ricocheted around the dinner table at these "Black Shirt" gatherings. If Peter would allow it, she'd stay home.

"I'll probably fly to Berlin next week," Peter told her when they were settled in the Rolls-Royce. "I've been invited to dinner at the home of Magda and Joseph Goebbels. And I'll go to Munich the next day. It's likely," he said with pride, "that I'll be lunching with Hitler himself at the Osteria Bavaria."

In the car Iris made a pretense of listening to Peter's tirade against Ramsay MacDonald. How could she persuade Peter to go to Palm Beach in January? She was anxious to see Laura and the children. *It had been so long.*


In the remaining months of Hoover's presidency conditions grew worse. Unemployment continued to climb. Over 15 million were out of work. Desperate farmers in

187

the West were fighting bank foreclosures with shotguns; some committed suicide in their anguish at losing land that had been in their families for generations.

Early in 1933 the number of banks that were closing across the nation was terrifying. Depositors lined up in panic to withdraw their life's savings before the banks ran out of money. On February 14 the governor of Michigan declared a bank moratorium in his state to forestall runs on the banks. Now other states were taking the same action. New Yorkers were convinced their own great banks were safe.

Late in February—on a day when Bernie insisted that Laura skip classes to fight a heavy cold—Mrs. Goldstein appeared at the door late in the morning. She was pale and trembling, her eyes glazed in shock.

"Laura, my bank," she gasped. "I went over this morning to take out a few dollars. There was a line halfway down the block. Before I could get inside, they closed the doors." She clutched at Laura's arm. "Every cent I have in the world was in that bank!"

Gently Laura drew Mrs. Goldstein into the apartment and to the kitchen, seeking for words of comfort while she poured coffee for Mrs. Goldstein and herself, trying not to reveal her own consternation.

"All our lives Milton and I worked hard, we put away every penny we could. We'd been married forty-one years when he died—and we never took one day of vacation. I wore the same winter coat for ten years. We went to a movie once a month. Not until Milton was gone did I let myself spend a few dollars for a radio—because I had to have a voice in the house or go crazy." She rocked back and forth in remembered grief. "We saved for emergencies and for our old age. And for what did we deny ourselves?" Her voice grew shrill. "So the bank could take our money and not give it back?"

"The bank hasn't officially closed." Laura clutched at hope. "Nobody came out and said the bank was bankrupt."

"The bank will not open again." Mrs. Goldstein seemed to age before Laura's eyes. *"Laura, it's not right for something like this to happen.*"

"Maybe the bank closed this morning to stop a run and will reopen tomorrow or the next day. Let's see what the evening newspapers have to say."

"They will say the bank is *kaput.*" Mrs. Goldstein closed her eyes in anguish for a moment. "Since their father died, my girls keep telling me to come and live with them. I always said 'no.' I wanted to be independent. Now I'll have to go. But not until you graduate law school, Laura," she stipulated. "Somehow, I'll manage to pay the rent until then." Tears welled in her eyes. "I'll miss you and Bernie and the children."


Mrs. Goldstein's bank had not reopened and at the end of the month she moved into the Hunter apartment. She sold her furniture, and with Bernie's help packed up the memorabilia of a lifetime for shipment to her youngest daughter's home. A couple with two small children moved into Mrs. Goldstein's apartment.

Laura marveled that outwardly Borough Park — like many other communities — seemed untouched by the deepening Depression, yet behind neatly curtained windows lives were being turned upside down.

On March 4 Franklin D. Roosevelt was to be inaugurated as president. Describing Pennsylvania Avenue in Washington D.C. on this cloudy morning, a newscaster reported on the line-up of soldiers with mounted machine guns on the parade route, and Laura remembered that just over two weeks ago an unemployed bricklayer had tried to assassinate the president-elect.

It was a magical moment when President Roosevelt addressed the nation after taking the oath of office:

"Let me assert my firm belief that the only thing we have to fear is fear itself . . ."

Listening to the vigorous voice of Roosevelt, a people drowning in despair felt a surge of fresh hope. The country faced terrible problems, but here was a leader to take needed action. Already tomorrow seemed less desperate.

The most urgent problem facing Roosevelt was the

banking situation. The day after his inauguration he declared a national "bank holiday," and at the same time issued a ruling that forbade the export of gold. On Sunday, March 12, President Roosevelt spoke to the people via radio, in what he labeled his first "fireside chat." On Monday the banks opened their doors. Deposits exceeded withdrawals. The new president had brought about a resurgence of hope and faith in the hearts of Americans.

With Laura's graduation from law school approaching, Iris sent her a magnificent mink coat.

*"Darling, you know my problem. No cash, just chits. Feel free to hock this at any time. I'm so proud of my sister, the attorney!"*

The night before her graduation, Laura struggled futilely to sleep. Fearful of waking Bernie, she left the bed and went out to the kitchen. Her mind was a kaleidoscope of memories. Nine years ago today Iris and she had boarded the Seaboard Airline train for New York. So much had happened—so much that was good. Yet tonight—hours away from receiving her law degree—she felt as far away from clearing her father's name as on the day Iris and she arrived in New York.

"Laura?" Bernie hovered in the kitchen doorway. "You can't sleep."

"I'm too excited." Laura managed a rueful smile.

"Both of us." Bernie sat beside her.

"Now I worry about passing the bar exams."

"You'll pass them. And these rotten times won't last." His eyes pleaded with her to believe him. "When conditions are better, we'll get out of New York. We'll go down to Magnolia to live." *It amazed her the way Bernie so often read her thoughts.* "Laura, I've told you. We'll work together to set the record straight down there. Not just for you and Iris—for the children, too. They have to know their grandfather was a fine man."

"I wish Papa could have been here for graduation tomorrow. I wish Iris was here." For so many important events in her life Iris was far away.

Bernie reached for her hand.

"I know," he said compassionately. "But Jonnie and Katie will be there." He grinned. "How many children have

190

the pleasure of attending their mother's graduation from law school?"

Laura waited until she was convinced Jonnie and Katie were asleep before she turned on *Voice of Firestone* and began to wrap the Hanukkah presents, to be doled out—according to American-Jewish tradition—nightly during the eight days of the holiday. The presents from Iris—always special—would be given to them on Christmas day.

They didn't observe Christmas as a religious holiday, Laura comforted herself. Christmas to the Hunters was a time to pray for peace on earth. This allowed the children not to feel themselves outsiders in the Christmas holiday season.

Earlier Laura had polished the small brass Hanukkah menorah. Four *dreidls*—spinning tops with Hebrew letters—were tucked away in a drawer, to be given to Jonnie and Katie along with Minna Levine's two little ones at the Hanukkah party Minna planned for tomorrow afternoon. A Hanukkah card from Mrs. Goldstein was propped against the sugar bowl on the kitchen table.

Laura glanced at the clock. Bernie should be home any minute. He'd phoned from the office an hour ago to say he was headed for the subway. She gathered together the presents and hid them on a high shelf in the kitchen cabinet—beside the bottle of inexpensive champagne Bernie had bought when just a few days ago the last of the thirty-six states needed had ratified the Twenty-first Amendment, repealing Prohibition. The champagne was to celebrate their eighth wedding anniversary in February. Now she began to set the table.

The kitchen was comfortably warm on this cold December night. The aromas of onions, spices, and vegetables simmering with the pot roast on the range lent an aura of well-being to the atmosphere. Once a week she bought a pot roast and stretched it out for three dinners. Spaghetti, noodles, and rice dishes served as main courses the other nights.

Bernie kept insisting she have her diploma framed.

*"Laura, we can afford it."* But she tried to save every possible penny. Still, it was an enormous satisfaction to know that at last she was a full-fledged lawyer. Despite her fears she had passed the New York bar exams on her first try.

It would be more satisfying if she had a job. Minna Levine, whose husband was in civil service, had offered to care for Jonnie and Katie along with her own two if a job came along. Today employers were reluctant to hire women in any capacity when so many men — heads of families — were without work.

Laura crossed to the range to check on the pot roast. With a cheaper cut, the longer it simmered the more tender the meat. It was fine. At twenty-nine cents a pound, steak appeared on the table only on Bernie's birthday and their wedding anniversary. She thought about the slaughter of six million young pigs in the stockyards just a few weeks ago — an effort of farmers to keep up the price of pork.

She had hoped to pick up some free-lance typing assignments from Bernie's office, since part of the clerical staff had been laid off. But Bernie said the office had no funds available for this; when the one remaining typist was overloaded with work, the lawyers did their own typing. *But conditions would improve.*

Laura's face lighted as she heard Bernie's key in the door. She switched off the radio and hurried out in the hall to greet him. She felt an urgency in him when he kissed her.

"Bernie?" she asked, suddenly fearful when she saw the anguish in his eyes. "What happened?"

"Laura, how can I tell you?" He spread his hands in a gesture of helplessness.

"Tell me," she said with shaky calm, drawing him into the kitchen.

"Laura, I can't believe it. Mr. Weinstein told me at closing time. We're getting one week's notice. What's left of the staff is being laid off. No," his voice soared, "fired. Laid off sounds temporary. This is final. *One week's notice.*"

"The firm's going out of business?" *What had happened to so many was finally happening to them.* The rent had to be

192

paid at the first of the month. The gas and electric, the phone, the children's doctor. "Why didn't they give you all some warning?" Laura's anger disguised her panic.

"I should have seen it coming." Bernie pulled off his coat, tossed it across the back of a chair and slumped into another. "I saw it," he berated himself, "but I backed away because I was scared. Not one of the partners has drawn a salary for four months. The office rent is three months behind. The furniture will be sold off next week. Mr. Schiffman is retiring. Mr. Weinstein and Mr. Elkin are starting out on their own."

"If they're selling off the furniture, Bernie, it'll be cheap," Laura said quietly. "We won't need much. Two desks, a file cabinet, a few chairs." Bernie stared at her in shock. "We'll find a tiny office somewhere — office space is going begging these days. We'll be all right," she insisted, knowing that at this moment Bernie needed reassurance above all else. Forget that she, too, felt sick with fear. "Hunter & Hunter, Attorneys-at-Law. Just the way we've always planned. I'll sell my mink coat. It'll bring in a chunk of money. Mrs. Grafton upstairs loves our Wedgwood — she'll grab it at a good price. And we have our money in Postal Savings. *We're going to be all right.*"

Bernie found tiny quarters in their old building. In two weeks *Hunter & Hunter, Attorneys-at-Law* were in business. Laura came into the office each morning after she had deposited Katie with Minna Levine and had taken Jonnie and Betty's little boy off to school. She left the office each afternoon in time to pick them up at dismissal.

Laura had known it would be difficult to acquire clients. But she had not suspected that they would be grateful for the sordid divorce cases that came their way. Bernie and she were ever conscious of the need to meet their bills. Each month was a battle for survival.

She gritted her teeth and remained silent when clients referred to her as Bernie's secretary. Their emergency savings had grown perilously slim and she appointed herself their personal collection agency, belaboring delinquent clients to pay their bills or face court actions.

Relief rolls across the country had grown to include many whose savings and other financial resources had been drained by the years of the Depression. The great American dream of rags to riches had been obliterated.

By the end of 1934 Bernie was fearful. Hitler and his Nazis proclaimed the Jews were responsible for the impossible peace terms forced on Germany, that Jewish financiers were responsible for Germany's economic chaos, its social and moral disintegration. German leaders declared "we would have no crime if we had no Jews."

"Jewish doctors are losing their practices. Jewish judges removed from the courts. Jewish lawyers can't even enter a courtroom!" Bernie railed over a late dinner. "Don't they realize that of thirty Germans who have won Nobel prizes, eight have been Jews!"

"Iris wrote that Sir Oswald Mosley's British Union of Fascists has over twenty thousand members. Including her husband," Laura said grimly. She understood that Iris remained with him only for the security his position provided. Now she was relieved that Iris had never told Peter she was Jewish. Sir Oswald Mosley and his British Union of Fascists were holding marches right in the Jewish areas of London—their theme song, Iris wrote in secret rage, "the Yids, the Yids, we've got to get rid of the Yids."

"England has Mosley, and here at home we have Father Coughlin." Bernie shook his head in recurrent bafflement. "He receives over eighty thousand letters a week from radio listeners. Ten million people hear his program. He feels so strong he even ignores his church. The man's as anti-Semitic as the Nazis!"

On May 27 the New Deal faced its own "Black Monday"; the Supreme Court killed a farm mortgage relief act, condemned the entire National Industrial Recovery Act as unconstitutional, and issued a personal rebuke to Roosevelt for what it considered an illegal exercise of his removal power.

That evening Laura and Bernie listened with somber intensity to the radio newscaster reporting on the Supreme Court's three sweeping decisions.

"It's always the same," Bernie protested. "Big business is out to grow even bigger. Roosevelt *knows* that small businesses are the soul of this country. They make our economic society work."

"How could the Supreme Court do this?" Laura was shaken.

"Everybody thinks the Supreme Court is sacrosanct," Bernie said in rage. "They forget the times it has been wrong. Remember the Dred Scott decision, denying blacks their human rights? The Supreme Court justices are only nine old men — not God!"

"What happens now?" Laura asked.

"New laws will be passed to protect the workers," Bernie predicted. "Next year is the presidential election year. The Democrats know they have to prove themselves on the side of the common man."

"Bernie, when will the country get back to normal?" Laura reached forward to switch off the radio after the newscaster summed up the situation abroad.

"Soon things will be better," he encouraged. "It's not just here. The whole world is in chaos. I don't know the magic formula," he tried for a light note. "I hope to hell all those people in Washington find it soon."

"Jonnie's talking about a two-wheeler for his eighth birthday," Laura told Bernie. "You know, the ones with training wheels."

"We can't afford it." Bernie frowned. "He's a baby. He can wait another two years." His face tensed. "I didn't have a bike until I was fourteen."

"Maybe an important case will come in before the children's birthdays. Katie is just asking for a party."

Bernie glared at her.

"Who's got money for parties? Katie thinks she's Barbara Hutton?"

"I'll bake a cake. I'll make crepe paper decorations. We'll have just five little girls," Laura cajoled. "It won't cost much."

"Damn it!" Bernie slammed a fist against his thigh. "We work like dogs. Why can't we afford to buy a bike for Jonnie? Why can't we give Katie a fancy birthday party?"

"It's not just us. Everybody's scrimping."

"Not the Rockefellers and the Huttons and the Dukes," Bernie said with a new bitterness.

"We'll make Jonnie understand he'll have to wait for a bike. We'll buy him another set of tinker toys, and the two of you will build a whole city." Laura fought back the tears.

When a fine English bicycle arrived from Iris three weeks before Jonnie's birthday, Bernie was suspicious.

"You told Iris he wanted a bike!" Bernie accused.

"Bernie, no," she reproached. In every marriage there were times when a small lie was necessary. "Iris guessed. Every little boy starts asking for a bike around his age." On those rare occasions when she used a small lie to cover a traumatic situation, she felt guilty. But Jonnie's face when he saw the bike had told her she had not done wrong.

"Maybe it's time for us to start handling some assigned cases." Bernie's voice betrayed his humiliation that it was his sister-in-law who gave his son his first bike.

"Become jail lawyers?" Laura was shaken that Bernie would even consider their joining that group of attorneys who took on cases gratuitously in the hope of persuading the defendant or his family to come up with some cash in order to guarantee more attention to the case. "Bernie, no."

"All right, forget that," Bernie capitulated. "But it's time we became realistic. We'll expand. In addition to divorce cases and civil suits, we'll move into criminal law. Not assigned cases," he emphasized. "In these times we can't afford to work for nothing." Laura remembered his earlier determination to devote part of his working hours to the poor. "We'll take on criminal defendants who can afford to come up with a respectable fee."

"Bernie, we'll have to be selective." Her throat was tight with anxiety.

"Laura, every defendant has a right to the best lawyer he can afford." He avoided meeting her eyes. "Who are we to judge who's innocent and who's guilty? That comes out at the trial."

"You always said you wouldn't want to represent petty criminals." She tried to keep her voice even. *What was happening to her husband?*

"We broke our backs to get through college and law school. We have a right to earn a living as attorneys!" A vein in his forehead was distended now. "Even petty criminals have a right to a fair trial."

"Bernie, you went into law to be able to defend those who were being denied justice. Not to help some crook — or worse — to escape the law."

"I didn't expect a stock crash. I didn't expect a Depression," Bernie said harshly. "We have two children to raise. We owe them a decent life. I'm tired of seeing you scrimp on the table, deny yourself a new dress or a new pair of shoes. I'm tired of being scared to death of next month's bills." Bernie exhaled a long, painful breath. "I'll let it be known we're expanding into criminal law."

# Chapter 17

In a black satin slip that emphasized her slenderness without detracting from her voluptuous breasts, Iris sat at the dressing table in her bedroom at Cranford Hall and gazed searchingly at her reflection. In five months — in August — she would be twenty-nine. Thirty was terrifyingly close. She searched for telltale lines, at last conceding she saw none. *How would she bear being old?* Elaine and Sandra talked about a marvelous doctor in Switzerland who gave mysterious injections that chased away the years. They'd almost persuaded Peter to give it a whirl.

She reached for the bottle of her latest Paris perfume and absently dabbed a drop behind her ears, at her throat — and then, with an anticipatory smile, at her cleavage. Reginald's replacement — Sandra declared he reminded her of their favorite American movie actor, Clark Gable — would drive her into London shortly. They would stop at their secluded rendezvous point along the road, and Donald would join her on the back seat of the Rolls. Peter was off again to Germany. He was due back in a day or two.

Donald was smart — he knew he'd lose his job if any word got back to Peter. In these times nobody wanted to join the unemployment rolls. Peter was forever coming to her with weird invitations — let him watch while she made love with some young boy or with another woman. Or watch with him while "these two beautiful young boys" made love. She suspected he was picking up his ideas from the nightclubs he visited in Munich and Berlin.

He had not been to her bed for months. Not since she had blackened his eye when he tried to get brutal again. All of a sudden she had known she couldn't take that anymore, not even for the jewelry he gave her afterwards. She warned him she'd go to the editors of the London *Daily Mirror* and tell them the "inside story of the marriage of Lord and Lady Cranford" if he ever tried that again. She should have used that threat right from the beginning—but she'd been so young and naive then.

"Thank you, Edwina." Iris smiled as her personal maid laid the freshly pressed Schiaparelli Irish tweed suit across her bed. "I'll wear the mink jacket with it."

She glanced at her diamond-studded watch. If Donald and she were to have any playtime at all, she'd better dress. She was to meet Sandra and Elaine at the Savoy for lunch. Diana was off with her husband at a houseparty at some baron's castle in Tunisia. They'd all meet in Paris next month.

Iris felt a flicker of excitement.

She dressed quickly and hurried downstairs, the mink jacket over one arm. Donald was waiting in front of the house with the white Rolls-Royce. He leaped from behind the wheel to open the door for her. Couldn't Peter guess she got the "hots" just looking at Donald? Maybe he didn't care. All that interested him these days were gambling, hunting, and his weird political friends. And his weird sex parties.

"You're looking beautiful," Donald murmured, his face impassive, lest one of the servants was watching them. "That scent absolutely sets my teeth on edge."

"That's what the copy writers promise," Iris drawled.

She settled herself on the back seat while Donald hurried to take his place behind the wheel again. She lived a fairy-tale life since she married Peter but not until Donald replaced Reginald five months ago had she realized how bored she was much of the time.

Some women hated sex. Some tolerated it. Others—like herself—needed it to be fully alive. She'd never told any of her friends—she'd never even told Laura—about Peter's depraved approach to lovemaking.

The corners of her mouth lifted in amused recall. The other three girls in what those in their circle dubbed the "gorgeous quartette" had taken young lovers within months after their marriages to titled men. Over cocktails at Fouquet's in Paris last spring she had confessed she had slept with no one except Peter since their marriage.

*"Darling, I can't believe it."* Sandra had gasped at her in shock and wonderment. *"Is Peter that good?"* Elaine and Diana had waited open-mouthed for her reply.

*"Peter is a disaster,"* she'd admitted. *"But I'm not giving him grounds for divorce."*

Though Peter still adored showing her off among their acquaintances, she suspected that at times he regretted his hasty marriage. Some doors in stuffy England had been closed to him before he brought her home with him. But more doors had slammed shut when he married what his children considered "a cheap American adventuress."

Donald was slowing down now. They were approaching the grounds of a closed-up little house with a vine-covered porte-cochere — both hidden behind twelve-foot privet hedges. Their rendezvous spot.

Iris was already unbuttoning her blouse when Donald opened the rear door of the car. She felt defiant and triumphant at the same time. Why shouldn't she have this? Peter wasn't faithful to her. When he was drunk, he openly boasted about his bedroom encounters with other women — and men.

"That shouldn't be wasted on an old man," Donald murmured hotly, as he prodded her across the seat, one hand cupping the rich spill of her breast while the other manipulated her skirt above her thighs. "You travel for action," he noted with approval. A silken strip of bra and matching panties were concealed in her purse. Later she would be properly dressed for London.

"I don't want to waste a minute." Her smile was dazzling. He'd known she was prepared for this encounter. "Let's get this show on the road." Her hand reached to his crotch, and she felt a surge of anticipation. He couldn't wait to get in.

Her mouth was at his earlobe — her tongue probing — while he freed himself, reached into a pocket for the protection Iris insisted upon.

"Donald, it's going to be fabulous," she whispered, fingers moving with featherlight swiftness between his taut thighs.

"You'd drive a eunuch frantic!" he swore and thrust with impatient haste. "Oh, God, Iris!"


Iris straightened her stockings, made sure her blouse was properly buttoned. She reached into her purse again — bought at Schiaparelli's newly designed boutique in Paris — for her compact and lipstick. She felt exhilarated and refreshed. And Peter would never know.

Starting up the motor, Donald drove slowly from the porte-cochere down the driveway towards the road. At the opening between the privet hedge he stopped with a suddenness that almost unseated Iris.

"Donald, what the devil!"

"We have to wait a few minutes," he told her, his voice uneven.

"Why? I have a luncheon appointment in London."

"Didn't you see the Bentley that just passed?" He swung about to face her. "Dobkins was at the wheel. He was coming from London with Lord Cranford." When Peter went to Munich or Berlin, he traveled without his manservant. Dobkins met him with the Bentley at the airport.

"Peter wasn't due back until tomorrow." All at once Iris was trembling. "Dobkins didn't say a word about a change in schedule."

"Why should he?" Donald shrugged. "He takes his orders from the old man."

"We can't do this anymore," Iris said after a moment. "I'll miss it, but I can't take a chance on Peter's finding out." *It was a close call.*

"No," Donald agreed. "I don't want to find myself on the dole."

She lived in a silken prison, Iris tormented herself. She was Peter's chattel. And he was getting more difficult every day. Ever since he met Hitler personally in Munich last year, all he talked about was how Hitler was managing to put new life into Germany again. He derided newspaper reports of Hitler's atrocities against German Jews.

She hoped Peter would manage to keep this admiration silent in Paris. Ten days ago Nazi troops had moved into the Rhineland to set up a barrier against France. Peter privately predicted that in ten years Hitler would rule all Europe.

"I think it's safe to leave." Donald punctured her introspection. He sounded chipper again. "They're too far down the road for him to recognize the car even if he happened to look behind." He drove cautiously onto the road and headed towards London. "I say, Iris, do you think there's anything to all those stories floating around London about His Majesty and that woman from America? Wallis Simpson?" He looked over his shoulder for an instant. "You're American, aren't you?"

"Oh, yes."

"That's what Edwina said. You sure as hell talk like high-tone British."

"That was acquired," Iris told him, her smile ironic.

If she had dropped her Southern accent eight years ago, she would be a Hollywood star today.


Laura left the children's school and hurried towards the subway. This morning Jonnie's class had presented a play in the school assembly. As always she was among the attending mothers. Sentimental tears filled her eyes. He was so sweet and serious about the project. Thank God for Jonnie and Katie. They made life worth living.

The first forsythia of the season blossomed in golden splendor in small gardens. She was grateful that the New York winter was past them. The way the children were growing she'd been afraid she might have to buy new coats before the warmer weather arrived.

She should be grateful, Laura admonished herself at regular intervals, that they were managing to survive, yet it was agonizing to accept why they were so fortunate. Bernie tried to hide his bitterness, but he, too, loathed the small-time gangsters they were reduced to defending. It was not the kind of law practice they had envisioned for themselves.

She had to wait only moments before a train pulled into the station. The rush hour was past — she found a seat. Now she remembered the letter to Iris that was in her purse. She'd mail it before she went up to the office.

Iris wrote gaily about trips to Paris and Vienna and St. Tropez, yet Laura sensed her sister was bored and homesick. If conditions were not so bad, she would encourage Iris to come home. But what was there here for her?

It alarmed her when Iris talked about a possible war involving England. Already there were two wars in progress — in China and in Spain. Now Mussolini's troops had invaded Abyssinia. *"Everybody pretends war is unthinkable, but we all know the new German air force is a real threat."*

If there was any sign of war, she'd insist Iris come home. They'd manage somehow. Better poor than dead.

Laura left the subway, stopped to mail the letter to Iris, and went up to their tiny office. Her eyes dwelt for an instant on the gold lettering on the glass door: *Hunter & Hunter, Attorneys-at-Law.* How excited they had been at starting their own office.

She opened the door and walked inside. Bernie was alone, hunched over the phone in absorbed conversation. He glanced up, beckoned her to the chair beside his desk. There was an aura of excitement about him.

"Yes, it's all settled," he assured whoever was at the other end of the line. "The file's coming over by messenger now. As soon as Jerry is able to talk with me, I'll go over to the hospital and discuss what he's come up with so far." Bernie paused to listen. *What was he so keyed up about?* "Yes, sir. We'll stay in touch." Bernie put down the phone, exhaled eloquently. "God, what a morning!"

"Who was that?" She sensed a blend of jubilation and unease in Bernie. "What's happened?"

"First of all, the phone was ringing when I walked into the office. Jerry Abrams was in a car accident this morning." Abrams was a flamboyant young lawyer addicted to sensational cases. Bernie had known him in law school. Laura detested him. "He'll be all right, but he'll be out of action for at least six or seven weeks."

"He's handling the DeVito case," Laura pinpointed. She knew that the case was coming to trial next week. Ray DeVito, the son of a big-time racketeer, was to be tried for the rape and murder of a seventeen-year-old girl. For weeks the tabloids had been playing up the sensational details of the rape and murder of Peggy Williams, the only child of a forty-seven-year-old mechanic whose wife had died when his daughter was four. Every time such a case was splashed across the headlines Laura relived her father's trial and his death. "But what has that got to do with us?" All at once her heart was pounding.

"Jerry's partner is on a case—he can't touch it—" Bernie was striving for calm. "He talked with Jerry at the hospital early this morning. Laura, they've suggested to Vincent DeVito that I take it on—"

"Bernie, you can't!" At twenty-three, Ray DeVito had already been arrested for drunken driving and leaving the scene of a fatal accident. Only his father's money and connections had got him off. "Everybody's convinced he's guilty."

"Nobody is guilty until he's been convicted," Bernie reminded her. "Jerry's partner spoke very highly of me. He said if

203

anybody could clear Ray, I would be the lawyer to do it."

"Bernie, you can't defend somebody like that! All the evidence is against him. *He raped and murdered that sweet little girl.*"

"Jerry has done all the ground work," Bernie said evasively. "All I have to do is go into court and plead the case. He'll split his fee with me."

"I know you, Bernie," she pounced. "You'll dig day and night for more angles until the minute you're in court. How can you defend a man like that?"

"I'd have to approach Judge Claiborne and ask for a three-week postponement," Bernie conceded. Judge Claiborne looked upon Bernie as one of the most promising young lawyers practicing in New York. *Jerry was counting on that.* "I'd need that much time to familiarize myself with the case."

"Bernie, you'd be defending a man we're both convinced is guilty of a terrible crime," Laura protested hotly.

"Vincent DeVito left the office fifteen minutes ago," Bernie said, avoiding her eyes. "I've already accepted the case." Laura was dazed. "I couldn't turn it down. Laura, if I can get an acquittal, Vincent DeVito will pay me an extra twenty-five thousand dollars."

"Oh, my God—" Laura gasped.

"I know what you've been thinking," Bernie said. "It's going against all our beliefs. We were never going to defend someone whom we thought was guilty. But I can't turn down the chance of earning twenty-five thousand dollars. If I clear that boy, we can afford to leave New York, buy a house down in Magnolia and set ourselves up in practice. You know the depressed prices in real estate. We can invest down in Magnolia. In coming years it'll be worth a fortune. Laura," he reached for her hands. "This could give us and the children a real future."


Laura went to court each morning with Bernie, when the DeVito case came to trial. She could understand what had pushed Bernie into accepting the case. Nonetheless her cherished image of her husband was destroyed. She detested the arrogant young defendant. Detested his father, who was convinced Bernie was the best his money could buy. Yet every waking moment she was guiltily conscious of what an acquittal could mean to them.

Despite her reluctance to be involved she sat in the kitchen far into each night and worked with Bernie to ferret out angles that would help to clear their client.

"Laura, think," Bernie urged her repeatedly. "There are three women on the jury. How do we make them feel that maybe — just maybe — Ray's innocent?"

Their initial fee itself was the largest they had ever received. The bonus would change their lives. They'd live in Magnolia. And in time they would clear Papa's name. But how would she live with the knowledge that they had cleared a man guilty of rape and murder?

Bernie and Laura focused totally on the case during the three painful weeks that the trial dragged. Laura realized Bernie was subtly creating doubts in the minds of those three women jurors. Still, there were nine men to convince.

On the last day of the trial aura sensed a new confidence in Vincent DeVito. He was almost jovial when the jury filed out of the courtroom.

"How long do you think they'll be out, Bernie?" the senior DeVito asked. The stocky racketeer — in an expensive Brook's Brothers suit — dropped an arm about his son's attorney. "A few hours? A couple of days?"

"Not long," Bernie guessed, exchanging an uncomfortable glance with Laura. They both suspected DeVito had done some jury tampering. "But I could be wrong."

At eleven the next morning — with the handful of people in the courtroom suddenly alert — the jury filed back to report their verdict. Laura saw Bernie's knuckles go white as he clenched his fists. The judge asked the traditional question. The foreman of the jury replied:

"We find the defendant 'not guilty.' "

Laura's eyes shot to Peggy Williams's father. He bowed his head for a moment as though in prayer, then rose to his feet and left. She could feel his anguish. Today his daughter's murderer had been set free. Justice trampled on once again — as with her father. Tammy Lee Johnson's murderer still walked free.

The courtroom was in pandemonium as reporters rushed towards Ray DeVito, arrogant and self-assured again. Vincent DeVito — radiating triumph — sat at the table, pulled out his checkbook, and began to write.

"You came through, Bernie!" Vincent rose to his feet,

slapped Bernie on the back as he handed over the check. "Come on out to lunch with Ray and me. We have to celebrate!"

"Go on, Bernie," Laura said quickly before he could remind DeVito that she had been part of the defense team. "I'll take the check to the bank." Vincent DeVito considered her Bernie's secretary.

"Let me endorse it," Bernie said, his eyes caressing Laura. "Vincent forgot to make it out to the firm."

Laura took the check, gazed at it with mixed emotions, then folded it and put it into her wallet. The three men were charging out into the sunny June morning. She walked slowly, struggling to digest what had just happened in the courtroom behind her.

All at once the sounds of what she thought to be those of a car backfiring jarred the usual morning sounds. But it wasn't a car backfiring. She heard the screams and the shouts and rushed ahead in sudden terror. Ray DeVito and his father lay sprawled across the steps. Bernie—clutching his chest—had turned to face the courthouse.

"Laura! Oh my God, Laura—"

She rushed to Bernie's side as he collapsed to the steps, pulled him into her arms while blood stained his immaculate white shirt. She was vaguely conscious that Williams had turned the gun on himself while the terrorized onlookers huddled close by.

"Laura, I'm sorry. You were right—" his voice trailed off.

"Bernie, don't talk," she pleaded. "You're going to be all right." *He had to be all right.*

While a crowd gathered about them, Bernie closed his eyes with a convulsive shudder.

"Bernie?" He was breathing, but he was unconscious.

"Someone phoned for help." A stranger leaned compassionately over her. "The ambulance will be here soon."

It seemed hours rather than minutes before an ambulance crew lifted Bernie from her arms and onto a stretcher. A police officer helped her into the ambulance. In moments the ambulance was racing through the busy city streets. Let them get to the hospital in time, Laura prayed.

While a team of doctors and nurses worked over Bernie in an operating room, Laura paced in the deserted waiting area.

*This wasn't real.* It was a nightmare. She'd wake up and Bernie would hold her in his arms and soothe her. They'd laugh about it together.

But reality pierced her numbness. The children! They'd be frightened when they got out of school and she wasn't there. Call Betty, her mind ordered. Ask her to pick up Jonnie and Katie. Her eyes darting around the room, she spied a public phone booth a dozen yards down the hall. She hurried towards it, at the same time fumbling with trembling hands in her change purse.

Her voice harsh with anxiety she told Betty what had happened.

"Stay with Bernie," Betty said. "I'll bring Jonnie and Katie to my apartment. I'll keep them as long as necessary. And Laura, I'll be praying for Bernie with you."

When Laura returned to the waiting area, she saw a doctor waiting to talk to her. His somber face sent alarm charging through her.

"Mrs. Hunter?"

"Yes," she whispered. "Is my husband out of surgery?"

"I'm sorry, Mrs. Hunter. There was nothing we could do to save him. He never regained consciousness."

"Oh my God —" She would have fallen if the doctor had not reached out a hand to steady her.

A nurse came forward solicitously.

"May I get you something, Mrs. Hunter? Would you like me to call someone for you?"

"Thank you, no." She summoned strength from some unknown source. "I — I'd just like to sit down a few moments."

In the tailored blue dress that was Bernie's favorite — stained now with his blood — she sat in a corner of the waiting-room sofa. Bernie was gone. Two hours ago they'd sat side by side in the courtroom. He'd been so excited about the check. And now he'd never smile at her again in that special way of his. He'd never hold her in his arms. She would have to be both mother and father to Jonnie and Katie. For their sake she must go on living. . . .

*Part 3*

# Chapter 18

Laura knew that for the rest of her life she would never erase from her mind the disbelieving, terrified expressions on Jonnie and Katie's small faces when she told them their father had been murdered. There was no kind way to tell them. She remembered Papa telling Iris and her that Mama was dead. Even now she could remember their grief. But she remembered, too, how Papa's love and tenderness had carried them through the days and weeks that followed.

Laura was grateful for friends and neighbors — some of whom she knew only from casual encounters — who rushed forward to offer their help. Hearing about the triple murder and suicide over the radio, Mannie Schwartz — who had been Bernie's best man and whom Laura and he had seen irregularly through the years — rushed to the apartment, took charge of the funeral arrangements. Mannie and his wife went with the children and her to the cemetery. It was Mannie — the accountant — who deposited the twenty-five-thousand-dollar check that had been signed by Vincent DeVito and endorsed by Bernie minutes before they were gunned down.

Minna Levine insisted Laura give her Iris's address. "Your sister will want to know," Minna insisted. *But Iris was in London. What could she do?*

Iris and she had not been able to sit *shivah* for Papa. The children and she would sit *shivah* for Bernie. It never should have happened — these murders were a kind of terrible retribution that should not have touched Bernie. In normal times he would not have been part of it.

To walk into the bedroom she had shared with Bernie for eleven years was to grapple with recurrent pain. How could she sleep in the bed where the warm imprint of his body would never rumple the sheet again? She would lie there and reach out to emptiness. Each night she brought sheets and a pillow to the sofa, lay in wait for sleep to bring release from the anguish of living.

Slowly, steadily, as the days dragged by, Laura brought herself to deal with reality. She was a widow with two children to raise. She must find the strength. She must learn to make decisions. Except for the DeVito case, she and Bernie always had made decisions together.

Mannie assured her that Vincent DeVito's check would be honored by his bank. They were not destitute—as Iris and she had been. But she must plan for their future, she told herself each day.

On the last day of their sitting *shivah* Laura went to the door at the sound of the bell.

Iris was standing there.

"Laura, I can't believe it." Tears flooding her eyes, Iris pulled her sister into her arms. "I came on the first available ship. Swearing all the way," she managed a shaky laugh, "because it was taking so long. When the hell are they going to begin trans-Atlantic plane service?"

"I was praying you could come," Laura confessed, hugging Iris, "though I was afraid Peter might object."

"I didn't ask him," Iris said. "I just packed up and came. I left a note for him—he must have found it when he returned from another of his endless trips to Munich." A sudden smile lighted her face as Jonnie and Katie came into the hall, curious to see who was at the door. "Don't tell me those two are my precious nephew and niece? My God, how big they are."

Laura and Iris talked far into the night. It was as though they were reliving the awful hours after their father's death. This fresh tragedy was a match that rekindled Laura's impatience to clear her father's name. She could take no practical steps towards this without returning to Magnolia. Yet the prospect of going back without Bernie at her side was unnerving.

Iris pleaded with her to move to London. What was there here for the children and her? With the money from the DeVito case they could live comfortably in London for years.

"I can't move to London." Laura frowned in rejection, determined to bring up her children in their own country despite her grief. "Jonnie and Katie would be homesick." She paused, anticipating Iris's objections. "We'll stay here for a while. Until I'm able to think clearly again. Then I may take the children down to Magnolia to live." She was tired of the frenzy of daily life in New York. She longed for the slow-paced existence she had known in Magnolia.

"Laura, how can you go back to the town that allowed Papa to be convicted of murder? A town where a lynch mob strung him up? How could you live there? Maybe it's thirteen years behind us, but people will remember. You've never told Jonnie and Katie! How will they feel when they find out?"

"They won't find out." Laura's face tensed. "I won't be going back as Laura Roth. I'll be Laura Hunter. Do you think anybody will look at me and know? When I left Magnolia I was fifteen. A skinny little girl with flaming hair. I'm fifteen pounds heavier now. My hair has changed color. I don't have a Southern accent—" She paused in sudden astonishment. "Neither do you, Iris."

"I lost it somewhere in London. Deliberately." Iris sighed. "A few years too late. Maybe nobody will recognize you," she conceded. "You're not Papa's little string bean anymore. You've filled out in the best places. You've learned to wear clothes. You're a beautiful woman, Laura. I never realized it until just now."

"No compliments," Laura admonished tenderly. "Just moral support. I've wanted to go back to Magnolia for such a long time."

"I don't understand you. I hate every inch of that town. Even thinking about it I feel such rage."

"I remember the happy years, Iris. The years when Mama was alive. The warm and tender years when Papa tried to be both father and mother to us. Bernie made me understand that the Jewish community was frightened for their lives. Magnolia was in the hands of a powerful clique. They railroaded Papa for their own purposes."

"Do you think it's any different today?" Iris shot back.

213

"I'm older and wiser," Laura told her. "They won't frighten me. Those crowds in the courtroom each day—ignorant and out for blood—don't represent Magnolia to me. Before those last nightmare weeks Magnolia was a town I loved. I hope to find that town again. I *need* to find that town—and to clear Papa. Iris, that's why I fought my way through law school."


Laura knew she could never practice law in New York without Bernie. She would arrange for the closing of their office. She worried that the children clung to her with such desperation. They were reluctant to return for the final week of school—feeling alien among classmates who had fathers at home. But Laura would not allow herself to coddle them—they must understand that life goes on.

While the children were at school each day, Laura and Iris shared the routine housework, sat talking over endless cups of coffee about the years when they had been apart. Laura was increasingly upset at the ugliness of the marriage Iris refused to abandon.

"Iris, I have money," she coaxed. "Leave Peter. Come live with us."

"I've stayed with him for six years. Most of the time he's off somewhere on his own. I'm used to high living, Laura. I'd hate to give that up. And he's getting on. When Peter dies, I'll be a rich woman in my own right. I can't throw away that chance. Of course, he may live to ninety-five." Her smile was wry.

"If you change your mind, Iris, you know there's always a place with us for you." But Laura understood. Iris had moved into the world of the ultra-rich.

In good-humored defiance Iris hocked the diamond earrings she'd brought from London.

"Why not?" she shrugged. "I'll tell Peter I lost them aboard ship. Serves him right for refusing to insure my jewelry. I had to borrow from Elaine in London so I'd have money for tips on the ship and for a taxi from the pier to the apartment. Now I feel rich. And you know what?" she reached to pull Katie into her arms. "Tomorrow we're going to Radio City Music Hall to see that marvelous new Walt Disney film. What's it called?" She squinted in thought. *"Snow White and the Seven Dwarfs."*

Jonnie and Katie turned hopefully to their mother. They knew the family was still in mourning.

"Take the children," Laura agreed. Bernie would be pleased that they were provided this diversion. "I have to meet somebody at the office about buying the furniture."

For the first time since Bernie died, Laura was alone in the apartment. She moved slowly from room to room, remembering special moments. It was almost as though Bernie were here beside her—except that she couldn't touch him, he couldn't talk with her.

Today she was able to make peace with herself for having been privately resentful of Bernie's actions in these last two years. *He had behaved as he felt he must for the sake of the children and her.* He was no less a man for having pushed aside his ideals to battle for survival.

Lugging bags of delicatessen cold cuts and a cake from the bakery, Iris and the children returned in a relaxed mood. Jonnie and Katie bubbling over with reports about the film. It was right that Iris had taken them to the movies, Laura comforted herself. It was wrong for children to mourn every waking moment.

"Can we listen to the radio?" Jonnie asked tentatively while Laura and Iris set the table for dinner.

"Of course," Laura told him tenderly.

Iris took Katie on a shopping spree at Saks Fifth Avenue and Bergdorf's. Afterwards Katie, ecstatic at the experience, solemnly modeled the clothes Iris had bought for her. They brought home a Buck Rogers pocket watch, a fielder's glove and ball, and a fine chess set for Jonnie. A set of luggage was to be delivered shortly for Laura.

"I'm still hoping you'll come home with me," Iris confessed. "But whatever, you can always use good luggage." Laura knew Iris recoiled from the prospect of her living with the children in Magnolia. Ostensibly she was making no immediate decision about their future.

Iris remained in New York for almost three weeks—until Peter cabled, ordering her to return immediately to accompany him to the Lido for a month's stay.

"Laura, remember, any time you change your mind, I'll help you get settled in London. It'd be so wonderful to be together." Iris was close to tears. Laura and the children were seeing her off on the elegant new *Queen Mary.* Jonnie and Katie were fascinated by the awesomely large ship.

"We'll be all right here, Iris." Laura said nothing to her sister about the decision she had just arrived at to return to Magnolia before the opening of school. Bernie would approve, she told herself. And fresh anguish surged in her as she remembered their dream of going to Magnolia together.

Laura was pained by the grief she felt in Jonnie and Katie. Listening to a favorite radio program one or the other would turn as though to their father—and realize suddenly he was gone. *They were so young to suffer such a loss.* Living in a new town would be a diversion.

The children didn't know that she had been born and raised in Magnolia. For their own protection she had contrived a background in a mythical small South Carolina town. Nobody in Magnolia must know she had been Laura Roth before her marriage. The children must never be tainted by the shame wrongly thrust upon the family.

Now Laura focused on preparing for the return. It would be impractical to try to set up practice there in these times. She must find a firm in Magnolia who'd be willing to hire her, provide her with local legal experience. She was grateful that her law school records were in the name of L.R. Hunter. She knew the unlikelihood of a Magnolia firm hiring a woman lawyer—no matter how fine her qualifications. But they wouldn't know that until she arrived. They'd be furious at discovering they'd hired a lawyer who happened to be a woman—but if they had made the commitment they would have to honor it.

Laura wrote to every law firm in Magnolia, Georgia, offering her services as an attorney. She explained that she wished to "resettle in the South" as a "fine place in which to rear children." As a member of the New York bar she was confident that she would pass the Georgia bar examinations. Her law school was well-respected in the field.

She indicated that her law school records showed that she had graduated third in her class. And to prove her decision to become a permanent resident of Magnolia, she told her prospective employers that she meant to buy a residence on her arrival in town. This also hinted at a successful — though brief — law practice in New York.

She sent out her letters and waited, conscious of each passing day. It was urgent that they be settled in Magnolia before the opening of school. Georgia schools, she remembered, gratefully, opened later in the year than those in New York.

In mid-August — when she was fighting panic at the lack of any replies — she received an offer from the firm of Slocum, McArdle, and Winston. Pale and trembling, she sat down in the kitchen to read the letter. Judge Slocum had presided at her father's trial. Her initial reaction was rejection. But from the dozen letters she had sent out, this was the sole reply.

Slocum, McArdle, and Winston was the most prestigious, and largest, law firm in town. They were offering her a two-year contract at an outrageously low salary. A contract that would hold up in court. They suspected that L.R. Hunter was so eager to return to the South, that "he" would accept any offer. They never guessed the applicant was a woman attorney.

Could she learn to look at Judge Slocum and not see him in that courtroom over thirteen years ago? He had only been the presiding judge, she forced herself to concede. He was not the prosecuting attorney — who had connived to frame her father. Still, the presiding Judge Slocum had sided with the prosecution all through the trial.

If she wished to work as an attorney in Magnolia, she had no choice but to accept Slocum's offer. It was her only offer. He thought he was being crafty in insisting she sign a two-year contract. She would sign the contract. Judge Slocum would countersign and return it, and she and the children would travel to Magnolia.

Jonnie and Katie were ambivalent about leaving New York. They had never even been out of the state. One moment they regarded the move as an exciting adventure. The next, they were unhappy at leaving friends and a familiar school.

"We'll travel by Pullman," Laura promised on impulse. *Why not?* Let them enjoy this small extravagance. Bernie would approve. And it gave her a certain satisfaction to return to Magnolia by Pullman with a bank check for twenty-four thousand dollars in her wallet. Iris and she had traveled from Magnolia in a drab day coach with twenty-five dollars to their name.

She arranged that they would stop in Atlanta—only fifty-three miles north of Magnolia—for two days. There she would open a bank account and initiate a Georgia corporation with an Atlanta mailing address. She would take to Magnolia sufficient funds to buy a modest house, furniture, and to establish a local checking account. If she opened an account in Magnolia with twenty-four thousand dollars, this would soon become public knowledge. Instinct warned her to keep her finances confidential.

The final hour at the apartment threatened to destroy her composure. She roamed about the near-empty rooms with a stifling sense of loss. So much had happened to Bernie and her within these walls. They had moved here with such joy. Such hopes and ambition. This was the only home Jonnie and Katie had ever known. Leaving here today meant embarking on another life. A life Bernie never knew and could never share.

She was grateful that the children were caught up in the excitement of a long train trip. Minna Levine, bless her, would admit the movers, who'd be arriving this afternoon to pick up the last few pieces of furniture for the new owners.

She started at the sound of the downstairs buzzer. That would be the neighborhood man she had hired to drive them to Penn Station.

"All right, kids." Her throat tight, she tried to smile as she summoned them to her side. "Let's get our luggage downstairs. The car is here." Earlier she'd said good-bye to

Minna. It was easier that way.

At Penn Station they waited at the gate with the gathering crowd until it was time to board the Pullman. Jonnie was absorbed in his newest "Buck Rogers" book, Katie admired their expensive new luggage from Aunt Iris. Laura was belabored by conflicting emotions. Would the children adjust to life in the South? Would they be happy there? Would there be someone who recognized her as Laura Roth? *No.* And with poignant pleasure she visualized their finding a pretty little house with a small garden. Real estate was low in Georgia—she ought to be able to buy for well under two thousand dollars.

Finally, the gate was opened. They followed the porter with their luggage to their Pullman car. Jonnie and Katie were intrigued by the prospect of sleeping in berths tonight, Jonnie in the upper, Katie with her in the lower. And she'd promised the children they would eat in the dining car.

Laura had known the return to Magnolia would be traumatic. She was relieved that Jonnie and Katie were engrossed in the excitement of the trip. *"Mom, are we really in Washington, D.C.?" "Mom what're all those white balls they're kicking in the fields?" "Mom, did you know we're in North Carolina already?"* Most of the time she could pretend to read the magazines she had brought along with her while she struggled to cope with reality. The stop off in Atlanta would be a welcome respite.

When the train pulled into Union Depot in Atlanta, Laura remembered their father bringing Iris and her there for a two-day holiday when they finished grammar school. They had stayed at the Piedmont Hotel—feeling so grownup and special.

"Mommie, are we really going to stay at a hotel?" Katie asked avidly.

"At the Ansley," Laura told her. The Piedmont would be too painful with memories of Papa. Katie and Jonnie didn't know she'd ever been in Georgia before, Laura cautioned herself. They must never know until Papa had been declared innocent of Tammy Lee Johnson's murder.

Admiring the fine new Union Depot, Laura hurried the

children out to a taxi with their luggage, and instructed the driver to take them to the Ansley Hotel. Within their brief stay in town she had much to accomplish, but she would manage to take Jonnie and Katie to see some of the local sites. Atlanta was one of the great cities of the South.

Two mornings later Laura and the children checked out of the Ansley Hotel. They took a taxi to Union Depot, then boarded a train for the fifty-three-mile ride to Magnolia. At moments, Laura thought, it seemed as though she had been away a hundred years. At other moments, the memory of Iris and herself walking into the Magnolia Depot—while Mrs. Tannenbaum's chauffeur watched to make sure they were on the New York-bound train—was so vivid it might have occurred only a month ago.

What had happened to their graduating class in these past years? Andrew Miller had planned on going on to medical school. Two others were going to law school. Jean Perkins was going to teach. How many had married? What about Perry? Iris and he had such a crush on each other their senior year. Would any of them *believe* that Iris was now Lady Cranford, of London, England?

"Mom, you're sure school hasn't started yet?" Jonnie asked anxiously. "It'd be awful to miss the first week."

"I checked before we left," Laura reassured him tenderly. "School won't open until Monday a week."

When Iris and she had left, Magnolia had three hotels. One catered to drummers, which Laura dismissed as not a family-style hotel. One faced the Courthouse Square. She had phoned last night to make reservations at the Briarcliffe, half a dozen blocks north of the Square. She was not emotionally prepared to face the courthouse where Papa had been tried and convicted.

They would have to stay at the hotel until she could arrange to buy a house. In the midst of the Depression she would have her choice, Laura surmised. And paying cash assured a fast closing. She could hear Bernie's voice: *"You buy property when the market is low. You sell when it's high."*

"I wish we could have brought my bike," Jonnie said

220

wistfully as the train pulled into Magnolia Depot.

"We'll buy another," Laura soothed. "And one for you, too, Katie," she forestalled the inevitable question.

The train chugged to a stop. Across the aisle from his mother and sister Jonnie leaped to his feet in a spurt of exuberance.

At the exit Laura froze, hurtled back in time at the sight of the turn-of-the century depot. Her throat tightened in recall. All those years ago Iris and she had walked in such pain from that depot to the waiting train on the tracks. With a sense of impending suffocation she remembered the police pulling Papa from the house on that awful night. The insanity in the courtroom day after day. Those last moments with Papa. The cemetery.

"Mom?" Jonnie's voice jolted her back to the present.

"Coming, darling." She would have fallen down the steps except for the quick hand of their porter.

She waited with the children while their luggage was loaded on a hand truck. *Why did I come back to Magnolia? I hate this town for what it did to Papa. How can I look at these people without screaming at them? How can I work in the same office with Judge Slocum?*

With a monumental effort Laura pushed away panic. She was here because she once loved Magnolia. She had to be here if she were ever to clear Papa's name. She could hear Bernie's voice: *"Laura, don't be bitter at the whole town. It was a rabble-rousing mob that made that courtroom into a circus, that dragged your father out of jail. The Jewish community was afraid to support him openly. But you told me they'd brought a team of lawyers down from New York to appeal the case."*

"You-all bein' met, ma'am?" the porter asked politely.

"No. I'd like a taxi, please."

Flanked by Jonnie and Katie, Laura followed the porter into the depot. How little it had changed! A new clock hung on one wall. There was the same enormously high ceiling. The same black ceiling fans. The same rows of mahogany stained benches. The same ticket windows. Perhaps the same ticket sellers.

"Wow, it's a teensy station," Jonnie said while they followed the porter through the doors that led to several

221

waiting taxis.

Laura remembered how Papa and Mama—and then Papa alone—had brought Iris and her here as little girls to watch with awe and excitement as the trains arrived and departed.

"Mom, look at the pretty flowers." Out of the depot Katie stopped, dropped to her haunches before a bed of colorful, velvet soft petunias, and the smiling black porter obligingly paused, too.

"Let's go to the taxi," Jonnie chided his sister. "It won't wait all day."

"Jonnie, we're in the South now," Laura laughed. "People aren't in a rush all the time."

"You folks from New Yawk?" the porter asked politely.

"Yeah," Jonnie told him. "We're going to live here now."


Settled in their hotel room, Jonnie and Katie giggled about the Southern accents they were encountering.

"If we stay here," Katie asked, "will we start to talk like that?"

"I did," Laura told her. "Until Daddy told me I'd better lose my Southern accent if I wanted to plead cases in the New York courts."

An hour later they left their hotel room and walked out into the torpid heat of the early afternoon. September was still a brutally hot month in Georgia.

"I'm hungry," Katie said, reaching for her mother's hand.

"You're always hungry," Jonnie said but his smile was hopeful. "Are we gonna have lunch now?"

"We'll go right over to Broad and find a restaurant."

They paused at the corner of Broad and Thirteenth Street while Laura pretended to survey the area. She was conscious of few physical changes. From the taxi that took them to the hotel she had noted that the Presbyterian Church was buff-colored now—it had been white all those years ago. The houses seemed little different.

"The streetcar tracks have been taken up," she said in astonishment, and Jonnie and Katie looked up questioningly. "I thought all these Southern towns still had street-cars," she covered up quickly. "I guess Magnolia is served by buses."

Laura allowed her eyes to rest on the First National Bank across the street. The bank where Papa had kept his money. It was pristine white now rather than the dingy gray she recalled.

"Let's turn down here." *Not* the Blue Moon Café, she told herself as she spied the small family type restaurant where Papa had taken Iris and her on special occasions.

Her smile grew tight while they walked past a barber shop and she recognized the graying man talking with a young boy. *It was Mr. Cappelli, who used to cut Papa's hair.* For an instant his eyes focused on her with quiet approval. The glance of a man who appreciates a pleasant-looking woman. He didn't recognize her.

Her heart pounded absurdly when a waitress came to their table to take their orders. It was Sally Lou Edmonds, who had gotten pregnant her junior year at vocational high. She'd bleached her hair and had a bad permanent. She looked older than her age.

"What'll you-all be havin'?" Sally Lou asked politely. "My, what a pretty little girl! That one's going to grow up to be a heartbreaker."

Nobody in Magnolia would recognize her, Laura concluded in satisfaction. Just as she had told herself. After lunch she'd go over to the First National Bank and open up a checking account. And then the three of them would look for a real-estate office. Somebody new in town.


The real-estate broker was eager to show them houses—especially when Laura explained she would require no mortgage. He talked about a beautiful new area called Wildwood Gardens.

"Folks have been moving out there for the last couple of years," he said expansively. "It's real pretty."

"I don't have a car," Laura said. "I'd like something in town and not far from the grammar school."

She was astonished to be able to find a house that same

afternoon. It was the kind of house that Bernie would have loved, she thought with fresh grief, visualizing his pleasure if he were standing here beside her. A yellow-shuttered, white clapboard with three bedrooms, a sunny kitchen, dining room, and a living room that looked out on a rose garden. A wide porch presided over a patch of front lawn edged with summer flowers. The owner—an elderly widow—had vacated some months ago. It was available for immediate occupancy.

"It's rather small," Laura said politely, gearing herself to negotiate as Bernie would have done, ignoring the children's wide-eyed reproach. They liked the house at first sight. "The price is higher than I would have expected, considering its size and the condition of the real-estate market."

"It has steam heat," the broker pointed out respectfully. Most houses in Magnolia depended upon fireplaces and coal stoves. "It was built just six years ago. The Emersons expected it to be their retirement house. Then he died, and it was just too much house for her alone."

Within ten minutes of low-keyed bargaining, the price had been readjusted to twenty-seven hundred dollars, and Laura confirmed the sale. The real-estate broker was fighting to hide his elation. Commissions were hard to come by these days.

"I gather you're a stranger in town, ma'am," the broker said politely. "Would you like me to put you in touch with a local attorney?"

"I *am* an attorney." Laura smiled at his amazement. "I'll represent myself at the closing."

The closing was scheduled to take place late the following week. Meanwhile, Laura shopped for basic furniture. At intervals she choked with fear that she was about to be recognized.

She had written to Judge Slocum that she would present herself at the law firm on Monday morning. She dreaded the initial encounter, bracing herself for his rage. But she would point out that it was he who insisted on a two-year contract. *A contract that would hold up in any court of law.*

224

Over the weekend Laura walked with Jonnie and Katie along the wide avenues of the town. She enjoyed their delight in the beautiful surroundings, though she meticulously avoided walking down Third Avenue—where Iris and she had grown up—or down lower Broad, where Papa had had his shoe-repair shop.

Laura showed Jonnie and Katie where they would go to school. *Where Iris and she had gone to school.* The three wandered along Broad Street, stopping at The Oasis—an attractive new ice-cream parlor—for huge scoops of their favorite coffee ice cream. On Sunday afternoon she took the children to the Edison Theater to see Disney's *Snow White and the Seven Dwarfs* for the second time.

With the guidance of the sympathetic desk clerk Laura hired a friendly young colored girl to take care of the children while they remained in residence at the Magnolia hotel. When they moved into the house at the end of the week, Jewel, a big, heavy-set girl oozing friendliness, would become their maid.

Since she was fourteen, Jewel had worked as a washerwoman—like her mother. She picked up bundles of laundry, brought them home to wash in a black tub behind the family shack, and returned them to her "customers." For small batches she was paid twenty-five cents, large laundries earned her fifty cents. Jewel was delighted with this new job, for which she was to be paid the gratifying sum of three dollars a week.

On Monday morning Laura left the children in Jewel's care. Instinctively she knew this was the beginning of a long-term relationship. The children liked the affectionate, high-spirited Jewel. Their laughter followed her reassuringly from the hotel room and down the hall to the elevator.

The offices of Slocum, McArdle, and Winston were located in the new six-story office building that was the most imposing structure in Magnolia. Though the day was hot, she had chosen to wear a smart black-linen suit with a white-linen blouse. It was unlikely that anyone at Slocum, McArdle, and Winston would recognize it as a Paris original. It had been a gift from Iris.

She was nervous as she waited for the elevator to take her up to the sixth floor, occupied solely by the prestigious law firm. Slocum's father — a judge, also, in his time — had opened law offices in Magnolia over sixty years ago, Laura recalled. An earlier Slocum had been one of the founding fathers of Magnolia.

In the elevator, she formed sentences in her mind to counteract the recriminations Judge Slocum was sure to hurl at her. He was not expecting his new staff member to be a woman. He must be smug at having insisted on a two-year contract at a salary that — even in these troubled times — was shockingly low. It was no more than he would pay a beginning typist.

Striving for a poise that she didn't feel, she left the elevator and approached the double doors that led into the firm's offices. It was clear that the firm was not suffering from the Depression. The floor was carpeted, the reception-room furniture suitable for the living room of a luxurious home.

"I'm L.R. Hunter," she said politely to the receptionist, sitting behind the desk in a simple black dress and pearls. The image, Laura guessed, that Judge Slocum demanded. "I'd like to see Judge Slocum, please."

The girl's eyes skimmed Laura's exquisite suit in approval.

"Do you have an appointment?" She reached for the phone.

"He's expecting me this morning," Laura said.

"Is that Miss or Mrs. Hunter?"

"Does it matter?" Laura smiled faintly. "I'm L.R. Hunter, the new attorney on staff."

"Yes ma'am." The receptionist's eyebrows shot upward. Laura caught a glint of amusement in her eyes. "I'll tell him you're here."

Laura waited while the receptionist announced "L.R. Hunter."

"Just go straight down the hall to the double doors," she instructed. "That's the Judge's office."

Laura hesitated at the heavy oak door, struggling to wash away ugly memories of Judge Slocum presiding at her father's trial. *That was another lifetime.* She knocked lightly.

"Come in," a crisp Southern-accented voice ordered, and Laura complied.

Judge Slocum sat behind a huge desk in an oversized carpeted office furnished with elegant antiques. A black lacquered ceiling fan whirred softly. A tall, slender, prematurely white-haired man with a permanent air of hauteur, he had aged slightly since she had last seen him. Laura waited for him to look up from the legal papers he was perusing, understanding he wished his new attorney to know that Judge Matthew Slocum hurried for no man. Or woman.

Finally Judge Slocum laid aside the papers, gazed up with what was meant to be a welcoming smile. The smile froze.

"I was expecting Mr. Hunter." His eyes narrowed. "Are you his wife?"

"I'm L.R. Hunter," Laura said, her eyes meeting his. "I'm the attorney from New York."

His face flushed.

"You said nothing in your correspondence about being a woman!"

"You said nothing in yours about being a man," Laura pointed out.

"You misled me!" He pushed back his chair and rose to his feet. "We don't have women lawyers on our staff."

"You do now, Sir. For a period of two years commencing this morning." She held her hands firmly at her side lest Judge Slocum see that they were trembling. "Unless, of course, you prefer to buy out my contract." She paused. "For face value."

"Damn it, this is pure deceit!"

"Judge Slocum, it was at *your* insistence that I signed an ironclad contract."

"The contract is void if you fail to pass the Georgia bar exams." He struggled for composure. It would be unseemly for a Slocum to engage in a shouting match.

"There is no chance that I won't pass the bar exams. I was graduated third in my class at New York University

Law School. I passed the New York bar exams. I've already made the necessary arrangements to take the Georgia bar exams." She paused for an instant. "Judge Slocum, I doubt that any male lawyer would have accepted the salary you'll be paying me."

She stood motionless while he weighed the situation in his mind. She tensed at the glint of triumph she read in his eyes as he sat down again and reached for one of the phones on his desk.

"Maisie, get in here," he said tersely and turned to Laura. "Do you take dictation?"

"No." She had been forewarned about women lawyers who admitted to knowing stenography.

"Maisie is my secretary. She'll provide you with assignments." His voice was as cold as an Arctic winter. "You will report to her each morning." He reached for papers on his desk and proceeded to ignore her until the door opened to admit a small, pretty, slightly plump woman in her early thirties. "Maisie, this is L.R. Hunter," he said with sarcasm. Laura saw Maisie's start. "See that she's provided with work. We won't be replacing Beth."

In the privacy of her own office Maisie Rawson explained that she had been Judge Slocum's secretary since she had graduated business school sixteen years ago. She had come to Magnolia from Columbus. Her husband Everett was an accountant. She radiated a warm Southern graciousness that was a relief after the hostile meeting with Judge Slocum.

"The Judge won't make life easy for you around here," Maisie warned compassionately when they went out to lunch together three hours later. "Beth's leaving next week—she's getting married. She's been the clerk and typist who fills in wherever she's needed. Don't count on any legal work, Laura."

# Chapter 19

In the bedroom of her suite at Cranford Hall Iris stirred fretfully beneath the white velvet comforter. She would have to start to dress soon for the drive into London. If she had known she'd be feeling rotten again, she would not have promised to meet Diana for luncheon. Why did Peter insist on being here at Cranford Hall in dismal January?

Elaine and her husband were en route to Jamaica for six weeks. Sandra and her husband were off to Bali. Going to the Riviera or to Switzerland for skiing wasn't really traveling anymore — not when planes took you there so fast.

She frowned at the knock on the door.

"Yes?"

The door opened and Edwina approached with her breakfast tray. The pungent aromas of fresh coffee turned her sick.

"Take that damn tray out of here!" she shrieked. "I don't want breakfast this morning. Go on, Edwina," she insisted because Edwina was upset that so many mornings lately she rejected her breakfast tray. "Go on," she said through gritted teeth.

She lay back against the pillows in a fight against fresh surges of nausea. It was humiliating to throw up. And frightening. Women as young as she were known to develop ulcers. Or cancer. She remembered the talk at last night's dinner party about how the Earl of something-or-other had to have half his stomach removed — and he was still in his thirties.

At last confident that the queasiness was past, Iris reached into the drawer of her night table and brought out Laura's last two letters. She always kept the last two until yet another arrived. She could not reconcile herself to Laura's living in Magnolia again.

How long would Laura stay in Judge Slocum's office when all she was allowed to do was routine office work? Laura was a *lawyer* — she'd passed both the New York and Georgia bar exams. She didn't have to take that kind of treatment from Slocum. She had money now.

Laura's move to Magnolia had put up a barrier between them. She had always clung to the knowledge that if she decided to walk out on Peter, she could go home to Laura. *But not to Magnolia.* She'd die before she'd go back there. She pulled the earlier letter from its envelope and re-read the familiar lines.

*"Iris, you should have seen Slocum's face when he found out I was taking off for the high holidays. Not only had he hired a woman but a Jew!"*

Laura wrote that she had joined the Reform temple rather than the Orthodox synagogue — where their father had been a founding member — because Katie rebelled at the separation between men and women in an Orthodox congregation. Also, Laura confessed, it was less traumatic for her.

*"In New York we'd never bothered joining a synagogue or temple because there the children knew they were Jewish. Here we're a minority. But, thank God Jonnie and Katie are adjusting.*

Iris rang for Edwina. She'd soak in a tub for a little while, then dress. She was feeling better. That was because she knew she would be away from this mausoleum for a few hours. Peter would carouse with his hunting cronies until high tea. Why couldn't Peter take off to hunt in Kenya?

He was developing such a phobia about his age. Sandra said it hit some men at fifty, others at sixty. Peter waited until his sixty-seventh birthday before becoming a nervous wreck. After staying away for over a year he'd come to her bedroom four times in the last three months. She'd told herself that part of their marriage was over — though she was still afraid to take on a successor to Donald.

The last time they'd made love, Peter cracked her rib. He was abject afterwards — especially when Dr. Rathbone questioned her about the bruises, showing disbelief when she said she'd fallen down the stairs.

When Iris arrived at the Savoy, she found Diana already at their table.

"You look dragged out," Diana commented. "Late night?"

"No more so than usual." Iris sat down with an air of exhaustion. "I'm just feeling rotten."

"The rib acting up?" Diana asked solicitously. Finally she

had told Diana about Peter's weird lovemaking. There was almost nothing that the members of "the gorgeous quartette" kept from one another.

"No, I'm sure it's not that." Iris tried not to appear apprehensive. "I'm just so damn queasy so often. All I have to do is smell fresh coffee in the morning and I'm ready to heave. I keep thinking about ulcers or cancer—"

"Iris, are you late?" Diana interrupted.

Iris stared without comprehending for a moment.

She squinted in thought.

"Oh! Maybe a few days. Or maybe two or three weeks." Alarm shot through her.

"You're probably pregnant. Make an appointment with Sandra's obstetrician." Sandra had been pregnant twice, had suffered two miscarriages, the second induced.

"Diana, how the hell could that happen?"

"The usual way," Diana said bluntly. "Don't you take care of yourself?"

"At Peter's age the thought seems ridiculous." The possibility of her being pregnant was unnerving. "God, I don't want to have a baby!"

"Go to Sandra's obstetrician, Diana prodded. "If you don't want to be pregnant, then you won't be for long."

Their waiter arrived and they lapsed into luncheon discussion. Should they have the poached salmon or the duck confit? The carrot soup or the celery soup with lobster? But part of Iris's mind had bolted into the past. She remembered going with Laura to see Dr. Fink—when she was sure she was pregnant by Lance. That seemed a lifetime ago.

"Well?" Diana probed when the waiter left them alone. "Are you going to call Sandra's obstetrician?" Her eyes were a peculiar blend of compassion and wistfulness.

"Sandra's in Bali."

"I have the number," Diana told her. "Ring me up later, and I'll give it to you."

"Of course, if I am pregnant," Iris said slowly, "Peter would be out of his mind with excitement. A baby would make him feel thirty years younger."

"Yeah, it's like saying to the world—'See, I can still do it.' Iris, you'd have Peter eating out of your hand. Particularly if you can manage to have a boy."

"Can't you just imagine Peter's son and his two daughters if I *am* pregnant?" Her laughter was touched with malice. Peter's children always managed a few bitchy remarks on the rare occasions when they were together. "One more to share in the estate when Peter goes." If she gave Peter a child, she'd be Lady Cranford forever.

"I'll ring up the obstetrician and make an appointment in your name," Diana said briskly. "And I'll go with you."

"It may be a false alarm," Iris reminded. "It's happened to me before." But instinct told her she was pregnant. Laura would be happy, she thought wryly. A cousin for Jonnie and Katie.

Iris listened with part of her mind to the obstetrician's instructions. She was about nine weeks pregnant. When would she start showing? She'd have Molyneux design her a maternity wardrobe. She didn't have to look grotesque just because she was pregnant.

"I anticipate your having a normal pregnancy," Dr. Kingsley wound up with a gentle smile. "And an uncomplicated delivery at the Royal Northern Hospital."

"Could I have a Caesarean delivery?" she asked, recoiling from the vision of herself in labor. "I know it's becoming quite popular." Barbara Hutton had a Caesarean.

Dr. Kingsley frowned.

"We don't like to perform a Caesarean section unless it's necessary. We prefer a normal delivery. A section is major surgery."

"Whatever you think, of course," Iris capitulated. *This was unreal.*

Diana was waiting for her in the reception room. Iris nodded, and Diana hugged her enthusiastically.

"Let's go to the Ivy for cocktails. I can't wait to see Elaine's face when they hear the news!"

"I can't wait to see Peter's." Belatedly she was uneasy. Would he be ridiculous enough to think the baby wasn't his? "Oh God, we're leaving for St. Moritz next week. I won't dare ski. And I've bought all those gorgeous ski outfits."

Iris was relieved that this was one of the rare nights when Peter and she would be dining at home. She was impatient to give him the news. He wasn't going to make some silly accusation, was he? She hadn't been near another man since that last time with Donald. *Almost two years ago.*

She had meant to tell Peter after dinner; but when she heard the Bentley drive up before the house late in the afternoon, only minutes after she had arrived home, she decided not to wait.

"Edwina," she called from her sitting room, "please bring me a pot of tea. When it's ready, knock on Lord Cranford's door and tell him I'd like to see him."

She changed into a white-velvet robe and matching slippers, pausing for an intense inspection of her figure. Was she imagining that her skirt had fit a teensy-weensy bit tighter than normal? She was simultaneously revolted at the prospect of a swelling figure and sentimental at the knowledge that she was carrying a child.

She had never envisioned herself with a child. Of course, she'd have little demands made on her. There'd be a baby nurse early on, then a governess, then boarding school. That was the English way. It might be fun to design the nursery, shop for baby clothes.

Iris settled herself before the cozy blaze in her sitting-room fireplace. She'd write to Laura tonight. Dr. Kingsley said she would give birth in late July or early August. Perhaps she could persuade Laura to come to London to be with her. All at once she felt an overwhelming urge to see her sister.

Edwina brought her tea tray and left with clothes to be taken down stairs and pressed. Moments later Peter arrived.

"Edwina said you wanted to see me." He stood in the doorway, arrogant and impatient. "You know we're having dinner at the Ashcrofts' tonight." *Oh God, she had forgotten.* "Iris, we can't just not show up."

"I know, Peter." Peter was testy these days because some upper-class British were alarmed by German aggression. Peter's friends seemed to believe that the stories of Hitler's atrocities against the Jews were not true or much exaggerated. The Ashcrofts—like Peter—were convinced the new prime minister, Neville Chamberlain, could negotiate peacefully with Hitler. "Sit down and have tea with me." He brushed aside the suggestion with a curt gesture but sat in the needlepoint-upholstered wing chair opposite her own. "I have something rather breathtaking to tell you."

"Well, tell me, Iris." His eyes were wary.

"I'm pregnant."

He stared at her in calculated silence. Her heart began to pound.

"Who's the bastard you've been sleeping with?"

"Only you!" she shot back, her high cheekbones stained with color. "How dare you talk to me like that! I saw Dr. Kingsley this afternoon—he's Sandra's obstetrician. He said I'm about nine weeks' pregnant. You're going to be a father again, Peter."

She sat motionless, teacup suspended in one hand, her head high, eyes defiant, while Peter deliberated.

"You mean to sit there and tell me you haven't been fucking around behind my back?" Doubt battled astonishment.

"Only with you, darling," she said sweetly, and returned the teacup to its saucer. "If I'd been having an affair, I'm sure your children would have reported it to you. Nothing is secret in our circles."

Unexpectedly Peter chuckled.

"You're afraid of them. You've a right to be. They're dying to run to me with some story about you making a disgrace of our marriage."

"I'm as amazed as you are about this. I suppose I'd got rather careless."

"You're pregnant with my child." His voice deepened with pride. "When will you deliver?"

"Late July or early August. In time," she suddenly realized, "for your birthday."

"I'm dumbfounded," he admitted. But his face betrayed an inner jubilation. "Damn it, that'll tell the world there's plenty of juice left in the old man!"

Iris felt suffused with relief. It was going to be all right. Peter would be the most solicitous father-to-be ever on this earth. And after the baby was born, she'd make sure he took her to Cartier's for a diamond necklace that would dazzle everybody in London.

"I'll need a maternity wardrobe," Iris said with a new self-confidence. "By Molyneux, I think."

"Make sure it's ready in the next six or eight weeks." Peter smiled smugly. "I want to show off my pregnant wife to some

234

friends in Vienna. We'll stay at this magnificent castle close to the city. You won't overdo," he promised. "There'll be a ball or two, a few dinner parties. You'll relax all day while I'm involved in some political situations." He was choosing his words with care, Iris noted. "There are those in the German government who value my advice. My knowledge of affairs in London."

"By then I'll be showing," Iris warned.

"My pleasure. My pride." He reached for her hand and lifted it to his mouth. "You've made me very happy, Iris."


Laura switched on her desk lamp in the waning February afternoon and tallied up the real-estate tax figures before her. Logic told her it was absurd to feel such exhilaration at having been assigned a real-estate closing to handle. But for the past months she had gritted her teeth and performed only routine clerical assignments. She knew Judge Slocum and his partners were waiting for her to quit.

She couldn't allow herself that luxury. She had promised herself the time would come when they'd be so shorthanded they'd be pushed into giving her legal work. She needed law experience here in Magnolia before she went out to open her own law office. People had to know she was more than a clerk here.

"How long are you staying?" Maisie hovered in the doorway of Laura's cubicle, her face compassionate. The others had left at five-thirty. Maisie had remained to retype a brief for Judge Slocum. They were the only two of the staff who ever worked beyond the scheduled hours. Maisie had no children, and her husband Everett was "understanding" when she remained late at the office.

"I'll be another hour or so, I guess. I phoned Jewel early in the afternoon and asked her to give the children dinner and stay until I get home."

"That could wait until tomorrow," Maisie pointed out.

"I want everything ready before I leave the office." Laura was firm. "I don't want the Judge coming in tomorrow morning and saying he'll take over. Everything will be *ready*. I'll be at the bank with our client at 2 P.M. tomorrow afternoon. And it wasn't the routine closing Judge Slocum said," she said with a touch of satisfaction. "There were problems, and I solved them."

"I hate them for the way they treat you, Laura." Maisie had been here for sixteen years, but she harbored little respect for the partners. "Anybody else would have walked out by now."

"I can't afford to walk out. Nobody else in Magnolia is going to hire a woman lawyer." Laura was matter-of-fact. "But after I handle that closing tomorrow, I figure the word will circulate around town. Slocum, McArdle, and Winston has a woman lawyer on their staff."

"I'll stop off at the soda fountain downstairs and tell them to send up coffee for you," Maisie said. "Black, no sugar."

When the boy arrived with Laura's coffee, she pushed aside work for a few minutes to sit back and sip the hot black liquid. The heat was going down for the night and she welcomed the warmth of the coffee. At nine o'clock the building closed up. It remained open that late to accommodate the evening hours of the three doctors who were tenants.

Tomorrow night she was going to Maisie's house for dinner. She looked forward to spending the evening with Maisie and Everett. With his deep concern for the world, Everett reminded her of Bernie. Maisie and Everett were the only friends she'd allowed herself to make in town. She maintained a polite relationship with their neighbors on the block without becoming socially involved, ever fearful of being "found out."

Each encounter with someone she remembered was a fresh emotional shock. She'd learned that Mr. Massey had moved away from Magnolia twelve years ago. Mr. McKinley and Mrs. Bernstein had both died within the past three years. Her much-loved Latin teacher was in a nursing home.

Thank God, the children were adjusting. And they adored Jewel. They liked their new school and their teachers.

With a sudden need to hear the children's voices she called the house.

"Hunter residence," Jonnie responded ebulliently to the ring of the phone.

"You have dinner yet?"

"Jewel said we could wait to eat until after we hear 'Easy Aces.' "

"And after you eat, you do your homework," Laura ordered.

236

"Yes ma'am. Jewel already told us. When will you be home?"

"Around nine," she promised. "Any mail?"

"A letter from Mrs. Levine. That's all."

"Let me talk to Katie for a minute." She was pleased that Minna had written. She'd hoped, too, that there'd be a letter from Iris. She was both astonished and pleased when Iris had written that she was pregnant.

Katie reported on the day's activities at school—until Jonnie summoned her to the radio. It was a nightly ritual for the two of them to listen to "Easy Aces." Laura drained the last of her coffee and returned to the papers for tomorrow's closing.

It was close to nine when Laura slid the papers relating to the closing into a manila envelope. She was exhilarated by the prospect of representing a client tomorrow. She started at the sound of the elevator stopping at their floor. Someone was coming into the reception room, down the hall now.

All at once uneasy, she rose to her feet and peered into the hall.

"Hey there." Derek Slocum, the Judge's youngest son who lived on the family's plantation in south Georgia, was walking towards her. She had seen him in the offices this afternoon. He was about her age, good-looking, ingratiating. He was in town for a few days, Maisie had explained. Laura suspected that Maisie disliked Derek Slocum.

"Hello." Laura was relieved. It was silly to have been nervous.

"Is my father around?" Derek asked with a friendly smile.

"No. He left the office around five-thirty."

"Perhaps Mother and he went over to my brother's house for dinner." Laura knew about the Judge's two older sons, one an adopted nephew, who headed up a real-estate empire. *"They're vultures,"* Everett had scoffed. "What are you doing here so late?" Derek teased.

"I had to finish up some papers," she explained. "I was just about to leave."

"Have pity on the family ne'er-do-well," he coaxed charmingly, "and have dinner with me. Any place you like."

"Oh, thank you, but I have to get home." Laura was startled by the invitation.

"Why?" He moved closer, a hand at her arm.

"My children are expecting me."

"Phone and tell them you have a date." His hand traveled up to her shoulder in a slow, caressing gesture. "How old are they?"

"Eight and ten." She tried to hide her discomfort and growing fear.

"You look too young to have children that old." His eyes focused on her breasts. "Too sexy."

"Perhaps you'd like to call your father at your brother's house," she stammered while he spread his other hand on the wall, effectively imprisoning her.

"I saw you when I was here this afternoon." His eyes were disturbingly aroused. "I was just driving around town tonight, and then I passed the building. I saw you standing by the file. Such a gorgeous baby."

"I have to leave now," she told him, her heart pounding now with terror.

"Oh, no, you're not!" Suddenly he seemed enraged. "I came here just to see you!

He pulled her into his arms, drew her tightly against his body, thrusting his hips against hers while panic surged in her.

"Derek, let me go," she pleaded. "Please—"

"You're like all the others! Rotten little bitch!" His mouth closed in on hers, his tongue trying to push its way past her teeth. One hand moved inside her blouse, clutching roughly at a breast.

"Derek, stop it!" a male voice ordered, and Derek seemed to freeze. "Derek, let her go." The voice was firm but quiet. "Let her go." Trembling, Laura turned to the newcomer as Derek released her.

"You always spoil my fun," Derek complained, his voice hoarse.

"I'm sorry, ma'am. I'm Derek's nurse. He sneaked off while I was in the bathroom. Are you all right?" he asked solicitously.

"Yes," Laura told him. *Derek Slocum was a mental patient.* "Thank God you tracked him here."

"He took off with the car. I figured he was coming here. He kept talking about the beautiful girl at his father's office." Derek stared at the floor in sullen anger. "Derek, you know you promised to behave if your parents let you come home for a while."

"Let's get out of here! Come on, Stu!" But he waited, his eyes wary, for his male nurse to make the next move.

"I'm sorry, Miss," the nurse apologized again. "Judge Slocum keeps thinking Derek has recovered from his 'illness.'" Sarcasm crept into his voice. Laura remembered that the Judge's youngest son was supposed to be asthmatic and unable to live in Magnolia's climate. They kept Derek hidden away on the family plantation in preference to committing him to a mental institution. "Come on, Derek," the nurse wheedled. "We'll go home now."

Laura stood in the hall and watched them leave. When she heard the elevator go down again, she hurried out to lock the office door. Shaken, her stomach churning, she went back to her desk and reached for the phone, dialed Maisie's number.

"Hello." Maisie's voice warm and reassuring.

"Maisie, you won't believe what just happened. Derek Slocum came up here. *Maisie, he tried to rape me.*" It was a shrill wail. "He would have if his nurse hadn't arrived."

"Stay there," Maisie ordered gently. "I'll drive right over."

Her coat around her shoulders, Laura waited on the sofa in the reception room. Maisie would have the downstairs door key if the building was locked up already. *Why was her life always touched by rape?* Tammy Lee Johnson, all those years ago. Then Peggy Williams. If Derek Slocum had raped her, would he have killed her afterwards?

Maisie, who believed that coffee contained a magic potion, arrived with a thermos from home.

"Maisie, I was so scared," Laura told her, shivering in recall. "It was useless to scream. There was nobody in the building except the doctors on the third floor. Nobody would have heard me. *He could have raped and killed me and gotten away with it.*"

"I've known about Derek since the first year I worked for the Judge." Maisie was somber. "He was in and out of 'special schools' and sanitariums since he was eight. Every once in a while the Judge tries to bring Derek back into the family — he doesn't want to accept the truth. Fourteen years ago he even managed to enroll him in a military school up in Virginia."

"How was he able to do that?" Laura was appalled.

"He didn't stay long. He was thrown out before the end of his first month there. For molesting the thirteen-year-old daughter of a teacher."

"Judge Slocum has to know about tonight." How could she pretend it never happened?

"The nurse will tell him," Maisie assured her. "The Judge will be furious that you know about Derek, but he'll apologize. Only a handful of people in town know. Derek was always presumably away at boarding school. Because of his asthmatic condition. And then he was supposedly managing the plantation." She searched Laura's face. "You're all right, honey?"

"Shaky but fine." Laura managed a smile. "I was just so stunned."

"I'll drive you home." Maisie squeezed her hand in reassurance.

"It's only five blocks."

"I'll drive you," Maisie insisted. "Haven't you noticed how nobody walks anymore?"


As Laura had anticipated, Judge Slocum summoned her to his office immediately after arriving in the morning. He was courtly and apologetic as he discussed her "unpleasant meeting with Derek."

"I hope you will help the family maintain the secrecy about Derek's condition. His mother was most distressed about what happened. There'll be no further effort to bring him home again."

"I'll say nothing about it, Judge Slocum," Laura said quietly. "And I do sympathize."

Laura saw him bristle involuntarily. He hated being beholden to her. She sensed this only increased his hostility towards her. And he knew that if she ever tried to make the incident public, he had only to deny it happened. He was a highly respected member of the community; she was a Yankee newcomer. Judge Slocum's word would be accepted over hers.

Now she turned the conversation to business. She brought out the problems she'd encountered with the closing and how she handled the situation. He deliberated a moment.

"There's another closing coming up that you might as well take over," he said casually. "Maisie will brief you on the details."

At two o'clock Laura met with their client at the offices of the seller of the property under negotiation. She sensed the client's grim hostility at being represented by a woman. By the time the property had been transferred, Laura knew she had earned his respect. People in Magnolia would hear that Slocum, McArdle, and Winston had a woman attorney on staff and that she had saved their client money. That would be important in a year and a half, when she opened her own office in town.

Laura walked briskly in the crisp February night to the small, red-brick house the Rawsons had bought four years ago. She sniffed the aromatic smoke emerging from the chimney. Though Maisie was proud that the house had steam heat, both Everett and she enjoyed using the living-room fireplace.

Maisie refused to allow Laura to help in the kitchen.

"Sit in the living room and talk with Everett until I call you to the table," she ordered.

Laura and Everett discussed the problem of soaring unemployment again after a reduction in government spending. Again, many Americans were going to sleep hungry.

"Do you think the Wages and Hours Act will go through?" Laura asked. There was talk in Congress of raising the minimum wage for workers engaged in interstate commerce from twenty-five to forty cents an hour.

"I'm more anxious to see new government spending." Everett shook his head in bafflement. "Cities like Chicago and Omaha and Toledo are running out of relief funds. Chicago had to close down all nineteen of its relief stations. The conservatives are declaring there's no way the New Deal can work. And no matter how you look at it, the South is getting the worst of it. We're the nation's number one economic problem."

"To the table," Maisie called ebulliently from the dining room. "Let's eat while everything is hot."

At dinner, much of the conversation revolved around Laura's encounter with Derek Slocum. Deviously — some inner instinct directing Laura to probe this point — Laura questioned Maisie about Derek's being at a military school.

241

"Oh, no doubt about his being there," Maisie confirmed. "I got the phone call from the outraged principal at the school when Derek was caught trying to pull down the girl's bloomers." She laughed. "Later we wore panties."

"When did this happen?" Laura contrived to sound merely curious.

"Oh, I know exactly when." Her eyes strayed tenderly to Everett. "It was on May 12, 1924. Our second wedding anniversary."

"What did the Judge do?" Laura asked. "Did the school try to prosecute?"

"The Judge drove right up to the school that night and brought Derek home. The school didn't file any charges — they didn't want that kind of publicity. Three nights later the Judge took Derek down to the plantation."

All at once Laura's throat was tight.

*On May 12, 1924 Derek came to Magnolia. Three days before Tammy Lee Johnson was murdered. The same night her body was found he was hustled off to the plantation.*

Laura's mind was in tumult. Derek had been here in Magnolia when Tammy Lee was raped and murdered. Was it *Derek* who dragged Tammy Lee into that alley, raped and then murdered her? And afterwards Judge Slocum sat there presiding at Papa's trial — while Derek was safely hidden away on the family plantation.

*Was that they way it happened? How could she prove it? She had to.*

# Chapter 20

Iris gazed into space as the plane lifted off the ground at Croydon Airdrome. She was unnerved by Peter's insistence that they go ahead with the trip to Austria even though the Nazis had taken over the country just twelve days ago. Peter appeared jubilant about the situation. He kept saying that Hitler was the man to maintain peace in Europe. What Chamberlain referred to as "peace in our time."

Normally all she read in the London *Times* was the society news. Now, with a fearful sense of doom, she turned first to the foreign news pages. She'd listened with Peter to the wireless reports of Chancellor Schuschnigg's departure from Austria. Peter pointed out with pride that this had been a bloodless invasion. *Had it?* News on what was happening within Austria was sparse. But only this morning she had read a story in the London *Times* that sickened her. In Vienna the Nazi storm troopers were forcing Jews — men and women, the young and the aged — to scrub away the portraits of Chancellor Schuschnigg and the Teutonic crosses that had been painted on the pavements while watching crowds shouted: "We thank our Fuhrer for finding work for the Jews."

"Why so serious?" Peter turned to her with a mocking smile. "We're going on a holiday. You should be pleased."

"It seems strange to go on a holiday in a country that's just been taken over by an enemy nation." She feigned ironic amusement. *They would be staying in the castle of an Austrian Nazi while German refugees were flooding London, talking about the awful atrocities at the hands of the Nazis.*

"Germany is not the enemy." Peter frowned in irritation. "Many Germans live in Austria. They welcome this changeover."

She didn't know a word of German. She always felt so awkward when she didn't speak the local language, though she had been astonished to discover that she remembered sufficient high school French not to feel entirely lost in Paris or on the Riviera. Peter spoke German and French and a bit of Italian.

"Will we go directly to the castle?" Iris asked. Papa had been German. What would have happened to him if he had stayed in Germany instead of moving to America? But could it have been worse than what happened to him in Magnolia, Georgia?

"A limousine will be at the airport to take us there. But you'll have a chance to see something of Vienna before we leave," he promised. "At dinner tonight you will meet some of the most powerful men in Austria. The ones who understand what Hitler can do for the world. Wear something exquisite. And your diamond necklace and earrings." Peter had replaced the earrings she had hocked in New York. "Every man at the table will be envious of me."

In moments Iris drifted off to sleep. Peter shook her awake when the plane began its descent.

"We're at the Vienna airport, Iris."

A Mercedes limousine was waiting for them. Now Iris felt the lively curiosity that usually assailed her in a strange country. Nobody—not even Peter—knew she was Jewish.

"This is beautiful country," Peter said as the Mercedes left the airport and traveled in the direction of the castle. "We'll be only about twelve miles out of Vienna. Just below Klosterneuburg."

Iris admired the surrounding hills, crowned with vineyards and orchards. She surveyed the streams, the fishponds, hunting lodges, quaint small houses they were passing. Peter pointed out the medieval Greifenstein castle and the twelfth-century Augustine Abbey.

244

Then they approached a baroque country castle—once a twelfth-century stone fortress—that was situated in a rocky crag right above the Danube. Though the moat had been widened to become a charming lagoon surrounded by a sweep of elegant formal gardens, the castle evoked an atmosphere of foreboding gloom. This was the residence of their host, Herr Wahl.

They were greeted at the door of the castle by the housekeeper, Frau Fischbein.

"Herr Wahl has been detained in Vienna on business," she explained in guttural English. "He begs you to forgive him. He will be here in time for dinner."

Frau Fischbein ordered servants to handle the luggage. She herself escorted Iris to her rooms while a manservant was ordered to show Peter to his suite. Frau Fischbein was almost obsequious in her eagerness to please. She withdrew when the maid arrived to unpack for Iris.

At last Iris was alone. She walked from her sitting room into the bedroom, then crossed to a window. The view was magnificent. She looked down upon the swift-flowing Danube, then lifted her gaze to the view of Vienna in the distance. Peter had promised she would "see something of Vienna." Frau Fischbein's face had told her it would be wiser not to see the once-gay city now that it was in Nazi hands. She was impatient for this week at Herr Wahl's castle to be over.

With obvious pride Peter introduced Iris to their host while they settled themselves in a lower floor drawing room for pre-dinner wine and to await the other dinner guests. She knew that she was dramatically attractive in the gray velvet caftan designed for her by Molyneux, the diamond necklace and earrings lending her a regal air. Her pregnancy was only slightly discernible.

She sat in a Louis XV armchair, upholstered in Beauvais tapestry, and sipped her wine while the two men talked. Out of deference for his guests Herr Wahl spoke in English, though Peter prided himself on his knowledge of German.

When the other guests arrived, Iris was startled to discover she was to be the only woman at the table. After dinner—while brandy was being brought to the men—Peter asked that his wife be excused.

"It's been a tiring day for her," he said, proud of being an expectant father. "I'll see her to her rooms."

Iris was relieved that both Peter and Otto Wahl were away from the castle much of the time. She saw the two men only in the evening—at dinner parties at the castle or at elegant private mansions in Vienna. In Herr Wahl's limousine they were driven to their parties through the night-darkened Vienna streets that betrayed little of the upheaval that had infected the country. Iris saw the enormous swastika flags flying over public buildings. German cars. A tank. Clusters of men in Nazi uniforms and jackboots.

Iris encouraged Frau Fischbein to spend time with her over coffee several times during the course of each day.

"You're not happy about the Nazis taking over Vienna," she said compassionately while they sat in her sitting room and ate the delectable sugar cookies that Frau Fischbein herself had made.

All at once Frau Fischbein was trembling. Her face drained of color.

"How can you believe that?" she stammered. "Please, I—"

"I think it's terrible," Iris said with sudden passion. "I hate sitting down to dinner every night with Nazis."

"You understand." Frau Fischbein's smile was tremulous. "All the time I am afraid. Herr Wahl is my cousin—we share a grandmother. He insists I will not be harmed. He says the Fuhrer knows about his Jewish grandmother and is willing to overlook this because of Herr Wahl's devotion to the party."

"Your grandmother was Jewish?" Iris was startled to feel a new closeness to the housekeeper.

"My grandmother and my mother and father," Frau Fischbein whispered. "My cousin's parents were Protestants, like the grandfather we shared. He insists I will be safe here with him. So far our village has been spared."

"Let me help you leave here," Iris said impulsively. "I'm sure my husband could arrange for a British visa."

"Bless you," Frau Fischbein interrupted, "but I could never bring myself to leave Austria. No matter what happens, it is home to me."

"If you ever change your mind, I'll be ready to help," Iris promised. "Just send me word."

While Jonnie and Katie changed into proper clothes for Friday night services at temple, Laura settled into her favorite chair in the living room. The children were disappointed at having to miss "Death Valley Days"; but it was time, she told herself, that the three of them shared a religious experience. It was not enough that they were attending Sunday school.

Iris's latest letter—she'd re-read it three times since its arrival yesterday—made her starkly conscious of the fate of Jews in Germany and Austria.

*Laura, it's so frightening to see firsthand. Here in London most people seem to believe Chamberlain is right in his appeasement plans. They don't want to believe what Hitler is doing to the Jews. But Laura, I saw in Vienna. I wish I had the nerve to be part of the protest meetings that are popping up in London."*

She had written Iris in detail about her job with Slocum, McArdle, and Winston. She had told her, too, about Slocum's sons and his nephew Eric, who were doing so well in Magnolia real estate. Iris remembered Eric Slocum.

*"Eric was a senior when I was a freshman. Folks in town gossiped about his not being a nephew but the Judge's son. His son by that high yallar girl he used to keep a few miles from town."*

She had not told Iris of her suspicions about Derek. She had debated about confiding in Maisie, then dismissed this. Maisie—sure to sympathize—might inadvertently let it slip. She was not prepared to have the town know her real identity or to have Jonnie and Katie learn what happened to Papa. The time would come when they could be told.

Iris was so anxious for her to be in London when the baby was born, but how could she take off that much time? She worried, too, about a possible outbreak of war. She wished she could persuade Iris to come back to America. Everett predicted that within a year or so they'd hear a radio news flash that German planes were bombing London.

"Mom, do I *have* to wear a tie?" Jonnie came into the living room, struggling to make the appropriate knot.

"You have to, and I'll fix it for you." How handsome he looked, she thought tenderly. "Katie, darling," she called, "hurry up. We don't want to be late."

In the early May evening, fragrant with the scent of magnolias, Laura and the children walked to temple. At painful moments—like now—she remembered that they would soon be observing the first anniversary of Bernie's death. There were nights still when she subconsciously reached out in her bed and then realized with fresh anguish that Bernie was gone.

"Mom, when are we going to have a car?" Katie asked wistfully. "Everybody we know has a car."

"Not everybody," Laura corrected. "Lots of people don't."

"Well, when will we?" Katie persisted. A few weeks short of nine, Katie already had the kind of drive that promised to take her far, Laura thought with pleasure.

"Soon," Laura promised. Within the next few weeks. She could afford to spend six hundred dollars for a Pontiac. Not a used car, she remembered Bernie's admonition. You never knew what you were getting when you bought a secondhand car. And she'd have to learn to drive. Iris had been driving for years. Iris had traveled all over Europe. She felt so backward sometimes when she thought about Iris.

People were standing in front of the temple in lively conversation as they approached. Katie released her hand to run off joyfully to join a school friend. Jonnie stayed at her side while she paused to talk with Cecile Berger, the vivacious and friendly mother of one of Jonnie's classmates. Seeing Chet Berger Jonnie, too, defected.

"You're looking beautiful," Cecile commented. "The pageboy is new, isn't it?" Cecile inspected the new hairstyle with approval.

"Katie persuaded me to try it."

"The dress is smart. You didn't buy that in town," Cecile surmised.

"No. My sister sent it from Paris. It's old, but with skirts getting shorter, I decided to bring it out again."

"Let me warn you," Cecile said with conspiratorial amusement. "After services Mrs. Tannenbaum is going to speak about contributions to the fund for Jewish refugees." Laura involuntarily tensed. In all the months she had been back in Magnolia she had not encountered Mrs. Tannenbaum. She had known that it would happen eventually. "The old bitch ought to send a thank you note to Hitler for providing her with a new philanthropy. This gives her a lot more mileage than the free lunch program at the elementary schools."

"You don't admire Magnolia's 'Queen of Philanthropy,' " Laura laughed. She'd thought everybody in town revered Mrs. Tannenbaum.

"She's vicious," Cecile shrugged. "She broke up her daughter's marriage, you know. After seventeen years Ted Weinberg took off for parts unknown." Laura had vague recall of the Weinbergs. "Old lady Tannenbaum was always on his back—he wasn't successful enough to satisfy her. Her housekeeper is my maid's mother—we get the blow-by-blow accounts of the fighting in that family. Mrs. Tannenbaum was always complaining how Enid had 'married beneath her.' "

"I've never been a member of Mrs. Tannenbaum's fan club," Laura confessed. Until the day she died she'd remember Mrs. Tannenbaum coming to the house three mornings after they buried Papa. *All she'd cared about was getting Iris and her out of town.*

"Now she's trying to run Phil's life. That's her grandson. He left college to go to Spain to fight with the Abraham Lincoln Brigade. Grandma put a stop to that. He's back in school again, and she's talking about the wonderful career he'll have in banking." Cecile drew Laura off to the side. "Speaking of the devil," she whispered. "Here she comes."

"It's time to go inside," Laura said. Why did she get this suffocating feeling whenever she encountered someone else from that earlier life in Magnolia? Mrs. Tannenbaum would not recognize her. Nobody did.

"That's Phil with her. They must have drafted him to come to services with her tonight. They take turns."

Walking up the path to the small portico that led into the temple, Laura allowed herself one swift glimpse of Mrs. Tannenbaum. She was little changed by the years. But Laura was startled by the intense gaze of the young man at Mrs. Tannenbaum's side. Dark-haired, slender, he had handsome features and an ingratiating smile. He was still in college, Laura recalled. He couldn't be over twenty or twenty-one, but there was an arresting maturity about him.

All through the services Laura was conscious of Phil Weinberg's glances in her direction. They were flattering but disconcerting. He probably thought she was a new girl in town. He never guessed she was a widow with two children.

After the services Mrs. Tannenbaum was introduced and made her plea for contributions. Listening to the fund-raising speech Laura was conscious of her own financial situation. She was uneasy that she was drawing on principal for their daily expenses. It was impossible to live decently on what Slocum, McArdle, and Winston paid her.

Bernie would expect her to buy real estate in these

depressed times. He'd want her to invest. Each time she considered buying rental property, she brushed this aside. She was nervous about property lying unrented or with tenants unable to pay. But it was almost a year. She couldn't keep on allowing the money to sit in the bank and collecting such little interest.

She would have to stop being so cowardly about investing. She should put a solid chunk of the money lying idle in the Atlanta bank into rental property. People kept saying that "prosperity is just around the corner." Now was the time to buy. That was what Bernie would do.

In early July Peter insisted that Iris take up residence in the London house in order to be close to the hospital when labor began. She was restless and irritable as July passed with no indication of imminent delivery. She knew, too, that Peter's children by his first wife were trying to instill doubts in him about the parentage of this child. *Please God let the baby have one feature like its father.*

Early in August Iris went into labor. Peter hovered at her side, trying to hide his impatience that delivery was slow. He would have followed her into the delivery room if the doctors had permitted this.

"I'll never have another baby!" Iris swore through clenched teeth between pains. "Why does it have to be the woman who goes through this?"

Eleven hours after her first contraction Iris gave birth to a son, to be baptized Noel Percy Cranford. She gazed at him with astonishment as she held him in her arms for the first time. *Her son.*

"Peter, he has your eyes," she said in sudden triumph. "Look at him."

"All new babies have blue eyes," he said, but she sensed his pleasure. "But you're right," he conceded complacently, "he has the Cranford eyes."

Young Noel was immediately swept up into the British upper-crust system of child raising. Iris's sole maternal obligation was to breast feed Noel for the first three months of his life. Peter presented her with a superb triple strand of pearls and a diamond and aquamarine tiara. Within three weeks he was on his usual rounds of hunting, gambling, and odd sexual pursuits.

In September—for more than two weeks—the world's attention was focused on the insane ravings of Hitler and Mussolini and on Neville Chamberlain's futile efforts at appeasement—while the Czech leaders denounced the threatened dismemberment of their nation. The public watched while Chamberlain rushed to Berchtesgaden, to Godesberg, to Munich.

Americans listened to the radio reports by H.V. Kaltenborn in New York, Edward Murrow in London, William Shirer in Godesberg, Germany and later in Berlin and Munich. On September 29 Americans heard William Shirer announce that the Big Four—Germany, Italy, France, and England—had come to an agreement over the partition of Czechoslavakia. Without consulting the Czech leaders, or Russia, Hitler, Mussolini, Chamberlain, and Daladier had decreed that Czechoslavakia must cede the districts of Bohemia and Moravia to Germany. Peace had been bought at the cost of the Czech nation.

Peter was smug about the results of the Munich Conference, pleased that Chamberlain had returned home a hero. He ridiculed Winston Churchill's warnings that Nazi Germany was a threat to the world, that it was urgent Britain build a powerful air force. Charles Lindbergh was right; war in Europe could not be won by England even if the United States came to their aid. Now Iris listened to the more serious dinner conversations, where once she had ignored them. Not everyone believed that Chamberlain's policy of appeasement would keep world peace. Some wealthy British talked about stockpiling gold, buying retreats across the Atlantic.

Again, Iris played the social scene with her three close friends. It soon became clear that any foray into the nursery that lasted for more than ten minutes was considered an intrusion by Noel's nanny, chosen personally by Peter. At intervals she accompanied Peter to country houseparties or on a trip to the Riviera. Though friends were making the trek to Palm Beach or Jamaica or Mexico, Peter preferred to remain on their side of the Atlantic.

At one restless soul-searching moment Iris remembered her first weeks in Palm Beach as Mrs. Latham's companion. She remembered her envy of the ultra-rich women who lived in that world. And she remembered her sudden realization that these women were not happy. As she was bored and unhappy now.

By early 1939 France was already preparing for war. Late in February Britain and France recognized the Franco government in Spain. On March 15 Nazi troops seized the Czech territories of Moravia and Bohemia. Sixteen days later Britain and France agreed to support Poland if Hitler attempted to invade that country. A week later Italy invaded Albania.

While still attempting to discourage Hitler from further military expansion, Chamberlain began to prepare for war. The first peace-time military conscription was introduced in Great Britain. English planes were on constant patrol. Gas masks were being issued in France. Begonias were planted above the bomb shelters under the Champs Elysées in Paris.

Working late at the office on an unseasonably cool Monday in April, Laura paused for coffee and took advantage of these few minutes to peruse the current issue of *Time*. She rejoiced with other Americans in the improving business conditions—though it was disturbing to realize this was being brought about by fears of war in Europe.

She swigged down the last of the coffee, put aside the magazine, and reached for her notes on tomorrow's closing. Suddenly she realized that Judge Slocum was still in his office. She heard his voice in heated conversation. He was talking with his two sons about one of their real-estate projects, she realized in a moment.

"You've got definite word Stephens Industries is interested in coming down South?" the Judge demanded. "From Pittsburgh to Magnolia, Georgia is a drastic move. I've been going along with you on this—but keep in mind we're laying out a hell of a lot of cash without a real commitment."

"They're coming," his older son insisted. "But like I've been telling you, they'll want a big tract close to town. We'll be able to name our own price if we can deliver."

"All right," the Judge said, "let's assume Stephens is our buyer. The next step is to approach Chuck Donnell."

"You're sure that the bank is about to foreclose on the Donnell place?" the Judge's younger son asked.

"I got it from Bill Davis himself," the Judge said. Bill Davis was president of the Third National Bank, Laura recalled. "Donnell has close to two hundred acres. Right next to the sixty-two we've already bought up. That's the only tract that size left close to town. And there's no way the old bastard can pay off. Now the way I figure it, with foreclosures hanging over Donnell's head, we'll be able to buy him out for peanuts. A little something over the mortgage."

"Sounds good. I'll run over and talk to Donnell in the morning." His older son's voice deepened with anticipation.

"Wait two or three days," the Judge cautioned. "Nobody's running over to buy it. Bill says they'll be ready to pounce by the end of the week. Let Donnell sweat it out. Then he won't give us any back talk when you make him an offer."

Laura sat motionless, listening to the three men—in smug high spirits—leave the offices. They were not even aware she was here. Her mind was charging ahead. She could hear Bernie's voice: *In real estate everything is in the timing."* With business improving prices would go up. Now was the time to buy. Particularly, now was the time to buy the Donnell farm.

She checked her watch. Farm folks went to bed early, but it was just past 7:30. She could be out there in an hour. She reached for her jacket and purse in sudden decision. She'd come in early in the morning to finish up the papers for the closing. Right now she was going home, pick up the car, and drive out to the Donnell place.

Jewel smiled in relief when she arrived at the house. It was time to leave, but Jewel liked to see her home before going off for the night.

"Yo' dinnuh's warmin' in the oven, Miz Laura," Jewel reported. "And Ah started a fire in the grate. It's awful cool for April."

"I have to run out on an errand," Laura explained to Jewel and the children. "But you go on home, Jewel. The kids will be fine. Back to your homework," she ordered Jonnie and Katie. They liked to desert homework to sit with her at her delayed dinners. Sometimes she felt guilty that once or twice every week she stayed late at the office. Too late to sit down with them for dinner.

"Homework's all done," Katie said triumphantly. "We'll listen to 'Burns and Allen.' I just love Gracie."

Behind the wheel of the car Laura concentrated on her approach. She sympathized with the Donnells. The small farmers had been through a rough siege despite government aid. She would offer to buy the property—allowing them to keep the house and five acres—for a thousand over the mortgage. Judge Slocum would take the whole farm—including the house—and probably offer them five or six hundred over the mortgage. At least, if they sold to her they'd still have their home.

She watched carefully for the road that led out to the farm. The houses were far apart now. She felt faintly uncomfortable driving at night in an unfamiliar area. Thank God, she'd learned to drive. She squinted into the

255

poorly lighted night. There, that was the Donnell house, situated close to the road and with close to two-hundred acres behind and to the north.

Laura parked. Hearing the car come up, somebody had switched on the porch light. A slightly stooped man in his late sixties, in worn but clean overalls, stood on the porch, a poignant sadness in his eyes that told Laura he was anxious about the future ahead for his wife and himself. The Donnell house was small, modest, showing a need for paint. A broken window pane had been neatly closed up with cardboard.

Laura introduced herself and was invited inside. Mr. and Mrs. Donnell didn't know her. They were politely curious about her mission. She explained that she understood they were having problems with the bank.

"Yes ma'am, we are," Mr. Donnell conceded warily and reached for his wife's hand.

"I'm a lawyer," she said, and saw Mrs. Donnell's eyes widen with respect. "I have a client in Atlanta who would like to buy your place. Not the house," she said quickly and saw the quick, relieved exchange between husband and wife. "He'd be happy to exempt the house and five acres from the sale." Laura took a deep breath. "I've been authorized to offer to pay off your mortgage and pay you an additional thousand dollars for the property." Her heart was pounding when she finished.

"And we keep the house and five acres?" Mrs. Donnell stressed.

"You keep the house and five acres," Laura reiterated. "I can draw up the agreement tonight, bring it over first thing tomorrow morning for you to sign, and talk to the bank."

"That's all we have to do?" Mr. Donnell asked.

"You'll probably want to be represented by a lawyer," Laura said.

"No ma'am," Mr. Donnell said firmly. "As long as that piece of paper says we get to keep the house and five acres and you give us a thousand dollars cash, no need

256

to be spendin' money on a lawyer. We got a deal, Miz Hunter."

Laura arrived at the Donnell house before eight the next morning. After the preliminary papers were signed Laura handed over her own check for one thousand dollars—"on behalf of my client, who'll reimburse me"—to Mr. Donnell as contract deposit.

She went into the office to finish up what needed to be done for the 11 A.M. closing she was handling. Judge Slocum was in court this morning. The other two partners were away from the office on business. At 9:30 she presented herself to an officer at the Third National Bank and explained her mission.

"You'll be needing a certified check for the closing," the bank officer informed her.

"I know." Laura smiled faintly. "My client is located in Atlanta. I'll go up tomorrow to have him sign the necessary papers and turn over the bank check. We'll be ready to close day after tomorrow."

"A mite fast, wouldn't you say?" He lifted his eyebrows in surprise.

"Mr. Donnell tells me there are no liens against the property. I trust him. Shall we say 3 P.M. on Thursday, here at the bank?"

Laura knew that it wouldn't be long before Judge Slocum discovered that the property had been bought by "an Atlanta corporation." She had not expected it to happen so quickly. She was clearing up her desk for the day when he stormed into her office.

"What the hell are you up to?" he demanded through clenched teeth. "I just had a call from Bill Davis at Third National. He told me you're representing somebody in Atlanta who wants to buy the Donnell farm!"

"We're closing day after tomorrow." Laura refused to relinquish her calm.

"You hid here in your office, and you heard the boys

and me plan to buy that property," he seethed. "That's unethical! I'll take you up before the Bar Association!"

"I doubt it," Laura bluffed. "If anything is unethical, it's that contract that brought me down here. You pay our receptionist more than you pay me."

"I don't know who you're doing business with in Atlanta, but tell him to stay out of the way of my sons and me. We don't tolerate outsiders in this town. And you're fired. Get the hell out of my office!"

The following morning Laura boarded the train for Atlanta. Instinct told her to continue the pretense that she was representing an Atlanta client. Last night Maisie and she had talked for almost an hour on the phone. Maisie was encouraging. It was time Laura opened up her own law office.

Both Maisie and Everett approved of the deal she had pulled off. She had provided the Donnells with some security, which Slocum would not have done. And Maisie and Everett encouraged her to contact the Stephens people in Pittsburgh. With a tract of almost two hundred acres, Everett had assured her, she'd have land enough to make a sale.

But Laura was not closing her eyes to the fact that Slocum and his sons had been buying up other acreage. It was possible that they had sufficient acreage of their own to offer to Stephens Industries. And she had no inkling of their special requirements — which obviously were known to Ted Slocum.

Had she been too hasty in striking the deal she made for the Donnell property? Paying off their mortgage and adding another thousand would leave a considerable dent in her capital. If Stephens Industries didn't buy, how long would she have to hold on to the property before she resold it?

# Chapter 21

Iris had come to Cranford Hall with Noel and their usual entourage three days ago at Peter's instructions, phoned from Vienna. He was arranging some secret conference at the country estate on behalf of Goebbels. Several times Peter had been guest of Magda and Joseph Goebbels in Berlin. *"A charming man, Iris."* How would Herr Goebbels react if he knew his hostess at Cranford Hall was Jewish?

She had been instructed to see that eight bedrooms were made ready for their guests. Peter told her he would be arriving with Ernst Wahl. *"He remembers you with much admiration."*

Peter was sure Britain couldn't win a war with Germany. Did he truly expect to accomplish something with this stupid conference at Cranford Hall? He felt so important at bringing people together, but he had no official status. Some highly placed Germans and two French officials were to be among the guests, Peter said. Everything must be kept secret. The guests would be flying to London by private planes.

Early in the afternoon Peter phoned from London. He had arrived from Vienna this morning with Ernst Wahl. A plane from Munich and another from Paris had just deposited their other guests at the airport. They would all arrive via two limousines in time for dinner.

"There will be ten for dinner, Iris," Peter said crisply. "Wear black. And your tiara."

Iris played the gracious hostess when she welcomed their guests to Cranford Hall, though she recoiled from the German presence in her home. What did the two

259

Frenchmen—appearing wary and reproachful—hope to accomplish here?

Iris thanked Ernst Wahl for the tin of cookies sent by Frau Fischbein.

"She remembers your visit with much pleasure," Ernst Wahl told Iris. *Ernst Wahl was a traitor to Austria.* "She hopes you will honor the castle with another visit soon. I myself will be in Munich for the next two or three months, but please, consider my castle to be your castle."

Conversation at dinner was both apolitical and in English, out of respect for their hostess. It was as though the men were deliberately allowing themselves some levity before retiring to serious business. The Germans talked nostalgically about visits to Paris. Relaxing now, the French recalled visits to Berlin and Vienna.

"We hope that tourists from your country will honor us this summer again," Ernst Wahl said to Iris with a show of Viennese charm. She recalled that Peter said he owned hotels in Salzburg and Graz. He was greedy for the American dollars. "Especially now that Pan American Airlines will start regular flights between New York and Europe next month."

"I'm sure they will," Iris smiled, thinking what American in his right mind would want to visit Europe this summer, when Austria and Czechoslavakia were in the hands of the Nazis, Spain ruled by Franco, and Mussolini in control of Italy? In Paris there was no music or dancing after 10 P.M. The police kept a close watch. It was almost like Prohibition, Iris thought with a flicker of humor. And in London the government was busy building air-raid shelters and determined to distribute gas masks to every resident.

At a signal from Peter, Iris excused herself and went up to her suite. Edwina brought a tea tray to her sitting room. On impulse she reached to the table beside her chair for the handpainted cookie tin Frau Fischbein had sent to her. Was Frau Fischbein as safe at the castle as her cousin believed?

Iris untied the carefully knotted red velvet ribbon and opened the tin. Frau Fischbein had made the luscious-looking array of concoctions of chocolate, nuts, and marzipan herself. Frau Fischbein remembered how Iris loved the homemade cookies.

She had eaten almost nothing, though the staff had prepared a gourmet meal. She was robbed of appetite when Nazis sat at her dinner table. But now—her appetite whetted by the tin of cookies—she dug in. On the fifth foray she became aware of something other than cookies beneath her fingers. Curious, she pulled out a folded sheet of violet note paper.

A note from Frau Fischbein, she realized. Smiling in anticipation she unfolded the paper. Her smile ebbed away as she read.

*"You were so kind to offer me help. I come to you now on behalf of seven children being hidden in the town. I have heard Herr Wahl talk with the town council. Before the summer is over we must expect spot checks by the Gestapo. The children will be found and taken away."* To be thrown into German camps, Iris thought, suddenly cold. *"Talk with Willi Czinner. He runs a bookstore in Chelsea. The Book Corner. Please! For the children!"*

Iris sat motionless, almost overwhelmed by the urgency of the situation. Seven innocent children from the village near the castle. Now she picked up the cookie tin and poked her fingers searchingly about the bottom. She pulled forth another folded sheet of paper. Opening it, the faces of seven young children stared up at her. Passport photographs, her mind pinpointed.

Clutching the photographs and the note, Iris walked into her bedroom and locked the door. Her mind was in chaos. How could she help bring the children out of Austria? And simultaneously she knew that she just might pull it off. Being the wife of pro-Nazi Lord Cranford gave her a real advantage.

The following morning Iris was having her morning tea in bed when she heard cars pulling away before the house, returning their guests to the airport for their flights home. Peter said he'd be "involved in business" in London for a week or ten days, but he'd insisted she remain at Cranford Hall. It was better for Noel this time of year than London. At convenient intervals he was a fatuous parent.

Peter would spend an hour in the nursery with Noel, Iris guessed. He'd have luncheon with her and then Dobkins would drive him into London. She'd wait a half hour or so and then have Collins—the new chauffeur—drive her into the city. She'd shop something for Laura and the children at Harrod's. From Harrod's she'd have Collins take her to the bookstore. She'd buy a copy of *Rebecca*, that novel Laura liked so much. And she would talk to Willi Czinner.

She shopped with unusual swiftness at Harrod's, then instructed Collins to take her to the Book Corner in Chelsea. Her heart was pounding as she walked from the Rolls to the entrance to the small bookstore. From the titles in the window she understood the bookstore catered to artists and theater people. She'd pick up a copy of a Noel Coward play.

There were two male clerks in the store. Which was Willi Czinner? The older, she decided. She found a copy of Coward's latest play and approached him. He was talking with another customer. He spoke perfect English. Instinct told her he was not Czinner.

As though remembering another title she wished, she walked to the bookcase against the far wall, where the other clerk was straightening a shelf.

"Mr. Czinner?" she asked softly.

"Yes." His accent was German.

"Can we talk somewhere? I have just heard from Frau Ania Fischbein. She told me to go see you."

His face tensed. He was ashen.

"Please. Come with me."

Czinner led her to a tiny room behind the store that served as an office. He closed the door, hesitated, then

262

locked it.

"Please, tell me what Ania said."

"It's urgent to get seven children out of Austria. Some time before the end of the summer." Iris reached into her purse to pull out the photographs. She handed them to Czinner. "She sent me these."

He shuffled through the photos and then seemed immobilized as he gazed at the face of a pretty little seven-year-old.

"Ilsa," he whispered, his face luminous with love and pain and incredulity. "My daughter. I was in Switzerland on business when the Nazis marched into Austria thirteen months ago. I had been active in the underground—the Nazis were looking for me. I couldn't return. They took away my wife. Ilsa was at school—friends have been hiding her. Occasionally word comes through to me—but for the last five months nothing." His eyes were searching Iris's now. "How do you know Ania Fischbein?"

"My husband and I visited the castle last year. I offered to help her get a British visa after the Anschluss, but she refused to leave Austria."

"You're British?" Czinner seemed uncertain. Her accent was a blend of American South and British.

"American. My husband is Lord Peter Cranford." For an instant she was startled by his air of sudden withdrawal. Then she understood; some of the more sensational papers had written about Peter's frequent visits to Berlin and Munich and hinted at perverted sexual interests that drew him there.

"My husband and I have completely different viewpoints about the Nazis." About almost everything—except for their mutual appreciation of high living. "I've loathed Hitler for years. He's a psychotic monster. But I don't know how I can help these children." *But she had come here. He knew she wished to help.*

"Ania sent the photographs so that I could obtain false passports for them," Czinner said, frowning in concentration. "But how do we get the children across the border? It would be useless for me to go back." He paused for a moment. "There is one way. If they were spirited out by an American woman supposedly showing Europe to a group of American children. A tour by motorbus," he pinpointed. "That would be safer than by train or plane. Do you drive?"

"Yes. But how could I—" But already initial bewilderment was giving way to determination to play this game. "Mr. Czinner, how could I do this?"

"Forgive me," he said, "but as the wife of Lord Cranford you would not be suspect in either Austria or Germany. It will take much planning, much work—but these children—my Ilse—have no other chance."

"Tell me what we must do," Iris said with an unfamiliar exhilaration.

"Meet me tomorrow at four for tea at the little restaurant across from the Tower of London. It will appear a casual encounter," he emphasized. "Your husband must not discover you know an Austrian refugee wanted by the Gestapo."


Iris came to her second meeting with Willi Czinner with fresh confidence. She knew how to lend legitimacy to the touring venture. She would urge Laura to allow Jonnie and Katie to come to London for a visit. Laura was involved in business and couldn't leave Magnolia herself. She would pay all expenses, Iris plotted. Not only for the children but for a companion for them. In Paris she would rent a motorbus, as Willi had instructed. They would be two carefree American women showing Europe to a group of American children. They would go into Austria with two and come out with nine.

"This is not without risk," Willi warned. "Even with your husband's connections, it can be dangerous. But once the children are in England, I can guarantee care for them. Organizations are standing by to help out in

264

such emergencies."

"I may have trouble with my sister," Iris cautioned. "She's upset about what's happening on this side of the Atlantic. But my nephew and niece are Americans—they're the perfect front for us. And they'll be in no danger. American tourists are being courted by the Austrians and Germans." She *must* convince Laura to allow Jonnie and Katie to come.

"You can't tell your sister what this is all about," Willi reminded.

"No. Just that I'm terribly homesick, and that it'll be such a wonderful experience for the children to see London and Paris. And it will be." Later Laura would learn about their more extensive itinerary.

Willi focused on working out a time slot. Georgia schools closed in late May. As soon after that as possible Jonnie and Katie should arrive in London. Now Willi and Iris faced the critical problem of communication with Laura.

"Letters back and forth will be impossibly slow," Willi realized in consternation. It was possible to phone from London to New York City, but Laura lived down in Magnolia, Georgia. "Can you convince your sister by cable to allow the children to come to you?"

"I doubt it," Iris conceded. Now she remembered the new Pan Am Clipper service. "I'll fly to New York by Pan Am Clipper, then fly down to Georgia. First I'll write and plead. Then—without waiting for an answer—I'll fly over."

"Your husband will allow you to fly to the United States?" Czinner appeared skeptical.

"He'll be amused," Iris reassured Czinner. For an uncomfortable moment she envisioned a tragic plane crash over the Atlantic. Noel without a mother. *Stop being melodramatic.* "And Peter knows I adore flying. Everybody flies these days."

When she returned from Magnolia, she would tell Peter that her sister and the children were coming over for two weeks. He would make sure to be absent.

"You must spend two days sightseeing in London, another two days in Paris, Willi plotted. "You'll stop at the usual tourist towns en route to Vienna. It must appear a legitimate European tour. You'll write to Ania that you're bringing the children to see Vienna but wish to stay at the castle. Give her the specific date. You said Herr Wahl will be in Munich until the end of June?"

"Yes."

"Ania will understand. She'll have the children at the castle. You'll drive away at dusk. No one will question a busload of children with two American women. You will have proper passports for each child. The children—my Ilsa among them—understand what is happening in their country." His face reflected a sadness that blended with tenderness. "They will do exactly what you tell them."

"Willi, do you think I can do it?" Iris's throat was tightening with anxiety.

"You can and you must," he said gently. "You're the children's only escape."


Laura waited impatiently for the train from Atlanta to pull into the Magnolia depot. Iris had phoned from the airport in New York to tell her the plane had arrived safely. She'd phoned again from the Atlanta airport.

She shouldn't have told Jonnie and Katie about Iris's invitation. They'd become so excited at the prospect of crossing the Atlantic on a huge liner and then seeing London and Paris. But she was well aware that it wasn't advisable to dash around Europe in these times.

Both Jonnie and Katie wanted to take the afternoon off from school to meet the train. They were hoping Iris could persuade her to let them make the trip. Iris would be in town only for two days. She said she'd been dying to fly on one of the new Pan Am Clippers; and once she was in New York, she couldn't fly back without seeing them.

266

Iris had been right in suspecting that Laura couldn't take time off to go overseas with the children. While clients were slow in coming to her, she had to keep the office open. And in ten days a team from Stephens Industries was coming down to Magnolia to look at the property. They were candid in admitting they would look at Slocum's land at the same time.

She was glad Everett had suggested she check into the products Stephens Industries were producing. She could talk intelligently about the advantages of buying her tract rather than the one being offered by the Slocums. If war should break out in Europe, and she prayed it wouldn't, American factories would be swamped with orders. Both Slocum's acreage and hers allowed for large expansion — but her land was closer by two miles than Slocum's to the major highway used for truck deliveries. A mile closer to the railroad. This could represent a substantial annual savings.

When the stationmaster announced the train was approaching Laura hurried out of the depot into the warm early May afternoon. Her anticipation at seeing Iris was colored by the painful memory of their last meeting right after Bernie's death.

She knew that this return to Magnolia would be distasteful for Iris. She remembered her own feelings when she arrived here with the children. Iris had always sworn she'd never set foot in Magnolia again.

The train pulled to a stop on the tracks. Laura watched the passengers emerging from the Pullman car, impatient for sight of her sister.

"Laura!" Iris called while a Pullman porter handed down her two valises to a station porter.

"Iris!" Her face incandescent, Laura darted forward to embrace her.

"Oh, baby, it's so good to see you." Iris clung to her for a moment, then released her. "Only for you would I ever come back to this bastardly town."

"The car's right outside," Laura told the porter. "The

maroon Chevvie." She linked an arm through Iris's as they followed the porter.

Driving home Laura sensed Iris's tension as they passed familiar locales.

"It hasn't changed much," Iris said contemptuously. "Same stupid Magnolia. Pretty on the outside, ugly on the inside."

"It's just beginning to change," Laura acknowledged. "Some people are beginning to build houses further out. Lovely homes."

"I don't know how you live here." Iris withdrew her gaze from the aged red brick structure that had been their elementary school. "Knowing what this town did to Papa. Except for the fact that you live here now, I'd be happy to hear the whole bloody place had burnt to the ground."

"It took a long time before I was comfortable here," Laura confessed. "But it's a beautiful place to raise Jonnie and Katie. And if I'm ever to clear Papa's name, I must live here." She smiled compassionately at her sister. "And I will do that, Iris." She paused. "Iris, I'm sure I know who killed Tammy Lee Johnson."

Pale and shaken, Iris listened while Laura told her about Derek Slocum. Her smile was bitter when Laura finished.

"Laura, how the hell will you ever prove that? The Slocums have always been one of the most powerful families in this town."

"One day I will prove it," Laura promised. "The time will come when all the small pieces will fall into place."

"When Laura Hunter is as powerful in Magnolia as Judge Slocum and his sons are, maybe you'll prove it," Iris jibed, but her eyes were bright with love.

"That day will come, Iris. For Papa I have to make it come."

Laura and Iris had an hour alone before the children returned from school. Jewel brought them coffee and hot-from-the-oven pecan pie, scolding Iris when she hesitated

268

at accepting a second wedge.

"Miss Iris, you and Miss Laura is so skinny you could eat the whole pie between you and no harm done."

Iris showed off the latest snapshots of Noel, laughed at Laura's reproach that she didn't know Noel's current weight.

"Darling, Nanny Worth takes care of all those things. That's the British way," she shrugged.

Iris was candid about her now celibate marriage and about Peter's pro-German attitudes, which were beginning to cause a ripple of disapproval among their acquaintances.

"Of course, Chamberlain is still trying to do nothing to provoke Hitler—even though he's started this peacetime conscription. Peter is sure there'll be nothing this summer but what he calls a war of nerves. Hitler's all involved with some secret negotiations. Laura, this may be the last summer when Americans can come to Europe without the fear of war breathing down their necks. And believe me, plenty of tours are coming over. I wish to God you could come, but at least let the children have the trip. I'm sure there's some woman here in town— somebody you trust—who'd be delighted to bring them over to London and then tag along for the ride until it's time to take them home again. They're not babies anymore, darling," she teased. "And if anybody asks," she laughed, "I'll say they're the children of my much older sister."

"Iris, it's so far away. And I'd worry about them. I worry about you over there."

Shortly past three Jonnie and Katie arrived from school. Iris dug out gifts from her valise, answered all their questions about the flight from London to New York.

"Kids, it was fantastic! Real beds, a five-course dinner—with strawberry shortcake for dessert. The lounge was decorated by Norman Bel Geddes," she told Laura.

"Aunt Iris, how big was it?" Katie demanded.

269

"Eighty-five-feet long." Iris gestured eloquently.

"I was scared to death about your flying," Laura admitted.

"Your mother is such a worrier," Iris laughingly told the children.

But by the time Laura chased Jonnie and Katie off to do homework, she knew Iris had won. She was confident that Maisie's schoolteacher sister Doris Rainey, who lived in Columbus, would be thrilled at the chance to see London and Paris.


With Collins at the wheel of the Rolls, Iris met the children and Doris Rainey at Southampton early in June. She was fighting to conceal her dismay that Peter — whom she had been confident would take off rather than meet their guests from Magnolia — would be at the London house when they arrived. Doris Rainey, Laura had told her, was third generation Georgia Baptist. *Let Jonnie and Katie say nothing about their being Jewish.*

Iris was touched by the children's excitement at having sailed on the *Queen Mary,* the largest ship afloat. They were such warm, sweet kids, she thought with a proprietary pride. While in Austria, children like these — Willi Czinner's daughter among them — faced being thrown into Nazi camps solely because they were Jewish. Her distaste for Peter and his beliefs these days was so strong that any time they spent together was painful for Iris.

"Were you able to fill my shopping list?" Iris asked Doris when they were all settled in the Rolls. Her smile was apologetic. "It probably sounded absurd." Later Doris would understand.

"I was able to pick up everything in a small shop near the hotel in New York," Doris told her. "A dozen Dodger and Yankee baseball caps, a dozen New York World's Fair T-shirts in several sizes, a dozen assorted comic books, and three inexpensive cameras. I hope they're appreciated here."

"They'll be appreciated," Iris promised. What better disguise for seven little Austrian Jews? "And tomorrow," she said in convivial tones, "we'll all go sightseeing to the Tower of London."

She was tense and wary when they arrived at the house. *Peter must suspect nothing.* The safety of those seven children depended upon that. The seven false American passports—"borrowed with consent," Willi explained, and with substituted photos—were concealed in the false bottom of a jewelry box Willi had provided. It was unlikely, he kept reassuring her, that any custom's inspector would give them more than a cursory glance considering the façade the group would present. And at last, she had secretly acquired her British driver's license, along with an international driving permit.

While Iris was settling Jonnie and Katie—along with Doris Rainey—in the three-bedroom guest suite that was normally opened up only for royal visitors to Cranford House, Dobkins arrived to tell her that Peter had been suddenly summoned to Berlin.

"He said to tell you that he will probably remain for at least three weeks. His Lordship can be reached at the Hotel Adlon."

"Thank you, Dobkins." Relief surged through Iris. The first hurdle had been passed.

Mindful of Willi's exhortations, on the following day Iris escorted her three guests on a morning tour of the Tower of London. The children were surprised that the Tower, actually a medieval fortress, was comprised of not one but a cluster of buildings. They were fascinated by the picturesque red, black, and gold uniforms of the Yeoman Warders of the Tower. Iris was relieved that Doris had read up on the major attractions of the Tower and played guide to them.

Doris and Jonnie climbed up the stairs to the Bloody Tower; by then Iris and Katie were happy to settle themselves on a bench. They'd visit the Jewel House, Iris decreed when Jonnie and Doris returned, and then go back to Cranford House for luncheon.

In the afternoon Iris showed them Westminster Hall.

"Wow, what a place to play baseball!" Jonnie was oblivious for a moment to the history that had transpired within this huge, medieval structure.

From Westminster Hall they detoured to St. Margaret's Church, where Sir Walter Raleigh is buried, and then moved on to awesome Westminster Abbey, where Doris was enthralled by the Poets Corner. Here were the graves of Spenser, Chaucer, Johnson, Dryden, Tennyson, Dickens — the list was endless. Katie was eager to see the place where Florence Nightingale was buried.

Finally Iris insisted they go back to the car and have Collins drive them to the Savoy for afternoon tea. She was pleased to notice that despite conditions abroad, an impressive number of Americans were in London this summer. Her group of "American children" would not be conspicuous.

Over an early dinner Iris suggested — seemingly on impulse — that they leave in the morning for Paris and catch up on London on their return.

Doris was simultaneously enthralled and terrified when Iris said that they would go to Paris by plane — and ambivalent about Laura's reaction to their flying.

"It's so timesaving," Iris persuaded while Jonnie and Katie listened in ecstatic anticipation. "I want to show you as much as possible in the days you'll be over here. Laura knows I fly between London and Paris constantly," she said and the children nodded.

"Whatever you say," Doris capitulated. "I can't believe I'm actually in London. Wait till I tell my sixth-grade class that I climbed all the way up to the Bloody Tower!"

In the morning they flew on an Air France plane to Le Bourget airport outside of Paris, where a rented limousine waited to whisk them the seven miles to the Hotel Crillon in Paris. Jonnie and Katie were recurrently awed and delighted by their aunt's luxurious mode of living. Not until they were settled in their elegant suite at the

Crillon did Iris confide that their touring was to include a motorbus trip from Paris to Munich and on to Vienna.

"There's more I have to tell you," Iris said, including the two children in her confidence. Her voice serious now. "This is not just a pleasure trip." She paused, gearing herself to explain to the other three, wide-eyed with expectancy. "In a village near Vienna there are seven young children whose lives depend upon our taking them out with us." She paused. Doris was pale with shock. Jonnie and Katie were flushed with excitement. "I'm sure the three of you are safe—American passports are still highly respected in Austria. If anything goes wrong—if we're stopped and questioned and the truth comes out—I'll explain that the three of you know nothing. That I've plotted the rescue on my own. The Nazis in Austria are aware of some British hostility." She managed a wry smile. "Despite all of Chamberlain's efforts at appeasement he did sign an agreement to help Poland if Hitler decides to invade it."

"That's why you wanted the caps and the tee shirts and all," Doris said. "Camouflage."

"That's it," Iris confirmed. "We'll be two American women taking a group of American schoolchildren on a tour. A Georgia teacher and the wife of Lord Peter Cranford, well known for his pro-German feelings," she said with an ironic smile. "If you're nervous about accompanying us, Doris, you can stay in Paris until we rejoin you."

"I wouldn't miss it for the world!" Doris exulted. "Nothing so exciting has ever happened to me in my whole life. I'm grateful for the chance to help those children."

Iris turned to Jonnie and Katie.

"How do you two feel about this?" She was serious, talking to them as to two adults. "Do you want to help me with this?" Instinct, and their expressions, told her they were avid to share the experience. "It's your decision."

273

Katie nodded enthusiastically.

"What do Katie and I have to do?" Jonnie was endearingly solemn.

"I'll explain as we go along," Iris promised. "Meanwhile, tomorrow and the next day we'll sightsee in Paris. Every step we take must appear normal. I've already arranged for the motorbus and our accommodations along the way." Everything had been scheduled by Willi Czinner. "We'll arrive in Vienna in five days. We'll sightsee for two days, then visit the castle where I've stayed with Peter. The children will be hidden there. Dressed in their baseball caps and New York World's Fair T-shirts they'll pass for American tourists."

"Do they speak English?" Katie asked.

"They won't talk," Iris said, fighting anxiety. Her greatest concern had been over the communications problem. "The four of us will carry on any necessary conversation. When we're around people, the children will pretend to be engrossed in their comic books or taking snapshots. We'll work it out carefully before we leave the castle."

"I understand a little German," Doris told Iris. "My grandmother was German. She lived with us when Maisie and I were little."

"That'll be a big help," Iris was relieved. "We'll spend money freely. We'll be welcome everywhere." For once Peter had put cash at her disposal.

They played at being tourists for two days. Iris showed them the Eiffel Tower, the Cathedral of Notre Dame, took them through the Louvre Museum and on the Metro, the Paris subway. They had lunch at a sidewalk café on the Champs Elysées, dinner at a bistro on the left bank. Jonnie and Katie sent postcards home to their mother, then went with Iris and Doris to shop a present for her at the huge Galeries Lafayette—the venerable Paris department store.

Early on their third morning in Paris they left by motorbus for their first destination. Iris was intent on making this an exciting holiday for Jonnie and Katie; but when they arrived in Munich, she sensed their tension. Young as they were, they understood what was happening to Jews and political dissenters in Germany. They struggled to conceal their distaste for the strutting storm troopers, seemingly ever present. They gaped in disbelief at rouged and powdered Nazi officers walking in pairs.

Right on schedule, they left Munich and headed for Salzburg, the music festival city loved by tourists of all nationalities. They were too early in the season for the Mozart Festival, but as Doris pointed out, American children—unless music students—would not be upset by this.

Lying sleepless in her bed in their aristocratic hotel suite, Iris asked herself—in delayed trepidation—what she was doing in Salzburg with Laura's kids and that sweet teacher from Columbus. *What possessed her to take on this insane trip?*

In the stillness of the night her mind was stripped of pretense, the small daytime subterfuges. She was thirty-one years old, and she had never done one worthwhile thing in her whole life. This was a chance to prove to herself that she was more than a parasite. If she handled herself right, she could save those children. There was no one else to do it.

## Chapter 22

From Salzburg the party headed north for Linz. They remained briefly in the ancient city on the Danube, and then followed the river south towards Vienna. Iris was ever conscious that it was the returning trip—with their added "tour members"—that could be hazardous. But Doris and the children were Americans, she coddled herself—no harm could come to them. She refused to consider her own fate if she were caught.

Iris planned that they would arrive at Ernst Wahl's castle at dusk, when the bus would be shrouded in shadows. Ania Fischbein welcomed them with poignant relief. To minimize the number of people who would see them, she had given the staff an overnight holiday.

"The children will be brought here close to midnight, when others in the village are asleep," she explained. "You must leave with them early in the morning. It will not look suspicious. American tourists always try to see so much in a short time. Where do you go from here?"

"Willi told us to go to Graz," Iris told her. "His daughter is all right?"

"Ilsa is fine. But thank God, you've come. Each day we grow more anxious. The Gestapo is everywhere."

"I thought they wouldn't be here until the end of the summer." Iris was cold with alarm. So far she'd felt safe as a group of four touring Americans. But when they left the castle, they'd be fugitives. "That's what you said." Her voice was involuntarily sharp.

"That is what Ernst believed," Ania apologized. "But they come already to—" she searched for the proper English phrase, "to spot check. A Gestapo party was here in the village two days ago. It is not likely that they will return for another few days. You must leave early in the morning," she reiterated, a tic in one eyelid revealing her apprehension. "But come. You must be hungry after your drive."

To alleviate the tension, Frau Fischbein took Doris and the children on a tour of the castle after they'd finished their superb dinner. Iris sat in the smallest of the drawing rooms, sipping at a glass of wine, and mentally rehearsed what lay ahead of them.

The children—five of them Jewish, two of them the offspring of Christian political dissenters—must be coached in the roles they were to play. They must do nothing to betray their true backgrounds. Willi had mapped out the roads that would be safest. Their next "point of interest" would be Graz. From Graz they would go to Klagenfurt and then to a small town on the Italian border. Willi's voice echoed in her mind.

*"You're Americans. The inspection by the Austrian officials will take minutes. The same for the Italians. Once you've crossed the Italian border, you'll be safe."*

Shortly before midnight, at five-minute intervals as planned, the children began to arrive. Iris fought back tears. They were so little, so scared. The three women settled them in bed for a few hours' rest before they would leave, but Iris doubted that they would sleep. Ania packed the small knapsacks each child had brought along into the pair of Vuitton valises Iris had provided for this purpose.

"I saw your father in London, Ilsa," Iris gently told Willi's seven-year-old daughter and reached to hold the trembling little girl in her arms. Then she realized Ilsa spoke no English. "Doris," she called across the room. "Tell Ilsa I saw her father in London."

"Your friend is good with the children," Ania said while they watched the poignant joy that glowed in Ilsa's eyes and smile when she understood. "Thank God, she knows sufficient German to communicate with them."

277

Iris and Doris took turns at napping during the next few hours. Before sunrise the children were awake. Ania served them breakfast. Then the little Austrians — seeming less alarmed because of Jonnie and Katie's presence — were dressed in the New York World's Fair T-shirts and given Dodger and Yankee baseball caps and comic books. American brownie cameras were draped about the necks of the three older ones.

With a glorious June sun rising over the mountains, Iris and Doris prodded the children into the motorbus.

"God will bless you for this," Ania Fischbein told Iris as the group prepared to depart. "I'll pray for you."

*You* brought us here," Iris said softly, her throat tight with misgivings. How long would Ania Fischbein be safe? She hesitated. "Is there some way for you to come to London? I heard somewhere that for domestic employment Austrian women are—"

"Earlier that was possible. Not now — not for Jews," Ania said. "But Ernst is sure that I will be all right because of him." Yet her face betrayed her fears.

"Iris, let's move," Doris called. "We have a long drive ahead."

They passed few people as they made their way towards the road that led to Graz, about 130 miles south. Then, as Doris made a sharp turn to the left, they spied an approaching car carrying several Nazi officers. In her shaky German Doris issued instructions as rehearsed the previous night. The seven little Austrians focused on their American comic books or their cameras. With admirable coolness Jonnie and Katie waved to the Nazi officers as the cars passed.

"We made it!" Doris chortled. But Iris knew that Doris's heart, like her own, was pounding from the close encounter.

Iris was conscious of pride in her nephew and niece. They'd handled themselves well. And she was startled to feel a sudden urge to hold Noel in her arms. *Her son.* Damn Nanny Worth for keeping her distant from her

278

own child!

To ease the tension in the motorbus, Iris began to read from the guidebook. The children might not understand the words, but instinct told her that her own calm would be reassuring.

"The second largest city in Austria, Graz lies on both banks of the Mur River, on the eastern boundary of the Alps. It is known as the 'Garden City' because of its many beautiful parks."

When they arrived in Graz, Doris inquired directions to the Wahl Hotel. Iris had reserved the suite usually occupied by visiting royalty or high-ranking Nazi officials. With so little sleep the previous night, and to avoid as much exposure as possible, Iris decreed that they would have their luncheon sent up from the hotel restaurant and then nap for two hours.

Slowly, it appeared to Iris, the children were relaxing. They seemed to be comforted by Jonnie and Katie's exuberant spirits. When they left the hotel for their compulsory sightseeing, Katie positioned herself between the two smaller girls, a hand of each in her own.

Conscious of the need for cover, Jonnie boasted about the prowess of the Brooklyn Dodgers. Taking their cue from him the others smiled and nodded. No one would guess they couldn't understand one word of what Jonnie was saying.

They climbed a winding path to the Schlossberg, the castle hill, with its magnificent view of the city, saw the Clock Tower and the Bell Tower. Then they made their way down again to roam through the town. They saw the Gothic cathedral, the Mausoleum of Emperor Ferdinand II, and the amazing Provincial Armory—the Landeszeughaus—which houses armor for 5,000 soldiers, most of it from the sixteenth century.

Within four hours they returned to the Wahl Hotel. Again, they ate in their suite. Doris promised that tonight everyone would sleep well.

"Tomorrow," she told the children in her uneven German, "we'll go to Klagenfurt."

And from Klagenfurt they would go to the small town where at last could cross into Italy — and freedom.

A persistent knock at the door of their suite aroused Iris reluctantly. But reluctance was swiftly replaced by alarm. She leaped from her bed, reached for her robe, and hurried from the bedroom to the door of the suite. *It was just past 5 A.M.* Her throat was tight with fear.

"Who is it?" she demanded imperiously.

*"Geheime Staatspolizei!"* a harsh masculine voice replied. She didn't need an interpreter, Iris told herself, to know this was the Gestapo. *What had they done to appear suspicious?*

Iris pulled the door wide, looked up with a polite inquiring smile at a tall Nazi officer.

"Heil Hitler." He raised his right arm in the Nazi salute.

"What is it?" she asked again.

He replied in German. She gestured her incomprehension, indicated for him to wait. She crossed to the door of the bedroom Doris was sharing with Ilsa and the five-year-old girl.

"Doris, you'll have to interpret." She tried to appear casual. The two little girls were huddled beneath a sheet on the other bed, their eyes bright with terror. Damn him! He must have awakened everybody.

"The Gestapo?" Doris asked while she pulled on a robe.

"It's not the hotel porter."

Doris walked with her to the door and spoke to the Nazi in German. He replied.

"He wants our ID," Doris said with the air of a bored tourist.

"I'll get them," Iris said. For convenience sake all passports were kept in one folder.

Iris returned with her passport and Doris's. If he asked

280

for the children's passports, *then* she would bring them out.

As the Nazi continued to question Doris and she fumbled to reply in German, Iris ordered herself not to antagonize him. With each question, Doris interpreted for Iris before answering.

*"What are you doing in Graz?"* . . . *"Sightseeing with my tour groups."* . . . *"Do you know people who live here?"* . . . *"No."* . . . *"How long are you staying?"* . . . *"We leave in the morning for Venice."* . . . *"How many in your group? Are they all American and British?"*

The Nazi was growing testy, Iris sensed nervously. In one of the bedrooms a child began to cry. The little five-year-old, Iris identified with a surge of panic. *Let her not speak in German.*

"Doris, tell this man we're annoyed with his impertinence," Iris said loudly, anxious to cover the sounds from the bedroom. Doris was startled. "Tell him he's upsetting the children, that Herr Wahl—who owns this hotel—is a close friend of my husband and myself. We've just come from Herr Wahl's castle. He will be furious about this intrusion!"

Doris began to stammer in German. Iris saw the officer's face tense at the mention of Herr Wahl! *Why didn't Doris talk louder?*

"My husband is with Herr Goebbels in Berlin right now," Iris shot at the Nazi. At the mention of Goebbels he paled. "Tell him we will phone Herr Goebbels if he doesn't stop this inquisition immediately."

The Nazi mumbled a nervous apology and withdrew before Doris finished her translation.

"Oh, Iris, you were wonderful!" Doris reached to embrace her. "I was scared to death."

"Is it okay now?" Jonnie appeared in the doorway of one of the bedrooms. "We heard the door close."

"It's all right," Iris reassured him. "The Gestapo makes random checks in the hotels. They won't come back again."

But no one could go back to sleep. By a few minutes past 7 A.M. they were in the motorbus en route to Klagenfurt for a day of ostensible sightseeing. The morning was cloudy and unseasonably raw. Rain began to pelt the motorbus before they'd driven a mile. Iris was at the wheel, Doris studying the road map. But still shaken by their earlier encounter with the Gestapo, neither woman was conscious of the sudden drop in temperature.

By this time tomorrow morning they would be at the Italian border, Iris reminded herself. She dismissed the impulse to bypass Klagenfurt and head straight for the border. They must follow Willi Czinner's instructions to the smallest detail. He was a master at taking refugees out of Austria.

"Aunt Iris, everybody's cold," Jonnie's anxious voice brought Iris to attention. "Can we stop and take out sweaters?"

When they reached the twelfth-century city they registered at a deluxe hotel, again ordered luncheon sent up to their rooms, then, with the rain over, spent the afternoon strolling about the Alter Platz with a show of almost frenetic gaiety. Even the youngest among them knew that tomorrow morning they would wake up and drive to the Italian border. In Italy they'd drive to Venice and on to Paris, where the motorbus would be returned.

Long after the children were fast asleep Iris and Doris sat talking in whispers about what lay ahead. Katie had been delegated to watch over the three little girls. The four boys would be Jonnie's responsibility. *No word of German must pass their lips when they lined up for inspection at the border crossing.*

The next morning was warm and sunny again when on schedule they boarded the bus. To a casual observer they were a convivial group of Americans avid to sightsee. Only Doris and she would notice the scared young eyes that belied the smiles the children had been instructed to keep pasted on their faces, Iris told herself.

There was little activity on the city streets at this hour

of the morning. Now and then someone stopped to smile at the motorbus's occupants. As coached, the children waved to them. Willi had told her they would have the least trouble at the Italian border, Iris reminded herself. They'd come this far—they mustn't fail now.

They paused briefly in Villach, fifty miles east of Klagenfurt, so that Doris might make inquiries about the approach to the pass through the Alps that would take them to their destination. Iris knew the children were at last growing less tense when—for the first time—they giggled at Doris's accent when she struggled to explain that they would soon be at the border. But they were serious and attentive when she emphasized that they must not talk when they were at the inspection point.

"We'll make it," Iris told Doris when they at last arrived at the Austrian border patrol. It was a prayer more than a statement.

"Jonnie and Katie, start singing 'Three Little Fishes,'" Doris ordered. Immediately they complied. Now she told the Austrian children to clap in tune.

The Austrian inspector grinned, nodded in approval, and passed them through with a superficial glance at their papers. Their performance elicited a similar response from the Italian inspector.

"We did it!" Iris turned to the children. Triumph blended with relief in her voice. All the terrible fears that had haunted her evaporated. "It's all right, we're in Italy!"

Without understanding Iris's words but comprehending the meaning, the children joined Jonnie and Katie in a whoop of joy. Tears filled Doris's eyes.

"Wow, is Mom gonna be surprised!" Katie chortled. "Can we send postcards home from Venice?"

# Chapter 23

In her elegant gray-linen dress by Molyneux—an earlier gift from Iris—Laura sat at a damask-covered table in Magnolia's choice restaurant with the two men from Stephens Industries in Pittsburgh. The men were perspiring in their well-tailored jackets despite the ceiling fans that spun overhead.

"Mrs. Hunter, you're asking considerably more for your tract than the Slocum people are for theirs," Clark Stephens, Jr., son of the president of Stephens Industries, said with an effort at jocularity while he stabbed at the excellent pecan pie Laura had suggested for dessert. "That presents a real problem."

"I have a lot more to offer." Laura had expected this horsetrading. Instinct told her to play this in a low key. She could envision the hard sell of the Slocums. "Twice the number of acres plus—"

"We don't really need that much land," Stephens's associate interrupted. "You should be prepared for major expansion," Laura pointed out, "considering the strong possibility of war. You'll need acreage for warehousing as well as for shipping facilities. And you've seen my figures on your savings in transportation by building on my tract." She took a deep breath and geared herself to grandstand. "I'll need your decision within the next week if you want to tie up the property at my present figure. A cotton mill in Lowell, Massachusetts, is flying down in ten days to confirm the availability of trained labor." In truth, the Lowell mill had not yet responded to her initial correspondence. "Of course, in Georgia that's no problem." She chuckled indulgently. "Workers here have been in the cotton mills for four generations."

"That's your best offer?" Stephens made a show of disinterest.

"That's it. It could go up. The land is ideally suited for a cluster of cotton mills and warehousing facilities. We've—"

"Mrs. Hunter, you drive a hard bargain," Stephens scolded. "But we'll go along with it. Have your lawyer draw up the papers. We'll sign in the morning before we leave for Pittsburgh."

Giddy from excitement Laura returned to her office. The Donnell farm, except for the house and five acres, had cost her fourteen thousand dollars. A fair price for farm land. She had just sold it for seventy-five thousand. More than five times what she paid. Now she sat down at her desk to draw up the necessary papers.

Earlier than normal, Laura left the office and went home. She had no appointments for the balance of the day. Clients were not exactly breaking down her door, she mocked herself wryly. She was exhausted from the nervous tension plus the torpid heat of the past few days.

She walked into the house and called to Jewel, singing exuberantly if slightly off key out in the kitchen. Each time Laura came home she was conscious of the children's absence. The rooms seemed so empty.

"You come out here, Miz Laura and lemme give you some cold lemonade," Jewel ordered. "I ain't puttin' nothin' in the oven in this heah weather. You gonna have cold chicken and some fresh butter beans for dinner. And I made a big bowl of skillet sweet potato pudding that'll last a few nights."

"Thank you, Jewel." Laura sank into a chair at the kitchen table with an air of supreme satisfaction. "I had a great day. I sold that piece of property I've been worrying about."

"I knew you would." Her smile was tender and proud. "You is a special lady, Miz Laura."

"I'm raising your wages starting Monday. Another dollar a week." *She had just made sixty-one thousand dollars.* No doubt in her mind that the representatives of Stephens Industries would go through with the deal. She had exactly what they needed.

"Miz Laura!" Jewel suffused her perspiring face. "Now ain't that somethin'! I can send my Mama to the dentist for her teeth. He say for one dollar a week he'll start to make 'em." Now her mouth dropped open in dismay. "Now what's the matter with me? You got some postcards this mornin'. From Katie and Jonnie. Some funny writin' on 'em." She reached into a drawer to bring out the postcards.

"Thank God." Laura reached eagerly for them. "I was getting worried at not hearing, though my mind kept telling me they were just too busy sightseeing." She read the hasty scribbling on each of the four postcards with a sense of closeness to Jonnie and Katie. God, she missed them! They were in Paris again — and they'd been in Venice! Iris had said nothing about Venice.

"When the kids comin' home?" Jewel asked. "Ain't it about time?"

"Their ship docks in New York day after tomorrow. They'll take the train the next morning and be here the next night. Oh, Jewel, I can't wait to see them!"

While Jewel fussed over Jonnie and Katie as though they were at the point of starvation, Doris conscientiously briefed Laura on all the details of their trip. Laura was shocked and angry.

"How could Iris do that? To lie to me that way! To use the children and you without asking me first!"

"Mom, it was so exciting," Jonnie soothed between spoonfuls of ice cream. "And we got those kids out of Austria. Aunt Iris said it would have been awful for them if we hadn't."

"They hadn't seen their mothers and fathers for months," Katie said softly. "Two of them had nightmares every night."

"Laura, we were in no real danger," Doris insisted, but Laura found this difficult to believe. "I'm so grateful to have been able to help. It's something I'll remember the rest of my life."

"Me, too," Katie chirped. "Wait till we tell the kids at school."

"Iris would have liked to send us home on a Pan Am Clipper, but she figured you'd be scared to death," Doris laughed.

"I'm proud of you all," Laura said after a moment. "But Iris should have asked me first."

A few weeks after the children and Doris returned from their trip, the Soviet Union and Germany signed a nonaggression pact, lining themselves up against Great Britain and France. Appeals for peace ricocheted around the world.

Still, there was optimism in England. There were those in high places who were sure Germany would back down, would not invade Poland. Then, at five o'clock in the morning on September 1 German troops marched into Poland. Warsaw suffered its first air raid. On September 2 general mobilization began in Britain and the evacuation of one million children was launched. And at 11:15 A.M. on Sunday, September 3, Chamberlain declared war on Germany.

A letter from Iris made the declaration of war intensely personal to Laura:

*"We were listening to the wireless on Sunday morning after Chamberlain's speech when the air-raid sirens went off. We all went down to the shelter in the basement of the house. Later that night the sirens went off again. They were both false alarms. But now we all have more respect for that damn shriek. It isn't a dress rehearsal anymore. We're at war."*

In letter after letter Laura pleaded with Iris to come back with Noel to the United States—if not to Magnolia, then to New York. She told Iris about her real-estate windfall—she offered whatever financial aid Iris would

287

need.

Iris refused to leave London, though many women had been evacuated along with their children.

*"Darling, you wouldn't believe how busy I am. It's very chic to be involved in national defense work. This month I'm doing the all-night canteens. But really, Laura, everything's back to normal after that horrible first announcement, though the best restaurants have cocktail-bar shelters, and everybody is home by eleven."*

Iris wrote that Noel was permanently based now at Cranford Hall. Peter spent most of his own time there, coming into London at intervals to present himself at the Admiralty or 10 Downing Street to offer his services to the government. He felt personally betrayed by the Nazis. So far he had rejected the positions offered him as being unworthy of his status.

Laura tried to convince herself, as months passed, that the American press was correct in calling this "the phony war," but she worried about Iris's safety. Once each week she had dinner with Maisie and Everett, and conversation inevitably focused on the war in Europe.

In April Germany invaded Norway and Denmark. That evening Maisie good-humoredly scolded Everett when he carried the radio into the dining room while Laura and she brought dinner to the table.

"Hell, let's listen to what's going on in the world!" Everett shot back. "Maybe now the British will dump Chamberlain and bring back Winston Churchill. And maybe isolationists like Lindbergh and Hoover will realize we have to take sides in this thing."

On May 7 Chamberlain resigned and Churchill became prime minister. Three days later the "phony war" was real. The Nazis bulldozed their way through the Netherlands, Belgium, and Luxembourg. A week later Germany invaded France. On May 27 began the heroic evacuation of 300,000 British and Allied forces from Dunkirk.

Iris wrote that Cranford House had been closed up "for the duration" and she commuted between Cranford

Hall and a suite at the Dorchester. In London, shop windows were boarded up. At night traffic lights were adjusted to a match-thin green or red cross. Still, Laura thought, Iris sounded almost gay.

In Magnolia the only real sign of war was the increasing business in the local cotton mills. Across the country relief rolls were dropping. Laura spent little time at her law office — people in Magnolia shied away from women attorneys. Remembering Bernie's exhortation about buying real estate when prices were depressed she drove about the area in a frenzied search to buy up houses before prices began to soar. And before Stephens Industries' new facilities went into operation.

On this bright early June morning Laura closed up her office and headed for a meeting with Clark Stephens, Jr. in his temporary quarters. With their building close to completion, Clark was spending most of his time in Magnolia. He was being entertained by the best families, though Laura guessed the Slocums were not among them.

The town was jubilant about the rash of new jobs Clark would shortly be offering local workers. She was interested in the thirty-two families who would make the move from Pittsburgh to Magnolia with the company. They would require houses. It wasn't generally known around town yet that key employees were being brought down to Magnolia. The Slocums would be on their trail the moment word leaked out.

"Laura, what are you up to now?" Clark had adopted an amused benevolent attitude towards her ever since she'd helped him locate an elegant colonial that had pleased his wife, somewhat reluctant to make the move to the South. A house conveniently close to the Magnolia Country Club, where Daphne Stephens could play tennis and swim when the weather was right. "Something that's going to cost me," he clucked.

"Not at all. I've brought together a brochure, loaded with photos, that I'd like to present to your Pittsburgh people who're coming down here." Laura handed over the carefully planned four-color brochure. "Houses that I own, and will redecorate according to the wishes of the buyers." She'd had all the basic repair work done already. She'd brought in several yard men to make the grounds of each house presentable. "All they have to do is choose from color swatches. Everything will be ready—including new gas ranges and GE electric refrigerators—when they arrive. They'll just have to move in."

"They'd been planning to spend some time at a local hotel while they looked around." Clark squinted in thought. "I don't know if you're going to sell houses from a booklet." He flipped through the brochure, studied its content.

"Let them come down for a weekend at the hotel," Laura pursued. "I'll take them on a personal tour of my houses. I'll—"

"On the other hand," Clark interrupted, "you've set this up to look damn good. And it'll be real convenient to be able to move right in. Send a batch—say about fifty—up to the office in Pittsburgh, along with a note to the old man. You might just do some business." He grinned. "What's in it for me?"

"I'll handle your closing next week without a fee." Clark had already hired her as attorney for this. "And take you and your wife out to dinner when she comes down again."

Laura left Clark's office to drive back to town. Then on impulse she swung left at the next corner and headed for the undeveloped area close to the city dump. Ever since she'd returned to Magnolia, she had been aware of the *For Sale* sign posted on a straggly tree that fronted the property.

She never drove past without painful recall. *From one of those trees her father had been lynched.* She was going to buy those seven acres, she suddenly resolved. Have them cleaned up, planted with flowers. With fresh anguish she visualized her father on his haunches before the petunias, the pansies he loved so much. It would be a secret memorial to Papa.

She was recurrently haunted by the knowledge that she was doing nothing to track down and confirm her suspicions about Derek Slocum. Driving back to town she remembered a bit of conversation with Maisie last night. Maisie was dreading the chore of rearranging the Judge's storage closet. She had to move twenty-eight years of day books to higher shelves in order to accommodate files being brought over from the real-estate office. *"The Judge is paranoid about having everything right at his fingertips."*

What had Judge Slocum been doing on the day Tammy Lee Johnson was murdered? Was there some little detail on his day calendar that would lead her to evidence against Derek? She was convinced that Judge Slocum had sat there at the Judge's bench knowing it was his son who should be on trial. Iris thought she was out of her mind.

After dinner—while Jonnie and Katie listened to "Mr. Keen, Tracer of Lost Persons" in the meager comfort of the dining-room ceiling fan—Laura drove over to talk to Maisie. She found her sprawled on a glider on the front porch and sipping iced tea in the sweltering dusk. Everett was working late.

"I keep telling Everett we've got to have this porch screened in," she said, swatting at a persistent mosquito. "I tell you," she laughed, "he prays over every dollar we spend that isn't absolutely necessary. Can't he see we're moving into good times?"

"Because of the war," Laura said somberly. "Isn't it sad that we're benefitting because people are being killed in Europe?"

"Let's not be morbid tonight," Maisie scolded. "Every couple of years the Judge starts up with this 'rearranging the storage closet' routine, and I hate it. So tonight let's be lighthearted and cheerful because tomorrow I'll be cussing."

"Maisie, would you have the Judge's day book for 1924

291

in that storage closet?"

Maisie gazed at her in curiosity.

"Yeah, it should be there. Why?"

She hesitated.

"Maisie, can you get it out of the office for me? I just want to flip through the pages, then I'll give it right back."

"I can do that," Maisie conceded. "But why on earth do you want to see it?"

"If I find something there that confirms what I'm thinking, I'll tell you," Laura promised. She was conscious of the pounding of her heart. *Was she on the track of clearing Papa's name?*


Laura blamed the heat for her insomnia. She was impatient for the night to be past, for tomorrow to pass—until she was with Maisie and going through Judge Slocum's day book for the month of May, 1924. Lying awake in her bed, staring into the dark she relived that last day in the courthouse, the noises in the night that had sent Iris and her running from the house to the jail. That was sixteen years ago, and it was as real and as painful as if it were yesterday.

She awoke early, went into the office earlier than usual. Every hour of the day seemed to drag. Shortly past six Maisie phoned her at home.

"Come over tonight," she said briskly. "I've got your book."

Leaving Jonnie and Katie to clear away the dinner dishes, Laura left the house to drive over for her conference with Maisie. Everett was in the dining room digging into an oversized wedge of sweet potato pie and listening to a radio newscast. He gestured Laura to the table with a welcoming smile.

"Later," Maisie told him. "I want to show Laura the new dress I bought at lunch time."

In silent conspiracy the two women climbed the stairs

to the master bedroom. Maisie drew a manila envelope from a dresser drawer and handed it to Laura.

"Sit down and look at it now. I'm a little edgy about taking it out of the office."

"It won't take long." Laura reached with tense hands for the envelope.

"You're sure of the year?" Maisie asked.

"I'm positive.

Laura sat at the edge of the chintz-covered boudoir chair and opened the day book, praying she would find some important clue, fearing that she might not. Her eyes ran down the appointments on the first two pages, then with her throat tightening in anxiety, she flipped forward into May. Maisie went to the closet to bring out the new dress, pretending to be involved in removing a bit of lint.

In a rush of impatience Laura pushed ahead to mid-May, studied each page. Only seemingly innocuous business appointments, she tormented herself. *What had she expected to find in an attorney's day book?* Reluctant to abandon hope, she turned back to the day of Tammy Lee's murder. As before, she scanned the usual list of meetings with clients. But now she noticed a phone number scrawled in pencil at the top of a page. It was faded, barely visible. Before the number was the name "Way-cross." A town in south Georgia, Laura recognized.

"Maisie—" Her voice was distorted in her excitement. "May I make a phone call? It's long distance—I'll pay you back."

"Go ahead," Maisie said.

Laura dialed the long-distance operator and gave her the number. Her mind warned that the number might have changed hands a dozen times in the course of the years. Her heart pounded as she heard the ring at the other end. Then someone was responding.

"Good evening, Maynard Sanitarium."

"I'm sorry, I have the wrong number," Laura stammered and put the phone down. She sat motionless, her

293

face drained of color.

"Laura, are you all right?"

"Maisie, have you ever heard of a Maynard Sanitarium in Waycross, Georgia?"

"It's well known." But Maisie was suddenly alert.

"Has it been there a long time?"

"I know it's one of the sanitariums where Derek Slocum spent time when he was younger. Laura, what are you after?"

"I have something to tell you. I'd like Everett to hear it, too." No one could have better friends than Maisie and Everett.

*Judge Slocum called the Maynard Sanitarium the day Papa was arrested. To make arrangements for Derek's commitment.* Had Derek tried to rape Tammy Lee, panicked when she cried out, then murdered her? If his male nurse had not intervened, Derek would have raped *her.* But how was she to prove Derek Slocum had murdered Tammy Lee Johnson?

# Chapter 24

Iris glanced at the clock on her sitting-room mantel—between the gas mask and her tin hat—in the Dorchester suite. She was anxious to finish the letter to Laura and post it before she reported for her night shift at the canteen. The post was irregular these days, and she knew Laura worried about her.

She'd taken the night shift because she found it impossible to sleep once the antiaircraft guns and the planes and the bombs went into action. She'd be damned if she'd go down into the Dorchester basement to sleep on one of those cots set up for guests.

Up until a few days ago London had been spared direct enemy fire, though the suburbs had been badly hit. She worried about Noel at Cranford Hall, but Peter said the house remained untouched. *"And remember Iris, the shelter here is absolutely bombproof. It's only a matter of time, anyway, before we have to make peace with Hitler."*

Iris swore at the sound of the phone. God, she missed Edwina, but Edwina was in the age group called up for war work.

"Hello."

"Darling, why didn't you show up for Buffy's birthday luncheon at the Ritz?" Sandra reproached. "He looks so gorgeous in his uniform.

"I slept straight through till dinner," Iris confessed. "We had a rough night."

"I wish now I'd gone to the States with Diana," Sandra sighed. "These damn raids every day are driving me out of my mind. Do you know, yesterday the air-raid warning went off seven times? That's not including the night craziness. During the day one usually starts up when I'm in the midst of an important phone call."

"Very inconsiderate of them," Iris laughed. "But I have to dress and rush off to the canteen — "

"Cocktails tomorrow?" Sandra asked. Despite the air raids life went on in London.

"I'm not sure." Iris was unfamiliarly evasive.

"Iris, have you got some lover stashed away that I don't know about?"

"I'll tell you about that tomorrow," Iris said. "Last night I met this RAF officer on convalescent leave. He's from Liverpool and stationed at a fighter field near Dover. He's only twenty-six," she said self-consciously, "but so good looking. And *not* incapacitated," she anticipated Sandra.

"Darling, in the RAF they age six months for every mission. He's old enough for you." Her voice crackled with interest. "Promise to buzz me tomorrow and tell every fascinating detail."

"I worry a bit about Peter's finding out," Iris admitted.

"He's sitting out the war up there at Cranford Hall. How can he find out? Besides, he can't expect you to spend the best years of your life sleeping alone. It's your patriotic duty to keep the RAF in good spirits," she giggled.

"Talk to you tomorrow. 'Bye now."

Iris finished up the letter to Laura, turning down her sister's invitation to take Noel for the duration of the war. Peter kept saying that some MPs were arguing for an early peace with Hitler. Still, she was furious at Peter for refusing to allow her to send Noel to stay with Laura. Since June, the upper class in London had been sending their children out of the country.

*"Iris, I don't give a damn that Duff Cooper has sent his son to Canada!"* Alfred Duff Cooper was the Minister of Information. *"My son is English — he remains in this country. He'll be perfectly safe at Cranford Hall."*

Noel was his son, but she was Noel's mother. In the eyes of the Nazis Noel was Jewish. More than a year later she still remembered the terrified eyes of those seven little Austrian children. *People talked so much about a German invasion.* If it happened, Peter wouldn't be able to help Noel and her.

When the supply of petrol permitted, she took the train up to the country, to be met by Dobkins with the Rolls. She'd fuss over Noel for a day or two, avoiding Peter, who was in such a bastardly mood about the war, as much as possible, then return to London. Despite the ghastly raids these last few days, with no end in sight, she preferred being in town.

For a few moments she was immobile, her mind churning. Could she, in effect, kidnap Noel and go to the United States with him? Noel was British — a child born in England of an English father. If she applied for a British passport for Noel, word would filter through to Peter. He'd never let her take Noel.

Iris thrust her letter into an envelope, reached into the drawer of the writing table for a stamp. Stop thinking like this — she'd just end up with another rotten headache. Sandra was right — the only way to survive was to live day by day. Squadron Leader Randy Wickersham was dying to have a fling with her. Why not? Who was to say they'd be alive tomorrow?

For a moment she debated about changing from her canteen uniform of slacks and blouse into a smart summer suit. No. Every woman at the canteen didn't have to know she was seeing somebody when she went off duty.

She left the Dorchester and walked in the direction of her canteen. Taxis were almost impossible to find in London these days. She strode briskly into the darkness alleviated only by the spill of moonlight and the shifting fingers of the searchlights darting across the sky. The night was hot.

Even in the dark she was conscious of the destruction caused by the raids. Of the barricades and barbed wire. And every night the ghastly fires. It amazed her that so much of London remained standing.

At the canteen the conversation always focused on the raids. Why did *she* stay here, Iris probed while she walked through the night—subconsciously awaiting a fresh shriek of the air-raid sirens. Noel, she pinpointed. If the Germans did invade England, she meant to be with her son.

Two hours after she began her shift, Randy appeared, handsome and debonair in his RAF uniform. His left arm was still in a sling. Yesterday he'd stayed at the canteen until the 7 A.M. crew arrived. He'd taken her to breakfast at Claridge's. They'd talked—knees touching under the table—until the air-raid signal sent them down to the shelter. She'd fallen asleep on his shoulder. He had to waken her when the "All Clear" sounded. He said he'd be back tonight.

Twenty minutes later the sirens began to wail. The "red alert" light flashed, meaning "planes overhead." There was an orderly exodus towards the shelter.

"Let's not go to the shelter." Randy reached for her arm, his eyes amorous.

"You have a friend up there?" she laughed, pointing skyward.

"I have a hotel room very close by," he said. "And a bottle of decent champagne on the table by the bed." Now his eyes were serious. He seemed strangely vulnerable.

"All right," she agreed after a moment. In some weird fashion, she thought, it was fitting that she make love with this RAF pilot—still carrying the wounds of war—while British antiaircraft guns cracked away at the Luftwaffe droning overhead.

Hand in hand, Iris and Randy hurried into the night. A red glow in the sky told them an incendiary had set off at least one fire already somewhere near the docks. Heavy explosions wracked the East End as the Luftwaffe dropped their bombs.

"The Germans are getting desperate," Randy said while he drew her into the tiny lobby of his hotel. "I figure there must be about a hundred planes up there."

"I can tell the difference now between theirs and ours,"

Iris said with an air of small triumph. "Their engines have a kind of uneven beat. Ours are even.

The desk clerk had gone to the shelter. The elevator was unmanned.

"How far up?" Iris asked.

"Three flights," he soothed. His uninjured arm closed in about her waist.

Randy's room was modestly furnished, neat, and clean. On the night table sat a bottle of champagne and two stemmed glasses.

"I'm a bit awkward with this bum arm," he apologized, freeing himself of the sling and preparing to remove his jacket. "I'm afraid the champagne isn't chilled."

"Neither am I," Iris laughed. At this moment—with bombs and incendiaries raining down from the sky and the antiaircraft guns in action—it was as though Randy and she were alone on earth. "I'll pour," she offered. "If you can get out the cork."

"You'll have to help," he warned.

But before they could approach the champagne, Randy had drawn her to him with his working arm. His mouth reached for hers with an impatience matching her own. Without releasing her mouth he prodded her backward until she felt the edge of the bed against her legs.

"Oh God, you taste good!" He allowed his fingers to trace the outline of her mouth.

"There's lots more of me to taste," she taunted in sudden impatience. *It had been so long since she felt this way.*

"You know what I hate most about this war?" He reached now to unbutton his jacket. "The way the women all run around in pants. I like to see them in skirts, with plenty of leg showing. I want to see all of you," he said with sudden intensity. "This minute."

In a rush of heat they stripped to skin, then swayed together, for a few moments content with erotic closeness.

"If I had to get shot up, thank God it was only my arm," he chuckled and pushed her playfully across the bed.

"Randy, hurry," she coaxed, reaching to touch him. She

299

hadn't felt this crazy in a long time.

"Usually women complain about too much hurry," he scolded, but he was pleased.

Her hands closed in about his shoulders, her body straining to meet him. She was conscious only of the need to draw him within her, to touch, to explode in dizzying excitement.

"Oh, baby, baby," he groaned, and thrust with an urgency that matched her own.

Later, much later, they sprawled against the pillows and sipped the tepid champagne. One of his legs rested across hers.

"How many missions have you flown?" Iris asked, remembering Sandra's comment about missions and age.

"Forty-eight," he said. "I've been shot down twice. Once twenty miles at sea. I'm a cat," he mused. "I have nine lives. Seven to go."

"Let's go up on the roof," Iris said on impulse. "I want to see what it's like up there in the midst of a raid." The "All Clear" still had not gone off.

"You're a cat, too?"

"Let's find out." She left the bed and began to dress, feeling oddly exhilarated at the prospect of defying death.

A few minutes later they stood alone on the roof while dozens of searchlights darted about the sky, vying with the splash of stars. Perhaps a dozen incendiary bombs — some with green, some with whitish flames — flared in the distance. No roof watcher on duty.

"It's the Fourth of July in the States!" Iris laughed and then clutched at Randy as a bomb hit close by.

"We're up there, too, along with the Boche raiders," Randy said softly. "I can hear our engines."

"Randy, when do you have to go back on duty?" All at once Iris didn't want to think about Randy up there in what he called his "vicious little hurricane."

"I have another ten days," he told her. A hand at her breast. "Two hundred and forty hours."

"We'll spend them together," she promised. "Every minute. At my suite at the Dorchester," she stipulated with a hint of laughter. "I'm a woman who likes to be comfortable."

"Have you ever made love on the roof of a hotel in the midst of a raid?" he asked, drawing her close.

"Not until now," she conceded, ignoring the whistling scream of a bomb uncomfortably close.

"Since you're a woman who likes to be comfortable," he mocked, "I'll lend you my jacket for a pillow."

Oblivious to descending bombs, the fire engines shrieking in the distance, Randy drew her down with him to their improvised bed, folded over his jacket and slid it beneath her head. Tonight's air raid became a symphonic background for their lovemaking.

As Iris had promised Randy, she took ten days' leave from the canteen. They spent every moment together. Day and night they ignored the air raids. They went to the theater, saw Sadlers Wells's *Sleeping Beauty* with Margot Fonteyn, went to the cinema to see a rerun of *Gone With the Wind*.

One afternoon Iris helped Randy choose gifts for his family at Selfridge's, the huge plate-glass windows shattered. She tried to imagine what his family was like. They knew he was convalescing in London. Did they wonder that he didn't come home to Liverpool? Or did they understand?

Iris and Randy paused for meals at erratic intervals. Claridge's was busy as ever at luncheon, the Ritz still a favorite for drinks. On two evenings they had dinner at the Dorchester — when they were impatient to return to their bedroom upstairs.

Occasionally they paused to listen for a few somber moments to the wireless. On the night before Randy had to report for duty Iris had a sudden disconcerting suspicion that Randy and she were being followed.

A middle-aged man in a bowler had sat across from

301

them at Myers earlier in the day while they had excellent coffee—though no cream—and delicious pastry. Now the same man sat two tables away from them at L'Escargot and pretended to be interested in his glass of wine. The restaurant had few diners and he stood out.

Iris suspected that Peter had hired this grubby little detective and she said nothing to Randy. She'd worried about Peter's finding out—but why should it make any difference? Peter and she had no marriage anymore.

Did Peter think he could divorce her? He hadn't touched her since Noel was born—but there were all those ugly times when he had physically abused her. Dr. Rathbone hadn't believed her stories about falling down the stairs the time he taped up her cracked rib, nor the time she said she'd tripped in the dark and fractured her wrist. He knew.

She'd see Randy off tomorrow at Victoria Station, and then she'd go up to Cranford Hall and warn Peter never to have her followed again.


Iris sat on the train en route to Cranford Hall and stared at the passing scenery without seeing the craters made by German bombs, the houses reduced to rubble, trees scorched from incendiaries. She felt outraged that she had been followed. It was a kind of violation.

Already the days with Randy seemed unreal, part of a fantasy. This morning he had kissed her passionately in Victoria Station and promised to write. She suspected he wouldn't. They'd shared his convalescent leave as though they were two alone in the world; but if he were lucky enough to come back home, he'd return to his family in Liverpool and marry some pretty, leggy young girl.

She wasn't going to worry about Peter trying to divorce her. He wouldn't dare—not when she got through talking with him. But she would not be followed around the way Randy and she had been trailed by the stupid detective.

When the train pulled into the station in the sunny

302

afternoon, she saw Dobkins sitting behind the wheel of the Rolls. When he saw her, he hurried from the car to open the door. There was a sadness about him these last two years. It disturbed Dobkins that Peter was so ridiculously pro-German, she thought in sympathy.

"His lordship is pheasant shooting," Dobkins reported while they drove away from the station, not quite muffling his sense of disapproval. "The season has begun."

Who but Peter would go pheasant shooting when the country was under attack, Iris asked herself in irritation.

"And Noel?" she asked, all at once eager to swoop her son up in her arms.

"He's in a fine fettle." A hint of affection seeped into Dobkins's usually impassive voice. "Growing like a weed, he is."

"There's been no trouble at Cranford Hall from the bombs?" she asked after a moment.

"The left wing was damaged last week, but everyone was safe in the shelter. We've had some bad moments," he conceded after a brief pause. "But we can put up with all of that so long as the Germans don't invade." As Hitler was constantly threatening.

At Cranford Hall Iris lingered briefly in her suite, then went to the nursery She was disappointed that Noel was napping. Of course, Nanny Worth wouldn't allow him to be disturbed. She left the nursery wing of the house to return to her own rooms. Approaching Peter's quarters, she heard him shouting into the phone.

"I don't care that Savile Row is battered to bits from the bombs! When I order a suit to be made up for me, I expect delivery as promised! You'll see no more business from me!"

Iris debated for an instant, then knocked at Peter's door.

"Come in," he yelled.

Iris opened the door and walked into the sitting room. Peter was sprawled in his leather armchair with the morning's newspaper on the floor at his feet.

"My, you're in a foul mood." Maybe she ought to wait

until later.

"Damn it, my tailor's two weeks late with the suit I ordered. The phone's out in my shoe shop on Regent Street. There's a rotten chill in the air already, and we're running into a shortage of coal because of the blasted war."

"We can't expect things to be normal." This wasn't the moment to confront Peter about the detective. "A lot of places in London are without electricity, water, and telephones. Sandra tells me Claridge's is rationing bath water. She says she swears at the Nazis every time she gets into the tub."

"Don't blame the Nazis," Peter shot back. His eyes vindictive. "Blame Churchill for dragging us into this mess."

"Chamberlain declared war against Germany," Iris reminded. "Not Churchill." Peter hated Churchill because he'd warned against the Nazis before anybody else.

"It's the fault of the bloody Jews!" Peter shouted. "They're the bastards to blame for what's happening to this country!"

"Peter, stop being paranoid," she said through clenched teeth. She thought about Ania Fischbein at the castle near Vienna. Was Ania still alive? She thought about those seven little kids Doris and she had smuggled out of Austria. She thought about Papa, who'd died because a lynch mob thought like Hitler. "Hitler started this war." She struggled to keep her voice even. "Hitler keeps it going!"

"It's the Jews, like Mosley said!" Peter leaped to his feet, his face flushed a dark red. "We should have shipped them off to Africa or somewhere! Hitler's right. They're trying to take over the world!"

"How dare you talk or even think like that!" Pale, trembling with rage, Iris took a step towards him. "I'm Jewish, Peter. Your wife is Jewish," she taunted him. Watching with defiant satisfaction while his mind assimilated this. "Your son is half Jewish."

"You bitch—" His voice was a weird shriek. His eyes unnaturally bright. "I'll kill you for this!"

Instinctively she stepped back as Peter lunged towards

304

her. But all at once he seemed immobilized. Then his shoulders jerked convulsively and he fell to the floor at her feet.

"Peter?" She gazed at him in disbelief for one frozen moment. "Peter?" Now she darted to the door and called down the hall.

"Dobkins! Dobkins, phone for Dr. Rathbone!"


In the damp chill of the October dusk Iris, in one of her elegant black frocks by Molyneux and her pearls, stood with Peter's two daughters and his son by his first wife in his London hospital room. Peter lay motionless on the bed, under heavy sedation. The head of his team of doctors had just informed them of his condition and prognosis.

"He remains paralyzed from the neck down. He's unable to speak. We're concerned that he is not responding to treatment," the doctor acknowledged. "On the other hand, he's in no immediate danger of losing his grip on life."

Iris frowned as Roland began to ask a series of questions of the doctor. She was fearful in Peter's presence, as though at any moment he might open his eyes and glare accusingly at her. What would happen when he regained his power of speech—or was able to write notes? He would blame her for his having the stroke. It wasn't her fault—he goaded her into saying those things. *All true.* If he hadn't had the stroke, he might have killed her.

"There's nothing we can do?" Peter's daughter Melinda brought Iris back to the present. "Just stand by and wait?"

"We'll watch him closely," the doctor said. "But we have little hope of any substantial recovery."

Iris returned immediately to Cranford Hall. Noel was too young to be told about his father's illness, yet she had an unexpected compulsion to be with him. It wasn't like Jonnie and Katie when Bernie died, she reminded herself. They loved their father. Peter fussed over Noel at convenient intervals—he didn't share his younger son's life. Noel would scarcely be aware of Peter's absence from the house.

Two days later Roland appeared at Cranford Hall. Obviously, his father could no longer handle his financial affairs, he pointed out. Long ago Peter had made provisions for any such occurrence. Roland would take over the reins of his father's affairs. He would pay all the bills, as his father had done in the past, and make any necessary decisions about investments.

"Life will continue as usual," Roland told Iris, but she was aware of a speculative glint in his eyes. Was he already thinking ahead to his father's death? Peter must have included Noel and her in his will. The title, of course, would go to his older son—but Noel and she would share in the estate. "We hope, of course," he said with a perfunctory smile, "that Father will gradually improve to the point where he can at least share in these duties."

"Of course." Iris suppressed a smile. Roland was such a stuffed shirt, but he wasn't above undressing his stepmother with his eyes. "I'll go into London once a week to visit him and talk with his doctors." Let Roland remember that she was Peter's wife. But the prospect of walking into that hospital room and facing Peter with his faculties restored unnerved her.

*How long had that bastardly detective been following Randy and her? Had he turned over his reports to Roland?*

# Chapter 25

Laura was elated when the Stephens Industries employees began to show interest in her houses. She arranged a "house showing weekend," with Hunter Realty picking up the tab for a night at the Magnolia Hotel plus breakfast at the hotel restaurant, after which she conducted a tour of her properties.

By the end of the weekend she held binders on six of the houses. Five other couples were dickering over prices. She was confident these would be eventual sales. The window dressing that she had added — attractive exterior paint jobs, colorful shutters, foundation plantings — had paid off handsomely.

On Monday she made a series of phone calls to Pittsburgh, set up another "house showing weekend." With the first buyers about to apply to local banks for mortgages, she knew Magnolia realtors, and particularly the Slocums, would rush into the market. She countered by offering the Stephens Industries employees "rental with option to buy" deals.

When Roosevelt was elected for an unprecedented third term, and the economy was on an upward spiral, Laura geared herself for further expansion. She was determined to plunge most of the funds coming in from the house sales back into real estate. Already prices were rising.

Maisie, and particularly Everett, had become what she called her Board of Directors.

"Laura, every morning you take yourself over to the county recorder's office," he instructed. "Check out which properties have a default notice." Despite the improvement in business conditions there were always some people on the point of losing their houses. "Make a list of the properties in foreclosure, go over and take a look. If what you see on the outside appears interesting, go knock on the door and talk to them. It's the Donnell farm situation all over again. I'm sure Slocum's got a network of folks in the banks who keep him posted. You beat him to the draw."

Laura discovered herself in competition with the Slocum combine, but frequently she was able to buy before they approached. Maisie laughingly attributed this to her "fast-moving Yankee attack." She relished beating out the Judge, even while she was nervous about her fast-diminishing liquid capital.

"Go to the banks, Laura," Everett encouraged. "They'll give you mortgage money. With your holdings you're a good risk. Grab the property while it's available. Foreclosures will soon be nonexistent."

But moving into 1941, Laura was uneasy at the size of the mortgage payments due each month. She waited anxiously for closings that would replenish her funds. Her law practice was forgotten in her absorption with real estate. On paper she was already a wealthy woman.

She sensed a new respect for her among the local townspeople. Little remained secret among the middle- and upper-class residents of Magnolia, Georgia. Though Judge Slocum, Laura tormented herself at regular intervals, had managed to hide the truth about the murder of Tammy Lee Johnson. She was now totally convinced that Derek had killed Tammy Lee.

She worried constantly about Iris, though Iris insisted she was safe — she was spending most of her time now at Cranford Hall, which had not been touched by German bombs except for one minor incident.

*"Hitler keeps announcing his invasion dates, but he never seems to make it. At any rate, considering Peter's condition, I couldn't leave for New York even if I wanted to. I wouldn't trust his older son to keep me in funds if I were out of sight. Roland's managing the estate now — and according to the doctors this could*

go on for years. I was in London yesterday, picked up a smart tweed suit at Molyneux's salon on Grosvenor Square. Another is en route to you—I hope it arrives in time for you to wear it this season." Transatlantic mail was becoming unpredictable.

It amazed Laura that Iris could be so casual about the war. Every night that she could arrange to be home in time she listened to Edward R. Murrow, broadcasting live from London with a background of air-raid sirens, the shriek of German bombs and the rumble of British antiaircraft fire. *Why wouldn't Iris come home?*

Katie was unhappy that her teacher was leaving at the end of the term to be married. She was convinced she would hate the replacement.

"Katie, give the new teacher a chance," Laura scolded tenderly. "You'll probably like her once you get to know her."

"It's not a 'her.' " Katie was grim. "It's a 'him.' "

"Then give him a chance," Laura insisted. Her small daughter could be so intense, shifting moods with lightning speed.

At the end of the first day of the new school term in early February Katie came home to report that her new teacher looked "just like Tyrone Power."

"Only Mr. Weinberg has light hair," Katie said ebulliently. "I can forgive him for that." Katie had just seen Tyrone Power in *Zorro*.

At a dinner party at the home of Cecile and Barry Berger two months later, Laura met Katie's new teacher.

"A year and a half in Atlanta was all Phil could take," Cecile joshed while the slender, handsome young man gazed down at Laura. "Excuse me, new arrivals—" She walked to the foyer.

"My daughter is in your class," Laura told him. Until Cecile introduced them, she had not realized Katie's teacher was Adele Weinberg's son. *Mrs. Tannenbaum's grandson.*

"You're Katie's mother?" Phillip asked in astonishment. "You look far too young." He studied her face. "But I can see the resemblance now. Same beautiful features. Same expressive eyes."

"Katie was so upset at getting a new teacher in the middle of the year, but you won her over the first day." Laura was disconcerted by his obvious admiration. Now she remembered seeing him with his grandmother at the temple three years ago.

"It's a pleasure to have Katie in my class." His smile was mesmerizing. "I love teaching. It's what I've wanted to do since I was ten. For a while I allowed myself to be derailed. As soon as I heard there was an opening at the school, I applied. I missed Magnolia." His voice was a caress. She, too, had missed Magnolia, Laura remembered nostalgically. "I hated banking," he grunted in distaste.

"Magnolia's gain," Laura said while the maid offered them tiny wedges of caviar pie. Born and raised in Boston, Cecile adored offering her guests sophisticated fare. "From what Katie tells me, I know you're a dedicated teacher."

Laura was pleased that she was seated next to Phillip at dinner. She enjoyed his light witty conversation. She had not laughed like this for years. It was incredible that he was Mrs. Tannenbaum's grandson.

Gradually, as often happened during these times, conversation became more somber, focusing on the war.

Laura talked about Iris, dividing her time between London and a country house in Kent. Refusing to leave England despite the constant German raids. In an effort to brighten the mood she recalled the British cartoons that poked fun at those Britons who abandoned their posts over the weekends.

"Iris says the heaviest attacks are always over weekends because Hitler knows how the British cherish these. He hopes the British weekend will bring down the Empire."

"Your sister must be devoted to her husband to insist on remaining in England," Phillip said quietly to Laura.

"She has a son who's almost three. I'm hoping her

310

concern for Noel will bring her home."

"You don't have a Southern accent," Phillip pinpointed. "Where are you from?"

"Originally a small town in South Carolina." She parroted the familiar story. Only in the last few months had she felt truly safe from exposure. "But I lived in New York from the time I was fifteen until I came here close to four years ago." She was uncomfortably conscious of being drawn to Phillip. As he was to her. *This was ridiculous.* She was eight or nine years older than he.

"The Community Theater is giving a production of *The Late Christopher Bean* next weekend. May I take you to see it?" She realized he knew she was a widow. "We could have dinner first—"

"I'm really awfully busy," she stammered.

"If the British can take off their weekends in the midst of the war," he teased, "surely you can take off a few hours while we're still at peace."

"Do you expect that we'll get into the war?" She recalled Cecile saying the night she first saw Phillip that he had wanted to fight in Spain. Bernie, too, had been emotionally involved in the Loyalists' fight to keep their country a democracy. She had suspected that if Bernie had been single, he would have joined the Abraham Lincoln Brigade. "Roosevelt keeps telling American parents 'Your boys are not going to be sent into any foreign wars.' "

"Famous last words," Phillip said. His eyes troubled. "Eventually we'll have to get into it."


Laura was astonished at the way Phil moved into their lives. First she was drafted as Katie's mother to participate in the extracurricular activities he fostered. She had enormous respect for his warmth and imagination, and Katie took such pride in her participation that she couldn't refuse him. Then he infiltrated her personal life.

He appeared on a balmy Saturday afternoon, when

Jonnie and Katie were off with their respective friends, to take her on a picnic on the shore of a nearby pond. He drove up to Atlanta to buy theater tickets for the road company of a Broadway play that he was confident she would enjoy. Soon he was coming to the house for dinner once or twice a week, taking her to the movies over protests that she should be working.

"I can't believe that a slip of a girl like you is an important real-estate operator," he teased. "You belong on a college campus."

"This slip of a girl is a widow with two children to support," she laughed. Subconsciously she wished that Phil were ten years older. She must never allow herself to forget the years between them.

Phil and she were kindred spirits, she told herself. He could talk to her the way he couldn't talk at home. Like his father must have been, he was intense and compassionate, fighting against the iron will of his grandmother. His mother and grandmother couldn't understand that he could find joy in teaching. They couldn't understand his tossing aside a financially promising career for the limited salary of a school teacher.

Katie was delighted that Phil was so often at the house. She was endearingly possessive. After an initial wariness, Jonnie accepted Phil as part of their lives. He was Katie's teacher and Mom's friend.

Phil made her feel young again, Laura analyzed. She was almost thirty-three years old, but alone with Phil she felt like twenty.

She knew Phil had been hurt when his father walked away from his family. She sensed he understood his grandmother had been responsible. On the first Sunday of every month, Phil explained, he had to be by his telephone during the evening hours; this was when his father called.

Laura tried to ignore the glow in Phil's eyes that told her he regarded her as more than a friend. He was afraid to push too far. At tenuous moments when he appeared on the verge of declaring his true emotions, she managed a light jest about his youth. He automatically switched to a safer topic. Each time she told herself she should be relieved. Why did she feel disappointment?

How could she consider anything deeper than friendship between Phil and herself? She was a woman with two children — one already a teenager. Phil was twenty-four.

When she was serving with Cecile at a temple bake sale, Cecile pointed out a pretty young visitor from nearby Atlanta, who had been guest of honor at a series of parties during the past week. The war had not stopped the rounds of parties that was the birthright of every Southern girl and woman of comfortable circumstances.

"Mrs. Tannenbaum and Adele are trying like mad to bring Phil and her together," Cecile confided. "Wouldn't you think they'd know by now that they can't control his life?" There was an oddly questioning glint in her eyes.

"She's lovely," Laura admitted and immediately looked away from the Atlanta visitor. It was unnerving to think of Phil moving out of her life.

"They figure if he's married, he won't be drafted," Cecile guessed. The first peacetime draft had gone into effect last September. It frightened Laura to think of Phil in uniform. "Also, Flora comes from a well-connected family," Cecile drawled. "That would suit Madame Tannenbaum."

"Do you suppose Phil's being a teacher will keep him from being drafted?" Laura tried to sound casual.

"With his grandmother's influence in this town, I'd count on his being safe from a draft call." Cecile chuckled. "I can't imagine our local draft board tangling with the old lady."


Laura was alert to the increasing activity at the cotton mills, with the war orders piling up. Instinct told her that farm workers would soon be deserting the outlying farms for more lucrative jobs in the mills. Only one of the seven mills in town provided houses for their workers. The other workers would need living quarters.

Laura drove endlessly about the area in search of properties that she might buy up and rent out at affordable prices. The search seemed futile. With school closed for the summer Phil appointed himself her chauffeur. He seemed fascinated by the real-estate field, asked her endless questions.

"One of these days I'd like to see houses built here in town for the elderly and the handicapped," he said zealously, and Laura felt a surge of tenderness. In so many ways Phil was like Bernie in the first years of their marriage. "You know how they get stuck away in cheap rooming houses."

Laura's mind charged into action.

"Apartments might be more practical. They would be much less expensive but could be comfortable. Not quite like Regency Court," she conceded humorously. The one apartment house in Magnolia was an elegant red-brick structure catering to those with substantial incomes.

"Why not build an apartment house for new workers?" Phil challenged. "You know there'll be a market."

"The way prices are going up, that would cost a fortune," she protested. Yet the possibility was intriguing. She visualized an unpretentious but pleasant development — something Magnolia had never seen. "Maybe I can find some unoccupied building that could be converted into apartments." Excitement took root in her. "Phil, a conversion! Not only would it be less expensive, but it would take far less time than starting from scratch."

"All right, let's scout for a building." Phil's enthusiasm matched her own. "I have time on my hands."

Day after day Laura and Phil explored the area they'd settled on as being suitable. Their frustration soared. Every manufacturing facility that had been closed down during the Depression years was being reactivated. Magnolia was booming.

Laura was fearful of starting a full-scale building project in the face of escalating costs. She might start a building next month and find costs doubling before it was completed. Just when she was at the point of abandoning the contemplated venture, Phil phoned late on an August night.

"Laura, I'm driving over—I think I have a lead for you on a terrific piece of property."

"Something we've missed?" They'd covered every inch of this area.

"A deal that's just fallen through for somebody else. I'll be there in ten minutes."

Laura and Phil sat on the white wicker sofa on the front porch in the sticky hot night, with a pitcher of iced tea handy for refills, and talked in muted tones. The air was sweet with the scent of honeysuckle. The porch light was off lest it draw mosquitos.

"I heard my mother and grandmother talking with their lawyer," Phil explained. "Grandma owns the big warehouse at the south edge of town—you know, the one that was supposed to become a shirt factory. The deal fell through. The bank won't give the shirt manufacturers the money. Grandma's lawyer, Barry Berger, suggested he talk to the Slocums about a possible sale."

"I'll talk to Barry first thing in the morning." Laura was elated. "I don't suppose you know how much your grandmother was offered for the warehouse?"

"I'll find out at breakfast," Phil grinned. "I'll call you right away."

"You're such a good friend," she said softly.

"I'd like to be a lot more than that." He reached for her hand. The atmosphere was suddenly electric. "Laura, when are you going to stop holding me off?"

"Phil, I'm so much older than you," she stammered. Why couldn't they go on the way they were? Comfortable and safe.

"What's a few years one way or another?" He reached

315

to pull her close. "I knew I loved you the first time I saw you at the temple over three years ago."

"We're out of our minds," she protested as his mouth reached for hers.

"Sssh," he ordered and kissed her. At first tenderly, then with passion.

"I didn't mean for this to happen," she whispered. *It had been so long since she had felt this way.* She had been sure that part of her life was over.

"It had to happen. Laura, we're so right together."

"But I'm so much older than you—" How could she feel this way about Phil after being married to Bernie for eleven years? What about Jonnie and Katie? Would they be upset? The children came first.

"You'll stop having birthdays right now," he ordered. "I'll catch up with you soon enough." In the spill of moonlight Laura saw the aura of exhilaration that radiated from him.

"Phil, I don't know—" Yet her eyes pleaded for reassurance.

"I want to spend the rest of my life with you," he said quietly. "I want to help you bring up Katie and Jonnie."

"You know so little about me—" He'd been six years old when Papa died.

"I'll learn through the years," he promised with a flicker of humor, and then moved suddenly away because a car was turning into the driveway of the house next door. "I'd better get the hell out of here before we shock the neighbors."

Laura lay sleepless far into the night. She had built her life around Jonnie and Katie and the business. She had convinced herself she needed nothing else—until Phil came back to Magnolia.

Did people here in town know she had been seeing him? She searched her mind. Usually they were off somewhere away from their own social circles. Except for the time he'd taken her to the Community Theater. And once they'd run into Cecile and Barry coming out of the movies. Maisie and Everett knew. She'd taken Phil to dinner there one night. But neither Cecile and Barry nor Maisie and Everett would have gone to tell Phil's mother and grandmother that Phil was seeing her beyond school activities. Wouldn't that rock Mrs. Tannenbaum and Adele?

In a spurt of restlessness she left her bed and went out to the kitchen for a glass of lemonade. It was absurd to be upset because Phil was Mrs. Tannenbaum's grandson. That nasty old woman had nothing to do with how they felt about each other.


Laura debated about phoning Barry at home so early in the morning. But it was important to catch him before he talked to the Slocums about the warehouse. *Call now.*

"Cecile, I'm sorry to be buzzing you so early," she apologized, "but this is business. May I talk to Barry?"

"He's just finishing breakfast. Hang on, Laura."

Barry listened to her offer for the warehouse and chuckled.

"Things get around this town fast." He probably suspected Phil had told her. "I'm sure we've got a deal as long as you'll match the other offer." He hesitated. "Depending, of course, that there's no mortgage problem."

"I'm buying for cash," Laura told him. It would be tight; but if she delayed to put through a mortgage, something might go wrong. "I'll be ready to close as soon as I can get title insurance."

"Great," Barry approved. But his curiosity seeped through. "What are you planning on doing with that old warehouse? Not going into manufacturing, are you?"

"You'll see," she laughed. "I'll drop by your office this morning with a check and to sign the contract. Good enough?"

"Good enough."

Two weeks later Laura was at a conference table in Barry Berger's office for the closing. She was grateful that

317

Mrs. Tannenbaum wasn't there in person. She still felt a strong hostility on those rare occasions when she encountered Mrs. Tannenbaum, though they'd never exchanged a word.

Laura knew it was a big gamble to put most of her liquid capital into an outright purchase of the warehouse. She was depending upon a first mortgage at the bank to make the extensive renovations that would convert the property into apartments. Without that mortgage she'd be in serious trouble.

That same afternoon she sat down with Phil in her office, after ordering her newly hired secretary to hold all calls, to work out the costs of the renovations along with estimates of the projected rentals. Tonight they would go over to discuss the figures with Everett. He was the accountant for two local builders—he was familiar with the cost of labor and materials. Tomorrow she would approach a bank for a first mortgage.

The following morning she sat across the desk from Bill Carlton, president of Third National Bank, and asked for a mortgage on the warehouse. Third National held the mortgages on the cluster of houses she had not yet sold.

"Laura, you're taking on a whale of a deal," he said cautiously.

"I own the property outright," she pointed out. "The rental potential as apartments is terrific."

"Provided this boom doesn't bottom out," he reminded. "If Hitler makes peace in Europe, the economy could go into a tailspin."

"Peace, Bill?" Laura scoffed. "When Germany's just invaded Russia?"

"You're asking for a lot of money, Laura." He shuffled some papers on his desk.

"Do you realize what that property will be worth when I finish the renovations?" she challenged. But her initial confidence was eroding. *Was Bill Carlton turning her down?*

"It won't be worth a damn if you can't rent it," he said

bluntly.

"I steer all my potential buyers to you," she reminded. True. "I've brought a lot of business into this bank."

"We've been badly hurt in the past. We have to remember how we sat with properties through the thirties." He squinted in thought. "I figure we can work out a deal, Laura." His smile, meant to be reassuring, put her on guard. Bill Carlton had a reputation for being shrewd. "We'll advance you the money you want. But you'll have to put up all your properties—including your own house," he stipulated, "as collateral."

Warning signals shot up in her mind. "That's a lot of collateral."

"That's it," Bill said briskly. "Take it or leave it."

She hesitated for only a split second.

"I'll take it."

## Chapter 26

Iris subconsciously leaned towards the wireless as the announcer reported on the meeting between Churchill and President Roosevelt, somewhere on the high seas.

"Damn!" She scowled at the shrill ring of the telephone, reached to pick it up with one hand and switched off the wireless with the other.

"Hello."

"Elvira here," Roland's wife announced crisply. "Roland and I would like to run up tomorrow morning for a chat. Will you be home?"

"I will now." Iris strained to be polite. "Will you arrive in time for luncheon?"

"Earlier," Elvira said. "And don't bother with luncheon, we won't be staying."

Why the devil were Elvira and Roland coming up tomorrow morning? Iris leaned back in her chair and tried to ferret out the reason for their coming to Cranford Hall. Had Peter recovered his speech, and they were coming here to confront her? She wasn't responsible for Peter's stroke—it was his rotten temper getting the best of him.

Another thought struck her. Had Peter died? No. She was Peter's wife. The hospital would have called *her*. Restless, with nothing to do but wait till they arrived, she reached for the phone and called Sandra in London where she and Elliot were still in residence at the Claridge. The two women talked for almost an hour over a range of subjects—clothes, increasingly difficult to find; the theater, such as it was; and, inevitably, about the war.

After they rang off Iris spent an hour with Noel in the nursery—until Nanny Worth decided it was time for his supper. With nothing else to do she returned to her own rooms and fretted over the arrival in the morning of Roland and Elvira. There was something ominous, she warned herself. They would not make the long drive up to the house just to pass the time of day.

Over dinner on a tray in her sitting room, she listened to the news on the wireless again. Though newscasters seemed to be elated about the Atlantic Charter, she sensed a covert disappointment that Roosevelt hadn't declared war against Germany. Didn't they understand the president couldn't do that on his own?

The night was uneventful. No raids disturbed her slumber, yet sleep was elusive. These past weeks she had seriously considered taking Noel and going back to New York. It wasn't unnatural to want to see her son out of England—many British children had been sent to America. But as always there was the question of money; she didn't trust Roland to send her funds if she were out of the country.

Earlier than normal she was dressed and listening for the sounds of a car coming up the driveway. Had Roland decided his father should be sent up here with a nurse rather than to remain in the hospital? God, how she'd hate that!

At a few minutes past ten Iris heard a car pull up before the house. Grim but determined to appear casual she hurried downstairs. Collins was at the door with Roland and Elvira.

"Good morning." Iris managed a polite, though chilly smile. "Collins, will you bring us coffee in the library, please."

"No coffee," Roland dismissed this. "Let's just go into the library."

"No coffee," Iris repeated to Collins. Roland's hostility proved that something *was* up. "Have you seen your father this morning?" she asked Roland while they walked

321

down the long hall to the library.

"I saw him yesterday morning." There was a faint reproof in his voice. Roland saw Peter every day. Iris made it clear that she drove into London once a week to visit Peter in the hospital. She hated the few minutes she spent in his room. Usually she contrived to be busy arranging flowers at his bedside. There was no communication with him. He lay immobile, seeming to be unaware of her presence, his eyes expressionless. "I'll be at the hospital this evening," she said a trifle defensively.

"Roland, close the door," Elvira told him. "The servants don't have to hear."

"Don't have to hear what?" Iris asked with an air of amusement.

"About your affair with the British flyer," Roland shot back. So the little man with the bowler was in his employ. "It was outrageous. But that's beside the point now." He smiled maliciously.

"Your father is hardly in a position to hear your ugly reports." Why bother to deny it at this point? What she'd shared with Randy had been sweet and exciting. She had not received as much as a postcard from him since he rejoined his unit nor had she expected to hear. "And that's all you have — some notes from a sleazy detective." That stupid little man had never seen Randy and her making love — what could he prove?

"That doesn't concern us any longer. But this does." Roland pulled an envelope from his jacket pocket. "It's a letter from an important law firm in New York City. My father told me the amusing story of your so-called marriage." *What did he mean, so-called marriage?* "How the so-called captain of a cruise ship to Havana performed a marriage ceremony. We've checked the records. The man was not the captain. The real ship's captain was sleeping off a drunk in his cabin that night. Nor was the marriage ever recorded. Therefore you are not Lady Cranford. Nor does your son bear the Cranford name." His eyes glittered in triumph.

"You are out of your mind!" Iris was dizzy with shock. "Your father and I were legally married!" This was a weird nightmare. "Everybody in London knows that!"

"You are not my father's wife. These papers prove it. Show them to your attorney," he ordered, extending the envelope. Iris made no move to take it. He dropped it onto a table. "You will have one week to vacate this property. Two weeks to clear out of the suite at the Dorchester. Orders will be left at the hospital that you are not to see my father."

Iris's mind careened backward in time. She remembered Mrs. Tannenbaum standing in the living room of the little house in Magnolia ordering Laura and her out of town. *Nobody wants you here.* But times had changed. Nobody pushed Iris around anymore.

"My barrister will be contacting you shortly." She managed an air of faint amusement. "I'm your father's wife. I'm Lady Cranford. Noel is his son. Noel Cranford. Now will you please leave *my* house?"


Iris stood at the window of the bookshelf-lined law office and stared down at the Londoners en route to their flats or houses after the day's work. Sandra sat on the sofa while her husband—a barrister before joining the War Department—studied the papers Roland had left with Iris.

"Elliot, what is taking you so long?" Sandra scolded while her eyes moved sympathetically to Iris.

"This is a serious matter, Sandra. Come sit down, Iris. I have to ask you some questions."

Iris crossed to the chair at his right and sat down. As soon as Roland and Elvira had left Cranford Hall, she had phoned Sandra in panic. Sir Elliot Forbes had a reputation for being a wily barrister. Thank God, he'd agreed to meet with her right away.

Straining for patience she replied to Elliot's flood of questions.

"Everybody in London knows I'm Peter's wife," she burst out in exasperation as Elliot continued the seemingly endless questioning. "How can Roland and his sisters get away with this?" Throwing her out on the street with Noel. Cutting her out of Peter's will when he died.

"We need some blackmail." Elliot was blunt. "Peter has a reputation around town for being something of an odd duck. We need something to fight against what appears to be a rather unfortunate situation from your point of view. I know he was too chummy with the Nazis—" He squinted in thought. "But I don't think that's strong enough."

"You can tell Roland that I will go to all the tabloids and tell how Peter physically abused me. Damn, it was true until I was pregnant with Noel. Dr. Rathbone treated me for cracked ribs, a dislocated shoulder, a fractured ankle. He was suspicious, though I denied Peter beat me. He loathed Peter—he'll be happy to testify." Iris paced the room in a fury. "And further Peter tried to involve me in his perverted sexual encounters—I refused to degrade myself that way. Elliot, you tell Roland I'll drag the Cranford name into the mud and across every scandal sheet in London if he doesn't forget this craziness."

"It just might work," Elliot said thoughtfully, refusing to commit himself. "I'll arrange an appointment with him tomorrow." He hesitated, his eyes compassionate. "Iris, why the hell did you put up with that?"


On the last Saturday before school was to reopen, Laura and Phil left for a day's outing at the Warm Springs summer house owned by his grandmother but rarely used in recent years. Mrs. Tannenbaum and Adele had been at a resort hotel in North Carolina for the past three weeks. Jonnie and Katie were at a temple-sponsored picnic.

She needed a day away from business. Even with Nora

to help in the office, she rarely left before seven o'clock most days—and she was at the renovation site by 7:30 most mornings. And she worried, too, about Iris's situation in London. Why was her lawyer taking so long to work out a settlement with Peter's children? She wished Iris and Noel were away from England. Every time she read about London's being bombed yet again, she was terrified.

The morning was hot and humid, but Laura and Phil ignored the discomfort as they drove towards the cottage. The trees were lushly green on both sides of the road, though the grass was burnt brown from the sun. Ruddy patches of Georgia clay showing through at intervals. They were alone, Laura thought with pleasure, away from curious eyes. Maisie had told her people were talking about Phil and her. Because she was ten years older than he and a widow. At unguarded moments she worried about this.

She was playing at being a wide-eyed young girl in love, perhaps making up for a girlhood she had never had. From the day Iris and she left Magnolia right up to her marriage to Bernie, she had worried about their survival.

"Thirsty?" Phil asked. "We could stop and have some lemonade." The thermos sat on the back seat of the car, sandwich makings and fruit packed in an ice bucket.

"I just want to get there," she said, leaning her head against his shoulder. "Country air and the scent of pine trees. That's what you promised."

"I can't believe the summer's almost over." His eyes left the road for an instant to rest on Laura. "You'll have the renovation finished by the end of the year." He knew she was anxious to have the apartments on the market, to see some cash flow again. "You won't have to worry about tenants—not with the way the mills are planning to increase production. I hear the Merrick Mill just picked up a huge contract to make army shirts and pants."

"Let's don't talk about the war," Laura scolded. "This is

our great escape."

"I'm for that." He chuckled, but his eyes were serious. Though he hadn't been called for the draft yet, they both knew this was inevitable. She didn't want to think about his being in service — away from Magnolia.

The cottage, a four-bedroom white shingled house that had been in the family since before Phil was born, was nestled among an acre of fragrant pines. Modern conveniences such as a refrigerator and electric fans had been installed in recent years. They put the food they'd brought along in the refrigerator, and Phil took her to see the room that had been his as a child.

"We used to spend every summer up here," he reminisced. "No matter what happened, we had to come out here the day after school closed — and here we stayed until school opened. Mother and Grandma used to sit out there on the porch and talk. They never seemed to run out of words. Dad came up for the weekends. The two of us used to go for long walks in the woods."

"Were there other children around for you to play with?" Laura had a sudden vision of lonely summers for Phil.

"Occasionally. I used to read an awful lot in those summers. Dad would bring up several books every weekend. Then — when I was fourteen — Dad took off. I couldn't blame him. My mother and grandmother didn't give him space to breathe."

"You miss your father," she said softly.

"Laura, when can we stop playing games?" Phil asked. "When will you marry me?"

For an instant she stood immobile beside him. It wasn't fair of her to keep avoiding the subject. To keep him waiting this way when they were so in love.

"Give me some time, Phil," she pleaded. "There are things I have to work out in my mind. I have to make sure the children understand —"

"It's awful waiting this way —" He pulled her close, his mouth reaching for hers.

"We don't have to wait," she told him with sudden decision in her voice. She wasn't some wide-eyed young girl—she was a woman. Her heart pounded when she saw the joyous comprehension in his eyes. "Today belongs to us, Phil."

After they had made love, Laura lay in the curve of his arms and told him in halting detail about her father. He winced when she related the encounter with his grandmother.

"I heard the talk about the trial—and the lynching—when I was a little boy. Then people stopped talking about it. Nobody in Magnolia ever gives it a thought anymore. And the Jewish community prefers to leave it buried."

"Phil, I can't leave it buried."

Now she told him about Derek Slocum and her frustrations at not being able to come up with concrete evidence to clear her father.

"Laura, we'll work on this together," he promised. "You're not alone any longer."

"You know how powerful the Slocums are in this town," she reminded somberly. "I found out only a few months ago that Judge Slocum owns stock in the *Magnolia Journal*—that was the newspaper that attacked Papa so terribly. Judge Slocum wanted Papa lynched—because he thought that would close the case forever."

"It won't be closed until your father's name has been cleared." Phil's face tightened. "We'll start by going through the old newspaper files. We'll just say you're working on a law case," Phil decided. "We'll go through the papers for every day of the trial."

"I need to talk to the witnesses against him." The years kept rushing past, but she had accomplished nothing. "How could they have all lied that way. Why?"

"It'll take time, but we'll dig up evidence to reopen the case. I know you're busy as hell with the contractors right now, but I'll go over to the *Herald* office after school each day and make notes. We'll compile a list of every person who testified against your father." He was silent for a moment. "Laura, are you prepared to drag this out into the open right now?"

Laura gazed at him with incomprehension for a moment. Then she understood. Phil knew that she had never told Jonnie and Katie about what had happened to their grandfather in Magnolia. They thought she had grown up in South Carolina. The whole town would be shocked to discover that Laura Hunter had been Laura Roth.

"When we can track down a substantial number of witnesses that I need to question," she searched for the right approach, "then I'll consider how to handle the situation."

"It'll be tough to make any one of them refute their testimony," he warned. "Even if we can contact them."

"I have to make the effort," Laura insisted. "And at the same time I have to build a case against Derek Slocum—and that will be tough."

"If Judge Slocum has any suspicions of what you're trying to do, he'll be out to cut your throat. We have to play it low key all the way. Actually, the Judge is an accessory."

"Phil, you do believe it was Derek?" Her eyes searched his.

He nodded slowly. "Yes. But we'll have to bring up strong evidence to have the case reopened. It won't happen overnight," he reminded again.

"I've waited seventeen years." Laura tingled with fresh hope. "I can wait a little longer."


Iris sat across the desk from Elliot and tried to hide her impatience while he ran over—for the fifteenth time, it seemed—the various facts Roland's New York lawyers had produced. Damn it, she knew all this! For almost three months he had been negotiating with Roland's attorneys, insisting she was Peter's wife, Noel his legitimate son. She had not been put out of the house yet, but her nerves were frazzled. Roland's attorneys had told him not to pay her bills around town—not even the rental for the suite at the Dorchester. She'd had to hock her pearls to stay afloat.

"But," Elliot continued, a glint of triumph in his voice, "your blackmail threat has finally gotten through to them. They've come up with an offer." Iris tensed—simultaneously hopeful and wary. "It entails your leaving the country," he said with an air of apology.

"Elliot, what about the money?"

"They've agreed to provide you with a monthly allowance provided you take Noel and leave England. I can draw up a contract that will set up an arrangement with the bank that will prohibit their reneging on this. And when—"

"How much money?" Iris demanded. "I have no intention of lowering my lifestyle to please Peter's children. Noel has a right to the kind of background their own children enjoy."

Elliot mentioned a figure and Iris smiled. She should have realized Elliot would not let them send her off to poverty. Already she envisioned making the resort circuit in the States with Diana. Palm Beach in January, she planned with fresh optimism. Then in the spring Diana and she would go to the Greenbrier or the Homestead. Maybe they'd take off for Maine Chance, the Elizabeth Arden resort, for two weeks.

"Of course, I insisted on provisions for you—and for Noel—at Peter's death," Elliot brought her back to the moment. "The doctors agree that this could happen tomorrow or, perhaps, not for ten years. The agreement includes a clause that will give Noel and you jointly one-third of the estate. I think that's fair, Iris."

"I knew his children would share in the estate." Iris was candid.

"I've studied the papers from their attorneys, made a few changes they've accepted. All you have to do now is sign the agreement." He cleared his throat self-consciously. "This won't go in effect until they have proof you've left the country."

"I'll cable them from New York," she drawled. "Is that good enough?"

"That should do it," Elliot nodded.

"How do we travel to the States under current conditions?" Iris asked.

"I'll make the arrangements for you." His smile was wry. "My connections with the War Department will be helpful. You'll go by special train to a port that must be nameless." Lisbon, Iris assumed. "You'll fly to New York on the Clipper."

"When do we leave London?" All at once Iris was buoyed by a sense of adventure. "I must run over to Izod's to buy sweaters first!"

Exhausted from a twelve-hour day, Laura sneaked a glance at her watch while Avery Bishop, her electrical contractor, tried to alibi the delays in finishing his share of the renovation project. Jewel said Iris had phoned in midmorning from New York and would call again this evening. Mail was coming through so slowly these days — just yesterday she'd received a weird letter from Iris that hinted she'd be returning home. She surmised that Iris was not allowed to mention time or places because of the war.

"Honest, Laura, I'm doing everything I can to finish up the work," the contractor wound up. Laura knew he kept pulling men off her project to work for the Slocums. "But you know how slow deliveries are with so many plants busy with war work."

"Avery, I can't afford to keep this renovation going much longer," she warned. "My costs are running way over all estimates. You complete the first dozen apartments by the end of the month, or I may have to call off the whole project." This was not true, but he was milking her for labor costs. Why did men have so little respect for women in business? "I have to leave the office now." She pushed back her chair and rose to her feet. "I'm expecting a long-distance call at the house."

"You moving out into new territory?" he kidded, but she saw his mind clicking.

"In time," she shrugged. If she built away from Magnolia, she wouldn't be hiring a thief like Avery Bishop. "See you in the morning."

She heard the phone ringing in the house as she pulled into the driveway.

"Mom!" Katie yelled from the doorway. "It's Aunt Iris in New York. Jonnie's talking to her. He won't let me say a word!"

Laura rushed into the house, eager to hear Iris's voice. Had it really been four and a half years since they'd seen each other?

"Baby, I'm home!" Iris chortled. "Noel and I landed at La Guardia this morning. Along with Bridget, a darling young cockney girl who was thrilled to come over as Noel's nursemaid."

Laura listened while Iris briefed her on what had happened. She knew it would be futile to try to persuade Iris to move in with her. Iris lived in another world. But thank God, she had come out of this with financial security. Again she thought, Iris is a survivor.

"Diana keeps an apartment at Sutton Place. I'll hole up there temporarily. With plenty of heat, please God! This was the coldest November I remember in England — and top of that we've had the fuel rationing. Anyhow, we'll probably be heading for Palm Beach some time after the first of the year. I know I swore I'd never set foot in Magnolia again. I hate the place. But for you and the kids I'll do it. We'll stop off on our way down to Palm Beach."

"Oh Iris, I can't wait."

"You might drop a line to the society editor of the Magnolia papers," she laughed. "Lady Iris Cranford, sister of Laura Hunter, will visit Magnolia briefly after the first of the year. Wouldn't that set the local bitches back on their heels!"

Laura went out to the kitchen to talk with Jewel for a few minutes, but her thoughts remained with Iris. It would be wonderful to see her. And Noel, she thought tenderly. Her only nephew was past three and she'd never seen him. And while Iris was here, Laura told herself with pleasure, she'd meet Phil.

She wouldn't say anything to Iris about how Phil and she were trying to track down the witnesses who had testified against Papa. Not yet. So far they were having abominable luck. It was as though every witness had disappeared from the face of the earth.

"What's for dessert, Jewel?" Laura asked, reaching for the oven door.

"Miz Laura, you knows better than to open the oven door when I's bakin'. That's my lemon cheese cake, since Mist' Phil is comin' for dinner. That's his all-time favorite." On Friday evenings Phil was always at their dinner table. Occasionally — when his mother was involved in some social affair — he was drafted to escort his grandmother to Friday evening services at the temple.

While Laura and Phil dawdled over second cups of coffee at the dining table, Jonnie watched impatiently for his friend Chet to appear. They were going to see *Sergeant York* at the Beverly. Katie had already escaped to her room to pack for her slumber party two houses down the street.

"I heard in the news earlier that the Russians are keeping the Germans from Moscow," Phil contributed. "That heavy snow isn't helping the invasion.

"That's Chet." Jonnie's face brightened at the sound of the doorbell. "See you later." He darted from the dining room and out to the hall closet to take down his jacket. Laura and Phil heard him talking with Chet about the movie they were to see.

"One down and one to go," Phil whispered, his eyes making love to Laura.

"Mom, I'm going over to Annabel's," Katie announced from the doorway. "I packed my toothbrush and my hairbrush," she anticipated her mother's admonitions. "And my new pajamas and robe."

"Have fun, darling."

"I will!" Katie trilled, running down the hall.

"I know — we have to clear the table," Phil teased, rising to his feet. "But we'll let the dishes soak."

With the dinner dishes out of the way Laura and Phil walked into the living room. While Phil pulled down the shades, Laura turned on the radio. If neighbors should wonder, let it appear that Phil and she were listening to the Cities Service Concert.

"I thought dinner would never be over," Phil said, reaching for her hand.

"Lock the front door," Laura reminded. She was always scared to death that Jonnie or Katie would walk in when Phil and she were making love.

"When you finally decide to make an honest man of me, you'll still insist we have to lock the bedroom door," Phil chuckled but he was going to the door.

Hand in hand they walked into her bedroom, closed the door behind them. Instantly Phil pulled her into his arms. If Iris were here, Laura thought, she'd say, "Marry him, for God's sake. To hell with what people may say!"


On Sunday Phil came over for an early afternoon dinner. It was understood he'd be going home to wait for his father's call. His mother maintained the pretense that Sunday evening was the time he scheduled for correcting papers. Though Phil said nothing to her, Laura knew that gossip had gotten back to his mother and grandmother. Cecile had told her they were furious.

Midway through dinner Maisie phoned.

333

"Laura, turn on the radio!" Maisie ordered. "Pearl Harbor has just been attacked!"

Along with millions of Americans, Laura and Phil and the children clung to the radio with the awareness that the war had become intensely personal. The belief of so many Americans that the United States would provide financial and material aid but would never participate in the fighting was punctured. American blood had been spilled at Pearl Harbor.

Late in the afternoon Laura ordered Jonnie and Katie to their rooms to finish off postponed homework.

"Mom, we're in the war," Jonnie protested.

"You still have school work to do. We're not going to be invaded." Laura struggled to sound matter-of-fact.

The war had from its beginning been ever present in her mind because of Iris. Now it hung over her with fresh foreboding.

As though reading her mind, Phil talked about the imminent escalation of the draft.

"Laura, I'll be drafted for sure now. Why wait? I'll enlist. How can I not fight? The rest of the world has to stand up against Hitler and Hirohito."

"Maybe something will happen," she said irrationally, out of alarm for Phil's safety. "Maybe our armed forces will finish off the Japanese in one gigantic effort. Phil, wait," she pleaded.

"Don't count on a miracle." His face was somber. "But I won't enlist immediately. I can't leave the school until they've found a replacement."

A few evenings later—while they sat at Laura's dining table and studied Magnolia almanacs in their ongoing effort to track down witnesses at Jacob Roth's trial—Phil confided that his mother and grandmother were fighting with him to take a job as a supervisor at the Mei  k Mill.

"The mill is filling army contracts. Making army uniforms. I'd probably be exempt from military service," he said wryly. "Grandma owns a chunk of stock in the mill."

"And you said 'no,' " Laura guessed.

"I talked with Henderson this morning." Henderson was the school principal. "As soon as I can be replaced, I'll enlist. I couldn't live with myself if I didn't, Laura."

"I can't believe this is happening." She recoiled from the painful reality of Phil's going off to war. "I thought we'd be able to stay out of this mess."

"You wanted to believe that." He took her face between his hands, his eyes searching hers. "Laura, marry me before I leave for basic training. Nobody has to know. We'll go up to Atlanta and have a civil ceremony. Afterwards we'll have a real wedding."

When Phil told her five days later that a replacement for him had been found by the school, Laura knew she would marry him immediately. She arranged for Jewel to stay at the house with the children for two days while she went up to Atlanta—presumably on business that required her remaining overnight.

Phil was to leave Magnolia on an earlier train than she. He phoned her from the depot while he waited for the train to arrive.

"When we return, you'll be my wife. This is the most wonderful day of my life."

"I hope you won't be sorry—" She tried for laughter. "When you're forty and I'm pushing fifty."

"Train's pulling in," he said. "I love you. I'll love you forever."

On the brief trip to Atlanta—her hands cradling the boxed corsage of fragrant sweet peas she had bought at the florist shop—she fought against an unanticipated sense of guilt that she was remarrying, as though this was an affront to Bernie's memory. But this was another life, she told herself. One life ended with Bernie. Another was about to begin with Phil.

Her face lighted when she spied him waiting for her at Atlanta's Union Depot. How could she let him go away without their being married? When he came home again—when this awful war was over—then they'd face his family and Jonnie and Katie. And the townspeople. So she was nine years older than Phil, she thought defiantly. Did that matter when they made love? Did it lessen their pleasure in just being together?

Phil's eyes swept over her smart prewar Chanel cotton print—a gift from Iris.

"You're wearing my favorite dress," he said, drawing her into his arms. "My beautiful bride."

"Phil, I was thinking on the train," she said, faintly breathless. "They won't draft married men right away. Maybe you could wait a while."

"The war won't wait," he objected. But he understood. "Come on, we've got a date with a judge."

Laura stood beside Phil while the judge read the short ceremony. It was as if she were playing a role in a play. She gazed at the slender gold band Phil slid on her finger with the realization that she must not wear it when they returned to Magnolia.

"I now pronounce you husband and wife," the judge intoned and Phil reached to kiss her.

"Feel any different?" he whispered when they left the judge's chambers hand in hand.

She laughed.

"It's legal now."

"Let's hurry to the hotel." His hand tightened on hers.

For these precious hours she promised herself, she would not allow herself to think about Phil in uniform. Phil fighting in the war. These hours must sustain her until he was safely home again.

# Part 4

## Chapter 27

Magnolia was caught up in the spirit of the season. Christmas lights were strung across the major street crossings. Shop windows were festively decorated. Christmas trees adorned front lawns. It was as though everyone was making a special effort to celebrate this year, Laura thought, because so many Magnolia boys were going into service.

When Phil walked into the house two days before Christmas, his face unfamiliarly somber, Laura knew he had enlisted. Her throat tightening, she tried not to show her fears while he told her what she already knew. She had known since Pearl Harbor that it was inevitable. Why did she feel as though her world had just collapsed?

"When do you have to report to the induction center?" she asked.

"The day after New Year's." He reached for her hand. "Honey, I'm glad I'm going right into uniform. The sooner we get this war over, the sooner we can begin to live again."

"You'll just miss seeing Iris," Laura said shakily. She'd phoned Iris and told her about the secret wedding. Iris had been so pleased. "She'll be arriving on the fourth." Iris would stay for four days and then leave to join her friend Diana in Palm Beach.

"I noticed in this morning's *Herald* that the mills are advertising for help," Phil told her. Laura understood he was trying to divert her mind from his enlistment. "Your apartments are almost ready for occupancy. Why don't you alert the mills that you'll be renting in another week or so?"

"Two or three weeks," Laura pinpointed. "But you're right—I should go over to talk with the mill people." It was unreal to be talking business with Phil when in ten days he'd be on his way to basic training. "Families coming from the farms will have to find places to live."

With his departure for Texas imminent, Phil found himself involved in family dinners at home. While he was an only child—like his mother, there were great-aunts and great-uncles and a stream of cousins. Two draft-age cousins had already gone into the Merrick Mill to assure themselves exempt military status.

With a new urgency Laura and Phil sought to spend every possible moment together, impatient at other demands that eroded these interludes. When New Year's Eve was at their heels, Laura invented an excuse to spend a day in Atlanta. While the children were still at breakfast, she left the house, ostensibly to collect some papers from the office before heading for the depot. Phil was waiting for her.

In the crisp, cold end-of-December morning, they drove from town. Not until they were five miles north of Magnolia did Laura bring out her wedding ring and slip it on her finger. They drove in anticipatory silence in the cozy warmth of the car, her head on Phil's shoulder, her left hand on his knee.

"We're staying at the Ansley," he told her when they approached Atlanta. "In the same room where we spent our wedding night."

"Phil, I'm scared." Her voice was an anguished whisper.

"I'll come out of this fine," he promised. "We've a lot of living to do."

On the morning of January 2, 1942 Laura stood on the sidewalk before her office and watched the civilian-clad recruits march to the depot where they would board the train that would take them to their camp in Texas. With a determined smile, her vision blurred by tears, she waved to Phil, as others waved to their departing men. And like the others, she asked herself, "When will they

340

return?" *How many would return?*

The remainder of the day, Laura tried to focus on business, but already she was aware of the void created in her life by Phil's absence. When she arrived home, Katie charged towards her with the evening edition of the Magnolia *Herald*.

"Mom, Aunt Iris's picture is in the paper!" Katie reported. "They know she's coming tomorrow!"

In astonishment, and then amusement, Laura read the notice on the society pages about the arrival of "Lady Iris Cranford, stopping off en route to Palm Beach to visit her sister, Mrs. Laura Hunter." She wasn't Laura Hunter anymore, Laura realized subconsciously. She was Laura Weinberg now. But although a Weinberg marriage would have rated a mention, the society editor had never been informed of her marriage to Phil.

"How did they know?" Jonnie joined them with an air of curiosity.

"Aunt Iris must have sent in the notice," Laura told them. Iris knew she would never bother to send in a society page item. "She probably thought it would shake up the town to have 'Lady Iris Cranford' here. Titled ladies don't often appear in Magnolia."

The phone rang as they sat down to dinner.

"You character!" Cecile effervesced. "You just said your sister would be visiting for a few days. You never said she'd married to a British lord!"

"Does that make her any different?" Laura laughed.

"It creates some excitement in town. That title rubs off on you, sweetie. Look, Adele Weinberg is going to call you later about giving a tea in your sister's honor. Right now she's on the phone with the Magnolia Women's Club about reserving the Waterford Room. I imagine she'll call you when she's sure she has the room."

"Cecile, Iris will be here for only four days." A tea given by Mrs. Tannenbaum's daughter? God knows what Iris might say. "I don't think so," she demurred.

"What about a small tea at my house?" Cecile coaxed.

341

"Just a dozen guests. Come on, Laura, let me have the pleasure of winning over Madame Tannenbaum and Adele," Cecile wheedled.

"All right," Laura capitulated after a moment's inner debate. After all it was Cecile who had brought Phil and her together. "But no more than a dozen guests." When Phil's mother got around to calling, she'd politely explain that Iris had time for only one social engagement.

"Très select," Cecile said with relish. "Anybody special I should include?"

"Risa Bernstein." She was married to Mrs. Bernstein's son — now a local pediatrician. "And Maisie. Iris met her sister Doris in London."

"Sure thing. Our token Christian." Cecile giggled. "I do so enjoy ruffling Madame Tannenbaum and Adele."

Laura was at the depot half an hour before Iris was due to arrive. She knew the train would be crowded. With gas rationed, most people traveled by train rather than by car these days.

Restless in this unfamiliar idleness she left the bench where she had been sitting to cross to a phone booth. She phoned Nora to check on incoming calls, phoned the temporary office set up in Columbus. While she talked, she became aware of people coming into the depot, of the air of excitement that always foretold the arrival of a train.

Then the station master announced the train was approaching. Laura finished her phone call and hurried from the depot to wait before the tracks. When the train began to disgorge its passengers, she searched eagerly for Iris.

"Laura!" In absurdly high heels and a magnificent mink coat Iris was walking towards her.

"Iris!"

They kissed, clung, both caught up in the pleasure of being together again.

342

"You look marvelous," Laura said. "What's that perfume?"

"The last of my Chanel No. 5," Iris told her and looked over her shoulder. "Bridget, bring Noel over here."

The small, pretty cockney girl shyly approached, was introduced to Laura. In his impeccable British clothes Noel observed her with a wariness that Laura found touching.

"Noel," Laura said softly, stooping to kiss him. "Iris, he's so handsome." She gazed at Noel with recurrent wonder that Iris was a mother. This was her nephew.

"And he's so spoiled," Iris laughed. "Noel, this is your Aunt Laura. And you'll meet your two cousins at her house."

Iris and Laura were cautious in their conversation before Bridget; presumably Iris had visited Magnolia only once before—briefly. Iris instructed Laura to drive to the hotel, where she would register for Noel and Bridget. Noel was to have a nap, then Bridget was to ask for a taxi to bring them to the house.

Laura glanced at her watch. It was past two.

"Did you have lunch on the train?"

Iris nodded. "The dining car was rather decent."

With Noel and Bridget installed at the Magnolia hotel, Laura and Iris drove home. Jewel fussed over Iris, brought them coffee and freshly baked sweet-potato pie, then hurried out to the kitchen to begin preparing her elaborate dinner. Laura reveled in Iris's stream of questions about her real-estate operations, with obvious pride. The children, too, were proud of her recognized accomplishments.

"Now tell me about Phil." Iris kept her voice low.

"I love him, Iris." Laura's face was luminous. "I never thought it could happen for me again. Nobody knows," she reminded with a cautious glance towards the kitchen. "Only you—and Maisie and Everett."

"Darling, I'm so happy for you." She leaned forward to kiss Laura. "When do I get to meet him?"

343

"Right this minute he's on his way to basic training." Laura's voice became somber. "Hopefully he'll be sent to Fort Benning to the new Officer Candidate's School after boot camp. At least, he'll be close then."

"Laura, are you happy here?" Iris was suddenly serious.

"I would be if Phil were home."

"I don't know how you can stay in this town. I'll never forgive Magnolia for what it did to Papa—and to us." Her face was rigid for a moment with fresh rage. "But I can handle it for a few days. What I'm trying to say," she laughed, "is how the hell can you breathe in a town this small? I know—I spend a lot of time in small resort towns. But that's different. Anyhow, New York is my home base now. We never knew New York, Laura. Not the important people, the exciting places. This time around it'll be different."

"Are you all right financially?" Laura probed. The cost of Iris's lifestyle unnerved her.

"Darling, I'm fine," Iris assured her, then paused. "I don't know how well off I'll be when Peter dies and the government comes in with the new death duties." She shrugged. "Peter's awfully rich. I'll manage."

"Oh, a friend of mine is giving a tea for you tomorrow afternoon at the Women's Club. Cecile Berger—she's married to Barry Berger, who was a senior when we started high school. Do you remember the Bergers?"

Iris frowned, ignoring Laura's question.

"Oh God, I don't want to be put on display for a bunch of creepy women here in town. Who put her up to that?"

"It just kind of happened. You did send that notice to the *Herald*." Laura was upset. She should have understood Iris would be irritated. "Cecile phoned and said that Adele Weinberg was calling the Women's Club to reserve the Waterford Room. Her mother and she were planning a tea in your honor."

"Without bothering to consult you?"

344

"I'm not exactly a favorite of the Tannenbaum women. They've known for a while that Phil and I were seeing each other."

"But to entertain Lady Cranford they could overlook that," Iris drawled.

"Cecile asked if she could give a small tea—sort of jumping the gun on Mrs. Tannenbaum and Phil's mother. I guess the word spread around town fast—I never heard personally from the Tannenbaum ladies." Laura's voice faded. She had meant for this to be a pleasant visit for Iris, despite her feelings about Magnolia.

Unexpectedly Iris laughed.

"All right, we'll go to Cecile's tea." Her eyes lit with malicious amusement. "So long as Tannenbaum and daughter are not among the guests."

"They won't be," Laura promised, smiling. "I'd love to see the old witch's face when she discovers one day that her granddaughter-in-law is the 'former Laura Roth.' "

Iris hesitated. "Does it bother you that she's Phil's grandmother?"

"Only at first," Laura acknowledged. "I love Phil. I don't have to love his family."

"Is anybody I know coming to the tea?" Iris appeared in high spirits, but Laura sensed her tension at being here in Magnolia. "Not that anybody would remember Iris Roth."

"You knew Irene Fishman," Laura told her. "She was Irene Wendroff. A year ahead of us in school. She went off to the University of Georgia and married a dental student." Laura paused. "Iris, stop worrying. I told you, nobody recognized me. They won't recognize you."

Laura was grateful for Iris's presence, dreaded her leaving even while she understood that Magnolia was full of ghosts for her sister. On a gray, chilly afternoon, after Iris and she had deposited Noel and Bridget at their hotel, Laura drove her sister to the plot of land where their father had been lynched. It was fenced in now and

345

landscaped, with a stone bench placed beside a bird bath.

"I bought it as a secret memorial to Papa," Laura said. "One day, when Papa's name has been cleared, it'll be a public memorial. When I'm especially upset about something, I come out here and sit on that bench. I feel very close to Papa then."

For the first time in many years Iris sobbed openly.

"One day I'll clear his name," Laura said again, holding Iris in her arms. "One day this town will know it murdered an innocent man."


Cecile's tea was a huge success. Iris charmed their guests. She was beautiful, warm, and unpretentious.

"Were you ever in the movies?" one guest asked avidly.

"For a while," Iris conceded.

"I thought I recognized you!"

There was a fresh surge of excitement. Not only was Laura's sister married to a British lord, but she had been a real Hollywood actress.

The morning after the tea Laura accompanied Iris, Noel, and Bridget to the train for Palm Beach.

"You'll put the jewelry somewhere safe," Iris reminded as the train pulled into the depot. Last night she had given Laura several pieces of her jewelry for safekeeping. "I know the London bank will send my remittances according to the arrangements, but I like to know I have something special laid aside."

"I'll put it in my bank vault," Laura assured her. Why must they always be separated this way? "Take care of yourself, Iris. And Noel. We all love you."

"I love you all, too." Iris clung to her for a poignant moment, then followed Noel, Bridget, and the porter who carried her bags to the train.


After Iris's departure, Laura forced herself to concentrate on the business. As she had anticipated, the apartments—modest but comfortable—were being grabbed up by new mill employees. She was planning another renovation—in Columbus—if the property owners would accept her offer. Doris had scouted around town until she discovered an abandoned bottling plant. Columbus was booming, with over 45,000 troops at nearby Fort Benning. There was an enormous need there for housing.

Phil wrote regularly, phoned when it was possible. He sent her snapshots of himself with a pair of army buddies. She fought back a rush of fear at the sight of him in army uniform, a gun at his waist. She was upset when he wrote that he had rejected Officer Candidate's School. He was impatient to be overseas. Nothing was going well for the Allies.

On January 2 the Japanese had driven the Americans under General MacArthur's leadership out of Manila. On March 17 the Japanese drove them out of Bataan. In April the "Death March" of American and Philippine prisoners taken at Bataan began. The prisoners were forced to march eighty-five miles in six days with no food other than one bowl of rice each. At the end of the march over five thousand Americans were dead.

In early May, already steamy hot in Georgia, Phil phoned Laura and asked her to meet him in Atlanta the following morning.

"Register for us at the Ansley. I'm catching a ride on an army plane. We'll have a few hours for ourselves before I have to go home." He tried to sound casual, as though this were just a pleasurable interlude in a busy schedule, but Laura sensed the urgency underneath his casualness.

"Shall I meet you at the hotel? Or at the airport?" There was no question but that she would be there. Tomorrow's appointments with contractors who had submitted estimates would have to be shifted.

"The hotel," Phil told her. "I don't know when we'll be landing. Laura." His voice dropped to a caressing whisper. "I love you."

347

"I love you, too," she said. "I can't wait to see you. It's been so long."

She sat immobile before the phone at the sound of the click at the other end. She was cold with shock, knowing that this was Phil's last leave before being shipped out. He wouldn't dare say this over a public phone, but she knew. He wasn't being transferred to another camp, he was going into action.

She had been terrified of guns ever since Bernie had been shot down. Even now the sound of a car backfiring turned her stomach sick. How would she survive if anything happened to Phil? He teased her when she admitted to being afraid for him. *"Honey, you know the old cliché — lightning never strikes twice. Married to you I'm leading a charmed life."*

Laura was on the early morning train to Atlanta. The minutes seeming to drag until the train pulled into Union Depot. At the Ansley she registered for "Corporal and Mrs. Phillip Weinberg" and went upstairs to their room. She thought she saw a glint of compassion in the eyes of the desk clerk when he handed her the room key. With Fort McPherson at the edge of the city such meetings at the Ansley must be frequent.

When at last she heard a knock on the door, she rushed to reply, willing herself not to show her inner anguish.

She opened the door, for an instant mesmerized by her first sight of Phil in army uniform. Then he reached for her, and kissed her with a hunger that matched her own.

"Baby, you don't know how I've counted the hours." He swayed with her, his face against hers.

"You need a shave," she laughed.

"I didn't dare take the time. I was standing by since before reveille to hitch this ride. I'll have to grab a train back to Texas tomorrow morning — it's a long haul."

"Are you hungry?" she asked solicitously. "Shall I call for room service?"

"Later," he said tenderly. "Much later."

348

Close to five o'clock they checked out of the hotel and headed for the Greyhound bus terminal. Phil had phoned his mother to say he was on his way home. When would he be home again, Laura asked herself in pain. He was certain his company was headed for the Pacific. *"We know from the gear we've been issued."* Arriving in Magnolia Phil called a cab.

"I'll drop you off on the way," he said while they waited. He hesitated. "Should I stop off to say hello to the kids? I'd better not," he said quickly before she could reply.

"No," she agreed.

"I'll take the first train out in the morning." His eyes clung to her face. "I'll tap on your bedroom window before I go to the station."

"I'll be waiting," she promised. "I wish you didn't have to go home—"

"How I wish it too."

"Here's the cab." She reached for his hand. It was unlikely that anybody would see them. Except for strangers waiting for buses, everybody in Magnolia was at home for dinner or working on the swing shift.

"Where to, soldier?" the cab driver asked good-humoredly, and Phil gave him their two destinations.

Before six in the morning—before Jewel arrived at the house and while Jonnie and Katie still slept—Laura heard a faint tapping at her bedroom window. She hurried to pull up the shade, smiled in welcome.

"I'll be right there." She knew Phil could read her lips.

Already dressed for the day, she hurried out in the blessedly fresh morning air that later would become humid.

"I have Mother's car." Phil pointed to the Packard at the curb. "I'm to leave it at the station."

"I'll go with you to the train," she said and saw his face light up.

349

"This rotten war won't last much longer," he told her. A few days ago the Allies won the Battle of the Coral Sea—an important victory. But at the same time General Wainwright had to surrender Corregidor and other Philippine islands to the Japanese. "I'll come home, and we'll have a splashy wedding at the temple. Jonnie will give the bride away and Katie will be your very young maid of honor."

"Phil, be careful," she pleaded. "I love you so much."

# Chapter 28

Ten days after Phil's departure for Texas, Laura received a card giving her his APO address. He was en route to the Pacific. Wistfully, she wished that she was close to Phil's family so they could share the anguish of his being at war.

Each night Laura wrote to Phil. She clung to the radio to hear the latest newscasts about the fighting in the Pacific. In early June Americans repulsed the Japanese effort to seize Midway Island. Later in the month they attacked the Japanese at Salamaua, New Guinea. On August 7 U.S. marines landed on Guadalcanal in the Solomon Islands. It was soon clear that fighting here would be bitter and long.

Each morning Laura embarked on a long day of business activities, determined to immerse herself in work. But she made a point of being home for dinner with the children each night.

After dinner Jonnie and Katie settled themselves at the dining room table to do their homework. Laura sat with them doing work she had brought home from the office. On most nights she spent close to an hour on the phone discussing business problems with Everett—now a salaried consultant with the firm.

The renovation in Columbus—desperate for living accommodations—was progressing with frustrating slowness. The Slocums were building in Columbus, also. David Slocum, the Judge's oldest son, had connived to hire away half the workmen assigned to her job.

Iris wrote spasmodically, phoned at intervals. From Bar Harbor, Acapulco, Lake Arrowhead, she was following the resort circuit, only slightly touched by the war. *"Everybody thinks I did the right thing in taking Noel away from all the bombing. You 'd be amazed how many people I knew from London and Paris and Rome are here in the States now."*

In the early autumn, at Everett's urging, Laura became active in the local Chamber of Commerce and in local politics. She understood the high value of the right political connections, an advantage Slocum Realty had mined for years.

The renovation in Columbus was finally completed and the apartments rented out in record time. Laura began to search for more suitable property, widening her horizon to include the whole state along with neighboring Alabama. Training camps and airfields were mushrooming in the Southern states because of their climate and extensive tracts of open space.

Laura enlarged her staff. Maisie enraged Judge Slocum by resigning as his secretary to become Laura's personal assistant while Everett was devoting more time to Hunter Realty than to his accounting clients.

Laura had hoped that Iris would stop off in Magnolia en route to Palm Beach for the season, but Hanukkah and Christmas arrived and passed without any indication of her arrival. Iris and Diana were holiday houseguests of Jimmy Harris, the only son of a chemical products tycoon, at his villa in Acapulco. *"Jimmy's 4-F. Some very minor heart condition his father managed to have the authorities consider serious."*

Letters from Phil were intermittent and hastily written, on occasion marked by the censor's scissors. She knew he was somewhere in the Pacific theater. He wrote wistfully about his longing for the war to end and to be home again with her. *"After being out here I'll never complain again about Georgia summers."* He'd written about the torrential rains, wading knee deep through thick, black mud. And always he told her how much her letters meant to him.

Early in January, 1943 Laura received a letter from Iris. Diana and she had just flown with Jimmy from

Acapulco to Palm Beach in his father's private plane. "*You know how hard it is to get reservations these days, so we grabbed at the chance. Do you own any properties in Atlanta? Jimmy says his father is talking about moving some of his operations down there because labor is less expensive than in New York. I thought it might just be something you'd want to follow up on.*"

Laura's mind charged into high gear. Could Iris be talking about Harris Chemicals? She immediately phoned Iris at The Breakers, where she was staying. Iris—as she had feared—was not in her suite. Bridget promised that she would call back. "But it may be late, ma'am," Bridget apologized.

"Tell her to call no matter how late it is," Laura instructed. "Everyone's fine—this is just business."

Long past midnight Iris phoned.

"Iris, is Jimmy Harris's father Harris Chemicals?" Laura asked her.

"Yeah," she said after a moment. "That's what Jimmy calls the firm. Interested?"

"You bet I am. Harris Chemicals is one of the biggest in the field."

"Then you have property in Atlanta," Iris pinpointed.

"Not yet," Laura admitted. "But I will have within the next two weeks. Do you suppose Jimmy can give me some idea of what his father would require?"

"Darling, Jimmy knows absolutely nothing about the business," Iris laughed. "But you're smart. You'll figure out all the angles. I'll tell Jimmy to phone his father up in New York. Right away. He'll ask his father to talk with you."

"Let me know when he's spoken to his father. I want to get on this deal fast."

"I'll call you the instant I know," Iris promised.

Despite the hour, Laura began to plot this new venture. Again, a gamble, but what possibilities! She would have to go out on a limb and buy up property. With her holdings now she'd have no trouble lining up a mortgage. She wouldn't have to lay out much cash. First thing tomorrow she'd start boning up on Harris Chemicals.

Everett worked up a report for Laura on the Harris operation so that she would know what their requirements would be. Maisie was doing an in-depth financial check. In addition, Everett came up with the information that Harris Chemicals was currently involved in government contracts. The financial reports that Maisie tracked down were awesome.

"This would be a major move for them," Everett pointed out. "If you can find quarters suitable for quick conversion for their needs plus land for expansion, you could make a killing. You've got the contact," he conceded, "but if Harris is serious about the move, he'll soon start inquiries in Atlanta. You can't sit on this."

"I know. Can you do a cost breakdown for me on per foot construction costs? There can't be much difference between costs in Atlanta and Magnolia."

"I'll check out Atlanta. We want to be as close as possible in our figuring. Laura, this could be a sensational operation."

After five days of frenzied searching in Atlanta, Laura came up with a couple of possible sites, neither of which generated real excitement in her. But when Iris phoned to say that Jimmy had finally contacted his father, Laura moved into action. She spoke with Arnold Harris in New York, arranged to meet with him there ten days later to outline her still frustratingly elusive "available properties." Maisie immediately embarked on the task of arranging train reservations—difficult to come by since the first days of the war.

At her Atlanta bank, where she continued to maintain a corporate account, Laura learned of a bank auction to be held the next day. A fast inquiry about what would be offered followed by a careful inspection of the property convinced her she had located what she needed to present to Harris Chemicals. At 8 A.M. the following morning she was back in Atlanta and en route to the auction.

Refusing to consider that Arnold Harris might reject the property, Laura bought it. This was by far the most expensive transaction she had ever negotiated. Her profit, if she had gambled right, would be awesome.

Right on schedule she left for her New York meeting with Harris. When hotel accommodations seemed impossible to find, Laura called Iris in Palm Beach. With her contacts among the very rich, Laura assumed, Iris would come up with something. An acquaintance wintering in Palm Beach maintained a suite at the Waldorf Towers. The suite was put at Laura's disposal during her three-day stay in New York.

Leaving the train at Penn Station, Laura was assaulted by bitter memories—of her arrival with Iris right after Papa's death, of her departure with Jonnie and Katie after Bernie's murder. But she had no time for morbid recall, Laura told herself. Tomorrow morning she was to meet with Arnold Harris. She must be bright, self-assured, confident. She was pleased to give a Waldorf-Astoria tower suite as her temporary address when she spoke with Harris's secretary. Ten minutes later he phoned to suggest they meet for lunch the following day at Le Pavilion.

Iris had said that in the old days they'd never really known New York. Settling herself in the two-bedroom, two-bath suite in the Waldorf Towers, Laura understood what Iris meant. She ordered dinner from room service, dined by a window that looked out upon much of the city. A light snow was beginning to fall, blurring the skyline. Laura was conscious of an unexpected serenity— a sense of being removed from the rest of the world for this quiet time.

After she had eaten, Laura phoned home and talked with the children and with Jewel, who was living in during her absence. Guiltily aware of the phone bill she was running up as Katie gregariously reported on school ac-

355

tivities.

Too tense to sleep she wrote a long letter to Phil, to be mailed in the morning. Then she planned her wardrobe for the crucial luncheon appointment. She had brought along one of the exquisite suits Iris had sent her through the years, and she had worn the timeless Burberry tweed Chesterfield Iris had sent her three years ago. She knew the importance of appearing highly successful. She phoned Iris down in Palm Beach and learned that Le Pavilion—across the street from the St. Regis—was New York's newest ultra-chic French restaurant.

Laura knew within ten minutes after meeting Arnold Harris that she had a deal. He admitted to having spoken with two Atlanta realtors, who had quoted astronomical prices for property that would require extensive conversion.

"They looked me up in Dun & Bradstreet and figured they'd take me to the cleaners," he chuckled, and Laura remembered that Everett said Harris was a self-made millionaire. "You and I can do business, little lady."


Katie hovered before the radio while Jewel washed, dried, and put away the dinner dishes. She knew she should have started her homework twenty minutes ago, but she adored the radio plays. Jonnie was sprawled on the floor, concentrating on his geometry assignment.

"You kids doin' your homework?" Jewel called from the kitchen.

"I am," Jonnie called back. "Katie isn't."

"Snitch!" Katie reproached and reached to switch off the radio.

"You do your homework, young lady!" Jewel yelled firmly from the kitchen. "This minute."

With a sigh of reluctance, Katie reached for her books. With Mom out of town, it was kind of a vacation. Jewel could be wheedled into a second piece of pie or a double scoop of ice cream at bedtime—as long as they promised to clean their teeth before they went to bed.

When she told the kids at school that Mom was up in New York on business, she'd thought it sounded kind of exciting. Patty said her mother thought it was "sad that Laura Hunter had to be away from her children so much." But, when home, Mother spent a lot of time with them. She even took them to the office every now and then, so they could see where she was much of the day.

"Katie, you're daydreaming again," Jonnie jeered.

"I'm doing my French," she countered. "You stop it, or I'll tell Mom you were picking on me all the time she was away."

"Do you think she'll phone tonight?" Jonnie was wistful.

"She's on the train tonight, stupid. She'll be home tomorrow."

Both Jonnie and Katie ignored the sound of the front doorbell.

"One of you kids answer that," Jewel ordered from the kitchen. "I'm up to my elbows in soapsuds. Pronto!"

"Okay, I'm going," Katie grumbled. It was probably Patty—she said she might have trouble with the French assignment.

With a sidewise glance at the reflection in the hall mirror of her delicately blossoming figure, Katie walked to the door. Patty had been wearing a bra for almost two years. Mother promised they'd go over to Glover's on Saturday and buy her some bras.

Katie frowned as the doorbell rang again.

"All right, I'm coming!" She pulled the door wide and stared at the Western Union messenger who stood there.

"Telegram for Mrs. Weinberg," he said, extending the small yellow envelope.

"Nobody by that name lives here," Katie said.

He squinted at the address.

"1402 Maple Avenue?"

"Yeah—"

"Mrs. Laura Hunter Weinberg," he enunciated carefully.

"Laura Hunter—" Katie stared in shock. Laura Hunter *Weinberg?* Mom had married Phil! "Yeah—"

"Sign here—" He held out a pad and pencil.

Katie scrawled her name on the pad and reached for the envelope.

"Thank you—" The messenger's voice trailed away. He abandoned hope of a tip.

Clutching the envelope in one hand Katie walked down the hall into the living room.

"Who was it?" Jewel called.

"Western Union—" Mom had gone and married Phil without telling them. She was going to keep it a secret from them—she didn't want Jonnie and her to know.

"From your mama?" Jewel hurried from the kitchen. "Did she miss her train?"

"It's for her. I think." Katie felt sick. "I don't know," she burst out desperately.

"What are you talking about?" Jonnie jumped to his feet and reached for the telegram. "Mrs. Laura Hunter Weinberg," he read aloud and then stared open-mouthed from Katie to Jewel. "Weinberg?"

"Mom married Phil before he went away!" Katie's eyes blazed with anger and hurt. Mom was pushing Jonnie and her out of her life. That's why she hadn't told them.

"Katie, now don't you get all upset," Jewel scolded, her face serious.

"Did you know she was married?" Katie challenged.

Jewel shook her head, her eyes fastened fearfully to the telegram.

"Jewel, who do you think it's from?" Jonnie asked. "From Phil?"

"From somewhere in the Pacific?" Katie scoffed. The atmosphere was suddenly oppressive. "Could it be from the War Department?" When her friend Donna's brother was captured in the Pacific, his mother received a telegram from the War Department.

"We don't know who it's from, and we ain't gonna

worry," Jewel said firmly. "Your mama will be home to-morrow. Put it on the hall table with her mail."

"It's about Phil! He's been wounded, or he's a prisoner of war, or he's dead," Katie said and broke into tears. "Why didn't Mom tell us Phil and she were married? Didn't we have a right to know?"


Laura waited with simmering restlessness for the train to pull into the Magnolia depot. She needed the reassuring presence of the children after the trauma of returning to New York. There she had been hounded by memories. Still, she was coming home with the most important deal she had ever negotiated. She wished Phil were here so she could share it with him.

"Next stop Magnolia, Georgia," the conductor announced, and passengers for Magnolia began to collect their belongings.

A smiling porter lifted Laura's small valise from the luggage rack while she gathered the parcels from Saks that contained presents for the children and Jewel. Gifts for Maisie and Everett and for Nora were being mailed out by Saks. She had filled the empty hours after seeing Arnold Harris by shopping.

The train pulled into the depot. With her coat over her arm, because the day was sunny and warm for the end of January, Laura followed the porter to a taxi. She glanced at her watch. The children would be home from school in an hour. She was eager to see them.

Walking into the house Laura sniffed the enticing aromas of fresh bread baking.

"Jewel?" she called with a lilt in her voice. "I'm home."

She reached for the mail that sat on the hall console table, then started at the sight of the Western Union envelope. From Iris? No, Iris phoned—she never wired. Suddenly cold with fear, she picked up the telegram. *"Mrs. Laura Hunter Weinberg."*

"Miz Laura—" Jewel was walking down the hall towards her.

It was about Phil, Laura guessed, terrified to open the envelope. Yet she knew she must. With a swift rip she opened the envelope and pulled out the small sheaf of paper. The words etched themselves into her brain. Not again. It couldn't be happening again.

"Miz Laura?" Jewel said anxiously, as Laura sank into a chair and buried her head in her hands.

"Jewel, he was killed in action. He's dead. Phil's dead."

Dazed, Laura allowed Jewel to pull her to her feet and prod her down the hall to her bedroom. All the time murmuring sympathetically, Jewel persuaded her to take off her jacket, to lie down. She pulled off Laura's pumps.

"You stay right there. I'll go fix you a cup of hot tea. You jes' rest, Miz Laura, you hear?"

Laura lay back against the pillows and remembered those last hours with Phil. He had been so sure he'd be all right. What was wrong with her that every man she loved—Papa, Bernie, Phil—all died violent deaths? Was she marked in some way? Why?

Jewel brought her a cup of tea, inspected her solicitously.

"I'll be all right, Jewel," she murmured, too stunned to cry. "Let me just be alone for a while."

Later she heard Jonnie and Katie come into the house. She heard Jewel talking with them in whispers, telling them not to disturb their mother. Had they seen the telegram? They'd be upset—they'd been so fond of Phil. They must know Phil and she were married before he was shipped out. Were they angry with her?

With night settling, Jewel knocked on her door.

"Miz Laura, I'm putting dinner on the table. The kids want to see you."

Laura took a deep breath. "I'll be right there," she promised. "As soon as I've made a phone call."

She had to call Phil's mother. The War Department had notified his wife. His mother didn't know about the telegram.

360

Still in the rumpled skirt and blouse she had worn on the train, Laura went into the living room to phone Phil's mother. She could hear the subdued voices of the children in the dining room.

"The Tannenbaum residence," a maid said.

"May I please talk to Mrs. Weinberg." Laura fought to keep her voice even.

"Who's callin' please?"

"Laura Hunter." Laura Hunter Weinberg, but Phil's mother didn't know.

"Hello." A cold, wary voice greeted her. "This is Mrs. Weinberg."

"I'm sorry to have to tell you this way," Laura stammered. "But there's no other way. Before Phil was shipped out, we were married. I—"

"Phil wouldn't keep something like that from me!" Adele Weinberg's voice was shrill. "Just what are you after?"

"I'm Phil's wife," Laura reiterated, her head pounding now. "He wanted us to be married before he went away—"

"Don't expect my mother and me to believe this until Phil tells us himself," Adele said arrogantly. "You're a widow with two children. He's a boy."

"We were married, Mrs. Weinberg. I've just received a telegram from the War Department. I'm sorry to have to tell you this. Phil was killed in action at Guadalcanal." Quickly, as though to shut out the truth, she put down the phone and went into the dining room.

Their eyes reflecting shock and hurt and questions, Jonnie and Katie sat at the table.

"I have so much to tell you," Laura said softly. "Phil loved you both. We had to keep the wedding a secret because—" she sought for a reason that would be acceptable to the children—"because we both knew his mother would be upset. We-we figured we could deal with it easier after the war—" Her voice broke. Phil wouldn't be here after the war. "And I was trying to gear myself to

361

face people when they heard we were married. I mean, the difference in our ages—"

"That was nobody's business," Katie said fiercely. "Just yours and Phil's."

"For a little while he was our stepfather," Jonnie said, his eyes overly bright. "I'm glad about that."

Later in the evening Laura talked with Iris, down in Palm Beach.

"Do you want me to come up?" Iris asked immediately.

"There's no need for that." She knew how Iris hated being here. "I'll be so busy on this new project—running back and forth between here and Atlanta—that I wouldn't even see you except at dinner."

"You change your mind, you let me know. You hear?" It was endearingly strange to hear her very British sister fall back into a local expression.

Now Laura geared herself to talk with Maisie and Everett. With the feeling that this was a terrible dream she dialed their number. Her heart was pounding.

"Hello." Maisie's usual cheery response.

"I'm back, Maisie—" All at once the necessary words refused to come.

"Everett's been sitting here stewing all evening," Maisie confided. "Dying to know how you made out with Harris. I told him—"

"Maisie, something awful has happened," she interrupted.

Her voice faltering she told Maisie about the telegram from the War Department. She listened—only half hearing—to Maisie's shaken efforts at condolence, and then she spoke with Everett. Tomorrow she would tell Everett about the deal with Harris. Tonight she could remember only that Phil lay dead somewhere on a battlefield in Guadalcanal.

# Chapter 29

Laura gripped the phone with such intensity that her knuckles whitened.

"Laura, they're outrageous!" Cecile railed at the other end of the line. "Both Mrs. Tannenbaum and Adele. They're telling their friends that you pushed Phil to enlist, that you married him for his insurance money."

"They're sick," Laura whispered, recoiling from such ugliness.

"I can't believe they can be so stupid. Everybody knows how successful you are. But not everybody agrees with what they're saying," Cecile comforted. "You know Southern women. They'll 'yes' Adele to her face because that's the polite thing to do, but privately they think she and her mother are just awful."

"I've got another rumor for you to circulate." Why was she trembling this way, Laura reproached herself. "Not a rumor," she corrected. "Phil's insurance money will go to establish the Phillip Weinberg Library wing at the high school."

"Set it up with the Board of Education, Laura. Let the whole town know."

"Barry's on the Board, isn't he?"

"Right," Cecile pounced. "Drive over after dinner and talk with him about it. He'll take it to the Board."

That would silence old Mrs. Tannenbaum and her daughter, Laura promised herself. How terrible that Phil's mother and grandmother could feel this way about her. Phil's death should have drawn them together. But she was a woman now—not a frightened fifteen-year-old girl. This time she could fight back.

The library would be a fitting memorial to Phil. But in no way would it lessen her devastating sense of loss. Again, she was alone. Alone as a woman, and alone in her fight to clear Papa's name.

She sought solace from grief in work. She plotted to be embroiled in the business almost every waking hour. At bedtime she brought a folder of statistics to her night table and analyzed the figures until her eyes began to close from exhaustion. The nights, she thought, were the worst time of all.

She spent three full days a week in Atlanta now. Ever guilty at not being an "at-home" mother — though in these war years more women were leaving the home to work — she religiously spent her evenings at the house, even holding business conferences here. She was pleased when Jonnie asked questions about the business. Katie seemed disinterested.

She knew Katie had been badly hurt by Phil's death and at intervals she worried about the wall Katie seemed to have erected between them. She suspected her daughter had still not forgiven her for keeping the marriage a secret. Under prodding Jewel had admitted Katie's reaction to the telegram addressed to "Laura Hunter Weinberg." How could Katie believe she had meant to shut her precious daughter out of her new life?

In an effort to draw Katie out of her unhappiness, Laura decided they would move into a new house. A fine house that would reflect her burgeoning success. A change of scenery would be good for all of them. This house was full of taunting memories of Phil.

Late in May an elegant four-columned colonial in a charming, outlying area came onto the market. The house was more expensive than she'd planned, physically larger than they needed, but Katie adored it. Laura bought it with the bittersweet realization that Phil had once pointed out the house as one he particularly admired.

Now Laura decided that Jewel would become their

live-in housekeeper, with a cleaning woman to come in by the day. A part-time gardener was hired. How Papa would have loved the rolling lawns, the flower beds, the rose-covered trellises. How proud he would have been of the children.

In September Jonnie began his senior year at Magnolia High—already he was arguing with his friends about where to go to school. She dreaded the prospect of his being away at college. And she tried to stifle her growing fears that the war might continue past Jonnie's eighteenth birthday.

In the past weeks the Allies had driven the Axis troops out of Sicily and invaded the Italian mainland. Mussolini had been dismissed from office. After the Allied landing at Salerno, the Italian government surrendered. In the Pacific the Allies were advancing, with heavy losses to the Japanese. Still, Laura worried.

By early fall the house had been redecorated and furnished. Laura gave a lavish reception, though neither Mrs. Tannenbaum nor Adele was invited. It was what Maisie good-humoredly called a "cross-the-board" party that included Laura's Jewish and Christian friends. At the reception Barry Berger drew Laura into an active discussion of the Chamber of Commerce's drive to entice more out-of-state businesses into town.

"That's a project everybody will approve," Laura said. "You know how busy I am, but I'll do what I can."

"Not everybody approves," Craig Meyers, who operated a menswear factory, said with an acerbic smile. "We're getting a lot of flack. Particularly from the Slocums."

"Why?" Laura was astonished. "They were eager enough to bring Stephens Industries into Magnolia."

"Because they stood to make a killing on the Donnell farm," Barry reminded.

"But new businesses are important to Magnolia. They'll enlarge our tax bases. We'll be able to—"

"We'll be able to offer more jobs," Barry interjected drily. "The Slocums might have to pay higher wages."

"They can't be allowed to get away with that!" Laura turned to Craig. "Can the city offer new businesses a tax break, some really strong incentive?"

"We need to get some fresh voices on the city commission to do that," Craig said. "Right now it's packed with men controlled by Slocum."

"Barry Berger," Laura pinpointed. "Any time you decide to run, I'm behind you."

"What about Laura Hunter?" Barry challenged. "We've never had a woman commissioner."

"You first," Laura chuckled, but she was startled. "Later we'll talk about running a woman for city commissioner."

But all at once Laura's mind crackled with excitement. For as long as she could remember, both socially and politically, Judge Slocum and his inner circle had ruled this town.

The Judge was old-line society. His two sons and the nephew he adopted as a small boy had followed his example by marrying society women who led genteel lives involved with lavish entertaining and not too demanding charity committees. On the social level the Slocums moved in a tight, inbred clique of their own kind. But the Judge and his sons were mired in dirty politics, aimed at maintaining their power and increasing their wealth. Perhaps it was time to change that through an insidious campaign by people like Barry and Craig and herself.

Beating the Slocum machine — acquiring political power of her own — would be a tremendous asset in her efforts to clear Papa. But, Laura amended mentally, there would always be some doubt unless the real murderer was convicted. That meant fighting the Slocums to a bitter climax. It meant bringing Derek to trial.

With political power on her side she'd be able to cut through much red tape. She'd be able to build a strong case against Derek and make sure the case was retried before a judge who wouldn't knuckle under before Judge

Slocum. There were new people moving into Magnolia in surprising numbers. Let them hear Laura Hunter.

The months were racing past. In late January American and British troops landed at Anzio and Nettuno in Italy. A few days later Allied troops advanced in the Pacific, for the first time setting foot on Japanese territory. Four weeks later eight hundred Flying Fortresses dropped two thousand tons of bombs on Berlin. Americans began to feel a surge of optimism.

For Phil this turnaround in the war came too late, Laura thought with a wrenching pain while she sat with Everett and Maisie in her sun-drenched living room after a mid-afternoon Sunday dinner and discussed this new sense of hope that peace would come within the next dozen months.

"Before Jonnie's old enough to be involved," Maisie read Laura's mind.

"What have you decided about school?" Everett asked Jonnie when he appeared with their after-dinner coffee tray.

"I'll probably go to the University of Georgia if I'm accepted," he said, depositing the tray on a strategic table. "It's close enough to come home most weekends."

"Of course you'll be accepted," Laura said with pride. With his grades he'd be accepted anywhere. Thank God, he chose to be near home.

"Jewel wants to know if anybody wants whipped cream with the pie," Katie said, bringing in a tray with wedges of hot pecan pie.

"You tell Jewel to stop trying to fatten me up," Maisie ordered. "She's ruining me. All I have to do is look at whipped cream, and I gain two pounds."

"I've been thinking, Laura," Everett said in that casual tone that warned her he was deviously plotting. "With the war women have moved into a new era. They've been pushed out of the kitchen. Don't you think it's time Magnolia women took a stronger role in local politics?" With an ingenuous air he turned from Laura to Maisie.

"Like what?" Maisie demanded, exchanging a swift glance with Laura.

"Like organizing a professional women's club in Magnolia."

Laura frowned.

"Doesn't that sound kind of elitist?"

"Honey, in Magnolia any woman who earns a regular salary is a professional," Maisie chuckled. "Whether she's a lawyer, teacher, saleswoman, or typist."

"I think it sounds terrific," Katie approved, digging enthusiastically into her pecan pie. "I mean, women go out to all kinds of jobs these days. Even into the army."

"Women don't realize the power they wield. The women's vote could control an election," Everett pointed out. "Right now a lot of them just vote the way their husbands do—if they bother to vote at all. But organize them into a group—and wow, would that change things!"

"Laura, you're the one to organize a women's group here. How many women in this country have made it in law and in real estate?" Maisie challenged, and Laura lifted an eyebrow in reproof. Law was still a difficult field for women. "All right, you're a terrific success in real estate—a man's world. And you practice law. Women in this town—particularly the young ones just moving out into the world—have tremendous respect for you."

"It never hurts a real-estate developer to have friends in public office," Everett said meaningfully. "A strong-minded women's club could throw its weight around in this town. Elected officers can be real grateful."

"You may not have a big law practice, Mom," Jonnie grinned, "but I'll bet nobody has more grateful clients." It was well known around town that Laura Hunter's clients rarely paid a fee—though Laura herself was silent about this.

"I'll invite a few women to join me for lunch next week," Laura said after a moment of inner debate. "We'll launch the professional women's club of Magnolia."

She remembered Barry's remark at the housewarming about her running for city commissioner. When the time looked right, she might do that.

The Harris project in Atlanta was moving ahead on schedule. Laura bought additional property at another Atlanta bank auction—immediately aware of its potential despite its depressing present state. The secret in buying property, Bernie had taught her, was to see ahead to what it could become.

She was wary of expanding in Magnolia in the face of a barrage of difficult new rulings passed by the city commissioners. Barry told her that these had been instigated by Judge Slocum to keep out new businesses. Laura participated in heated Chamber of Commerce meetings, where many of the members were pitted against the Slocums. Laura welcomed the undercurrent of revolt she sensed.

Early in the spring the Phillip Weinberg Memorial Library was dedicated at Magnolia High School. At Laura's insistence the donor was announced as anonymous—but the whole town knew who had made it possible. Mrs. Tannenbaum and Adele contrived to be in White Sulphur Springs at the time of the dedication.

Fighting tears—conscious of covert, sympathetic scrutiny—Laura sat among the guests and tried to focus on Phil's dedication to teaching. Their marriage had never been openly acknowledged, either by Phil's family or herself. She remained Laura Hunter, but Phil would remain forever in her heart.

"You okay?" Jonnie asked solicitously and reached to cover her hand with his.

"I'm fine," she whispered back. Bless Jonnie and Katie.

Late in May Jonnie was graduated from Magnolia High, the same school where—in the tumult of her father's arrest—Laura herself had been denied the right to make a commencement speech. Jonnie was making it for her, she told herself with defiant satisfaction.

Iris sent Jonnie an outrageously expensive watch from Cartier. She was in New York and planning to leave in two weeks for a borrowed house in Bar Harbor. She had hired a governess who would be able to tutor Noel. *"Laura, I can't believe he'll soon be six and ready for schooling. He's so handsome, and so damn spoiled. I keep telling Bridget not to let him run over her the way he does."* Bridget would become her personal maid with the arrival of the governess.

Iris urged Laura to come up to Bar Harbor for at least a week or two with the children in the course of the summer. But it would be impossible for her to spend even a few days at Bar Harbor, Laura reminded herself, as much as she would have enjoyed it.

At the same time that Judge Slocum's oldest son David announced he would run for city commissioner in the fall, the town was split wide by the discovery that it was losing a major new industry because the commissioners had rejected an application for an adjustment of newly passed and absurd zoning regulations.

"That's Slocum again!" Barry Berger voiced the sentiment of other Chamber of Commerce members gathered around the restaurant luncheon table for a hastily convened informal meeting. "He's costing this town at least fifteen hundred new jobs. Not to mention what the industry would have meant to our tax rolls."

"A lot of people in this town are angry," Laura said. "When they go to vote in the fall, they won't vote for David Slocum."

"The Slocums still throw a lot of weight around," another member warned uneasily. "The Judge is determined to replace Fred Peterson with his son." Peterson would not run for reelection because of poor health. He was one of two men among the commissioners who weren't manipulated by the Slocums. "He'll spend money like water and twist arms along the way."

370

"Barry, when do you announce your candidacy?" Craig Meyers asked. "We don't want to lose a day of campaigning."

"I don't think I should run," Barry said, and the others stared at him in shock. "I want to see Laura run. She'll bring out every woman voter in Magnolia. The timing is right," he emphasized. "Let's get out and make Laura Hunter the first woman commissioner in this town."

"The voters may complain that I'm a comparative newcomer," Laura hedged, but the prospect of beating out a Slocum was exhilarating. "And how many men will go to the polls and vote for a woman?"

"Laura, you've done more in this town in six years than most men do in their lifetime. And you've won a lot of friends along the way. You've earned a reputation for fairness and compassion. And for being a damn smart woman, Hank Richards, the Chamber of Commerce's long-time president, said with conviction. "And you may not take credit for the Weinberg Memorial Library at the high school, but everybody knows you put up the money for it. We'll have a better chance with you than with anybody I can think of. Begging your pardon, Barry," he apologized.

"Laura, will you run?" Craig asked. "Like Barry said, the time is ripe for change."

"I'll run," Laura agreed. *Laura Hunter vs. David Slocum.* For Papa she would do it.

Laura's announcement that she would run for Peterson's seat on the Commission generated an excitement in town that astonished her. Jonnie and Katie quickly became embroiled in the campaign. They handed out flyers, ran errands at campaign headquarters. The Professional Women's Club was immediately involved. Cecile — who briefly had been an advertising account executive in Boston before moving into interior decorating — took on the job of Laura's publicity director.

Despite the demands of business, Laura spoke before groups around town whenever the occasion arose. Iris phoned constantly to ask how the campaign was progressing. She found malicious delight in the prospect of Jacob Roth's daughter becoming a political power in Magnolia.

*"I know you won't do it, Laura, but I'd love to see you take office and run that bloody town right into the ground. Make them pay for what they did to Papa."*

Perspiring and in shirt sleeves, Judge Slocum pulled away from the back of his leather-upholstered chair and reached to adjust the electric fan on his desk. Eric was reporting on the New York phone call from the private detectives hired to dig into Laura Hunter's past.

"That's all they have to say?" he demanded when Eric finished. "We pay the fucking bastards a small fortune, and they come up with what we already know?"

"It's a prestigious detective agency," Eric said aggrievedly. "They were highly recommended by people in Washington."

"Where the hell is David?" The Judge reached to buzz for his secretary. Damn Maisie for quitting on him like that and going to work for Laura Hunter. The bitch knew more than she should about Derek, though she was too smart to spill her guts. "He should have been here twenty minutes ago."

The Judge's secretary opened the door, and behind her trailed David Slocum.

"It's all right," the Judge waved away his secretary. "Get in here, David."

David shut the door behind him and shot a swift glance from his father to Eric.

"The detectives came up with nothing," he guessed.

"They traced her back to New York Law School and Hunter College. She married a young law clerk who went into practice with her and got himself murdered by some nut. She left New York and came down here," Eric

372

reported. "As far as they can see, she wasn't running away from any criminal background."

"How did she come up with all that cash to start up down here the way she did?" the Judge challenged. "Not from that two-bit practice you told me about."

"The story was that the husband defended the son of some big-time racketeer in New York. The father came across with a fancy fee."

"What about before she went to New York? When she was living in that town in South Carolina?" the Judge pushed.

"They say there's no such town as Bickford, South Carolina," Eric reported. "We must have been mixed up on that."

"No," the Judge rejected. He rose from his desk and crossed to the row of files at one side of the room. "I'm sure it's in her letter of application." He pulled open a file drawer, rummaged among the folders, plucked out a letter. "Goddamn it, here it is. Bickford, South Carolina. I tell you, she's hiding something," he said with triumph. "Eric, you get on the phone with those fucking detectives. You tell them we want some real answers—and we want them fast!"


Rumors reached Laura regularly about the Judge's rage that she was conducting such a strong campaign. He was vowing to cut her down. First she had dared to challenge him as a real-estate developer. Now she dared to run for political office against his son.

The Slocum wives gave small teas and talked lightly about David's run for office. Their photographs appeared with calculated frequency on the society pages of the *Journal* and the *Herald,* along with stories extolling their philanthropic efforts.

Laura spoke with impassioned eloquence before business groups, women's clubs, on the local radio station. She was the new young voice pleading for much needed change in city government. She canvassed personally in the colored section of Magnolia and in the mill section. She was blunt in her assessment of the Slocum machine, but everything she said was based on truth.

With the imminent approach of the election Laura's campaign committee was confidently predicting victory.

"It won't even be close," Barry chortled. "There's a change coming in this town. The war has brought in new people, brought about new thinking. The Judge sees the handwriting on the wall. It's the end of a dynasty."


At the elegant white colonial built by Judge Slocum's grandfather before the Civil War, the Judge sat in the library with his sons and villified Laura Hunter.

"That woman has been trouble since the day she lied her way into my office." A vein pounded in his forehead. "She stole the Donnell farm right out from our noses. She's connived and cheated and pushed her way up to where she thinks she can run this town. *This is my town—I'll run it the way I want!*"

"It doesn't look good for David right now," Eric Slocum, the Judge's adopted nephew, said somberly. "She's got a strong element behind her. The detectives have dredged up nothing we can use against her. We can't come out and say, 'we sure as hell don't want a woman or a Jew on the Commission.' "

"You boys go out and make it clear—in the right places—that I want David to win," the Judge ordered. His poised, patrician image shattered in the privacy of his home. "I don't give a shit how much it costs!" He glowered at the intrusion of a knock on the door. Didn't Josiah know after all these years not to disturb them when they were in the library? "Come in."

The door opened. A tall, slender, smartly dressed woman with impeccably coiffed white hair came into the library.

"We're ready to sit down to dinner, Matthew," Mrs.

Slocum told the Judge with a hint of reproach in her genteel voice. "Lily Mae can't delay much longer."

"We'll be right there, Betty," the Judge promised and pushed back his chair. The sky might be falling down, but his wife had to entertain their sons and daughters-in-law every Thursday evening.

The men joined the three Slocum wives in the high-ceilinged dining room. The lace curtains at the tall, narrow windows swayed slightly in the hot summer breeze.

"I don't know why we didn't go to the mountains this summer," David's wife sighed. "We always do."

"You didn't," the Judge said brusquely, "because your husband is running for city commissioner."

Betty lifted a hand to indicate to Josiah that dinner was to be served. "Matthew, you've always said in the past that politics was not the concern of women. Why are we being involved this time?"

"Because, Betty," he said with the strained politeness he used towards his wife outside their bedroom, "we're running into strange times. It's not at all clear that David is going to win this election." He stared from woman to woman with grim satisfaction. That shook them up a bit. "Laura Hunter is causing us a peck of trouble. She and all those other Northerners coming into town since the start of the war. They don't understand how we run things in Magnolia."

"Matthew, Slocums always win." Betty Slocum's smile was arrogant, but he sensed she was nervous. "But enough of politics. This weather is just awful. I think maybe we ought to run down to the plantation for two or three days," she turned to her daughters-in-law. "Tomorrow's the day I visit Miss Pearson at the nursing home, but—"

"Stay away from the plantation until after the election!" the Judge interrupted. It amazed him that Laura Hunter hadn't dragged out the truth about Derek. He'd had to tell her that time when Derek tried to jump her in the office. And Maisie knew, too. Maybe Hunter wasn't as smart as he'd thought she was. "You're all part of the family image," he said, striving for casualness. "Let's be visible."

"How is Miss Pearson?" David's wife asked her mother-in-law. "I think it's so sweet of you to visit her every month."

"Oh, she's doing very well," Betty said. "Her memory is not always so clear, but she recalls everything from the years she taught at Magnolia High. All of us took French with Miss Pearson. Well, not you, Matthew." For a moment she was the flirtatious Southern belle. "You were out of high school by the time she began to teach. Miss Pearson might not understand the country is at war, but she remembers her pupils."

"Eric, you go down to the colored church on Sunday." The Judge squinted into space while his mind plotted. "Talk to them about getting out to vote in this election. And tell the minister we're presenting the church with a memorial plaque in honor of that young Negro who was some kind of hero in the Solomon Islands."

Seemingly undisturbed by the morning heat, Betty Slocum waited in her chauffeured limousine until Josiah appeared with a bouquet of flowers for her to present to Miss Pearson. She was still unnerved by what Matthew had said at dinner about David's having a bad time in his first campaign for public office. Matthew always said that David would be mayor of Magnolia by the time he was forty. That was only one year away.

"Thank you, Josiah." Betty smiled and accepted the flowers. Several magazines and the morning's *Journal* lay on the seat beside her. On each visit to Miss Pearson for the past seven years she brought flowers, magazines, and the morning's newspaper.

At the nursing home she found Miss Pearson in her wheelchair in the garden.

"Betty, how sweet of you." This was one of Miss Pearson's good days. "I thought it was about time you'd be visiting me again."

Betty listened to Miss Pearson's small cache of gossip while part of her mind focused on Matthew's concern about the election. All Miss Pearson wanted was a willing ear. A show of interest was all that was required.

"And you remembered to bring me today's *Journal*," Miss Pearson said archly, reaching for the paper and unfolding it. "Oh my, another picture of Laura. Such a bright child, and so pretty."

"Laura Hunter?" Betty asked involuntarily. Was Miss Pearson slipping into unreality? Up till now everybody had been so amazed at her memory for her students.

"Oh, when I knew her she was Laura Roth. Pupils like Laura I always remember. I always said, 'we should have more Lauras in this school.' " "Already Miss Pearson had that vague smile on her surprisingly unlined face that said she was creeping back into yesterday.

Miss Pearson was making a mistake. Laura Hunter had not gone to school in Magnolia. Matthew said she'd originally come from South Carolina. What had Miss Pearson called her? Laura *Roth*? Why was that name familiar? She searched her mind for a moment. *Jacob Roth. The man who raped and murdered little Tammy Lee Johnson.* He'd had two daughters. Laura and Iris Roth.

Excitement charged through Betty Slocum. All at once it was urgent to talk to Matthew.

"I'll see you next month, Miss Pearson," she said politely, though she suspected her former teacher was no longer aware of her presence.

She hurried from the nursing home to the waiting limousine.

"To the Judge's office, Noah," she instructed the chauffeur.

If Miss Pearson was right, Laura Hunter would never be elected to anything in this town. David would become the new commissioner. Now she was attacked by doubts. Would Matthew laugh at her? But she had to tell him what Miss Pearson said.

Twenty minutes later Betty sat in her husband's office and reported on the meeting with Miss Pearson.

"Betty, Miss Pearson is senile." Damn it, did she have to interrupt his day with this stupidity? But she was upset. Slocums never lost an election in this town.

"I know it sounds ridiculous," Betty conceded, "but Matthew, everybody knows she has this phenomenal memory. When we gave that party at the nursing home for her on her eightieth birthday, she recognized Suzanne Evans, whom she hadn't seen in twenty-eight years. Suzanne couldn't believe it."

This might be worth some digging, Slocum considered. Why would Laura Hunter want to hide her birthplace? "That could be why the detectives couldn't locate her home town in South Carolina. Why would she come back here?" he pursued aloud. He smiled with malicious pleasure. "To get revenge on the town? If she is Laura Roth, we've got the election sewed up. But first I have to prove it—"

"How will you do that?"

"Watch me, Betty." He left his desk and strode to the door of his office, swung it wide. "Mary Lou, I want you to drive over to the high school and ask whoever is in the office to loan you a copy of the high-school yearbook for—" He squinted in thought for a moment. "For 1924. Tell them it's for me—and get back here with it fast.

At her husband's instructions Betty phoned around town on his private line until she located David.

"Tell him to get his butt over here quick," the Judge ordered, "and now try to locate Eric." He stood at his desk and ripped out photographs of Laura Hunter from a collection of old newspapers.

When Mary Lou returned with the yearbook, the three men were gathered about the desk inspecting newspaper photographs of Laura. Betty Slocum sat at one end of the green-velvet sofa and sipped at an iced cherry Coke.

"Thank you, Mary Lou. That'll be all," he dismissed

her.

David began to flip through the pages of the yearbook.

"Have you got a magnifying glass somewhere?" David asked. His voice was thick with excitement. His father supplied this immediately.

"Is she Laura Roth?" the Judge demanded after a few moments.

"It's hard to tell," David faltered. "The school picture was taken twenty years ago.

"Let me have that." Eric took the glass from David and peered at the photographs. He frowned, seeming ambivalent. "Like David said, this was twenty years ago—"

"Let me see." Impatiently the Judge took the yearbook and magnifying glass from Eric and inspected the photograph himself. "Look at this, and then at these newspaper photographs." He grunted in satisfaction. "Forget that her hair is darker now and she's wearing it differently. The mouth, the nose, the eyebrows, the eyes—they're the same!"

"We need some proof," Eric cautioned. "If she isn't Laura Roth, this could backfire."

"Wait a moment," Betty rose from the sofa and walked to the desk. "Her sister was here recently. There was something on the society pages about her. Lady Cranford—she married some British lord. Lady Iris Cranford," she pinpointed. "Wasn't the other Roth girl named Iris?"

"That's it! Laura and Iris. It can't be just a coincidence." The Judge slammed a fist on his desk. "It's all here in front of our eyes."

"We should have irrefutable proof," Eric argued.

"Fuck irrefutable proof," the Judge dismissed this. "Pardon my language, Betty. We've got all the proof we want right here. We'll run with it. Call Mike over at the *Journal*. Tell him to get over here fast—and clear the front page for a new headline story for the afternoon paper: LAURA HUNTER DAUGHTER OF CONVICTED RAPIST-MURDERER JACOB ROTH."

# Chapter 30

As soon as the car approached Magnolia, Laura began to relax. The day in Atlanta had been hectic, hot, and humid. It was so generous — so typically sweet — of Maisie and Everett to share their gas coupons with her so that she could enjoy the luxury of driving to and from Atlanta now and then. It was so much more pleasant than traveling on the overcrowded train, where more often than not she had to stand.

She smiled as the pungent scent of honeysuckle, blending with the aromas of the pine forests, seemed to charge towards her. Coming home after a strenuous day in Atlanta, she always felt herself enveloped in an aura of cherished serenity. She enjoyed the stimulation of Atlanta for a few hours — it was a small version of New York, but Magnolia was home.

Laura debated about her first destination. She would stop first at campaign headquarters — Jonnie and Katie would be there — and go to the office later. Her face lighted with maternal love and pride. They were spending their whole vacation working for her election. But in a couple of weeks, she remembered wistfully, Jonnie would be going off to college.

She swung left now into the center of town, heading for the vacant store that had become their campaign headquarters. At the store she parked and left the car. What was happening inside? Why was everybody gathered around Ethel Lynch's desk? Ethel was their one full-time paid helper.

Katie was crying, she realized in sudden alarm. Cecile had her arm over her shoulders trying to comfort her.

Jonnie was talking excitedly to the others. With a premonition of disaster she hurried across the sidewalk to the store. Everybody looked up with strangely hostile faces as she opened the door and walked inside.

"Mom!" Katie picked up a newspaper from Ethel's desk and rushed towards her. "Mom, tell them this is all lies!"

Feeling as though she had been hit across the head with a sledge-hammer, instinctively knowing she had been unmasked, Laura took the newspaper from Katie and read the headline that stared at her. "LAURA HUNTER, DAUGHTER OF RAPIST-MURDERER." Her eyes skimmed to the photographs below. The picture of her from her high school annual—and a current newspaper shot. The resemblance was hardly striking but they knew. The Slocums, of course—to get her out of the race.

"I phoned Barry," Cecile said, her eyes somber and questioning. "He's calling an emergency meeting here at six."

"Katie—Jonnie—please wait for me in the car," Laura told them, her heart pounding, her mind in turmoil.

Katie stood still, waiting for her mother to deny the headline. Jonnie reached for her hand.

"Come on, you heard what Mom said."

Laura watched them walk out the door, then turned to Cecile. She was conscious of the volcanic atmosphere as Ethel and the half-dozen volunteers waited for her to deny this bombshell, even as Katie had waited.

"Cecile, tell Barry I'm withdrawing from the race." Laura flinched before Cecile's startled comprehension.

"Maybe there's some way we can handle this," Cecile tried, but Laura shook her head.

"Not after this—" Involuntarily her eyes settled on the newspaper headline. She could survive withdrawing from the race. At this moment it was unimportant. But how would she make Jonnie and Katie understand about Papa?

"It's true!" Ethel Lynch shrieked into the leaden silence. "You're Laura Roth! That monster's daughter!"

"My father was not a monster!" Laura lashed back, trembling in rage. "My father was a kind, gentle, intelligent man who was railroaded to his death by people in this town who didn't want the truth to be known."

"What truth?" a volunteer asked avidly.

Despite her shock Laura's mind was sharp. She must say nothing to alert the Slocums to her suspicions about Derek. She was not prepared to make accusations. Not yet.

"One day the people in Magnolia will know they convicted an innocent man." She fought to keep her voice in control. *And then they lynched him.* The real murderer will be brought to justice one day. I know this."

"Why did you come back here?" demanded an elderly woman who had joined the campaign "because it gives me something to do with my afternoons." "Why did you lie to everyone?" Her voice held a shrill reproach.

"I didn't lie," Laura said. "My husband's name was Hunter—I was Laura Hunter." She hesitated. "I came back to Magnolia because I'd always loved this town— and because I'm convinced that one day someone here will speak out and clear my father's name." She paused, her breathing suddenly labored. "If you'll excuse me, I have to go to my children."

Laura walked out of the store and crossed to the car. How did the Slocums find out? Aside from Phil, only Maisie and Everett knew—and they would never have told the Slocums. Where had she slipped up?

Still crying, Katie was huddled on the back seat. Pale and somber Jonnie sat up front. Laura slid behind the wheel and reached for the ignition key.

"Mom, do you want me to drive?" he asked, touchingly protective.

"Thanks, but I'll drive." She needed to do this to keep from falling apart. What she had always promised herself could never happen had happened.

With deliberate slowness Laura told her children about the nightmare of her father's arrest, conviction, and lynching. Subconsciously, she was aware of a newsboy embarking on his route, spreading the ugly disclosure. She told Jonnie and Katie how Iris and she had been driven from the town. That she had gone to college and law school in the conviction that a law degree would help her to prove her father's innocence.

"I'd swore I'd come back here one day and prove he had not been guilty of that awful crime. Phil knew—he was working with me. We had some leads." She chose her words carefully. She mustn't say too much—the children mustn't know her suspicions about Derek Slocum. "But above all else, remember that my father—your grandfather—was a wonderful man. He could never have killed that little girl."

"You shouldn't have come back here!" Katie blazed. "Why did you do this to us? It was dumb to think nobody would ever find out!"

"Katie, shut up," Jonnie said through clenched teeth. "It's all a bunch of lies."

"He *was* convicted," Katie shot back. "That mob lynched him."

"That doesn't make them right," Laura reminded.

"How do we even know you're our mother?" Katie challenged. "You've lied to us about everything else!"

"Katie, shut up!" Jonnie repeated, half leaning over the back of his seat in his rage. "Don't you ever talk to Mom like that again."

"I want to go back to New York," Katie sobbed. "Nothing like this would have happened there. You shouldn't have brought us here."

The instant Laura brought the car to a stop in the driveway, Katie darted for the house. Following behind her, Laura paused at the stairway leading to the second floor. She winced at the sound of Katie's bedroom door slamming shut. Jonnie hovered anxiously at her side. They heard Jewel singing in the kitchen while she prepared dinner.

"Miz Laura, you want a cup of coffee before you sit

down to eat?" Jewel called.

"No thanks, Jewel." Later she would have to explain what had happened. Jewel was like a member of the family.

"Mom, I don't have to go to college this term," Jonnie said. "I mean, I can wait a year—"

"You'll go to school as planned," she told him. What had she done to Jonnie and Katie? She loved them so much—and she was bringing them such hurt. "Nothing has changed, Jonnie. Except that I'm not running for city commissioner. But I won't let them drive me out of Magnolia a second time. We're *staying.*"

Jonnie went to his room to read until dinner. And to try to cope with the terrible revelations that had just assaulted him, Laura tormented herself. She knew not to approach Katie, locked in her room. She reached for the phone to call her office.

"Laura, are you all right?" Maisie asked anxiously at the sound of her voice.

"You saw the newspapers." Oh God, she was so tired. So drained.

"I figured on working a little late tonight. Everett went out to get coffee for us. He saw the *Journal.* Laura, how did they find out?" Laura heard her anguish. "You know we didn't tell them."

"I'm sure of that. I keep asking myself, how did it happen?"

"Do the kids know?"

"They know. Katie's distraught. You know Jonnie—he always keeps everything inside. But he's very supportive."

"You're still running for commissioner," Maisie said, but Laura sensed she was trying to convince herself of this.

"That's impossible now. Probably Barry will replace me."

"Everett and I will be over after dinner. Honey, remember you're not alone."

384

Laura knocked lightly at Katie's door waited for a reply. The silence was ominous.

"Jewel is ready to put dinner on the table," Laura cajoled through the closed door.

"I'm not hungry," Katie's voice was muffled, as though she had pulled the bedspread over her head despite the warmth of the evening. Katie always ran from hurt by burrowing under the bedclothes.

"All right, darling." Laura knew not to press. She had been only a few months older than Katie when Papa died, but somehow Katie seemed so much younger.

"Mom, Mrs. Berger's on the phone," Jonnie called. "Jewel says should she hold dinner?"

"No, tell her to go ahead—I'll be right there."

Laura talked for a few minutes with Cecile. It had been agreed that Barry would replace Laura, though chances of his being elected were meager considering the situation. Cecile made it clear that nothing had changed in their feelings towards her. She reported that Barry's mother said the Jewish community had been convinced Jacob Roth was innocent.

"Some folks are concerned that with the case resurrected this way, we might have a fresh outbreak of anti-Semitism."

"Cecile, it happened twenty years ago!" Laura was astonished that anyone could harbor such thoughts.

"I know." Cecile managed a wry chuckle. "But this is the South. You lived in New York for a lot of years. I grew up in Boston. Being Jewish in a large city is a whole different ballgame from the rest of the country. Jews here never totally forget that their assimilation is on a 9 A.M. to 5 P.M. basis. You'll never see Jewish guests at the homes of the Slocums or the Lowells or the Pendletons."

"I keep asking myself, how did the Slocums dredge this up? I was so certain nobody knew—except for Maisie and Everett, who certainly would never tell them."

Cecile hesitated.

"Laura, I discovered how it happened. You know how everybody gossips around town. Betty Slocum was at the nursing home this morning—visiting Miss Pearson. That sweet old lady had no inkling what she was doing to you. She recognized you from the newspaper photos. She told Betty Slocum how you'd been in her class years ago. Betty ran to tell the Judge. They got the 1924 school annual and put your annual photograph beside the newspaper pictures. You could have denied it. They probably never could have proved it."

"No," Laura said softly. "They would have kept digging until the truth came out."

"Miz Laura, that pot roast is gonna get cold," Jewel called loudly from the dining room, and Laura excused herself. Thank God for friends like Cecile and Barry and Maisie and Everett.

After dinner Maisie and Everett arrived. Maisie refused to be pessimistic.

"People will talk a lot, sure," she conceded. "But it'll blow over fast. Laura, you're providing a lot of jobs in this town. You donate money to every charity drive that comes up. So you won't be city commissioner. You still throw a lot of weight around. People respect that."

"What about the kids?" Everett asked.

"Jonnie goes away to school in less than two weeks. He'll be all right. It's Katie that I worry about. She's been through the horror of her father's death. I uprooted her from all her friends and dragged her down here. Then there was my secret marriage to Phil—and his death. Now this."

"Give her some time," Everett said. "Kids are resilient. She'll snap back."

"How will her friends react to this?" Laura demanded. "Kids can be so cruel." She remembered how their friends had shunned Iris and her at the time of their father's trial. Her best friend had ignored her at school. Would that happen to Katie?

"It'll be rough for a while," Maisie said gravely. "But there are people here who love her—she'll be all right."

Laura stared into the darkness of her bedroom knowing it was impossible to will herself to sleep. She was too conscious of Katie, awake and miserable in the bedroom across the hall. And torturous memories of the weeks of her father's trial, his death, assaulted her.

All at once it was urgent to talk to Iris. She left her bed and went downstairs to the room that had become her office at home. Iris had been in Washington for the past three weeks, though she complained about the awful heat. But Newport and Bar Harbor were dead these past three summers, Iris wrote. Diana and she were playing hostesses for Arnold Harris and Jimmy in their borrowed Georgian mansion on R Street. From a recent business luncheon with Arnold in Atlanta, Laura knew he was having problems buying raw materials for the company. That had sent him to Washington.

Impatient to hear Iris's voice, Laura called the number in Washington, D.C. She waited, listening to the ring at the other end. Nobody answered. It was late—the servants were off for the night and the others off partying, no doubt. Iris had written that despite the war, Washington, D.C. was still a partying town. In the capital partying was important business.

All right she'd try again in half an hour. She'd keep trying until she reached her sister.

# Chapter 31

At an Embassy party—wearing a chic black crêpe gown with slit skirt, Iris feigned amused interest in Ernie Castello's gossip about Evalyn Walsh McLean's last Sunday dinner. Around them three monarchs deprived of their thrones, a pair of congressmen, and a host of government bigwigs and their ladies talked animatedly and consumed much champagne. The true object of her interest was a pair across the room, Arnold Harris, in deep conversation with Ernie's business representative. Arnold wanted Ernie distracted while he tried to make a deal for the raw material he needed badly. If the business representative gave his word, Ernie would accept it, even though he felt his company should explore other offers. Arnold had delicately suggested that she take Ernie off to the China benefit and handed over a pair of high-priced tickets.

"Ernie, why don't we get out of here? This party was dead two hours ago." Iris's smile was a blatant invitation. She was convinced the wealthy South American would not be intrigued by two tickets to the latest China benefit.

"There's a party at the Brazilian Embassy," he offered, though his eyes made it clear he had another destination in mind.

"Let's go some place we can be alone." Iris slipped an arm through his. He had been making a play for her for the past week without receiving a hint of acceptance. "You're a most attractive man, Ernie." Darkly handsome, still trim in his early forties, it was true. Probably passionate as hell. Everybody said South American men were hot. And Ernie was very rich, she remembered with a flicker of interest. Not that she would ever give up being Lady Cranford. But there was no harm in fantasizing.

"I keep an apartment not far from here," he said, a glint of victory in his eyes.

In silence they quickly left the party and walked out into the sultry night. Moments later Ernesto Castello's chauffeured Mercedes drew up at the curb, and he handed Iris inside. Why did rich men always excite her? Rich was sexy.

In his charming Portuguese-accented English, Ernie talked about his rubber plantation in Brazil and about his pride that Brazil had sent troops to fight with the Allies—the only South American country to do so. Then the chauffeur pulled up before Ernie's elegant apartment house, and they left the car to walk to the entrance.

"I am here in Washington more often than at home," he said humorously, an arm about her waist.

The elevator door opened in the lobby to reveal a pretty young girl in an amorous embrace with a naval ensign. They separated with sudden realization, and the girl giggled as they emerged. Iris tensed as she intercepted Ernie's approving inspection of the curvaceous young figure. Damn it, why did every man look hungry at the sight of a twenty-year-old body?

She was thirty-seven years old. Three years from now she'd be forty. Where did the years go? She didn't feel like thirty-seven. She felt like twenty-seven. Diana said that after the war they both ought to go to that place in Switzerland where the doctors did marvelous things with injections.

When the elevator door closed behind them, Ernie pulled her into his arms for a heated kiss.

"I've been wanting to do that since I first met you," he admitted when they separated. "You Englishwomen are so—what is the word?" He squinted in thought. "Standoffish."

389

"I'm an American," she corrected him. "I'm married to an Englishman, who's unfortunately in very bad health."

"My wife, too, is in bad health," he told her. He didn't believe what she said about Peter's health. Nor did she believe it about his wife. But he felt comfortable in the knowledge that this would be no more than a brief fling.

"Tell me more about Brazil," she encouraged. She was still fighting against resentment at the way he had looked at that girl in the elevator. Did he think someone that young and inexperienced could please a man the way she could? So she wasn't twenty. Neither was he.

Ernie unlocked the door to the luxurious penthouse and gestured to her to enter. She understood; the servants were gone for the night.

"Champagne?" he asked, already walking to the Louis XIV cabinet that obviously masked a bar.

"I don't need champagne," she mocked. What the devil was she doing here? Would it make her feel young again to sleep with Ernie Castello?

"I was being polite," he shrugged, but she felt his arousal when their eyes clashed.

"Stop being polite," she ordered. "Make love to me."

With three strides he stood before her. She lifted her face to his, her mouth parted. In a sudden gesture she kicked off her shoes, knowing how he enjoyed towering above her.

"You are the most provocative woman I've ever met," he said, taking her face between his hands.

Iris closed her eyes while his mouth came down upon hers and his tongue probed, his hands at her breasts, his hips moving against her own. He wasn't thinking about that young slut in the elevator now.

For a few moments they were content to move against each other. Then his hands were inside the deep neckline of her dress, fondling one nipple, the hardness of him arousing her. She was never passionate until she was convinced the man couldn't wait. It gave her such a feeling of power.

"Let's go into the bedroom," he said thickly.

"We'll shower first." It was an order. "Together."

"The tub." His smile was enigmatic. "There's this enormous black marble masterpiece in the master bathroom."

Hand in hand they left the living room, walked with taunting slowness down the hall to the master bedroom suite. He reached for the wall switch, and the bedroom was bathed in soft light.

"It's a real showplace, yes?" He smiled with pride while Iris admired the magnificent antiques, the priceless Aubusson rug at their feet. "It was decorated by Syrie Maugham for some mideast ruler who was deposed. I bought it as soon as it came on the market."

"It's charming," Iris conceded. "But after England I find flats so confining." He might be a multimillionaire South American, but she knew he was impressed that she was Lady Cranford.

"You'll forget that in a few moments," he promised.

He stripped with an economy of motions that excited her. She dawdled, aware of the erotic portrait she provided. At last she stood nude before him, small without her ridiculously high heels, as voluptuous and firm as she had been at twenty.

"The bath?" she drawled.

"Later," he said and cursed in Portuguese. "Stop tormenting me!" With one startling sweep he lifted her from her feet and tossed her across the bed. In another moment he hovered above her, his hands encircling her hips as he prodded between her thighs. It was going to be great, she told herself as he found his way and began to thrust within her.

"Hold my breasts," she whispered. "Hold them in your hands, and it'll be wonderful for both of us."

In a few minutes the bedroom echoed with the sounds of their passion. Then he swung over on his back. They were both content to lay motionless against the mound of satin pillows, both caught up in the pleasure of the ultimate emotion.

"What is that scent?" he asked, lifting himself on one elbow to gaze down at her.

"*Tabu*," she said, and he laughed.

"I'll run us a tub." He sat upright and swung his legs to the floor.

Iris lingered on the bed, one leg flexed provocatively. Damn him for staring that way at that girl. Too often now she remembered the years. Forty sounded like a death knell. But she wouldn't become one of those women in their sixties and seventies who dashed about with lovers half their age.

What would happen to her when Peter died? Everybody in England with money was petrified about the huge death taxes. What would be left for Noel and her to divide with Peter's other children? She'd be too old to marry rich again. Rich men wanted young wives.

Jimmy was funny sometimes, the way he talked to her about their growing old together. He had never made a pass at Diana or her. Diana said he was neuter. She always felt comfortable with Jimmy—no playing games the way she did with everybody else. He said that his father and she were a lot alike—neither of them respected anything except money.

"Madam—" Ernie strode into the bedroom. "Our tub awaits," he announced with mock courtliness. "Champagne now?"

"Why not?" Her smile was dazzling. *Why did she play these stupid games?*


Laura awoke, for an instant bewildered to find herself sitting in an armchair in the office. Then the memory of the day's bizarre happenings swept over her with the intensity of a tornado. She had come down here to phone Iris. Only Iris could know what she was feeling.

What time was it? She leaned forward for a view of the clock on the mantel. It was past 3 A.M. Was it too late to phone Iris? No, in her world the evening was just drawing to a close.

A strange relief rushed through her when Iris picked up at the other end. With sentences already formed in her mind she told Iris what had happened.

"Laura, get out of that town!" Iris's voice was strident. "In Magnolia you'll always be Laura Roth, whose father was lynched. Look what they did to us. Do you want that to happen to Katie and Jonnie, too?"

"Iris, I can't just walk out," Laura protested. "I've built up a very successful business. I never dreamed I'd do so well."

"You can move your business anywhere. You can build a national real-estate empire with what you've learned. You're smart. Remember what Papa used to say? 'Laura could become president of the United States if she was a man.' I know you've made a lot of money," Iris was conciliatory now. "But I'm talking about Laura Hunter, multimillionaire real-estate tycoon."

"I have to stay in Magnolia," Laura said slowly. "I'm on to something about Tammy Lee's murder."

"Laura, grow up," Iris ordered. "So you had a young girl's fantasy about clearing Papa's name. You're a woman now. You know it's not going to happen."

"I've never for one moment thought that," Laura said quietly. "More than ever I have to make this town know — because now it's affecting the children."

"You're obsessed, Laura." Iris's tone verged on exasperation.

"It will happen," Laura said stubbornly. "I don't know when — but the day will come when Papa's memory will be honored in this town. I live for that day, Iris."

Exhausted from too little sleep, Laura settled herself at the breakfast table. Jewel was determined to be cheerful, though her eyes betrayed her distress.

"Don't you pay no mind to that cloudy sky, you hear, Miz Laura? I feel in my bones it's gonna clear befo' you

393

leave for the office."

"Hi, Mom." Jonnie came into the breakfast room. "Hi, Jewel," he called into the kitchen.

"Good morning, darling." Had Jonnie lain awake half the night, worrying about how his friends would react to the newspaper headlines?

"Mom," he asked somberly, sliding into his chair, "do I have to work at campaign headquarters today?"

"That's up to you, Jonnie," she said after a painful moment. Was Katie right? Had she been terribly wrong in bringing the children here? "Why don't you talk to Chet about it?" she encouraged. Chet Berger was his best friend. They would be roommates at the University of Georgia.

"Okay. I'll call him now. His mother doesn't mind early calls," he said.

"You get back here quick," Jewel ordered. "I'm putting up French toast. And yell upstairs to Katie to get herself down to the table."

A few minutes later Jonnie returned, his expression more relaxed.

"I'm meeting Chet at nine o'clock," he reported. "We're distributing circulars. His father had them run off overnight." He sat down and reached for his orange juice. "Mom, I think I want to go on to law school after college." The love that she could feel between Jonnie and her brought tears to Laura's eyes. "I want to help you clear our grandfather."

"I think that will be very nice. But you don't have to decide your first year at college. Give it some serious thought."

"I will," he promised. "But I know I'll go on to law school." Laura watched while he seemed involved in some inner debate. "Mom, when Daddy was killed after he cleared that man in his last case, did he believe the man was innocent? The newspapers all sounded as though everybody was sure the man was guilty."

"Jonnie, how did you know what the newspapers said?"

Her voice was involuntarily shrill. She thought she had kept those horrible tabloid stories from the children. The whole week they were sitting *shivah*, no newspapers came into the apartment. After a week the stories about the murders and suicide were replaced by another sensational case. Jonnie and Katie saw only a handful of people. *"How did you know?"*

"I took old newspapers from garbage cans," he confessed. "I'd heard people in the house talking. They looked at us in that funny way—"

How little you knew what went on in children's minds. They knew—they observed—so much more than you gave them credit for. All these years—since he was ten years old—that question had been festering in Jonnie.

"Did he, Mom?" Jonnie pressed.

"Ray DeVito was Daddy's client," Laura said carefully, remembering her own anger, her hurt and disappointment, when Bernie took on the case. "It was his job to defend him."

"But he didn't have to take the case if he thought the man was guilty," Jonnie persisted.

Laura paused. It would be wrong to lie to her son.

"Daddy and I thought Ray DeVito was guilty," Laura acknowledged. "I admit I was upset when he took on the case. But Jonnie, that was in the middle of the Depression. Ray DeVito's father promised Daddy twenty-five thousand dollars if he won an acquittal. You don't know what it was like in those days." She felt afresh the agony of never knowing if they would be able to pay the rent, buy needed clothes, terrified of some medical emergency. "That money was a fortune. Daddy was fighting for our survival."

"But the man was guilty!" Jonnie accused. "Maybe he'd go out and kill somebody else after that."

"Jonnie, remember—your father loved us all very much. He was afraid for our future. He couldn't bring himself to turn down the case. Somebody else would have taken it. With the DeVito money behind him any sharp

395

lawyer would have won an acquittal."

"I won't ever do that," Jonnie said with heated conviction. "I won't defend anybody unless I'm sure he's innocent."

"Jonnie, don't blame your father," Laura pleaded. "He did what he thought was best for us." She paused. "Did you ever discuss this with Katie?"

"No." Jonnie was startled. "She's younger than me — and she's a girl."

"Where's your sister?" Jewel asked Jonnie as she brought out the first batch of French toast to Laura, always the first out of the house in the morning.

"Oh, she said she wasn't coming down," Jonnie reported.

Laura and Jewel exchanged an anxious glance.

"I'll go up and talk to her," Laura said, pushing back her chair.

Laura knocked lightly, steeling herself for rejection. She still recoiled from the rage she'd felt in Katie last night.

"Come in." The low, disinterested voice told Laura that Katie was still angry with her. Had she expected Katie's hurt to evaporate overnight?

"Darling, I'd like you to come down and have breakfast with me before I leave for the office."

"I don't want breakfast." Anger crept into Katie's voice. "I'm going back to sleep. This is vacation time, isn't it?"

"There must be something you'd like to do today." Laura strived to sound casual. "After all, school opens soon — you won't have all this time on your hands."

"I'm not going back to school," Katie said defiantly. "Not in this town."

"Katie —"

"They all hate me now! No one called me last night!" Usually Katie talked on the phone for hours every evening. "Not even Annabel! My best friend." Oh God, Laura thought, it was happening again — the way it happened to Iris and her. "I won't go back to that school."

396

"But Katie—" Laura began.

"I want to go to boarding school," Katie said. "Far from here. You can afford it," she challenged. "Everybody in town knows we're rich. I want to go to boarding school in New York," she pinpointed and then hesitated. Her father had been murdered in New York. "Not New York—but somewhere far away—"

"We'll have to talk about this, Katie," Laura said after a moment. She was shaken. It was unnerving to visualize Katie away at school for months on end. Yet for Katie perhaps it was the only way. "I'll have to talk to some people." Her eyes told Katie this would be given serious consideration. Was Iris right? Should she take the children and move to another town? Or did Katie need distance from *her* at this point in her life? It was a painful supposition.

Laura fought to cope with the realization that she had created this crisis in Katie's life. What was that line from Oscar Wilde? "And all men kill the thing they love." Had she killed Katie's love when she meant only to protect her?

She remembered that Cecile and her sister had gone to boarding school for two years after their mother's early death. She'd call Cecile from the office, Laura decided, and ask her to have lunch. Cecile would help her.

At the office Laura was relieved to be caught up in work. The staff—except for Maisie—was subdued this morning. Still, Laura thought, she felt no hostility. And Maisie, bless her, behaved as though this were just any other morning.

Walking into the crowded restaurant for lunch with Cecile, Laura was conscious of cold stares from several tables. But Cecile was waiting at their table with a warm welcome. They talked for a few moments about the campaign, then about the liberation of Paris by Allied troops just forty-eight hours ago.

"I've been so caught up in private troubles I don't know what's going on in the world." Laura chastised herself.

"Barry says we shouldn't be hanging out 'welcome home' signs yet, but we've got the Nazis on the run. One of the radio newscasters said that Patton sent Eisenhower a message from France: 'Dear Ike—Today I have spat in the Seine.' "

"Cecile, Katie wants to go away to boarding school," Laura said quietly. "Somewhere up north. I thought you might be able to help." Instantly she felt Cecile's compassion.

They talked about the boarding school Cecile and her sister had attended. Laura understood that it was late to be applying for this school year, but Cecile offered to phone the headmistress at the Madison School for Girls and try to make arrangements for Katie.

"You're dying at the thought of her being so far away," Cecile surmised, and Laura nodded—fighting tears. "It may be what she needs right now. She can come back home whenever she likes. There'll be no problem about her returning to Magnolia High."

"It's just that she's so young—and hurting so much."

"You weren't much older than Katie when Iris and you went up to New York with no help in sight from anybody. I think each generation grows up later. Oh, the latest dirt!" Cecile shook her head in distaste. "Madame Tannenbaum is talking about how she personally helped the Roth girls when the whole town was against them. Of course, then you had the brass to come back and marry her grandson."

"Cecile, Mrs. Tannenbaum—working with a committee of ladies—collected money for train fare and twenty-five dollars, and ordered Iris and me to leave town." She felt sick with recall. "I remember her exact words: 'Your name is Roth. Don't you understand? Nobody wants you here! You're putting the whole Jewish community in danger.' We paid back every cent—such as it was—within a year."

A smiling waitress came to their table. "You ready to order, ladies?"

The waitresses wouldn't be cold to her, Laura thought with a new cynicism. She was known as a good tipper.

Laura postponed all future meetings until she could arrange for Katie to be registered at the Madison School for Girls, situated just outside of Boston. With Cecile's help and after a series of frenetic phone calls to the school, Laura told Katie that she was to go to Madison.

"Cecile went there," she said with a show of cheerfulness, even while she recoiled from the vision of her baby all the way up in Boston, surrounded by strangers.

"Okay." Katie was noncommittal. She still blamed her for being Laura Roth and coming back to Magnolia.

"You'll need a school wardrobe," Laura said. "I'll take off tomorrow from the office—" Did Katie resent her involvement in the business? Did her children think she belonged at home—like most mothers? "We'll go over to Glover's and—"

"No!" Katie said defiantly. "I'm not leaving this house until we go to the depot."

"Katie, you'll want some pretty new clothes," she cajoled. "We'll drive over to Atlanta and shop. Everett gave me his gas coupons. We can make it there and back."

"Okay," Katie shrugged listlessly. "If you insist."

In the Atlanta shops—yearning to see a glimmer of pleasure in her daughter's eyes—Laura spent with compulsive extravagance. At intervals Katie's face lighted with approval. But that approval, Laura tormented herself, did not extend to Katie's mother.

Laura paused to buy a cashmere sweater for Jonnie, and then they went back to the car, their arms full of packages, and headed back to Magnolia. Laura was pained by the way Katie clung to her side of the car, as though putting as much distance between the two of them as possible. After a few attempts at making conversation, Laura gave up. Katie gazed out the window in silence for the entire trip home.

On the day when Katie was to leave for Boston, Laura awoke with a devastating conviction that she had failed as a mother. Katie was running away not only from this town but from her.

Jewel made Katie's favorite strawberry pancakes for breakfast, fussed over her as though this were a festive occasion. But Laura saw the tears in Jewel's eyes when Katie pointed out shortly after breakfast that it was time to leave for the train. Laura remembered Iris and herself traveling in the dusty, hot day coach to New York twenty years ago. With his ever useful connections, Everett had managed to acquire a Pullman compartment for Katie.

"I'll bring down your suitcase," Jonnie said self-consciously. "Your trunk went off yesterday, didn't it?"

Katie nodded. For a fleeting moment Laura thought Katie was ambivalent about going away. But Katie rose to her feet and crossed to a pile of magazines.

"Is it all right if I take this copy of *Vogue?*" she asked politely. Katie might have been talking to a stranger, Laura told herself.

"It's yours, darling," Laura reminded. Iris had sent Katie a subscription several months ago.

Katie kissed Jewel good-bye, clung to her for a moment, then walked out of the house to the car. Not one of her friends had phoned since the day the *Journal* ran its lurid front page story, Laura thought with fresh anger. Why must Katie pay for what this town did to Papa?

Laura lingered for only a moment in the Pullman compartment. She was determined not to let Katie see her cry. If Katie chose to leave her home and her family, then so be it. But Laura remained inside the depot, gazing at the Pullman until it began its slow chug out of the station. *Her baby was going away.*

The following morning Laura went with Jonnie to the depot. She knew he was upset that both Katie and he were going away to school.

"I'll be home every weekend," he said earnestly after he had kissed her good-bye.

400

"Darling, hurry inside so you can get a seat," Laura urged.

"Mom, it's not that far," Jonnie laughed, but his eyes were troubled. "I'll phone as soon as I get a chance." He hesitated. "Is it all right if I call collect?"

Again, Laura watched until the train bearing her eldest child moved out of the depot. Squaring her shoulders she returned to the car to drive to the office. Tonight she would go home to her big, beautiful house that was now far larger than she needed.

Except for Jewel she would be alone in that house.

## Chapter 32

Desperately missing Katie and Jonnie, and ever conscious of the wall between Katie and herself, Laura sought a new project in which to lose herself. She devoured the business pages of a dozen periodicals and of *The New York Times*. She became aware of the tax-loss—carry-forward laws. She sat down with Everett and plied him with questions about these laws.

"What you're saying," she said at last, her mind charging ahead, "is that a company with a backlog of losses is given a period of tax-free years until its profits match the losses on its books?"

"That's it," Everett said, his face lighting up. "I think I see where you're headed."

"If I buy a company that's been losing money and merge it with a profitable one, I'll save a lot of taxes—"

"It's a legal tax shelter," he nodded. "Used by the sharpest businessmen."

"Then I know our next venture." Excitement kindled in her. "Everett, find me a company with heavy losses on their books—and one that'll be happy to sell cheap. Then I'll buy these commercial properties in Atlanta I've been considering, and merge the two. I know Atlanta is going to expand like mad. With renovations the properties ought to show terrific profits over the next two or three years."

"Profits that will be sheltered by the losses on the books," Everett confirmed. "Go to it, Laura."

Two or three times each week Laura invited Everett and Maisie for dinner at the house. She told herself these conferences were most practical outside of office hours. In truth, she dreaded sitting down to dinner alone.

She blamed herself when Barry was defeated in the local elections, though he pointed out they had expected this. Cecile and he insisted that their faction—mostly younger generation residents of Magnolia plus the steady influx of new people—was growing stronger with every passing month. The three of them were convinced Magnolia would continue to expand in dramatic proportions even when the war was over.

Ten days after the local elections Cecile stormed into Laura's office—after waiting in the reception room for twenty minutes—with outrage etched on her face.

"Cecile, I'm sorry I kept you waiting," Laura was contrite. "I was on an important long-distance call."

"I'm not angry at you, sugar," Cecile said grimly. "For no reason at all the houses on our block were just reappraised. Our taxes have been doubled. This has to be the fine hand of the goddamn Slocums."

"You'll fight it," Laura surmised.

"Oh, sure. But it won't do any good," Cecile predicted. "The Judge is after our hide because Barry dared to run against David. We can't win against the Slocum machine any more than Everett can. But believe me, we'll have plenty to say—loud and clear."

"What about Everett?" Laura asked, suddenly ice cold.

Cecile looked nervous. "I didn't mean to say that, Laura—"

Laura pushed a button on her desk and waited for Maisie to join them. What were Maisie and Everett protecting her from?

"Laura, I shouldn't have said that," Cecile reiterated unhappily. "I'm just so damn furious."

"Yeah?" Maisie hovered in the doorway.

"Come inside and close the door, Maisie."

"Something wrong?" Maisie gazed from Laura to Cecile.

"Our house has just been reappraised. Our taxes were

403

doubled. Not the taxes of the people on either side of us. Not those of the people across the way." Cecile sighed. "I made a crack about Everett having problems, too. It just slipped out—"

"What are they trying to do to Everett?" Laura asked.

"He lost his two major accounts. Other than Hunter Realty," Maisie said with an effort at humor. "He figures Judge Slocum pressured them to move somewhere else. The Judge never forgave me for quitting and coming to you. Then Everett and I added insult to injury—in his vicious mind. We dared to support your campaign against David."

"I want Everett to join my company on a full-time basis," Laura said firmly. "You tell him I won't take 'no' for an answer. Tell him to name his price. And the sooner he can arrange to join us, the happier I'll be."

In mid-October Jonnie came home for a weekend. He seemed content to lounge around the house, but Laura asked herself if he were afraid to face the town. When she mentioned this to Maisie after seeing Jonnie off on the train for Athens on Sunday afternoon, Maisie scolded her.

"Laura, stop being paranoid. Jonnie came home for the weekend because he wanted to see his mother. Besides, all his friends are away at school, too—nobody's here. Don't go looking for trouble, honey."

Jonnie phoned every Sunday night—and Laura remembered how Phil had always waited for a call from his father on the first Sunday in every month. For a precious little while Phil had given her the young girlhood she had never known. Now—at thirty-six—she felt like an old woman, alone in her fine, big house.

Laura phoned Katie once a week, always frustrated and guilty when she hung up. Katie remained polite and impersonal. *"I like the school. Everybody's nice."* This was not her high-spirited, vivacious Katie. This was a little girl afraid to allow anyone to get close to her.

At Thanksgiving Jewel prepared a sumptuous dinner

before leaving to spend the rest of the day with her family. In a need to fill the house with voices Laura had invited Maisie and Everett, along with the Bergers, to share Thanksgiving dinner with Jonnie and herself. But amidst the festivities she was ever conscious that Katie was not at the table. Katie was right, of course; the Thanksgiving holiday was too short to make the long round trip between Boston and Magnolia.

Now Laura allowed herself to do what had been impossible when the town knew her only as Laura Hunter. Through town records she tracked down the site of her father's unmarked grave, arranged for a simple headstone and perpetual care. The rabbi who had replaced Rabbi Simon at the synagogue where Papa had been a member conducted a brief memorial service, unannounced and attended only by Laura. Even all these years later, Laura told herself, it would be prudent to do this quietly.

Over coffee with Everett and Maisie—after a conference at the house on a wintry December Saturday night—Laura turned the conversation from business to her personal obsession.

"I know the terrible odds against my proving that Derek Slocum murdered Tammy Lee Johnson," she conceded, "but I have to try. I'll never be truly at peace until I can do this."

"I'm not normally a vindictive man, but I would take pleasure in helping to topple the sacrosanct Slocum family," Everett admitted. "But I don't even know how to start."

"Every day I spent in Judge Slocum's office after that incident with Derek was a private hell for me." Laura gripped the fragile china coffee cup with perilous intensity. "Judge Slocum had sat there and presided at my father's trial—knowing he was innocent."

"Laura, you've never said specifically what efforts you've made." Everett squinted in thought. "Beyond pinpointing Derek's presence here in Magnolia on the day the murder was committed—after he'd been expelled

405

from school for molesting a young girl."

"Phil and I tried to track down the witnesses against my father. It was as though they had all disappeared from the face of the earth. Probably paid off by Slocum," she guessed bitterly. "Then came Pearl Harbor, and Phil enlisted. I let things ride after that."

"Let's go back and retrace those steps," Everett suggested. "Maybe we should concentrate on one witness for a start. If a witness left Magnolia, where would he be likely to go? We can check the census records of neighboring towns—"

"I never thought of that." Laura's voice crackled with fresh hope. "Slocum paid them off to leave Magnolia—but it's reasonable to believe they settled close by. Everett, help me with this and you can name your own fee."

"I'll do it because you are our very dear friend," he said gently.

"You realize it'll be hard to reopen the case," Maisie said.

"Hard, but not impossible," Laura pinpointed. "As Barry keeps saying, the old order is being challenged. If we come up with concrete evidence, we'll be able to go into court and see justice done. I have to do this. Not just for Papa—and Iris and myself. For Jonnie and Katie." Her face glowed with a messianic zeal. "My children have to be able to walk in Magnolia and hold their heads high."


Katie made self-conscious efforts to remain at the school over the Christmas vacation. There were several foreign students who would not be able to go home. But Laura held firm. Katie must come home. She could bring anyone she liked with her, Laura cajoled. But Katie replied she would come alone.

Laura waited with eager impatience for the children to arrive. Suspecting it was futile but propelled by a longing to see their small family reunited, Laura phoned Iris in

New York. With Noel registered at a posh private school—*Noel in the first grade*—Iris was staying at the Sutton Place apartment. She was scheduled to leave for Palm Beach, along with Noel, his governess, and Bridget, late in the month. In January Noel and Miss Brisbane would return to the New York apartment. Iris would rejoin them there in early March.

"Darling, you know how I feel about Magnolia," Iris chided when Laura phoned. "But why don't you come down to Palm Beach in January? Don't tell me you can't take off a few days."

"I'll see how things work out," Laura hedged. It would be exciting to run away from everything for a little while. To be with Iris. In a corner of her mind she worried that Iris would be leaving Noel alone with the governess for two months. Iris insisted she was raising Noel in the fashion of the British upper classes. But wouldn't she miss him? "We'll talk about Palm Beach after the holidays."

Now Laura was caught up in the children's imminent arrival. Despite her frenetic schedule she had shopped extravagantly for slightly belated Hanukkah presents, to be presented on the children's first night home. She planned a small New Year's Eve dinner. Katie wouldn't object to having Maisie and Everett and the Bergers at the house. They were all like family. Just the five adults and three teenagers. But eight at the table would be festive. How empty the house seemed with Jonnie and Katie away at school!

Laura was at the depot almost half an hour before Katie's train was due to arrive. Too restless to sit, she left the depot to wait before the railroad tracks in the crisp, cold late afternoon.

Already she was trying to cope with summer vacation, knowing Katie would balk at coming home for those long weeks. She would buy a summer house at Warm Springs, she plotted. Katie would be thrilled at being so close to President Roosevelt's Little White House. And maybe in the course of the summer she could convince Katie to go back to Magnolia High.

Laura waited expectantly as the train pulled into the depot and drew to a stop. The atmosphere in the area, crowded with other parents waiting to welcome home-coming students, suddenly became electric when passengers began to disembark.

"Katie!" Laura called out joyously and darted forward to embrace her daughter, conscious all the while that Katie accepted this without actual participation. "Darling, you look marvelous. So grownup." She chose her words carefully, fearful of saying the wrong thing.

Laura kept up a stream of lively conversation as they walked to the car, with a porter carrying Katie's valise. Driving to the house she was aware of Katie's covert inspection of the passing scenery. Katie had been home-sick, Laura realized.

"Jonnie will be home this evening," Laura told Katie. "I was hoping Iris would be able to stop off on her way to Palm Beach, but she can't make it." At Iris's urging the children had abandoned calling her "Aunt Iris."

"She sent me a bottle of Tabu from Saks," Katie reported. A hint of pride in her smile. "The perfume. I just love it."

"She sent Hanukkah-Christmas presents for you and Jonnie. They're waiting at the house." Laura remembered the large bottle of Chantilly, the eau de toilette, that she had included in Katie's presents. That would pale before the sophisticated perfume that Iris sent.

At the house Jewel swooped Katie up in her arms.

"It's so good to have our baby home!" Jewel chortled. Now she held Katie away for a close inspection. "They ain't feedin' you good up at that school. You is skinny, young lady."

By evening—after Laura had gone to the depot and picked up Jonnie—the house buzzed with conviviality. Jonnie asked Katie all the questions about the school that Laura had been afraid to ask. Did she like her teachers?

Did she like the food? Had she made friends among her classmates? Did she like her roommate?

"They've got a nutty rule," Katie said with the first indication of hostility. "Christian girls room with Christian girls, Jewish girls with Jewish girls. My roommate is a spoiled brat. Cindy Rogers and I wanted to switch so we could be roommates, but they wouldn't let us."

"They do that in my dorm, too," Jonnie shrugged. "But I wanted to room with Chet. Not because he's Jewish—because he's my friend."

Laura was disappointed when Katie decided to go to bed early. Still, she understood the long train trip had been tiring. Then Jonnie settled down to a long phone conversation with Chet as though they'd been separated for weeks rather than hours. It felt so good, Laura told herself, to have both children home with her.

The last few days seemed to have flown past, Laura thought when she stood again at the depot and watched Katie's train pull out. Jonnie would be home for another two days. Then she would be alone again. Business would keep her from brooding over the children's absence, she promised herself. But she knew that each night when she settled in her bed, she would be conscious that Katie was all the way up near Boston and Jonnie in Athens. And she worried constantly because Jonnie would be eighteen in August and old enough to be drafted.

The new project was proceeding with only minor complications. Everett made a trip to Washington D.C. to check into the tax laws that could make Laura a very rich woman if her plans went through on schedule. But they faced continual frustrations in their efforts to find witnesses who had testified in Jacob Roth's trial.

In March Laura found a charming five-bedroom summer house in the mountains midway between Columbus and Magnolia. She was enthralled by the views, the

409

splendor of the pine forests. She arranged to buy it immediately. The five bedrooms would be necessary because both Jewel and their maid who came in by the day would be in residence for the summer—and she envisioned Jonnie's friends coming up at regular intervals.

Cecile—who was a fledgling interior decorator when she met and married Barry—undertook to furnish the house. Laura was too occupied by business to handle this herself, but determined to have the house ready for summer occupancy. Laura took dozens of photographs of the spacious colonial cape and sent them to Katie. At Laura's instructions, Cecile consulted with Katie about how she would like her room furnished.

Though Katie seemed pleased that the family would spend the summer at Pine Mountain, she hedged at coming home for the spring vacation.

"I'd just get there and then have to take a train back to Boston two days later," Katie insisted when her mother phoned to discuss this. Not quite true, Laura taunted herself—Katie could spend five days at home. "Besides, school closes in May."

On April 12—with the Axis on the run—the world was shocked to learn of President Roosevelt's death in Warm Springs, Georgia. For many young Americans the only president within their memory was gone. In cities and villages alike grief-stricken people gathered on street corners to mourn FDR, considered to be as much a casualty of the war as the men who died on the fighting front.

Then on April 28 Mussolini was assassinated by Italian partisans. Allied troops were closing in on the Nazis from all directions. On May 2 Berlin fell to the Russians. On May 7 the Germans signed the terms of unconditional surrender. The war in Europe was over. It was only a matter of time, most Americans were convinced, before the Japanese would surrender.

Jubilance over victory in Europe was shadowed by the grim discovery of Nazi atrocities as Allied armies cap-

410

tured concentration camps. On a hot May evening—drained by a long day at the office—Laura sat beneath the ceiling fan in her bedroom and read the sickening reports of the horrors suffered in the Nazi camps. She remembered the seven children Iris and Maisie's sister had spirited out of the country. Thank God they had been saved from such horrors. She felt a fresh sense of pride that Jonnie and Katie had helped in this.

Engrossed in her reading she started when the phone rang. Glancing at the clock on her night table, she walked to the phone, picked up the receiver. Late night calls always alarmed her.

"Hello."

"Laura, isn't it awful about those concentration camps in Germany?" Iris's voice was shrill in outrage. "I've written to Ania Fischbein at the castle in Austria. I don't know if she was ever sent to a camp. I tried to persuade her to come to London or America, but she wouldn't hear of it!"

"Iris, you did what you could," Laura soothed. "It's possible she sat the whole war out there at the castle."

"And these were the people Peter admired." Iris sizzled with contempt. "He was so proud of knowing Goebbels and the others. I wish he were able to know what the world thinks of the Nazis now."

"How is Peter?" Laura asked.

"Still the same. The lawyer sends me quarterly reports. I have to hope he lives a long time," Iris reminded. "I don't want to think what the death duties will do to my inheritance."

"Where are you calling from?" Laura asked. "Are you still at Maine Chance?" If she gained five pounds Iris grew frantic and headed immediately for the spa.

"No, I'm at Lake Arrowhead," Iris reported. "Staying with Debbie Macmillan. She has a gorgeous house here. We ran into each other at Maine Chance."

"Ian Macmillan's wife?" Laura was suddenly alert. Ian Macmillan had instigated inquiries into the operations of

411

a dozen major real-estate developers who were acquiring illegal FHA loans. He was considered the champion of honest real-estate entrepreneurs with vision. "The congressman from Colorado?"

"That's right," Iris confirmed. "Can he do you some good?"

"Possibly some time in the future," Laura said. Rumor was that shrewd Bill Zeckendorf of Webb & Knapp was interested in Denver. If he was interested in a city, Laura thought—then certainly she should be.

"Let me know when you'd like to meet him."

"How's Noel?" Laura asked. She worried that Iris left him alone with the governess for such long stretches of time.

For a few minutes they talked about Iris's small son. Because of Noel's temper tantrums and physical attacks on his governess he was being seen by a psychiatrist two afternoons a week.

"Laura, I don't know how to cope with him," Iris admitted. "And Miss Brisbane wouldn't stay unless I put him in therapy. He's simply out of control." Laura heard a woman's voice in the background now. "I'll be right there, Debbie. Darling, I have to run. Talk to you soon."

Laura was delighted when Cecile phoned to report that the final pieces of furniture for the summer house had been delivered, the curtains and drapes hung.

"I'll pick you up first thing in the morning," Cecile said, "and drive you up."

"I'm dying to see the house," Laura confessed, "but I should go to Atlanta to check on the renovations there." The office building with its street-level stores was in the midst of extensive renovations.

"You'll go to Atlanta tomorrow," Cecile coaxed. "It's been hot as hell for the past week—you can use a few hours in the mountains. I just want to be sure you like what I've done." Cecile had been ecstatic at the lavish budget Laura had allowed her.

Immediately after an early breakfast Laura and Cecile were en route to the summer house. The heat seemed to grow less intense as they left the town behind. Laura abandoned herself to the morning quiet, enjoying the lush summer greenery, the cloudless blue of the sky, the morning sounds of the birds.

For no reason that she could comprehend Laura suddenly thought back to the day when, the children still babies, Bernie and she had fled the hot city and had driven out to Montauk in his boss's car. The sky then had been this same cloudless blue. There the only sounds had been those of the gulls cawing in flight and of the waves crashing against the sand. That was the day Bernie had promised her they would eventually live in Magnolia.

"We should have brought along bathing suits," Cecile broke their companionable silence. "The lake must be wonderful on a day like this."

"Katie loves the water," Laura remembered. "I figure she and Jonnie will swim a lot." She squinted in thought. "What do teenagers like these days? It's funny—they used to be adolescents. Now they're teenagers. Records," Laura pinpointed suddenly. "I'll buy phonographs for each of the kids' rooms, so there'll be no private war, and let them load up on records. What else fascinates girls Katie's age?" Laura probed.

"Boys," Cecile laughed.

Laura sat immobile, her mind in high gear.

"Cecile, Jonnie will expect Chet to come up often during the summer. And some of their other friends—" Katie couldn't tell Jonnie not to have his friends up to the house.

"Hmmm-hmmm." Cecile nodded knowingly. "Katie's a gorgeous kid. They'll be drooling over her. She'll begin to understand that the kids have forgotten all about what happened last summer."

"Cecile, do you think it'll work? Katie won't just close

413

herself off in her room, will she?" *Had the kids forgotten?* "I think you ought to try it." Cecile's matter-of-factness was encouraging.

"She'll be sixteen in July." Sixteen should be a wonderful experience. It had not been for Iris or her—but she'd envisioned Katie euphoric at reaching that very special age. "We used to talk about a splashy 'sweet sixteen' party. But I'd be afraid to give her a surprise party. That might drive her even further away."

"Laura, take one step at a time," Cecile advised. "Let Katie be exposed to Jonnie's friends. She was fine at your New Year's Eve party, remember?"

"None of the kids were there. Just Chet. He's like family." But Laura felt cheered. "You're right. I'll take one step at a time."

Laura was relieved that Katie seemed happy at the summer house. Jewel reported that she swam in the mornings with Jonnie and Chet, spent hours playing her records, playing cards with the two boys. Katie was teaching Chet to Lindy. But she understood that the house was Katie's protective cocoon against the outside world.

Laura stayed in town on Wednesday and Thursday nights and Cecile went up to the summer house to supervise in her absence. Late in June Jonnie was allowed to invite two additional friends to the mountain house. Cecile would chaperone because Laura had to be in Atlanta on business for several days. Laura refused to admit even to herself that she had plotted to be in Atlanta when the two other boys would arrive. She was terrified that Katie would be upset. Her presence would only make it worse.

Restless in her hotel room and anxious about Katie's reaction to the new guests, Laura phoned the mountain house. Cecile answered. Laura heard the strains of "Besame Mucho" in the background.

"How's everything going?" she asked with a show of

cheerfulness.

"Sugar, relax," Cecile told her. "For the first three or four minutes Katie looked as though she were facing a firing squad. But the boys set her straight right away. The five of them are listening to records in Jonnie's room."

"Thank God." Relief blended with pleasure in Laura. "Maybe this is the breakthrough, Cecile."

"Laura, when is Katie's birthday?"

"In two weeks. And I'm wracking my brains for something special to give her."

"Give her a surprise birthday party," Cecile urged.

"Oh, Cecile, I'm scared—"

"She might be upset for a few moments. Like when the two boys arrived," Cecile conceded. "But I suspect she's very lonely. Take a chance. Invite five of the girls that were her friends when she was at Magnolia High. If they accept, you'll know they've forgotten all that business. They probably forgot two weeks later—"

"They didn't have to drop her as though she had leprosy," Laura said with fresh anger, remembering how Iris and she had been ostracized by their classmates.

"Laura, that's in the past," Cecile said quietly. "Give them another chance. For Katie."

"I'll make some calls when I get home," Laura said after a moment. Cecile was right. If the surprise party went off well, Katie would come back to Magnolia High.


The early morning sunlight darted between the drapes in Katie's pine-paneled bedroom and lay in a ribbon of gold across the patchwork quilt needed in the cool mountain nights. Katie opened her eyes in a sudden awareness that this was her sixteenth birthday.

When she was back at Magnolia High, all the girls used to talk about finally being sixteen. It was the most important birthday in the world. At sixteen you could wear makeup and date. But at Madison there were all those nutty rules.

Chet had come up again yesterday. She'd seen him whispering and giggling with Jonnie. It had something to do with her birthday, probably. Jewel pretended she didn't remember, but she was sure Jewel would be making a birthday cake today.

It was Friday—Mom would be coming up tonight. Not to spend her birthday with her, Katie thought aggrievedly. Because Mom always came up on Friday nights. Couldn't she take a whole day off from the office for her daughter's sixteenth birthday?

When she came downstairs for breakfast, Katie discovered the boys had already gone off to swim. She glanced around the kitchen for some sign of baking. Was she wrong? Had Jewel forgotten it was her birthday? Had everybody forgotten?

Today Katie didn't walk over to the lake to swim with Jonnie and Chet. She sprawled in a hammock and started *A Bell for Adano*. Cissie had given it to her the last day of school. All the while she listened for sounds in the kitchen that would tell her Jewel was baking a cake. Jewel never forgot any of their birthdays.

In the afternoon she played cards with Jonnie and Chet. Still there were no indications in the kitchen that Jewel was making a cake. Maybe she'd been wrong when she'd thought the boys were whispering about her birthday. She went off to school for one year, and everybody just forgot all about her.


Laura glanced up from a phone call towards the door as Nora knocked lightly and came inside.

"The bakery just delivered the cake," Nora said and brought the large box to Laura's desk. "It looks just beautiful." She pulled up the lid to show off the concoction inside while Laura hastily ended the phone conversation.

"Oh, it's lovely," Laura approved, admiring the triple-layer chocolate cake filled with white chocolate mousse and covered with white chocolate frosting adorned with delicate bittersweet chocolate roses. Since she was seven, Katie always insisted on a chocolate birthday cake. "Considering this heat I'd better get moving fast. It'll go up in Maisie's car. Two of the girls in the back can hold the cake across their laps."

It was arranged that Maisie would drive up with the five girls. Cecile would bring up the three boys. She would arrive in the second-hand Chevvie she had managed to buy last week and would leave at the summer house. Jonnie could drive Jewel to the country store for supplies whenever she ran out of something.

"Are you here?" Nora asked as the phone on Laura's desk rang.

"If it's somebody important," Laura stipulated, reaching into a desk drawer for her purse. The presents were already locked in the trunk of Maisie's car including the mink jacket Iris had sent. It was much too grownup for a sixteen-year-old, but Laura knew that Katie would adore it.

"It's Everett," Nora reported and extended the receiver.

"Thanks, Nora." Laura reached for the phone with a flicker of excitement. Everett had gone to Macon today to follow a lead on Lily Melrose, the rooming house owner who had testified against Papa. "Just leave the cake there on my desk." When Nora left the room, Laura spoke with Everett.

"Now don't get all excited yet," Everett cautioned, "but the Lily Melrose in the Macon census used to live in Magnolia. She left Macon about two years ago to move to Augusta. I think it would be smart for me to stay overnight here and run over to Augusta first thing tomorrow morning. There's nothing coming up at the office that can't wait twenty-four hours." Laura's pulse quickened.

"Please follow it up, Ev. This is the first real lead we've come up with so far. And I won't count on anything

417

happening," she anticipated him. "I know she may still be scared to talk—but it's a start."

"Tell Katie I'm sorry to be missing her birthday," Everett said. "But she knows we love her."

Off the phone with Everett—transferred now to Maisie—Laura called Cecile.

"The boys are all here," Cecile reported. "We'll be leaving in about ten minutes."

The cake in tow, Laura stopped by Maisie's office.

"Ev just told me about Lily Melrose," Maisie said, her smile jubilant. "And I'll leave in a few minutes to pick up the girls. Laura, it's going to be a great party.

It would be a great party if Katie didn't climb into her shell, Laura thought nervously as she headed for the door. The girls had all been so pleased and excited. Especially Annabel, who had been Katie's best friend. Oh, dear God, let everything go right tonight.

On the road to the house Laura mentally went over the plans for the party. Jewel had hidden the party decorations and the favors. As far as Katie knew, Jewel was preparing dinner for the family. Jonnie had bought records as his present, but he wouldn't give them to Katie until later. Her own presents, she thought wryly—a beautiful wristwatch, a subscription to *Seventeen,* and a set of special teenage makeup—would seem insignificant beside the mink jacket Iris had sent.

Laura was tense when she at last turned into the dusty dirt road that led up to the house. As always she was aware of the pleasant drop in temperature here on the side of the mountain, of the scents of pine and honeysuckle and roses. This was a timeless oasis of peace and quiet. The days were long this time of year; the sun would not be setting over the lake for at least another hour.

She followed the final bend in the road, and the house appeared before her. The three sprawled on the floor of the porch were too intent on their card game to give more than a moment's recognition of the arrival of an unfamiliar car.

"Gin!" Katie chortled, and at the same moment Jonnie realized who was behind the wheel of the car.

"Mom!" He darted down the porch stairs towards the car. "Did you bring the presents?" he whispered while his mother kissed him.

"In the trunk," she said softly.

"Your car break down?" he asked, inspecting the Chevvie.

"I bought this for up here," she said casually while Katie and Chet approached.

"It's neat," Chet admired.

"Anything that rolls is neat these days," Laura laughed, dropping a kiss on Katie's cheek, sensing her bewilderment that her birthday was being ignored.

Laura contrived to keep Katie on the porch with her while Jonnie and Chet went inside to set up the party decorations. She emphasized that the Chevvie was to stay up here for the summer.

"Everett offered to teach you to drive," she smiled. "But of course, not in this heat." She made an effort to sound casual. "Wasn't that sweet of him?"

"Yeah." Katie's eyes strayed to the Chevvie.

Now they saw Cecile's car turn into the road.

"She's bringing up three of Jonnie's friends for the weekend."

"Again?" Katie frowned, but Laura sensed she wasn't displeased.

It was obvious the boys had been coached to pretend this was just a casual visit with Jonnie. Not until Maisie arrived with the girls—and the birthday cake—would Katie know what was happening. The boys talked about their respective colleges, football, the newest movies. All agreed that Betty Hutton was sensational in *Incendiary Blonde*.

Laura tensed when she heard yet another car approaching. She began to talk animatedly about Cecile's plans to open an interior decorating shop in the fall.

419

From Katie's slack-jawed stare Laura knew Katie had spied the cluster of girls in the car with Maisie. Katie was pale, seeming immobilized in shock.

"Hi!" Annabel effervesced, climbing out of the car and hurrying towards the porch. A gift-wrapped box was clutched in her arms. "Happy birthday! Surprise, surprise!"

"Hi—" Katie managed a convivial smile. "Wow! I am surprised!" She gazed cautiously at the four other girls in party dress, all carrying colorful, gift-wrapped parcels, charging towards her.

"You really didn't know!" Frances was happily astonished. "Whenever my mother has tried to give me a surprise party, I knew every little thing about it a week before."

All at once an awkward silence hovered over them. Laura's throat went dry. Were they remembering last summer? Was the party an awful mistake?

"I think you grew an inch while you were away at school." Annabel scrutinized Katie. "Maybe two inches."

"Not just in height," another giggled, and the five erupted into laughter. Laura's eyes clung to Katie. *Was* it going to be all right?

"Thank God, I had my tonsils out last summer," Annabel clutched at her throat in eloquent recall. "Remember how many things I used to miss because I was always coming down with tonsillitis?"

"The class picnic on Decoration Day," somebody remembered.

"And Mary Beth's July 4th swimming party," Katie contributed. Laura glowed. Katie wasn't running away.

"You're coming back to Magnolia for our senior year?" Annabel made it more statement than question. "I mean, you'll want to graduate with us, won't you?"

Laura's heart pounded at Katie's barely perceptible hesitation.

"Oh sure," Katie shrugged. "It wouldn't be legal if I didn't."

Three of the boys pushed open the screen door. "Happy birthday! Come into the house and let's get this party moving!"

# Chapter 33

On Saturday afternoon Everett phoned Laura from Augusta to report that Lily Melrose had died two years earlier.

"We knew it was a long shot." Laura struggled to hide her disappointment. "But I don't have to tell you how much I appreciate your efforts."

"Sugar, we're just beginning," Everett said. "We've got another ten people to track down. Some of them have to be alive. Some of them may have the courage to speak the truth all these years later. Oh, I just heard something that'll make you sizzle. Slocum is trying to have the property at the corner of Maple and McDowell condemned because he wants to develop in that area, and he figures the old house is an eyesore."

"The Waters house?" Laura's voice soared in rage. "That sweet old couple in their eighties?"

"That's it. It was the first house built in Magnolia, back in 1837. It's stayed in the family all these years. Most of the acreage has been sold off but they've kept the house and a two-acre plot. What upsets them most is that the family cemetery, going back almost a hundred years, occupies over an acre of their property."

"Slocum can't get away with it!" Did he think he was the dictator of Magnolia, Georgia? "Everybody in town knows and likes Mr. and Mrs. Waters. They'll stop Slocum."

"Don't count on that," Everett warned. "The city commission is in his back pocket."

"He *has* to be stopped."

"How?" Everett challenged. "Barry's going around in

422

circles trying to find a legal way to prevent it."

Laura searched her mind for some legal loophole. But Barry had come up with nothing, and he was diligent and knowledgeable.

"We'll form a new group." She clutched at a fresh approach. " 'The Committee to Save Magnolia's Historic Landmarks.' We'll collect funds towards setting up an historic district," she pursued. "It's long past due. I'll make the first contribution. Five thousand dollars."

"Laura, if you were a man you'd be governor of this state in time," Everett chuckled. "But we'll have to move fast on this."

"Talk to Barry about setting up a public meeting. I'll contact members of the Professional Women's Club. You talk with the Chamber of Commerce people who're on our side." There were some who bowed down before the Slocum machine. "And Everett," she said gently, "tell Mr. and Mrs. Waters they're not alone. We'll be fighting with them."

At dusk Laura sat on the porch glider and tried to relax in the beauty of her surroundings. She felt a joy in the knowledge that Katie would be returning to Magnolia High in September. She would make every effort to be a "normal" mother, she promised herself. While it was impossible for her to be a "stay-at-home" mother, she would turn over much of the out-of-town work to Everett and cut down on her night hours at the office. In this final year before Katie went away to school, she must make her daughter understand that her children came before all else.

She hadn't shirked her duties as a mother, Laura analyzed. She may have skipped some PTA meetings, but she was always there for school plays and debates and Little League games. She was always available in any emergency. Yet it still rankled when she remembered how Katie reported that she was "the only kid in the class with a working mother." It hadn't bothered Jonnie, she thought defensively—he was proud of her success.

423

Again, her thoughts focused on the Slocums. They wanted to build a development out near the Waters house — where the Judge owned a large tract of land — because they knew that the war would surely end within months, though the Japanese were fighting with a fanaticism that was terrifying. Everybody knew that many American lives would be lost in an invasion of Japan. But once the war was over, the country would face a tremendous demand for housing.

It was time to plan for a whole new village, Laura plotted. A community of pretty, comfortable yet inexpensive homes that homecoming GIs would be able to afford. She would talk to Iris about meeting with Congressman Macmillan. A substantial FHA loan would be essential.


By early August the Magnolia Historic Association was a working organization, arousing enthusiastic support. The pressure on the commissioners was sufficient to delay — and hopefully forestall — the condemnation of the Waters property. But local projects faded into the background when the world learned on August 6 that the first atomic bomb had been dropped on Hiroshima. Eighty thousand people were killed, the city reduced to rubble. Three days later — when Tokyo made no move towards surrender — a second atomic bomb was dropped on Nagasaki. The next day Japan requested peace negotiations and President Harry Truman spoke to the nation via radio.

V-J Day was a joyous occasion across America — yet for Laura, as for many thousands who had lost loved ones to the war, it held painful overtones. It was a reaffirmation of Phil's death. But Laura was grateful that the war was over before Jonnie could be drawn into military service.

In September Jonnie went off to college. Later in the month Katie began her senior year at Magnolia High. It was a recurring source of astonishment to Laura that her children were fast approaching adulthood. Jonnie, lean and handsome, towered above her, with his father's dark hair and her blue eyes. Katie, already two inches taller than she, wore her lush auburn hair shoulder length, her eyes the same blue as Jonnie's. Beautiful and bright, both of her children.

By early October it was clear that the Magnolia Historic Association would save the Waters house. The Slocum machine had lost for the first time. Laura exulted in this victory. A new era was beginning in Magnolia, Georgia.

Through Iris's connivance, Laura was invited to attend a houseparty at an Aiken, South Carolina plantation, where Congressman Ian Macmillan was to be among the guests. Laura battled against guilt that she would be away from home for the weekend, when she had promised herself that she'd be constantly available for Katie. But Jewel would be at the house, and Maisie and Everett would come over for dinner one night and Cecile and Barry the following night. The meeting with Congressman Macmillan was critical. She needed to know how to handle herself in a project of this dimension. And it would be wonderful to spend even a couple of days with Iris.

Faintly nervous at joining Iris's ultra-rich circle, Laura was relieved that her sister had arranged to pick her up at the depot and drive her to the plantation, currently owned by Claudia and Charles Calloway.

"You'll love Calloway Place," Iris assured her when they were in the car. "It's been in the Calloway family for over two hundred years. The gardens are breathtaking."

"What about Ian Macmillan?" Laura asked. "Has he arrived?"

"He's due this afternoon," Iris told her. "Debbie is already here. They both know you're very active in Georgia and Alabama real estate. It'll be easy to lead into talk about the best approach to acquiring a large FHA loan."

"I remember what you said about wardrobe and I won't disgrace you. Most of what I've brought are dresses you've sent me," Laura laughed.

"Darling, I never suspected you would. You're a beautiful, clever woman. You'll charm everybody."

Laura was amazed at how quickly she relaxed at Calloway Place. The house was a masterpiece of quiet elegance. The gardens were magnificent — a symphony of velvet-leaved magnolias, live oaks, cypresses draped in Spanish moss, Cherokee roses still in bloom. The guests were not at all intimidating, as she had feared.

The following morning she spent an uninterrupted hour in conference with Ian Macmillan. She marveled at how much she had learned from the congressman. Iris was so right. Contacts were a most important part of any big business deal.

To Laura's astonishment Claudia Calloway insisted that she be flown to the Atlanta airport in the Calloways' plane.

"Darling, the pilot is always on call. Why should you waste time on a train?" Laura hid her fear of flying from the others. Iris was forever flying somewhere, she reproached herself. It was part of the modern world. And wouldn't Katie be impressed to learn she had flown to the Atlanta airport in a private plane?

Iris returned from shopping at Bergdorf's in preparation for her departure for Palm Beach next week to find Noel throwing another of his temper tantrums.

"This child is impossible," Miss Brisbane declared, her breathing labored as she struggled with Noel. "I don't know how I can stay on with him."

"I know he's difficult," Iris cajoled while Noel screeched in rage because the governess had pinned his flailing hands to his side. "But he's going to the psychiatrist three times a week now. I'm sure he'll be better soon. And meanwhile I'll raise your salary by another ten dollars a week."

"I'll try it for another month," Miss Brisbane agreed after a thoughtful moment. Though she complained regularly about Noel's behavior, she was proud that — as the son of a lord—he could put "Honorable" before his name. "Oh, a cable arrived for you about ten minutes ago," she told Iris. "I put it on the dresser in your bedroom."

"Thank you, Miss Brisbane." She sighed as Noel began to cry. In a few minutes he would stop, throw himself on the floor and fall asleep. Before Diana left for London, she'd insisted the best thing for Noel would be to send him off to school. But he was still a baby—only seven. How could she send him away to school? Of course, Peter said *he* had been sent away to boarding school at seven.

In her bedroom she picked up the cable and slit the envelope. She paled as she read the message from Elliot Forbes. Peter was dead. Her presence in London was required for the settling of the estate.

There was no point in taking Noel with her, Iris told herself. He'd stay here with Miss Brisbane and go to school. She'd call Laura to stand by for any emergency, though the governess could handle any situation that arose. Still, she'd feel more secure if Laura were on call. No doubt in her mind that Laura would rush to New York if Noel needed her.

She wouldn't have to stay in London more than a week or two, would she? She could give Elliot her power of attorney or whatever it was called in England. It would be hypocritical to pretend to grieve. Except perhaps for herself, she thought with bitter humor. What was her financial status now that Peter was dead?


The phone ring shattered the early silence, bringing Laura instantly awake. Something had happened to Noel! She pulled herself up against the pillows and reached for the receiver. She'd pleaded with Iris to send Noel down here with the governess. At his age it wouldn't be a tragedy to miss a week or two of school.

"Hello." Her voice was shrill with alarm.

"I know you're always up early, and I just couldn't wait any longer to call," Iris said, plainly distraught.

"Iris, what's happened?" It was still dark outdoors. Her eyes sought the clock. Just past 5 A.M.

"I arrived back in New York six hours ago. I couldn't fall asleep. Laura, I won't know for months what I'll receive from Peter's estate — but meanwhile, my checks have been stopped. And Elliot says not to expect more than a pittance after the death duties are paid. And of course, I gave up claim to the two houses when we made our deal."

"Iris, come stay with me," Laura urged. "There's plenty of room here. And we'll work out —"

"I won't set foot in that town again!" Iris broke in, on the verge of hysteria. "I changed my reservations down in Palm Beach before I flew to London. I'm scheduled to arrive there the end of the week. Noel will stay in New York with Miss Brisbane."

"Do you need immediate cash?" Laura asked anxiously. Iris could be so impractical.

"For the moment I'm all right. I talked with Jimmy a while ago. His father is flying down to Atlanta in the family plane on Wednesday, and Jimmy and I will go with him. Then we'll go down to Palm Beach. Laura, will you meet me in Atlanta and bring my jewelry? Jimmy's smart about those things — he'll be able to get good prices for me."

"When shall I be there?" Thank God, Iris had stashed away the expensive jewelry Peter gave her. That would carry her for a while.

They talked for a few minutes longer. Now Iris was fighting yawns.

"I'll try to sleep for a few hours. I want to dash over to Bergdorf's before they close to pick up another bathing suit. See you in Atlanta on Wednesday, darling."

"Iris, remember," Laura said tenderly, "you'll always have a home with me. It isn't Cranford House or Cranford Hall, but we're comfortable." By Magnolia standards both the house in town and the one in the mountains were luxurious.

Laura made no attempt to go back to sleep. What

428

would Iris do when she ran through the money her jewelry brought? It was obvious she had no intention of retrenching. She'd be able to help her sister, Laura reminded herself, but she couldn't help her maintain the Lady Iris Cranford lifestyle.

In Atlanta Laura had a brief reunion with Arnold Harris, in the city for a business meeting, then went off for a lengthy lunch with Iris and Jimmy. Iris casually accepted the parcel of jewelry and proceeded to talk about the season at Palm Beach as though she had not been close to hysteria about her financial situation a few days earlier.

"Was that houseparty at Aiken helpful to you?" Iris asked. "I mean, were you able to use what Ian Macmillan told you?"

"It was a marvelous help," Laura said. "And he's saved me months probably on getting my loan through." Twice Iris's social contacts had been important. As Lady Iris Cranford her sister was a distinct business asset.

"Why don't you join us for a few days in the Bahamas in March?" Jimmy invited. "I've rented a house in Nassau, and there's a yacht to take us island hopping."

"Laura, you're always working," Iris scolded. "Come down and play for a few days."

"It sounds enticing," Laura conceded. "I'll have to see how tied up I am with the business."

Laura pushed ahead with the new village on the outskirts of Atlanta. Together she and Everett plotted ways to cut back on costs, to accelerate construction without sacrificing an image of quality. She was convinced the market would be strong for low-cost housing.

Prodded by Iris on one side and Maisie and Cecile on the other, Laura gave in to Iris's tempting invitation. She was tense and tired—she'd worked so many years without even the pretense of a vacation. Katie, too, encouraged her to go. And in the back of Laura's mind lurked the bonus of Iris's social contacts.

Again, a private plane was at Laura's service. Arnold

Harris was stopping off in Atlanta, then flying on to Miami.

"You'll hop a ride with Dad," Jimmy wrote. "He'll be expecting a call from you on Monday."

Laura enjoyed the flight with Arnold Harris. He talked casually about million dollar deals here and there, and about acquaintances that she knew only from the newspapers. She marveled at the comforts enjoyed by Iris's international set. Jimmy had ordered a chartered plane to stand by to take her on to Nassau. She was his houseguest, he insisted—it was normal hospitality.

She arrived in Nassau in mid-afternoon and was whisked off to Jimmy's rented castle at Emerald Beach. His other two houseguests—Peggy and Bob Westcott—were off at the golf course. She would meet them at dinner. Tomorrow, Jimmy told her, they would go for a sail among the islands, and on the following day they would have tea at the Emerald Beach Club.

While an ingratiating colored maid unpacked for her, Laura sat with Iris on the deck off her room, basking in the magnificent stretch of beach and emerald ocean on display. Iris assured her Jimmy had done well in selling her jewelry, but Laura sensed an undercurrent of uncertainty in her.

"Iris, how long will it be before Peter's estate is settled?"

"Elliot says these things go on forever. And the death duties will eat up most of it." Fear glowed in her eyes. "I never should have signed away my rights to the houses. I don't know why Elliot told me to do that!"

"Iris, come stay with me," Laura coaxed yet again. Beneath her air of constant frivolity Iris was bright. She realized she couldn't keep up this lifestyle for much longer. "Noel could go to public school. You wouldn't need an expensive governess—you know how cheap domestic help is in the South. We could—"

"No!" Iris recoiled in pain. "I'd rather die than live in Magnolia." But with chameleon swiftness Iris discarded this mood. "Darling, I want to know all about Katie and

Jonnie. Tell me every little detail," she ordered blithely.

Finally—with a glance at her watch—Iris pointed out that it was time they dressed for dinner.

"You'll like the Westcotts. Peggy and Bob are both so sweet. He's a multimillionaire oil man who deserted Dallas for Denver when the doctors decided that a higher altitude would be better for Peggy's health."

Laura tensed in alertness. Just a few days ago she'd read in a trade journal that Bill Zeckendorf of Webb and Knapp was out in Denver and working on a major deal.

"Denver's always been a great health resort," she recalled.

"Both Bob and Peggy are in their sixties and childless," Iris elaborated. "Technically he's retired since the move to Denver, but I understand he still dabbles in business deals when something interesting comes up." Iris gazed speculatively at her sister. "This could be another great business contact for you, Laura."

Over a sumptuous, impeccably served dinner, Laura listened attentively while Bob Westcott—a big bear of a man with a perennial tan and snow-white hair—talked about Denver.

"There she sits, on a mile-high plateau at the foot of the Rockies. As pretty a town as you'll see anywhere—and with the driest, cleanest air in the world," he boasted.

"But what I like most," Peggy said tenderly, "is to wake up in the morning, open the drapes, and look out on those magnificent mountains. It makes me feel so good inside."

"In its day," Bob said complacently over dessert, "Denver was one grand town. In the days when Horace Tabor—he owned all those silver mines—built his opera house."

"I hear Denver is in for some revitalization," Laura said. Instinct—and the Zeckendorf interest—told her this was the time to build in Denver. Excitement charged through her as she contemplated the potential. With its central location and with plane travel what it was today, analysts predicted Denver would become one of the oil capitals of the nation.

"That fellow from New York—I think his name is Zeckendorf—is trying to buy the Court House Square. All kinds of protest groups are fighting it," Bob told her. "They don't want some stranger from the East building in their town. And they like Denver just the way it is."

"That has to change," Peggy insisted, "what with so many new people moving into town. Right now Denver pulls in its sidewalks by 11 P.M., when the movie theaters close for the night."

"I understand there's a tremendous need for housing. If I were not so tied up financially with Hunter Village—my new development near Atlanta," Laura explained casually, "I'd head straight for Denver."

"Now I think that would be a mistake, Laura." She could see Bob's shrewd mind working. "Oh, sure, we need housing in the worst way. But building has got so damn high in Denver not even middle-class folks can afford a decent home. What's going up now will be blight for years to come. Tiny boxes—each one just like the other—set on tiny lots with not a tree in sight."

"Why is building so expensive there?" Laura was not yet ready to abandon thoughts of Denver residential development.

"All kinds of black and gray markets," Bob explained grimly. "Inefficient workmen. And make-work rules set up by labor. And special costs tacked on today. When did a Denver builder ever have to pay for freight until now? Don't try building in Denver," he reiterated. "Not now."

Laura understood—even before Jimmy shot her a warning glance—that this was not the moment to push a Denver deal. But surely there was a way to get around Denver's building problems. She must contrive in the course of the evening to channel the conversation back to Denver.

Later, in Laura's room, she and Iris probed into the possibility of drawing Bob Westcott into a deal in Denver.

432

And Peggy Westcott's interest in change would be helpful.

"Peggy is a lady accustomed to having her own way. She's sweet and charming—you know Southern women. But in her own soft way she'll connive for what she wants."

"I see something far bigger than Hunter Village. The Denver population is growing—it'll really take off in the next year or two. The people coming out will be in the top-executive category. They'll want expensive homes with terrific views of the mountains. Strikingly modern homes," Laura pinpointed. "Oh Iris, I can see those houses being built at the edge of the city but with a feeling of being almost in touching distance of the Rockies. Maybe along the lines of the houses by Frank Lloyd Wright."

"You could build those houses with Westcott money behind you," Iris said softly.

"I can't push him too hard," Laura warned.

"How would you like to handle this?"

"It would be useful to meet him again on a social basis. Not right away. Maybe in a few weeks." Laura's eyes were questioning.

"The Broadmoor at Colorado Springs." Iris's voice was suddenly electric. "In early June. Peggy and Bob are going to be there for four weeks. I'll arrange to be there, too. You'll join me." She glowed in triumph. "Peggy and I will work on him before you come out. Laura, we can rope him in."

"If I make a deal with Bob Westcott," Laura told her, "the firm will pay you a hefty commission. You'll be working for Hunter Realty."

# Chapter 34

Katie was caught up in the excitement of approaching high school graduation and registration for college in the fall. Annabel and she would be roommates at the University of Georgia. Though Katie seemed happy to be home again, Laura understood she had blocked from her mind all she had learned about her maternal grandfather.

Katie couldn't believe he had been guilty of that awful murder, could she? Did doubts lurk in her young mind? At painful intervals these possibilities plagued Laura. One day — when Papa's name had been cleared, she promised herself — she and Katie would sit down together and talk about the fine man he had been.

Late in May Laura sat in the high-school auditorium — with tears of pleasure filling her eyes — and saw Katie graduate. Early in June Katie and Annabel left with a group of Magnolia girls on a six-week bus tour across the country. Jonnie and Chet — both planning to go on to law school after college — would be working for the summer in Barry's law office.

Though she was actively involved with Hunter Village, Laura was impatient for the next meeting with the Westcotts in Colorado Springs. She was stimulated by the possibilities of expanding into a much broader field. Always ambitious, she was now consumed by visions of buying up properties and rebuilding in all the great cities across the nation. Of changing the skylines of those cities. To lay this kind of success at Katie's feet would, perhaps, make up for the pain she had caused her daughter.

Laura briefly considered hiring detectives to try to track down the witnesses at her father's trial. Intuition warned her against this. The Slocums must never suspect that she was out to clear her father's name, out to bring the real murderer to trial. She and Everett—at every opportunity—must do this alone. She knew it would be arduous and slow.

On a dazzlingly sunny afternoon Laura arrived at the elegant Broadmoor. A lakeside, pink-stucco nine-story Mediterranean masterpiece, it faced Cheyenne Mountain.

"Iris, the view is spectacular." Laura stood mesmerized until her sister prodded her into the hotel's elegant interior.

"The view that will excite you even more," Iris promised, "will be watching Peggy at the dinner table tonight. She's going to lay a trap that Bob won't be able to resist. We figure the strategic time to do this is when you're there to pick up the ball and run with it. But we'll talk about that when you're settled in your room."

In the elevator en route to Laura's room, she and Iris exchanged gossip about the children. Noel was enrolled at a posh summer camp for six weeks—to provide Miss Brisbane with a much-needed vacation.

"I don't know how I'd survive without that woman," Iris sighed. "Noel is impossible. She's worth every dollar I pay her." But how long could Iris afford Miss Brisbane?

Alone with Iris in her room, Laura focused on the business that lay ahead.

"What have Peggy and you conjured up?" Laura chuckled indulgently as she dropped into a chair, but her eyes were all business.

Iris pulled another chair closer to Laura's.

"Between the appetizer and the main course Peggy will tell Bob how hurt she is that they were not invited to the big shindig at the Evans' farm on July 4. Bob gets very upset if Peggy is snubbed. They've never been accepted by the so-called first families of Denver despite all their money. So-o," Iris drawled, "you remind him that the 'first families' are still living in the old Denver. Maybe they ought to be shaken up by some modernization in the city."

435

"A little thing like that can change one of the sharpest business minds in the country?" Laura was skeptical.

"He knows how the old families feel about Texans. They just might accept members of an old line Eastern or even Midwest family—but not oil-rich Texans. I gather he's ignored that so far, but Peggy means more to him than anything in this world. If he feels the Old Guard in Denver has snubbed his wife, he'll do anything to get back at them."

"Even to financing a multimillion-dollar project?" Logic told Laura that Iris was fantasizing, but her intuition said Iris could be right. On the strength of some small quirk many major deals had been consummated.

"You come down to dinner tonight with some great ideas to throw before Bob," Iris instructed. "You *have* been thinking about this?"

"Ev and I have dug up everything possible on Denver," Laura confirmed. "Maisie researched in the library for us. She wrote to the Chamber of Commerce and to the Denver Historical Society for information. Denver is still living in the last century. There hasn't been one important new building constructed in the center of Denver for over thirty years. That's sad, considering its potential." All at once she glowed. "And I think I know how to sidestep the hazards of building houses in Denver."

"We'll pull this off," Iris predicted jubilantly. "And wear something spectacular tonight. Bob loves being surrounded by beautiful women."

Peggy and Bob were waiting for Laura and Iris at their table in the hotel's dramatic dining room. Bob's eyes lighted at the sight of the two women.

"Peggy, don't those two look like a pair of movie stars?" he said admiringly.

"Iris was a movie star," Peggy reminded. "Of course, she was very young then."

Laura sat quietly listening to the playful conversation between Iris and Bob. She sensed he was pleased to be in the company of someone he considered British aristocracy.

436

Even multimillionaire Texans seemed impressed by titles.

"Honey, what do you think we ought to do about July 4?" Peggy asked ingenuously at a break in the table talk.

"Celebrate it, Peggy," Bob chuckled. "We'll be back at the Denver house. Why don't you two came out there for the July 4 week?" Bob invited. "We've got the greatest view of the Rockies in the city of Denver."

"I feel just awful that we weren't invited to the big shindig at the Evans' farm." Peggy's eyes were wistful. "Almost everybody important in Denver will be there. And I did serve on the garden-club committee with Avis Evans. You gave them a huge check in their last fund drive, Bob."

"Who the hell do they think they are?" Bob exploded, then quickly lowered his voice at a reproachful glance from his wife.

"They're old line Denver, I gather," Laura said with distaste. "They love their big old mausoleum homes and the depressing old office buildings and stores in town."

"They die every time a new house goes up in the suburbs just because it's new," Peggy's voice was scathing.

"They think they even own the Rockies," Iris laughed.

"I think the mountains are Denver's greatest asset," Laura said. "If I had the capital, I'd like to build a hundred new houses—all of them on one floor with huge windows looking out on the Rockies. Expensive houses with perfect views that would put the old homes to shame." In the price range she had in mind, building costs would be no object. The added expenses that plagued average Denver builders would be lost in their price tags.

"That Zeckendorf fellow isn't thinking about houses." Bob's eyes narrowed in a quizzical stare. "He's talking about commercial property."

"And from what you tell me he's going to have the devil of time going ahead with his urban development program." Laura knew she had Bob Westcott on the line. Could she bring him in? "He'll be so tied up with court actions—trying to buy *city* property—that he probably won't be able to start construction for years."

"And what would you do?" Bob challenged.

Deliberately Laura paused. She knew this was not a casual question.

"I would buy land in what I knew I could convert into 'Tiffany' locations," she began. "Residential purchases won't create hostility if they're handled quietly. All privately owned acreage," she emphasized. "And when I had my land, I'd build the most exciting homes Denver has ever seen. With every possible luxury touch. There's big money coming into the city—and a market for those houses."

For a moment Bob squinted in thought. Then he slammed a fist onto the table.

"Peggy, we're going to show those 'first families' that we don't need their blasted parties." Bob's face radiated pleasure. "We're going to create a whole new elite community that'll put theirs to shame." He turned to Laura.

"Laura, let's build those houses. I'll phone my lawyer to come up from Denver and start the ball rolling. That is," he grinned, "if you're willing to take me on as a partner.

Laura smiled brilliantly.

"You bet I'm willing."

"It'll be such fun," Peggy effervesced. "After a few weeks at the Denver house, we always get restless. But not anymore."

"Hell, we might even set up an art museum out there when Westcott Acres is finished." He leaned ingratiatingly towards Laura. "You got any objections to calling our new community Westcott Acres?"

"None," Laura assured him and reached for her wine glass. "Let's drink to Westcott Acres."

# Chapter 35

Bob Westcott was amused and pleased to discover Laura was an attorney. Within forty-eight hours Westcott's attorney and she had worked out the details of the new corporation. Westcott would supply the financing, Laura the know-how. They would be equal partners. The filing would be rushed through as swiftly as possible and the corporate bank account established, the other attorney assured Laura. Westcott & Hunter was a reality.

Laura knew that Bob was a shrewd manipulator who had fought his way up from worker in the oil fields to owner of one of the largest independent oil companies in the country. She valued his input in their operation. Yet his enthusiasm, his emotional involvement in the project made her increasingly uneasy. How would she handle him if he tried to take over control? That could be disastrous.

She mustn't let that happen. She was moving into the national field—this was the most important step in her real-estate career. She'd make Bob Westcott understand that she must make all final decisions. Laura brushed aside doubts. Westcott Acres would become a landmark in residential building.

"When you come back to Colorado, you're staying with me at the Westcott house," Iris reminded her at the airport. "I'll be there until I find an apartment." Iris was to settle into a small apartment near the fashionable Denver Country Club, her rent paid by the corporation. She was now officially employed.

"I should be able to fly back out here within a week," Laura estimated. With Katie away on the tour and Jonnie engrossed in his job, she'd be free to commute between

439

Denver and Magnolia for the rest of the summer. "I want to start buying land as soon as possible."

Back in Magnolia she'd do some hasty reorganizing. She'd enlarge the staff, assign much responsibility for Hunter Village to Everett and Maisie.

"Iris, am I going to have trouble with Bob?" She trusted Iris's instincts. "He's beginning to come up with a lot of suggestions. Some are good. But most are impractical."

"He'll be chasing off to Palm Springs or Palm Beach or someplace," Iris shrugged. "Right now Westcott Acres fascinates him—it's a new toy. Just play along with him for now. He'll be out of your hair soon. Laura, this is going to be fun!" Iris relished her first assignment: to contact local brokers and inform them she was interested in purchasing land in order to build a house. Behind this front Laura would choose the properties that fitted into her plans.

"Until it's too late to stop us, nobody will realize that a pair of outsiders are buying up a lot of choice Denver property," Laura pointed out.

She enjoyed the challenge ahead. She knew the choice areas in town that could be parlayed into "Tiffany locations." And she would find an architect with the imagination and creativity to build the houses she envisioned.

Back in Magnolia she focused on reorganizing the Magnolia operation. By the end of the month both she and Everett considered this accomplished and she phoned the Westcotts to say she was heading for Denver. She learned that Bob and Peggy were flying out to Palm Springs for a long weekend. Iris would pick her up at the airport.

As her plane approached the modest Denver airport—which Bob insisted would soon have to be replaced by a larger one, Laura was conscious of the burnt, brown, treeless plains that surrounded the city. Bob and Peggy had told her that between 1905 and 1912 thousands of elms, poplars, and oaks had been planted in Denver, making the city today an oasis of greenery.

Iris was waiting for her, the Westcott chauffeur standing by to collect her luggage.

"Darling, you look indecently young," Iris chided high-spiritedly. "Don't you dare tell anybody that you have two children in college."

Ensconced in the Westcott's gray Rolls-Royce, Iris reported on the properties being shown her. None of the brokers was aware that she was working with any other. Iris had a list of sites to show Laura.

"Bob's concerned about the terrain in some cases," Iris told her, "but I said you'd know which would be good."

"If the views are spectacular, we'll design to fit the lot," Laura said calmly.

"There won't be a problem when the brokers find out at the closings that they're not selling to Lady Iris Cranford?" Iris asked with a touch of anxiety.

"Your lawyer—me, if I'm in town," Laura laughed, "will explain that for tax purposes the sale is to go through the corporation. We'll be paying cash—they won't ask questions. It'll take a while before people catch on."

"I've told Jack to take us on a short sightseeing tour before we go to the house," Iris explained. "I know you. Once you're involved in business, you'll have time for nothing else."

"Oh Iris, these views!" Laura gazed out the car window to the west. "I know I saw the mountains at the Broadmoor, but I'm impressed all over again. I feel as though I could reach and touch them." Endless foothills climbed skyward into huge, craggy peaks.

"That's the marvelous air here. Everything seems incredibly near."

The chauffeur drove them past the beautifully classic Civic Center, the gold-domed Capitol—a carbon copy of dozens of others across the nation—and the United States Mint. Then they were driving along Sixteenth Street and Iris pointed out the large department stores, the smart shops.

"Don't buy anything silver unless I'm with you," Iris

441

warned. "Most of it is factory made for the tourists."

They crossed to Seventeenth Street, known as the Wall Street of the West, the home of Denver's large banks and brokerage firms. Then Iris instructed Jack to take them through the wide, tree-shaded residential streets, where small brick homes and low, modern apartment houses sat back on brilliantly green lawns, amidst well-tended gardens and shrubs.

"It's a magnificent city," Laura said. "Isn't there anything unpleasant to see?"

"Some of Denver you don't want to see," Iris conceded. "But why bother seeing what isn't lovely?"

Laura thought about the inadequate new houses built at the edge of town, the Denver families squeezed into a single cubicle in a rooming house, the desperate few who had moved into abandoned streetcars. She ought to be building for these people. Guilt, she thought wistfully, was a way of life for her.


Laura looked forward to the long weekend alone with Iris in the Westcott mansion, furnished with elegant antiques Peggy had collected from around the world. It resembled one of the great Fifth Avenue houses built in New York at the turn of the century. Iris herself drove her — in Peggy's just-off-the-assembly-line Cadillac — to see the acreage that was up for sale.

On Laura's first evening in town she went with Iris to Central City to see a play. Every summer for three weeks such stars as Ruth Gordon, Lillian Gish, and Gladys Swarthout appeared at the Central City Play Festival. The following evening they were to be guests for dinner at the home of one of the old-line families, whom Iris knew from Palm Beach. Laura was delighted that Lady Iris Cranford was being accepted socially where even the Texas-rich Westcotts were denied entry.

"They love entertaining titled English," Iris drawled as they left the car to approach the huge stone palace that was similar to the Westcott house. Most of these had become quarters for prestigious schools or charitable organizations. "How could I ever marry again and give up being Lady Iris Cranford?" she wailed, half in jest.

When the Westcotts returned to the city, Laura sat down with Bob to formulate their strategy. Bob was happy to be involved in setting up their construction team. The wily Texan agreed with Laura that they should do their own contracting. The money would be better spent on luxury details.

An unpretentious office was set up in downtown Denver. Iris's job was to bring to Laura's attention high-powered young men with impeccable connections who might be recruited as salesmen. The prospective commissions selling the most expensive houses available in Denver would be alluring.

Laura was pleased with the construction team she had put together in Denver. She had acquired the best available by offering top salaries and emphasizing that this was to be a quality development.

Her first serious impasse arrived when she began to interview architects. Thus far, she had built homes in a low-price range. Now she was reaching for the heights. Bob and she had agreed not to hire a Denver architect—they preferred one who approached the splendor of the mountain backdrop with fresh eyes. For weeks she interviewed in Magnolia and Atlanta without encountering a single architect who seemed to understand the kind of houses she visualized for the Denver hills and how each custom-designed house must fit into the pattern of a very special community.

The situation was becoming critical. Impatient to break ground on the first homes, Laura discussed the situation far into a November night with Everett and Maisie. Early in the new year, she vowed, they'd have their architect.

"Maybe you should reconsider hiring a Denver architect," Maisie said.

"Hire somebody young," Everett urged. "Not many

years out of architectural school and not beaten into formula designing."

"I'll do some screening when I'm out in Denver the beginning of next month," Laura decided. She'd be back in Magnolia when Jonnie and Katie arrived for the Christmas break from college. "But I still have this crazy feeling that a Denver architect might be so used to those views that he won't appreciate what they mean to Eastern or Middle West buyers."

"Let's get out of here so Laura can get some sleep," Everett chuckled. She was still the first one in the office when she was in Magnolia. "And I could use some myself."

"Laura, remember you have that dinner tomorrow night," Maisie said while Everett went to retrieve their coats. "Cecile is counting on you."

"I'll be there," Laura promised. Cecile was chairman of the fund-raising dinner. "I may fall asleep midway through the speeches, but in body I'll be there."


While Laura was dressing for the dinner, Cecile called.

"Barry and I will pick you up," Cecile told her. "Then we'll stop off to pick up the Goldmans. You haven't met them yet, have you?"

"No. I've been out of town so much the past few months. They're the couple from Boston?" Cecile had mentioned them several times.

"Rhoda met Seth when he was at school up there. Actually he's a New Yorker. She was born right here in Magnolia, but moved to Boston when she was twelve or thirteen. Rhoda's a few years older than us — you probably didn't know her."

"What brought them back to Magnolia?" Instinctively Laura tensed. Did Rhoda Goldman remember Papa's trial?

"Rhoda said she couldn't bear another rugged Boston winter, and Seth was disenchanted with his job. Since

444

they have no children it was easy for them to pick up stakes and move. Seth and she plan on opening up a fine gift shop in Magnolia. He's looking for a location."

Ever punctual, Laura was waiting in the foyer—her lavishly designed mink coat over one arm—when Cecile and Barry pulled up before the house in their Packard. She knew Cecile—with her eye for line and color—would like the olive green velvet Mainbocher that Iris had sent her from London seven years ago and that was still smart. She'd bought the mink in Denver at Iris's insistence. *Laura, mink tells them you're successful—think of it as a business investment.*

The night air was sharp. Cecile prodded Laura into the back seat and settled herself beside Barry.

"You'll be happy to know that Mrs. Tannenbaum and Adele won't be at the dinner," Cecile told her. "They bought tickets, of course; but since neither of them was on the committee, they can't be bothered with attending."

"Listen to my catty wife," Barry teased. But he understood, Laura thought, that she still recoiled from encounters with Phil's mother and grandmother.

Several minutes later they turned into the driveway of the charming house rented by the Goldmans. Barry pressed on the horn.

In the light from the porch lamp that the Goldmans left on, Laura saw that Rhoda Goldman was a small, slender, dark-haired woman with a quick smile. Her husband was of medium height, prematurely gray, and handsome in an understated fashion. Laura immediately understood why Cecile was so fond of the Goldmans. They radiated warmth.

"Thank God, I've finally lost enough weight to get into this dress," Rhoda said when she and Seth had joined Laura on the back seat, and they'd been introduced. "I bought it for an affair ten years ago—and I've never worn it since."

"It's lovely," Laura told her. "It's one of those ageless dresses that are so wonderful."

445

"Seth picked it out for me," Rhoda confided. "I remember when I bought it. It was at B. Altman in New York. We were going to a formal dinner given by Seth's firm. He was an architect before we escaped from Boston and came down here to live." She exchanged a tender smile with Seth. This was a good marriage, Laura decided.

"And now Seth and Rhoda are going to open a gift shop," Cecile said with an appraising glint in her eyes. Cecile knew she was searching for an architect for the Denver deal, Laura thought. Surely she wasn't trying to promote Seth Goldman? He was opening a business here in town.

Over dinner in the Magnolia Hotel ballroom — the customary setting of local charity affairs — Laura discovered that Seth had been with a successful Boston architectural firm for the past eighteen years; but until the day he resigned, he had been at odds with the rest of the staff.

"Seth was always ahead of his time," Rhoda contributed, and Laura began to feel a stir of excitement. She was after an architect who had not been forced into conventional thinking. She'd harbored an image of an architect somewhere between twenty-eight and thirty-five, and Seth was somewhere in his mid-forties. Still, she suspected Rhoda was right. Seth was creative and original in his thinking.

"They tolerated me at the firm. I would grumble and complain, but eventually I did what they wanted. I knuckled down to the almighty dollar," he mocked himself. "I hated designing those dull, pretentious houses. But there have been architects who've managed to defy convention and take off in a new direction."

"Like Frank Lloyd Wright," Barry picked up.

"Nobody could put a harness on Wright. Look how he changed the face of architecture with his idea of harmonizing a structure with its surroundings." Seth glowed with an inner radiance. "When he designed the Imperial Hotel in Tokyo, he was criticized for so-called violations of sound construction. But in the earthquake of 1923, the

Imperial Hotel was one of the few buildings that wasn't damaged."

Laura and Cecile listened as though mesmerized while the other three discussed Wright's work.

"I haven't seen the 'Falling Water' house at Bear Run, Pennsylvania," Laura admitted during a pause in the conversation, "nor his 'Taliesin West' near Phoenix. But the photographs are fascinating. And of course, I appreciate his use of local stone. We used Georgia granite in our Atlanta building."

"You're a real-estate developer?" Seth gazed at her in astonishment.

"A damn successful one," Barry said, beaming. "Ask anybody in town about Laura Hunter."

"I was kind of pushed into real estate," Laura said wryly. "I came down here to work as a lawyer, but women lawyers aren't hugely popular. I moved out into real estate. So far we've operated mainly in Georgia and Alabama, but now I'm involved in a major project out in Denver."

"What are you doing out there?" Rhoda asked.

Laura talked about the prospective Westcott Acres and the kind of houses she hoped to build. She saw excitement welling in Seth while she described the spectacular views of the Rockies from the land she had bought.

"And you mean to use those views," Seth surmised with relish.

"To the limit." Laura arrived at a spontaneous decision. If Seth Goldman was still interested in architecture, he was the man for the Denver project. "We plan to offer the most luxurious housing—modern in every detail—that has ever been sold in Denver."

"All on one floor," Seth stipulated, "with great expanses of glass facing the mountains."

"Oh, yes." Laura nodded enthusiastically. "Natural woods, never painted—but perhaps stained."

The others listened attentively while Laura and Seth talked about the kind of houses that would fit into the

447

environment—until dinner was over and speech-making about to begin. Laura heard little of the speeches, mentally visualizing Seth Goldman at the head of their architectural staff.

On the drive home from the dinner Laura said nothing more about her own ventures. She listened while Rhoda talked about the gift shop the Goldmans planned to open in Magnolia. She sensed that Rhoda was more enthusiastic about the shop than her husband. This was Rhoda's opportunity to utilize her feeling for beautiful objects, Laura understood. For Seth it was a means of earning a living away from the frustrations of his former firm.

"I'm so glad I persuaded Seth to come down here to live," Rhoda said warmly when Barry drove into the Goldmans' driveway. "For all Boston has to offer in the way of culture, I've always missed Magnolia."

Seth helped Rhoda out of the car and then leaned towards Laura.

"It's been great to talk shop with you, Laura. Wonderful to know there's somebody here who thinks the way I do."

"Let's have dinner together soon," Rhoda invited the others. "I'll call tomorrow," she turned from Laura to Cecile, "and let's set a date."


As always when her mind was highly stimulated, Laura struggled through hours of insomnia before she fell asleep. But her last waking thought was the decision to approach Seth about taking on the assignment of designing for Westcott Acres. He wouldn't have to live out there, she reasoned. A week's stay in the beginning and then three-day trips as the construction moved along. Denver was most accessible by air.

In the morning she lingered longer than usual under the shower where she humorously claimed she did her clearest thinking. She was excited about the prospect of working with Seth, yet she recognized the conflict this

448

would cause in his plans. Although it was obvious that Rhoda looked forward to buying, to setting up displays, designing the shop windows, would she be able to run the shop on her own?

At the office Laura went through her routine morning conferences with Everett and Maisie, then told them about her encounter with Seth Goldman.

"I know he and his wife plan to open a gift shop here in town, but he's so right for this assignment. I have to make him an offer. I'll ask him to go out to Denver and check over the site, submit some rough sketches."

"Shouldn't you do some checking first with the Boston firm?" Everett pressed. "Talking and performing are not always the same."

"Ev, I know this is the architect for us," Laura insisted. "I'll ask them out to lunch today. We need Seth Goldman on our team."

Rhoda answered the phone when Laura called. Laura was candid — she was eager to have lunch with them and to talk about Seth's designing the Denver houses. She was aware of a fragment of hesitation before Rhoda accepted the lunch invitation. Though the Goldmans had never considered the possibility of Seth's working as an architect in Magnolia, she suspected that Rhoda would be on her side.

Wearing one of her smart London tweed suits on a December day reminiscent of spring, Laura was waiting at their table when Rhoda and Seth arrived. Rhoda had told him, of course, the purpose of this lunch. She was radiant; Seth seemed oddly serious.

"I haven't seen you in such a long time," Laura laughed as the other two sat down. "Rhoda, you can't complain about our Magnolia weather."

"Oh, it's glorious. We still have roses blooming beneath our dining room window. Seth can't believe it," Rhoda said affectionately.

They talked first about Boston, then New York. Seth conceded he would miss the cultural scene they'd enjoyed

449

in Boston and on frequent trips to New York, but he was philosophical about this.

"Magnolia is a beautiful town. I'm sure I'll come to like it as much as Rhoda."

A waitress arrived at their table. While they debated about what to order, Laura was conscious that Seth was concerned about abandoning their plans for the shop. Because of Rhoda, she interpreted.

When the waitress withdrew, Laura launched into her offer. Seth listened without interrupting. Rhoda exuded approval.

"I know you can make Westcott Acres what I envision," Laura told Seth. "Each house custom-designed and fitting uniquely into its grounds. You're the first architect who understands what I'm trying to do."

"I'm very flattered, Laura." He smiled, but his eyes were somber. "Fifteen years ago I would have given my soul to the devil for a chance like this."

"These are expensive homes," Laura pushed. "You can be as lavish and innovative as you like." She hesitated, then mentioned a fee that she knew would meet with his approval.

"We've made up our minds to become shopkeepers." Seth tried to appear cheerful. "It'll be a casual, pleasant life. But I do appreciate your offer."

"Seth, this is a dream come true," Rhoda scolded. "How can you turn Laura down?"

"We're committed to something else." His voice was strained. "I'm sure you'll find someone soon, Laura."

"Can you hold this open for a week?" Rhoda asked her. "I think Seth should give it some serious thought."

"Of course." They were still closing on acreage. She had allotted herself another month to settle on an architect. Then it would become a crisis situation. "Are you planning to go to the Community Theater production of *Claudia?*" Laura deftly switched topics. "I know it isn't Broadway, but the group is talented. I think you'll enjoy it."

Two nights later — minutes after Laura talked with Bob in Denver about the possibility of having found their architect — Seth Goldman called.

"Laura, if your offer is still open, I'm available."

"Seth, that's wonderful," Laura was exultant. "Would you be able to go out to Denver within the next few days? The company will arrange for accommodations for both Rhoda and you," she added quickly.

"I'll go out alone. Rhoda hates traveling. Besides, she'll be busy redecorating the house. We came down here and moved in without doing much to the place. Now she'll be able to concentrate on that."

"Will you drop by the office tomorrow morning?" Laura was exhilarated by his acceptance. "We'll start moving right ahead."

Three days before Seth's scheduled departure Laura left for Denver. She wanted to sit down with Bob for serious talk before he and Peggy left for a month at Palm Beach.

Stepping off the plane in Denver, Laura was enthralled by the sight of the snow-covered Rockies. She felt the kind of happiness she'd experienced at the sight of the magnificent beach and ocean at Montauk all those years ago. A beautiful sense of peace settled about her as she hurried forward to meet Iris.

"Bob rented a Cadillac for me to use," Iris reported after a warm embrace. "I'll drive you to the apartment via the scenic route."

"Great." Laura was in an unfamiliarly carefree mood. Was it the altitude? "I always prefer the scenic route."

"You know what the mountains look like?" Iris laughed. "Like a series of giant ice-cream sundaes."

"That's sacrilegious," Laura teased, noting that Iris had abandoned her smart British tweeds and her elegant furs for ski attire. It was difficult to imagine her glamorous sister interested in sports.

"Sorry. It's all this fresh air. I'm living such a clean life

451

out here," Iris drawled.

"When did all this happen?" Laura asked while they drove away from the airport. The road had been cleared, but snow lay everywhere else. All at once her mind hurtled back through the years. She saw Jonnie and Katie laughing on their sleds in Prospect Park, exuberantly struggling to stay vertical on their ice skates while Bernie and she encouraged them on with promises of hot chocolate later.

"We had about ten inches yesterday, but the snow never lasts more than a day or two in the city, I understand." Iris brought her back to the present. "Remember, Denver has three hundred days of sunshine every year."

"But Bob and Peggy are still dashing off to Palm Beach," Laura said wryly.

"If you don't ski, you can get bored fast out here," Iris admitted, and Laura sensed a restlessness in her. "Jimmy came out to ski for a few days last month. I went out on the slopes with him a couple of times."

"I didn't know you skied." Laura gazed at her in astonishment.

"I put in an appearance," Iris shrugged. "The way I did at St. Moritz and Kitzbühel before the war. It's always the same—those gorgeous young men with fantastic tans." She uttered an exaggerated sigh. "Darling, I can't bear it—I'll be forty in a few months. Where did all the years go?"

"As I recall, you've lived well a lot of those years." It was a gentle rebuke. Was Iris involved with one of those "gorgeous young men"? Jimmy Harris, she knew, was a devoted friend. Nothing more. "Iris, are you having an affair with somebody out here?" She was faintly uneasy. Although this was acceptable, even expected, in Iris's international set, she suspected Denver would be less approving.

"Laura, at thirty-nine a woman doesn't hand in her license to fuck," Iris said sharply. "Why shouldn't I enjoy myself? Even if I wanted to remarry—and you know I'll never give up my title—rich men all want young girls. I

452

don't qualify," she said with a hint of exasperation.

"Please be discreet. And be careful," Laura added. Would she ever stop worrying about Iris? "You don't want to get pregnant at thirty-nine."

Unexpectedly Iris chuckled.

"Nobody out here thinks I'm more than twenty-eight," she said complacently. "Noel's only eight. He could have been born when I was eighteen." She hesitated. "I suppose I should give up the New York apartment and bring him out here with Miss Brisbane. I'll probably be out here for at least a year—"

"Oh Iris, yes! Do bring Noel here." Laura beamed in approval. Perhaps the boy would be less difficult if he saw more of his mother. It always upset her that on those rare occasions when she saw her only nephew, she felt a kind of wariness rather than love. He looked enough like Jonnie and Katie to be their younger brother—except for those cold gray eyes. Peter Cranford's eyes. Arrogant, almost contemptuous. It was unsettling to see that in such a small boy.

"You know I've never stayed anywhere for a whole year—not since I married Peter," Iris said with an air of discovery. "I hope I don't get cabin fever." Laura felt a sudden ambivalence.

"You'll be making side trips," Laura comforted. "Company expense trips to keep up contacts. And when you go off the Westcott & Hunter payroll, you move over to Hunter Realty."

"I'm a business woman," Iris laughed. "I can't believe it."

"Hold on to the Sutton Place apartment," Laura said. "Hunter Realty will pay the rent. It'll be our base in New York."

"I'll put in an appearance there from time to time, give a party or two." Iris nodded in comprehension. "Jimmy's invited me to a houseparty in Acapulco in February," she recalled now. "He said he'd love to have you come, too. You'll be getting one of his crazy little notes soon."

"Let me check on my schedule. If I'm out here then

and everything's going well, I should be able to fly down for a couple of days." Within the next six months, once Westcott Acres was well on its way, she'd begin to look for something new. Bob and Peggy were enjoying this deal, but she doubted that their interest would extend beyond that.

"That would be marvelous," Iris enthused. "Stay as long as you can."

"You took care of the reservations for Seth Goldman at the Brown Palace?" Laura asked.

"It's all set. There'll be a car for his use, too." Iris's eyes left the road for an instant. "He must be something special, the way Bob tells it."

"When Seth finishes up the designs for Westcott Acres, he'll take on Hunter Realty's next project. I'm not sure yet just what that'll be, but I want Seth to head up our architectural staff."

Iris brought her up to date on what had been happening around town in the past few days. Word was circulating that much choice residential acreage was being bought up by Westcott & Hunter. Yesterday they'd heard that a local group was preparing to fight to prevent some of the closings from going through.

At lunch with Iris and Bob at the Westcott estate, Bob expanded on this situation.

"There's no way they'll be able to do it," he assured Laura with rage in his voice. "Peggy and I are going on to Palm Beach as planned. She's down at Daniels & Fisher, buying out the store again," he chuckled. "But if the lawyers run into any trouble, I'll be right back. Nobody's stopping Westcott Acres. These so-called 'old families,' he scoffed. "Not one of 'em goes back more than fifty or sixty years. There're too many new people coming into Denver for them to run it anymore."

"Politics here are like in Magnolia, only on a much larger scale," Iris told Laura with bitter humor. "A small clique runs everything."

Bob grinned. "I may be an old codger, but I've got

young ideas. Oh, Peg said to tell you — we're taking you girls out for dinner. Nothing fancy," he cautioned. "Some real local color. We're going to Buckhorn Lodge down by the railroad tracks for the largest steaks and the biggest display of taxidermy anywhere in this city. And don't dress up," he cautioned. "It's not the place for it."

At Buckhorn Lodge restaurant the Westcott party was greeted warmly by a little white-haired man — quick to say he'd passed his eightieth birthday. He personally settled the newest arrivals at a cozy corner table with checkered tablecloth and lingered to chat.

"You tell these two ladies from back east about how you headed here from Kansas City with an ox team, and how you scouted for Buffalo Bill himself," Bob ordered good-humoredly. He'd heard Dietz's reminiscences many times and still enjoyed the telling.

"Oh, that ain't the half of it," Dietz boasted. "For a while I was a guide for Teddy Roosevelt himself. But the day that always stays in my memory is when Chief Red Cloud came in and brought me a sword he had taken from General Custer's body. I got it right here on the wall," he said with pride. "Got Custer's name carved on it."

Then their enormous steaks arrived and Dietz left them to enjoy their dinner. Laura sensed Bob had something tugging at him tonight. Not until their hot apple pie arrived did he admit what concerned him.

"Laura, you're sure about this architect you're hiring?" Bob pressed. "I mean, we've got a helluva lot of money going into those houses. What about one of those big-wheel firms up in New York?"

"I want Seth Goldman to design Westcott Acres," Laura said firmly. "I don't think there's an architect in the country that could do a better job. He sees Westcott Acres the way I see it. And he didn't come seeking the assignment," she emphasized. "I had to persuade him to abandon going into business to take this. If we brought in one of those prestigious New York architects," she pointed out, "we'd be paying a fee five times as large."

"Sometimes you have to pay top dollar." Bob squinted into space. Was he going to make trouble? Laura was shaken.

"Bob, I want Seth Goldman to design Westcott Acres," she reiterated. *She had borrowed to the hilt to build Hunter Village. She was in no position to buy out Bob.* "Do you trust my judgment, or are we at a stalemate?"

The atmosphere was suddenly super-charged. Laura managed a quiet, inquiring smile, but her heart was thumping.

"Hell, you're the builder, little lady," Bob said. "Keep your architect. But if he can't deliver, we're going to have egg on our faces. And a lot of red ink on our books."

Had she made a stupid, impulsive decision, Laura asked herself. They wouldn't know, she forced herself to acknowledge realistically, until Seth's designs for Westcott Acres were in work.

# Chapter 36

On a dazzlingly sunny Wednesday afternoon—a few hours after Bob and Peggy left for Palm Beach—Iris drove Laura to the airport to meet Seth. The snow had disappeared from the ground but was on spectacular display on the mountains at Denver's back door.

After a warm exchange of greetings with Laura and his introduction to Iris, Seth paused beside the car and gazed with rich appreciation at the majestic Rockies.

"Why do Americans—including me," he added humorously, "run to Europe to see the Alps when we have such splendor right here at home?"

"I knew you'd love these mountains." Laura felt a surge of pleasure at his admiration.

"Several summers before Pearl Harbor Rhoda and I rented a house for a month in a Swiss village called Bougy Villars, midway between Geneva and Lausanne. Each morning we'd rush from bed to stand at a window and look out at Mont Blanc. Such an exhilarating feeling. It's almost a confirmation that 'God's in his heaven—all's right with the world,' if I may quote Robert Browning."

"An awesome experience," Laura concurred. "That's what our houses at Westcott Acres will provide."

"I'm eager to see the sites." Seth opened the rear car door for Laura and climbed in beside her. "Each plot will offer a special challenge." Laura felt his excitement. "All on a hillside facing west."

Laura nodded. Yes, she was certain that Seth was the architect for this project. "It always irritated me," he confessed, "that at my firm in Boston we were assigned houses to design without any consideration of the sites. I see these mountains, and I know each house must be designed with its specific view in mind."

"Would you like to drive out there before dinner?" Laura asked. "Or would you rather rest up at the hotel?"

"I'd like to see the property right now," he said instantly. "Let's just stop at the hotel so I can register, leave my luggage and we'll go."

After a brief stop at the hotel, they headed out towards the edge of the city to the locale that would become Westcott Acres. Iris parked at the first site, and they left the car to inspect the rugged terrain. After a few minutes of contemplation, Seth pulled out a sketching pad and began to make a rough drawing.

"You don't know what a pleasure this is," he said with relish. "To design a house without worrying about how to keep the costs down."

"I do know," she laughed. "I've never been able to build on such a lavish scale before. I've lost many a night's sleep struggling to work out a budget that would allow for at least an aura of quality. I love working with Hunter Village," she acknowledged, "but this is a dream come true."

"I won't go absolutely crazy," he promised.

Laura was to return to Magnolia on Sunday morning. Seth would remain another three days, conferring with their construction staff at the downtown Denver office. But in these days Laura came to feel that she had known Seth for years.

At intervals during the long hours of work-related talks, they discovered how much they had in common. Seth talked eloquently of his love for the rocky coast at Gloucester, a short drive from Boston.

"It was my escape hatch," he told her. "When things got too frustrating at the office, Rhoda and I would rush off to Gloucester for the weekend—winter or summer. There's nothing like sitting at a candlelit table in a fine seafood restaurant and gazing out at the Atlantic."

"Montauk was like that for me," Laura said in nostalgic recall. "I was only there once, but I'll always remember the stretch of magnificent deserted beach and the rush of the waves to the shore. Keep in mind," she chuckled, "that

458

the only beach I really knew was Brighton Beach in the summer."

Both had fond memories of New York's great museums and the theater, yet each relished the quiet charm of Magnolia.

Seth ferreted out information about the Jewish district in Denver, and Laura and he explored the area on a quiet Saturday morning.

"I knew that Jews were among the early settlers," Seth explained, "and that they've contributed much to the development of Denver. The first big tubercular hospital—free and nonsectarian—was established here back in 1899. I remember hearing my parents talk about it."

Laura and Seth walked along W. Colfax Avenue where kosher restaurants, poultry stores, and a variety of shops were closed for the Sabbath. They saw the Jewish motion picture houses and the headquarters of the Jewish newspapers.

"I would never have expected this in Denver," Laura said softly as they returned to the car.

"We Jews do get around," Seth chuckled.

That night Seth and Laura dined alone at his hotel. Iris was attending a dinner party at the home of one of Denver's elite families. Her escort was one of the "gorgeous young men" who would be selling Westcott Acres houses as soon as plans were available.

They lingered over coffee—both reluctant to call an end to the evening. Without meaning for it to happen, Laura told Seth about her father. Sooner or later, she reminded herself, someone in Magnolia would bring it up and she'd rather he heard it from her.

"What a terrible ordeal for the three of you." Seth was white with shock. "But you came through it well," he said gently. "We don't know how much we can endure until we're faced with a problem."

"There are homes in Magnolia where I'm sure the children and I are not welcome," Laura conceded. "Like every small town, Magnolia has its layers of society. We tend to stay within our own layer."

"I had trouble accepting the colored situation in Magnolia," Seth admitted. "Having to ride in the back of the buses, having their own restaurants and movie theaters—I find the whole scene disturbing. I spent three years in the army during the war—most of it overseas. Colored soldiers died over there just like whites—bullets and bombs were color blind. Laura, you wouldn't believe the bigotry in the army. Not just against colored and Jewish soldiers—there were Catholic priests who were hostile towards the Protestant chaplains, and vice-versa. It startled me. But about the colored situation—" His voice was troubled. "We're going to see great changes demanded in the years ahead. It's inevitable. I hope Magnolia copes with it sensibly."

"There's intolerance in the North as well," Laura reminded. "Iris has an apartment on Sutton Place in Manhattan. There's an unspoken rule in her building that they don't rent to Negroes or Jews." Her smile was wry. "Of course, nobody there knows Lady Iris Cranford is Jewish." Suddenly she was uncomfortable with this inadvertent admission. She glanced at her watch and stood up. "I have an early flight tomorrow. I should be getting back to the apartment."

"See you in Magnolia in a few days," Seth smiled. "I'm so happy to be working with you on Westcott Acres."

In the guest bedroom in Iris's smart apartment Laura packed for tomorrow morning's flight with a mellow satisfaction. These few days had been almost a vacation, she thought whimsically. No constant phone interruptions, no meetings or conferences. Just working with Seth on the immediate problems. It was relaxing to be with him, she realized. He reminded her so much of Bernie. Not physically but in his thinking, his compassion.

She started at the sound of footsteps in the entrance foyer.

"Iris?" She walked into the hall.

"Right," Iris called back and strolled towards her. "In Denver parties end early. How was your evening? Full of business talk," she guessed.

460

"Up to a point," Laura agreed.

"You miss the kids." Iris dropped herself across the foot of Laura's bed. "You're anxious to be back in Magnolia."

"Iris, they're off at school," Laura laughed. She kicked off her shoes and sat in a slipper chair close to the bed.

"And you miss them like hell," Iris said sympathetically.

"At first, yes," Laura said after a moment's contemplation. "I couldn't bear walking into that big, empty house. I hated to sit down to dinner alone. But something happened. I discovered I had a new freedom."

"Laura, I never expected to hear you say that!" Iris gazed at her in good-humored astonishment.

"I never expected to feel that way," Laura said slowly. "But it was good. I didn't have to worry anymore because I wasn't at home with the kids like a normal mother. I don't love them any less—and I can't wait for them to come home for school holidays. Maybe if all I had was the house and the kids I'd be desolate—but of necessity my world expanded. Life doesn't end when the kids grow up. Of course, they're always there in a special corner of my mind. I'll see something in a shop window and think, 'Oh, Katie would adore that—or Jonnie could really use that.' And I thank God I have them." How sad that Iris never truly enjoyed Noel.

"What about men?" Iris prodded.

"Iris, I've had two husbands." All at once she was defensive. "Twice is enough for one lifetime."

"Darling, I'm not talking about marriage," Iris reproached indulgently.

"I know what you're talking about." All at once Laura was self-conscious. "I have no room in my life for a man. I have the children and the business. That's all I need." She rose to her feet and faked a yawn. "Iris, I'll never get out of bed when the alarm goes off if I don't get some sleep."

In the months ahead Laura worried at intervals that Seth was spending so much time in Denver, though

Rhoda appeared to accept this with equanimity. Once her house was redecorated to her satisfaction, Rhoda allowed Cecile to persuade her to become involved on a part-time basis in the interior decorating shop.

Laura shuttled between Magnolia and Denver, contriving to be in Denver to attend some of the small dinners Iris gave. On occasion the dinners were for friends of her international set. More often the guests were local lawyers, judges, political figures who could be useful to Westcott and Hunter.

On her company expense account Iris took off for long weekends at Acapulco, Mexico City, and Palm Springs, her objective to pick up leads about possible buyers for the Westcott Acres houses and to promote the pleasure of maintaining a house overlooking the Rockies.

The bright young men Iris brought into the sales force were selling the well-publicized Westcott Acres houses from floor plans.

Hunter Village, too, was doing well. The attractive but modest homes were drawing buyers from ex-GIs eligible for home loans. At a conference with Laura and Seth, Everett suggested they plan a second section — Hunter Village II.

"At higher prices, of course," Everett pinpointed. Inflation was everywhere. "And schedule some for a higher-earning group."

"Truman lists the housing shortage a major problem in the country," Seth reminded. "In every price range."

"The market is there, Laura," Everett pushed. He reached into a folder to pull out a report. "Look at these figures."

"All right, we'll do it," Laura agreed after a moment. As fast as she was earning money, she was pushing it back into the business. But the banks were ever eager to extend her loans and her holdings were impressive.

Laura was pleased when Iris brought Noel and Miss Brisbane back with her to Denver after a brief trip to New York in the late spring.

*"Noah's still being terribly difficult,"* Iris wrote. *"I was asked*

*to take him out of that damnably expensive school he was attend-ing. I hope he behaves himself in the Denver school that's accepted him. I don't know if it was Bridget or Miss Brisbane that made him so aware of being the son of a British lord. When we're not together, Miss Brisbane makes him write me a little letter once a week. He signs it 'the Honourable Noel Cranford.' I ought to tell the arrogant little brat about his grandfather on his mother's side. But he's not always like that. One minute he's absolutely ador-able—and the next he's a little monster. Peggy says it's because I've had to bring him up alone."*

She had brought Jonnie and Katie up alone for a lot of years, Laura remembered—but they were fine, sweet kids. Papa had brought Iris and her up alone. Maybe Noel just needed more of his mother. But how would she ever make Iris understand this?

At each of those cherished intervals when Jonnie and Katie came home from school, Laura made a point of having a small dinner party that included Maisie and Everett, Cecile and Barry—and Chet if he were available, and Seth and Rhoda.

The conversation at these dinners invariably focused on world events. Laura enjoyed the way the children became involved. Katie was articulate but emotional, Jonnie and Chet analytical, cool. Laura prided herself that her chil-dren would never be bigots.

Laura knew Jonnie was going into law. Katie talked vaguely about social work or library science. Whatever she decided, Laura told herself, she would do well.

In July Iris was to fly to Paris with Peggy Westcott for Dior's second collection and a reunion with several of her international-set friends at a villa in the south of France. She pleaded with Laura to allow Katie to go with them.

"Katie didn't really see Paris that last time," Iris pointed out. "We owe her this."

"Iris, she's so young," Laura protested. "And how will she fit in with your friends at that houseparty in the south of France?"

"She'll be spoiled to death," Iris laughed. "They'll adore her. It'll be a marvelous experience for her. Laura, we never had such chances at her age. Let her enjoy what we couldn't."

With some trepidation Laura consented, in a corner of her mind happy that she could give her children such advantages as this. Next summer, she promised herself, she'd send Jonnie on one of those student tours of Europe.

Laura was delighted that this summer Jonnie asked to be allowed to work for Hunter Realty. He became her official driver, accompanying her to construction sites each day. Chet was working at his father's law office, along with the daughter of one of the other partners. Laura surmised that there was no real job open for Jonnie in the law office.

Katie returned from France in a haze of euphoria, bubbling over with anecdotes. Now she pleaded to go to Denver with her mother, and Laura acquiesced. At moments she was disturbed by Katie's façade of charming sophistication. Inside Katie was still a young girl.

In the fall Jonnie began his senior year at the University of Georgia. Katie was a sophomore. Both reported the campuses were overrun with ex-GIs returning to school under the new GI Bill of Rights. Next September Jonnie would go off to law school. He had applied to Harvard and at Emory, but appeared to be leaning toward Emory because it was closer to home.

Everett continued to make sporadic efforts at tracking down the witnesses who had testified against Laura's father, striking out every time. Laura and he discussed the situation after a late meeting in the Magnolia office soon after New Year's.

"Maybe we ought to try to contact the members of the jury," Everett said while he and Laura waited for Maisie to return from a nearby restaurant with sandwiches and hot coffee.

"You think we might unearth some jury tampering?" Would a member of the jury suffer from attacks of conscience this belatedly?"

"It's all we have to go on at this point," Everett said

gently.

"The names of the jurors were all mentioned in the local papers," Laura recalled. "I remember how Iris and I went through the list hoping to find somebody there that was Papa's friend. He was well liked in this town. Many a time he wouldn't take money for shoe repairs he did for mill families who were out of work. He was always doing something to help elderly people in our neighborhood. But nobody stood up for him," she said with fresh bitterness. "Ev, I'll never rest until his name is cleared."

"I'll start with the members of the jury," Everett told her.

Ten days later Everett came into her office and tossed a sheaf of papers before her.

"Here's the list of the jurors. Two are dead. One is in the state asylum. Seven have moved away. Two are still in Magnolia. You've got a breakdown on their backgrounds there."

"What are the names of the two here in town?" Laura was trembling. That awful time might have been yesterday.

"It's a long shot," Everett cautioned, pointing out the local residents. "Would you like me to talk to them, or shall we go together?"

Laura took a deep breath, warning herself not to allow emotion to overrule logic.

"I'll go alone, Ev. It might be more effective that way." She glanced at her watch. "I have to drive up to Hunter Village now. Tomorrow morning I'll call on them."


Everett's earlier research indicated Ralph Dixon was a retired carpenter, widowed and living with a daughter and son-in-law in a comfortable older house only five blocks away from where Laura had lived with her father and Iris. Laura made the necessary morning calls to the Atlanta construction office, then left to approach the first of the two jurors.

As she neared the house she saw smoke billowing from

the chimney. Mr. Dixon was home. She parked in front, left the car, and walked to the front door. Through a window she saw a gray-haired man sitting in a chair before the fireplace and reading the morning's *Journal*. In a corner of her mind she remembered this was the paper the Slocums controlled.

She knocked, gearing herself to ask the questions she had formulated in her mind.

"Yeah?" Dixon opened the door and stared down at her.

"I'm Laura Hunter," she began.

"I know," he interrupted, clearly hostile. "What do you want with me?"

"I'd like to talk to you about my father's trial. He was—"

"I know who he was," Dixon interrupted again. "I got nothin' to say to you." He slammed the door shut.

Laura stood immobile for a moment while her mind tried to deal with this encounter. Somebody had warned Ralph Dixon not to talk about the trial. Probably after the Slocums spread the word of her identity around Magnolia. Ralph Dixon had been a carpenter all these years. Working for the Slocums, she surmised. *What could he have said that would have helped her clear her father?*

Next Laura drove to the rundown residential district close to the railroad tracks. She located the small house where Daniel Matthews lived with his wife of thirty-one years. She worked as a saleswoman in a local shop. He did odd jobs—when he was in the mood.

Her hand was perspiring despite the chill of the morning when she reached to knock on the door. A rundown, ancient Ford sat in the driveway—she assumed Matthews was home.

A tall man in his early fifties, with a beer belly and weathered skin, pulled open the door. She saw the look of recognition on his face and caught the scent of cheap whiskey on his breath.

"May I come in?" It was a polite, impersonal inquiry.

He shrugged and gestured her inside. But his eyes were bright with curiosity.

She walked into the small living room, furnished with wicker garden furniture and a shabby rug. Coal heaped high in the fireplace grate lent warmth to the room. She fought against a sense of intimidation.

"You served on the jury that convicted my father, Jacob Roth," she said quietly. "I'd like to ask you some questions."

"That happened a long time ago." His belligerence battled with his curiosity. "What you after now?"

"The jury was out only a matter of hours." She managed to sound almost detached. "Wasn't there any one of you who had some doubts about his guilt?"

"Yeah," he drawled. "We had a woman on the jury. Dumb little chippie. What's a woman doin' on a murder trial anyway?" The woman had been a teacher at the trade high school. "She had some crazy ideas. But we set her straight. If she wanted to make it a hung jury, she'd pay for it. They'd throw her right out of her job."

"Who're *they?*" Laura demanded.

"None of your business!" he shot back. "Let's just say it's the folks who run this town. But don't you go spreadin' the word around," he ordered, "because I'll say you made it all up. I don't know nothin' about a crazy woman tryin' to hold out against a 'guilty' verdict. Now get out of my house."

Laura sat behind the wheel of her car for a few moments. She knew from the list of jurors and their present addresses that the woman who could have made it a hung jury had been incarcerated in the insane asylum at Milledgeville for the past nineteen years. Was she there because she couldn't live with the verdict of that jury?

Laura was grateful for the few close friends she had made through the years in Magnolia. Maisie and Everett, Cecile and Barry — and now Rhoda and Seth. They understood the frustration that plagued her despite her material success. They knew her suspicions about Derek Slocum, which seemed impossible to pin down. Yet,

467

somewhere, there must be a weak spot in the armor that protected him.

On a spring afternoon, standing with Seth before a unit of Hunter Village II which would go on the market within the month, Laura thought about the hollowness of her success. She had been back in Magnolia for almost eleven years. Why had she been so helpless in all that time to clear Papa's name?

"You're looking at the houses," Seth's voice intruded compassionately, "but you're not seeing them."

"No," Laura confessed. So often Seth was able to read her moods. "I was thinking about my father—and about Derek Slocum hiding in his protective cocoon."

"Laura, you can break your neck trying; but if the time isn't right, it'll come to nothing. One day—out of nowhere—something will happen. And then you'll know the time has come. You'll be able to prove that Derek Slocum—and not your father—killed that little girl."

"I'm convinced that somebody in this town could crack this wide open. The Slocums are losing that sacrosanct power they held over Magnolia for so long—people should not be afraid to talk."

"That's a hard-to-break habit," Seth said quietly. "Despite the business with the Historic Association a lot of folks here are afraid to ruffle Slocum feathers." ·

"Remember when we were kids?" Laura's smile was painful. "We were so sure that right always won. Perhaps it's wrong to raise children to believe that," she said with rare cynicism.

As always when in deep despair Laura thrust herself into planning fresh expansion in the business. By early fall, she plotted, she ought to be able to launch a major development of expensive suburban houses in Washington, D.C. Seth's designs were attracting national attention. A suburb of the Capital would be the perfect site for his talents. They'd start looking immediately for land.

But with the Washington, D.C. project still in discussion, Laura was caught up in local politics. Once again Magnolia was divided over the prospect of bringing new

468

industry into Magnolia. The Slocums were determined to keep out a New Jersey cement plant eager to locate in Magnolia because of its deposits of clay and its mild climate. The Slocums were heavily involved in another cement plant that had close to a monopoly in Magnolia. Laura dealt with a company based in Montgomery. She paid less, but the transportation costs ate up the savings. Still, she would not do business with the Slocums.

At an emergency meeting at Laura's house, a special committee from the Chamber of Commerce considered the situation.

"We're not going to get that company without some incentive," Barry pointed out. "We've got three other towns dying to have them locate in their areas."

"The Slocums still control the city commission," Cliff Meyers grumbled.

"They won't get any tax abatement. Not if we yell until we're blue in the face," another member of the committee warned. "When do we have to offer our proposal?"

"We've got forty-eight hours." Laura was grim, her sharp mind racing. "I have two thoughts," she said after a moment. "First, I'll personally channel all my business for the next five years to them, provided they're selling at fair market price. And for one dollar," she added slowly, "I'll sell them a parcel of ten acres of land suitable for their needs." Thank God for her obsession for buying up vacant land as it came onto the market. Nobody realized how much acreage she owned within a twenty-mile radius of Magnolia. Only the Slocums, she surmised—furious that she often jumped the gun on them. They, too, were land hungry. "Gentlemen, how do you think they'll react to my offer?"

"They'll buy it," Barry guessed jubilantly. "That's damn decent of you, Laura: Slocum bites the dust again."

"He never forgave you for spearheading the Historic Association drive, Laura," Cliff chuckled. "Now he'll really be out for your hide."

Several days after the papers were signed with Osgood Cement, Laura received an early morning call from Bill

469

Carlton at the Third National Bank.

"Laura, I'm sorry as hell to have to do this." He cleared his voice in embarrassment. "But the bank has to call in your note."

"Bill, are you out of your mind?" Laura's voice was strident with shock. *Calling in a note of that size with so little warning would throw her into bankruptcy. No time to sell off properties to bring in capital. And how could they?* "I'm not in arrears. Neither on interest nor principal!"

"I know," he said unhappily, "but under the 'boilerplate' there's a clause that says the bank can demand full payment if you fall behind with any one creditor. You're thirty days behind with Edgewater Corporation."

"I never heard of the Edgewater Corporation," she gasped. "Bill, this is some insane mistake."

"You've been doing business with one of their subsidiaries for the past three years," Carlton told her. "Montgomery Cement. And if I don't call in this note, I'm open to a stockholders' suit."

"Wait a minute." Facts were jumping into place in her mind. "I have a sixty-day arrangement with Montgomery Cement. I have another thirty days before their bill is due. And there's no way I won't meet it on schedule." Had Jack Mitchell at Montgomery learned about her commitment to Osgood and was getting back at her this way? No, she dismissed this. She was a good account, but losing Hunter Realty wouldn't put him in serious trouble.

"A stockholder has complained that you're behind with Montgomery Cement," Carlton said. "Even if you paid up your account with them today, it wouldn't help. He's brought an affidavit from Montgomery that you're a delinquent account. I have to call in your note. You've got twenty-four hours, Laura."

"I'm not in arrears," she reiterated hotly. "I'll have Jack Mitchell from Montgomery call you and verify that. We're on the best of terms, Bill."

"I've got a statement from Edgewater saying that's not the case."

"Who is Edgewater Corporation?" Laura demanded impatiently.

"I'm not free to disclose that." Laura understood; somebody was pushing him.

"All I have to do is send someone over to the Montgomery courthouse to look it up," she reminded. "It's on file."

"Then I guess you better do that. I'm sorry as hell, Laura," he said and hung up.

Laura phoned Jack Mitchell.

"I'm sorry, Mrs. Hunter, but Mr. Mitchell is no longer with Montgomery Cement," his secretary reported. "Mr. Langley is handling his accounts now. Would you like to talk to him?"

"I want to talk to Jack," Laura said tersely. "Where can I reach him?"

"He left yesterday on an extended vacation. He didn't say where he could be reached."

Laura sat at her desk, trying to piece together what had happened. Somehow, the Slocums had to be involved in this. She summoned Nora to her office, instructed her to drive immediately to Montgomery and check out the Edgewater Corporation.

"When you've got the facts, phone me—I want to know immediately. And Nora, if there's any problem in getting the records, call me. Barry Berger has a brother-in-law in Montgomery. We'll contact him if necessary."

Now Laura called for an immediate conference with Everett and Maisie—and on impulse phoned Seth at Hunter Village and asked him to join them as soon as possible. *How could Hunter Realty be on the threshold of bankruptcy?*

"This is insane!" Laura reported the crisis situation to Everett and Maisie. "Who set us up like this?"

"It has to be the Slocums," Everett said, jumping up from his chair in a burst of frustration.

"Sit down, Everett," Maisie ordered calmly. "We won't know that until Nora phones from Montgomery."

"Judge Slocum owns a chunk of Third National Bank," Everett pointed out. "Who else would pull something like

471

this?"

"Our assets far outweigh our debts," Laura was grim. Hunter Realty's holdings were worth many millions of dollars. "If we had to do it, we could sell off some properties at giveaway prices and pay off the loan—but not in twenty-four hours."

"Somebody is out to break you, Laura. We ought to bring Barry in on this." He reached for one of the phones on Laura's desk.

"He's in Macon on a case," Laura said. "He'll be back tonight."

"All right, let's go over all the figures." Everett was struggling to remain calm.

"What we have to do is find Jack Mitchell," Maisie said bluntly. "He has to back up the deal he made with Laura." Maisie squinted in thought. "Isn't there a paper somewhere that sets our terms with Montgomery Cement?"

"I've been doing business with Jack ever since I built my first houses here in town. We never needed to put everything in writing." Laura shook her head in disbelief. "Every time I was in Montgomery we had lunch together. He never said anything about being taken over by Edgewater."

"Maisie, try to locate Jack at his home in Montgomery," Everett instructed. "I know his secretary said he's left for an extended vacation," he mocked, "but let's try."

"I'll bring in the Montgomery correspondence," Laura said. "Maybe somewhere in there we'll find something to support my arrangement with Jack."

Maisie conceded defeat in trying to track down Mitchell. Now the three of them concentrated on going through the heavy Montgomery Cement file, triple-checking every letter, every invoice, every bill of lading. Seth arrived as they finished up the last few papers in the file. As calmly as possible Laura briefed him on what was happening.

"That son-of-a-bitch Slocum has been after you for years, Laura." Everett's face was flushed. "And the deal with the Waters house burned him up."

472

"Nora's driving to Montgomery to check out Edgewater," Laura told Seth. "Not that knowing it's Slocum will make a difference," she acknowledged. "Where the hell is Jack? I can't believe he'd put me in this position!"

"He may not even know," Seth said thoughtfully. "They may have bought him out with the stipulation that he leave town for a while."

"Wouldn't he know something crooked was up?" Maisie scoffed.

"If he was paid a high-enough price," Everett said, "he wouldn't ask questions. The problem is, where do we find him?"

"I have one place I'd like to check out," Seth said. "Jack's proud of his vacation house on Pine Mountain. It's all concrete. He showed me a batch of photos of the house once. I gave him some ideas for a new wing. Laura, let's drive out. If we find Jack and he confirms your terms with Montgomery Cement, you're off the hook."

"And what if he won't?" Maisie asked uneasily.

"We'll face that when we have to." Seth reached for Laura's jacket, draped across the back of her chair, and held it for her. "Let's go, Laura."

# Chapter 37

On the drive to Jack Mitchell's Pine Mountain retreat, Laura and Seth explored every facet of the situation. Both were oblivious today to the glorious display of dogwood in bloom along the road.

"I believe we make a left just ahead," Seth said, frowning in thought. "Jack's house is about a hundred yards beyond."

"It's a magnificent day to be out here." Laura fought against recurrent panic. Why hadn't she insisted on that clause being deleted from the contract? She was a lawyer—she should have been more careful. Yet it was a clause that was never enforced. Until now.

Seth turned off the highway onto the side road, his eyes searching for the house.

"There it is," he said in relief as he sighted the sprawling Spanish-style concrete-block house shaded by tall evergreens and flowering dogwoods.

"Seth, somebody's there! See the car in the driveway?"

Seth swung off the road into the long circular driveway. A pair of beagles, barking vociferously, charged into view.

"Shut up, Hannibal," a male voice ordered good-humoredly. "You, too, Harry." Jack Mitchell strode towards them with a welcoming smile. "What are you two doing out this way?"

"Looking for you," Laura said grimly, emerging from the car. "Seth thought you might be here."

"You're a man of leisure," Seth chuckled. "We're envious."

"Jack, when did you sell Montgomery Cement?" Laura asked while Seth bent to pat the friendly beagles.

"Oh God, it was the fastest deal on record. The Edgewater Corporation came to me three days ago and made a fantastic offer. But they insisted it had to be signed, sealed, and delivered within forty-eight hours. With that kind of money dangling before me, I didn't fight them. I'm sorry I didn't get around to calling my choice customers—like you, Laura—but they made it clear they didn't want me mixing in with their new setup." Curiosity glowed from him. "But what happened to bring you two out here?"

Succinctly Laura briefed him on what had happened, explaining her own critical situation.

"The lousy sons-of-bitches!" Jack swore. "Excuse me, Laura, but that's the lowest thing I've heard in a long time!"

"Jack, will you give me a notarized statement that Hunter Realty is on a sixty-day agreement with Montgomery Cement, and that I am not in arrears?"

"You draw it up legal-like and I'll sign it." Jack was grim. "I've got a typewriter in my office here at the house. We'll drive down to the notary at the country store. Laura, it'll hold up, won't it?"

"It'll hold," she told him and exchanged a smile of relief with Seth.

"If Bill Carlton wants me to come down to the bank," Jack said while they walked to the house, "you tell him to call me, you hear?"

Laura was shaken by the realization of how close she had come to losing her real-estate empire. And at the same time, she was unnerved by the closeness she felt to Seth, sharpened in this crisis. The men to whom she was drawn were in all one mold—warm, creative, crusading, she reflected unwarily. Then she was suffused with guilt. How could she think of Seth in the way she had thought of Bernie and then—for a precious little while—of Phillip? Seth and Rhoda were cherished friends. Yet there were unguarded moments when her eyes met Seth's, and she knew he felt more than deep friendship for her as well.

Sitting at dinner on Friday evening Laura tried to cope with what Cecile and she had discussed earlier on the phone. Why did Rhoda—obviously a bright articulate woman—pretend to be a mindless social butterfly? She'd just told Cecile that she "simply didn't have time" for the interior decorating shop any longer, what with all her committees. But she wasn't that involved in the local social whirl.

Did Rhoda suspect that Seth felt something for her that he had no right to feel? Was that why she was behaving this way? The possibility was shattering.

"Mom?" Laura started at the unexpected sound of Jonnie's voice in the hall.

"Darling!" Her face lighted with love. "I'm in the dining room."

Jonnie charged into the room, leaned forward to kiss her exuberantly. Chet hovered at the entrance. All at once Laura realized this was the time when law school acceptances came through. *That's why they were here.*

"May I use your phone to call my mother to come and get me?" Chet asked.

"Of course, Chet. She'll be so pleased you're home."

"Take my car and go on home," Jonnie told him. "I won't need it tonight."

"Naw," Chet kidded. "Not now that Corinne's back in Boston. Good night, Mrs. Hunter."

"Anything special to report?" Laura asked expectantly when they were alone, part of her mind focusing on the banter between Jonnie and Chet. Who was Corinne?

"Jonnie!" Jewel screeched from the doorway. "I musta known you'd be home this weekend. Guess what's for dessert?"

"Hot pecan pie," he gloated, exchanging a hearty hug with Jewel. "All the way home I kept sending that wish to you."

"Set yourself down at the table, and I'll bring you dinner." To Jewel the children were still "my little kids."

"Jonnie, what's special?" Laura prodded again. "Did the law school letters come in?"

"Should I tell you?" he teased.

"Tell me," she ordered, dinner forgotten.

476

"I've been accepted at Harvard!"

"Jonnie, how wonderful!" She glowed with maternal pride.

All at once he turned serious. "I know I was leaning towards Emory so I'd be close to home; but by gosh, I made Harvard Law!"

"There are planes flying these days," she laughed, hiding her disappointment that he'd be all the way up in Boston. That was selfish of her. "You'll be able to come home for Thanksgiving and the winter and spring breaks. And summers, of course. What about Chet?" she asked. "Did he make Harvard?"

"He didn't even apply." Jonnie smiled wryly. "His father went to Emory, so, of course, he has to do the same."

"Talk to Seth about Boston. He used to live there, you know." Was Jonnie so excited about Harvard because Corinne lived in Boston? But she mustn't pry, she warned herself. In his own time Jonnie would tell her if he were seriously interested in a girl. She knew the day would come—but now it was oddly disconcerting.

"You giving me a job this summer?" Jonnie asked with mock seriousness. "I'll build up a great tan running around to construction sites with you."

"You're hired, boy," she flipped.

With Jonnie in and out of the house with Chet the weekend sped past. The next time she would see Jonnie would be at his graduation, Laura thought, while she stood on the porch on Sunday afternoon and watched him slide behind the wheel of his car. How proud Bernie would have been to know that their son was going to Harvard Law School. Bernie used to say that a degree from Harvard Law was like a trust fund.

" 'Bye, Mom—" Jonnie waved a hand as he backed out of the long driveway.

" 'Bye, darling—"

She envisioned him in politics within ten years. One day he might be in the state legislature, later, in Congress. A living memorial to his father and grandfather.

* * *

Laura and those close to her were candidly upset over the hysterical antics of the House Un-American Activities Committee, which gave no indication of letting up and which were causing such chaos in the movie, radio, and television industries. They worried, too, about the reactions of the Deep South to President Truman's outspoken dedication to civil rights.

On a dazzling sunny late May day Laura and Iris sat together at Jonnie's graduation while Katie and Annabel flirted with two male classmates across the aisle.

"I couldn't make your college graduation," Iris laughed, "so I had to make damn sure I'd be here for Jonnie's." Iris still made a point of not coming to Magnolia. Laura and she had met in Atlanta and driven to Athens together.

After the post-graduation festivities, Katie and Annabel drove home with Jonnie and Chet, Laura headed for Atlanta with Iris. They would spend the night at the Biltmore, and in the morning Iris would fly back to Denver. Laura sensed, understandably, that Iris was restless in Denver. Every house at Westcott Acres was now sold before construction was completed. And there were no plans to expand since Bob Westcott preferred to keep the new elite community small. At the Biltmore Laura and Iris shared a two-bedroom suite. Prior to retiring they gathered together in Laura's room for still more talk.

"I've put off telling you my ugly news," Iris confided, dropping across the foot of Laura's bed. "Noel was expelled from that fancy private school in Denver."

"Oh Iris." Laura was appalled. "Why?"

Iris sighed. "He was caught cheating on a test. And he's not at all remorseful—that's what kills me. Oh, it wasn't the first time. He'd been warned if it happened again he'd be expelled. I don't know what in God's name is wrong with that kid. We can't be together for ten minutes without fighting. Is it me, Laura?" Her eyes were troubled. "Have I been such a terrible mother?"

"You've been raising him in the British fashion." Laura smiled evasively. She was often upset by the way Iris raised Noel. "The way his father was brought up."

"Sometimes I look at Noel, and I don't see even the slightest trace of *us* in him. Oh sure, he looks enough like Katie and Jonnie to be their younger brother—but he's a miniature Peter. Peggy says it's genetic," Iris said defensively. "I know I'm not the maternal type, but remember those kids I got out of Austria? I felt something for them. I feel love for Katie and Jonnie. Maybe I can't get close to my son because he's so much like his father."

"Noel's my only nephew," Laura said with an effort. She had told herself she would never admit her feeling towards Noel to anyone, but now it was necessary. "I've never been able to feel any real love for him. And it upsets me. But you're right. He's all Peter. And you're not to blame for that."

Iris sighed, yet Laura sensed a kind of relief in her.

"The problem now is where will I send him to school in the fall? He's got some screwy idea about boarding school in England, but that's out of the question."

"Think in terms of Washington, D.C.," Laura said.

Iris brightened. "You have a project scheduled there?" She'd always liked Washington.

"I'm beginning to move in that direction. A huge expansion in the suburbs. Most likely in Georgetown."

"It's a smart place to live," Iris approved.

"We'll find a house there, and you'll move in with Noel," Laura plotted. "We'll do what we did in Denver. It's a quick flight for me—I'll be able to come up often. You'll give a splashy party when you're settled in. Be sure to look up Debbie and Ian Macmillan."

Now Laura and Seth—with Everett masterminding the financial details—were caught up in the new venture. Still, Laura contrived to spend time each morning at the Hunter Village II construction site, always with Jonnie at her side. They shared a communal joy in watching the operations of the giant machines—like prehistoric monsters—that victoriously battled with tree stumps and stubborn boulders, gouged into the red Georgia clay to make way for construction.

When she went up to the Atlanta construction site, Jonnie was with her. Often Seth made it a trio. On impulse late in the summer she took Jonnie with her on one of her trips to Washington. Katie was at St. Simon's Island for the month of August with Annabel and her family.

She and Jonnie stayed at the Mayflower, where Iris was ensconced in a private apartment until she had found a Georgetown house, complaining that she would collapse in the Washington heat except for the respite of brief escapes to Newport. Jonnie was impressed by the history of the venerable hotel, was eager for sightseeing, though their time in town was limited.

Between the rush of business Laura took Jonnie to the Mall, and in the fashion of summer tourists—ignoring the torpid heat—they walked the long length from the Washington Monument to the Capitol. The afternoon before their departure for Magnolia, they followed a group of tourists into the Capitol, and sat respectfully in the empty congressional gallery—Congress, of course, was not in session in August.

"I thought it would be bigger," Jonnie said in surprise, yet he shared her sense of awe. "But think of everything that's happened here since the first session of Congress!"

Some day Jonnie might sit down there as a congressman from Georgia, Laura thought sentimentally—and then reality punctured this image. An ugly headline charged across her brain: GEORGIA CANDIDATE GRANDSON OF CONVICTED RAPIST/MURDERER.

All her wealth, her prestige—and she recognized the extent of both—meant nothing until she erased the shame of her father's false conviction and lynching.


Early in September Laura saw Jonnie off for Boston—caught in a mixture of pride and wistful regret that he would be so far from home. But she clung to the knowledge that he would fly home for Thanksgiving. A few nights later Katie was packing to leave for her junior year at the University of Georgia.

Sitting at the desk after dinner in her elegantly furnished at-home office, while the perky strains of "Buttons and Bows" drifted downstairs from Katie's record player, Laura flinched at the prospect of an empty house again, even while logic told her she would be so involved in Hunter Realty's new projects she'd have little time to be lonely.

The night was hot. Through the parade of tall, narrow, open windows the scent of roses and honeysuckle drifted into the room. From habit Laura had settled at her desk to look over reports Everett had brought together for her to review. Not tonight she told herself suddenly and reached for the pitcher of iced coffee Jewel had set at the corner of the desk twenty minutes ago—the ice now melted down to tiny pellets.

"Mom—" Katie hovered in the doorway, small and lovely and unfamiliarly serious. "Can I talk to you for a while?"

"Darling, of course." Laura beckoned her into the room. "Are you all packed?" Katie was driving up to school with Annabel and two other Georgia coeds in the morning.

"Just about—"

The two settled themselves in a pair of chairs positioned to catch the meager night breeze.

"Mom, would you think it was crazy if I said I wanted to go to law school after graduation?"

Pleasure managed to override Laura's astonishment.

"Katie, I think it would be wonderful!" How little parents knew what went on in their children's minds. "Your father would have been so delighted." She paused, reaching over for Katie's hand. "And proud."

Laura prodded herself to point out the hazards that lay ahead of a woman law student. In truth, the situation in 1948 had changed little since she received her law degree from NYU fifteen years ago.

Katie listened attentively, yet Laura knew that nothing would turn her determined daughter away from pursuing a career in law. Instinct told her that what had happened

481

to her grandfather played a role in Katie's decision to become part of the judicial system.

"I know it's rough for women." Katie's eyes glowed. "But I won't let anything stop me. And times *are* changing. The war made women realize they could make real contributions in every field. They won't take a back seat any longer."

"Katie, less than two hundred women were graduated from law schools in this country last year."

"So in five years—if there're no new figures in the meantime, I'll make it two hundred and one," Katie flipped, and Laura suddenly heard Bernie's voice, the night he asked her to marry him: *"It's very rough for a woman in the legal field. There are less than eighteen hundred women lawyers in the whole country—"* And she heard herself answering, *"I have to become a lawyer . . . If eighteen hundred women have become lawyers, then why can't I?"*

"You'll help make a difference, Katie." Laura leaned forward to hug her daughter. "It's time women lawyers took their rightful place in the system."


On November 2 Laura left the house at shortly past 7 A.M., to vote before going in to the office. She was angry at the public-opinion polls that predicted an easy Republican victory.

President Truman had called the 80th Congress "the worst in our history." The Congress had fought him on many major domestic policies, passing bills—including a major tax reduction—over his veto. He deplored the resurgence of conservatism.

"Laura," Seth called to her as she headed for her car after voting. "I thought you'd be here early."

"I'm scared to hear the results," she confessed. "We need Truman in the White House. I shudder to think what'll happen to this country with Dewey as president."

"Dewey won't win despite all the predictions," Seth comforted. "Oh, Rhoda asked me if you'd stop by some time today. She needs you to settle a difference between Cecile and her about the new wallpaper for the dining room." Rhoda had become addicted to redecorating various rooms in the house.

"I'll run over this afternoon," Laura promised. "How's that cold?"

"She's still not up to par," Seth said somberly. "But she'll come over to vote later in the day."

In midafternoon—remembering her promise to Seth—Laura left the office to drive over to the Goldman house. She had close to an hour free before a meeting with the construction bosses at Hunter Village II. The meeting would probably continue until close to dinner time.

She parked before the house and walked up to the door.

"Good afternoon, Miz Hunter," Georgia, the Goldman maid, greeted her warmly. "Miz Goldman's up in her room. She's feelin' poorly today."

"Thank you, Georgia. I'll run upstairs—"

"I'll bring up some coffee directly," Georgia promised and headed down the hall towards the kitchen.

Laura climbed the stairs to what she knew was Rhoda's room. Both she and Cecile had been startled to learn several weeks ago that Rhoda and Seth no longer shared a bedroom. Rhoda said she was an insomniac and liked to read suspense novels until all hours of the night. *It's silly for me to spoil Seth's sleep when he's always up by six-thirty.*

"Rhoda?" Laura called, pausing before the slightly open door.

"Laura—" Rhoda's air of synthetic gaiety was oddly disturbing today. "Come in, sugar."

"Seth said you had some decision to make," Laura reported lightly and walked to the chintz-covered chair drawn up beside the bed. Rhoda seemed thinner, tired. But she'd been housebound with a cold for several days.

"The wallpaper for the dining room." Rhoda pulled swatches from a drawer of her night table. "Tell me which you like best."

For a few minutes they discussed the wallpaper. Then Georgia rolled in a serving cart with steaming cups of coffee and plates of finger sandwiches.

"Oh, they look delicious, Georgia." Laura leaned forward playfully to choose from her plate. "As always."

"Georgia, if there are any calls, will you please take the numbers and say I'll call back later," Rhoda said with an unexpected sharpness. "I don't want to be disturbed right now."

"Yes ma'am." Georgia smiled and left the room, closing the door behind her.

"Rhoda, is something wrong?" Laura's throat tightened. Was Rhoda upset because Seth spent so much time on field trips? More than was necessary, she sometimes suspected.

"Laura, the time has come to be honest with you." Her tone turned serious. "Your friendship has meant so much to me — and to Seth." She seemed to be searching for words. "We didn't come to Magnolia to live because I hated the cold winters of Boston — or because Seth was disenchanted with his job. Although that part is true," she conceded wryly. "But he wouldn't quit. We came here because I wanted to die in Magnolia."

"Rhoda—" It was a shaken whisper.

"Seth and I agreed we'd keep it a secret as long as possible. I didn't want people looking at me with pity — but I wanted to die in the town where I was born and spent my happy young years.

"Rhoda, there must be something that—" Laura began desperately, but Rhoda shook her head.

"I've been through all the tests three times. In Boston first, then in New York. I'm grateful for the time I've had, but it's running out. With luck I could go on for another three or four years. But I can't play the game anymore."

"I can't believe it," Laura whispered.

"I'm not taking an ad in the *Magnolia Herald,*" she said with an effort at lightness. "But will you get the message across to people we see? I might accept an invitation for dinner — and then discover it falls on a bad day. I want our friends to understand."

"I'll tell them." Laura struggled to suppress her anguish

and remain strong. Later she would cry.

"I'm so happy that Seth found himself here. He's never been so happy in his work. It's been hard on him, knowing what lies ahead for me. I hope he'll remarry. He's a fine man, Laura."

"I know," Laura said shakily. Rhoda hoped Seth and she would marry one day. But, thank God, Rhoda didn't know the feelings they shared, she comforted herself. Not one word had ever passed between them — only unguarded glances betrayed them. "You're both very dear to me," Laura filled in the pregnant silence.

"Seth and I always regretted that we had no children. Katie and Jonnie have helped fill that void in our lives." She leaned back against the pillows, seeming exhausted. "They're such warm, sweet kids."

"You're tired," Laura said compassionately and rose to her feet.

"There are good days and bad ones," Rhoda said with a semblance of her old conviviality. This isn't one of the best. You'll explain to Cecile and the others?"

"I'll explain," Laura promised.

Laura walked slowly down the stairs, struggling to cope with what Rhoda had told her. How awful for Rhoda to have her life cut short this way. How awful for Seth. She remembered her own agony at Bernie's death, and again when Phil was killed in action. The devastating sense of loss, the anger that this could happen, the feeling of helplessness.

Whatever she could do to make this last period easier for Rhoda and Seth, she must do.

# Chapter 38

After a solitary dinner Laura sat in a green velvet club chair drawn close to the living room fireplace — where chunks of wood crackled cozily in the grate — and tried to concentrate on the election returns being reported by a radio newscaster. She was straining to escape for a little while from the heartbreaking news of Rhoda's illness.

Truman was holding an early lead, but Laura remembered the widespread predictions that Dewey would win by a landslide. She'd listen for a while and then go on up to bed. Returns would be coming in all through the night.

"Miz Laura, I brung you some fresh coffee," Jewel said solicitously. Her tell-tale red eyes said that she knew about Rhoda. "You feel like somethin' else, you just yell for me. I'll be up in my room workin' on my quilt."

"Thank you, Jewel." The phone rang and Laura frowned. "You go on, I'll answer it." She rose to her feet, lowered the volume on the radio, and crossed to the phone. "Hello."

"You listening to the returns?" Katie asked.

"What else tonight?" Laura chuckled. Later she'd have to tell Katie about Rhoda. This was not the time. "How are you, darling?"

They talked about the new television station — WSB-TV — just dedicated in Atlanta. It was the first in the South. Then Laura said, "Now tell me about school."

Laura listened while Katie reported on school activities.

"My English Lit teacher — Mr. Granger — is just great. He's had two plays produced on broadway. Neither made it commercially," she conceded, "but they were considered artistic successes. He's young — he'll be an important playwright one day. And I'll be able to say that I sat in his classes."

"I hope you do more than sit," Laura laughed, grateful for the sound of Katie's voice.

They talked for another few minutes until Katie was summoned by her roommate. Moments after she put down the receiver, Laura heard the phone ring again. She reached to respond.

"Hello."

"Rhoda said she told you." Seth's voice was strained. "I wasn't sure she could."

"Seth, I can't believe it." Laura was caught up in fresh anguish. "It's unreal."

"It's very real, Laura. Rhoda and I have both finally accepted it. I couldn't for the longest time," he admitted. "I was almost out of my mind with grief and anger. But working with you—with the company—has held me together."

"Anything I can do, Seth, tell me," she urged.

"Are you listening to the returns?" Laura understood; Seth was deliberately changing the subject. "Of course, we won't know the results until morning."

"I don't think I'll stay up to listen." Laura struggled to sound casual. "I'll hear the results on the 7 A.M. news."

Despite the public opinion polls' predictions, Harry Truman awoke on Wednesday to discover he had been elected. An election "extra" distributed by the *Chicago Tribune* had erroneously declared Dewey the next president. This was one of the greatest upsets in political history. Laura arranged an impromptu celebration dinner, and then was tormented by guilt that she was giving a party when Rhoda was so ill.

She focused now on the projected development in the Washington, D.C. area. Looking ahead to the traveling the business would soon require of her, she bought a company plane and hired a permanent crew so that she would take off with little waste of time for Washington or New York or Houston—where she was dickering over the building of a major shopping mall. At first appalled at this extravagance, Everett soon applauded the decision.

"Laura, you've got the magic touch."

When Iris took off for a week of partying in Palm

Beach, Laura decided to fly down in the company plane, along with Katie and Jonnie, now home for the holidays. She was always proud to appear socially with the children. It gave her pleasure to know that she could give them so much that Iris and she had never had.

Now Iris took up residence in a charming early American house in Georgetown and began to entertain lavishly. Debbie Macmillan was introducing her to various congressmen and senators and their wives. Aware of the importance of these contacts, Laura strived to be in Washington at least once a month.

Iris was running into fresh difficulties with Noel. Miss Brisbane, who acted as Iris's part-time social secretary and Noel's part-time governess, had walked out. In a fit of rage Noel had given her a black eye. Now her replacement was threatening to leave.

Iris had returned from an afternoon of shopping with Debbie Macmillan at Garfinkel's to discover Miss Brisbane's replacement grimly packing.

"That child is a monster," she hissed. "I don't want any part of him. He needs to be spanked till he can't sit down for a week!"

Reluctantly Iris cancelled a dinner engagement and sat down to consider her options. She could hire yet another governess—or she could ship Noel off to boarding school. Was that why he was acting up this way, she asked herself with sudden prescience. Did he think if he made himself sufficiently obnoxious she'd send him off to school in England? Damn it, he was only ten years old!

Iris heard the sound of the television set she'd bought him just last week—a bribe to make him behave with the new governess—as she climbed the narrow stairs that led up to Noel's room. Noel was *not* going off to boarding school in England. Period.

Ordering herself to be calm but firm, she pulled open the door of Noel's bedroom and walked inside. He swung around to confront her, his face contorted in anger.

"Why don't you knock before you come in? At least, act like you're Lady Cranford."

"I *am* Lady Cranford!" What the hell did he mean?

488

"You weren't born a lady," he taunted. "I heard you talking with Aunt Laura once out in Denver. You were a Jew girl down in some Georgia hick town before you married my father."

Iris recoiled from the malicious triumph in his eyes.

"And you're half-Jewish, Noel Cranford! Don't you ever forget it!"

"I'm not!" he screeched. "You don't count! I'm British like my father!" He raised his hands like a vicious cat's claws, reaching for her face.

"Stop it!" Iris caught at his wrists, breathless with the effort to subdue him. This was insane! "Stop it, Noel!" She imprisoned his hands, but with one foot he aimed blows at her ankle. "Damn you! What do you want from me?" she screamed. *This was Peter all over again.* "What do you want?"

All at once he was still.

"I want to go to boarding school. In England, where I belong," he said with an unnerving victory. "I'm the Honourable Noel Percy Cranford. Find me a boarding school near London."

Iris sent off a series of cables to people she knew in London. Within a few days a school was found that would accept Noel immediately. A male companion would be hired to escort him to the school. Once delivered into the hands of the school authorities, he would be their responsibility.

But watching Noel board the plane that would take him to London, Iris was astonished to feel a sense of loss. Her son—her one real accomplishment in this world—was walking out of her life. Was he a "bad seed"—or had she failed once again?


In one of her fine cashmere sweater sets and matching gray wool slacks, Katie darted across the spring-green campus to the parking area. She checked her watch as she slid behind the wheel of her late-model Dodge. Even if she ran into traffic driving downtown, she'd arrive at the coffee shop before Keith. She was greedy for every moment she could share with him.

He was right, of course. They couldn't afford to have the faculty know they were seeing each other. Not only because he was a teacher and she was a student. His divorce hadn't come through yet, though there was no question that it would. How sad that his wife had walked out on him and their little girl. But Keith had admitted their marriage was dead by the time Gina was two—and she was seven now.

Sometimes—when they were walking somewhere or just sitting over coffee—Keith's eyes would grow so sad. He was unhappy that he couldn't have Gina with him. Katie had tried to talk to him about bringing her here. It would be easy to find someone to come into the house and look after her, but Keith insisted it was better this way. Between preparing for his classes and working on his screenplay he'd have no time to give to Gina.

A jewelry store clock told her she was ten minutes early when she'd parked and was walking towards what had become "their place." Sometimes she couldn't believe she'd known Keith only since the beginning of the school year. They hadn't started seeing each other until right before Christmas.

Katie hurried into the coffee shop and to the rear booth that was their regular meeting place. She wished they didn't have to hide this way. At least, in another five weeks, Keith's divorce would be final. It was his wife who had wanted it so she could remarry. What kind of a woman could walk out on her little girl that way?

She sat down and the waitress automatically brought her coffee. When Keith got here, they'd order an early dinner and dawdle over it until night fell. Then under cover of darkness they'd drive to the tiny cottage he'd rented for the school year.

Her face brightened when she spied Keith. He looked more like a graduate student than a teacher. A lot of girls in his classes had crushes on him. He was only thirty and so good-looking, so intense. She was unhappy that he was abandoning playwriting, but he felt that he could earn real money writing for the movies—and then he could keep Gina with him. That was why he took this teaching job after the last play closed — so he'd be earning money and still be able to squeeze in writing time.

"Hi —" Keith smiled and sat down across from her. "The dogwoods are budding. I can't wait to see them in full bloom."

"That's right," she teased. "All the flowers you've known grew in window boxes in Manhattan."

"Oh, I got up to the Bronx Botanical Gardens every now and then," he drawled.

"I wish spring break wasn't coming so soon," she said wistfully. "I'll hate not seeing you for all those days."

"I'll miss you." His hand — tanned and graceful — reached over to cover hers.

Someone had just dropped a coin into the jukebox, and the popular "So In Love" filtered into the coffee shop. Keith had not once said "I love you," but she knew he did. He had betrayed himself endless times. They weren't just a teacher and a student having a fling. This was real. She wouldn't be sleeping with him if she didn't think that.

"You'll be going up to New York to see Gina," Katie guessed.

"Yeah, I'll head for New York." He was oddly somber.

Their waitress sauntered over to their booth, and for a few moments they were occupied with ordering dinner. Katie knew it upset Keith, but she always insisted on paying her own check. Keith had to send money every month to his aunt to cover Gina's care.

"Keith, you're worried about something," she said anxiously when they were alone again.

"It's Gina," he said after a moment. "I have to find a new place for her to live."

"Your aunt can't keep her any longer?" Katie was solicitous.

"Gina's not with my aunt." His voice was taut. "I don't have an aunt. I've been alone in the world since I was eighteen. I think that's one of the reasons I rushed into marriage — I was so damned lonely."

"Then who has Gina?" Katie was bewildered. Keith had made it clear his almost ex-wife wanted no part of her.

"She's in a school," he said slowly. "A school for disturbed children. From the time she was three we knew she—she had problems. She began to have violent temper tantrums. She'd refuse to eat or talk—and when she did talk, she was irrational. We took her to doctors. They all agreed. Katie, I should have told you before. Gina's schizophrenic."

"Oh, Keith, how sad. But surely there's something that can be done for her. I mean, in these modern times," she stammered.

"We went from doctor to doctor, but nobody seemed to help. I was holding down two jobs plus the playwriting, and Edith worked as a secretary so we could pay the insane medical bills. Then two years ago Edith just packed a valise and walked. She couldn't take it anymore. I tried keeping Gina with me. The women I hired to take care of her never lasted more than a few weeks. Then I tried to enroll her in school." Keith closed his eyes for an agonized moment. "That was a disaster. I couldn't lie to myself any longer. Gina can never live a normal life. I've had Gina in a home for the past year and a half. There've been times when we were sure she was responding to drugs, then she regresses. That's why I've got to finish this screenplay and sell it. I have to be able to afford decent care for her—and it comes high."

What could she say to Keith that would help his hurt? All these months he'd suffered in silence.

"Let's hurry through dinner and go to your house," Katie whispered. She could comfort him in her arms.

While early dusk overtook the day, Jonnie sprawled in a lounge chair in the living room of his apartment on the second floor of a well-preserved red-brick Federal house a few blocks from Harvard Yard. He tried to focus on the textbook in his hand. The floor was cluttered with books that lay where he had dropped them earlier.

The radiators clanked with a fresh rush of heat. The day had been cold, and the night would probably be colder. Subconsciously he reminded himself he ought to start up a blaze in the bedroom fireplace. Corinne loved to lie in the dark with the firelight fanning rosy color across the minuscule room that allowed for only the bed and a dresser.

His mind rejected study. In a gesture of defeat he slammed the book shut and dropped it to the floor. What had given him the weird idea that studying at Harvard Law would be one sensational deal? Whatever gave him the idea he wanted to be a lawyer? He stared into space and appraised his situation.

He was three quarters through his first year of law, and he hated the stuff. So his mother and father had both gone to law school and had practiced law. That didn't mean he had to follow in their tracks. Hell, Mom hadn't practiced law in years.

He just never forgot when she told him about his grandfather and how she'd worked her way through law school — even though she had Katie and him to raise — because she thought that would help her clear their grandfather's name. He'd never been so impressed by anyone in his whole life. He'd never loved Mom more than at that moment. *But what made him think he wanted to be a lawyer?*

He untangled himself from the chair and went into the kitchen to put a light under the percolator and then into the bedroom to start up a fire. Corinne ought to be here soon. The corners of his mouth lifted into a smile. Being here at law school kept him close to Corinne — Harvard Med was just ten minutes away on the "T".

Mom would be upset when she discovered Corinne and he were serious. Corinne wasn't Jewish. Her father was a lapsed Catholic and her mother a Unitarian. They couldn't get married until she was out of med school and he — out of what? How could he tell Mom that what he honestly wanted to do was to go to architectural school? Corinne kept telling him he was out of his mind even to think about a switch.

Jonnie enjoyed the brief routine of coaxing the kindling wood around the three small logs in the grate into a blaze. He waited and watched until he was sure the fire would continue, then went back to the kitchen to pour himself a mug of coffee and carried it into the living room. What about Corinne's parents? Were they upset that she was running around with a Jewish kid from Georgia? They probably figured it didn't mean a thing. They knew how dedicated she was to becoming a doctor. She felt about medicine the way he felt about architecture.

His first few weeks in Cambridge he'd walked around in a haze of awe, overwhelmed at being here at Harvard, all caught up in the history of the college, founded in 1636. Its law school, the first continuous one in the nation, dated back to 1817—its first class consisting of six students. He'd relished the atmosphere of intellectual excitement that seemed to infect everyone.

He stood before the huge, multipillared, limestone Langdell Hall—the Law School—and thought about how proud his father would have been to see his son a student at Harvard. How proud Mom was that he was here! But he was ever conscious that minutes away stood the Graduate School of Design. Too often he lingered—guiltily eavesdropping—at a table at the Wursthaus or in an aisle at the Coop because a cluster of architectural students were talking absorbedly, dissecting a lecture by Walter Gropius or discussing the innovative ideas of I.M. Pei, who had been a professor at the architectural school until he abandoned teaching to become a practicing architect.

At intervals his feet took him—seemingly of their own volition—to stand before the 1895 building that housed the Graduate School of Design. So close to Langdell Hall—yet a million miles away. He envied those who studied there. Even all these years later Seth talked with proud nostalgia about his years at Harvard.

Still nursing his mug of coffee, he jumped to his feet at the sound of the doorbell and rushed to respond.

"I thought you'd never get here," he chided good-humoredly, reaching with one arm for the classic-featured, slender blonde who hovered in the doorway. "God, you're beautiful, Corinne!"

"How many cups of that garbage have you had today?" she said as she approached and kissed him lightly.

"It keeps me going when you're not around." Jonnie drew her inside, deposited the mug atop a bookcase, and pulled her into his arms.

"Caffeine is terrible for your health. And I want you healthy," she reminded. "I'm healthy, I'm healthy," he chuckled. "Let's go into the bedroom and I'll prove it."

"God, you've got a one-track mind." But she nuzzled heatedly against him. "Oh, I almost forgot, you're invited to dinner with my folks tomorrow night." Corinne was a medical school day student. She lived with her parents in a nearby suburb.

"Ah-hah, you're showing me off to the family," he grunted in approval.

"They feel better when they know who I'm seeing." She began to unbutton his shirt.

"Whom," he corrected. "A doctor should speak grammatically."

"That's for male doctors," she giggled. "Women doctors are rebels, don't you know?"

"When you start focusing on your specialty, I want you to think of obstetrics," he said with mock seriousness.

"Why?"

"I don't want you messing around with good-looking male patients."

"Let's get this show on the road," she laughed, "before I fall asleep. I was studying till past three last night, and I had a nine o'clock class this morning."

"I'll wake you up," he promised, pulling off his shirt and reaching to unzip his slacks. "I'm great at that."

"Braggart." But she was shedding her cardigan. "You Southern men think you're so hot."

"Aren't we?" he challenged.

"I haven't tried that many," she conceded and pulled the sweater that had been beneath her cardigan over her head.

His throat went dry. When he was with Corinne, all he could think about was making love.

"I'm going to miss you during spring break." He reached behind her to unhook her bra, then caught her small, high breasts in his hands.

"You don't have to go," she said, pushing her skirt and panties to the floor in one swift gesture. "It could be wonderful for us here with no classes, no studying."

"I could never explain that to my mother—" He cleared

495

his throat in passion while his eyes swept over the tall, slim length of her covered only in lacy garter belt and nylons.

"Try," she coaxed and lifted her mouth to his. "But enough talk. It's time for action."


"I won't need you any more today, Pat," Laura told her newly hired chauffeur when he pulled up before the house shortly past 6 P.M. It was early for her to leave the office but Jonnie was home and she cherished every moment with him.

She hurried into the house and up to her room. Katie had gone back to school already, leaving an emptiness in her wake. She'd talked about a trip out to California this summer with a couple of classmates. But most of the time she'd been home Katie had seemed to be off in another world, Laura thought. Was she debating now about going on to law school? Was that what concerned her? How did you know what went on in their young minds?

Tomorrow Jonnie was flying back to Boston. He was leaving early because of some research he wanted to do before school started again. He'd seemed tired when he first arrived. He'd needed this rest from the rough law-school grind.

"Mom?" Jonnie called through her half-open doorway.

"Come on in, darling."

"You mind if I cut out after dinner?" he asked apologetically. "Chet's got some party going over at his house."

"Go to the party," Laura smiled.

Jonnie hesitated.

"Mom, I was thinking maybe I'd go to summer school this year. There are a couple of special courses in international law that I'd like to take."

"All right, if you think it'll be useful." She tried to hide her disappointment, having so looked forward to having Jonnie working with her this summer again. "When do you have to register for them?"

"Not for a while yet. I'll let you know later."

"Fine." She managed a smile. "Let's go down to the dining room. Jewel's serving dinner early tonight. You won't miss a minute of Chet's party."

In the midst of dinner Iris called from Washington.

"You know I always have my ear to the ground," Iris reminded. This was part of her usefulness to Laura's business. "I don't know exactly what it means, but congressmen and lobbyists are buzzing about an urban redevelopment bill that's due to come up soon. Interested?"

"Of course I'm interested," Laura said, her mind in high gear. "Do you have a dinner party scheduled in the next two or three weeks?"

"Tomorrow night," Iris told her.

"Can you fit me into the table arrangement?"

"Consider it done. I always have a list of extra men on tap," Iris said and Laura sighed. It irritated her that parties in Washington were always assembled in pairs as if for Noah's ark. "When will you arrive?"

"I'll fly up in the morning." Urban redevelopment meant a lot of government aid, Laura pinpointed. Much money, much prestige for the companies involved. "Will Ian Macmillan be there?"

"Debbie and he are down in Bermuda for three days. But I have a senator and a bank president coming," Iris said triumphantly. "Plus a gorgeous diplomat from Spain."

"Seat me between the senator and the bank president," Laura ordered. "And have the maid press my gray-satin Dior." Laura kept a designer wardrobe in the Georgetown house for such occasions as this. "Oh, Iris—" Her voice was all at once electric. "Don't bother about an extra man. I'll ask Jonnie to come up with me and go on up to Boston the next day."

"Does he have a dinner jacket?" Iris asked.

"Have a tailor standing by. Tell him to bring a size thirty-seven jacket. A thirty waist for the pants. It'll be good for Jonnie to be exposed to one of your dinner parties."

But Jonnie appeared upset when Laura issued the invitation to the dinner party.

"Darling, you'll cancel your flight arrangements for tomorrow. You'll fly to Washington with me in the company plane, and then take a flight out of Washington airport to

Boston the following morning."

"I'm kind of expected in Boston tomorrow afternoon," Jonnie said apologetically, yet Laura sensed he was intrigued at the prospect of flying in the company plane to Washington.

"Jonnie, you'll meet some fascinating people," she coaxed. Was he rushing back to Boston to be with Corinne, she asked herself in sudden curiosity. He pretended to be casual about her, but her name was always seeping into his conversation. "You'll enjoy it."

"I don't know, Mom." All at once Jonnie was self-conscious. "I mean, the important people Iris knows. I'd feel funny sitting down to dinner with them."

"The people Iris and I both know," Laura explained. "It's time you began to expand your circle of acquaintances." In a few years from now these people could be important to his career. "Katie went with Iris to Europe summer before last and had a marvelous time."

"You sold me, Mom." Jonnie sounded low-keyed and casual, but she felt his anticipation. "I'll have to make a phone call to Boston—"

Later, preparing for bed, Laura thought about Jonnie and Corinne. He made a point of not sounding serious, but obviously he was seeing much of this girl up in Boston. He was proud that she was in medical school. He knew from talk at home through these years how difficult it was for women who went into law or medicine. He knew, too, that both Corinne and he had years of school ahead of them.

It was strangely unnerving to think of Jonnie as being in love. Thinking of marriage. Children. Tenderness lent a glow to her face. She would adore Jonnie's children. And Katie's. She sat at her dressing table and brushed her hair without seeing her reflection in the mirror.

But suddenly she was assaulted by familiar anxieties. She had allowed Katie and Jonnie to be hurt by the discovery of what had happened to Papa. She had failed them. Each had reacted differently, but so often she asked herself how this was affecting their lives. Now she must look ahead to another generation. How could she protect

Jonnie and Katie's children?

She'd tried to accept Seth's conviction that the day would come to clear Papa's name — and she would seize it. But this shadow that hung over their lives had become a demon that haunted her. She had been in Magnolia for almost twelve years. What had she done to show the world that Papa had been unjustly convicted? That his town had killed an innocent man.

# Chapter 39

At the Magnolia airport Laura left the plane and hurried to the waiting car.

"Good to see you back, Miss Laura," Pat greeted her with a genial smile as he opened the door of the gray Cadillac limousine that whisked her from one construction site to another these days.

"It's good to be back, Pat."

While Pat drove away from the airport, Laura reran the past twenty-four hours in her mind. She had been proud of the way Jonnie handled himself at Iris's dinner. He'd looked so handsome in his hastily acquired attire. He had displayed the proper amount of deference to the other guests, had been articulate and intelligent in conversation. And he'd even confessed that the evening had been exhilarating.

From a business standpoint the trip had been a huge success. She had a clear understanding of this act that was coming up before Congress. A city—working with the federal government—could buy land and turn it over to private developers at less than cost with the provision that they build low-income and medium-income housing, all situated in inner city slums. She saw the opportunity to earn enormous profits, but more than money drew Laura to this project. She envisioned the excitement of revitalizing major cities.

Over and over again she had been shocked to discover how yet another American inner city had fallen into devastating disrepair. Title I should be an important step in turning this around. She must launch a major campaign to be part of it. Everett would be their advance man. He'd go into the cities they'd pinpoint as likely areas and screen each carefully. Once they'd made a choice, she would move into action with a formal offer. All details would be worked out carefully with Everett and Seth.

Though convinced that the Title 1 Urban Redevelopment Act would go through, Ian Macmillan had warned her that a lot of cities would not take advantage of it.

"*They know most major developers will steer clear of something so complicated and politically touchy. You'll have trouble raising money, Laura. And FHA will be slow in coming up with mortgage insurance in slum areas.*"

Still, Laura was determined to become involved. She recognized the prestige in replacing urban blight with decent apartments.

As soon as it was feasible, Laura plotted, Hunter Realty would approach prospective targets. Ian had suggested Minneapolis, whose housing situation was desperate, and—again—Denver.

Suddenly the hot Southern summer arrived full blast. Laura utilized the mountain house as a weekend retreat, where she could combine business and pleasure. On Friday evenings she drove up with Jewel. A local cleaning woman came in twice a week to keep the house presentable. On Saturday mornings Maisie and Everett drove up for the weekend. Usually Seth would come up for the day, either on Saturday or Sunday.

She had offered Rhoda and Seth the use of the house for the summer, since signals were coming through that neither Katie nor Jonnie would be home for more than a week or two at a time. But Rhoda insisted she'd be more comfortable in their house in town despite the valley heat that descended on Magnolia for painful stretches.

Occasionally Rhoda felt well enough to come over for dinner. Despite her efforts to pretend that she was all right, those close to her knew her life was slowly ebbing away. It disturbed Laura to see the faint bickering that occurred these days between Rhoda and Seth over trifles that normally both would have ignored. Cecile and Barry, too, were conscious of this undercurrent of tensions between them.

"Look, it's natural," Cecile said after an evening when the bickering between Rhoda and Seth had become almost hostile. "You know the strain they both live with night and day."

"There must be moments when Rhoda rails against fate," Laura said somberly. "Sometimes I look at her, and I want to cry." And there were moments, Laura suspected, when Rhoda wished the travail was over.

Katie sprawled on the sofa and read Keith's screenplay while he sat jackknifed in an adjacent chair. She knew it was important to be objective. So much was riding on Keith's making it in Hollywood.

"Well?" he demanded while her eyes seemed frozen to the last few lines.

"Keith, I think it's terrific," she said, her face serious. "I'm not a real authority, but I think you have a winner."

"This is a great time for newcomers in Hollywood," he said and winced. "It's awful how the House un-American Activities Committee is crucifying all those people out in Hollywood. I cringe at benefiting from their anguish. But Hollywood is looking for fresh writers—and here I am," he said with a touch of bravado. "Of course, they may not like my work. They may offer me peanuts."

"Why can't I go with you to Hollywood?" Katie asked for the dozenth time. "I could tell my mother I want to take some special film course at UCLA. I could rent a little house and you could stay—"

"When I know I've got some kind of security in Hollywood, then we can talk about being together. About being married. I can't saddle a new wife with my problems. I have to know that I can afford to keep Gina in a private institution."

"When are you leaving for the Coast?"

"The day after school closes," he told her, though she already knew this. "And you won't be teaching here next term," she said mournfully. "Keith, how can you walk out of my life this way?"

"Hey, is that all the faith you have in me?" He extricated himself from the chair and crossed to sit beside her. "We can survive three or four months until I get moving out there. And the minute I've got some kind of decent contract in my hands—and the times are on my side," he reminded with a sigh, "then you'll come out, and we'll be married. I need you, Katie," he said, drawing her close. "You don't know how much I need you."

"Sometimes I don't think you need anybody. You're the strongest person I know." She hesitated. "Except for my mother. She's like that, too." Keith knew about the way

Daddy was gunned down. He knew about her grandfather. He probably knew her better than anybody alive. How would she survive away from him? "I'll go crazy just sitting around in Magnolia," she warned.

"You said Annabel and Jodie are going off to Italy and Switzerland for six weeks with a group of students. Why don't you go with them? Your mother won't mind." He knew Mom was generous with money—and that she was forever tied up with some major project. Maybe Mom would be relieved to have her set for a good chunk of the summer.

"Maybe I'll go to Italy this summer," Katie shrugged. Mom would just die if she knew about Keith; one, he wasn't Jewish; two, he was divorced; and three, he had a schizophrenic child.

"But don't get involved with one of those hot Italians," Keith teased. "Remember, you're promised to me."


At a table in the coffeehouse that was their rendezvous point during the school day, Jonnie gazed with a mixture of anger and dismay at Corinne.

"What do you mean, you won't be in Boston for the summer?" The only reason he was registering for summer courses was to be here with her.

"Jonnie, you never have to worry about money," Corinne said in exasperation. "You live in a whole different world from my middle-class, middle-income parents. I have to earn money towards next year's tuition. This job working on a cruise ship for the summer will pay me more than I could get anywhere in Boston. I don't try to work during the school year—classes are all I can handle. But I have to do what I can during the summer."

"My mother's not all that rich," Jonnie said self-consciously. "I remember the rotten years in the Depression, before we moved to Magnolia. I—"

"Jonnie, don't get defensive," Corinne scolded. "Your mother has become one of the wealthiest women in America. My father reads about her in all those business magazines he's addicted to. Hers is a modern-day Cinderella story. And don't knock it," she laughed. "My parents are impressed. Their daughter running around with Laura Hunter's son."

"What am I supposed to do this summer?" he countered. It would be rotten not to see Corinne until school opened again.

"Take those courses in international law," she urged. "You're not going to be content to practice law in a grubby little Southern town. It'll come in handy."

"Corinne, Magnolia is not a grubby little town. It's a beautiful city, and it's growing like mad. And I've told you—" He was suddenly serious. "I don't want to practice law. I don't know what the hell I'm doing at law school. I ought to sit down with Mom and explain it's not for me. It's just that I know what a terrible disappointment it'll be to her. My father was a lawyer. She has a law degree. Katie plans to go on to law school—"

"Jonnie, don't talk like an idiot!" Corinne blasted. "You'll have a great career as a lawyer. Your mother has marvelous connections. Look at those people you met down in Washington at that dinner party. How many law school students sit down to dinner with a senator and a Supreme Court judge?" She reached for his hand. "Darling, we've got it made. I'll intern in New York City while you join a prestigious law firm. The only place today for young people on their way up is Manhattan."

"I'll go home for the summer," Jonnie said, retreating from further argument. "I'll work for the company again."

He didn't want to live in Manhattan. He didn't want to practice law. But the only way he'd hang on to Corinne was to play the game the way she called it.


Laura was delighted that Jonnie had decided against summer school. Instead he wanted to work for the company during vacation. He said he'd enjoy the change of pace after the rugged first year of law school—the toughest year of all, she reminisced tenderly.

She worried that Katie would be chasing off to Europe again this summer, though Annabel's mother assured her the student tour group was in the hands of a fine Atlanta woman. She recoiled from the prospect of Katie's ever becoming another playgirl in the international set. Despite the wealth she was accumulating, she meant for Katie and Jonnie to lead responsible lives.

Laura was scheduled to spend four days in early July with Iris — along with other guests — at Bar Harbor aboard a yacht belonging to an Arab prince with whom Iris had become friendly in Washington. Laura was somewhat uneasy when she realized the prince was a student at Georgetown University, though Iris pointed out that he was "pushing thirty."

*"Darling, I know I'm a dozen years older than he, but he's charming and sensational in bed. And knowing Abdul is so useful — he has entrée everywhere, with all that oil money in the family."*

Laura was pleased that Jonnie and Seth were growing so close. Jonnie was intrigued with many aspects of architecture, and Seth was delighted to be his mentor. In time, Laura told herself with relish, Jonnie would become not only Hunter Realty's attorney but one of its owners. He should know the business. And involuntarily she asked herself if Corinne was aware of the money Jonnie would one day inherit.

In July she flew up to Bar Harbor for the yacht party, then dallied briefly in New York and Washington before returning to Magnolia. Iris was urging her to buy a house at Southampton, though she suspected it was more out of an eagerness to be part of the Southampton summer social life than for its business potential.

Laura filed the thought away in a corner of her mind. A Southampton house would be a solid investment — and she loved the seashore. She remembered how Seth talked with such nostalgia about Gloucester — and Jonnie, too, had spent joyous weekends at Gloucester with law school friends. Yes, she'd ask Everett to make some inquiries in the fall about properties that were available.

Early in August Katie returned from Europe. The girls had loved Italy and Switzerland. They had been tourists, Laura told herself — enjoying the sights of Rome and Venice, Geneva and Lausanne and Berne. The Europe they saw was not the one familiar to Iris and her set.

Katie reported that Noel had been cold — "really obnoxious" — when she visited him at his camp near Lausanne.

"It was a nutty idea for me to make the trip out to the camp to see him," Katie shrugged. "He's such a twerp. I only did it because Iris asked me to."

Katie had been home less than a week when she broached the possibility of flying out to Los Angeles to spend time with a friend from school who lived out there.

"Katie, you've just got back from six weeks in Europe," Laura protested. Was she giving Katie too much leeway? Was Katie outgrowing Magnolia? *This was their home.*

"I know, Mom." Katie was her most beguiling. "But my senior year is coming up, and it's going to be a grind. I thought it might be fun to take a peek at Hollywood and the movie studios."

"Who is this classmate?" Laura stalled. "Why does she come all the way from Los Angeles to attend college?"

"Mom!" Katie reproached. "I'm twenty—I'm not a little kid anymore. Why are you asking these silly questions? I'll stay at the Beverly Hills Hotel—that way I won't be intruding." Laura suppressed a smile—kids today were so independent. "If it's boring, I'll just turn around and come right back home," she shrugged.

"All right," Laura capitulated. "Talk to Nora about making hotel and plane reservations for you."


Katie slept through much of the overnight flight from New York to Los Angeles. She awoke to hear a couple across the aisle exclaiming over the magnificence of the Rockies. She was instantly awake. The Rockies below meant they were nearing the end of their flight. Again, she tried to thrust aside guilt at not being truthful with her mother. But Mom would never understand. Mom still saw her as a little girl.

Mom had run off and married Phil without telling Jonnie and her, Katie recalled defiantly. They discovered she'd married Phil when that awful telegram came from the War Department. If Mom could keep a secret, why couldn't she?

Keith didn't know she was coming out to California. If she'd told him, he would have insisted she wait until he sold his screenplay and was under contract for another. He wouldn't let himself think beyond providing for Gina.

She paused at the airport, debating about phoning Keith from here. No, she rejected. She'd settle in the hotel and then call him. His agent had found him a one-room apartment in a rundown building off Sunset Boulevard, which he loathed — but it was cheap. He nurtured every cent, because if a check didn't go out to the home for Gina's care every month, she would be transferred to a public institution.

In her room at the posh Beverly Hills Hotel, Katie sat down at the edge of the bed and reached for the phone. Her heart was pounding. Would Keith be angry at her for coming out? But she had to see him. The phone calls were so frustrating. There had to be a life for them beyond Gina.

Trembling, Katie waited while the phone rang in Keith's apartment. Let him be there. Please, God, let him be there. She'd talked to him from Magnolia just three days ago — he must be in California.

"Hello —" Keith's voice, warm and deep.

"Keith," she murmured in relief. "I was afraid you'd left."

"Katie, where would I go?" he chuckled. He'd given up the house in Athens. His books were being stored by another teacher.

"I thought you might have gone to New York to see Gina." Why was she stammering this way?

"I can't afford to spend money that way," he reminded, yet there was an unexpected lilt in his voice. "At least, not yet. Katie, Al Rosen sold the screenplay! He just called me twenty minutes ago! I'm waiting for him to phone back and tell me when he'll have the contract."

"Oh Keith, that's wonderful! Did he get a good price for it?"

"Enough to take care of Gina for a year. Not at that shitty place in New York state. At a place I've screened near here — where I can see her every week, and know what the hell is happening. We haven't signed yet, but Al says it's a firm commitment."

"Keith, guess where I am," she said unsteadily and then rushed ahead. "I'm at the Beverly Hills Hotel. I couldn't stay away any longer. It's been so awful, not seeing you for all these weeks."

"Give me your room number," he said in elation. "I'll leave here as soon as Al calls back. We'll celebrate together."

Katie hastily unpacked, hung away her clothes. Keith was coming over. He'd sold his screenplay. Probably they'd want to sign him for another. There would be no reason for them not to get married. What did it matter that he was ten years older than she and had a child?

Forty-eight hours after her arrival in Los Angeles Katie sat beside Keith in his beat-up Chevvy while the car sped towards Las Vegas. The air was sweet with the scent of the red roses that made up her bridal corsage. Al Rosen and his wife — who would be witnesses at their wedding — followed in Al's white Cadillac. Keith had chosen Las Vegas because they could be married there immediately. No waiting period was required.

Katie sat with her head against Keith's shoulder and fought off recurrent guilt that she was deceiving her mother this way. But it was the right thing to do. Keith and she loved each other — needed each other.

Keith's hand left the wheel to rest reassuringly on her knee for an instant while they waited at a traffic light at the approach to town.

"In an hour," he told her with an elated smile, "we'll be husband and wife."

They were married by a justice of the peace in a three-minute ceremony and then were swept off by Al and his wife for a wedding luncheon, Al making ribald remarks about the amount of Dom Perignon Keith was consuming. Katie was giddy with happiness. After the festivities Katie and Keith headed for a three-day honeymoon in a borrowed cottage at Malibu.

Tomorrow, Katie reminded herself while Keith struggled with the key to the Pacific-facing cottage, she must phone and tell Mom that she was Mrs. Keith Granger.

# Chapter 40

Laura gripped the phone with such intensity that her knuckles were white. *This was a nightmare.* Katie hadn't gone out to California with a classmate—she'd rushed out there to marry that teacher she'd talked about so much.

"I tried to call and tell you yesterday, but Maisie said you wouldn't be back from Washington until tonight. Mom, Keith and I love each other. Please be happy for us." It was a poignant plea.

"But why couldn't you tell us about him?" Laura fought against recriminations. That would only drive Katie away. "Darling, why couldn't you come home and be married?"

"Mom, I'm sorry." Laura was touched by the desolation in Katie's voice. "First we had to wait for Keith's divorce to come through—he wouldn't let me talk about our being married until the divorce was final—"

"You said you were married in a civil ceremony?" That meant he wasn't Jewish. Divorced and not Jewish. But Katie loved him, Laura rationalized. He had to be special for Katie to love him.

"He's not Jewish. But he'll convert. Later we'll come home and have a religious ceremony," Katie promised. Because that would make Mom feel better. "But right now we have to stay out here because he's in the midst of negotiating for a contract. There's one thing more—" Katie paused and Laura braced herself. "Keith was married while he was still in college. He has a little girl—she's almost eight."

"She's with her mother?" Laura asked. Katie was twenty and she had an eight-year-old stepdaughter?

"No." Katie's voice was so soft now that Laura had to strain to hear her. "Gina's in a home for disturbed children. Mom, it's so sad—she's schizophrenic."

"Oh, Katie—" Her twenty-year-old daughter saddled with a schizophrenic child? Was schizophrenia hereditary?

Did this mean Katie and Keith should never have children? "Keith's first wife couldn't take it after a while. She walked out two years ago." Laura sensed a reluctant compassion in Katie for Gina's mother.

"Katie, what about school?" Laura pressed. Where was all that determination to become a lawyer? "You can take your senior year at a college in Los Angeles—" Don't push her about law school just yet, Laura cautioned herself. Katie was too infatuated with this man to think that far ahead. "I'll send you whatever money you need." Her baby was married to a man she had never met.

"Mom, I don't think this is the time for me to worry about school. Later I'll go back for my senior year," Katie hedged. *She said nothing about law school.*

"Darling, when will I see you?" Desperation crept into Laura's voice.

"Keith and I will try to come home for Thanksgiving," Katie said. "Mom, you'll love him. He's a fine person. He cares about people. And he's so talented and bright."

"You'll write?" Laura was dizzy with shock. "And call me," she urged. "Call collect," she laughed shakily. Keith had sold a screenplay, so she assumed they were not poverty-stricken. But care for a disturbed little girl must run high.

"I'll call. And I'll write. Mom, tell Jonnie and Iris for me? And Jewel." Katie managed a giggle. "Jewel and Annabel are both going to be mad at me for depriving them of a big wedding. I'll write both of them," she promised. "Mom, I love you—"

"And I love you, darling."

Laura put down the phone and lay back against the pillows, the papers she had been studying abandoned now. She brushed aside her instinct to go to Jonnie's room and tell him that Katie was married. He'd been out in the hot sun for ten hours today—he was probably sound asleep by now. And Iris was again en route to Bar Harbor with Jimmy.

Where had she gone wrong, Laura asked herself, that Katie would run off this way and marry without telling her family? Was it because Katie was afraid she'd try to stop the wedding? Why hadn't she noticed the small signs along

510

the way? But she had thought Katie was just enthralled at having a teacher who was a professional playwright. Katie had talked about his talent, his sensitivity—and she had not recognized that her daughter was falling in love.

Had Katie felt justified in running off to get married because of her own secret marriage to Phil? She'd set the wrong example, Laura chastised herself. But she mustn't reproach Katie. She must do nothing that would erect a wall between them again.

While a stubborn mosquito buzzed annoyingly outside a window screen, Laura considered her options. Katie might be married, but she was still her daughter. The best wedding present would be a substantial check—Katie could buy whatever she liked. Right now they might be living in Keith's one-room apartment, but knowing how Katie cherished her physical comfort, she suspected this would soon change. She'd send Katie a check for ten thousand dollars.

Late in October she was scheduled to be in Phoenix on business. How could she not fly out to Los Angeles to see Katie when she was that close? She had been so happy to see Katie after the European trip—and now she wouldn't see her again until late October. But God bless Alexander Graham Bell. Katie and she would talk often.

Jonnie sat across from his mother in the new breakfast room designed by Seth and featured recently in a national magazine. His forkful of scrambled eggs frozen midway to his mouth, he listened in shock to the news of Katie's marriage.

"She's out of her mind!" he exploded when his mother paused. "A divorced guy with a schizophrenic kid!"

"I won't pretend I'm not upset," Laura conceded. "But they're married, and we just have to hope for the best."

"What about her last year of college?" Jonnie demanded. "And law school?" He hadn't girded himself yet to tell Mom he wanted to switch from law to architecture. He was still fighting with Corinne about it. But he'd counted on Katie going to law school. "She has to register in two weeks."

"For now she's forgetting about law school. But that

511

doesn't mean she won't go back," Laura said with conviction. "Women go back to school after marriage." She managed a wisp of a smile. "You and Katie were at my graduation from law school."

"I remember," Jonnie said and grinned at her openmouthed astonishment. He was six years old when Mom graduated. "How could I ever forget? Daddy was so proud. He kept telling Katie and me, 'Your mother is a lawyer!' "

"He would have been so proud of you, Jonnie. His son, going to Harvard Law. Neither of us ever dreamed of such grandeur."

"Mom, what are we going to do about Katie?" he pressed. How could he tell Mom he wanted out of law school when he knew that Katie was never going to be a lawyer? Corinne was winning, after all. "We can't let her throw away her whole life like this."

"When Keith and she are settled down, then she'll probably go back to school."

"I hope so." Did Mom truly believe that? He hesitated. All at once he felt an obligation to tell Mom about Corinne. "Mom, I'm kind of going steady with a girl up in Boston—"

"Corinne?" she asked.

"How'd you guess?" He was startled.

"Jonnie, you mention Corinne often enough," Laura laughed tenderly.

"We're not officially engaged." He cleared his throat in tension. "We both realize we've got a lot of schooling ahead of us. Did I mention Corinne's in medical school?"

"Yes, you did." He saw the unspoken questions in his mother's eyes. What was Corinne like? Was she Jewish? What did her father do? But he wasn't ready to deal with that yet.

"So we can't even think about getting married." He was trapped. He couldn't hurt Mom after this business with Katie—and if he tried to switch to architecture now, Corinne might walk out on him. He didn't want to think about a life without her. "I mean, don't start ringing wedding bells."

"I'd love to meet Corinne," Laura said. "Why don't you bring her home during one of the school holidays?"

"If I can tear her away from the school books." Jonnie grinned. "She's like you must have been at law school. If she doesn't walk off with top grades, she's sure she's a failure."

"Women in law school and medicine start off with two strikes against them," Laura said grimly. "They have to be the best." Her face softened. "Corinne must be strong minded."

"That she is," Jonnie agreed. Sometimes he wished she was less so. "She's working like a dog this summer to pile up money towards next year tuition."

"You've worked hard too," his mother pointed out. "You've been putting in ten- and twelve-hour days."

"But I like it," he said with involuntary enthusiasm and felt his face grow hot. "It's fun to shift gears this way." He tried to sound casual. "Corinne hates this cruise job."

"Jonnie, a lot of us have to work at times at jobs we hate. Most people spend their whole lives at meaningless jobs. We're among the lucky ones. We know what we want to do." Sure he knew—but how would he tell Mom now? "Intuition tells me that Katie will come to realize this—and she'll go back and finish college and then on to law school."

"Yeah, Mom." He understood she had to believe that. Now he hesitated. "Would you mind if I headed back to Boston a few days ahead of schedule? Corinne was hoping we could spend a little time at Gloucester before classes begin."

"You go right ahead, Jonnie. Whenever you like."

"Thanks, Mom." He knew it was a point of pride with Mom not to hang on to Katie and him—which made it all the more difficult to do something that would hurt her.


In late October Laura phoned Katie from Phoenix. Seemingly on impulse, she said she'd run out to Los Angeles for three days before returning to Magnolia if Katie had time to play tourist guide for her.

"I've never been further west than Denver," Laura laughed. "Isn't that absurd?"

"Please come, Mom," Katie said ebulliently. "Right now Keith's tied up at the studio all day—I have plenty of time

513

to show you the town."

"Great." Laura's voice was electric with anticipation. She was going to see Katie. "I'll make reservations at the Beverly Hills Hotel for—"

"Mom, you will not!" Katie interrupted indignantly. "You'll stay here with us in Benedict Canyon. We have two bedrooms. Keith can move his typewriter into our bedroom while you're here. It's not gorgeous," she warned. "Not like our house in Magnolia—or even the summer house," she laughed.

"Katie, all that matters is that I'll be with you. But are you sure Keith won't mind being thrown out of his office? I could stay at the hotel and—"

"No deal," Katie insisted. "Keith will be so pleased you're coming to us. And Mom, you'll like him. I know you will."

"Darling, are you happy?"

"I never thought I could be so happy. Of course, we both worry about Gina," Katie said conscientiously. Katie was so young to have to deal with a disturbed child. "And the whole movie colony is a mess right now with all the red scare craziness. Keith feels bad that he's working when so many fine writers are being blacklisted."

"Oh Katie, I can't wait to see you."

"How's Jonnie?" Katie seemed wary.

"He's fine. He's seeing a lot of a medical student named Corinne Wells."

"I figured something was going on there," Katie admitted. "When will you be arriving, Mom? Did you fly to Phoenix in the company plane?"

"No, Seth and Everett are practically commuting between Magnolia and Washington at this point—I came out on a commercial airliner. I'll have a hotel clerk make my reservations, then call you back. Darling, I'm dying to see you."

Off the phone Laura sat immobile for a few moments. Katie wasn't pregnant, was she? Surely Keith and she would check into the situation before they even considered having a family. Katie was only twenty—she didn't have to rush into having a baby. But she would be afraid even to broach the subject with Katie. She mustn't be an interfering mother and mother-in-law.

* * *

When Laura suggested she take Katie and Keith out somewhere sumptuous for dinner, Katie rejected this.

"I'll cook for us," she said gaily. "Jewel sent me loads of her recipes. All printed out so I wouldn't have any trouble reading them. You two go sit down in the living room while I make like a chef."

In less than an hour Katie—in her much-loved dungarees and ballet slippers—ordered her mother and husband to the table. Laura marveled at Katie's efficiency. At home she had never so much as made coffee. Now she was bringing out a platter of Country Captain—pieces of baked chicken drenched with a curry-spiced tomato sauce and topped with toasted slivered almonds and currants, a bowl of steaming rice and another of tossed salad.

"I never had Country Captain until Katie made it," Keith said, digging with relish into the generous portion Katie served him.

"You haven't had chicken until you've had Country Captain," Katie laughed. "I remember the first time Mom made it for us. We hadn't been in Magnolia for long, and Jonnie and I were having some trouble getting used to everything." Laura listened in astonishment; she'd thought the children had adjusted so fast and so well. "Then Mom told us if we liked Country Captain, we were Southerners at heart."

"I think you miss Magnolia," Keith teased.

"A little," Katie confessed. "But wherever you need to be, that's home now."

"Katie's been telling me how well you're doing," Laura told Keith. She was astonished to realize how much she liked him. He was a warm, caring human being. "She's so proud of you."

"I'm working because of the damn red scare that's tearing Hollywood apart." All at once Keith was somber. "Normally my agent would have a hard time selling me. I have no prior screen credits. I have a background of two failed Broadway plays—"

"But you have talent," Katie said zealously. "They wouldn't buy your scripts if you couldn't deliver."

"I read what's happening, and it's frightening." Laura, too, was serious now.

"It's painful to write for films today." Keith's eyes darkened in rebellion. "The great gods to appease are the DAR and the American Legion. But the worst thing is the way decent, talented people are being trodden into the ground. Anybody who ever signed a petition for Russian relief or against the atom bomb is a Commie."

"And it's going to get worse before it gets better," Laura said with fatalistic calm. "Before the guns of World War II were cold, we were into this hysterical confrontation with the Communists."

"But it won't touch Keith," Katie said, her face alight with optimism. "Nobody can ever point a finger at him," she turned to her mother. "He's a World War II veteran. He was decorated for heroism in battle."

"Don't count on that to protect me," Keith said with unexpected pessimism. "Not in this climate."

"Keith, you're not a Communist!" Katie reproached.

"Nor are a lot of people who've been labeled that," Keith shot back. "But *Counterattack* or *Red Network* labels somebody a red, and they don't work."

"It won't happen to you," Katie insisted.

"Katie, the way things are going in this country, it could happen to anybody." Keith's face tensed. "It could happen to me. Not because of anything I've done — but because of the crazy hysteria that's screaming on every side. But for now —" he forced a smile. "For now let's be happy that I'm working."

# Chapter 41

During the next few months Laura spent much time in Washington because of bureaucratic red tape. She abhorred what Everett called the essential back scratching, but she forced herself to play the game. The stakes were dazzlingly high. Iris and she entertained at glittering dinners at the Georgetown house, with Seth often in attendance. Under the expert guidance of Laura's public relations firm he was becoming an architect of national prominence.

Laura was disappointed when Katie phoned a few days before Thanksgiving to say that she and Keith would not be able to come to Magnolia for Thanksgiving week as planned. But Jonnie was coming home—though without Corinne. He explained that her mother insisted on her presence at the family dinner.

Laura gave her usual Thanksgiving dinner for their close small circle—and was grateful that Rhoda was well enough to attend. As always she was uncomfortable listening to the mild bickering between Seth and Rhoda, even while she understood the tensions under which they both lived these days. Seth confessed in one dark moment that he was inundated by guilt that his own health was good when Rhoda was so clearly losing her battle for life.

Katie wrote enthusiastically about the premiere of the movie based on Keith's screenplay, released in time to be a candidate for the next season's Academy Awards.

In Washington early in the new year Laura persuaded Iris to go with her to see the film.

"If it's nominated for an Academy Award," Laura decided as they emerged from the movie theater into the first snow of 1950, "we'll both fly out to Hollywood. Katie is so excited about Keith's success."

"You'll go to the Academy Awards alone," Iris said tersely while the chauffeur hurried from behind the wheel to open the car door. "I won't even listen to the radio reports."

"Iris, why?" Laura asked in astonishment.

"Because it'll just remind me of what I missed out on." Iris drew her Somali leopard coat—bought from her commissions on an earlier project—tightly about her, though the car was warm. "I should have become an important movie star. As big as Ava Gardner and Rita Hayworth. My stupid Southern accent ruined everything for me." Her voice was harsh with recall.

"You'd never have become Lady Cranford if you'd stayed in Hollywood," Laura reminded gently. Iris always pretended this was the ultimate accomplishment. It unnerved Laura to discover Iris harbored such bitterness. "That's earned you a fancy lifestyle."

"I'd turn in the title any day to be a successful movie star." All at once Iris seemed to age ten years. "But not for any man," she added quickly. She had long ago ruled out remarriage. "I should have divorced Peter as soon as I realized what he was like, and gone back to Hollywood with my new English accent. I could have had a real career. Why do we always see the right approach when it's too late?"

"Iris, you're an important asset to the business." Laura was anxious to ease her sister's pain. "You've carved a special place for yourself with Hunter Realty. You're part of its success."

"So maybe—for Katie—I'll listen to the Academy Awards," Iris said with an attempt at humor. "Now let's go home and soak in hot, perfumed tubs before we have to go to that Embassy ball tonight."


In January, President Truman ordered the Atomic Energy Commission to work for the development of a hydrogen bomb, which promised to be more deadly than the atomic bomb. Hysteria over possible Communists in the United States was escalating to frightening proportions. The world knew that the Soviet Union—after grabbing off half of Europe—had three times as many combat planes as the United States.

In the film studios and in the radio and television industry fear reigned. Any hint of Communist connections—documented or not—was sufficient for firings. Careers were being terminated on the strength of letter-writing campaigns.

Katie and Keith watched with shock as the blacklisting forged ahead. They took meager comfort in the firm conviction that Keith could never be a victim of the nefarious blacklisting. His first screenplay had been nominated for an Academy Award. His second was the basis for a high-budgeted film. And now Al was negotiating for a major contract.

On this sunny March morning Katie paced restlessly about the living room. She wished now she had signed up for classes at UCLA. Maybe she would go to summer school. She was so bored with doing nothing but taking care of the house. But she didn't want Keith to think it wasn't enough just to be his wife. He needed to feel she would always be there whenever he wanted to reach out for her.

Keith was sure that with his first screenplay nominated for an Academy Award, Al would come up with a great new contract. When he had that kind of assurance—when he knew the money would be there for Gina for years ahead—then she'd go back to school.

Katie paused to glance at the clock. It was past 10 A.M. How was the meeting going at the studio? At shortly past seven this morning Ted Bromfield himself had called the house and asked Keith to come over to the studio immediately. Probably some rush assignment, Keith assumed.

He hadn't even paused for breakfast. She'd put up a fresh percolator of coffee, she decided, and hurried into the kitchen. While she debated about preparing to make French toast for him, she heard the sound of a car in the driveway. She left the kitchen and walked down the hall to the front door.

The car was Al Rosen's late-model Cadillac. Keith and he were just emerging. Had their car conked out again at the studio, she asked herself in impatience. They really ought to buy a new one. Keith hated to make any major investment with the monthly bills at Gina's sanitarium so high.

519

"Hi," Katie called out as the two men approached. Why did they look so serious? Was Bromfield giving them a hard time about contract terms?

"I'll have to send a mechanic to pick up the car," Keith said, kissing her lightly. "Damn thing wouldn't start up again."

"Hi, Al." She smiled tentatively. "They got you up early, too?"

"Keith called me at the office to come pick him up," Al explained while the three of them walked into the house.

"I have fresh coffee perking." All at once Katie was apprehensive. The eyes of the two men were foreboding. "What about French toast to go with it?"

"Just coffee." Keith dropped an arm about her waist.

"Something's happened." She couldn't restrain herself from questioning them. "What's wrong?"

"Pour us coffee and sit down," Keith said with uncharacteristic sharpness. "Then we'll talk."

Silently, conscious of the grim communication between Keith and Al, she poured coffee and joined them at the table.

"Katie, how the hell can I tell you this?" His face betrayed his inner agony. "I've been blacklisted. The studio wants no part of me. Nobody will want me now."

"Why?" Katie demanded in a blend of disbelief and rage and shock. "You've never belonged to the Communist party. You've never been a union organizer. You've never signed petitions—"

"Some smear group sent in a rash of letters. In my first screenplay—the one nominated for an Academy Award—I dared to talk about respect for human labor. Nobody noticed it till now," Keith said with blistering contempt. "But the letters pointed out that the screenplay—written by Keith Granger—was infiltrated with Communist doctrine. There's not a studio in Hollywood that will touch me now."

"Al—" Katie turned pleadingly to Keith's agent. Their *friend*.

"Katie, it's a crazy situation." Al stared into his coffee cup. "But I figure I can line up some work for Keith. Under a pseudonym," he conceded unhappily. "And the money will be shitty. But this can't go on forever—"

"How much money can you get for me?" Keith challenged, a vein pounding in his left temple. "How much, Al?"

"I'll have to do some digging," Al admitted. "I've got a writer—I don't dare mention his name, but he was drawing three thousand dollars a week—who's working on flat rates. Look, it's not good, but it's better than nothing."

"How much?" Keith demanded again.

"Seven hundred and fifty dollars," he said reluctantly. "We got some greedy bastards in the business—they'll look away if they're saving money. Use Katie's name."

"How far will seven hundred and fifty dollars go?" Keith's face was taut with apprehension. "Al, you know what it costs me to keep Gina in that sanitarium."

"I'm sorry, Keith." Al spread his hands in frustration. "It's the best I can do."

Katie watched fearfully while Keith struggled to accept reality.

"Okay, Al. Get me some flat-rate deals. I'll write damn fast. Our bankroll won't last long."

And Keith wouldn't allow her to ask Mom to help them with money, Katie reminded herself. He insisted Gina was his responsibility.


Jonnie sat arguing politics with Chuck Anderson—a buddy since his first day at Harvard Law—at a booth in a long-favored coffeehouse. He was killing time until Corinne arrived and they could go out to dinner. Normally he would have gone home to Magnolia as soon as school closed, but this summer Corinne's cruise job wouldn't begin until July 1.

"I know there are all those crazies running around in Washington who see a Commie behind every bush," Chuck agreed with Jonnie, "but the trouble in Korea is real. I don't trust all those skirmishes between North Koreans and South Koreans near the 38th parallel. And don't give me that crap about their being guerrila attacks. That's the North Korean Commies attacking soldiers of the Republic of Korea. Why the hell did we pull most of our army out of South Korea?"

"Chuck, you know why." They'd battled over this before. "Both General MacArthur and Secretary of State Acheson say South Korea lies beyond what they call the American defense perimeter in the Pacific. If South Korea is attacked, then the UN will have to move into action." Jonnie sighed. "It's too damn hot to talk about a shooting war. Did you catch *The African Queen yet?* It's great."

"Since school closed I've been working fourteen hours a day at that paralegal job. You know, piling up money towards next year's tuition." At intervals Jonnie felt guilty that some of his friends—including Chuck and Corinne—had serious financial problems.

"Hey, there's the future Dr. Corinne Wells," Chuck drawled, nodding towards the entrance. "All set for a big Saturday night."

But Corinne's demeanor was hardly festive. Her expressive face was somber. She clutched at her purse in a gesture Jonnie recognized as indicating anger.

"Have you heard the news?" she asked as she slid into the booth beside Jonnie.

"What?" Jonnie exchanged an anxious glance with Chuck.

"It just came over the radio. North Korean armed forces have crossed the parallel in three columns. With Russian T-34 tanks on the ground, Russian artillery for support, and Russian combat planes overhead. They're heading for Seoul."

"Oh, God!" Chuck clenched a fist until his knuckles were white. "I'm a marine reservist," he reminded Jonnie. "What do you want to bet I get called up for active duty within the next sixty days?"

"They won't pull you out of school," Corinne said quickly. "By the time you finish your last year, the fighting will be over. This is a United Nations action."

"If I'm called, I'm going," Chuck told them. "And don't worry about me, old buddy." He grinned at Jonnie's open-mouthed shock. "I'm a survivor. I'll be back."

The UN passed a resolution condemning the North Korean invasion. Two days later President Truman ordered U.S. forces to the aid of South Korea. On July 1 a battalion of the all-black U.S. 24th Infantry Division—with a permanent base at Fort Benning, close to Magnolia — was flown to Pusan in South Korea.

Jonnie returned to Magnolia and to his regular summer job with Hunter Realty. But this wasn't like other summers. He sensed his mother's anxiety about Katie. After writing in January that she would be home for three weeks in April, she had switched this to "sometime during the fall."

"I worry about Katie," his mother confessed on a drive back from Atlanta in a waning mid-July dusk, fragrant with the scent of pine and summer flowers. Jonnie, rather than the chauffeur, was at the wheel. "When I casually mentioned that I might be out in Houston in May — close enough to fly out to L.A. for a day or two — she fabricated some story about going along with Keith on location on his latest picture. I didn't believe her for a minute. Jonnie, she's trying to keep something from me."

"Maybe she's fighting with Keith," Jonnie said after a minute. "And she doesn't want you to know."

"She surely must understand that whatever is wrong we're here to help. I've tried to get that message across." Laura rebelled at her sense of helplessness.

"Relax, Mom. Katie will work it out. The first year of marriage can be rough, I hear." If Corinne and he got married while they were in school, they'd probably be fighting like crazy. They'd wait till they were out of school — that was one point on which they both agreed.

"I feel so frustrated not knowing what's wrong." Laura sighed. "But you're probably right. Whatever it is, Katie will work it out. She's very much in love with Keith."

Jonnie was learning much about the business — and from Seth he was absorbing details about architecture that instinct told him were valuable. Yet he could not bring himself to talk to his mother about abandoning law school — with his last year just ahead — and trying for admission to Harvard School of Design. He didn't dare consider Corinne's reaction.

Corinne insisted stubbornly — and irrationally — that she would be a doctor and he a lawyer. She refused to believe that after all his talk about the legal profession, he didn't want it any longer.

He remembered Chuck's blunt assessment. *"You're so damn*

hot to hop into bed with Corinne, you're not thinking for yourself anymore. Me, I'm sold on law. I was a little kid during the Depression, but I never forgot how my old man sweated to keep food on the table and a roof over our head. How he humiliated himself for that. And I swore it would never happen to me. I can practice law and live well. But Jonnie, you've got it made. You don't need the money. Your mother's loaded. Do what you want with your life."

On August 4, sixty-two thousand reservists were called up for twenty-one months' active duty. That same night Jonnie phoned Chuck in Boston. Chuck had to report for duty in ten days.

For Jonnie the summer seemed agonizingly long. Corinne mailed letters to him from each of the cruise's port of call, but there was no way for him to respond. With each letter she reinforced her conviction that fine careers awaited the two of them in the fields they had chosen. And Jonnie increasingly worried about Chuck, on active duty with the marines.

He spent long hours each day at the construction sites or holed up in Seth's office. At night he slept from exhaustion. He was impatient to see Corinne, yet he dreaded the return to school. This last year of law meant the death of his dreams of becoming an architect. He was trapped.


Jonnie arrived at his Cambridge apartment four days before classes were to begin. Corinne — back from her cruise ship twenty-four hours earlier — was there to meet him.

"You look marvelous," Corinne scolded after a long, thirsty kiss. "You've been lying on your back beside a swimming pool all summer, enjoying yourself too much to miss me for a moment."

"The only time I was horizontal was when I went to sleep at night. From eight in the morning till dinner time I was either working with an excavation crew digging into Georgia clay or working with the architectural staff." He suspected that the summers he had worked with Seth would have been useful in his gaining admittance to architectural school. "I had these wild erotic dreams about you."

"I'd be happy to know I'll never see another cruise ship."

She fastened her arms about his shoulders and lifted her face to his. "This year at school is going to be a real bitch. Let's run down to Gloucester for two days before classes."

"I was thinking along those lines, too. We've got a lot of catching up to do."

They stayed at a charming Victorian inn that overlooked the Atlantic Ocean and a stretch of rocky beach. They watched the sun rise over the water in the morning and set in rosy splendor at the end of the day. They made love before the fireplace in their bedroom. And they observed a silent pact not to talk about the future but to enjoy each moment of their togetherness.

"I hate to go back," Corinne confessed when they had checked out of the inn and were en route to the car. The brilliant blue sky matched the water. "I don't want to think about slogging through two more years of medical school. And then I have to worry about where I'll intern." Corinne was realistic about the hurtles that women physicians faced.

"Nobody's holding a gun to your head," he reminded, tossing their valises onto the back seat while an intoxicating vision danced about in his mind: he in architectural school while Corinne was content to be just his wife.

"*I'm* holding a gun at my head," she smashed the vision. "I don't care how I have to sweat, I'm going to be Corinne Wells, M.D. Did your father complain when your mother wanted to go to law school?" she challenged.

"No," Jonnie conceded guiltily. "But she's never had a real chance to practice law."

"We've been through a war. Times have changed. Women doctors are taking their place today. I know I'll run into a lot of brick walls; but Jonnie, I'll break them down."

"They're building a huge extension to Magnolia Hospital," he began tentatively. He had been thinking about this all summer—ever since Mom had mentioned it. "My mother throws a lot of weight around town. She should be helpful in landing you an internship at Magnolia."

"No," Corinne said flatly and climbed into the car.

"What do you mean, 'no'?" Jonnie asked, sliding behind the wheel.

"I don't want to intern in some sleepy Southern town." She grimaced in distaste. "There has to be some hospital in

New York that'll accept a woman. My grades are great."
Corinne said a woman had to be twice as good as a man to
earn the same respect.

"Corinne, Magnolia isn't some sleepy Southern town," he
mimicked. "Ignore the name. It's a city. And expanding
every year."

"That's no place for us." Her voice was harsh in rejection.
"We'd both have dull little practices with no real future
ahead of us. I've worked too hard to settle for that."

"Before we head for the apartment, let's stop off at
Chuck's house." Jonnie retreated from a possible battle with
Corinne. "I'd like to ask his mother if she's heard from
him."


While Jonnie grimly tried to settle down into his final
year of law, Corinne was excited at starting her clinical
years at medical school. Now she was spending most of her
time in the hospital. Between working in the medical
wards, attending lectures and studying, she had to scrounge
for time to spend with him.

He was trying to cope with the knowledge that Corinne
had this school year plus yet another ahead of her. She
talked about his staking out a job in New York after graduation, driving up to Boston to spend the weekends with her.
*Didn't he have a say about anything in their future?*

A call to Chuck's family told him that Chuck was en
route to Korea. Jonnie religiously followed the action of
what was being called "a police action" rather than a war.
On October 8, U.S. troops crossed the 38th parallel into
North Korea. North Korean forces were withdrawing towards Pyongyang, their capital. But on October 12 Chinese
Communist troops — with no warning — rushed to the aid of
the North Koreans.

While Jonnie was listening to a radio report of this latest
development, he received a phone call from Chuck's
brother. The family had received a telegram from the War
Department. Chuck had died in the recapture of Seoul.

Long after Chuck's brother was off the phone — with dusk
turning to night — Jonnie sat slumped in a chair in the unlit
living room and tried to understand that Chuck was dead.

Chuck had been so sure he was indestructible that this belief had infected Jonnie. He'd just assumed that Chuck would forever be part of his life — but for Chuck "forever" was over.

Remembered snatches of conversation tormented Jonnie. *"Okay, maybe to some people it's square to be a reserve officer, and I admit the money is important, but mainly I joined up because I want to do my part to keep the Commies from taking over the world."*

Like himself, Chuck hated what the House un-American Activities Committee was doing to the country, but Chuck was cynical about the Soviet aims for the future.

*"Look, the Russians have set up Commie governments in Albania, Bulgaria, Czechoslovakia, East Germany, Hungary, Poland, and Rumania. They swallowed up Lithuania, Latvia, and Estonia. They helped set up Communism in China, Vietnam, North Korea, and Outer Mongolia. Don't Americans have a right to be concerned?"*

Hell, how did you ever know what was right? Jonnie rose from his chair, walked to a lamp and switched on the light. But there was one thing he did know — he didn't want to continue with law school for another day. Every classroom, every lecture hall would taunt him with memories of Chuck.

Tomorrow morning he would look up the recruiting office in Boston. Tomorrow morning he would enlist in the Marine Corps.

# Chapter 42

Laura was hunched over the desk in her at-home office when Jonnie called. Her face lighted up at the sound of his voice. And then she listened — encased in ice — while he told her haltingly that he had enlisted in the Marine Corps. *What about law school?*

"Jonnie, why?" She clutched the phone in disbelief, her mind suddenly hurtling back through the years to the day Phil told her he was enlisting. With Phil she had known it was inevitable. But why must Jonnie go to fight in Korea? This country wasn't at war. "Why?" she repeated.

"Mom, it's something I have to do."

He told her that Chuck had died in Korea — and she felt his pain within herself. The government said we weren't at war, but American boys were losing their lives in Korea. The Cold War had become a shooting war — no matter that it was called "a UN police action." "I'm going to boot camp at Parris Island, South Carolina. I'll be there for six weeks. I'll write you, Mom — or call. And don't worry — I'm going to be fine."

Laura tried to convince herself that nothing would happen to Jonnie — they had endured their share of tragedy. She worried, too, about Katie. She perceived an undercurrent of hysteria in Katie's light chatter each time they talked on the phone, yet she didn't dare pry, fearful of driving Katie away.

For Katie's birthday — knowing her daughter's love for beautiful clothes — she had sent a designer dress she'd asked Iris to pick up on one of her quick trips to London and Paris. On instinct she'd sent, also, a substantial check — ignoring a taunting inner voice that said she was placing too much emphasis on money.

Jonnie was in uniform and Katie fighting some desperate battle of her own, Laura tormented herself. What could she do to help her children?

In their kitchen in the Benedict Canyon cottage, Katie listened for the sound of a car in the driveway while she checked the roast in the oven. Keith ought to be home any minute from his visit to Gina. No matter how hard he was working to meet a deadline, he was there at the sanitarium twice a week, spending most of the day — always frustrating and saddening — with his little girl. Occasionally she went with him — when he suggested this. But she sensed his need to be alone with Gina on most visits.

He worked so hard, Katie thought with recurrent rage, for a fraction of what he should be earning. He'd been nominated for an Academy Award, but in this insane era that meant nothing. He had to hide behind a pseudonym. Only the black market was open to him.

Any hopes they had harbored for his being cleared were destroyed when the filthy paperbound two-hundred-page rag called *Red Channels* hit the industry in late June. Keith was listed there, along with Lillian Hellman, Dorothy Parker, Judy Holliday, Luther Adler, and an endless list of the best in the entertainment world.

Keith refused to allow her to look for a job. He said he needed her presence in the house while he worked. She had taken a typing course during the summer so that she could help him in his frenzy to keep checks coming in. Thank God for the check Mom sent on her birthday. The sanitarium had been threatening to release Gina to a public institution.

Katie's face brightened as she heard the crunch of wheels on their pebbled driveway. Keith was home. She hurried to the door to greet him.

"Hey, that's a cool outfit you're wearing." His gaze swept appreciatively over her off-the-shoulder blouse and peasant skirt after a warm, unhurried kiss. On those days he went to visit Gina, she discarded the dungarees and shirt that were her uniform. She served wine with dinner. She fought to lift him from the depression that was part of those days. "Did I tell you yet today that I think you're gorgeous?"

"You may have mentioned it this morning," she drawled

and walked into the house with him, her arm about his waist while his encircled her shoulders. "You're in a good mood—" A question in her eyes. Had the doctors suddenly come upon some new treatment for Gina? Keith was ever hopeful of a miraculous discovery in the field of psychiatry.

"I stopped by Al's office. He's setting up a great deal for me. Decent money this time." He squeezed her shoulders with an air of elation.

"Keith, that's wonderful! Gina's bills were past due again. She'd felt the pressure building in Keith. And he kept refusing to allow her to ask Mom for money. *Gina's my responsibility, Katie.*"

"Maybe we ought to go out for dinner to celebrate," he said tentatively.

"I have a roast ready to pull out of the oven," she told him. "Tomorrow night we'll celebrate."

In the tiny dining area off the kitchen, Keith sat in his familiar place at the table and kicked off his shoes. Katie removed the roast from the oven, brought it to the table for Keith to slice. The Idahos could use another minute or two, she decided.

"Tell me about the screenplay," Katie ordered while she reached into the refrigerator for the bowl of tossed salad. "I'm dying to hear all the details."

She listened avidly while Keith reported on the new assignment. It was a small miracle. While he'd still be writing as Kate Hunter, he'd be paid decent money. Someday soon, she promised herself, this insanity would be over—and he'd write as Keith Granger again.

"That's about it," Keith wound up, faintly breathless, while they settled down to eat. It had been so long since she had seen Keith like this.

"Katie, this is a great time for you to fly home for a couple of weeks. You haven't seen your mother in over a year. And right now—with Jonnie in boot camp—she'll be especially happy to have you home for a little while."

"But I can't leave you when you're beginning work on an important assignment," she protested, even while she churned with excitement at the prospect of two weeks in Magnolia. And hopefully she'd see Jonnie before he shipped out. It was scary to think of Jonnie fighting in

530

Korea. "Later, Keith."

"No, I've made up my mind!" Keith was ingratiatingly firm. "Tomorrow morning I sign the contract. We'll have lunch at that French place Al keeps raving about. And tomorrow night you'll be aboard a flight heading for home."

"Keith, you're out of your mind!" she scolded.

"The first two weeks on this screenplay — when I'm plotting — I'll be in a foul mood. I'll be working twenty hours and sleeping four. I'll feel more comfortable knowing you're home and enjoying yourself." He transferred slabs of succulent eye-round roast from the platter to his plate. "You'll save me from a guilt trip."

"I think you're mad," Katie laughed. "But if that's the way you want it, then okay. I'll fly home. Provided I can get reservations at the last moment like this."

Keith reached into his pocket. "I've got your ticket east," he said in triumph. "I picked it up on my way home. I didn't ask for a return flight because I thought you'd rather leave the date open for now."

Katie searched his face for reassurance about her taking off so suddenly.

"Keith, you'll remember to eat? I don't want to come back and find you emaciated."

"I'll eat," he promised. "Probably nonstop," he warned. "You know how I nibble when I'm working hard. Katie, you're the most wonderful thing that ever happened to me." Under the table he extended one foot until it rested against her ankle. "From now on everything is going to be fine. Believe me."

"How was Gina today?" she asked, reaching for the salad bowl.

"Same as usual." His smile was wry. "In the morning, they told me, she'd been in agitated hyperactivity —" Katie nodded. She was familiar now with the terms used to describe childhood schizophrenia. "She refused to eat. I managed to coax her into eating a little ice cream. The rest of the time she sat jabbering away in that weird gobbledegook that nobody can interpret." He paused in pain. "And she's been hallucinating again. The new medication only made it worse."

"Keith, you know what you always say — the experts are

constantly experimenting with new medications." Katie struggled for a spontaneous optimism. "One day they'll come up with just the right drug for Gina. And she'll come home with us. We'll put the nightmare years behind us."

"You know what we're going to do after dinner?" Keith dismissed serious conversation. "We're going over to see Judy Holliday in *Born Yesterday*. And then," his voice dropped in amorous promise, "we're coming home to make love until dawn breaks through."

Keith stood watching from the ground long after Katie's plane had disappeared from view. Later she would know that he lied about the new assignment. There was none. His pseudonym had been penetrated.

During an unguarded moment, not realizing the impact, when Keith's name came into the conversation over a studio luncheon Al had mentioned that Keith's mother-in-law was the famous real-estate developer, Laura Hunter. It took the studio bigwigs only minutes to piece together the facts: Keith Granger was hiding behind his wife's maiden name. Shaken but honest, Al had to admit that he'd never be able to sell him in Hollywood again.

Keith went to the airport parking lot area, settled himself in the car, and headed home. He had much to do tonight. All of Katie's things must be packed and prepared for a pickup by Railway Express. He would leave the cartons with their kindly next-door neighbor, with an excuse about having to go to the studio. He had to write a letter to Al— with a list of instructions—and leave it under his office door.

His hands tightened on the wheel as he recalled the traumatic conversation yesterday morning with the director of the sanitarium. The director had made it clear. Unless he paid up the thirty-day delinquency plus two months in advance, within the next five days, the sanitarium would dismiss Gina from their care.

How could he allow sweet little Gina—his innocent little baby—to be committed to one of those public monstrosities? The image of Gina in those surroundings—living under those conditions—turned him sick. If Katie knew, she'd rush to ask her mother for financial help. But how could he let her do that? There was no end in sight. There was only one way out.

When he left the car and walked to the front door, he tried to gear himself to face the empty house — and what lay ahead. He had to see this through. He mustn't weaken now. His hands were clammy as he fumbled in his pockets for the door key.

Early tomorrow morning he would go to the sanitarium and bring Gina home with him. Nobody would ever harm his baby. She would never have to go to a public institution.


While a dreary, windswept rain hammered at the windows on her first afternoon home, Katie tried for the dozenth time to reach Keith.

"It's still busy." Katie was perplexed. "I've been buzzing the house for almost two hours."

"The phone's probably out of order," Laura soothed. "Ask the operator to check."

The operator reported that the line was "temporarily out of service."

"That means Keith has it off the hook," Katie said in relief. But she was annoyed that he had not realized she would be calling soon after her arrival. "He does that sometimes when he's deep into work."

"Try him again tonight," her mother encouraged. "You'll probably reach him then."

She had not slept well on the flight from Los Angeles. Now she was fighting off yawns.

"Katie, go up to your room and nap until dinner," her mother said tenderly. "You've had a long flight."

"All right." Katie rose to her feet. "It's good to be home, Mom." For her mother to have met her in Atlanta and to be taking off most of the business day told her how much her presence was valued.

"Darling, it's wonderful to have you home." Laura reached to draw Katie to her for a moment.

"I hope Jonnie gets to come home before I leave." Mom said he expected to be sent to Camp Lejeune in Jacksonville, North Carolina when he finished his basic training.

That should be any day now.

"Everything's so uncertain. Nora's nephew was shipped straight from boot camp to Korea. That's not enough training for those kids." Her mother's face was taut with alarm.

Mom lost Phil less than seven years ago. It wasn't fair for Jonnie to put her through this, Katie thought in momentary anger.

"Miss Laura—" Jewel's voice echoed down the hall. "The postman jes' brung a special delivery letter. It's for Katie," she reported with an air of surprise. "My, oh, my, that husband of hers must be missin' her already."

"Why on earth is Keith writing me?" Katie reached out a hand for the letter. A trickle of alarm darted through her. "Why didn't he just phone?"

"I bes' be gettin' back to my Country Captain if we's gonna have dinner tonight." Jewel's face was bright with pleasure because her "little girl" was home.

Katie ripped open the envelope and pulled out the typewritten letter. Her face drained of color as she read. Weak with shock she dropped into a chair while she tried to assimilate what she read:

*Darling Katie, I'm taking the only way out for Gina and myself. I hated to lie to you, but it was the only way. There was no great assignment. There'd be no more. By the time you receive this, Gina and I will both be at peace. I could never bear to see her in one of those horrible public institutions. I couldn't face leaving her alone if something should happen to me. Al will take care of all that needs to be done. Gina's body and mine will be cremated, and Al will sprinkle our ashes over our special stretch of the Pacific at Malibu. I know he won't fail me. I've packed up all your things and sent them on to Magnolia. There's no need for you to return to the house. Thank you for the most wonderful years of my life. You're so young, my love. You must marry again, have your own family. Promise me not to grieve too long. Yours, Keith.*

"Katie—" She heard her mother's voice, fraught with anxiety.

"Keith's dead," Katie whispered. It wasn't true. It couldn't be true. "He put Gina to a final sleep—and then he killed himself." It couldn't be happening this way. It was some insane nightmare.

"Oh, my God—" Her mother reached for the letter that

fell from Katie's nerveless fingers to the floor.

"I shouldn't have left him." A rope seemed to tighten about her throat, threatening to cut off her breathing. "If I'd stayed in California, I could have stopped him—"

"Katie there was nothing you could do."

"I told him you'd help us, Mom. I knew you would. But he wouldn't let me ask you. The checks you sent saved us for a little while. Mom, what is wrong with this family?" Her voice soared almost out of control. "What awful curse hangs over us? Daddy, Phil, our grandfather—and now Keith. Why, Mom, why?"

"Darling, I don't know." Laura reached to cradle her daughter in her arms while tears spilled over unnoticed. "Katie, you're so young to have lived through so much. But you have to learn to go on. Your life is just beginning. This is not the end. Katie, you must believe that."

"I'm going back to California," Katie insisted, white and trembling. "I have to go back."

"Katie, no. Keith didn't want you to face that. He loved you very much. He wanted you safely at home with family."

"But he can't die just like this. There has to be more." Katie sought for words to explain what she felt. "There has to be a memorial service. Something to show that he was once alive."

"He's alive in your heart. That's his memorial. But phone this man he mentions. This Al," Laura coaxed gently.

"I want to scatter Keith's ashes and Gina's myself," Katie said with sudden strength. "If it's not too late."

While her mother stood by, Katie phoned Al Rosen's office. His distraught secretary reported that he was with the police at Katie and Keith's little house in Benedict Canyon.

"Katie, I'm so sorry," she gasped. "We all are."

"Tell Al I'm flying out in the morning. Tell him—" She paused, fighting for breath. "Tell him I'm coming out to scatter my husband's ashes over the Pacific."

Laura refused to allow Katie to fly on a commercial liner. Katie would be flown out on the company plane. The crew would stand by to fly her home again. Katie rejected her mother's plans to accompany her to California.

"You can't leave Magnolia now, Mom," she insisted. "Jonnie may come home on a twenty-four-hour pass. He'll expect you to be here." She didn't remind her mother that this might be her last chance to see Jonnie before he was shipped out to Korea—but she knew this fear was ever present in her mother's mind. "I'll be all right. Don't worry about me."

"All right," Laura capitulated after a fleeting hesitation, and forced an acquiescent smile. Did Mom think she didn't want her to come along? It wasn't that at all.

Katie drove alone at sunset to Malibu. She was oblivious to the beauty of the orange-red sky and the ever-changing sea, ranging from peacock blue to a gleaming turquoise, remembering that Keith and she had spent their honeymoon in a charming borrowed cottage facing the Pacific.

They had been so in love, young and bursting with dreams about the exciting years that lay ahead, never suspecting that the blacklist would swoop down on them and make living unbearable for Keith. He was a victim of this awful plague as much as though he had been gunned down.

Now all that remained of Keith and Gina were the ashes in the small containers beside her on the front seat of the car.

Al was upset that she wouldn't allow him to come along with her—but this was a farewell she must say alone. To Keith and to poor, sweet, tormented Gina, whose life truly ended before her third birthday.

Katie parked by the sea. She kicked off her shoes, rolled up her dungarees. Carefully, she pried off the lid of one tin container. Her fingers brushed the fine, white ashes. Overhead a cluster of gulls cawed in their special language as they headed for the cliffs to her right.

Katie left the car, clutching a container in each arm. The white sand warm beneath her feet as she made her way towards the gentle surf. A poem of Tennyson's that Keith had especially loved surfaced from her memory.

"Sunset and evening star / And one clear call for me! / And may there be no moaning of the bar / When I put out to sea."

How easy to say—how difficult to obey.

# Part 5

# Chapter 43

Laura's soaring successes—in Washington, Minneapolis, and Houston—were a bitter mockery in the face of her personal anguish. Katie seemed immobilized by grief. She saw only Annabel—out of college now and a reporter on a new weekly newspaper in town, but even with Annabel she refused to leave the house.

Early in December Jonnie came home on a twenty-four-hour pass. He would not be stationed at Camp Lejeune after all. He was being shipped out to Korea. A little more than five years after V-J Day the world hovered at the brink of World War III. What did her successes mean, Laura railed, when Jonnie was going off to fight in a ridiculous war? Again, she lived for letters from a fighting front.

Laura and their small circle of close friends watched in pain while Rhoda's health deteriorated at an accelerated pace. There were rare days now when she left the house. But on New Year's Day, 1951, Rhoda insisted on giving a small dinner party. Laura was summoned to the house to help her dress for the occasion. Cecile and Maisie were helping Seth oversee dinner preparations.

"Laura, what should I wear?" Rhoda fretted. "It never seems warm enough in the house. I don't know why Seth can't have the furnace adjusted properly."

"Wear the winter white wool," Laura encouraged, knowing Rhoda was asking herself if this would be the last New Year's Day she would ever see. "You'll be warm, and it's beautiful."

Despite the effort it cost her, Rhoda rejected the wheelchair today.

"I'll walk to the dining room," she insisted, appearing heartbreakingly fragile. "We'll walk together." She reached for Laura's arm. "This is so hard for Seth," she whispered. "I'm so nasty to him sometimes, but that's because I have to vent my anger on someone and he's my nearest and dearest."

"Seth understands." Laura fought back tears. "We all do."

"When I'm gone, Laura, I want him to remarry," she said yet again. "He deserves some happiness."

"Rhoda, that's far off." Laura's laugh was tremulous. Most of the time they played a game about Rhoda's illness being more annoying than terminal.

"You're a dear friend, Laura. I bequeath Seth to you," she said with an attempt at frivolity. "I'm glad you came back to Magnolia. I'm glad Seth and I came back. You've given him the career he'd never had in Boston. You've made him an important architect."

"He's a major asset to the company, Rhoda. I don't think we would have come so far without him."

"I envy you," Rhoda said with a sudden, passionate bitterness. "You've done so much with your life. I have nothing to show for the years. Not even a child. A lot of women envy you, Laura."

"Happy New Year!" Cecile darted forward to meet them at the entrance to the dining room, and Laura brushed aside her astonishment at Rhoda's admission. "Rhoda, you look beautiful."


Early in February Iris flew to London to stay with Diana for a week at their Mayfair townhouse. She took a grim pleasure in the knowledge that Peter's children could no longer dictate her exile from London, though she was tormented on each trip to England by the reminder that she had signed away her rights to Peter's houses.

After several party-filled days and evenings Iris borrowed a limousine from Diana to take her up to Noel's school. It was her duty, she told herself grimly, to see her son. But Noel made it clear he was not happy to see his mother. He rejected her offer to take him into London for dinner.

"I wish you wouldn't come to the school," he said bluntly. "It's embarrassing. If you wish to see me, notify the school and they'll send me down to London in a car. After all, I'm Lord Peter Cranford's son. How would it look if my friends at school discovered who my mother really is?"

Iris stared at Noel, taller now than she, with impotent rage.

"You are a contemptible prick," she said through clenched teeth. "I won't bother to come to the school again."

"Just take care of my bills. After all, my share of my father's estate was turned over to you. It's coming to me," he said in triumph, his eyes daring her to deny this.

Two days earlier than planned Iris and Diana flew to Paris and settled in their suite at the Ritz. In the Ritz bar Diana introduced Iris to Greek shipping tycoon Niko Zolotas. Stocky, with penetrating dark eyes and thick hair streaked with gray, he was not handsome in the movie-star mold, but Iris was strangely attracted. And it was obvious the attraction was mutual.

"Niko, we see you so seldom these days," Diana scolded. "You weren't at Lady Mendl's party at Versailles or at that marvelous houseparty in Nice last month at—"

"Diana, I'm a working man," he scolded. "But I'll have my yacht at Nice next month. Why don't you two ladies join me there for a few days?"

"It sounds marvelous," Iris told him. "But I have to be back in Washington in ten days. Do you ever come to Washington?"

"I'll make a point of it," he promised, his eyes holding hers. "Are you in politics?" Now he was laughing at her.

"Only as it applies to real-estate laws that affect my sister's business," Iris drawled. "She's Laura Hunter." Would Niko Zolotas know of Hunter Realty?

"I'm not familiar with American businesses other than those that affect me," he conceded humorously. "But now I have a special interest in Hunter Realty." He withdrew his eyes from Iris for a moment to include Diana in the conversation. "Would you two gorgeous women take pity on a lonely man and have dinner with me tonight?"

"We'd adore it," Diana accepted for them. "We're staying here at the Ritz. What time shall we expect you?"

Iris tried to analyze her attraction to Niko Zolotas—whom she knew, of course, by name, though they'd never met. It was that aura of power he exuded that made him so sexy, she decided. And all that money. He'd made it clear he was interested in her, she thought with anticipation.

Times were changing. Women weren't so fascinated by titles anymore. It was money — mucho money — that was the strong attraction.

Not until she and Diana were inside their suite did Diana tell her that Niko was married.

"But he's always mentioned in the gossip columns as being involved with some celebrity or other." Iris was self-conscious at her ignorance of Niko's marriage.

"Oh, he and his wife have lived apart for a dozen years," Diana shrugged. "She's Catholic — she'll never give him a divorce. She doesn't need his money — she inherited millions when her father died several years ago. Niko goes his way, and Elita goes her way."


Staying at the Georgetown house with Iris late in March, Laura was conscious that Iris was drinking more than normal. Not merely at the endless cocktail parties and dinners but at home. On an evening when she and Iris were entertaining at one of their frequent parties, she watched unhappily as Iris sipped at a martini while they discussed the place cards. Seating at any Washington party was important.

"I was hoping the Cafritzes could come," Iris sighed and reached for the cocktail shaker sitting comfortably close on the dining room buffet. "But they're out of town. He built the new Ambassador Hotel, you know."

"Iris, you're drinking too much," Laura protested.

"Darling, what are you talking about?" Iris lifted an eyebrow in reproach. "I'm used to having a drink at five or six o'clock. If I happen to be at home and not at a party, I just naturally look around for a drink. It's something to pick me up."

"You're growing so dependent on a drink." Normally she would be more diplomatic, Laura thought — but she was worried about Jonnie. "That's dangerous, Iris."

"I don't *have* to have a cocktail," Iris flared. "I'm not a lush."

"I want to be sure you don't ever become one." Laura discarded discretion. "Every time I look at you, you have a drink in your hand."

"Don't lecture me!" Iris swigged down her martini with an urgency that unnerved her sister. "Oh, it's easy for you. You're rich and successful. What have I done with my life?"

Laura was startled that Iris echoed what Rhoda had said on New Year's Day. Didn't they understand she was a driven woman? She fought for success because work kept her from looking backward.

"You're an important part of the business, Iris. You live high. You have friends in the best circles —" She halted herself on the point of mentioning Noel.

"I'm shit," Iris said bitterly. "I have a title because I pushed Peter into marrying me when he was drunk. I live high because you're my sister. I haven't done a damn thing on my own. Even when we were kids, you were the smart one. Papa was proud of you — not me. I —"

"Iris," Laura protested, "Papa adored you. You were his little firebrand. I was the dull, dependable one. I used to wish I could be more like you —"

"Oh God, I don't believe this!" Iris's laughter was jagged. "I was always sure Papa loved you best."

"He loved us both," Laura reproached. "Each in a special way." She paused. How was she to make Iris understand it was urgent to cut back on her drinking? What was the right approach? All at once her mind clutched at Iris's most vulnerable area. "Iris, you've always been so careful about your looks and about staying slim." She forced herself to sound casually curious. "Don't you know liquor does awful things to your face? And to your figure."

Iris stared at her in disbelief.

"Nobody gets fat from cocktails. It's beer."

"And cocktails," Laura added with conviction. "Ask any dietician."

Iris's mouth dropped open in shock. Laura knew her mind was trying to cope with this warning.

"Oh God, I'm going out to Maine Chance after this round of dinners. Elizabeth Arden doesn't allow one drop of liquor on the premises. She's a real Carrie Nation."

"When you come home, you'll have to cut back on the cocktails," Laura reminded. "If you're smart, you'll cut out drinking altogether."

"Laura, how can I live in Washington and not drink?"

"Say you've discovered you're allergic to alcohol," Laura improvised. "Settle for a ginger ale or tomato juice."

"That could be something of a conversation piece." For a moment Iris appeared amused. Then she closed her eyes as though to blot out a sudden, painful image. "Laura, I can't believe it! I'm almost forty-four years old. I can't bear the thought of losing my looks, drooping everywhere. Ugh! But I'm scared to death of plastic surgeons."

"Iris, you look a dozen years younger than you are. If you take decent care of yourself, you'll go on looking younger. You're not a candidate for plastic surgery," she chuckled. "Go off to Maine Chance and be pummeled and pampered," she encouraged. She knew how Iris adored the pink and white splendor of Elizabeth Arden's baroque retreat that catered to the wealthy with the best of social credentials. "And come home feeling marvelous."

"I might meet somebody important there." Iris suddenly seemed less depressed. "For the business, I mean."

"I won't be surprised. You have a gift for collecting people who're important to the business. You do that so much better than I," she said with devious intent and saw Iris react pleasurably.

Yet she was still unnerved by Iris's declaration of envy. She would relinquish all of her success — all her wealth — if it would buy a lifetime of happiness for Jonnie and Katie. She would relinquish it if she could clear Papa's name.

Iris was convinced it was absurd to think she would do this one day. But Seth, bless him, was sure that the day would come — *'like the biblical quotation, Laura — 'to everything there is a season and a time for every purpose under the heavens.' "*

Laura drove up to the house on a hot Saturday afternoon in late May to the sound of laughter from the newly completed swimming pool. She listened intently, a hopeful smile lifting the corners of her mouth. Katie was in the pool with Annabel, both girls laughing. Hope surged through her. Was Katie finally coming out of that awful shell she'd built around herself these past six months?

Laura left the car in the driveway and hurried to the rear of the house. Katie and Annabel were carrying on a mock water battle amid much splashing and much laughter. She was glad both Seth and Maisie had encouraged her to have the pool put in.

"Hi!" Annabel waved and headed towards the edge of the pool.

"Come on in, Mom," Katie encouraged, a lilt in her voice.

"Later," Laura promised. "Right now I just want to collapse under an umbrella and have something cold to drink."

Jewel had heard the car come up the driveway. From the kitchen she'd seen her approach the pool, Laura realized. Now she was walking towards the umbrella-shaded table with a pitcher of ice-cold fruit punch.

"Jewel, that looks so good." Laura sank into a chair while they exchanged a relieved glance. Jewel had said all along that all they could do for Katie was to wait.

The two girls, patting themselves dry with the lush, jade-green towels pulled from the storage unit beside the pool, sat down at the table.

"Mom, Annabel and I have been talking," Katie said with an effort at casualness. "I'd like to go back to school in September."

"Fine, darling." Laura refrained from revealing her inner jubilation. Thank God!

"And after graduation I'll go on to law school. After all," she reminded slyly, "this family has a tradition to keep up. Daddy and you, and now Jonnie and me." Though Katie spoke lightly, Laura knew her daughter meant to assure her that Jonnie would come home when this madness in Korea was over.

Ever worried for Jonnie's safety, terrified when his letters were far apart, Laura devoured every news report from Korea. By June, UN forces had driven a short distance north of the 38th parallel. On June 24 Jacob Malik, the Russian delegate to the United Nations, proposed that truce talks begin. Laura clung to a hope that the fighting might be over. On July 10, truce talks were initiated in what was declared a neutral area, though fighting continued elsewhere. Reports that emerged as the days sped past were discouraging.

Returning with Seth and Everett from a brief trip to the

Midwest, Laura was upset that no letter had arrived from Jonnie. Each night she had called home to check. She was startled to learn that yesterday Corinne had phoned three times from Boston. She took the number Jewel gave her and returned the call. Nothing could have happened to Jonnie, she tried to calm herself, while she waited for someone to pick up the phone at the other end. Jonnie's *mother* would have been notified if he had been hurt. Unless Corinne and he had been secretly married before he left for Korea.

"Hello," a mature feminine voice came over the line.

"Hello, may I please speak to Corinne?" Laura hesitated a moment. "This is Laura Hunter. I'm returning her call."

"Just a moment, Mrs. Hunter."

Corinne's mother knew who she was, Laura recognized abstractly. Probably Jonnie had been to the house often.

"Mrs. Hunter, I hope you don't mind my calling you—" Corinne was faintly breathless. "But I haven't heard from Jonnie in three weeks—and that's unusual. I—I just wanted to know that he's all right."

"I haven't heard from him in about that time, also." Laura fought off panic. "But I'm sure he's fine. You know how crazy overseas mail can be sometimes." Jonnie and Corinne had reconciled before he left for Korea, Laura understood. He had told her in one of his early letters from boot camp that they'd split up—without saying what had come between them. Had Corinne tried to keep him from enlisting? "I'll phone you the minute I hear from him," Laura promised. "And if you should hear first, would you please call me?"

Now each day was a trial. Where was Jonnie? Was he all right? Plagued by insomnia, distracted in the midst of important business conferences, Laura propelled herself to take action. She phoned Iris in Washington to ask her to try to cut through military red tape and come up with information about Jonnie's whereabouts.

The morning after her impassioned conversation with Iris, Laura was summoned from a meeting by Maisie.

"It's Jonnie!" Maisie told her. "He's at Bethesda, Maryland!"

Laura darted from the conference room to her office,

frantic to hear his voice, to be told that he was all right, fearfully aware that marines injured in Korea were flown to Bethesda for treatment. *Had Jonnie been wounded?*

"Jonnie!"

"Hi, Mom—" This might have been a casual call from college.

"Are you all right?" she asked anxiously.

"I'm going to be fine," he soothed. "Just relax, Mom—"

"Tell me what happened," she demanded. But her voice was resonant with relief. "Tell me everything."

Laura listened while Jonnie explained that his leg wound was not serious, but he would be on crutches for two or three weeks. He'd be released from the hospital in three or four days.

"I had to enlist, Mom—but I'm glad as hell to be home."

"I'll be in Bethesda by dinner time," she promised. Bethesda was just ten miles northwest of Washington. "I'll call the crew to have the plane standing by. And Jonnie, call Corinne," she said gently. "She phoned me just yesterday. She's been worried at not hearing from you."

"Right away, Mom." Jonnie seemed pleased that Corinne and she had talked. "You'll like her."

Laura understood; Corinne was her prospective daughter-in-law. Was Corinne Jewish? What was her background? She knew only that Jonnie and Corinne were obviously very much in love. For now that would have to be enough.

Off the phone with Jonnie, Laura sat immobile for a few moments. Thank God, Jonnie was home. He was being discharged. The nightmare was over. Now she reached for the phone again to tell Katie and Jewel that Jonnie was back from Korea and would soon be home.

After she had spoken with Katie, Laura decided on impulse to phone Corinne. She was eager to be on warm terms with the girl Jonnie loved. But she was minutes away from heading for the airport before she was able to reach Corinne.

"Isn't it wonderful?" Corinne's voice exuded a blend of joy and relief and anticipation. "I'm flying down in the morning."

"Come down to Magnolia with Jonnie," Laura invited.

"He'll be discharged in three or four days."

"I'd like that," Corinne said softly. "This is my last day on the job. I'm taking a week off before heading back for my last year of med school. I'm just so relieved that Jonnie's back home. I—" she paused a moment, "I've been chastising myself ever since Jonnie enlisted. I'm sure I sort of pushed him into it."

"He told me it was because of Chuck's death, Corinne. I can't believe you wanted him to enlist."

"Lord, no!" She exhaled in eloquent rejection. "But I think if I hadn't leaned on him so hard about staying in law school, he wouldn't have rushed in that way. I've spent a lot of sleepless nights blaming myself—and being so scared that he wouldn't come home. I know I was wrong to push him the way I did when he wants so much to become an architect." *Jonnie preferred architecture to law?*

"He never said a word to me," Laura said after a moment. "He was afraid, too, of disappointing me. He knew how proud I was that he was following in his father's footsteps. But I want Jonnie to do whatever makes him happy. And nothing would make me prouder than to see Jonnie an architect. It's in the blood," she said humorously. "And we have a business waiting to use his talents. He won't go back to law school," Laura said with vigor. "He'll go to Harvard's School of Design."


Handsome in his marine uniform—cursing at the awkwardness of crutches, Jonnie waited with Corinne for the housekeeper at the Georgetown house to admit them. Iris was spending a week at a houseparty on some yacht anchored at Bar Harbor, but before flying home Mom had arranged for them to stay at the house tonight. Tomorrow the company plane would take them down to Magnolia.

"Jonnie, your mother's so filthy rich it's unbelievable," Corinne joshed.

"Sugar, you'll learn to live with it," Jonnie promised. He was proud of his mother's amazing success, and he enjoyed the luxuries this provided, remembering the rough Depression years in New York.

The housekeeper welcomed them warmly and showed

them to their rooms.

"Will you be wanting a snack before retiring?" she asked. "I can have it ready in no time."

"Thank you, no, Mrs. O'Brien," Jonnie smiled. "We've had a full evening, and we have to be at Washington Airport by eight tomorrow morning for our flight to Magnolia."

They decorously went to their separate bedrooms. Jonnie listened for the sound of Mrs. O'Brien's retreating footsteps, then left his room to go to Corinne's.

"What took you so long?" she laughed, closing the door behind them while Jonnie made his way on crutches to the bed.

"I'm hampered," he reminded high-spiritedly while he sat at the edge of the bed and handed Corinne his crutches. "But not now —" He reached to pull her beside him. God, he'd missed Corinne all these rotten months.

"Jonnie, it's all right?" she asked solicitously while he pulled her into his arms.

"Honey, it was my leg that got shot up," he laughed. "And it was worth it," he mused, "to bring me back home." It felt so great, just to hold her in his arms this way.

"The winter was a nightmare. We were frozen in foxholes, chopping away with our frost-bitten hands to dig ice-slivered beans out of a can. Everybody was sick with colds and sore throats. Then the hot weather arrived and we sweated like pigs, with no ice for drinking water, no way of relieving the heat. We'd have given a month's pay for a dish of ice cream or a bottle of cold soda. But don't get me wrong," he chuckled. "I didn't get shot deliberately."

"Jonnie, I kept blaming myself," Corinne whispered. "I pushed you into enlisting. I knew you —"

"Ssh," he interrupted, a long hunger suddenly ravenous. "We'll have plenty of time to talk later." His hands moved to unbutton his shirt while his eyes made love to her.

Corinne rose to her feet, kicked off her shoes, and reached for the hem of her dress. With one swift gesture she stood before him in panties and bra, her long lean legs tanned to a mellow gold. The creamy whiteness of her small, huge-nippled breasts were revealed as she ripped away her bra.

"Oh, baby—" Jonnie cleared his throat in a sudden surge of impatience. He remembered the endless stream of nights when he'd thought about Corinne like this.

Corinne dropped to her knees to untie his shoelaces and remove his shoes while he contrived to discard his trousers without standing on the injured leg.

"Jonnie, I was so scared," she whispered when they lay entangled along the bed. "The nights were worst of all—"

"For me, too." His hands roamed about her supple nakedness while his mouth reached to silence her, his body trembling with an urgency to fuse with hers.

"You're sure this is all right?" Corinne sought again for reassurance when he lifted himself above and thrust between the long, golden thighs that he thought the most exciting in the world.

"The greatest," he murmured hotly. "Oh, Corinne, how did I survive so long away from you?"


Jonnie lay back against the mound of pillows with Corinne nestled in his arms, her silken blond hair fanned across his chest. How many times he'd imagined this when he was rotting away in Korea!

"I can't believe I'm really back home. And that both you and Mom understand about my not going back to law school." A flicker of anxiety disturbed the perfect moments. "Now I have to worry about getting into architectural school. I'll never make it for the first term," he sighed. "I hate the thought of wasting time now."

"Jonnie, everything is going to work out." One slender hand caressed his hip. "You'll be at the School of Design in Boston, and I'll be at a hospital in New York for my internship and residency. We'll be together every weekend and all the holidays. We—"

"What about trying for an internship at a Boston hospital?" he asked. "So we can be together every night. Oh, we'll get married first," he grinned, "so your parents don't raise a storm."

"I think it's important for me to try for a New York hospital," Corinne told him. "After all, that's the city where we want to establish ourselves. I know it'll be tough for me to make it into an important hospital. The medical profession is still back in the nineteenth century when it comes to women doctors. But women *are* making it into New York hospitals. I'll carry on until somebody hires me," she said grimly. "And when you graduate from the School of Design, you'll move into an important New York architectural firm for your apprenticeship. Jonnie—" She lifted herself to gaze down at him in glorious anticipation. "We're going to have such a wonderful life together when we have the nonsense of school behind us!"

But in a corner of his mind—while he swung Corinne onto her back again in a fresh surge of passion—Jonnie tried to cope with the prospect of spending his life in New York. Corinne had accepted his switch from law to architecture. She would never accept their living in Magnolia. She couldn't understand what home meant to him. . . .

# Chapter 44

Laura sat tensely at her desk, drumming on the desk top with a forefinger while Seth carried on a lengthy conversation with one of the powers-that-be at the Harvard School of Design. She refused to believe it was too late for Jonnie to be accepted and registered for the fall term.

"Yes, he's done well on his summer jobs here with me," Seth said with conviction. "He has a real feeling for architecture. I think the field will be enriched by his presence in the years to come."

Laura waited, mentally inventorying their efforts to have Jonnie admitted to the architectural program. Ian Macmillan had prodded a Massachusetts congressman to talk to Harvard officials on Jonnie's behalf. She herself had spent a brutally hot day dashing around the Capital until she acquired an impressive letter from the War Department, attesting to Jonnie's service record in the Marine Corps.

"And let me point out one thing more, if I may." Seth reached for the letter from the War Department and read its contents into the phone while Laura watched anxiously. "Yes, he *is* an exceptional young man." Seth's eyes telegraphed victory to Laura. "We all appreciate this very much."

"Jonnie's accepted?" Laura barely waited for Seth to put down the phone.

"He's accepted. In eight days he'll be registered for his first year at the Harvard School of Design!"


Too stimulated by the activities of the day to sleep, Laura settled in a chair by a bedroom window and tried to focus on the current edition of *Architectural Forum*. She glanced up at the sound of a light tap at her door.

"Mom?" Jonnie called tentatively.

"Come in, darling." It was wonderful to have Jonnie home, she thought with recurrent gratitude. She wished that school would not begin so soon.

"I'm too excited to sleep." His grin was wry.

"Me, too," Laura smiled. "Come sit over here with me." Jonnie crossed to the chair across from her own, carefully lowered himself into it, and dropped his crutches against the wall.

"I can't believe I'm starting school this term. Only you could have pulled it off." His eyes glowed with love.

"A lot of people helped." Instinctively she knew he had come here to talk about Corinne.

"Corinne and I had thought we'd wait till we both had school behind us before we got married. But now that seems crazy. We want to get married in June, when she graduates from med school." He hesitated. "She isn't Jewish."

"I gathered that." Laura fought to appear calm, but her heart was pounding.

"Corinne isn't religious. Her father is a lapsed Catholic and her mother's Unitarian. Later—when we're ready to settle down and raise a family," Jonnie pushed ahead, "Corinne will convert. But for now we'd like to be married by a judge in a civil ceremony."

"That's for you and Corinne to decide," Laura said carefully, once again the old obsession surfacing in her mind. How was she to clear Papa's name? Not just for Jonnie and Katie—for their children. *How long must she wait?* "What about Corinne's parents?" Laura asked. "Will they be upset that she's marrying out of her faith?"

"Corinne doesn't think so," Jonnie said after a faint deliberation. "But whatever, we'll be married in June. She's going to talk to them when we're back in Boston."

"I want you to be happy—and fulfilled," Laura said. "For the children it's important that they know who they are. Sometimes I worry that I didn't give you and Katie a solid Jewish background."

"You did fine, Mom. Katie and I have always known we're Jewish—and we're proud of our heritage." He frowned in thought. "When Katie and I were kids we never thought about being Jewish—except for a couple of times when stupid red-neck students in the school here made nasty remarks. You didn't bring us up to look for segregation," he grinned. "You taught us to like people for what they are."

"That's the way it should always be." Laura felt the sting of tears in her eyes. "Until the world can learn to live without bigotry, we'll never be truly at peace."

"I realized that in Korea." Jonnie was somber. "I hated the racist attitudes of some soldiers towards Koreans—it didn't matter whether they were South Koreans or North Koreans. They weren't white-skinned. They were Gooks— animals, with no value placed on their lives."

"Let's pray the war in Korea ends soon," Laura said. World War II had to be fought. What would be gained when this one was over?

"Thank God, it's over for me." Jonnie managed a faint smile. "Selfish of me, sure—but I want to get on with my life."


Laura's pleasure that both Jonnie and Katie were back in school and in pursuit of careers they relished was overshadowed by the state of Rhoda's health. Shortly after the beginning of the new year Rhoda seemed hours from death. She rallied, but the doctors warned that the next such attack could mean the end.

Laura urged Seth to take time off from his exhausting efforts on the company's newest project, but he admitted it was work that held him together. By spring Rhoda was under around-the-clock nursing care. Seth confided that most of the time she was too heavily sedated to be aware of his presence at her bedside.

Laura was elated when Katie phoned from college to report she had been accepted at Columbia Law.

"Mom, I can't believe it's really happening," Katie bubbled. "I know it won't be easy, but I'm prepared to work my butt off. I want to go into criminal law," she pinpointed, suddenly serious. "Contracts and torts would drive me up the wall. But criminal cases involve people."

"I agree, darling. I'm so happy you were accepted at Columbia."

But off the phone Laura confessed to Maisie that she

dreaded the distance that Columbia Law School would put between Katie and herself. If Katie went to Emory, she could be home every weekend.

"Laura, you're flying off to some place or other half the time anyway," Maisie pointed out. "Look at all the time you're up in Washington these days. With the company plane always on call you can fly up to New York whenever you like. You'll see almost as much of Katie as if she were at Emory." Maisie chuckled. "You manage to see Jonnie up in Boston regularly."

"Katie can stay at the Sutton Place apartment. I'm glad I've held on to it all these years." At intervals she or Iris—or the two of them—lighted there for a few days at a time.

Jonnie phoned to say that after some initial anger, Corinne's parents were reconciled to her marrying him in a civil ceremony. "Corinne is trying to keep the guest list small," he reported in a later phone call, "but it's growing so large her mother insists the reception be held at their country club."

"Our side will be small," Laura reminded. "I'm glad Corinne has a bunch of aunts and uncles and cousins for you to share." And for their children to share one day. "It's beautiful to sit down to dinner in the midst of a large family." That was something she was unable to give Jonnie and Katie. "Does Corinne have any word yet about where she'll intern?"

"She's had only one offer." Jonnie's tone turned serious. "A small private hospital in the Boston suburbs. She's furious that she's having this kind of problem. Her grades have been great, and she's graduating from a prestigious school—but for a woman it's still rough."

"I know," Laura sympathized. This was what Katie would be facing when she graduated from law school. But at least Katie would be able to open her own office if need be. Corinne had to serve her internship and residency before she could go into practice. "People say the situation is changing for women, but we don't see it yet."

"I'm glad Corinne will be here in Boston with me," Jonnie said. Laura heard the undercurrent of guilt in his voice that he felt this way. "But I hate to see her so disappointed."

"It'll work out," Laura comforted. "Corinne's the kind

that will learn in any situation."

Laura and Iris attended Katie's graduation in Athens. Jonnie was unable to come down to join them. Three days later Laura, Iris, and Katie flew up to Boston for Corinne's graduation from medical school and the imminent wedding.

As the plane approached the Boston airport, Laura gazed out the window without seeing. To no one did she reveal her disappointment that Jonnie and Corinne would not have a religious ceremony. She thought back to her two marriages and those of Iris and Katie.

Her marriage to Bernie was a civil ceremony because it was the least expensive and they had so little money. Her marriage to Phil had also been a civil ceremony because they had so little time and a need for secrecy. Iris had married Peter at sea. Katie and Keith had been married by a judge. How ironic that Papa—once a Talmudic student—should have children and grandchildren married outside their religion.

For Laura the next seventy-two hours raced past with dizzying swiftness. Corinne's parents, her younger brother and sister, were pleasant, yet Laura sensed they were not entirely comfortable with Corinne's in-laws. They were impressed by the family money, she assessed, but having difficulty accepting their Jewishness.

Jonnie and Corinne were married by a local judge who was a friend and neighbor in the pleasant living room of the Wells's suburban colonial cape. The marriage ceremony was witnessed only by family plus Jonnie's law-school buddy, Marty Coleman. Laura intercepted the startled, nervous glance exchanged by Mr. and Mrs. Wells when Jonnie arrived with Marty. Obviously neither Jonnie nor Corinne had mentioned that Marty was a Negro. He was an intelligent, warm, close friend, and Jonnie and Corinne never thought of the color of his skin.

"It's a lovely reception," Laura told Corinne's mother.

Mrs. Wells's face lighted. "Corinne's so excited that you're giving them a European honeymoon." Jonnie and Corinne would spend three weeks in London, Paris, Vienna, and Venice, following the route Jonnie and Katie had taken with Iris thirteen years ago when they helped smuggle seven children out of Austria. "Though, of course, I'll be scared to death till they're back home again—what with all the flying."

"We're looking forward to having them home with us for the rest of the summer," Laura said. Jonnie would be working with Seth. And Katie would keep Corinne entertained. She was so pleased that Katie and Corinne had liked each other from their first encounter, both embarking on careers that were a challenge to women. That was a strong bond. "It was so good that Corinne landed an internship here in Boston."

"I wish they weren't so determined to settle in New York." Mrs. Wells sighed and Laura tensed. "They could have fine careers right here."


Laura was at home watching the presidential election returns on television with Maisie and Everett and Cecile and Barry when Seth called to say that Rhoda had fallen into a coma and was being rushed to Magnolia hospital.

"I'll meet you at the hospital," Laura said over the din of the election returns.

"Rhoda?" Cecile asked and Laura nodded, her throat too constricted for speech.

Immediately the five of them left for the hospital. They remained until almost two in the morning—when Rhoda's tenuous hold on life gave way.

"Seth, she'd suffered enough," Laura said gently. "She's at peace now."

His close circle of friends did everything that needed to be done. They were with him—along with those who remembered Rhoda from childhood—when she was laid to rest. Jewel moved in and out of the Goldman house with trays of food, grieving along with Laura. There was a pact among them not to leave Seth alone during the seven days he remained at home.

"I knew it was coming," Seth said exhaustedly to Laura on the seventh evening while she urged him to eat from the dinner tray Jewel had brought over a few minutes earlier. "I feel so guilty that I'm alive and she's gone."

"Seth, you're coming back to the office tomorrow," Laura

said resolutely. "Rhoda would want you to get on with your life." She took a deep breath. "I want to endow a small hospital in town to care for the indigent, without regard to race, religion, or color. It'll be called the Rhoda Goldman Hospital. And I want you to design it."

"Laura, what would I do without you?" The naked love in his eyes unnerved her. "Rhoda always said you were the best thing that ever happened to us—you and the kids."

As part of her efforts to draw Seth out of his grief, Laura invited him, along with Maisie and Everett, to the house once or twice every week for what she called "working dinners." She knew he agonized silently over the last troubled years of Rhoda's life. She suspected he was guilt-ridden about the feelings that neither Seth nor she ever voiced but nonetheless were always there.

The Rhoda Goldman Hospital was already on the drafting table. In addition Laura was surveying the possibilities of a housing development and a shopping mall in Long Island, New York.

In February Iris pressed Laura to fly with her to Paris for the spring collections. "Darling, you can stay just three days and fly back. I'll stay on for another four or five days. You have to show yourself in Paris originals, the way we're always being photographed for the magazines." Laura had long ago retained a prestigious public relations firm to keep her name and face—and Iris's—before the public. It was part of building a real-estate empire. "Let them be fitted properly in the Paris workroom this time. They're never quite the same when I bring them back and you take them to that little dressmaker in Magnolia."

"My schedule's too hectic to take off time right now," Laura refused.

"You need a few days away from the business, Laura. You're looking so drained these days."

Laura tensed. If she were looking drained, it wasn't because of the pressure of business. That was part of her lifestyle. She was exhausted from fighting her inner feelings for Seth. She was still stunned from Cecile's revelation last week. *"Sugar, I know nothing's happening between Seth and you, but half the town has thought for years that the two of you are having a passionate affair. Maybe because it's so obvious he's in love with you."*

She knew that Seth was only waiting for his year of mourning to be over to talk about their feelings for each other. But how could they marry? First Bernie, then Phil. To marry Laura Roth was to court a violent death. How could she allow Seth to take that chance, too?

After much cajoling—and mainly because she knew she needed to put distance between Seth and herself for a few days, Laura finally agreed to the Paris jaunt. Like Iris and Katie, she loved beautiful clothes, though so often she allowed Iris to choose for her because it was expedient. It would be exciting to see the Paris collections. She would allow herself to be madly extravagant.

Laura and Iris flew to Paris, installed themselves at the Ritz, and prepared to visit the couture houses. Laura adored Dior's tulip line, the dresses molded to the body from just under the bust to the hem, with off-the-shoulder necklines and waists gently emphasized. It was feminine and romantic.

In the elegant white-and-gray Dior salon, Laura and Iris encountered Niko Zolotas with his daughter Alexie, a sullen and arrogant divorcée at twenty-four. Instantly, observing the exchange of secret smiles, Laura knew that Iris and Niko had arranged this encounter. She remembered, too, gossip items that hinted that Niko had persuaded his wife to petition the Sacred Rota of the Vatican for an annulment of their marriage.

Before Laura and Iris left the Dior salon they had agreed to have dinner with Niko. Back in their suite at the Ritz, Laura confronted Iris.

"You knew Niko would be in Paris, Iris." Did she plan on marrying him if his wife secured an annulment?

"Laura, don't be angry." Iris switched on her charismatic charm. "He'd mentioned when I saw him in Palm Beach that he'd be in Paris with Alexie. I didn't want to show up alone, as though I was chasing after him. This way we're two sisters coming to Paris for the collections."

"Has he said anything to you about his wife's getting an annulment?" Laura was deliberately blunt. She was uneasy at the prospect of Iris's becoming seriously involved with Niko Zolotas.

559

"No. Those things can go on forever, even with people as rich as Niko and Elita. But in a crazy way Niko fascinates me. And it's not just all that money," she laughed. "It's Niko the man. I can see him screaming at a woman, but he'd never hit her. They could fight one minute and make passionate love the next. We have," she admitted eloquently. "But Niko's hard to pin down. He's always chasing from one part of the world to another. He's like you, Laura. Business takes first place in his life."

"Iris, that's not true!" Laura was stung by this assessment. "The business is terribly important to me, but family always comes first."

"Who knows?" Iris pushed ahead with a touch of bravado. "Maybe one day you'll have Niko as an investor."

"Iris, why would Niko Zolotas invest with Hunter Realty?" In truth, for tax purposes Laura's funds were divided among more than a dozen corporations. "He's one of the richest men in the world."

"And you're one of the richest women in America," Iris flipped. "God, Laura, when we climbed on to that Seaboard Airline train for New York, did you ever dream what would happen?"


Before flying home to Magnolia Laura spent two days at the Sutton Place apartment with Katie. It was exciting to see Katie's involvement with her law studies at Columbia. She was pleased that Katie and Jonnie kept in touch with each other, and that Katie and Corinne had become real friends.

In Cambridge for a day, Laura had an early dinner with Jonnie at the Wursthaus on Harvard Square—the darkly paneled, wood-beamed restaurant favored by Harvard students and faculty. Corinne was on duty at the hospital and probably would be tied up for the next twenty-four hours, Jonnie reported apologetically, while they settled themselves in a comfortable booth.

"Every once in a while she gets these back-to-back shifts and sleeps at the hospital."

"I imagine the first year is the roughest," Laura said sympathetically. "Like with law school."

"We knew it wouldn't be easy with me at school and with her at the hospital, but it'll be worth it. It wasn't easy for you and Dad, either."

"No," Laura smiled, "but it was worth it."

Laura arrived back in Magnolia the evening before what was to have been a very private ground-breaking ceremony for the Rhoda Goldman Hospital. Maisie was unrepentant about having allowed this to escalate. Sitting with Laura and Everett before an open fire in the Hunter living room while Jewel circulated among them with rich, fragrant coffee and wedges of her locally famous hot pecan pie, Maisie defended her stand.

"Laura, this is a major event in Magnolia. You're the best thing that ever happened to this town. Why do you have to hide every act of charity? Let people know what you're doing."

"I thought it would be easier for Seth if we kept it subdued," Laura alibied. Was it her personal reaction to old Mrs. Tannenbaum's much publicized philanthropies? For a moment she could hear Papa's voice: *"Mrs. Tannenbaum's compassion extends to how much newspaper space the charity will bring her."*

"Maisie's right," Everett intervened gently. "Let people know the good you do. It might be useful in paving the way for future projects you want to see through. And I'm not talking about business," he chuckled because he anticipated her reproof. "For instance, your stand on civil rights. Let your thinking help to shape what's going to happen here in Magnolia in coming years."

Laura's eyes caught the headline on the *Magnolia Herald,* which lay across a corner of the oversized coffee table. It was better to be proclaimed the benefactor behind a new hospital than the daughter of a convicted murderer, she told herself with bitter humor.

"This newspaper coverage of the hospital makes it harder for Seth to put Rhoda's death behind him," she managed a final reproach.

"Laura, the man's past his mourning period. Will you stop being morbid?" Maisie exchanged an exasperated glance with Everett.

"All right, I'll be there as scheduled," Laura agreed. "Now

tell me what's happening with the bids for the hospital equipment."

Only minutes after Maisie and Everett left the house, Laura received a phone call from Barry.

"Laura, we've got to take some action," he said without preliminaries. "Judge Slocum has just organized a White Citizens' Council here in Magnolia."

"Oh, God!" Laura was shocked.

"A lot of Southerners are scared to death of all the Supreme Court decisions that have been handed down in favor of the civil rights leaders. *Shelly* vs. *Kraemer, Sweatt* vs. *Painter*. The NAACP is moving into the courts like never before. Right now they're fighting against segregation at the secondary- and primary-school levels. *Brown* vs. *Board of Education*."

"Barry, these White Citizens' Councils could pop up all over." Laura flinched at the prospect.

"They will," Barry agreed, "if the Supreme Court rules in favor of Brown. They'll go after every Negro who tries to register and vote. They'll target every member of the NAACP. And any white who shows sympathy will be in for a rough time. That's the likes of you and me," he warned. "It's the Ku Klux Klan in new dress."

"What are you doing about it?" For a while the Slocums had lost some of their strength in this town. Now, by generating fear, they meant to regain that power.

"I've been feeling out people. We've set up a meeting for eight o'clock tomorrow night." He chuckled. "It was held up until you were back home."

"I'll be there. Where are we meeting?"

"At your house," he told her and she smiled. "Your living room can accommodate more people than mine. I took it for granted you'd be agreeable."

So it was to be Laura Hunter vs. the Slocums once again. But when would she be able to prove to the world that Derek Slocum murdered Tammy Lee Johnson? Would his father forever be able to shield him from justice?

Laura woke to a gloriously sunny morning, the air crisp but sweet with a promise of spring. By nine sharp she would be at the ground-breaking ceremonies for the hospital. Photographers and reporters from the local newspapers would be present—including the *Magnolia Journal,* controlled by Judge Slocum.

By 8 A.M. she was in the office as usual. This was her time to make calls to construction sites in the same time zone as Magnolia. At quarter of nine, while she sipped at the coffee Nora had brought to her desk, Seth appeared in the door of her office.

"We have to leave in a few minutes," he reminded.

"I'm ready." She rose from her chair, reached for the jacket to her suit. "Any more talk about a possible strike among the electricians?" she asked while Seth held the jacket for her.

"It won't affect us," he reported. "It's the Slocum construction jobs they're fighting."

"If we keep clear of strikes and have decent weather, the hospital could be finished in a year," she said with anticipation.

"That's right." But his eyes revealed a disconcerting frustration. "Then you'll come up with a new philanthropy for Magnolia. Laura, why do you punish yourself this way? You don't have to spend the rest of your life making amends for the crime people *think* your father committed."

"Seth, you know," she said unsteadily. "I won't be at peace until the whole world knows he didn't kill that little girl." Let Seth believe it was Papa who stood between them. It would be easier that way.

"It'll happen," he repeated. For the hundredth time. "One day—when you least expect it—someone will pull a thread that will unravel the whole cloth of duplicity which convicted your father. But you should enjoy each day that's given to you. Lord, Laura, I hate to see you denying yourself all that your father would want you to have!"

"Let's go in your car." Laura insulated herself from Seth's impassioned declaration. "Pat has the limo at the service station this morning."

A crowd had already assembled when they arrived. In her smart Chanel suit Laura took her place beside Seth. Her smile was radiant as she watched along with the others as Seth dug the shovel into the ground and lifted up the first earth from the site of the new Rhoda Goldman Hospital.

"Yeah, that's her," Laura heard a man standing in the road to the gathering say to a young boy at his side. "Buildin' a hospital for niggers and poor white trash. She thinks her crowd's gonna make us take them niggers into our schools." He spat on the ground. "Over my dead body."

Seth was right, she thought somberly. Magnolia had some tough years ahead.

After the heated meeting in her living room Laura called Katie in New York to tell her what was happening in Magnolia. She knew that Katie was following the cases that the NAACP was bringing before the Supreme Court. While she professed to be concerned only with criminal law, Katie was emotionally involved in the growing civil rights movement.

"Jonnie told me that Marty Coleman says it's wonderful that Eisenhower appointed Earl Warren chief justice of the Supreme Court," Katie told Laura. "Warren is a liberal."

Though Katie had lived in Magnolia since she was eight, she had early absorbed the family's Northern liberalism.

Laura told herself that not all the Magnolia citizenry would be taken in by Judge Slocum's rhetoric about the dangers that lay ahead for the South in the face of black aggression. Being close to Fort Benning—like Columbus, Magnolia was exposed to a more cosmopolitan world than many Southern towns. Military men from all over the country—and now an influx of foreign officers—were stationed at Benning, along with their families. They brought with them a cultural diversity. And since the war there had been an influx of civilian newcomers from the Northeast. Magnolia would handle whatever arose, she promised herself. Still, Laura and her group of concerned citizens carefully monitored the efforts of the White Citizens' Council.

In June, Jonnie and Corinne came home for a brief visit. His delight at being in Magnolia evoked fresh frustration in Laura. Jonnie wanted to live here. Was she being an interfering mother in wracking her brains for a way to bring Jonnie and Corinne home on a permanent basis?

Corinne was exhausted from the super-long hours spent in the hospital. She talked with rage—to Laura and Katie—about the hostility she often encountered as a woman intern.

"Not just among the doctors and other interns," Corinne emphasized. "On the wards. Some patients refuse to consider me as anything more than a nurse. Not just male patients!" She bristled in recall. "Women patients, too."

"I'll run into the same thing," Katie surmised and Laura nodded. "But times *are* changing. I mean, women proved themselves during World War II. Men can't expect them to be satisfied with the old ways forever."

Katie was working for the summer in Barry's law offices, along with Chet. Laura and Cecile reluctantly conceded that Katie and Chet would never be romantically involved—their relationship was in the sister-brother vein. Maisie and Jewel fretted over Katie's avoidance of the casual Southern summer socializing, but she seemed happy to be engrossed in work.

On July 27 the Korean armistice was at last signed by UN and Communist delegates at Panmunjon. The peninsula was basically back where it had been when the North Koreans had first advanced except for a minor shift in the dividing line. Laura was tuned in to a television newscaster late that evening when Jonnie called.

"It's finally over," he said somberly, and Laura knew he was thinking of Chuck.

"At what a terrible cost," Laura said in pain. "Do you realize, Jonnie, that in my lifetime American soldiers have died in three wars? When will the world learn to live in peace?"

"When the Soviet Union realizes the whole world doesn't have to be communistic," Jonnie said tiredly. "When they understand it's better to spend money on housing and schools and hospitals than on guns and tanks and fighter planes."

"Jonnie, I'll be up in New York next week on business." After intensive probing Everett agreed it was time for them to move into the luxury housing market in Manhattan. Prudent investigation showed a healthy market existed for this and was apt to increase in the decade ahead. "Why don't you meet me in Gloucester for a day? I think it would be a good investment to buy a house there. And you and Corinne could put it to good use." When Jonnie was home earlier in the month, she had listened to Seth and him talk about Gloucester with the same love she felt for Montauk.

"Mom, that would be great! Just tell me when."

Within a week Laura and Jonnie were being shown ocean-front property by a Gloucester real-estate broker, whom Maisie had contacted by phone. Laura wished to buy property that was immediately available.

"I think you'll like the Lawford house," the broker explained with low-keyed assurance as he drove them along endless rock-lined coves, with verdant hills rising to their left. "They're in the midst of a divorce and anxious to sell the place. It's a cozy four-bedroom house overlooking the Atlantic and it's available fully furnished."

She enjoyed being here with Jonnie, breathing in the salt air, admiring the view of green waves crashing against the dark clusters of rocks that jutted up with an air of omnipotence. Jonnie and Corinne would relax out here, even if they could come out for no more than a day at a time. They could drive from their Cambridge apartment in forty minutes.

Laura knew even before she emerged from the broker's car that this was the house she would buy. It was a hundred-year-old white-clapboard two-story colonial that clung to the edge of a low cliff overhanging a charming cove. Laura envisioned earlier generations of women standing on the widow's walk watching for their menfolk. Jonnie was intrigued by the house. Seth would love it, she thought subconsciously.

The broker was startled by Laura's insistence on buying it on the spot.

"Until such time as the closing can be held, I'd like to rent it," she compromised imperiously and dug into her purse for her checkbook. "Jonnie, you and Corinne might even be able to commute to Boston while the weather is good."

They left the broker to handle the business details and went off for an early dinner at a restaurant overlooking the harbor laden with fishing boats.

566

"Nothing can beat seafood or fish in Gloucester," Jonnie proclaimed when they had ordered and watched for the sunset that would soon lend glorious color to the harbor.

"Montauk," Laura teased playfully and was all at once awash with nostalgia. "One day I must show you and Seth the Frank Lloyd Wright houses out there."

"I miss working with Seth," Jonnie said wistfully. "I learn so much from him." Her children were on first-name terms with those close to her—a custom that shocked others in Magnolia. "How long has it been since Rhoda died?"

"It'll be a year in November. He's making arrangements already for the unveiling." A year after death in the Jewish tradition.

She didn't want to think about the unveiling because it would formally mark the end of Seth's period of mourning. She knew he was waiting for that before pressing her for a closer relationship. But how could she marry Seth? She loved him too much to expose him to the awful curse that seemed to hang over their family.

"Mom?" Jonnie's eyes asked the question he was afraid to voice.

"Jonnie, I've been secretly plotting a major project for Magnolia." She fought to derail his thoughts. "I haven't even discussed it with Seth or Everett yet. Several years ago I bought a large tract of land outside the city limits. It was going for almost nothing. Now, with the population growing the way it is, I envision a whole new town there." She was talking with compulsive swiftness, but she sensed Jonnie's interest. "If we play our cards right, we could see it annexed by the city."

"Then it would be able to utilize the city's services." Jonnie followed her thinking. "But haven't the Slocums been talking about a major development at the edge of town? Will the market be able to absorb both?"

"The Slocums are planning to move in the other direction, Jonnie. I think that's the wrong way to go. And they're talking about all luxury housing. I see a mixture of luxury plus middle-income houses and apartments, built around a huge shopping center. A model development." She paused, faintly breathless. "We'll call it Hunter Woods."

"You'll be bucking the Slocums again," Jonnie reminded.

"They play dirty."

"When have I ever been afraid of the Slocums?" Laura was almost defiant. "I know Seth will come up with a magnificent overall design. And you're going into your last year at Harvard." She was charged with anticipation. "By the time we get this project moving, you'd be able to come in with us. How wonderful if you could serve your apprenticeship with Seth!"

"Yeah, Mom." She saw the hunger in his eyes. "But where I'll be depends on where Corinne serves her residency."

"We'll see what comes up." Laura refused to relinquish her high spirits. Everett would be upset that she was overextending herself—but Hunter Woods just might entice Jonnie back home. It was time Corinne considered her husband's future. Magnolia was where he belonged.

## Chapter 45

Leaning back in the Cadillac limousine that had been waiting to bring her into New York from Idlewild Airport after her arrival from Paris, Iris thought for the dozenth time about Niko's odd preoccupation during their five days aboard his yacht, anchored in view of his newly purchased chateau on a Monte Carlo hillside. The house in Monte Carlo was now his official residence, meant to protect him from the heavy taxation he considered a personal affront.

Several times a year, at Bar Harbor, Palm Beach, St. Tropez, Monte Carlo, she was a guest on Niko's yacht. On all previous occasions Niko was host at a series of extravagant parties. This time—except for the crew—they had been in virtual seclusion. At first she had suspected he meant to bring up talk of marriage—since Elita had won the annulment. Not that Niko ever mentioned it. But it was splashed over all the gossip columns. He'd been so sweet, so tender, so solicitous of her comfort. They had not fought once. They had made love often.

It was the new business deal that was on his mind, Iris told herself. Would Niko never be satisfied? It wasn't the money that fascinated him—it was showing the world how brilliant he was. But up until now business had not interfered in their own relationship.

She hoped he'd be the old Niko when he came to New York late next month. She'd promised to come up from Washington, D.C. to be with him. Laura might disapprove of her affair with Niko—but she knew that Niko's presence at a party at the Sutton Place apartment assured a very monied guest list.

Iris found both Mrs. O'Brien and Katie waiting up to welcome her. Katie had come up from Magnolia a few days early because she was moving into an apartment close to the Columbia campus, Iris recalled. Was she having a fling with some man or just tired of commuting between Sutton Place and Broadway and 114th Street? Katie was twenty-five and beautiful—how long could she mourn that poor, unhappy husband?

"I'll bring you a tray," Mrs. O'Brien said warmly. "I know about airplane food. Coffee and Nova Scotia and cream cheese on pumpernickel?"

"That'll be lovely," Iris smiled and Mrs. O'Brien hurried off.

"Mom said you'd be in Paris for the Dior collection," Katie said avidly. Laura knew she was staying in Paris for two days before she joined Niko on the yacht. "I suppose the clothes were fabulous?"

"Katie, that man Dior has done it again," Iris said gaily. "He's raised hems up to the knees. At the Ritz all the women were sending out their dresses to be shortened. But we don't have to worry, darling. In this family we all have great legs."

"I don't know why I'm so fascinated by clothes," Katie laughed. "All I'll be wearing when school opens next week will be slacks and shirts."

"You graduate in June," Iris remembered in triumph. "I'll be there for sure."

"Oh, a friend of yours called several times today," Katie reported. "Debbie Macmillan. She thought you'd be arriving yesterday. She's at the Pierre. She said to phone even if it was late."

"They must have closed up the house at Bar Harbor, and she's in town to buy clothes," Iris surmised, glancing at her watch. "Maybe I'll give Debbie a buzz now. We can have lunch tomorrow and catch up on gossip. Tell Mrs. O'Brien I'll be right back."

Iris left the living room and hurried down the hall to her bedroom. Thank God for air conditioning, she thought. Manhattan was enveloped in one of its beastly heat waves. She sat at the edge of her canopied bed and reached for the phone. What was so important that Debbie wanted her to call even if it was late?

"Hello—" Debbie's gracious congressman's-wife voice greeted her.

"I just arrived at the apartment a few minutes ago." Iris

was slightly apologetic. "But Katie said I was to call even if it was late."

"Iris, I'm so upset. How could Niko do this to you?"

"Do what to me?" All at once she was ice cold.

"He said nothing to you in Monte Carlo?" Debbie's voice was strident in indignation. "For the past three days the columns have been full of it!"

"Full of what, Debbie?" Iris demanded impatiently.

"His engagement to DeeDee Metaxas!"

"Niko didn't say a word." She paused. "Debbie, maybe it's just gossip. You know how columnists make something out of nothing—" But her heart was pounding.

"Her father is giving DeeDee and Niko an engagement party next week at his chateau on Cap d'Antibes. Everybody's talking about it."

"I met her last year at a party on Niko's yacht. She was there with her father. Debbie, she's about twenty!" Pretty but terribly self-conscious, Iris recalled.

"The rumor is that DeeDee's father is anxious to link his fortune with Niko's billions. DeeDee was born when her father was fifty-four—she's his only child. I gather he wants to see her the richest woman in the world before he dies."

"And Niko can't wait to climb into DeeDee's bed!" That was why he was acting so weird on the yacht. Guilty conscience. "The fucking son-of-a-bitch! Tell me what else the columnists have to say about the fabulous couple."

At noon on this unseasonably cool, mid-September Sunday, in her tiny one-bedroom apartment in a brownstone on West 109th Street, Katie changed her clothes three times before she settled on the black pants—in the fashionable "capri" length—and a black-and-white striped T-shirt and Capezio flats. After all, she was only meeting Artie for a hamburger at the West End bar.

Last night—after they'd seen *From Here to Eternity*—they'd picked up the early edition of *The New York Times* and had come up to the apartment to read and snack. It was the first time they'd been alone together. He'd kept waiting for some sign from her that she wouldn't reject a pass. Why had she been so standoffish? She wouldn't next time.

571

It was funny, the way they had been in and out of the same classes for two years before they became friends. She knew Artie Kenmore was from the South from his accent, but not until they met at Ellen's party last May, when the school year was almost over, did she realize he lived in Atlanta. He'd talked with much bitterness about being with the army of occupation in Berlin. And she told him about Keith.

Being stationed in postwar Germany had been a traumatic experience for him. *"Up until then I had been able to accent my parents' conversion — before I was born — to Episcopalianism. But walking the streets of Berlin — knowing how the Nazis had slaughtered six million Jews — I couldn't accept that conversion. I wanted to learn everything I could about being a Jew."*

With a swift glance at her watch Katie reached for her purse and a gray cashmere cardigan, inspected her new Italian cut in the mirror above her dresser, and hurried to leave the apartment. She'd never thought she could be attracted to another man after Keith. But Artie invaded her thoughts constantly.

Slim, dark-haired, intense, Artie slouched outside the West End bar, his attention focused on a paperback.

"Hi." It was amazing how Artie and she thought alike on important issues. He'd listened with flattering seriousness when she told him about working this summer with the organization that was fighting Magnolia's White Citizens' Council. He suggested that they both look into the group on campus that was organizing in support of *Brown* vs. *Board of Education*. "Have you been waiting long?"

Artie's face lighted up.

"Just a few minutes. Let's go inside and eat before the mob descends." He shoved the paperback into his jacket pocket. "Then we'll head downtown."

Over hamburgers and coffee in their favorite booth Artie outlined their itinerary.

"We'll take the subway down to Delancey Street, then tour the Lower East Side. Down there businesses are closed on Saturdays but open on Sundays. When we're tired, we'll head for Ratner's for dinner. Okay?"

"Okay," Katie smiled.

The couple strolled hand in hand through the narrow,

crowded streets of the largely Jewish Lower East Side, unconcerned by the frequent jostling, the sounds of noisy curb-side bargaining that was part of the ritual of pushcart shopping. They enjoyed the exotic aromas that spilled forth from the delicatessens, the appetizer shops with their tempting displays of lox, karp, sturgeon, pickled herring, and the myriad foods foreign to Magnolia, Georgia—though to some extent available in the more cosmopolitan Atlanta.

"Let's walk up to Delancey Street and go in for dinner," Artie decreed at last.

"Great," she agreed blithely. She was touched by Artie's eagerness to sop up all the sights and sounds around them. "I'm starving."

In Ratner's on Delancey Street they waited fifteen minutes for a table, ordered their dinner, then reached with healthy hunger for the onion rolls that sat piled high in baskets before them. While they waited for their food, Artie talked about rediscovering his Jewishness.

"I think most Southern Jews were deeply affected by what was happening in Nazi Germany. Before then they were part-time Jews," he mused. "You can go by my immediate family, of course. From the day they arrived in Atlanta thirty-seven years ago, they were non-Jews. But I know I became acutely conscious of my Jewishness with the rise of Hitler. Maybe because each summer my parents took my sisters and me to spend two weeks at an uncle's cottage at Manhattan Beach up in New York. We went there," he conceded with sardonic humor, "because that assured that my Jewish aunts and uncles and cousins would not invade Atlanta. It was enough that they saw us once a year. From the time I was ten or eleven I remember their anxieties about what was happening in Germany."

"I remember all the fund raising for German refugees among Magnolia Jews during World War II," Katie said. "My mother always used to wonder if we had distant relatives among them. My grandparents on both sides had come from Germany."

"When I was sent to Berlin as part of the army of occupation, I hadn't expected it to be so traumatic. But for a Jew it's a city of ghosts. I was never comfortable there."

"I was in Austria just before the Nazis invaded Poland," Katie told him. "I don't think I ever want to go back."

Artie was mesmerized by Katie's report of her part in the rescue of seven Austrian children and she glowed at his interest.

"After that," he smiled, "you knew you were Jewish."

"I always knew it. I lived in New York until I was eight. Most of the kids in my classes through the third grade were Jewish. I didn't dwell on it," she pinpointed. "I never picked my friends for their religion." Keith had not been Jewish. "But yes," she probed her feelings, "after those weeks with the seven little kids who would have landed in concentration camps if they were caught, I was more conscious of being Jewish."

"During that long stretch in Berlin—and later in Munich—I couldn't believe the way Germans would insist that Hitler had no inkling that the Jews were being slaughtered. They still nurtured a strange affection for him. For a while I had nightmares about it."

"I think that being Jewish helps us understand that integration is inevitable." She smiled wryly. "Some Southern Jews—like other Southerners—are wistful about losing the old way of life. But they know it's only fair—and that it's coming."

"Katie, I can't believe I had to go to Columbia Law to meet you—when you were living all those years only fifty miles from Atlanta." His face was exultant. "Thank God, we both decided to study law."

"Amen," Katie said, teasingly solemn.

*She was beginning a whole new life.*


When Iris saw the chauffeured Rolls which Niko maintained, along with his suite at the Waldorf Towers in New York, sitting in front of the Georgetown house, she knew Niko was waiting inside. She emerged from the company limo in the early dusk and walked to the door of the Early American house that was now considered her permanent residence. This was the week she was supposed to have gone to New York to spend with him. Had he actually expected her to be there?

574

She rang the doorbell and fumed that one of the servants didn't instantly respond. The great Niko Zolotas was about to be thrown out on his somewhat over-padded rump.

The door swung open. Abigail stood there, her ebony face aglow with awe. Niko must have stuffed a fifty-dollar bill into her apron pocket, a winning little habit of his.

"Oh, Miss Iris, Mist' Zolotas been waitin' heah for 'most an hour," Abigail scolded.

"Where is he?" Iris asked.

"In yo' private sittin' room," Abigail said. "Shall I bring up coffee?"

"No, Abigail. He won't be here that long." Grimly she stalked to the stairs and headed upward.

Niko stood in the doorway of what had been labeled her private sitting room.

"Iris, you weren't at the Sutton Place apartment. Mrs. O'Brien told me you were in Washington. I drove straight down to see you." He managed to sound reproachful.

"You are not welcome here, Niko." She walked past him into the sitting room. Damn it, she didn't want the servants to hear her battle with Niko.

"Iris, don't do this to me." He followed behind her and closed the door. "Nothing's changed for us."

"Does your bride know about this?" Her voice was shrill despite her determination to remain calm.

"Technically she's not my bride yet." He moved closer, reached into the inner pocket of his Savile Row jacket. "She won't be for another seven weeks. But Iris, this is strictly a business arrangement. Her father's fortune joined with mine can control half the world," he chuckled and flipped open the velvet box he'd pulled from his pocket.

For an instant Iris was mesmerized by the magnificence of the diamond necklace Niko had picked up at Baily's — no doubt an afterthought as he drove into Washington.

"A wedding gift for your bride?" she drawled. Niko had put his private plane at her disposal, his apartment in Paris, his houses in Palm Beach and Bermuda. But he'd never given her expensive jewelry. "It's spectacular."

"Iris, stop being dense." He moved towards her in amorous intent. "It's for you."

"Take your jewelry and get out!" Iris lashed at him. Peter

had beaten her and given her jewelry. Niko was marrying another woman and trying to buy her back with jewelry. "I don't sleep with other women's husbands."

"You didn't worry about Elita," he shot back, his face flushed.

"That was different." How dare he put her in this position before all their friends! "That was no marriage."

"Nor will this be," Niko tried again. "It's a business deal with her father. DeeDee will go her way, and I'll go mine."

"What about Papa's fatuous promise of a castle in the south of France when DeeDee presents him with his first grandchild?" Tears of rage welled in her eyes.

"So the old man blows off steam," he shrugged. "DeeDee is cold as an iceberg. She's going along with the marriage to please him. We're booking two-bedroom suites for our honeymoon. Iris, no women ever excited me like you. We're alike in a lot of ways. We belong together." He moved cautiously towards her again.

"But you're marrying DeeDee Metaxas!" she shrieked.

"You never showed any interest in marriage!" he shouted. "Goddamn, you made that clear the first time we met!"

"Get out, Niko! Get out before I break a lamp over your head!" The servants could hear; she didn't care. "And may you rot in hell with your bride!"


In November, along with Seth and their small cluster of close friends, Laura attended the unveiling of Rhoda's headstone. Leaving the cemetery afterwards she was intensely aware that Seth's official mourning was over. Today, of course, his thoughts were with Rhoda and their beautiful years together before her illness. But he was now free to marry again.

Long past the hour when she should have been asleep, Laura lay awake, staring at the glowing embers in the master-bedroom fireplace. On cool nights such as this, after the heat had been lowered, she enjoyed reading in the cozy comfort of a fire in the grate. This was a small luxury that helped her fall asleep. Usually.

*She was forty-six years old.* Why did she feel like a twenty-year-old girl yearning to be loved? It was too late for her.

She had lost two husbands. She had a real-estate empire to control. And a debt still unpaid to her father. Seth and she must continue as always. She must make him understand that nothing would change.

In the days that followed the unveiling Laura was ever conscious of the question in Seth's eyes. But she ignored the question, pretending to be absorbed only in the business. Then Jonnie and Katie came home, and she could pretend to be concerned only with their presence in the house.

She was delighted when Katie casually mentioned one morning that a classmate from school, who lived in Atlanta, was driving down to take her out to dinner.

"Artie's in our campus group that's fighting racial discrimination. His parents would be furious if they knew." Katie smiled wryly. "They settled in Atlanta when they first got married, changed their name to Kenmore, and became Episcopalians."

"Kenmore—" Laura squinted in thought. "William Kenmore Plumbing Supplies?"

"I think so." Katie seemed startled. "Mom, do you do business with them?"

"Years ago," Laura recalled. "When I built my first Atlanta building. They weren't competitive—I moved on to other firms." Katie was seriously interested in Artie Kenmore. She wouldn't be talking about him this way if she wasn't. "You're saying the Kenmores are Jewish?" She tried to be casual.

"That's right. They can't change their roots by moving from synagogue to church. Artie grew up knowing the family was Jewish because of aunts and uncles who lived up in New York and made no secret of it. When he was stationed in Berlin with the army of occupation he tried to track down relatives who had lived there. They all died in Buchenwald."

"The holocaust has made many Jews conscious of their heritage," Laura said gently. Without seeing Katie's new friend she liked him. "We have over five thousand years of history behind us."

Laura suppressed her eagerness to meet Artie. When Katie was ready it would happen.

Laura continued to dodge the questions in Seth's eyes. She pretended to be totally involved in their plans for the still-secret Hunter Woods. She was obsessed by the conviction that to admit her love for Seth would be his death warrant, aching inside for the pain she knew she was inflicting on him. Her mind told her she was irrational. Her heart said otherwise. And she was selfish, too, she taunted herself. She couldn't bear to face another terrible loss.

As Laura had expected, Everett was upset that she was moving into such an enormous project as Hunter Woods when she was so financially involved with the New York high-rise apartment building, a totally new venture for Hunter Realty. Both he and Seth understood that she was emotionally committed to Hunter Woods because it just might bring Jonnie home after graduation.

On May 17, 1954—the last day on which the Warren court handed down decisions for the spring—the Supreme Court ruled in favor of Brown in the case of *Brown* vs. *Board of Education*. Segregation of students by race was ruled unconstitutional. The Supreme Court ordered action "with all deliberate speed." It was the second Emancipation Proclamation. Nobody in Magnolia was surprised when the White Citizens' Council called a meeting.

Three days later there was a very different meeting in Laura's living room.

"If we can hold down that bastardly Council," Barry declared, "we have a chance to survive the Supreme Court decision without violence. But Slocum is vowing that any Negro who tries to register and vote, who fights to have a school board desegregate classes, who dares to join the NAACP, will be fired from his job, have his rent jacked up to the sky. White farmers who're sympathetic won't be able to get farm loans. Other sympathetic whites will have their mortgages foreclosed, their credit cut off."

"Not my bank," a local banker with a realistic approach declared. "If it's the law of the land, then by God we have to respect it."

"It'll be a long, agonizing process," Everett said compassionately, "but integration will come about."

When Laura talked to Katie about the court decision,

she was surprised to discover that Artie planned to remain in New York for a few weeks after graduation to work with the NAACP.

"Katie, there's much to be accomplished right here in Georgia." Did Katie mean to stay on in New York, too? She was sure that Artie was more than a casual friend. What about Katie's future? Barry had offered to take her into his law firm. It had been a casual invitation, but Katie knew he was serious. As always, she was afraid to push Katie into any commitment. "I'm sure there's a branch of the NAACP in Atlanta."

"I know, but Artie feels he can be more useful here." Katie paused. "I think he's avoiding a confrontation with his parents." She cleared her throat in nervousness. "Mom, I don't see any reason not to tell you. Artie and I plan on getting married late this summer. He's been saying that we ought to wait and tell you and his parents at the same time, but I know you'll keep it a secret until we get around to telling them."

"Katie, I'm so happy for you." Laura was startled by the tears that suddenly filled her eyes. "You'll be married here at home." It was half statement half question.

"Oh yes." There was a lilt in Katie's voice now. "Just family. But a religious ceremony. Artie wants that, too."

"Katie, do you know this will be the first religious marriage in the family since Papa and Mama were married in London?" Laura was lightheaded with pleasure.

"I'll be coming home with you after graduation. I have to take the Georgia bar exams at the end of July," she reminded her mother. "Artie will come home for that, too."

"My wedding present will be a house for you," Laura decided. "Seth and you will sit down and discuss what—"

"Mom, I don't know for sure that we'll be living in Magnolia," Katie interrupted apologetically. "Not right away, at least—"

"We'll talk about that later, darling," Laura said quickly. "As soon as you and Artie decide on the wedding date, let me know so I can tell Dr. Schiff to reserve it for you."

Was she to lose both Jonnie and Katie to New York? She was greedy—she wanted to see her children more than once or twice a year. Katie and Jonnie were third-generation

Magnolia. Their children would be the fourth. She wanted her children—and her grandchildren—to have roots here in Magnolia.

And the time would come, she continued to tell herself with recurrent desperation, when the missing pieces of the puzzle would fall into place and she could prove in a court of law that Derek Slocum had killed Tammy Lee Johnson. She would build an office tower in this town, where no building stood higher than five stories. From every house in Magnolia people would look from their windows and see the twenty-story Jacob Roth Tower. Papa's eternal memorial.

In late May Laura and Iris gathered at the Sutton Place apartment to plan a dinner party at the Colony to celebrate Katie's and Jonnie's graduations. The guest list was eclectic, ranging from Marty Coleman and Chet Berger to Debbie and Ian Macmillan. The company plane would bring up Maisie and Everett, Cecile and Barry, and Seth. Laura always made it clear to Seth that his presence at family functions was important to her.

Several nights later, elegantly beautiful in an off-the-shoulder white silk gown by Dior, Laura sat at the festive table in the red-and-crystal main dining room of the Colony. She felt herself encased in a rare tranquility. This was an occasion to cherish. Yesterday she had attended Jonnie's graduation from Harvard's Graduate School of Design. Today she had fought back tears of happiness while she focused all of her attention on Katie, so serious at the Columbia Law School graduation exercises. Bernie would have been so proud of his son and daughter.

Katie and Artie sat at her left, Jonnie and Corinne at her right. She was aware that Katie was especially tender towards Artie tonight, to make up for his disappointment that neither of his parents—nor his two older sisters and their husbands—had attended the graduation, she surmised. They were showing their outrage for his involvement in the burgeoning civil rights movement. His parents had expected Artie to join the Atlanta law firm that handled his father's legal affairs. They couldn't understand his decision to become a public service lawyer.

Involuntarily Laura turned to Seth to meet his baffled gaze. Seth couldn't understand why she continued to hold him at a distance. He couldn't accept her inference that until she cleared her father's name, she wasn't free to reach out for personal happiness. He was too sensitive to pressure her. Sometimes she wished he would.

At last there had been a break in the sultry, enervating late July heat. Katie sat on the sprawling veranda of the house at sunset and waited for Artie to pick her up and drive her out to his family's house for dinner. Happiness lent a luminescent glow to her face as she remembered last night's reunion at a quaint little motel not far from the Atlanta airport.

Artie's parents thought he had just arrived this morning. She had driven up to the airport to meet him yesterday afternoon so they could have a little time alone. They'd been separated almost seven weeks, Artie working in New York and she cramming for her bar exams here at home.

Mom had made no comment when she explained she was driving up to Atlanta to meet Artie and that his parents thought he'd be arriving today. Sometimes Mom astonished her. She'd expected an indignant reproach that she would sleep with Artie before they were married.

Katie rose to her feet as Mrs. Kenmore's white Cadillac convertible, with Artie behind the wheel, appeared in the road. She dreaded this dinner tonight. Artie hadn't said so, but she was sure the Kenmores were furious that he was marrying a Jewish girl. That they would be married in a Jewish ceremony. Artie was supposed to tell his parents this morning that they'd just decided to be married the second Sunday in August.

"You look gorgeous," Artie said, his eyes sweeping over her exquisite Balenciaga—worn to impress her prospective in-laws. Normally these days she wore jeans and T-shirt or squaw skirts and Navajo blouses.

"Did you tell your folks about the wedding date?" she demanded, settling herself beside him in the car.

"We'll tell them together at dinner." He grinned. "They

581

didn't realize until today that your mother is Laura Hunter. It shook them up to know I'm marrying into the filthy rich." He paused. "Okay, I should have told them when we're getting married. So I'm pushing it off to the last minute."

"My mother has already ordered the wedding cake," Katie reported humorously. It had been decided to have the wedding dinner at the house, but Jewel would be too busy with the sumptuous menu to make a cake. "I just hope Dr. Schiff doesn't say something to somebody in Atlanta, and the word gets back to your parents before you tell them."

"They have no contact with rabbis," Artie reminded with ironic amusement. "We're safe."

Katie was relieved that only Artie's parents would be at dinner. His sisters and their husbands were off on vacations. Almost immediately she sensed the Kenmores' disapproval, though they were too consciously well bred to be overt about this.

It was obvious that the Kenmores lived well. Their recently built, spacious California ranch house, located in select Buckhead, carried an expensive price tag. Mrs. Kenmore mentioned having just returned from a bridge party at the exclusive Piedmont Driving Club. Where Jews were not welcome. As though to be perverse, Mr. Kenmore talked about a meeting last evening of his White Citizens' Council. Artie bristled. The Kenmores loved their son, but they didn't understand him.

The elder Kenmores and Artie and Katie sat down to dinner in the airy dining room, furnished in the popular Danish modern. They were served by a uniformed maid. Over their shrimp cocktails, served in Waterford crystal that matched their water goblets, Mr. Kenmore persisted in lambasting the Warren court. Artie stared doggedly at the opposite wall. Katie strained to appear interested in Mr. Kenmore's monologue.

Her voice edged with exasperation, Mrs. Kenmore finally shifted the conversation to a discussion of musical events scheduled in Atlanta in the coming fall. Katie felt a rush of relief; here was a safe topic.

Through a multicourse dinner they talked about current Broadway music hits, the comeback of Coco Chanel, and Ernest Borgnine's fine performance in *Marty*. Mrs. Kenmore firmly stamped out her husband's sporadic efforts to reintroduce politics.

"Artie tells us that you are originally from New York," Mrs. Kenmore said during an awkward pause in table conversation as dessert was being served.

"I was born there," Katie confirmed, "but my family moved to Magnolia when I was eight. Right after my father died. My mother was born in Magnolia."

"Oh?" Mr. Kenmore appeared mildly condescending. "What was her maiden name?"

For a fleeting instant Katie paused.

"Her name was Roth before she married." Again Katie hesitated. "She moved to New York with her sister Iris right after high school graduation."

"Katie's mother went on to graduate law school while her sister married into the British peerage." Artie was needling his father, Katie understood.

"But your mother gave up law for real estate," Mrs. Kenmore recalled with an effort at cordiality. And respect for the Hunter wealth, Katie surmised. "Not many women in this country have achieved her kind of success."

"The name Roth seems to ring a bell." Mr. Kenmore appeared to be searching his mind. "Was your grandfather an attorney, also?"

"No." Katie managed a shakey smile. "He ran a shoe-repair shop in Magnolia. Until his untimely death—"

Katie saw recognition drain Kenmore's face of color.

"Your grandfather was Jacob Roth? The man who was lynched in Magnolia thirty years ago?" His voice was raspy with shock. Mrs. Kenmore's mouth dropped wide. She turned in silent accusation to Artie.

"Yes," Katie said, almost arrogant in her defensiveness. "One day we'll prove that lynch mob killed an innocent man."

"And I mean to help," Artie said quietly. "Oh, Katie and I have settled on a wedding date." Katie gritted her teeth while an audible gasp escaped his mother. "It's to be on the second Sunday in August."

"We won't be able to be there," Mrs. Kenmore said quickly, exchanging a furtive glance with her husband. Her smile expressed polite regret. "We've already made reservations for that week at St. Simon's Island." It was as though they were discussing a patio barbecue, Katie thought in silent rage.

"Then the guest list will be two guests shorter," Artie shrugged, but his eyes showed his hurt. "You'll understand if we skip coffee. I have to drive Katie back to Magnolia. And we'd like to do some cramming for the bar exams day after tomorrow."

In the car Katie clung to the door on her side, refusing to cry, as though determined to put as much distance as possible between Artie and herself. She could feel Artie's fury at his parents. He drove in grim silence.

"Artie, it isn't going to work—"

"No," he agreed with an air of capitulation. "There's no way we'll have any relationship with my parents."

"I'm talking about our marriage, Artie. It can't work." She closed her eyes in pain for a minute. "You'd never have a chance in politics. My grandfather's name would drag you down. It happened to my mother when she was running for city commissioner." Even now she could feel her sick shock when she read that headline: "LAURA HUNTER, DAUGHTER OF RAPIST-MURDERER."

"Katie, we're being married the second Sunday in August. Nobody—not even my parents—will stand in the way. And if someday I decide to run for public office, then I will."

"No," Katie rejected. Artie dreamed of public service. He belonged there—he had so much to give. "Somebody would resurrect my grandfather's trial again. You won't stand a chance if you're married to me."

Artie pulled up at the side of the road.

"We're marrying each other. Not my parents. Not your grandfather." He reached for her hand. "I don't want to go through life without you. I need you, Katie, to be whole."

"Artie, can we make it work?" She lifted her face to his. "I'm so scared."

"We'll make it work," Artie promised.

At shortly past nine the following morning—while Katie sipped her morning coffee beside the pool—Jewel called from the kitchen window to tell her that Artie was on the phone.

584

"Coming!" Katie darted towards the house.

"Do you think your mother will object to a houseguest until the wedding?" Artie asked without preliminaries.

"She'd love it," Katie assured him. "It was that bad with your parents?"

"It was that bad. From now on we won't be seeing them."

"I feel awful to come between you and your parents this way," Katie said in anguish.

"Katie, it isn't you," he said gently. "They lost me a long time ago."

# Chapter 46

The regally beautiful Hunter living room was a fragrant arbor of red and white American-beauty roses when Katie and Artie stood beneath the improvised red velvet canopy for the wedding ceremony. The atmosphere one of subdued joy. How lovely Katie was in the flower-printed chiffon she had chosen for her wedding dress, Laura thought proudly. Artie so serious.

Subconsciously Laura allowed her eyes to move about the room, while Dr. Schiff conducted the service. Everyone dear to her was here today. Jonnie and Corinne, holding hands. Seth at her left, Iris at her right. Maisie, who had vowed not to cry, was gesturing to Everett for his handkerchief. Cecile and Barry, both absorbed in the ceremony. Chet was with Jennifer, the pretty little redhead he would marry in the fall. Katie's former "best friend" Annabel was not here. They had broken up over her siding with the integrationists. *"Katie, I can't believe you'd do such a thing—it's being a traitor to your class!"* And Jewel hovered lovingly at the door—ever mindful that her gourmet dinner demanded close scrutiny.

"I'll never have to go through this with Noel," Iris whispered in Laura's ear. Their only communications these days were through Iris's attorney. It amazed Iris that Noel had inveigled his way into a closeness with his half-brother and half-sisters. "I pity the poor girl who marries Noel."

"Sssh," Laura scolded tenderly. While Katie and Artie were leaving their life unstructured, she clung to the knowledge that they were excited about the house Seth was designing for them. The house they would, hopefully, soon occupy.

Now Dr. Schiff delivered the final blessing. Artie and Katie were husband and wife. Tears filled Laura's eyes as Katie turned around after kissing her husband and sought for her mother. Laura moved forward with outstretched arms. This time Katie would have a wonderful marriage.

The guests gathered in the dining room, the lace-covered table resplendent with Lenox china, Waterford crystal, Jensen silver. Today—at Laura and Katie's insistence—Jewel was to join the others at the dinner table. Laura, Katie, and Corinne would serve.

Jonnie and Chet disappeared at one point, and Laura suspected they were adorning the car that would take Katie and Artie to the airport. The company plane was to fly them to Gloucester for a week's stay at the house where Jonnie and Corinne spent as much time as they could manage. After the brief honeymoon they would live for the time being in Katie's apartment near Columbia. They'd insisted, Laura remembered wistfully, that they had no time for the European honeymoon she had offered.

"Mom, it was a beautiful wedding," Katie said exuberantly when she had changed into her tailored but feminine traveling dress. "Thank you for being my mother."

"Oh, darling—" Laura clung to Katie. "Thank you for being my daughter."

"The bridegroom needs to be rescued," Iris called blithely from the other side of the door. "Jonnie and Chet are issuing all kinds of threats if he doesn't do well by our little girl."

Katie pulled the door open and reached for her aunt.

"Iris, you know I couldn't have got married if you hadn't been here," she laughed.

"Darling, only for your wedding would I come to this rotten town. Or for your mother's," she said pointedly, and Laura felt color warm her face.

"We'd better hurry. The plane's standing by at the airport." Walking down the stairs behind Katie and Iris, Laura found her eyes colliding with Seth's. Everybody thought she was treating him shabbily. Perhaps—as Maisie insisted—she was being guided by illogical superstition, but she couldn't gamble with Seth's life. She loved him too much for that.


Iris shot a swift glance about her bedroom while she

587

reached for her jewel case. Her collection of Vuitton luggage had all been carried down to the Macmillan limo. A smile touched her mouth while she took a routine inspection of herself in the Dior suit. She was pleased that she had been able to arrange for Debbie and Ian Macmillan to be invited to the Callaway plantation this particular weekend. She had confided to Claudia Calloway that Debbie and Ian had just reconciled after a serious tiff—"it would be good for them to relax at the plantation just now."

Iris hurried downstairs and out to the waiting car with a pleasurable awareness that this was a perfect early October morning. Debbie waved from the car while the chauffeur moved to open the door for her. They were flying down to Aiken in the Macmillan's DC-3.

She loved Calloway Place. The huge estate provided a grandeur that reminded her of Cranford Hall, though physically they were very different. The house seemed right out of the movie version of *Gone With the Wind*. The Calloways, she thought in high good humor, made the Slocums seem like poor white trash.

"Most of the guests will be arriving tomorrow morning," Iris pointed out while she settled herself between Debbie and Ian. "Only two or three other guests will be there today."

"Great," Debbie approved. "The women will sit around and talk about clothes, and the men can yak all evening about what's happening in politics."

Iris normally enjoyed the flight to Aiken, but this morning she was fighting to block from her mind the knowledge that Niko and DeeDee were to be married on Sunday in a huge wedding in Athens. The newspapers were full of exotic details. She was relieved when Ian excused himself to join the pilot. Now Debbie and she could talk.

"If anybody mentions Niko's name this evening," Iris warned, "I'll probably shriek."

"No, you won't," Debbie rejected. "Everybody knows his marriage is a business arrangement. Two of the world's richest men out to make big deals together. Of course, I think Niko is a heel to go along with it. Everybody knows he's mad about you. When the annulment came through, we all expected the two of you to marry. And darling, he's a marvelous catch—"

"In less than three years I'll be fifty," Iris said bitterly. "I can't compete with a twenty-year-old. My God, where do the years go?"

"I was forty for seven years," Debbie reminisced. "I'll probably be fifty for at least ten. Darling, when you feel low, you run out to Maine Chance. After a while," she contemplated, "we'll cultivate softly lit rooms, long sleeves, and avoid swimsuits. I intend to grow old gracefully. But after seventy, I'll give up the face lifts. Have you seen poor Mimi lately? Her eyes are just slits between her eyelashes."

In the British tweeds she fancied, Claudia Calloway met them at the private airfield near Aiken.

"I've ordered perfect weather for y'all, as you can see," Claudia bubbled. "And we're going so political, Ian. Judge Endicott and his wife will be arriving later today, along with my cousin and Joe Weaver." Weaver was the long-time congressman from South Carolina with whom Ian was anxious to confer. "But I'm telling everybody to relax. You get enough of politics up in Washington."

Once settled in their rooms in the elegant Georgian mansion, the first three guests went downstairs for an excellent lunch served on the veranda. The two men took off on their own after lunch while the women settled down to exchange the latest gossip—Niko's wedding tacitly off limits—and projected travel plans for the months ahead.

"We'll have a houseful at dinner tomorrow night," Claudia confided. "It's Charlie's fifty-fourth birthday. He always pretends to forget about it." She chuckled. "But I've invited people down from New York and out from Dallas—and my distant Southern cousin to be your dinner partner, Iris. He doesn't run in our circles," she said ingratiatingly, "but Southern men are so romantic. And we'll all sing 'happy birthday' whether Charlie likes it or not."

While Iris was in her room dressing for dinner, she heard the arrival of more guests. She vaguely remembered encountering the Endicotts at diplomatic parties. The Judge might just be useful to Laura one day.

Beautiful in a pearl-gray satin Balenciaga with emerald necklace and matching earrings, Iris left her room and headed downstairs. She heard the light laughter in the drawing room, the exchange of convivial conversation. Debbie and Ian were downstairs already—and wasn't that Judge Endicott's voice? She'd seen him just yesterday on a telecast about the first televised cabinet meeting to be held next week.

"Iris, you bought that marvelous Balenciaga," Claudia trilled. "I loved it, but I'd have to lose twenty pounds before I'd dare try to wear it."

Iris accepted a glass of champagne, greeted the Judge and his wife with calculated warmth.

"Oh yes, we've met often in Washington." Iris radiated charm. "But Washington parties are so hectic—"

"Oh, here comes Eric." Claudia gestured to a man strolling into the drawing room with Charlie. "My cousin, Eric Slocum. If it wasn't incestuous I'd be attracted to him."

Iris froze. Eric Slocum from Magnolia? No, the South was full of Slocums.

"Eric," Claudia said flirtatiously, "you're very lucky tonight. This beautiful lady will be sitting next to you at dinner. Iris, I'd like you to meet my cousin, Eric Slocum. Eric, this is Lady Iris Cranford."

Eric stared at Iris. His face flushed, his eyes were contemptuous. Iris felt suddenly sick. She had spent most of her life dreading this moment. Eric Slocum knew who she was.

"Lady Iris Cranford," he mimicked his cousin. "Who was Iris Roth from Magnolia, Georgia. The little Jew girl whose father was lynched before he could be hanged for murder." Eric smiled at his hostess while Iris fought off a sense of suffocation. "My uncle presided at her father's trial."

"Not your uncle," Iris shot back in vindictive triumph. "Your father. I remember. You're his son by that 'high yaller' woman he kept three miles from town. Everybody knew, of course."

For an instant a stunned silence hovered over the small gathering. Then, white and grim-faced, Eric Slocum strode from the drawing room.

"Claudia, would you please excuse me?" Iris managed a brittle smile. "I seem to have developed a dreadful headache."

Iris lay across the bed in the dark room, ignoring Debbie's plea for admittance. Because of that rotten bastard, Eric Slocum, it was all over. Everything she had built up through the years.

"Iris, you open that door, or I'll have two strong men break it down," Debbie ordered. "Darling, we have to talk."

Iris left the bed and walked to the door, pulled it wide.

"Claudia is upset," Debbie said, reaching for the light switch with one hand and closing the door behind her with the other. "She had no idea her cousin could be so despicable."

"It's all true," Iris whispered. "Except that my father was innocent. And what I said was true," she added defiantly.

"Let's sit down and talk this through. Iris, nobody is going to breathe a word about what happened downstairs. Certainly not Claudia and Charlie—they're so upset that a cousin could behave that way. And everybody knows the Judge and his wife never have a bad word to say about anyone—I think they're Quakers. And you know Ian and I would never—"

Both women started at the sound of a shot somewhere down the hall.

"Oh, my God!" The words were wrenched from Iris.

Even before Ian arrived to confirm it, Iris knew that Eric Slocum had killed himself.


Laura was vaguely conscious that her hand that gripped the telephone hurt from the intensity of her grasp. She listened to Iris with an agonized sense of hurtling back through the years. First, to the nightmare of Papa's trial and death, and then to the newspaper headlines that told all Magnolia—including Jonnie and Katie—that Laura Hunter was the daughter of Jacob Roth, convicted of rape and murder.

"Laura, it was awful!" Iris wailed. "How am I going to face any of my friends after this?"

"Iris, you're not responsible for Eric Slocum's suicide," Laura said with forced calm. "And what he did to you was unforgivable. You—"

"I'm not talking about his killing himself!" Iris shrieked. "I didn't put a gun in his hand! But everybody at Calloway Place knows about Papa. In their eyes I'll forever be Iris Roth. She's dead," Iris said violently. "I killed her the day we set foot on that Seaboard Airline train for New York."

"Where's Debbie?" Laura asked. Iris was only a thread away from hysteria.

"Downstairs having dinner with the Calloways and Judge and Mrs. Endicott. The police have finally gone. Charlie Calloway convinced them Eric killed himself accidentally while he was cleaning his gun. Don't you know?" Iris made a pretense of bitter amusement. "Above all else we have to be civilized."

"Do you want me to come and take you back to Georgetown?" Laura asked gently, knowing Iris wouldn't come to Magnolia.

"Laura, yes—" Iris's voice broke. "Debbie keeps telling me nobody will talk about Papa—for reasons of their own. She says she'll bring me a sleeping pill after dinner, and tomorrow everything will be all right. *But it won't.* Nothing will ever be right again."

"It will be all right, Iris," Laura parroted Debbie. "We'll—"

"Laura, hurry up here," Iris interrupted. "I have to get away before the others arrive. I don't want to see the ones who're already here." Her voice rose into a high thin wail.

"Ask Debbie to arrange for the Calloway chauffeur to drive you to that little private airport at six tomorrow morning." Laura's mind was coping with what must be done. "I'll be waiting with the plane. We'll fly up to Georgetown together."

"Not until tomorrow morning?" Iris reproached.

"I have to notify the crew, have them service the plane, and get clearance for the flight," Laura pointed out, determinedly calm. "I'll be there at six. That's only nine hours away," she comforted. "Iris, everything is going to be all right," she reiterated, as though her sister were a small child.

"Oh, Laura, I love you," Iris whispered.

"And I love you," Laura said.

592

After she had checked with the crew, Laura talked with Seth on the phone.

"Do you want me to fly up with you?" he asked solicitously.

"I think it'll be better if I go alone." But she cherished his offering to fly up with her. "I'll stay with Iris at the Georgetown house for a couple of days. You and Everett will have to handle my appointments."

In his wood-paneled, bookcase-lined study in the Slocum family house, Judge Matthew Slocum — retired from the bench for four years now but retaining the title in the Southern tradition — sat at his antique mahogany desk and read again the brief letter left him by his late son Eric. This morning he looked his seventy-eight years. The lines in his face seemed deeper. His military bearing had succumbed to grief and shock and rage; his shoulders drooped with the weight of the years hitherto kept in abeyance.

He folded over the letter, meticulously shredded it, dropped the strips of paper into the deep ashtray atop his desk. While he held a lighted match to the paper, he relived that agitated phone call from his distant cousin, Claudia Calloway. She was family, and she knew how these matters were to be handled. To the world Eric Slocum died in a tragic hunting accident.

The Judge frowned at the light knock on his door.

"What is it?" His voice was sharp.

The door opened. David walked into the study. David knew about Eric. He'd known ever since he was seventeen. Betty had always pretended before the world that Eric was like another son to her, but within the walls of the house she abandoned pretense. She'd never accepted the Judge's explanation that Eric was the child of a profligate brother disowned by the family and now dead.

She hadn't slept with the Judge since the night her car broke down in front of Eulalie's house, and she'd come to the door to ask about a phone. He'd been stretched on the sofa in his shirtsleeves. Small loss; Betty had been a lousy lay. But she made the perfect wife for his public image.

"We have to leave for the church in fifteen minutes,"

David reminded. This morning—abnormally raw and gray for a Magnolia autumn—Eric was to be buried in the family plot.

"Come in and close the door, David," he ordered, pulling himself up in his chair.

"We just received a telegram from Claudia Calloway," David reported. "She and Charlie won't be able to attend funeral services."

"I didn't expect them to show up. They're too busy playing high society to bother with their Georgia kin. But I want you to remember something, David." He clenched one hand into a tight fist. "We're going to get those two Roth daughters. They'll pay for what happened to Eric. We'll wait for the right moment—and it'll come, as sure as God made little green apples. For years that bitch Laura Hunter has been in our way. We'll break her, David!"


In the ensuing weeks Laura was haunted by mental images of Iris's horrendous encounter with Eric Slocum. It could happen to Jonnie and Katie, she warned herself in recurrent terror. There were people in Magnolia who still regarded Jacob Roth's family as pariahs. She'd told herself it was all forgotten. But it wasn't.

She had made a terrible mistake in trying to live in this town. If she had remained in New York, Jonnie and Katie would have escaped the stigma.

Judge Slocum would be especially vindictive now. He would blame Iris for Eric's suicide. Damn it! Eric's death was on his father's head. For the Judge's illicit relationship with that woman who gave birth to Eric. For having contrived for Papa's conviction to save Derek's neck. Didn't the other Slocums know that Derek had been in town the day Tammy Lee Johnson was murdered? Didn't they know why he had been expelled from that school? Didn't they know why he had been spirited out of town so fast? They didn't want to know. It was more convenient to railroad Jacob Roth to his death.

Matthew Slocum was responsible for the grief of Eric's wife, his children. Laura had never liked any of the Slocums, but she knew the anguish Eric's family must be suffering and felt compassion for them. Had they been told the truth—or did they believe that Eric died "in a tragic hunting accident"?

Too often Laura remembered Iris's words when they met in the gray dawn at the airport near Aiken:

*"Laura, they'll never let us forget that Papa was convicted of murder. That will hang over our heads forever."*

Laura knew, too, that she had exacerbated an already tense situation when she announced her plans last week to begin construction almost immediately on Hunter Woods. The Slocum syndicate had just broken ground for a luxury development in the opposite direction—on acreage safely within Magnolia city limits, Laura acknowledged. But should the Magnolia city commissioners extend town boundaries to include Hunter Woods, it would have significantly less commercial possibilities.

Always thinking ahead, Laura had bought up contiguous land through the years so that now she was able to expand Hunter Woods into a total community. She meant to be able to cater to the American infatuation for suburban living. In addition to the ultra-modern shopping center, she had given Seth the go-ahead on a drive-in movie, despite Everett's apoplexy over the escalating costs. That, too, was infuriating the Judge. The Slocums owned three movie houses in downtown Magnolia, which would undoubtedly suffer from attendance at the drive-in.

Barry had initiated serious efforts to have the Magnolia city limits expanded to include Hunter Woods. Laura knew that those close to her in Hunter Realty were worried that this would not be accomplished. The Slocums still controlled four of the nine city commissioners and only three indicated interest in the city's annexing her new community.

Without city services Hunter Woods would become prohibitively expensive. Her entire empire could be in jeopardy. For the first time in all her years in business she had not heeded Everett's warnings. She was overextending herself financially and gambling on winning over the commissioners.

With the approach of Thanksgiving, Laura ordered herself to focus on the holidays. Jonnie and Corinne were coming down from Boston and Katie and Artie from New York. The four young people would remain for the long weekend. For those days, Laura promised herself, she would completely push business out of her mind.

It was tradition now for Laura to have Seth, Maisie and Everett, and the Bergers for a midafternoon Thanksgiving dinner. This year Chet and his pretty new wife, Jennifer, would be there, too. Iris—as Laura had expected—refused to come to Magnolia for the holiday. Just back from a week at the Homestead, she would spend the long weekend with Debbie and Ian Macmillan at their country house in Virginia. Then on Sunday Iris and Debbie would leave for a week at Maine Chance.

Katie and Artie arrived Wednesday night, full of talk about the spread throughout the Deep South of the White Citizens' Councils. They were delighted that Jonnie's friend, Marty Coleman, had moved to New York to work with their group.

"Marty's so bright," Katie said enthusiastically. "And he isn't one of those who expects overnight compliance with the Supreme Court ruling."

"Nor does he expect to wait twenty years," Artie pointed out. "Tell us what's happening down here," Artie urged Laura.

They explored the local situation—admittedly slow-moving—until Laura decreed it was time to go to bed. Too tense to fall asleep immediately, Laura sat before the fireplace, where a log burned brightly in the grate, and studied Everett's report on the New York high-rise.

She started at the sound of a light knock at the door.

"Come in—" She turned towards the door with a welcoming smile, suspecting it was Katie.

"I have some great news, Mom." Katie walked into the room and sat beside Laura. "Artie said I should wait to tell you until I've seen the doctor, but I just can't. I think I'm pregnant."

"Katie—" Laura's face was suffused with pleasure. "I'm so happy, darling." She leaned forward to kiss her radiant daughter. "What a wonderful Thanksgiving present!"

"Artie thinks maybe it's time we came home and worked here. He's been writing back and forth with Chet—and, well, you were right. We can be useful in Magnolia."

"Yes, of course you can! And work on the house is finished except for some trim. Katie, I'm so happy you're coming home." They would encounter no financial problems, Laura reminded herself in satisfaction. They could live comfortably on the income from Katie's trust fund, just as Jonnie and Corinne could live on income from his.

They talked for another few minutes, and then Katie returned to her room. Impulsively—despite the hour—Laura reached for the phone to call Maisie. She knew that Maisie would be happy that Katie and Artie would be living in Magnolia. But while she talked with Maisie about Katie's news, Laura churned with fresh helplessness. Papa's first great-grandchild would be born in late June or early July, and still she had not succeeded in clearing his name. Iris's experience at Calloway Place had emphasized the urgency of this.

Early Thursday morning Jonnie phoned from Boston to say that he and Corinne had missed their scheduled flight because she had been tied up at the hospital. They'd be taking the next flight out.

"I'll move dinner up a couple of hours," Laura said. "And the car will be waiting at the Atlanta airport."

When Jonnie and Corinne arrived only minutes before Thanksgiving dinner was scheduled to be served, Laura sensed they had been arguing en route. Corinne was polite but distant, Jonnie affectionate but tense, touchingly tender when Katie told him she was pregnant.

"Of course, the doctor may say I'm wrong," Katie laughed, but her aura of anticipation rejected this.

"The woman usually knows," Corinne said, seeming less withdrawn now.

But when Laura talked about the flourishing Rhoda Goldman Hospital, for which she and Seth were active in fund raising, she saw Corinne's mouth tighten. Corinne guessed rightly—that Laura hoped her daughter-in-law would complete her residency at Rhoda Goldman here in Magnolia. Self-consciously Laura shifted the conversation. She would have to be careful about what she said to Corinne.

After dinner Jonnie and Seth sequestered themselves in the library for absorbed discussion of Hunter Woods. Laura knew Seth was drawing Jonnie out about his own ideas for the new community. Bless Seth, she thought tenderly. But would Jonnie ever come back to work with Seth when Corinne was set on setting up practice in New York?

She remembered how Corinne had worried that she was responsible for Jonnie's enlistment. She had blamed herself for pushing him. *And she was doing that again.*

Didn't Corinne understand Jonnie wasn't happy working for that Boston firm? Jonnie wanted to live in Magnolia and to work with Seth. Why couldn't he make his wife understand that?

In her room in the preferred house at Maine Chance, Iris lay back, against the lace pillow-slips of the canopied bed. The maid had just removed her dinner tray. Unlike Debbie, she had been having all her meals sent to her room. She was here to relax and lose five pounds. Although she could cope with the impersonal group exercise classes, she was still too shaken by the encounter at Calloway Place for the evening socializing.

Iris glanced at the ormulu clock that traveled everywhere with her. The lights were turned off at ten. She'd read for a while, then Debbie would drop by for a late chat, and another day would have disappeared. She reached for a copy of *Vogue,* on her night table next to a bouquet of yellow chrysanthemums.

As she flipped the pages, she heard Debbie's special knock.

"Come in." Debbie was upstairs earlier than usual. She must have been bored by television or bridge—or both.

"Darling, I didn't know Mimi Edgewood was here!" Debbie rushed into the room, her face suspiciously triumphant. "She's been having all of her meals in her room since she arrived, like you."

"How is Mimi?" Iris was involuntarily defensive. Mimi Edgewood was the most notorious gossip in their set.

"Ten pounds heavier than at Bar Harbor and furious."

"What little goodies did Mimi come up with this time?" Iris pretended to be amused.

"Darling, she's just back from London. Niko's at Claridge's." Debbie settled herself comfortably at the foot of the bed. "She says that everybody knows Niko is terribly unhappy with DeeDee. They're still on their honeymoon and going their separate ways. Niko says if she ever has a baby it'll be another immaculate conception. She only married Niko to please her father. She idolizes that stupid old man."

"So why does Niko stay with her?" Iris challenged, conscious of a familiar stirring. It had been so long since Niko and she made love. There'd been nobody since him.

"Iris, you know why," Debbie clucked. "The Metaxas fortune makes him the most powerful man in Europe. And you know what else Mimi told me?" Debbie leaned forward conspiratorially. "Niko has been making discreet inquiries about your whereabouts. Not so discreet," Debbie amended. "He knows what an awful gossip Mimi is."

"He could have tried me at Georgetown or the New York apartment," Iris was skeptical. Had Niko been telling the truth? Was this marriage just a business deal?

"Iris, you've been dashing about from one place to another since Aiken," Debbie reminded. "And you've ordered Mrs. O'Brien in New York and the staff in Georgetown not to give out your whereabouts. They only take messages."

Iris sat upright in bed.

"Oh God, I haven't called the house or the apartment since we went down to The Homestead before Thanksgiving." Suppose Niko *had* been trying to reach her? Should she start up with him again while he was still married? She'd been so hurt and humiliated. She vowed she'd never see him again. But Niko and she had been great together. And not just in bed. Just *being* together.

"Nobody knows you're here except for Laura," Debbie broke in on her introspection. "And Laura wouldn't tell Niko."

"What about DeeDee?" Iris pressed.

"DeeDee is one of those women who thinks sex is disgusting. She likes to buy clothes, lunch, play bridge, and give small parties on Daddy's yacht. She likes male admiration—but on a vertical level."

"Poor Niko!" She paused for a moment. Her mind in high gear. Then, with a sudden smile, she reached for the phone.

"Iris, are you phoning Niko?" Debbie was intrigued yet anxious.

"You're damn right." Iris settled the phone beside her. "Laura will be furious with me, but I miss that old Greek like hell. I think I know Niko better than anybody else in this world," she said softly. "I know his weak spots, his crazy quirks, the tenderness he never shows to anybody else. We fight, we scream at each other, and then we make love. But I know, too, that his ambition for power takes first place."

"Can you handle that?" Debbie was serious.

Iris nodded. "I'm the one Niko needs. He doesn't have to play games with me. I never even let him give me jewelry," she confided with pride. "I think deep inside I wasn't just showing my independence. I was letting the great Niko Zolotas know I liked him for himself—not his billions."

"You know, Iris," Debbie smiled, "I think Niko will be a lucky man if you go back to him."

"Now don't start calling out the strolling fiddlers," Iris jeered. "We may have a rip-roaring battle and break up a week after we make up!"

# Chapter 47

New Year's Day, 1955, in Magnolia dawned invigoratingly cold, the sky a cloudless, serene blue. Sunlight infiltrated the tall, narrow, lace-paneled windows of Laura's formal dining room, where family and close friends had gathered for the traditional midafternoon dinner. Only Iris was missing at the table, Laura thought wistfully.

She worried that Iris was involved again with Niko. Iris was spending ten days on his yacht, anchored at Palm Beach.

Since the week at Maine Chance, Iris had limited her socializing to the diplomatic parties that were her business beat and where she felt safe from jet-set gossiping.

Katie, Laura thought as she ate with relish, was radiant in her early pregnancy, good-humoredly battling her expanding waistline. Artie was so loving and protective.

Laura's gaze moved to Jonnie and Seth, deep in earnest discussion about the progress of Hunter Woods. Corinne seemed tired and troubled. Jonnie said she was working horrendous hours at the hospital and fighting much prejudice at being the only woman on the staff. Yet Laura knew Corinne would consider her an interfering mother-in-law if she talked about the possibility of Corinne's transferring to Rhoda Goldman Hospital.

Today, Laura vowed, she would not think about business. The New York high-rise apartment had been plagued by a series of construction-worker strikes and with interest costs escalating wildly, the project would come in late. In Magnolia the city commissioners showed no indication of reaching an agreement on the annexation of Hunter Woods when it was completed, though Barry — working with a team that included Katie, Artie, and Chet — was fighting to push this through. Laura feared a financial crisis.

"Ever'body ready fo' dessert?" Jewel asked amiably, bringing in the pumpkin and sweet potato pies herself while the houseman and maid circulated with tea and coffee.

"Jewel, when you make pies, everybody's ready," Jonnie laughed. "Mom, you're in the wrong business. You ought to have a processing plant to freeze Jewel's pies and sell them nationwide."

"Mist' Jonnie, you just cut that out," Jewel giggled. In company she insisted on the formal "Mister" in addressing her "older baby," as Katie was "Miss Katie" in public. "You keep teasin' me and I ain't gonna bring in that hot pecan pie for second helpin's."

They'd left the table and gathered in the living room, where the men were eager to watch football on TV when Jewel summoned Laura to the telephone.

"I'll take it in my office," she told Jewel, guessing the caller was Iris.

"Hello." Her voice was expectant.

"Happy New Year, darling," Iris greeted her.

"I figured it was you. Happy New Year, Iris. How are you?"

"Smug as a Siamese with two saucers of cream," Iris bubbled. "We had a smashing party on the yacht last night. And Laura, not one word about that awful night at Calloway Place. I think you were right. It might never have happened."

But it *had* happened, Laura told herself with recurrent anxiety; and the Slocums were a vicious, vindictive clan. Eric's suicide had just added fresh fuel to their vendetta. Gossip drifted back to her. Judge Matthew Slocum would not be satisfied until he had destroyed her.


In March, Laura was unnerved by David Slocum's announcement that he would run again for city commissioner. He had served several terms in the past, withdrawing from another run when the climate seemed to be against the Slocums. But now with many Magnolia citizens incensed by the threat of integration, the Slocums seized at the opportunity to regain their power.

Laura called an emergency evening meeting at the house. In addition to Everett and Maisie, Seth, and Barry, she brought in the three young people—Katie, Artie, and Chet—who had become part of Hunter Realty's legal team. Of the nine city commissioners, four were outspoken now in their approval of annexing Hunter Woods. They recognized that the increases in the tax rolls would more than compensate for the services this new suburb would require. Four—long in the Slocum syndicate pockets—vowed to fight annexation. The incumbent commissioner was retiring because of ill health and the deciding vote would be cast by the commissioner elected in the fall. This was the seat David Slocum was out to snare.

Laura's inner circle settled themselves in her office and analyzed the situation. All of them were aware that the current climate favored the Slocum machine.

"David Slocum will run on a hate slate," Barry predicted. "Talmadge will back him for sure."

"Then we have to put up somebody to fight him," Katie said vigorously. Despite her advancing pregnancy, she insisted on being active. "You, Barry," she said in triumph.

"Katie, I have a bad track record in that area," he reminded wryly.

"That was years ago," Chet picked up.

"Barry, times have changed," Laura pursued. *It was imperative that the new commissioner favor annexation.* "If we get out after the black vote along with the liberals, you'll have a fighting chance." Of course, the White Citizens' Council—now headed by Judge Slocum—would threaten deadly reprisals against blacks who dared to register and vote. But since World War II the blacks—particularly the young—were fighting for their rights. "We have to put our own candidate into office," she said flatly. "He'll cast the deciding vote on annexation."

Magnolia was the scene of chaotic electioneering. There were those, including elected officials, who understood that the decision of the Supreme Court must be respected. The *Magnolia Herald* supported the decision, quoting Hubert Humphrey's declaration on the Democratic convention floor in 1948 when he was running for the United States Senate: "There are those who say to you—we are rushing this issue of civil rights. I say we are one hundred seventy-two years late." The Slocum-controlled *Magnolia Journal* vilified the Court, calling for defiance.

Late in June Katie went into labor. Nine hours later at Magnolia Hospital she gave birth to a daughter to be named Betsy. Joyously Laura phoned Jonnie. Two days later he and Corinne arrived in Magnolia. It was one of the beautiful times in her life, Laura thought sentimentally, while the family—except for Iris—gathered in Katie's hospital room. Iris had sent Katie her favorite American beauty roses and called to talk to her. *"Darling, I warn you, if anybody finds out I'm a great aunt, I'll say my niece gave birth at twelve!"*

Jonnie was so proud of being an uncle. Laura was glad he and Corinne had scheduled their vacation at this particular time.

"Betsy knew we'd be coming this week," Jonnie grinned. "She's a smart little kid."

"She's the image of Katie," Corinne smiled, yet Laura sensed she was troubled. "But she has your eyebrows, Artie." She squinted at Artie in an effort at levity.

Were Jonnie and Corinne having problems in their marriage, Laura asked herself anxiously. Though Jonnie professed to like his new job, she sensed he was restless within the confines that Seth, too—years earlier—had resented. Was that causing friction between Corinne and him?

Over dinner Corinne was irritated when Jonnie mentioned that she would not be able to go on into her specialty, orthopedics, at the Boston hospital. The hospital director had told her that she would be retained as a resident only through her current year, which would conclude in September.

"You would not believe the prejudice against women doctors," Corinne said bitterly. "Particularly if the woman doesn't choose pediatrics as her specialty."

"Corinne, I'm almost certain I could arrange for you to come into Rhoda Goldman in September." Suddenly the atmosphere in the dining room was electric. Laura tensed. *It was this moment or never.* She felt Jonnie's excitement at the possibility of coming home. And she was aware of Corinne's ambivalence. "Would you like me to look into the situation, Corinne?"

"It seems awfully unfair for me to take advantage of our relationship—" Corinne wavered.

"Corinne, it's okay if some things work out easily," Jonnie teased. "You don't have to break your back every step of the way to becoming a practicing physician."

"What about your job in Boston?" Corinne hedged.

"I'd give it up in a minute," Jonnie told her.

"I'm waiting to hear from a hospital near Lynne," Corinne told Laura. Corinne could commute from Boston to Lynne with no difficulty. "My father has some contacts there." She stared unhappily at her dinner plate. *She hated the thought of living in Magnolia.* "They have a great orthopedics department there."

"There's time." Laura forced a smile. There was nothing wrong with the orthopedics department at Rhoda Goldman Hospital. "If you'd like me to pull some strings, just let me know."

After dinner Jonnie took Corinne off to a downtown movie theater to see *The King and I.* Laura called Seth and talked in anger and frustration about Corinne's reluctance to settle in Magnolia.

"Seth, Jonnie told her right out he'd be happy to give up his job in Boston. Doesn't she care about his feelings?"

"Corinne has a warped vision of life in Magnolia," Seth said gently. "She doesn't know this town."

"Seth, she's been down here before," Laura said impatiently.

"What did she see?" Seth challenged. "Your house, the swimming pool, a few choice restaurants? Jonnie and Katie showed her Roosevelt's Little White House in Warm Springs, Fort Benning down in Columbus. Let her get a close view of our relaxed lifestyle. See how well she could live here. Show her how Hunter Woods is coming along."

"Seth, you're right. I won't urge her to go over to the hospital—but I know Jonnie can stress the fine building you designed for it and how well it's been received in town. I'll have Artie show her their house. Corinne will love it. And she knows I'd build a house for Jonnie and her if they settle here. Seth, they'll be here another ten days. In that time I have to sell Magnolia to Corinne."

"There's no guarantee she'll buy," Seth cautioned compassionately. "But I know you'll give it the best try possible."

All at once Laura was exhausted.

"Can't Corinne see what it'll mean to Jonnie to live here? Her career doesn't depend upon their living in Boston or New York. She could have a fine practice in Magnolia. And here—working for the company, with you—Jonnie will have a chance to soar as an architect. Seth, I have to make her understand this!"

The following morning Laura returned from the Hunter Woods site to learn that Artie had called her twice.

"He said to be sure and phone as soon as you could," Nora told her.

Laura sat behind her desk and reached for the phone, assuming Artie wanted to discuss some development in Barry's campaign. Instead, he reported that Marty Coleman had called from Atlanta, where he was addressing an NAACP meeting.

"Marty thought maybe I could drive up and have dinner with him in Atlanta tomorrow. He'd invited Katie, too, but I told him about the baby." Artie chuckled. "He said he bet Katie was still handing out voter registration leaflets the day Betsy was born."

"He was at Jonnie and Corinne's wedding."

"That's right. He couldn't believe Jonnie and Corinne were visiting down here just when he's in Atlanta. He'd like the four of us to have dinner together. Jonnie's chasing around town with Corinne, I guess. Jewel said they left right after breakfast. Would you please tell him about dinner tomorrow night?"

"Artie, call Marty back and tell him he's to be guest of honor at a dinner party at my house tomorrow night. I'd like him to meet Barry. And we'll ask Reverend Thompson and his wife to come." Thompson was the minister of the black Baptist church and active in black voter-registration efforts.

"Can you set up a party that fast?" Artie was startled.

"Artie, you arrange for Marty Coleman to come down

here. I'll handle everything else."

Laura called Jewel and worked out the menu for the dinner the following evening, then alerted Cecile. Nora tracked down Mrs. Thompson, and Laura explained the impromptu dinner party. Twenty minutes later Mrs. Thompson phoned back to say she had checked with the minister and they'd be delighted to come for dinner.

Over a business lunch with Seth, Everett, and Maisie in the company conference room Laura brought up the hastily arranged dinner party, to which the three of them were, of course, invited.

"Sugar, this could have some ugly repercussions," Maisie warned, her face serious.

"Because I'm having a civil-rights attorney to dinner at my house?" Laura laughed, but she understood what Maisie meant even while she rejected it.

"Laura, you're having a black man to dinner," Maisie said bluntly. Now—at least, outside of the South—Negroes were referred to as blacks. "If the word gets around town, there's going to be some nasty talk."

"The word will get around," Laura predicted, "because I also invited Reverend and Mrs. Thompson. Maybe this town needs to see that the sky won't fall in if white Southerners sit down to a dinner table with blacks."

The following afternoon Laura left the office earlier than normal. She stopped off at the hospital to visit Katie and to gaze lovingly at her granddaughter in the hospital nursery. She had known she would adore Katie's baby, but she had not suspected the depth of her love for this first grandchild. She had instructed Chet this morning to draw up papers to arrange for a trust fund in Betsy's name. When everything was set up she would tell Katie and Artie.

At the house Laura supervised the setting of the dinner table, arranged the flowers. Jewel was singing away in the kitchen, always happy when there was a party. For a moment—when she came home from the office last night—Jewel had seemed upset about this particular party. *"Miz Laura, I ain't so sure it's smart you bringing colored folks to the table. Not in this town."*

Within minutes of one another the guests started arriving. The house resounded with high spirits.

Jewel herself, rather than her kitchen help, appeared at the living room door to announce dinner. Her eyes filled with pride when Laura brought her over and introduced her to Marty Coleman.

Marty charmed everybody at the table. He admitted that on his first visit below the Mason-Dixon line he had been uneasy about his reception.

"I had the stereotypical vision of the South," he said humorously. "I was afraid if I walked out into town, I'd be cornered and beat up by a gang of whites. Wow, was I surprised when it didn't happen."

"And relieved," Jonnie laughed.

Much of the table conversation revolved around civil rights. Laura understood that Marty was gaining national prominence for his efforts.

"I wonder how many Georgia citizens realize that they're sending black college students on to graduate school?" Marty grinned, glancing about the table. "I mean, prestigious schools. Harvard, Yale, Columbia. Even Oxford University."

"Marty, how do you mean that?" Laura was intrigued.

"Not just Georgia," Marty added. "It's been happening in most Southern states for a lot of years. Black students are given state funds to pay for their graduate education outside the state. That's to avoid integration in lily-white state universities, since the state provides no graduate schools for blacks and, by law, they should be accepted as graduate students in white universities. I told my parents," he kidded, "that maybe they ought to move down South so they could save the cost of putting me through Harvard Law."

While the houseman and maid moved about the table serving Jewel's superb chocolate mousse and coffee, the conversation turned to Barry's campaign for city commissioner. Laura was worried about the fear tactics the White Citizens' Council was using to win support for David Slocum. She worried about Katie and Artie and other earnest young whites who were determined that blacks would vote in the coming city elections.

"Miz Laura!" Jewel's voice was shrill with terror. "Miz Laura!" Jewel appeared at the entrance to the dining room breathless and trembling.

"Jewel, what is it?" With one anxious movement Laura pushed back her chair and rose to her feet.

"I jes' went to the front door because I heard some cars stoppin' out front—" She struggled to continue. "It's a bunch of men in white sheets! Miz Laura, they's burnin' a cross on our front lawn!"

## Chapter 48

While the white-sheeted men in their anonymous black cars raced off into the night, Artie and Chet—grim with rage—hosed down the burning cross. Maisie had hurried indoors to phone the police. Marty and Corinne were quietly trying to calm Jonnie, who cursed under his breath in impotent fury.

"I can't believe this could happen in Magnolia." Laura was pale and trembling. "Not in 1955." Here again was the ugly, terrifying Magnolia that had dragged her father from the jail and lynched him. For a moment she was fifteen years old and dashing with Iris, terrified and helpless, across the courthouse square to the jail.

"There are bad pockets in every town in the South," Seth reminded, and Reverend Thompson nodded in agreement.

"I thought the times had moved beyond this," Mrs. Thompson said with gentle reproof for the intruders.

"I would never have exposed you to this if I had known," Laura stammered in apology, her gaze including Marty and the highly respected Thompsons.

Now Laura became aware that the two elderly sisters who lived across the road were standing on their veranda. As though feeling the weight of her gaze, they scurried into their house. In minutes the news would be flashing all over Magnolia. The KKK had burned a cross on Laura Hunter's front lawn because she had entertained a prominent young civil-rights leader and the Thompsons at her dinner table.

Marty refused to appear upset.

"Mrs. Hunter, it's all part of the integration process," he comforted. "We know there'll be nasty incidents, instigated by stupid, scared people," he conceded, his eyes pained. "We've already seen the needless deaths of men—both black and white—who fought to have the law respected."

"This won't make it easier to bring colored voters to the polls," Reverend Thompson warned. Barry's campaign crew had worked hard for voter registration among the blacks. They were exhilarated by their success, but they knew registered voters might not go to the polls on election day. Talk of retaliation by the opposition was strong and nasty. "Mr. Berger, you have a tough fight ahead."

"Miz Laura—" Jewel stood at the front door, outwardly placid now. "I got fresh coffee ready fo y'all."


Laura knew the morning newspapers would carry reports of the cross burning. Not waiting for one of the servants to bring in the *Herald*, she walked out onto the veranda and bent down to pick up the paper. Her eyes involuntarily strayed to the burned patch of grass where the cross had flamed last night.

The morning was already hot and humid. Thank God for air-conditioning, she thought as she walked back into the house. The familiar aromas of biscuits in the oven and perking coffee were comforting.

"Miz Laura, you downstairs already?" Jewel chided. Her gaze strayed to the newspaper. She knew what would dominate the front page. "It ain't seven o'clock yet."

"I want to get to the office early this morning." Laura tried for a smile. "We'll probably be having a meeting here after dinner. I guess you'd better do some baking." Reverend Thompson had been right about their having problems in getting black voters to the polls after what happened last night.

"Yes, ma'am. Now you git yo'self to the breakfast table. My biscuits are about ready to come out of the oven."

The *Herald* deplored last night's violence—"Magnolia has not so disgraced itself in the past thirty-one years"—and demanded that the culprits be caught and prosecuted. Little prospect of that, Laura inwardly raged, any more than the mob that had dragged Papa from the jail, thirty-one years ago, had been caught and punished. There was no doubt in her mind that Judge Slocum was responsible for last night's response to her entertaining Marty Coleman and the Thompsons in her home.

To please Jewel Laura forced herself to eat. She was upset that guests in her house had been subject to such treatment. She realized, too, that the burning cross was meant to remind Magnolia voters that Barry Berger — a Jew — was running against David Slocum for city commissioner. There had never been a Slocum defeat at the Magnolia polls.

Laura frowned at the intrusion of the doorbell sounding. Who'd be calling at this hour of the morning?

"I'm gittin' it, Miz Laura," Jewel called.

Moments later Seth appeared at the breakfast room entrance, attaché case in one hand.

"I'll bring you coffee, Mist' Seth," Jewel sang out. "You like some eggs and hot biscuits?"

"Just coffee, Jewel." He smiled at Laura as he sat down. "You manage to get some sleep last night?"

"A little." She watched while he reached into his attaché case and pulled out a newspaper. Instinctively she stiffened.

"The *Journal* is still taking orders from the Slocums," Seth told her, unfolding the newspaper. "Laura, they've dragged out the old story again."

"Papa?" Laura stared at him in disbelief. "How? What does Papa have to do with this?"

"You're 'Jacob Roth's daughter, entertaining rabble-rousing niggers —' " He flinched at his own words. "Don't read it," he pleaded. "But I had to warn you what you'd be facing."

"Slocum never gives up, does he? He knows that as long as I'm in this town, he has to face up to the fact that he's responsible for my father's death. That his own son should have been convicted of rape and murder." Laura fought for composure. "But he's not going to win, Seth. One day it'll be the way you keep telling me. Someone will pull a thread, and the whole cloth will unravel. The truth will come out."

"Laura, I don't believe Slocum ever thinks about the truth coming out," Seth said with rare cynicism. "You hurt him where it counts the most — in his business. When Hunter Woods is completed and becomes part of Magnolia, he'll have lost not only a lot of business clout but a bundle of money. His development will be sold off for less than his syndicate put into it. This is not the first time you've beat him in the real-estate market. And Judge Slocum is a bad loser."

"I don't care for myself," Laura said, fighting back anguish. "I can't bear exposing the children to this." She remembered Katie's traumatic reaction when she learned about her grandfather. And now there was Betsy. "How many generations must suffer for what Judge Slocum and his youngest son have inflicted on us?"

"I talked with Barry last night after we left. He's worried about the election. The *Journal,* of course," he said with contempt, "listed the guests. That cost Barry votes."

"Seth, how long can the South fight the law?" Laura asked exasperatedly. "Don't they realize that the day will come when we'll have black police officers, black mayors, black congressmen?"

"Laura, that outrageous exercise on your front lawn last night does not represent the thinking of every Southerner," Seth pointed out. "There are many people right here in Magnolia who are disgusted by what happened. They don't want to see a revival of the Ku Klux Klan. They know the KKK has brought only shame to the South."

"We'll have an emergency meeting here tonight," Laura said with resolve. "We need Barry Berger on the city commission. Not just so that Hunter Woods can be annexed to Magnolia. We need his voice in the years ahead. We need a lot of voices like Barry Berger's in Magnolia government."

The evening meeting at the Hunter house was well attended, filled with bravura statements and prophesies. But afterwards—lying sleepless in bed—Laura was caught up in troubled reflections. The burning of the cross on her front lawn, the resurrection in the *Journal* of her father's conviction were warnings from the Slocums that they meant one day to destroy her. Were all their lives—hers, Iris's, the children's, the grandchildren's—to hang on that moment when a fixed jury shielded the real murderer of Tammy Lee Johnson? Did human beings have no control—in the long run—over their own lives?

As Laura reached to switch off her bedside lamp, she was startled by a light knock at her door.

"Who is it?" she asked warily.

"Corinne—" Her voice apologetic. "I saw the light under your door."

"Come in, Corinne."

Her daughter-in-law opened the door and walked into the room.

"I know I should have waited until morning to talk to you, but I couldn't sleep tonight if I had."

"Come sit down," Laura encouraged, half hopeful, half fearful.

"I've been thinking about what you said. About helping me land a spot at Rhoda Goldman Hospital. I'd like that. I'd like to live in this town." She paused, seeming almost shy for a moment. Laura's heart pounded as she digested what Corinne had said. Jonnie was coming home to stay! "I'm glad Jonnie insisted I sit in on that meeting this evening. I respect the fighting spirit in those people. Jonnie and I can fit in here. I think we can be useful. I guess that's what I want most out of life," Corinne said. "To be useful."

Within three weeks Laura had made arrangements for Corinne to join the staff of Rhoda Goldman Hospital. Jonnie and Corinne would live with Laura while their own house—to be designed by Jonnie—was being built. Laura would have been ecstatically happy except for the alarming realization that she had overextended herself in the business.

She had ignored Everett's warnings, counting on a cash flow from other properties to see her through the construction of the New York high-rise and Hunter Woods. For the first time in her real-estate career she had made no allowances for the unexpected—and this was the time when expensive hurdles kept popping up.

She had made emotional decisions, she chastised herself. She had long wished to see her mark on the Manhattan skyline—and Hunter Woods would be the jewel in her real-estate crown. She had enormous equity, she reminded herself—if cornered, she could sell other properties. But nothing must stop the Manhattan project and Hunter Woods.

Everett's anxieties were infecting Seth, Laura realized while she was being driven home after a relaxing evening with Katie and Artie and tiny Betsy on a mid-August evening. This morning Seth had brought up the possibility of their cutting back on the initial plans for Hunter Woods.

*"We could break it down in two sections. The second to be delayed for a year or two. That won't affect an annexation."*

She had rejected that instantly. Hunter Woods must continue on schedule. Jonnie would work with Seth on the new units. It was important to Jonnie's career as an architect to be associated with a dramatic new community as originally planned.

All at once Laura knew what must be done. Everett would be upset. Seth, too, because he had tremendous respect for Everett's thinking. But the day after tomorrow she would fly up to New York for a conference with the bankers. She would do whatever was necessary to negotiate a huge loan.


Laura felt a surge of pleasure as the company plane came down for a late-afternoon landing at the Magnolia airport. She was coming home with funds to see her two major projects through to completion. She would not allow herself to think about the additional costs added to their budgets. Nor about Barry's chances of winning the imminent election, so important to the future of Hunter Woods.

Pat was waiting with the car at the airport.

"It's good to see you safely home, Miss Laura," Pat greeted her with a warm smile. He was nervous about her frequent flying.

"It's good to be home, Pat. Oh, let's stop for a few moments at Miss Katie's."

"You just gotta see that Miss Betsy," he teased.

Laura lingered briefly at Katie's house, delighted to catch Betsy in her bath.

"Ain't she somethin'?" Betsy's proud young nurse— Jewel's niece, Samantha—demanded.

"She's something," Laura agreed laughing.

Laura listened to Katie's report on her current part-time activity as legal counsel to the local civil rights group, nodded in approval when Katie said that she would be working full time again beginning next week.

"It's not as though I'm depriving Betsy of anything," Katie said and Laura smiled. How many times had she struggled to convince herself that she wasn't depriving Katie and Jonnie? "Artie agrees. Samantha is wonderful with Betsy."

As planned, Everett, Maisie, and Seth had arrived at the house for dinner. After an exchange of affectionate greetings Laura excused herself to go up to her room and change clothes.

"I'll just be five minutes," Laura promised.

"Well, if I knew you were dressing, I'd have brought out my new tux," Seth laughed.

Over dinner they kept the conversation light, yet Laura sensed a certain depression in the other three. They were upset that she had negotiated such a big loan. She knew the cardinal rule for success in real estate: keep control of construction costs and the cost of money.

After dinner the other three briefed Laura on what had happened at the office during her short absence. Everett and Maisie left early. He was to leave Magnolia at six tomorrow morning to drive to Montgomery on a deal with a supplier there. Seth lingered with Laura over a glass of white wine.

"Laura, you're driving yourself too hard," he scolded, his eyes saying much more.

"Seth, you know I flourish on pressure," she laughed. But he knew her too well not to sense her taut nerves. "I can't wait for Jonnie and Corinne to arrive. To see him working with you."

"Laura—" Seth hesitated, seeming to debate inwardly for a moment. "I hope you'll give serious thought to Everett's proposal to list some of the Texas properties for sale. You don't want to be caught short—"

"Seth, you're such a worrier! You and Everett are becoming a pair of old fogies. I'm not ready to sell the Texas property."

"It would be the easiest to move fast," Seth pushed. "If you could cut back the loan by a million or two, you'd save a bundle in interest."

"Seth, I don't want to sell!" Laura's voice was strident. "I have been running this business for twenty-six years. That Texas property will double in value within five years. I know how to run my business, Seth! I don't need you to tell me!"

Seth set down his half-filled glass of wine and rose to his feet. Polite and withdrawn, this was a Seth she had never known.

"I'm sorry, Laura. I'll remember my place in the future. Good night." He strode from the living room. A few moments later she heard the front door open, then close.

White and trembling she sat motionless. *What had she done?* How could she have spoken to Seth that way? Would he leave the company? She recoiled from the vision of a life without Seth—both professionally and personally. He was right. She was driving herself too hard. She wasn't functioning normally.

In sudden decision she rose to her feet, hurried into her office to find the keys to the Chrysler she had bought for those few times she preferred to drive herself. She was not too proud to go to Seth and apologize.

When she arrived at the charming country ranch house that Cecile had redecorated completely after Rhoda's death, Laura noted that the lights were on in Seth's study. He had come straight home, she realized in relief. She parked in the driveway, hurried from the car to the entrance to the house. The foyer lights went on now. Seth had heard the car pull up into the driveway.

"Seth, I had to come to you," she said with tenuous calm when he opened the door. "I behaved terribly—"

He reached out a hand to her and drew her inside.

"You were upset," he said tenderly, walking with her into the cozy living room. "I shouldn't have pushed you that way."

"Seth, I don't think I could survive if you walked out on me. You're such an important part of my life."

"I couldn't survive without you," he told her. "Laura, why do you keep fighting what we feel for each other?"

617

"Because I love you so much," she whispered. "I remember Bernie—and Phil—and I keep warning myself that to love me is an invitation to violent death."

"Laura," Seth chided, drawing her close, "how can a brilliant, educated woman fall prey to such childish superstitions?" But she saw the relief that welled in him. He knew now that she loved him—that the distance between them was created by her childish fears.

"Don't think Maisie and Cecile haven't read me the riot act about how badly I've been treating you." She managed a shaky laugh. "But when you walked out of the house that way, I knew I'd die if you walked out of my life as well."

"I've waited so long for you," he murmured, his mouth reaching for hers.

Her arms tightened about his shoulders while their mouths sought to relieve the passion welling in each. Her body rejoicing in the touch of his. So many nights through the years she had imagined herself in Seth's arms.

"Laura?" His eyes were beseeching.

"Oh Seth, yes." She was radiant in anticipation.

Hand in hand they walked from the living room across the small foyer that led to his bedroom. Beside the bed he reached to kiss her again, his hands moving hungrily about her slender body. In the pale light from the foyer he helped her undress, tossed back the light coverlet, and playfully lifted her from her feet and dropped her on the bed. She watched with an exquisite blend of tenderness and passion while he stripped. His body was lean and firm, his passion matched her own.

For a terrifying moment when he lifted himself above her, his mouth lingering at one taut nipple, she was afraid she would disappoint him. *It had been so long.* But then she felt the touch of him. The slow and ardent thrust of him. And she knew it would be all right.

Later she lay with her head on his shoulders, one hand in his. Relaxed. Incredibly content.

"Why can't you stay the night?" Seth persisted. "We have everybody's blessing."

"No one's to know," she stipulated. "Not for a while. Not until I've made peace with myself." How was she to rid herself of her childish superstitions? But she knew she must.

"I expect you to make an honest man of me," he chuck-led.

"In time, Seth," she promised. "We've waited this long. Before we tell the others—before we marry—let me convince myself that it's all right. That I'm not sentencing you to death."

"I'll exact blackmail." He swung a leg across hers. "At regular intervals."

"I'll be happy to pay," she assured him in a spurt of exhilaration.

"Oh God, Laura, I feel like eighteen again," he murmured. He reached for her hand, brought it down to show his fresh passion. "May we be greedy tonight?"

"I insist," she laughed, her hands at his shoulders as he lifted himself above her again.


At times Laura suspected that the others guessed about Seth and her. But personal feelings were being eclipsed by politics. The crucial election was almost at hand. Katie and Artie, along with Chet, were working to make sure registered local blacks voted in the election. Laura and Seth canvased in the black section of Magnolia to explain to those who were afraid to put in an appearance at the polls that they could use absentee ballots. Jonnie and Corinne, too, settling down into the Magnolia scene, were actively working for Barry's election.

On election eve Laura was at Barry's headquarters dispensing coffee from an urn along with massive amounts of Jewel's home-baked cookies. Seth sat comfortingly at her side because he knew she worried—as all of them did—about a possible outbreak of violence at the polls.

It was encouraging to Barry's campaign crew that they had garnered a large contingent of supporters. But until the votes were counted, no one could know if their support was strong enough to elect Barry.

"You know, Laura," Seth said seriously at a quiet moment, "I think that cross burning helped our cause. I suspect a lot of people in this town were shocked that something like that could happen in Magnolia these days.

They don't want it to happen again."

"When do you think we'll know?" Laura tried to hide her edginess.

"Probably not till morning," Seth surmised. "The polls will be open for another two hours."

Katie came running across the floor towards her mother.

"Mom, Judge Slocum was just on the radio station," she reported breathlessly, her eyes ablaze. "He claims David has won the election!"

"That's impossible to say at this stage," Laura pointed out. "We'll know tomorrow morning who's the new city commissioner. Barry!" she called as he came into the headquarters. "I'm giving a victory party tomorrow night! Spread the word around!"

Shortly past midnight Laura allowed Seth to drive her home. Jonnie was remaining at campaign headquarters till what he optimistically called "the triumphant finish." Corinne was on night duty at the hospital.

"Try to sleep tonight," Seth encouraged Laura. "Remember what I said. That cross burning made a lot of basically good people in this town realize they don't want a bunch of the KKK running Magnolia. Times are changing, Laura—but the Slocums aren't changing."

"Seth, we need that annexation ruling," Laura said tiredly. "Oh God, do we need it."

## Chapter 49

At shortly before 6 A.M. Laura stirred into wakefulness. Somebody was knocking at her door.

"Who is it?" she asked groggily, pulling herself up against the pillows.

The door swung open. Jonnie charged inside, followed by Jewel with a cup of coffee.

"Mom, Barry won!" Jonnie chortled, unperturbed by his all-night vigil. "It was close," he conceded, "but Barry Berger is the new member on the city commission."

"Oh Jonnie, that's wonderful!" Laura accepted the cup of coffee with a dazzling smile. "Jewel, we're having a bang-up victory party tonight. If you need some outside help, you know where to call."

"How many folks, Miss Laura?" Jewel relished these last-minute challenges.

"Count on at least a hundred," Laura said extravagantly. "Jonnie, will you please order the champagne?"

Before she dressed, Laura phoned Cecile, talked with her and Barry. Then she phoned Seth and told him the news.

"You were right, Seth," she said, her voice jubilant. "Times are changing. You're almost always right," she added tenderly.

"This clears the way for Hunter Woods," he said with satisfaction. "I feel much better about its future."

"Providing, of course," Laura forced herself to be realistic, "we hold on to the four votes promised." It was understood that the request for annexation would be considered before the end of the year. But they still had to cope with the staggering interest on the new loan, Laura reminded herself—at a time when costs of material and labor were spiraling. And there'd be no cash flow from Hunter Woods for at least a year. Perhaps Seth was right about putting up the Texas properties for sale. Everett was convinced it was wiser to reduce their interest costs now than to hold on to property in the hope that its value would soon soar. She'd talk to him about that this morning.

Judge Slocum sat at the breakfast table with David, his face taut as David briefed him on the election returns. This was the first Slocum defeat at the polls in forty-three years.

"It was close," David reached for meager comfort.

"We lost!" He'd thought he was blessed with his three sons. They were to carry on the Slocum prestige and power into another generation. He'd thought he was founding a dynasty that would one day include a governor and a president. But Derek lived in the shadows. Eric was dead. And David was a weakling, with his mother's empty head.

"We're not through with that bitch, David." The Judge jabbed at his grapefruit with unnecessary vehemence. "Ten to one she'll get her damned Hunter Woods annexed to the city. But we'll get back at her. We'll keep our eyes open, and we'll move in at the right time. No more mistakes," he warned. "We fucked up with Montgomery Cement—we should have finished her off then. We won't miss next time."

"No, sir," David agreed, humble for a moment. He glanced at his watch. "Hell, I have to drive over to Fort Benning. I've rented the Cole property to some young Arab studying at Benning." He grinned. "The son-of-a-bitch is paying a fortune for it."

"Why are you wasting your time on a deal like that?" the Judge scoffed.

"I went to school with Jim Cole," David pointed out. "I couldn't turn him down when he asked me to personally handle the rental while he and his wife chase off on some round-the-world tour. Besides," he drawled with a glint in his eyes, "this young guy just might be useful to us. He tells me his father—the old boy owns enough mideast oil to boggle your mind—is interested in investing in the United States. He'll be in New York in a couple of weeks. The kid went to British boarding schools and Oxford University, but he comes from one of the more backward Arab countries. He's worried his father isn't too sharp about the financial world. Still, he's sharp enough to know he needs a safety valve in case the mideast situation explodes."

"I thought those oil-rich Arabs were all addicted to Swiss bank accounts." The Judge narrowed his eyes in speculation. "He's getting greedy. He wants to see more than the shitty interest he gets from the Swiss accounts."

"That's what I figure. You got something in mind that might interest him?" David was hopeful. "Maybe our new development here in town."

"That's too small for Arab oil money." The Judge frowned in exasperation. "David, when are you going to learn to think big?"

"What do you have in mind?" David asked. A bully with outsiders, he was still insecure with his father.

"That office building up in New York." The Judge squinted into space. His tongue had been hanging out for that building ever since word leaked out that the builders were in trouble. You hadn't arrived in real estate until you owned important Manhattan property. It irked him that Laura Hunter had a major project going up there. "It's too rich for our blood," he conceded briskly, "but with oil money behind us we could sew it up."

"I'll feel out this guy," David promised and grinned. "Would you believe, they didn't want to let him into the Magnolia Country Club when I took him to lunch there? They thought he was a light-skinned black. I had some fast explaining to do on both sides."

"David, you don't just 'feel out' this guy. We're talking about the most important campaign we've ever tackled." His eyes glinted in anticipation. He might be seventy-eight years old, he told himself complacently, but there wasn't a shrewder manipulator in this country than he was. "We work out a step-by-step campaign. For starters, invite him to a small dinner party at the country club on Friday. Let him know he'll be meeting some of the South's finest old families."

"I don't know if he'll come." David was dubious. "He's about twenty-four. He'd probably be more interested if I told him some gorgeous twenty-year-old blonde was coming."

"He's a rich Arab," the Judge said. "They have respect for people in high places. Tell him Congressman Bill Raynor will be there."

"Will he?" David was skeptical. "Raynor's fighting on some committee up in Washington."

"We'll tell him Raynor was called back to Washington at the last minute — for a private meeting with Ike," the Judge fabricated. "The kid will be impressed."

On Friday evening Judge Slocum and his wife entertained handsome young Abdul Sabah at a Magnolia Country Club dinner party. The guests were all from Magnolia's self-appointed aristocracy. Over dinner, after apologizing for Congressman Raynor's absence, the Judge casually dropped important Wall Street names, hinted that his contacts reached right up to the White House.

"It's important to know what's happening behind the scenes in Washington as well as Wall Street when you're making substantial investments in this country," Judge Slocum told Abdul with a paternal concern. "I've had my ears to the ground for close to fifty years now, and I still check out every angle before I make a move. For instance, I've just been tipped off that a major office building up in New York is going to be offered for sale. I'll be going up there in about two weeks to form a syndicate to buy it."

"A syndicate?" Abdul grabbed the bait. "You mean other investors?"

"That's right," the Judge nodded indulgently. "Syndicating is routine procedure these days."

"My father will be in New York at that time," Abdul

said eagerly. "Perhaps he could become part of the syndicate?"

"I'll be delighted to talk with him about it," the Judge agreed. "Discuss it with him, and we'll set up a meeting."

"My father's English is not good," Abdul apologized, "but I'm sure you'll be able to communicate. He travels always with his business adviser, who is more fluent in English." Unexpectedly Abdul chuckled. "I think all he knows of America are Cadillacs and Coca-Cola."

Laura was relieved when immediately after the election Barry pushed the city commission to vote to annex Hunter Woods, though there were contingencies to be cleared. The commission would need to know all financial details about Hunter Woods before the annexation became official. At the same time she was upset that the Texas properties were attracting no offers. Despite the loan she was facing tight short-term money. A new union contract in New York was shooting the construction payroll to the sky.

"Maybe we ought to try to move other properties," Everett suggested at an after-hours conference at the office.

"We don't want word to get around that we might be in trouble," Laura came back. "You know what that'll do to offers. But damn it, Everett, our equity is tremendous."

"So are our interest charges and construction costs," Everett shot back and Seth nodded in agreement.

"Ev, I won't consider what you're thinking," she warned. Everett and Seth wanted to delay the second section of Hunter Woods until this cash flow situation was healthier. "We go ahead as planned. Cutting back on nothing." Jonnie was totally immersed in the project, ecstatic that Seth was giving him a free hand in the second section. It was a dream opportunity for any young architect. He'd even spent several nights in a sleeping bag in the area where ground had not yet been broken. *I want to get the feel of the place, Mom. I want to know everything about it.* Nothing must interfere with Jonnie's dream.

"We're going to be uncomfortably tight for the next six months," Everett punctured her introspection, "unless we unload something." He hesitated. "Or call in some favors."

"That might work," she conceded after a moment. "Talk with Phillips and with Randall." Both companies would be in precarious condition without Hunter Realty. Both had been rescued in the past from near bankruptcy. "Tell them we need to be carried for ninety days rather than our regular thirty. Just for the next six months," she emphasized. "That will give us breathing space."

"That's the route to take." Everett exchanged a relieved glance with Seth. "In six months we'll have money in the till. In a year we'll be riding higher than ever."


In his study Matthew Slocum checked each of the papers dealing with the Manhattan office building before slipping it into his attaché case. In the morning he was flying to New York. Late in the afternoon he would have a conference with the Madison Avenue brokers handling the sale. If he didn't move fast, he told himself, he could lose the deal.

He heard the sound of a car pulling up outside. That would be David, stopping by after his Chamber of Commerce meeting. One of the servants was opening the front door. He heard voices in the foyer, then a firm knock at his study door.

"Come in, David."

David walked into the room and closed the door behind him.

"I've talked with Robinson," he reported, his face grim. "Hunter Woods will be annexed."

"That's hardly news, David."

"He got some figures for us," David pursued. "The commission made Hunter Realty spell out every cent that's going into the development. How much they're spending, where they're spending it, how much they're borrowing. She's in heavy to the banks," he added maliciously.

The Judge was suddenly alert.

626

"Not the local banks or the ones in Atlanta. I'd know."

"In New York," David said.

"What bank?" the Judge demanded.

"I don't recall," David faltered.

"Damn it, find out! Tonight. I leave for New York in the morning." His mind was charging into action. Maybe he could wrap up two things at once. "I want to know the name of the bank, the amount she borrowed—and I want the name of every one of her creditors. You get on the phone with Robinson, and you tell him I have to have those facts by half-past seven tomorrow morning. They're all in the commission's files—he can get his hands on them. David, remind that bastard he owes us."

David reached for the phone. "He may not be home from the meeting yet."

"Keep trying until you get him. And tell him I want a copy of the note she signed. It has to be in the file. I want to see what's in the boilerplate." He frowned at David's look of skepticism. "David, we'll be dealing with a New York bank. If there's anything under the boilerplate, I'll run it to the ground. This isn't the same deal as before. *We won't fuck up this time.*"

David arrived a few minutes past seven the next morning while the Judge was shaving.

"What have you got?" the Judge demanded tersely.

"A copy of her agreement with the bank. It's all here," David said importantly, holding up a manila envelope. "And Robinson dug up a list of her creditors. It's here, too."

"Read the boilerplate?" the Judge reached for a towel.

"I didn't take time for that. You said you wanted me to drive you to the airport at half-past seven."

"I'll read it in the car."


In New York the Judge took a taxi directly from the airport to the Pierre Hotel. He had a late afternoon appointment with the brokers. He'd explained that he had Arab oil money connections. They were champing at the

627

bit to do business. Tomorrow he was meeting Abdul's father, Zaki Sabah, for a very private luncheon in his suite at the Waldorf Towers.

Bill Raynor had better not screw him on this deal. He'd told Sabah he was bringing Congressman Raynor to meet him — an unofficial governmental welcome to the United States. Over lunch he'd hint at a closeness with every American president since Harding. Abdul said his father was very uneasy with Americans, but that everybody — including himself — had told him the United States was the country to invest in.

As he was being driven to the real-estate brokers' offices in his rented chauffeured limousine, he plotted in his mind every angle of his campaign to make a deal with Zaki Sabah. The Arab oil money would come into the Slocum syndicate to buy the Manhattan office building — and then he'd give Sabah a private "insider" tip: invest heavily in the Garfield Bank of Manhattan before the stock began to shoot up sometime within the next six or eight months. It'd be almost a year before he'd find out the "insider" tip wasn't working out. But in the meantime he would be so grateful he would do his new partner a small favor. He'd push the bank into calling in Laura Hunter's loan. *This time it would work.*


Laura and Seth returned to the office in exuberant spirits after a business lunch with five local merchants. All five had been obviously impressed by Seth's presentation on the new shopping center under construction at Hunter Woods. With the official annexation to Magnolia now a matter of record, Hunter Realty was prepared to sign leases.

"Seth, they were absolutely awed by the way you foresaw their individual needs," Laura said while he held the door for her. "We'll be fully rented before the sidewalks are laid."

"Laura!" Maisie called from the entrance to Everett's office. An edge to her voice that sobered Laura instantly.

"Everett has to talk to you right away."

"Trouble," Laura told Seth. "What now?"

Laura and Seth walked into Everett's office. Maisie pulled the door shut.

"I've had a call from the Garfield Bank," Everett reported. His face was taut with rage. "Who said lightning never strikes twice in the same place?"

"What does the bank want?" Laura sat down, momentarily mystified by the phone call. Then all at once she was assaulted by a sense of déjà vu, remembering the call, years ago, from Bill Carlton at the Third National Bank on her so-called arrears with Montgomery Cement. But how could Matthew Slocum be involved with the Garfield Bank? "Everett, what the hell is going on?"

"Remember the boilerplate? We weren't happy, but you were afraid to haggle about the thirty-day calling in of the principal if the company was late with any creditor."

"We're not late!" She heard herself saying this to Bill Carlton. "Not with any creditor!"

"We're paying Phillips and Randall on a ninety-day arrangement. The bank considers that as being behind in our obligations. I don't know how they learned about that," Everett said tiredly, "but they did. The official notice is coming in the mail. They're demanding that the loan be repaid in full within thirty days."

"I've left word with Barry's office that you want to see him immediately," Maisie reported. "Katie and Artie are out of town today on some civil-rights business. Chet went with them." The four were Laura's legal team.

"We'll have a meeting at the house tonight." Laura struggled for poise. "I don't understand what's happening. The bank can't be within its legal rights to do this."

"I'm scared that they're technically within their rights," Everett admitted. "We'll have to unload at any price we can get. It's that or file for bankruptcy."

"How can we unload in thirty days?" Maisie demanded. "And who's behind this insanity?"

"I don't know how it's happened," Laura said slowly, "but I'll take any odds on Matthew Slocum."

While they explored the situation with mounting anxiety, Barry arrived. He listened absorbedly to Everett's summation of the situation, interrupting at intervals with a question.

"I know I shouldn't have jumped into signing so fast with Garfield," Laura acknowledged, "but I didn't want to quibble when we needed the funds so desperately. I saw no way that a New York bank would pull something like this."

"Slocum must be involved," Barry agreed. "I'm sure his boys on the commission gave him every detail of your deal with Garfield." Laura stared blankly at Barry. "Everett had to supply the commission with all the papers relative to Hunter Woods before the annexation could go through," he reminded, and Everett nodded.

"Does Slocum have the kind of power to manipulate a New York bank?" Seth asked. "This isn't some local deal."

"Matthew Slocum is pulling the strings," Laura insisted with fatalistic calm. "Now how do I raise that money in thirty days?" This was unreal. A nightmare.

Several hours later in the Hunter living room Laura and Seth listened while Barry and the three young lawyers — plus Jonnie, with his two years of law school behind him — dissected the loan agreement she had signed. At intervals she joined in the arguments being offered, but ultimately they admitted defeat. The bank was acting within its rights. Technically.

"Everything except Hunter Woods has to go on the block immediately," Laura decreed. "I know we have only thirty days; but damn it, our equity is many times the face of that loan!"

"We'll have to sell far below market value," Everett sighed. "Everybody will know this is a distress sale."

"Make it clear to all the brokers we have to close within thirty days. But we must save Hunter Woods. I won't lose that."

Laura walked through each day in a haze of unreality. The phones rang constantly, bringing in outrageously low bids on choice properties.

"They're vultures!" Seth blazed as Laura and he sat in Everett's office while prices were being argued.

"We have to save Hunter Woods." Laura clung to this. "We'll build again from there." But she knew if the bank moved in, she could lose everything.

## Chapter 50

On duty in Rhoda Goldman Hospital's orthopedic ward Corinne followed the harried young nurse to the room where a recently admitted elderly patient who was suffering from pneumonia in addition to a fractured hip insisted on seeing "my sweet young doctor." Because of the complications in his case, Corinne had been able to wangle one of the tiny private rooms for him.

"Now Zeke, what are you kicking up a fuss about?" Corinne scolded. "I want you to rest."

"I gotta talk to you," he pleaded. His eyes moved to the nurse. "Alone."

"It's okay," Corinne told the nurse. "I'll take care of him." She closed the door behind the nurse and went to stand beside Zeke's bed. "All right, tell me what's bothering you."

"You gotta help me. I can't go to my Maker with this awful lie hangin' over my head."

"You want to tell me about it?" Corinne said gently, trying to forget that she had been on her feet for fourteen hours. Another night Jonnie would sit down to dinner without her being at the table.

"I didn't wanna lie at that trial. I swear to God I didn't. But that Judge Slocum—he say he'd have the KKK string me up if I didn't do what he say."

"What did he tell you to do?" Corinne asked. *Judge Slocum?* Wasn't that the judge at Jonnie's grandfather's trial? All at once her heart was pounding. She remembered snatches of what Jonnie had told her. Was that the trial Zeke meant? "Zeke, if I'm to help you, you must tell me everything that happened."

"The Judge—he told me I hafta say I seen Jake Roth

leanin' over Tammy Lee Johnson—and her layin' there dead. But h'it wuzn't Mr. Roth. He wuz a good man. H'it wuz that Derek Slocum."

"Zeke, I'll help you clear your conscience," Corinne promised. She trembled with excitement, knowing what this meant to Jonnie and his family. "I'm going down the hall to phone some people who can set things right for you. You just relax now."

Corinne hurried to the phone. Jewel answered.

"Jewel, I have to talk to Jonnie or Miss Laura right away," she said, fighting for calm.

"They ain't here, Miss Corinne. They're probably still at the office."

"Thank you, Jewel. I'll try them there. And Jewel," she added, "please try to reach Katie and Artie. Tell them to come as quickly as possible to the orthopedic department at Rhoda Goldman. Tell them to ask for me."

"Somebody hurt?" Jewel was alarmed.

"No, everything's fine," Corinne soothed. "But tell them to hurry."


Laura stood beside Zeke's bed, Seth's arm about her waist, and hung on to every word Zeke uttered. Katie was scribbling on a legal pad and conferring with Artie. Jonnie exchanged exultant glances with his mother at intervals. After over thirty-one years Jacob Roth would be cleared of rape and murder.

"I wouldn'ta done it exceptin' Judge Slocum say he'd have me strung up by the KKK effen I didn't," he repeated. "An' he give more money than I ever seen to go up to North Carolina to live. An' he say I better not ever come back. But I's old and sick now—and I wanna die at home. I fell down some stairs and I broke my hip when I come back to Magnolia. I know I gotta set ever'thing right before I go to my Maker."

Katie and Artie drew up Zeke's statement, had it legally witnessed, then brought in the police so they could question Zeke further. With detectives interrogating Zeke, Seth insisted on taking Laura home.

"Let the kids stand by and handle what must be done," he said tenderly. "This is a landmark day for them, too."

"Yes, Seth." Her smile was shaky.

In the car Seth seemed to be involved in some inner struggle. Laura waited for him to speak.

"Laura, you must be realistic about this," he said at last. "In the eyes of the world your father will be cleared of a terrible crime, but the Georgia Supreme Court may refuse to exonerate him after all these years."

"It will happen." Her face glowed with conviction. "I can wait. At last I'm a free woman."

"Laura, now will you make an honest man of me?" he asked humorously. "And don't say we have to wait for the Georgia Supreme Court to clear him," he jested.

"No, Seth," she promised with exhilaration, "we don't have to wait."

While Jewel hurried out to the kitchen to prepare to serve a delayed dinner, Laura reached for the phone to call Iris. Though it was pre-season, Iris was on Niko's yacht with him at Palm Beach.

As they talked about Zeke's emotional confession, for Laura and Iris it was as though time had hurtled backwards and they were racing through the night to the jail where their father was being dragged out by a lynch mob.

"Change the name of Hunter Woods to Roth Woods," Iris ordered with vindictive satisfaction. "Let it be a memorial to Papa that Magnolia can never forget."

Brought back to ugly reality, Laura told Iris about the Garfield Bank situation, warned that she might lose Hunter Woods. And she told Iris she was sure Judge Slocum was behind the financial disaster that confronted her.

"He won't enjoy annihilating me," she interrupted Iris's instant tirade. "Not when Derek is named as Tammy Lee's murderer. And he himself implicated criminally by Zeke's confession."

"Derek Slocum will never see the inside of a courtroom, much less a jail!" Iris railed. "He'll be judged incompetent to stand trial. Laura, Judge Slocum is winning again!"

"No, Iris. Don't you understand? Slocum will be on the other side of the judge's bench this time. I don't know if a jury will convict him, but he'll have to stand trial for his part in framing Papa. He's not winning. Not with one son a suicide and another a murderer."

"I'm not like you, Laura. I'll hate that man until the day I die. I won't ever forgive him what he did to all of us."

"Iris, rejoice in knowing Papa has been cleared. We've waited thirty-one years for this. I feel reborn. And soon— very soon—I'm marrying Seth. I can live without my empire."

"It's not fair that you should lose what you've worked so hard to build. Laura, let me hang up and call you back." All at once Iris sounded tense. "Stand by the phone—I'll be back to you in a few minutes."

"All right, Iris—"

"What is it?" Seth asked when Laura put down the phone.

"Iris said she'd call right back," Laura told him. "Perhaps she wanted to tell Niko about Zeke's confession." She reached for Seth's hand. "I know she's pleased that we're finally marrying. She's told me so often that I treat you badly. And you know," she said with a sense of awe, "now that Papa's cleared, I can deal with losing the business."

"We'll start again." Seth squeezed her hand. "We've got a great thing going. Hunter Realty isn't finished. It's just beginning a new phase."

In a few moments Iris was on the phone again with Laura.

"Can you be down here in Palm Beach in the morning?" she asked.

"If you need me—" All at once Laura was anxious. A crisis with Niko?

"Come with lawyers," Iris ordered. "Katie and Artie can draw up the necessary papers. You've just acquired a new creditor, Laura. Niko Zolotas. He'll pay off the bank. Bring Jonnie and Corinne, too. And Seth. We'll have a family celebration!"


While Niko was closeted with Katie and Artie in his seaborne office and Seth swam with Jonnie and Corinne in the yacht's mosaic-bottomed swimming pool, Laura and Iris relaxed on chaises on the upper deck.

"Iris, how did you manage this?" Laura asked in awe. "Niko is loaning me a fortune."

"I convinced Niko it was a sound investment," Iris shrugged.

"In approximately three minutes?" Laura laughed.

"It helped that we're living together," Iris acknowledged, clearly jubilant to have rescued Laura in a crisis. "I don't know why I love that crazy old Greek — we fight like cats and dogs half the time. But in a weird way we're very much alike."

"What about his divorcing his wife?" She would have been sublimely happy at this moment except that she worried about Iris's future.

"When his father-in-law dies, Niko will divorce DeeDee. The marriage is a business arrangement. Maybe Niko will divorce DeeDee. Maybe he won't. But I'll be fine, Laura. I suppose I'm retiring from Hunter Realty," she said whimsically. "Maybe not living the life you'd like for me. But if anything ever goes haywire between Niko and me, I know I can always come home to you. We'll always be there for each other. The way Papa wanted."

"I'm going to build that memorial to Papa." Laura took her sister's hand in hers. "Together we've made this possible. A twenty-story office building designed by Seth and Jonnie — the tallest structure in Magnolia. The Jacob Roth Tower. The three top floors will be the offices of Hunter Realty. And from my penthouse office —" Laura's vision was blurred by tears, "I'll look down on all of Magnolia — and all of Magnolia will look up to Jacob Roth Tower."

"Hear, hear!" Iris glowed with satisfaction.

"I'll fulfill my promise to Papa," Laura said softly. "And Papa's children and his grandchildren and his great-grandchildren can hold their heads high in this town. It's as Seth always told me: 'To everything there is a season . . .' This is our season, Iris."

# THE FINEST IN SUSPENSE!

**THE URSA ULTIMATUM** (2130, $3.95)
by Terry Baxter

In the dead of night, twelve nuclear warheads are smuggled north across the Mexican border to be detonated simultaneously in major cities throughout the U.S. And only a small-town desert lawman stands between a face-less Russian superspy and World War Three!

**THE LAST ASSASSIN** (1989, $3.95)
by Daniel Easterman

From New York City to the Middle East, the devastating flames of revolution and terrorism sweep across a world gone mad . . . as the most terrifying conspiracy in the history of mankind is born!

**FLOWERS FROM BERLIN** (2060, $4.50)
by Noel Hynd

With the Earth on the brink of World War Two, the Third Reich's deadliest professional killer is dispatched on the most heinous assignment of his murderous career: the assassination of Franklin Delano Roosevelt!

**THE BIG NEEDLE** (1921, $2.95)
by Ken Follett

All across Europe, innocent people are being terrorized, homes are destroyed, and dead bodies have become an unnervingly common sight. And the horrors will continue until the most powerful organization on Earth finds Chadwell Carstairs—and kills him!

**DOMINATOR** (2118, $3.95)
by James Follett

Two extraordinary men, each driven by dangerously ambiguous loyalties, play out the ultimate nuclear endgame miles above the helpless planet—aboard a hijacked space shuttle called DOMINATOR!

*Available wherever paperbacks are sold, or order direct from the Publisher. Send cover price plus 50¢ per copy for mailing and handling to Zebra Books, Dept. 2806, 475 Park Avenue South, New York, N.Y. 10016. Residents of New York, New Jersey and Pennsylvania must include sales tax. DO NOT SEND CASH.*